D1394911

READER'S DIGEST

CONDENSED BOOKS

FIRST EDITION

THE READER'S DIGEST ASSOCIATION LIMITED
25 Berkeley Square, London W1X 6AB

THE READER'S DIGEST ASSOCIATION
SOUTH AFRICA (PTY) LTD
Nedbank Centre, Strand Street, Cape Town

Printed in Great Britain by Petty & Sons Ltd, Leeds

Original cover design by Jeffery Matthews M.S.I.A.

For information as to ownership
of copyright in the material in this book see last page

ISBN 0 340 24760 6

Reader's Digest
CONDENSED BOOKS

SUNFLOWER
Marilyn Sharp

THE PASSING BELLS
Phillip Rock

THE EDUCATION
OF LITTLE TREE
Forrest Carter

THE MOUNTAIN FARM
Ernest Raymond

COLLECTOR'S LIBRARY
EDITION

In this Volume:

Sunflower

by Marilyn Sharp (p. 9)

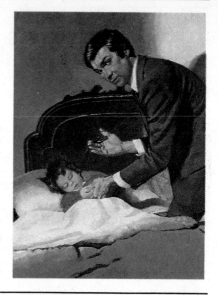

Somewhere, high up in the CIA, there was a traitor. And somehow, before he could do irreparable damage, he must be flushed out.

This was the difficult task in which top agent Richard Owen had a vital role to play. A curious role also, for his orders were to kidnap the President's young daughter. . . .

Sunflower is an expert, fast-paced thriller, full of surprises right up to its ingenious climax.

THE PASSING BELLS by Phillip Rock (p. 141)

The bells were tolling all through that summer of 1914. Few people heard them, but they rang for the coming death of a world that had seemed eternal. . . . The elegant world of Abington Pryory, the earl and his family taking their sunlit ease; the comfortable world of the earl's servants, well-fed, busy, secure. . . . Four years later that world had gone for ever, destroyed in the blood-soaked mud of the trenches, on the murderous beaches of Gallipoli. *The Passing Bells* is a brilliant story of men and women at peace and in war, unflinching, warm-hearted, vivid, unforgettable.

THE EDUCATION OF
LITTLE TREE

by Forrest Carter (p. 319)

In this intriguing and highly unusual book the author recalls his childhood in the 1930s, when he was orphaned and went to live with his Cherokee Indian grandparents in their Tennessee mountain home.

It was they who called him Little Tree. They were simple folk, but rich in the ancient wisdom of their people, and all that they knew they passed on lovingly to their grandson. Thus he learned not only the lore of the wild but also a disarming honesty in his dealings with his fellow men.

This is a truly remarkable memoir, illuminated throughout with gentle humour and rare human understanding.

The Mountain Farm

by Ernest Raymond (p. 403)

Any girl, living alone with her father and brother in a remote Cumberland farmhouse, may be forgiven for dreaming of love, of the handsome young man who will come and whisk her away to the big, exciting world beyond the mountains. Sometimes, indeed, such dreams may even come true. . . . Sometimes, also, fate may offer another happiness, closer to home: a different, unexpected, more lasting joy.

Sunflower

A CONDENSATION OF THE BOOK BY

MARILYN SHARP

A flower to be gently picked:
a child to be discreetly taken

ILLUSTRATED BY ROBERT CHRONISTER

PUBLISHED BY MACMILLAN

"We want you to pick us a sunflower. That's the operative code name, by the way. . . . We want you to kidnap President Easton's daughter."

Kidnap the child, but on no account harm a hair of her head. . . . For Richard Owen, top-flight CIA agent, it was the most incredible assignment of his whole career.

Admittedly his orders came from the President himself. But Anne was well guarded: the security net about her seemed impregnable. And were the reasons given him for the kidnap good enough?

Could he bring it off? And, even more importantly, *should* he?

Chapter One

Malcolm stood with his back to the castle, pacing uneasily and keeping an eye on the road where it curved up from the village of Knaresborough.

The castle rose up behind him, bleak and broken, a snaggle-toothed relic etched against the wet April dawn. The fortress stood silent, harmless, a brooding shadow of terror dimly remembered across the boundaries of time. But to Malcolm, the ghosts of Knaresborough Castle were strangely alive. Not that he was seeing things—no mute spirits clanking weightless chains. It was just a feeling he had, a sense of mystery provoked by crumbling walls and empty, staring windows.

And so he turned to face the present, keeping an eye on the road and an ear cocked for the hum of a motor. Instead, all he heard was the sound of water rushing over rocks—a gentle, hypnotic sound, like the steady scrape of the windshield wipers as he had made his way north from London through the lonely night. He turned his collar up against the chill of the air, then reached for the packet of sunflower seeds in his pocket.

It had to be sunflower seeds. Graham had been quite specific. Not peanuts or cashews, but *sunflower* seeds. The signal Graham would recognize. The code name for the project.

He tore open the cellophane wrapper and began to eat the seeds slowly, one at a time, careful not to drop any.

Malcolm was a tall man, but not tall enough to carry his overweight. His eyes were pinpoints in a florid face, surrounded by lines of age, yet watchful under the brim of his black bowler. His

9

coat was also black—surely the proper color for this sort of meeting. Under the coat, his shoulders sloped forward, collapsed after too many years of supporting his huge head. Yet, in spite of his bulk, his pale fingers were long and slender.

He yawned and shrugged off the fatigue of a sleepless night. He had worked straight through, rolling the last sheet of the report out of his typewriter just in time to be on his way. Now, with the report safely zippered into the black case under his arm, he felt like a man on the threshold of a new day. His full lips curved into a smile. It was appropriate that Graham had chosen daybreak for their first face-to-face meeting.

Malcolm didn't know precisely who Graham was, only that he was top echelon and rarely risked the cover of his own good name by venturing out into the field. Like Graham, Malcolm had a safe job; he worked behind the scenes, never on the front lines. But while the Grahams of the world sat in plush offices, issuing orders, the Malcolms worked out of drafty cubicles, plowing through tedious details, seeking out that rare morsel of information that was worth the attention of the Grahams. Or so Malcolm thought.

He pressed the black case closer, feeling the comforting presence of the report. It was his *pièce de résistance*, the crowning glory of a career his superiors had taken for granted too long. Now, at last, the honor would come. Not publicly, of course; it was all too top secret for that. But privately—new respect among the people who had ignored him all these years. Things would be different soon—and for that he had mostly himself to thank.

Of course, Graham deserved some credit, too. It was Graham, after all, who had asked for the best research analyst available, Graham who had chosen Malcolm for this key assignment.

For a moment, Malcolm stopped pacing, eyeing the ground at his feet with peculiar interest. He stooped to retrieve a single sunflower seed that had somehow escaped his grasp. As he straightened up, he caught sight of a man on the path that skirted the castle grounds. Even from this distance, Malcolm was grudgingly impressed. This stranger coming toward him did not appear to be Mr. "Top-Echelon" Graham, whose working clothes no doubt ran to Savile Row tweeds and shoes of Italian leather. This was a common man, in faded denims, with a blue seaman's cap pulled low over his brow. He was in character right down to the way he walked, with the rolling gait of a sailor.

Malcolm stuffed the sunflower seeds into his pocket. *"All human things are subject to decay,"* he said as the man approached him.

"And, when fate summons, monarchs must obey," Graham replied. He had lifted the lines from Dryden.

The two men fell into step, saying nothing as they made their way past the castle and down to the promenade, where the ground fell away sharply to the river below. "Well?" Graham asked at last.

It annoyed Malcolm to notice that Graham was younger than he—mid-forties, he guessed, as he studied the lean, unworried face.

"I've given this problem many hours of thought—" Malcolm began.

But Graham cut him off. "I'm not interested in technique, just results. Can it be done?"

"Yes, sir," Malcolm replied quickly. "It can be done."

"How?" Graham wanted to know.

"We begin by stealing this from the White House." He handed a folded newspaper clipping to Graham.

Graham unfolded the clipping. "You mean—"

"Yes, sir, that's what I mean."

For a moment, Graham's expressionless face came to life. He clearly liked the idea. But then he frowned.

Malcolm spoke up quickly, before Graham could verbalize his doubts. "We use the best possible person," he said, "a top-notch professional who can do a clean job, leaving no evidence behind. Not a single clue to who he is, nothing to—"

"Yes, yes, I know all of that," Graham broke in impatiently. "But what's the point of it all?"

"The point is, sir, that *we* provide the clues." Malcolm was all civil servant now, delivering his report efficiently. "We choose key trouble spots around the world, places where US prestige is already an issue, and we launch a campaign of befuddlement and apparent bungling. If we choose carefully, we might accomplish a few specific goals as well as the broader one. In any case, we give them nothing to help them recover the stolen item. In fact, we do all we can to prevent it."

"Ah, yes, I'm beginning to see where you're going." Graham

11

chuckled. "And in the end, we save the day and reap the rewards."

"Yes, sir. But not without placing blame where it's due."

Graham continued on down the path, stroking his chin thoughtfully. "It's good," he said at last. "I have to hand it to you, Malcolm. It's very good. But it's all predicated on one questionable point. Is it possible to steal the item you have in mind?"

"There's the rub, of course," Malcolm replied. "I should think it can be done. Nothing is ever completely impossible."

Graham stopped and turned on Malcolm with an angry glare. "I didn't tell you to bring me possibilities. I told you to—"

"There is one man who can do it," Malcolm broke in quickly.

No comment, only a raised eyebrow from Graham.

"His name is Richard Owen."

Yes, of course, Richard Owen. Whenever there was just one man for the job, it was always Richard Owen. Graham resumed his leisurely pace down toward the riverbank. "Convince me," he said.

Malcolm cleared his throat. "Well, sir, I should say he has all the necessary qualities. He's intelligent. He's extremely clever. Apparently, he's immune to fear. And frankly, sir, I'm not sure anyone else would accept this assignment."

"When I give an assignment, acceptance is not a question."

"Of course, sir. I didn't mean to suggest otherwise. But Richard Owen has one unique qualification: he's an absolute genius with languages. He speaks eight of them fluently, you know."

"Yes, I know that."

"Actually, to say he is fluent is rather an understatement," Malcolm added. "He's also a master of dialects. For example, he can speak English as an Englishman, or an American, a Scotsman, even an Australian, I daresay it's a gift, though it's not so surprising when you consider his background. His father was in the diplomatic service, and they lived all over the world."

"You don't miss anything, do you?"

"It's my job, sir," Malcolm replied. Graham merely nodded.

"Owen's value for this assignment is obvious, I think," Malcolm went on. "He is able to surface and resurface, over and over again, in the same place or an entirely new location, each time as a different person. Physical disguise helps, of course, and he does need the full line of false documents, but those can always be supplied by us. His command of languages is the main thing."

They rounded a curve in the path and Graham stopped, seeming to study the view. "Where is Owen now?" he asked.

"In Brussels. And I don't believe we'll have any trouble with him, sir. It's meeting the challenge that gives Owen his satisfaction. He has never failed. He's simply the best there is."

And that, thought Graham, summed up the problem of Richard Owen. Intelligent, Malcolm had said. Extremely clever. The words were hardly adequate. Owen was brilliant. More than that, independent. And that combination made Graham nervous.

He turned to Malcolm. "Tell me, what makes him function?"

"That's no simple question," Malcolm replied. "Owen is a complex sort of person—on the one hand amoral, on the other a moral purist. He's a master of deception, but incapable of hypocrisy. He'll kill one of our kind without remorse, but he doesn't like to hurt innocent people and tries to avoid it. In fact, he rather likes people, as long as they give him no reason not to. But liking and trusting to Owen, are two very separate things."

"Precisely," Graham said. "You're not easing my fears. If Owen should ask too many questions—"

"Ah, but he won't. He never does. He'll ask *some* questions because he likes to work from knowledge and not from ignorance. But policy doesn't interest him. Owen believes in one thing absolutely—the value of his word. If he gives you his word, he'll keep it." Malcolm glanced away to the river. "Of course," he added, "he may just turn you down."

Graham did not reply, but he knew Malcolm was right. There again was the problem: unlike most of his agents, Owen could not be predicted. Yet Owen was the only man for the job.

"On the other hand," Malcolm said, "Owen will do almost anything if it interests him. And this assignment, I think you'll agree, could hardly fail to do that." Malcolm's heart began to beat a little faster. He opened his black zippered case. "I've put together a complete dossier on him."

Graham said nothing. His placid features were frozen, his eyes glued to the document in Malcolm's hand.

Malcolm failed to notice. He dug deeper into the black case. "I've also put together a detailed outline of the plan we were dis-

13

cussing, sir. It's complete with suggested places where clues might turn up. And I've outlined my thinking on the climax and denouement. Of course, you didn't give me all the details of what you had in mind. I had to make some educated guesses, you might say."

Graham's expression ran from astonishment to outright anger. "You put all of that into writing?" he demanded.

"Don't worry," Malcolm assured him. "I worked at night and I shredded everything except what you see right here."

Graham glanced down at the neat, typewritten notes in Malcolm's hand. "Copies?" he asked.

"Just two, one for you and one for me. They're both right here—quite safe, I assure you."

Graham's face relaxed into a smile. "Good job, Malcolm. Let me see what you've done."

They continued down the path to the river's edge and sat down on a wooden bench. Graham took the report and began to read it. Malcolm glanced back over his shoulder. From this point, the castle was completely hidden by the steep slope of the riverbank. The rising sun began to burn off the mist and draw the chill from the air. Malcolm took a deep breath and reached into his pocket, then hesitated. One did not nibble in the presence of one's superiors. But was Graham still a superior? Malcolm thought not. He brought out the sunflower seeds and began to eat them. It was a new day, a new beginning, and he was glad to be alive.

Graham noticed the pathetic gesture of equality, but continued to read. When he was finished, he looked up, but not at Malcolm. He was looking at the river rushing by, breaking savagely over rocks. He was thinking about Malcolm—and his plan.

Malcolm had been a good choice. He was everything Richard Owen was not—a drone, a plodder who would never be credited with anything close to imagination. There would be no reason for anyone to connect him with this. But Graham had underestimated him, and now the old fellow knew too much.

Yet, it was an excellent plan.

Graham turned to Malcolm. "You're quite sure there are no other copies of this? Nothing left carelessly on your desk?"

"If you'll pardon my saying so, I'm not daft," Malcolm replied. "And I'm no newcomer to this business."

"No, you're not," Graham conceded. As he spoke, he took a fountain pen from his pocket, routinely removed the cap, and aimed it at the other man. A kestrel hawk dipped low in the sky and hovered motionless, seemingly without effort, over the river. That graceful, gliding action was the last thing Malcolm ever saw. He uttered a brief cry, but the sound was lost in the noise of the river. His arm jerked up to his face, but it was too late.

Graham quickly searched the dead man's pockets, then rolled the body over into the scrub growing beside the river. When someone stumbled onto it later, all traces of the poison would have vanished. Mr. Malcolm would be nothing more interesting than a government clerk on holiday, the victim of a heart attack.

Graham placed Malcolm's report back in the black zippered case, tucked it under his arm, and walked away into the trees. Behind him lay a cellophane wrapper with sunflower seeds spilling out over the ground. Soon, a stray wind scattered the seeds and lifted the wrapper into the river. For a moment, it bobbed along the surface, fighting to stay afloat. But finally, a swirl of foam washed over it, and the wrapper, too, disappeared.

Chapter Two

The Rendezvous Bar in Athens was all polished wood and old leather, small and cozy, with soft lights glowing under a crystal chandelier. At six o'clock on an April evening, the room was beginning to fill with groups of men in either business suits or the casual dress of tourists. There were women, too, in bright spring dresses as colorful as the sprays of gladioli that came from the flower stalls around the corner on Avenue Vassilissis Sofias. There was no music, only the sounds of subdued conversation, some laughter, ice clinking against glass. And one dignified waiter who moved quietly through the room, serving drinks.

Hovering over it all was the Grande Bretagne, the queen mother of Athens hotels, a stopping place over the years for monarchs and millionaires, and even Winston Churchill, who escaped an assassin through the subterranean corridors of the hotel's cellar.

Richard Owen smiled his approval as he crossed the lobby to

the bar. While the rest of Athens was going to neon and plastic, the Grande Bretagne had retained its charm. It was almost like coming home for a man who had no home. He chose a corner table with a view of the entire room and summoned the waiter.

"Glenfiddich on the rocks," Owen said.

The waiter nodded and moved away, sizing up his new patron. An American, quite obviously—mid-thirties, tall, with a slender, athletic build and brown hair cut fashionably long. His face had a rugged quality, but his features were well defined, and his eyes were young—full of trust and confidence. Yes, this was an American, the waiter thought, one with rare good taste, who ordered malt whisky by brand and his clothes from a quality tailor.

Only Richard Owen was not American. Or British, or French, or Russian. Or anything else. He belonged to no country beyond the one named in his current passport, and that would be different tomorrow. With each new name he became a complete new person. Between names he became Richard Owen, a person as carefully planned as the others. His real identity was buried in the past. All that was left was a solitary figure without friends or family and preferred it that way. For a reason. Attachments meant vulnerability. It was safer not to care.

The waiter brought his drink and Owen then focused his eyes on the wall across the room, over the heads of the other people. He wanted only voices floating to him, like so many points of information, to be rejected until the right sound came through. Mostly they were English. Some German. Hardly any Greek.

Some German. The voice was a man's, but it was followed soon after by a burst of feminine laughter, then her reply. Her accent was American; her German sounded book-learned.

Owen let his eyes move slowly to a table where a sleek young blonde woman was holding the full attention of a handsome *Deutschländer*. She smiled sweetly as the man held his lighter to her cigarette, then met his eyes with a look that could have melted the buttons off his shirt. She, alone among the women in the bar, was wearing a plain black dress—very chic and very expensive.

The German, made bold by drink, made no effort to keep his voice down. He was telling Blondie how beautiful she was. Beautiful, but smart. He hadn't met anyone like her for a long time.

16

American women have been liberated, Blondie told him. We're no longer chained to the kitchen.

I see. He nodded. That should leave you time for other rooms.

"*Aber natürlich,*" she replied with a knowing smile.

Owen listened a while longer and decided that Blondie's American accent was very good, but not good enough. She was a natural-born *Fräulein* if ever he'd heard one—a German woman pretending to be American and speaking her native tongue as if she had learned it in school. Owen smiled. A lesser ear for language would have been fooled; his was not.

Blondie was the right *Fräulein,* too. Even from across the room, he could hardly miss the splendid ruby earrings that adorned her lovely earlobes like a pair of polished red dice. As he watched, she raised her hand to one ear and slipped the ruby off. For a moment, she held it in her hand. Then she returned it to its rightful place and removed its opposite number.

Yes, Blondie was the woman he had come here to meet.

Owen tuned out the seduction scene and thought about the bland-faced man back in Brussels holding a pair of red dice in his hands. It had been a simple encounter. "Pardon me, sir, do you have the *time?*" this man had asked.

Time was the first key word.

As Owen answered, the man fell into step beside him, heading toward Owen's hotel. "I have *to* meet my wife in an hour," he said. "Are you *going* my way?" And when Owen said he was, "Well *now*, that's just fine."

Time to go now.

Then he had brought out the dice, and Owen knew the bland-faced man was no ordinary courier. It had been years since anyone had given him a double red alert. A double came direct from the top. No questions asked. Just follow orders until someone cares to enlighten you. And trust no one, not even your own granny, unless she's sporting a pair of something red.

Owen had listened carefully to the man, and by the time they parted three blocks later, he had acquired a new name, an American passport, a one-way ticket to Athens, and orders to go to the bar at the GB and wait for contact from a German woman traveling under cover as a young American socialite. Now, here

17

was Blondie, in her red ruby earrings, speaking German like a second language instead of the one she was born to.

Owen noticed her looking at him. But when their eyes met, she turned away. She repeated the performance a few minutes later, and finally she made her move. The German was paying the check when Blondie's voice floated across the room. *"Entschuldigen Sie mich, bitte."*—"Excuse me, please. I think I see someone I know." Without waiting for the German to reply, she stood up and came toward Owen's table. Owen watched her long, slender legs moving across the room in graceful strides. He started to rise as she approached him.

"Pardon me," she began, all American now. "Aren't you—" Then she answered her own unfinished question. "No, I'm afraid I've made a mistake." There was just the right touch of embarrassment in her voice, just the right shade of emphasis on the correct word. "I thought you were someone I met another *time*."

"I'm sorry I'm not who you thought I was," he said. "But do you have *to go now?*"

She flashed a smile, and for just a moment her hand lingered on the table. "My friend is waiting. I'm sorry I bothered you."

Owen and half a dozen other men watched her exit from the bar. Like the others, Owen was smiling, for her physical charms had not escaped him. But he was even more impressed by the skillful way she had dropped the small, folded piece of paper unseen on his table. He dropped the paper into his pocket. Then he settled back to finish his drink.

It was dark when Owen left the hotel twenty minutes later. The open cafés in the square across the street had filled with people, mostly couples. A warm breeze touched Owen's face, like the hand of a gentle woman, and for a moment he wished that the meeting with Blondie had been a little less professional, a little less brief. He crossed the avenue into Ermou Street, walking slowly, just another tourist on the lookout for a *taverna* with bouzouki music and gay *syrtaki* dancing. After a block, he stopped to light a cigarette by a shop window, and read the message: "No. 8 Kiristou Street. Tomorrow 9 a.m. Ask for icons, Saint Paul."

Owen moved on down the street. As he walked, he tore the paper into tiny bits and threw them into a sewer.

OVER BREAKFAST Owen studied a map of Athens. He didn't remember Kiristou Street, and it took some time to locate his destination in the Plaka, the old-town section of Athens that rambles up the slopes of the Acropolis. He glanced at his watch and decided to walk. The sight of the Acropolis sitting over the city in the morning sun was one that never palled.

Owen left the hotel and headed through Syntagma Square, the same direction he had taken the night before. In the distance, the pure Greek air gathered into a white haze through which he could see the tops of mountains where people still lived as they had for centuries. But here in the city, traffic buzzed along the busy avenue, and the air was full of the sounds of a modern city getting a start on the day.

Ahead of him lay the Plaka and an abrupt change of pace—primitive whitewashed houses nestled together like children's blocks along twisting streets that were hardly more than alleys. Owen passed the Orthodox cathedral at Plateia Mitropoleos, and leaving modern Athens behind, he followed a narrow street which ascended the hillside in a series of broad steps and plateaus. Here the only sign of life was a stray cat observing the siesta early in a bright patch of sunlight.

At the top of the steps, a path skirted the ruins of the Agora and led around to the entrance of the Acropolis. But Owen was not out to commune with the ancient gods. A block before the steps began their final ascent, he turned right into Kiristou Street.

The building at number 8 was sandwiched between a *souvlaki* stand and a tiny hotel. A sign over the door read THEODOROUS LIKAS, SOUVENIRS; Owen tried the door and found it unlocked. He paused in the doorway to let his eyes adjust after the bright sunlight. A small, stocky man came into focus. He looked at Owen across a countertop cluttered with cheap reproductions of ancient sculpture. On the wall behind him was a picture of King Constantine and his Danish bride.

Owen approached the counter. "Good morning. I wonder if you could help me," he said. "I'm looking for icons of Saint Paul."

A boyish grin broke over the man's face. Clearly, Likas was not Owen's contact. He was another innocent, one of thousands around the world who were called on from time to time to establish a one-shot cover for something they knew nothing about.

"You will find what you are looking for upstairs," the Greek said in carefully pronounced English.

Owen followed his gesture to a flight of narrow wooden stairs that led to the upper floor. The door at the top was open a crack.

"Go on," Likas urged him. "I know he is up there."

Owen unbuttoned his jacket and started up the steps, feeling for the revolver he carried nose-down in his belt. When he reached the top, he slowly pushed the door back against the wall. The room beyond was heavily shuttered, with packing crates along one wall. In the center was a table with two chairs. A slim man was standing behind the table, a silhouette against the shuttered window. He spoke out of the darkness. "Good morning, Owen."

The voice struck a note in Owen's memory, but he couldn't pin it down. "Are you allergic to light, or what?" he said.

"Just cautious," the man replied, without moving away from the window. "Come closer. Let me see your face."

Owen didn't answer. Slowly, he moved around the table, until he was at arm's length from the dark figure. He opened the shutter just enough to let a beam of light split the room and give shape to the unseen face. When he had seen it, he was not amused.

"Macklin, you rat," he said coldly.

Howard Macklin was some kind of junior assistant at the US embassy in Athens. That was where you looked for the professionals—among the junior officers. He had two sources of income Owen knew of and had managed to keep them from knowing about each other. One paycheck came from the US army, intelligence branch, the other from Her Majesty's Secret Service, Britain's MI6. Of all the people Owen didn't trust, Howard Macklin was high on the list.

"That's not a friendly greeting for an old friend," Macklin said as he held a match to a small oil lamp on the table.

"You're lucky I didn't kill you," Owen replied. "What do you want from me?"

"I don't want anything from you. I have something for you." Macklin pointed to a leather pouch lying unopened on the table. "We're working the same side of the street this time," he added.

"Whose street?"

"Yours. I'm here for your man Simon. He told me to tell you the *time is now*."

Owen didn't know Simon, at least not by that name, but he did recognize the variation on the code. Macklin then produced a deck of playing cards and turned up a pair of red kings. "All right, I'm listening," Owen said with a curt nod.

"You're being put on special assignment," Macklin said. "It's so top secret that your identity must be hidden even from your own people. In fact, in another ten minutes Richard Owen will have been dead for twelve hours."

Owen didn't comment. He waited for Macklin to explain.

"For the record, you left Brussels yesterday morning and flew to Oslo, but you met with an unfortunate accident on the way to your hotel. You died two hours later in a local hospital."

"Very neat," Owen said. He wondered who the lucky bloke was who got to stand in for him.

"It was a rented car—rented by you, of course. The point is, it's all official. Richard Owen is dead. Anyone trying to trace your movements will come to—pardon the expression—an abrupt dead end. Do you understand?"

"Certainly." Owen understood, all right. Someone, somewhere, was going to a lot of trouble to cover his tracks.

"You leave Athens this afternoon," Macklin went on. He opened the leather pouch and handed Owen an envelope. Inside, Owen found a Swedish passport made out to a fur trader named Lars Hansson. There were also letters, a driver's license, and a wallet-sized photo of a pretty young woman with two boys.

"Your family," Macklin said.

Finally, there was an airplane ticket, one-way from Athens to London. Departure date, that afternoon.

"I've taken care of everything you'll need," Macklin continued. "When you return to your hotel, you'll find new clothes—all from shops in Stockholm—luggage, shaving gear, the works. There's even a novel that's all the rage in Sweden now."

"Very thorough."

"I'll clean up after you've gone. Everything you brought into Athens stays behind. You must take nothing with you that might identify you as Richard Owen."

"And when I reach London?"

"Go to the Colony Hotel in Piccadilly. After that, your guess is as good as mine."

Chapter Three

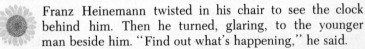 Franz Heinemann twisted in his chair to see the clock behind him. Then he turned, glaring, to the younger man beside him. "Find out what's happening," he said.

It was not a request but an order, delivered with all the courtesy of a military command.

Hans Müller hurried across the departure lounge to the desk where a man and woman in brown uniforms had finished checking in passengers leaving Vienna. As Müller approached, the uniformed bodies snapped to attention. Heinemann caught snatches of the conversation that followed. "So very sorry. . . . Unfortunately, can't be helped. . . . Is the maestro uncomfortable . . .? A lounge for our VIP passengers. . . ."

If the lounge were truly reserved for men of distinction, Heinemann might have been interested. But airlines calculated personal worth in numbers of miles flown. Very important had nothing to do with superiority or birthright; anyone could qualify. VIP lounge! Ridiculous! It wasn't worth the effort it took to move.

Heinemann's thoughts slipped back to an earlier time, when traveling had been a pleasure. Trains were slower, but they ran separate cars for people of class. Air travel had no place for passengers such as himself. Everything was so impersonal, everyone treated the same. The computer handed over your ticket. The machines told them you didn't have a gun in your pocket or a bomb in the sole of your shoe. Of course he had no bomb in his shoe! How dared they question that?

Yes, Heinemann preferred to travel by train. But between Austria and America, he had to fly.

But he did draw the line at one thing: the preflight inspection. "I will not have you putting my Stradivarius on that conveyor belt," he had asserted in a tone that left little doubt about the life left in his old bones. The young woman who worked for the

23

airport looked terrified, but she had agreed—and she handled his violin as gently as if it had been a bomb.

Müller returned to his seat. "It won't be long now, Maestro."

"That's what they said twenty minutes ago."

Müller started to speak, but Heinemann cut him off. "Never mind. If we must wait, give me my itinerary."

Müller unfolded a sheet of paper and handed it to the old man. Heinemann took it without a word, and looked it over with a critical eye. His first stop was in New York City, a recital at Avery Fisher Hall. Then on to Chicago, Denver, Los Angeles. He would play in Houston and Atlanta. And in Washington, DC at the White House, with all the trappings of a command performance. That, after all, was the prime reason for making this trip.

He glanced up at Müller. "There's no hotel listed for Washington," he said. "You know I insist on advance approval."

"Well, sir—" Müller cleared his throat. He didn't have time to explain. The uniformed man approached and spoke to Müller. "If you'll follow me, we'll get the maestro settled before the other passengers board."

Deference, Heinemann thought, was often very close to condescension. Nonetheless, he took Müller's arm and followed the uniform across the lounge.

It was after ten a.m. in Vienna when Heinemann's plane broke through the clouds and leveled off at thirty-five thousand feet. About the same time, in London, Richard Owen left the Colony Hotel on his way to Heathrow airport.

He had arrived the day before and settled in his room to wait for something, someone—for a small, dark Indian girl with a shy smile, and a set of fresh towels folded over one arm. Owen double-locked the door behind her when she was gone. He knew there was clean linen in the bathroom, and the Colony wasn't the kind of hotel where you could figure on extra service.

In the folds of the towels, he found what he was looking for—a manila envelope thick with new documents. There was a French passport in the name of André Bouchard, a freelance journalist. There was also an airplane ticket. And a locker key.

That night Owen wrapped Lars Hansson's personal belongings in brown paper and took a cab to Waterloo station. He matched the number on the key against the locker numbers until he found the right one. Inside, he found a worn canvas suitcase. The luggage tag said André Bouchard. He swapped his brown paper parcel for the canvas bag and left the station.

He walked back, choosing the scenic route that took him across the Thames, and he stopped on Westminster Bridge to admire the view—Parliament standing proud against the lights of the sprawling city. Big Ben was just striking the hour as he dropped the locker key into the surging black water below.

Owen stopped again at a pharmacy at Charing Cross, then returned to his room where he dropped the Swedish passport and Hansson's papers into the bathroom sink and set his lighter to them. When the flame died out, he turned both taps on full and watched the ashes disappear down the drain.

' Next, he propped the French passport open to the photo page and unwrapped the hair preparations he had bought from the druggist. The following morning he left the hotel unseen. At Heathrow, he boarded TWA's morning flight to New York City.

Six hours later Richard Owen was making his way through the crowded TWA terminal at Kennedy airport, where he stopped at a news stand for a copy of *The New York Times*.

Owen loved New York. More than any other city in the world, he thought, this one had a heart of its own—a cold heart, maybe, but one that never stopped beating. As he emerged from the terminal, he looked at the tangle of people fighting it out for a firm grip on the door handle of a passing taxicab and knew he had arrived in the New World. A yellow Checker cab came to a stop beside him, and he grabbed the door, claiming it for his own.

The driver leaned across the front seat and wound down the window. "Where you going, buddy?"

"Manhattan," Owen said. "To the Regency."

The cabby nodded and pushed open the front door for Owen to lift his bag in. This was a privately owned taxi, and it didn't have a bulletproof partition. One good thing about those partitions: they made driver-passenger conversations next to impossible. Owen could only hope this driver wasn't the chatty type.

He settled into the back seat and picked up the *Times* while the cabby pulled away. He scanned the headlines on the front page, then turned to the inside. Halfway through the first section, he stopped short. It was a small item, and Owen might have missed it if the name Howard Macklin hadn't jumped out at him.

ATHENS (AP)—Howard Macklin, 35, assistant first secretary of the US Embassy here, was accidentally drowned yesterday afternoon when he fell from a yacht in the Saronic Gulf off the Attic coast of Greece.

The yacht belonged to friends of Macklin who said the American official was known to be a poor swimmer. His body was discovered washed ashore near Lagonissi.

So, Macklin dead, one convenient day after he met with Owen on a double red alert. "Rest in peace," Owen murmured as he tossed aside the paper.

"What's that?" the driver asked.

"Nothing."

Without meaning to, Owen found himself staring at the driver's hack license on the dashboard. Anything was an improvement on the passing landscape: city streets fogged in under a drizzling sky. Suddenly, the license jolted him out of his thoughts. The name: Aaron Rosenberg. The picture: a man with thinning black hair and a good sixty years to his credit. Owen's eyes swung back to the driver. He was at least twenty-five years younger than the man in the picture, with wide shoulders and a strong neck. His hair was blond, his eyes blue, his features sharp—a perfect stereotype out of Hollywood war movies. From the look of things, Owen figured the driver's father might have led Aaron off to the ovens.

And where, Owen wondered, does he think he's taking me?

Then he noticed something else. The driver's hands were placed firmly on top of the steering wheel, and his shirt sleeves, extending beyond the cuffs of the plaid wool jacket, were fastened with a pair of flashy red cuff links. He was studying Owen through the rearview mirror, and the hint of a smile crossed his face.

"You happen to have the *time?*" he said matter-of-factly.

"I have *two* o'clock," Owen replied. It was more like ten a.m.

"Two o'clock," the driver repeated. "Bad *time to go* into Manhattan. Lot's of traffic right *now.*"

The man was German all right. His English was good, but Owen detected a distinct Prussian tone in the accent.

"Where did you send Rosenberg?" Owen asked. "Argentina?"

"That's close enough." The German smiled. "I slipped up on the license. Sorry."

Owen didn't return the smile. "Forget it," he said. But he filed the mistake away in his own memory bank.

"I'm Simon, by the way," the other man went on, extending his hand over the back seat without taking his eyes off the road. "The double red ends with me. I'm authorized to tell you why we've brought you here."

Owen gave the hand a perfunctory shake and waited for Simon to explain. But for the moment, Simon was busy with the cab. An accident on the road ahead had narrowed Manhattan-bound traffic to one slow-moving lane. Simon was in the wrong lane. He stepped down on the gas and forced his way into a gap between a Volkswagen and a long, black limousine. In that moment, Owen glimpsed a small, white-haired man sitting with a companion in the back seat of the limousine. The man's face was calm, even cold. And Owen recognized him as the famous violinist Franz Heinemann.

When Simon spoke again, there was a trace of amusement in his voice. "We're sending you out with your garden shears," he said. "We want you to pick us a sunflower. That's the operative code name, by the way—*Sunflower*."

As Owen listened to what Simon was saying, the German came up in his estimation. He seemed to be a friendly sort, with an easy manner and a ready smile. But Owen observed an edge of cold reality in Simon's blue eyes. He began to get a different picture of the man, a kind of X-ray view of a body where all the nerve endings connected up with a stainless-steel spine.

"Sunflower," Simon was saying, "is our code name for Anne Easton. I assume you know who she is."

"Of course," Owen replied. Anne Easton was four years old and an international celebrity. She was a real charmer, a tiny waif of a girl with big brown eyes and a dimpled smile.

She was also the only child of Matt Easton, the President of the United States.

Owen leaned forward. "So what's the job. Protection? I don't do protection."

Simon chuckled. "Hardly. But it's not what you'd consider your usual line of work." He glanced at Owen in the rearview mirror. "Ever read Mary Poppins? If you haven't, you ought to."

"Why?" Owen asked. "What is it you want me to do?"

"We want you to kidnap her," Simon replied, as calmly as if he were suggesting a good place for lunch. "We want you to kidnap President Easton's daughter."

THE APARTMENT where Simon dropped Owen was on Riverside Drive. It was spacious and tastefully furnished. Not quite the Regency, where Owen had planned to stay, but more private. Furthermore, the kitchen was well stocked and the bar offered three fifths of Glenfiddich and a fifth of Courvoisier VSOP.

Owen was pouring himself a whisky when he heard the sound from behind—the sudden creak of a floorboard muffled by thick carpet. His body tensed and his hand moved to the gun at his waist, but he didn't turn around. He stood motionless, seeming to study the lithograph hanging over the bar. Then he relaxed and reached for another glass.

"Not as light on your feet as you once were," he said, without turning around.

A man came up behind him. "How did you know it was me?"

"Not as observant either," Owen replied. He gave a nod to the lithograph, neatly framed under glass, reflecting back two faces. Then he turned to look at the man—at the faded jeans, the old cap, the day's growth of beard. He raised his glass. "To my old friend, Graham," he said. He tasted the whisky, then asked, "What can I get for you?"

Graham asked for the same and they settled themselves in the living room, where heavy drapes closed out the bleak day. Owen stared at Graham across the table between them. "So," he said, "you want me to kidnap President Easton's daughter. Why?"

"I thought you might ask." Graham picked up his drink but didn't taste it. Anger flashed in his eyes. "I can't tell you everything," he said. "I'm not authorized to."

"You're not authorized to? Or is it that you don't trust me to know?" Graham shrugged. "My loyalties have never been suspect."

"You're right, you've never betrayed us—but that's not the point. You'll do it because it's impossible."

Owen raised his glass. "And you'll trust me to do it because no one else is sufficiently foolish to try—or brash enough to succeed." It was not a boast, but a statement of fact. Owen smiled when Graham failed to reply. "What *can* you tell me?" he said.

Graham got up and began to pace the room. His face was troubled, his eyes still angry. "We have a security leak," he began. "Someone inside our agency passing classified data to the Soviet Union. Someone high level. *Very* high level."

Owen nodded, but didn't comment. This was not startling news. It happened from time to time in the CIA.

"In the beginning," Graham said, "we had four suspects. We set up tests for each of them, and they all passed. None of them is the leak. That meant we had to look to someone we'd not considered in the beginning because of his position. It was unthinkable! He's a man with instant access to the Oval Office—second only to the President himself!"

Owen didn't move. He stared at Graham, his expression hovering somewhere between amusement and disbelief.

"You're joking!"

Graham shook his head.

The amusement faded. *"Ed Nichols?"*

"Ed Nichols," Graham confirmed. Ed Nichols was the director of the CIA.

Owen leaned back in his chair. No wonder the double red! No wonder Graham was upset! The man they all worked for. And Ed Nichols was a lot more than that. He was the President's campaign strategist! His chief policy adviser. His hatchet man.

More, even, than that. He was the President's best friend.

"Touchy," Owen said.

"Touchy! It's dynamite! The President, of course, will require absolute proof. He's not going to take my word for this. Or yours. And that brings us back to his daughter."

Now Owen saw the connection. The trap baited with an irresistible lure.

"Yes," Graham confirmed, "the kidnapping is Nichols' test.

Anne Easton ostensibly in enemy hands. Nichols will have to find her." The hint of a smile appeared in Graham's eyes. "We'll give him leads to work on. Our own leads. They will all prove abortive. Confusing. Even disastrous. We must force him into a corner of desperation. We must force him to act."

"To contact the other side." Owen nodded slowly. "It's audacious," he said, "and it's also extremely dangerous."

"Precisely. It must be audacious. With his own daughter missing, the President will insist on exact information, as it develops, straight from Nichols himself. Furthermore, he'll accept no excuses. He'll permit no mistakes. He will require nothing less than total success. When failure occurs, as it will, everything Nichols values will be at stake. His relationship with the President. His job. His power. He will have just one choice left. His friends behind the curtain. He'll have to go to them for help."

Owen nodded. An excellent plan. And for him, the ultimate challenge. A greater risk than he had ever known. Graham was right. If he kidnapped Anne Easton, it would be for one reason. Because it couldn't be done, he would do it.

He drank his whisky, his mind already shifting from motives to operations. *How* was always of greater interest than *why*. "It will have to be done my way," he said.

"Naturally," Graham replied. "If I knew how to do it myself, I wouldn't need you."

"And without any harm to the girl."

"That goes without saying. Anne Easton must never be in any real danger. The same goes for the people around her. Family, servants, staff, Secret Service. None of them can be hurt."

Owen smiled. "You mean, don't kill off the President in the process."

"I'd rather you didn't."

Graham hardly needed to say so. The killing of innocents, Owen believed, was too often the easy way out. An intelligent person could find a different solution. Killing became an option only when the victim had forfeited innocence by choice.

"I do have one requirement," Graham said. "Once you have her, you must move her out of the country."

Owen looked incredulous. He was thinking about the White

House, its electronic security systems, its special police. Somehow he had to break through all that to kidnap the President's daughter. Then he had to sneak her across a well-guarded US border! "Don't make it too easy for me," he said. "I might get bored."

Graham smiled. "I know it's a tough order. But this thing has to look international. Otherwise, Nichols will have no reason to believe that Russians could help him."

Owen nodded.

"Take her wherever you want," Graham said, "as long as it's in Greece. I have people there I trust, in case you need help."

"All right, so I take her to Greece. Then what do I do?"

"You wait until you receive my signal, at which time we'll meet, you'll turn the girl over to me, and I'll take her home. In the meantime, you do nothing—just keep her out of sight. It will be at least two weeks, maybe more."

Two weeks! Simon wasn't kidding about Mary Poppins.

"What about the false leads?" Owen asked.

"Simon will handle those. As soon as he gets here, we can go over what you will need. Simon will be your contact with me, by the way. After I leave here today, I don't want to see you again until it's time to bring Sunflower home."

"You make me feel unloved."

"Yes, well, don't forget, you're supposed to be dead."

"It's not something I'm likely to forget," Owen replied. "I'm only sorry I didn't go to the funeral."

Graham smiled. "It was a quiet affair. Hardly anyone there."

"Pity."

The doorbell rang and Graham looked up. "That should be Simon now. Let him in, will you?"

Owen crossed over to the door and looked through the peephole. It was Simon, still wearing the plaid jacket he'd had on in the cab, and carrying a black attaché case. Owen let him in.

"How's the apartment?" Simon asked once he was inside.

He was tall and thin but powerfully built, and Owen could see a scar jagging down to his eye from his left temple.

"Comfortable," Owen replied.

Simon nodded. "We tried to accommodate all your needs," he

added, noticing the drink in Owen's hand. He dropped the attaché case on the floor beside a chair and sat down.

Graham was looking at Owen. "You can have whatever you want," he said. "Carte blanche. You have unlimited credit in terms of resources—personnel, false papers, technical services . . ."

"Money?" Owen asked.

"As much as you need."

"Thirty thousand dollars in cash."

"No more?"

"That's pin money," Owen said. "I'll let you know later how much more it will cost. Meantime, thirty thousand in a package compact enough to carry in a money belt."

Graham nodded to Simon. It would be done.

"I'll need a lot more than money," Owen said.

Simon pulled the black case up onto his lap. "This should be a good start," he said. "Our files on Anne Easton. Everything we know about her from the time she gets up in the morning until bedtime at night. Also a lot of material on security." He looked up at Owen. "Six Secret Service agents on permanent assignment. More as needed. They work in shifts. It's all there."

Owen took the files. "Now," he said, "let me tell you what else I want. The girl isn't my problem. It's the people around her. Those are the files I need. And I must have advance schedules for everyone in the family. Daily."

Graham glanced at Simon. "You'll have them."

"I also want a tap into the White House mail as far back as you can go without arousing suspicion."

Graham's forehead creased into a puzzled frown. "Why?"

Owen shrugged. "I don't know. If I did, I could tell you exactly what to bring me. Since I don't, I need it all."

"Can't you be more specific than that?" Graham asked. "The White House gets seventy-five thousand letters a week!"

"Then eliminate the fan mail and the hate mail, the photo requests, and letters on the issues. Bring me everything else."

Graham nodded to Simon.

"And I'll need to know how big Anne is. Her exact height. Her exact weight."

"Anything else?" Graham asked.

"Yes, one other thing. And it's critical."

Owen was thinking about the risk. Not the risk of his life; he faced that every day. But there was something Owen feared more than death—the loss of his personal freedom. And he didn't care to guess the years he would spend in jail if he were caught with the President's daughter.

Normally, the CIA gave him sanction to break the law. There were no threats of disavowal. On the contrary, he could count on extraordinary measures to prevent official action against anything he did on assignment. But this went far beyond the usual realm of the CIA. And the sanction, obviously, didn't come from Nichols.

He looked at Graham and said, "Who authorized this?"

Graham shook his head. "I can't tell you that."

Owen shrugged. "Then I must refuse the assignment. I won't take the risk, not on your say alone."

There was a long moment of silence. Finally, it was Graham who spoke. "I suppose you deserve to know what kind of protection you've got. And you've got it. The highest possible protection. From the President."

The President! Owen was stunned to silence. Whatever he had expected, it wasn't this!

"The *President?*" he said at last. "The President has agreed to have his *own daughter kidnapped? By the CIA?*"

"The President," Graham said, "understands what's at stake."

"I daresay he does!" Owen leaned back and took a drink of his whisky. Anne Easton, he thought, was about to learn an extremely valuable lesson. Trust no one.

"Well?" Graham said. "Will you do it?"

"Of course I will," Owen replied.

Chapter Four

Elizabeth Easton dropped her paintbrush into a jar of turpentine and stepped back from the canvas to study her daughter's face from a different angle. It wasn't quite right yet. She hadn't caught the smile that was uniquely Anne's.

She picked up a rag and started dabbing at the paint spots on her fingers, reminding herself that she'd never claimed to be a portrait painter. Her professional work ran mostly to landscapes and still lifes, which usually sold well. But she didn't intend to sell this portrait of her daughter. She was doing it as a gift for her husband to hang in his White House study.

Suddenly, she realized how quickly the light was fading. It was five o'clock. She pulled off her smock and headed for the bedroom she shared with the President of the United States.

An hour later she emerged, fresh from a hot bath and dressed for a state dinner. Short dark curls framed her face. Brown eyes, full of life, set wide over good cheekbones. Fair skin, and a smile that lit up her face with happiness.

She was happy here in the White House—with Matt, with Anne, with her work. Never mind what some people said she neglected! The White House was Matt's work, not hers. With little more than an hour before the official guests arrived, Elizabeth didn't know what was on the menu tonight. She didn't care who was sitting with whom. The social secretary was perfectly able to handle all that. She would attend the dinner and she would enjoy it—but for now she had better things to do.

She made her way down the hall to Anne's room and slipped quietly inside. Time with her daughter, plenty of time. That was a must every day.

Mrs. Haskins, the governess, looked up and smiled. So did Anne. Elizabeth saw the round little face surrounded by dark curls, a face so much like her own. Anne was delicate, petite, vulnerable. A sudden shiver of fear spread coldly down Elizabeth's back.

Dear God, she thought. She would die if anything ever happened to Anne!

"Do you take much interest in your husband's work, Mrs. Nichols?" the senator asked.

Vanessa smiled and glanced across the State Dining Room to the table where her husband was sitting between the Yugoslavian ambassador's wife and a famous columnist.

"Yes, of course," she replied. "But beyond generalities, I don't really know what he does."

It struck her once again that Ed didn't look like a CIA

34

director. Whatever that meant. Gray and distinguished? Small and furtive? Ed Nichols was neither.

He was a big, slightly awkward man with the candid face of a country lawyer; his eyes were bright behind loose-fitting bifocals in wire frames so old they had come back into style. It was a face quick to smile, suggesting a man for whom guile and cunning were as alien as foreign intrigue.

Vanessa smiled. She knew just how deep the apparent innocence ran. Guile and cunning were the staff of her husband's life long before he took over the CIA reins. Ever since Matt's first campaign a hundred lifetimes ago. For as long as she'd known him.

"But surely your husband shares some of his secrets with you," the senator persisted.

Vanessa looked at him. "May I ask you something? Why do you insist upon talking about my husband's work?"

The senator didn't reply. Someone drew his attention away. Vanessa glanced at the head table, in its usual place under the Lincoln portrait. Elizabeth was chatting easily with the Yugoslavian president, probably in Serbo-Croatian. Elizabeth, stunning as always, and so good at these things. And Matt, dark and slender, a naturally elegant man who wore the power of the White House as easily as he wore the well-cut formal clothes.

Vanessa felt a warm surge of affection. Grace and style were part of the Eastons' appeal; and yet she knew their life was seldom as easy as they made it seem.

As she watched, Matt's eyes scanned the crowd, stopped to look at someone at a table not far away. An expression passed over his face fleetingly—a dropping away of the public mask, a brief glimpse of the private man inside. Then he picked up his wineglass and turned, smiling, back to the guest of honor.

Vanessa frowned. She wasn't sure what it was she had seen in that moment. Was it anger? Suspicion? Hurt? But she did think she knew who the target had been.

Unless she was mistaken, Matt had been looking at *Ed.*

AT EIGHT O'CLOCK that same evening, Sam Wycoff, the head of the Secret Service, was working late in his office, approving the security plans for the President's Mexican trip.

The trip was routine, but the security plans were not. Two US businessmen had been kidnapped by terrorists in Mexico last year, and an embassy official had barely escaped the same fate. Wycoff, whose main concern was protecting the President, had recommended canceling the trip. But the State Department, whose concerns were broader than that, wouldn't have it.

Neither would the President, who didn't worry much about personal threats. He had sided with State. He was going. And it was Wycoff's job to make sure he came back.

Then Wycoff initialed another plan, assigning two special agents to the six who made up Anne Easton's Secret Service detail. Finally, he returned to the more pressing problems of the President's trip.

At the same time, in New York City, Richard Owen picked up a new batch of mail Simon had sent him. There were hundreds of letters, all addressed to, or written from, the White House.

Owen scanned them, discarding quickly. At last, one caught his attention. He read it again, and the others attached to it. Then he reached for a clipping he had torn from the Washington *Post* and matched one date with the others. It was perfect.

He would need more—dossiers for background, photographs for the face, movie film for the mannerisms, tape recordings for the voice. But those were easily had. The important thing was the set-up. The opportunity. The timing.

Owen smiled. He knew now how he was going to kidnap the President's daughter. He moved across the room to the stereo, selected an album and put it on to play. A Vivaldi violin concerto performed by the master Franz Heinemann. The music came to life—bold, dynamic, uplifting.

He also knew how he would smuggle her out of the country.

THE CAR was a plain black sedan with government plates. Owen parked it and made his way through the crowd to Pier 92, where the lights of the *QE2* brightened the night sky like a giant Yule log ablaze in its hearthside berth. Outside, the air was cool and damp, a wet spring night in New York. Inside the pier building, it was not just damp but chilling.

Owen pulled up his collar and took up a post outside the customs area. He was wearing a blue suit under a dark raincoat, his expression noncommittal, his manner and appearance designed to match the car outside. Standard government issue.

The passengers were disembarking. Owen studied them, looking for the one face that was etched into his memory by a few hundred feet of film. His mind scanned the man's dossier: Edward Drake. Born, Manchester, England, thirty-six years ago. Height, six feet. Weight, one eighty. Hair, black; eyes, brown. Occupation, photographer. Physically not unlike Owen himself. But Drake was also a gentle man, an artist, an unsuspecting man.

A camera bag was slung over his shoulder as he came off the ship, suitcase in hand. Owen headed him off.

"Mr. Drake? Mr. Edward Drake?"

Drake turned, surprised. "Why, yes—"

"Frank Jackson, US Secret Service." Owen flashed an ID.

Drake glanced at the card. "Is something wrong?"

"Nothing's wrong," Owen assured him. "But we need some more information before we can give you a clearance for Indian Springs. I have a car. If you're willing to answer some questions along the way, I'll drop you at your hotel."

"Be glad to," Drake replied as he fell into step with Owen. "I've booked a room at the Algonquin," he added when they were settled in the front seat of the car. "Is it far from here?"

"The Algonquin? Normally, no—but there's a big fire on Sixth Avenue. The streets over there are jammed. I'm afraid we'll have to go a rather long way around."

It was sufficient excuse for a circuitous route. Owen pulled out into the traffic. "We're interested in the period from 1967 to 1969," he began. "You weren't in England those years."

"No, I was in Australia."

"Doing what?"

"Mostly bumming around. Taking pictures, of course."

Owen listened enough to interject the appropriate questions. He knew the answers already. He was only interested in filling the time until he arrived at his destination.

Another fifteen minutes brought them to lower Manhattan, where the streets twisted into a maze that would disorient anyone but the most seasoned New Yorker. Owen turned left on Canal

Street. "I think that's enough," he said as Drake finished detailing his years in Australia. "We'll have to confirm it, but there shouldn't be any problems. Final clearance will come from Washington."

Drake nodded.

"We're getting into an interesting part of the city, by the way," Owen added. He made a right turn into a wide avenue lined with seedy bars and rooming houses. Derelicts shuffled along the sidewalk, the lucky ones clutching brown-bagged bottles. Others lay sprawled like dead men in the gutter. "The Bowery," Owen said.

Drake made no comment. All tourist now, he stared wide-eyed at the world's most famous skid row.

Owen turned right again. The street darkened dramatically. On the left, an abandoned warehouse. On the right, a row of shops closed and barred for the night. Straight ahead, tenement buildings with shades drawn, black silhouettes backlighted by the illuminated city beyond. Owen spotted the van parked at the curb.

"I hope we're not getting close to the hotel," Drake said. "This looks like a rough neighbourhood."

"It is," Owen replied. "We're nowhere near the Algonquin."

Drake turned to him sharply. There was no fear in his face. He was puzzled, confused. "Where are we? I thought we were—" He left the thought unfinished as the car pulled in behind the van.

Owen turned off the motor and looked at Drake, at the eyes that recognized an indefinable danger. Now the fear was plain.

"God, no! Let me out of here!" Drake swung around, groping blindly for the door handle. Owen raised his arm and brought his hand down hard against the Englishman's neck. Drake froze against the car door, and a sound escaped from his throat, a deep cry muted by rushing air. Then his eyes closed and his body slumped over sideways, hitting the dashboard hard.

He wasn't dead, just unconscious. Owen had no intention of killing Edward Drake.

Simon climbed down from the back of the van as Owen got out of the car. Simon was wearing two days' growth of beard and a thrift-shop suit that was shiny and shapeless from many years of wear. The two men said nothing, but quickly lifted Drake into the rear of the van. Simon sealed the door and switched on a light as Owen began to change clothes.

38

Then Owen turned to a black metal box from which he took a mirror, a comb, a towel, a bottle of black hair rinse, a pair of silicone pads to flesh out his cheeks, and a replacement for the photo page in Drake's passport. On it was a picture of a man who looked not quite like Edward Drake, but not like Richard Owen either.

Before long, Owen had become that man. He looked at himself in the mirror and smiled. He would have no trouble passing for Edward Drake.

Five minutes later Simon watched Owen drive away. Then he turned back to Drake, still unconscious on the floor. Just sit on him until the danger is over, Owen had said. And when would that be? Simon wondered.

Owen might not worry about being identified by Drake. But Simon didn't share Owen's confidence—or his mastery of disguise. Nor did he share Owen's weakness for the innocents of the world.

Simon moved quickly. He propped Drake against a wall of the van and brought out a bottle of whisky. He forced open the mouth, held the bottle to the lips. Then he pressed a knuckle against the throat, activating a natural reflex. Drake swallowed. The whisky began to go down in sips. Next, Simon pulled off Drake's suit, his shirt and tie, his shoes and socks, and replaced them with a suit of clothes like his own. Salvation Army rejects.

Simon turned and picked up a plastic syringe. There was nothing in it but air. The needle was finely ground steel, honed to a sharp point; it would leave no bruise. He inserted it carefully into Drake's arm, and released the bubble that would travel through the blood and into the heart. A tiny bullet of air.

By the time Owen was halfway to the Algonquin, Simon and Drake were slumped in a dark corner of the Bowery, staring at the passing world with sightless eyes, like so many others before them. Later Simon got up and walked away, leaving behind the nameless shape of a man—another drunk for the city morgue.

Edward Drake was dead. Irrevocably, untraceably dead.

THE DESK CLERK at the Algonquin Hotel accepted Drake's passport without question. Upstairs in his room, Owen locked the door and reread the files on the man he had become.

He had the dossiers, the photos, the FBI report, and the Secret

Service clearance which had been processed and signed three days before. And the letters, culled from hundreds of thousands, through which Owen had discovered Drake.

Dear Mrs. Haskins,

We've never met, but I am Rowena Drake's oldest son, and I have spent many hours listening to Mother's stories about her school days, and you. She insists I write to you now that I'm planning a trip to the United States.

I'll be arriving 19 April on the *Queen Elizabeth II* at New York City, where I've booked a hotel for two nights. After that, I'd like to come to Washington. I know you're governess to the President's daughter, and naturally I would love to see the White House, but if that's not possible, I'll be happy to meet you elsewhere.

In any case, please let me hear from you. I'm anxious to meet you. Mother sends her love.

Sincerely, Edward Drake

Mrs. Haskins' reply followed on a few days later:

Dear Edward,

Rowena's son! She's mentioned you so often in her letters, I feel as if I know you. Of course I would love to see you.

Unfortunately, I won't be in Washington during your visit. President and Mrs. Easton are going on a trip to Mexico, and I'm taking Anne to visit her aunt and uncle at their summer home on Lake Michigan, at Indian Springs. Is there any chance you might come to Michigan? I've asked Mrs. Wainwright, Anne's aunt, if she would object to your staying a night or two, and she says it's fine. I've also given your name to the Secret Service. I hope you don't mind—it's necessary, of course—and I assume you have no black secrets in your past to prevent immediate clearance.

Let me know if you can come.

Sincerely, Emily Haskins

There was an affirmative reply from Drake. Owen was satisfied; he knew everything he would have to know when he got to Indian Springs. But for now, two days in New York, he would do exactly what Drake would have done. He decided to start with the Statue of Liberty.

MARINE ONE appeared over the Washington Monument, blunt nose tilted slightly skyward as it moved in on the south lawn of the White House.

Clusters of people gathered against the black iron fence, unaware that the helicopter's landing pad was positioned to block their view of the President when he left the White House. Traffic was halted all the way back to E Street. No one could move until after the helicopter had taken off again. Its destination: Andrews Air Force Base, where *Air Force One* was fueled up for the flight to Mexico City.

Inside the White House grounds, press and staff assembled as the helicopter came to rest perfectly on target. Military aides opened the hatch and locked the steps in place. Two key staff men appeared through a break in the West Wing hedge, all busyness as they trotted across the lawn and climbed aboard.

Next, the First Lady emerged from the canopied Diplomatic Entrance. She smiled and waved for the cameras, then turned back to her daughter, who was standing with Mrs. Haskins. A few words, a quick hug, and Elizabeth Easton boarded the helicopter.

Finally, the President appeared to a round of applause. He flashed a smile, then reached down to gather the tiny Anne up in his arms. Cameras clicked.

The President's smile faded as he looked at his daughter's face for a moment. Then he glanced at Mrs. Haskins. "Take good care of her," he said.

The governess nodded. "I always do." Everyone in the White House knew how deeply attached the President was to his four-year-old daughter.

The President's eyes shifted back to Anne. "Behave yourself."

She nodded solemnly, smiled, gave him a hug and a kiss.

The President hugged her, too. Then he put her down and headed for the helicopter.

AS *MARINE ONE* LIFTED off its landing pad Inspector Martin Schweitzer, head of the Homicide Division for Manhattan South, was looking at the officer on the other side of his desk.

"Why should I care about another John Doe who killed himself on booze?" Schweitzer demanded.

"Because," the officer said, "there's something funny about this one. When was the last time you heard of a Bowery drunk wearing undershorts from a swank Regent Street men's shop?"

"Regent Street! Where's that? Brooklyn?"

"Regent Street. London. England! Listen, Inspector, this guy was dressed like he hadn't seen soap for six months. And yet there they were, underneath all that filth, a pair of clean undershorts. From London."

Schweitzer stared thoughtfully at the other man. "Interesting," he said. "I think we'll order an autopsy. And let's check his prints with Scotland Yard. I'd like to know who this John Doe really was."

Chapter Five

The Wainwright house was an authentic Victorian structure, of mismatched parts, full of gingerbread and turret rooms. It sat on the slope of a hill overlooking Lake Michigan and was enclosed by an iron fence running all the way down to the white sand beach below.

There were two points of access to the property—the beach and the front gate. With the President's daughter in residence, both were guarded around the clock by the US Secret Service.

It was Wednesday morning, two days since Owen had assumed Edward Drake's role. He stopped his car at the front gate and rolled down the window as a man came forward from the gatehouse.

A big man, in an ordinary business suit, with a small lapel pin painted red and white. There was no bulge under his arm, but Owen knew he was wearing a shoulder holster and a transmitter clipped to his belt.

"Good morning," Owen said. Another man, he noticed, watched them through a large glass window inside the gatehouse.

"May I help you?" the agent said.

"I'm Edward Drake."

The agent leaned forward, his eyes probing deeper into the car. "Yes, Mr. Drake. May I see your identification?"

Owen handed Drake's passport through the window. The agent

glanced at it, then said, "Just a moment, please," and walked back to the gatehouse. The agent there picked up a telephone.

This was a vulnerable spot, the primary point of acceptance, and Owen was unarmed. He didn't dare risk being caught with a gun.

The man on the phone finished his conversation, and now the first agent was coming forward again.

"Everything seems to be in order, Mr. Drake," the agent said as he handed the passport back, "but I'll have to take a look at your luggage."

"Certainly." Owen got out of the car and opened the trunk. The agent unzipped the suitcase and ran a practiced hand through its contents, then turned to the camera bag. He advanced the film on the cameras, one at a time. Finally, his hand came to rest on a bulky, paper-wrapped package in the back of the trunk.

"What's this?"

"A present for the President's daughter."

The agent pulled the package forward. "Good thing you didn't pay for gift wrapping," he said. "You'll have to leave it with us, I'm afraid. Procedure. We examine all gifts."

Owen shrugged. "Whatever you say."

The agent carried the package across to the gatehouse. Then he turned back to Owen. "You can go in now," he said. "They're expecting you."

INSPECTOR SCHWEITZER read through both reports and tossed them back on his desk.

The first came from Scotland Yard. John Doe was a British national, all right—a professional photographer by the name of Edward Drake—and his fingerprints were on file because he'd served in the RAF. He had no criminal record.

The second was the autopsy report. No evidence of death by unnatural causes. On the other hand, no evidence of heart attack or stroke. And while the alcohol level in the blood was well past the point of intoxication, there was no indication of anything that normally accompanied a pattern of heavy drinking.

The autopsy reached just one conclusion, in fact: a thirty-six-year-old man was dead, and the medical examiner couldn't say why. Or how. That alone was evidence.

Schweitzer knew who John Doe was; now he wanted more. He opened a drawer and pulled out a government form—a request for information from the FBI computer bank in Washington.

A HOUSEKEEPER MET Owen at the door and showed him to his room upstairs. She was a small woman with a pleasant face and a steady line of chatter. Mrs. Haskins would be pleased to know Mr. Drake had arrived. She was busy with Anne now, but would come as soon as she could get free. Anne slept from one to three most days. That part of the day and after seven—when Anne was in bed for the night—were about all the time Mrs. Haskins had to herself. Such a nice woman, Mrs. Haskins, and a fine lady.

Owen agreed.

"Ring if you need anything," the housekeeper added at the door. "And while you're waiting, feel free to wander wherever you like. It's a nice walk down to the beach."

"Thank you, I may do that."

Alone, Owen moved across to the window, which looked down over the lawn toward the lake. The housekeeper had confirmed two important pieces of information for him. First, the time Anne went to bed at night—seven o'clock. Second, that he was free to move about the premises at will, to see for himself what he had previously seen only on paper—the lay of the house and the land, and the position of each of the guards.

He turned back to the room and began to unpack his clothes. He didn't want one of the servants to examine the suitcase too closely. Not that a servant was likely to detect a secret that had already passed muster with the professional agent outside.

The suitcase had a second bottom that concealed a large, flat brown paper bag. Undetectable and not easily opened, the layer would require a knife to break the stitches.

Inside the brown paper bag was the one thing he had to have if his plan was going to work. It wasn't a gun, or any kind of weapon. On the other hand, neither was it a toy.

THE FBI REPORTS came back to Inspector Schweitzer: they'd never heard of Edward Drake until just three weeks ago, when the Secret Service ordered a security investigation on him. Drake had passed; the FBI had reported as much to the Secret Service.

The Secret Service? Schweitzer lit a cigarette. Where did channels begin with them?

OWEN'S GIFT was a great success.

It was waiting in his room after dinner the day he arrived, and he gave it to Anne the next morning. Her eyes widened with astonished delight as Owen tore the paper away. "A panda! He's bigger than I am!" she cried. She pounced on it with unrestrained glee, and Owen knew that whatever affection he hadn't earned for being Mrs. Haskins' friend, he'd obviously earned now.

He sat back to watch, smiling with pleasure and shrugging off Mrs. Haskins' objections to such a generous gift. "I saw it in the window at F.A.O. Schwarz and couldn't resist," he said.

Mrs. Haskins objected no more. "It was so thoughtful of you."

"My pleasure. Look, Anne, the arms move." Owen bent over to show her how they worked.

Anne flashed her dimpled smile and attacked the panda with new enthusiasm, bending the arms forward and backward. Owen turned to Mrs. Haskins. "Do you suppose you'll ever come home to England?" he asked casually.

"Probably not." The old woman's eyes shifted to the child. "I'm so attached to Anne now, you know. She's—"

A cry of alarm suddenly rose from Anne.

Across the room, a Secret Service man looked up sharply, then, assessing no danger, returned to his paperback book.

Anne, near tears, was holding one fuzzy black arm in her hand and staring unhappily at the panda. White stuffing protruded from a hole where the arm had been.

"Look at that, will you?" Owen said. "The arm's come off!" He got down on the floor beside Anne. "There's a good girl. Let me see." Owen studied the arm a moment. "Whatever this was attached to, it's gone now," he said. He tested the other arm, which came loose at his touch.

Anne was inconsolable.

"I promise we'll have him fixed," Owen assured her. Then he turned to Mrs. Haskins. "Fixed, my eye!" he added. "I'm taking it back. They can jolly well send her a new one."

Later the same day, when Owen knew Mrs. Haskins was outside with Anne, he brought the suitcase out of his closet, ran a knife around the false bottom, and removed the brown paper bag. Then he left the room and moved quietly down the hall.

Mrs. Haskins' room was adjacent to Anne's, with a connecting door. Owen stepped through the hallway door and crossed over to Mrs. Haskins' dresser, which he pulled out from the wall. He produced a roll of strapping tape from his pocket and fastened the paper bag to the back of the dresser. Then he shoved the dresser back and opened the door to Anne's room.

The armless panda was sitting on the floor at the foot of her bed, like a fat little Venus de Milo. Owen nodded it farewell and closed the door, then headed back downstairs.

AT THE Secret Service headquarters in Washington, Ken Russell found a message to phone an Inspector Schweitzer of the New York City police. Important, it said. Russell reached for the phone.

Then he glanced at his watch. His meeting with the deputy director was important, too. Schweitzer would have to wait.

OWEN spent two days inside the Wainwright house. He talked politics with Anne's uncle and theater with her aunt. He talked family with Mrs. Haskins. With Anne he took pictures. He was a charming and thoughtful guest. By the end of the second day, everyone in the house was sorry to see him go.

Anne's aunt and Mrs. Haskins were waiting for him in the front room when he came downstairs with his bags at eight o'clock. Mrs. Wainwright extended her hand. "It's been a pleasure to have you," she said. "I hope you'll come back."

Owen shook her hand. "I'd like that." Then he gave Mrs. Haskins a kiss on the cheek. "I can't wait to tell Mother all about our visit."

The governess smiled up at him. "Give her my love, Edward, and tell her to come with you next time."

"I will." He picked up his bags, then he turned abruptly, remembering. "I almost forgot the panda!"

"Oh, Edward, don't bother—"

"No bother," he replied. "We can't have Anne disappointed." He dropped his bags and turned to the stairs.

Anne was asleep as Owen entered the room. He closed the door and crossed the floor to the bed, pulling a fountain pen from his jacket as he went. He removed the cap and the writing point and pressed the pen against Anne's arm.

The pen concealed a tiny cartridge that worked like a hypodermic syringe. Sodium pentothal. The dose geared to Anne's precise age and weight. The effect immediate.

Anne's arm jerked at the sharp prick of the needle, but Owen held it firm. Her eyes opened, then instantly closed again as her brain dropped to a shallow level of unconsciousness.

Now Owen retrieved the brown paper bag from Mrs. Haskins' dresser. Inside lay a panda, armless, a replica of the other except for two features. This one had a long zipper opening, hidden deep in the plush. And this one was flat, unstuffed, with a balloon-like inner lining that was set to expand with pressure. It also had air holes punched into its plastic nose.

Owen spread the panda out on the floor and lifted Anne in, feet-first. Behind him, the door opened.

"Edward, I—"

Mrs. Haskins stopped where she was, eyes puzzled. Then her mouth dropped open and her eyes widened in horror.

"*Edward!*"

Owen leaped to his feet before the scream could emerge. He clamped a hand harshly over her mouth as he grabbed her around the waist. She fought against him vainly. Owen's thumb found the pressure point just below her jawline. Still she glared back at him, her face contorted with rage. Then, slowly, her eyes went dull, the muscles of her face relaxed. She felt no pain as her body sagged, deadweight in his arms.

IT WAS SEVEN THIRTY before Secret Service Agent Russell heard what Inspector Schweitzer had to say.

"You're right," he said when Schweitzer was finished. "It could be important. I don't know why we ran a security check on Drake, but I'll find out. Thanks a lot."

Russell called Records Division, gave Drake's name, and waited until the information came back. Edward Drake was a friend of Emily Haskins'. He'd been given clearance to Indian Springs.

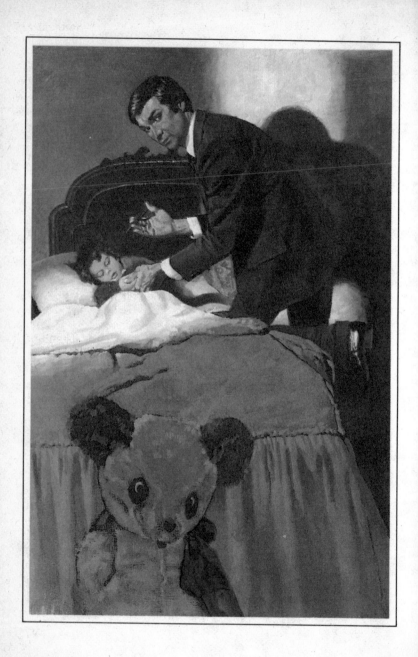

And the President's daughter was there.

Russell punched out another number, urgently now. "We've got a problem," he said to the chief of the Protection Service, quickly explaining what he'd learned about Edward Drake.

"But that's not possible," the other man replied. "Edward Drake isn't dead. He arrived at Indian Springs yesterday morning."

Then his eyes widened as the obvious became clear, and he grabbed up the direct line to Michigan.

ANNE'S AUNT was still in the front room, talking to one of the Secret Service agents, as Owen came back down the stairs, holding the panda. He stopped in the doorway.

"I'm afraid I awakened Anne," he said, "but Mrs. Haskins is with her."

Mrs. Wainwright smiled. "She's so good with Anne."

"Yes, she is, isn't she. Well, I must get on." With his free hand Owen slung the camera bag over his shoulder.

The agent moved toward him. "Let me help you."

Owen smiled. "Thanks, but I can manage. You might get the door, if you would." He picked up the suitcase. "Thank you again, Mrs. Wainwright," he added.

"We enjoyed having you. Good-by now."

Owen's car was waiting outside. He dropped his bags in the trunk and pushed the panda onto the back seat. Then, with a final wave, he got in and drove out through the gate.

Minutes later a phone rang in the guest cottage behind the Wainwright house, where the Secret Service maintained their operations center. It was the direct line from Washington. The agent in charge picked it up, listened a moment, then raced to the house.

"Where's Drake?" he demanded, bursting through the front door.

Mrs. Wainwright looked up, startled. "Why, he just left. Is something wrong?"

The agent brushed past her to the stairs, taking them two at a time. He pushed open the door to Anne's room and stopped suddenly, feeling a moment's relief as he saw the form of her small body under the bedcovers. Then a new fear gripped him when he approached the bed and realized there was no movement. Anne wasn't breathing.

Yanking back the covers, he recognized a truth more horrible than anything he'd confronted before. It wasn't Anne, but the panda! The President's daughter was gone!

THE IMPOSTER had a ten-minute head start, but a Secret Service car with four agents roared powerfully in the direction he had taken, along the only road that gave access to the Wainwright house. Six miles ahead lay Indian Springs and the first intersection offering a choice of route, but roadblocks were already being set up to stop all traffic. The man couldn't get away.

Then one of the agents gave a shout and pointed toward the sky, where a small airplane was just clearing the trees—a Piper Cherokee, dark against a dark sky.

The agent behind the wheel slammed on the brakes and the other three jumped out. In a moment, they were back. The imposter's car was there, all right, abandoned in the meadow from which the plane had taken off. One agent grabbed the radio and was already issuing orders to track the plane as the driver swung into a U-turn and headed back to the house.

From the trees by the side of the road, Owen watched the Secret Service car turn around. The crew at the house were on his tail; that was clear. But the ruse of the plane had worked. Now it was time to activate the plan for his own escape.

He switched on the radio transmitter left for him in the woods and spoke into it. "This is Sunflower. Make the phone call now."

Somewhere in the distance, a man—placed there by Simon—received the message. "Roger, Sunflower."

Owen then moved away through the trees, the panda under his arm. Half a mile back toward the Wainwright house, he found the car. And in it, a change of identity.

THE HOUSEKEEPER sat rubbing Mrs. Haskins' hands. They had found her in her own room, on the bed, unconscious. She was breathing, alive. She was going to be all right.

FATHER HEALY promised to come at once.

He jumped into his black Dodge Dart and headed north toward Indian Springs. The Wainwrights needed him. Some kind of big trouble out there. Someone sick? Someone dying? The man on the phone hadn't been clear. He rounded a curve in the road. Then, suddenly, he stepped down on the brakes.

A roadblock. Two state police cars, their crisscrossed front beams forming an arc of light that outlined the figures of three state troopers. One of the men came forward.

"Where are you going, Father?"

"To the Wainwright place. I've had a call asking me to come."

"Do you have some identification?"

"Yes, of course," He handed over his driver's license and a clerical identification card.

The policeman examined them closely. "All right, Father, you can go on."

"Thank you," the priest said. "What is this about?"

"Sorry, I can't tell you. But you'll know soon enough."

Half an hour later Owen pulled his car out of the trees and turned south, toward Indian Springs. The car was familiar there, a black Dodge Dart identical to Healy's even to the license plates. The only difference was that Owen's car had a ventilated trunk— with a toy panda inside it.

At the first intersection, he slowed the car to a stop just short of the wide circle of light. Two cars, three cops, all state police. One of the cops came forward. "Oh, it's you again, Father," he said. "How are they doing out there?"

"About as you'd expect," Owen replied sadly. "Any news yet?"

"Not that we've heard, but the Feds don't tell us much."

Owen shook his head grimly. "Well, I'd better be getting home. Good night."

He rolled up the window as he passed between the parked cars. Once he was past a curve and out of view, he pulled off the gray wig and the clerical collar. Then he stepped on the gas, moving fast through the night. He knew when the priest had been summoned to the Wainwright house. But he couldn't control the other man's departure. The real Father Healy might not be far behind.

THE MAN AT THE controls of the Piper Cherokee maintained a steady course, due west. He was somewhere over Wisconsin and bored. A clear sky, little wind, and a simple piece of machinery—

child's play for an old stunt pilot, hardly fair for the five hundred dollars he was going to be paid. On the other hand, for five hundred bucks in one night, he didn't have to ask questions.

THE SAC bomber, diverted from routine patrol duty along the Canadian border, was cruising at ten thousand feet. A small blip on its radar screen showed the Piper Cherokee heading west, five miles ahead and four thousand feet below.

The bomber's US air force pilot glanced at his co-pilot. "He's making no effort to lose us, is he?"

The co-pilot shook his head. Then, suddenly, he sat forward in his seat, staring at the radar screen. "He's gone!"

"Gone?"

"Completely. He couldn't have landed that fast."

"No," the pilot agreed. "At least not as a matter of choice."

THE AGENT in charge picked up the phone in the guest cottage behind the Wainwright house.

"Bad news," said the voice at the other end. "That Piper you had us tracking? It crashed in northern Wisconsin."

The agent gripped the telephone hard as he asked the inevitable question.

"Were there any survivors?"

"Hard to say," the voice replied. "You see, the plane crashed, but there wasn't anyone in it. The pilot must have jumped."

THE SIGN was impressive—KALKASKA AVIATION INCORPORATED: FLIGHT INSTRUCTION, HANGARS, TIE-DOWNS, AIRCRAFT FOR RENT OR LEASE. But the building looked like a temporary barracks, and the boy behind the counter was not yet of drinking age.

He stared at the customer on the other side. No one from these parts. A fancy black dude, probably up from Detroit.

"All we got is a Lear jet," the boy said. "And they cost plenty."

The customer brought out a money clip. "How much?"

The boy's eyes slowly widened as he looked at the size of the bills. Nothing smaller than a fifty! No black man he'd ever met made that kind of dough. No white man, for that matter.

"Just you?" he said.

"And my daughter," the black man replied. "She's asleep outside in the car."

The boy looked up sharply. He'd had a call from the state cops less than an hour ago. Be on the lookout for a man with a little girl. But this dude was making no effort to hide his daughter. And besides, the man the cops wanted was white. The boy relaxed and brought out a form. "Where you going?"

"The northern peninsula. I'll file a plan for Marquette."

The boy nodded. "Okay. If you've got three kinds of identification, including your pilot's ID, I think we can do business."

Twenty minutes later the Lear jet was off the ground, heading north until it was out of sight of the airfield below. Then it banked steeply to the east. Toward Washington, DC.

Chapter Six

 At eight forty-five, Ed Nichols was still at his desk in the massive CIA headquarters building at Langley, Virginia. A buzzer sounded. He flicked on his intercom.

"Excuse me, sir," said Nichols' staff assistant. "The Secret Service director is on the phone. He says it's urgent."

Nichols picked up the phone. "Yes, Sam."

In an instant, his attention was riveted to the words he was hearing, even as his mind rejected them as impossible. He sat frozen in his chair, his astonishment total.

Nichols asked one question. "Does the President know?"

"Yes. He's on his way back from Mexico right now. He wants to see you as soon as he arrives."

"I'll be there," Nichols said. He hung up the phone and sat without moving. The President's daughter *kidnapped?*

By whom? For what? He wasn't sure he really wanted to know.

At three a.m. the next morning, Nichols was sitting in the Oval Office with the President. Matt Easton brought his fist down hard on the desk. "Damn it, Ed!" he said. "The Secret Service had me wrapped in cotton down there. They imagined terrorists under every bed. What went on in Michigan? How did it happen?"

Nichols looked at his friend, a young president, not yet fifty years old. A man who throve on conflict, the tougher the better. But the man Nichols saw at the moment was full of anger, torn between lashing out and concealing intense personal fear.

Deep anguish boiling beneath the surface. Nichols knew it was there. And frustration beyond any political crisis. A man who was used to solving the problems of the world, now—like the father of any kidnapped child—had to rely on others. With all of his power, he could not go find her himself.

And something else, Nichols thought. There was something in Matt's face that caused a flash of memory. A nuance of expression that made him think of a campaign poster pose.

Nichols pulled off his glasses and passed a weary hand across his eyes. "Nobody *let* this happen," he said. "This was no crackpot scheme that might have been prevented with tighter security. The man who did this was a highly skilled professional."

"And the Secret Service?" the President demanded. "They're *not* professionals?"

Nichols sighed heavily. "I'm not talking about trained bodyguards. I'm talking about skilled intelligence agents. You can't blame the Secret Service."

"I can blame anyone I feel like blaming!"

The President leaned back in his chair and closed his eyes as the anger began to drain away. "I know," he said quietly. "Placing blame is counterproductive." He opened his eyes again. "Is that what you think, Ed? A foreign intelligence agency?"

Nichols pulled himself up straight. "It had to be someone with a sophisticated understanding of our security systems. The impersonation was flawless, the timing perfect."

The President pushed himself up out of the chair and began to pace the room—to the fireplace, with its carved antique mantel under a portrait of George Washington. Back again, to the broad sweep of windows behind his desk. His hand touched the thick partition of green-tinted bulletproof glass. "Foreign intelligence," he murmured. Then he turned to Nichols. "The Russians?"

Nichols shrugged. "The most and the least obvious."

"The least? How?"

"Because it's a hell of a risk, and they've got a lot to lose if we catch them."

"*If* we catch them? This is *Anne* we're talking about!"

No pose, Nichols decided. This was a man brought face to face with the high cost of power, and feeling guilty about it. "Whoever has her won't kill her," he said with more conviction than he felt.

"How can you be so sure?"

"Because she's not worth a cent dead."

"You can't think they're going to want money!"

Nichols shook his head. "A figure of speech."

The President thrust his hands deep into his pockets. "Well, they're going to want something big—and probably something I won't be able to give them."

Nichols nodded silently to himself. Matt Easton, the father, would do anything to get his daughter back. But Matt Easton, the President, had more than two hundred million people to worry about. If the kidnappers' demands ran contrary to the national interest—and it was hard to think they wouldn't—the responsibilities of father and president would meet on collision course. Both men knew who would die. In a democracy, the majority always rules.

The President moved back to his chair. "We've got to find her and fast," he said, "before they make their demands. That's why you're here. I don't trust anyone as much as I trust you."

Nichols leaned forward. "I'll do what I can, Matt, but you know the law says it's the FBI—"

"Because it's domestic? I don't know that at all. If it's a foreign intelligence agency, you've got authority there. Besides, I'm not talking about the FBI or the CIA. I'm talking about you, Ed. I want *you* to find my daughter."

Years of trust looked at Nichols across the desk. Years of deference looked back. Deference to Matt's needs, to Matt's goals. Years of handling the touchy stuff to keep Matt's political friendships intact, to keep his image pure.

"You'll have the CIA and the FBI," the President went on. "The Secret Service, if you want it. Treasury. Defense. The military. All the resources this government has to offer."

Nichols nodded slowly. He'd expected a major role in the search for Anne. But this? His hands were damp with perspiration. Enormous power. Enormous responsibility. Enormous risk.

And no choice. "I'll do my best," he said.

ELIZABETH EASTON'S press secretary felt sick, but she knew what she had to do. She inserted the paper in the typewriter, and pounded out the statement quickly.

> Anne Easton has been confined to bed with a virus while visiting her aunt and uncle in Indian Springs, Michigan. Doctors describe the virus as mild, but the President's daughter will not return to Washington for at least another week.

The statement would be released routinely from the East Wing tomorrow. The press corps would not give it much attention.

NICHOLS flipped over the last page of the thick report. Then he pressed a button in the brass panel on his desk.

"Tell Fleming I'm ready to see him now."

"Yes, sir."

Paul Fleming was Nichol's deputy director, a small man, thin and agile, with graying brown hair falling loose across his forehead. He was a former field agent who had made it his business to stay in good condition. He was in his forties, but appeared younger, and he was still known in Washington circles as the boy genius who worked in the woods at Langley.

Nichols glanced up as Fleming entered the office. "I've read the speculations, Paul," he said. "They're all right as far as they go. Sit down."

Fleming dropped into a chair. Like Nichols, he looked as if he hadn't slept for a week. "What do you mean, as far as they go?"

Nichols rested a hand on top of the report, two hundred and fifty-odd pages of conjecture and suggestions culled from the CIA's computers. "There's got to be something more immediately productive we can do."

"I don't know what," Fleming replied. "I've got the War Room on red alert, coordinating with the Pentagon and the National Security Council. I've alerted our station chiefs here and abroad. The military is playing bloodhound. We're tracing the leads—the panda, the getaway car, that plane—"

Nichols broke in. "We won't learn a thing from that airplane. The kidnapper was never in it. It was diversionary."

Fleming nodded sympathetically. "I know. It's frustrating. But unless we get a break on one of these things, we're going to be stuck waiting. First move, theirs."

Nichols sighed. "Like a game of chess where we can't see the board. No, Paul, I want action! I want our top field agents freed up from whatever they're doing." He pounded his fist against the report. "Damn! I wish we still had Richard Owen."

"We could certainly use him," Fleming agreed. "There are no others like Owen."

"I've known that every day since he was killed."

Then, abruptly, Nichols dismissed the thought. Wishing for a dead man was only a waste of energy. "You should also keep an eye on that greenhorn who thinks he's running the FBI. He doesn't understand who's got access to the Oval Office around here."

Fleming grinned. "I never deal with the director. I've got my own man at the FBI. He's been playing ball for years."

Nichols smiled back. Count on Fleming to have his own personal lackey, even at the FBI. "Good," he said. He moved across to the windows. Bright lights outlined the parking lot below, but gray light was beginning to show over the treetops.

"Just remember one thing, Paul," he said over his shoulder. "Everyone in Washington's going to want to be the hero on this." He turned. "But I intend to be."

DAWN was breaking as Owen turned east on Virginia Route 123, passing practically in the shadow of CIA's Langley headquarters. But he didn't turn in. Instead, he veered off onto a paved path winding back into the very woods that shielded the CIA.

He had landed the Lear jet routinely at Washington National Airport—a computer salesman arriving in town for a breakfast meeting, getting off the plane with an attaché case and a thick garment bag. No one had paid much attention.

Moving deeper into the trees, Owen spotted the mailbox with its freshly painted yellow sunflower. Simon came out of the house and signaled Owen back to a two-car garage.

"You made good time," Simon said. "How's your passenger?"

"Still sleeping."

Owen unzipped the oversize garment bag—his own design, the

parts custom built separately by Technical Services at Langley and assembled later by Owen. It was ordinary brown vinyl on the outside. Inside, it was a minor feat of engineering.

Steel stays held the shape of the bag against excess weight, and were padded to prevent injury to the occupant. The back of the bag was stiffened by a thin sheet of steel. Next to the steel sheet, a solid cushion of foam accommodated Anne. She was strapped to the steel sheet by padded belts around her waist and under her arms. A bar lower down supported the weight of her feet when Owen held the bag upright.

Another cushion lined the front side of the bag. It was made of thick, spongy, plastic mesh developed by NASA as space suit insulation for the Apollo probe. It was through this flexible mesh and vents built into the exterior of the bag that Anne was able to breathe without strain.

She lay there now, surrounded by cushioned comfort, as peaceful as if she were asleep in her own bed. Owen checked her pulse and breath rate and gave her another injection. He had switched to Valium, a tranquilizer that was safer than sodium pentothal for an extended nap. Again, the dosage was just enough to maintain a shallow level of unconsciousness for the period required.

At a gesture from Simon, he crossed over to the vehicle that occupied the other half of the garage.

"A beauty, isn't it?" Simon said.

Owen studied the long black hearse with the words UNITED STATES ARMY painted on its side door. "A good copy," he agreed. He pulled open the rear door and glanced inside.

There was a hole in the floor, coffin-shaped and dropping down maybe twelve inches to a second floor below.

"Where's the insert?" he said.

"Over here." Simon led the way to the front of the garage, to a long, flat box that stood a foot off the ground.

"Have you checked it for fit?" Owen asked.

"It's perfect. But there's one question," Simon said. He gestured back toward the hearse. "Graham wants to know just how you're planning to use this."

Owen smiled. "You tell Graham he'll know soon enough."

The next night, Saturday, a few minutes past six o'clock, Owen strolled into the lobby of the Hay-Adams Hotel, across from the White House. He made his way to the public phones and asked for William Hirsh's room.

Hirsh answered quickly. "Yes?" He was a busy man, the vice-president of Syntax Corporation.

"Mr. Hirsh, my name is Chandler," Owen began. "I'm a protocol officer with the State Department. I'd like to come up if you have a moment."

Hirsh hesitated. Then he said, "All right, but be quick about it. I'm going out soon."

Owen found William Hirsh standing in the open doorway of his room. He was wearing tuxedo pants and a formal shirt, and on his face was a look of mild annoyance.

"What's important enough to bring the State Department out on a Saturday night?" he wanted to know.

"A rather embarrassing problem, I'm afraid," Owen replied. He closed the door behind him, then turned to the other man. "We have received a formal protest from the Austrian government."

"What sort of protest?" Hirsh's voice was indignant.

"Regarding payments to certain Austrian officials. By your corporation."

Hirsh stared at Owen in disbelief. "What nonsense is this? Our relations with the Austrians are excellent."

"That may be, sir, but legal action is already under way."

"Is this a joke, young man?" Hirsh demanded. "Who are you?"

Owen opened his wallet and handed Hirsh a government ID with his picture on it. He was watching Hirsh's face, admiring its control. There was nothing to indicate that Hirsh knew what Owen knew, but Owen knew he did. For years, Syntax Corporation had indeed been bribing Austrian officials for favorable decisions on export quotas and tax matters. Of course, the Austrian government had not yet caught on, but that didn't matter. Knowledge of guilt was enough to make Hirsh cautious.

"In light of this," Owen added, "the Protocol Office feels it would be inappropriate for the corporation to be represented tonight at the White House."

"I see. So I'm to be ostracized on the basis of some vague charge. What charge, Chandler? Who made it?"

Owen shook his head. "I'm sorry. We're operating on a report from a foreign government. I can't tell you more."

Hirsh pulled off his bow tie and flung it across the room. "Get out, Chandler," he said. "I've got some phone calls to make."

Owen nodded and left the room. Let Hirsh try calling the State Department. He would only run into some Saturday night duty officer who would claim, honestly, no knowledge of the affair. And given time to think, Hirsh probably wouldn't try. More likely, he would be on the next plane to Vienna.

Just over an hour later a gray-haired, formally-dressed Richard Owen presented himself at the East Gate of the White House. He showed an engraved card to the gate guard, who checked Hirsh's name off his list.

Owen moved ahead into the East Wing and followed a broad hallway into a dimly lit, red-carpeted corridor with portraits of recent first ladies lining both walls. Owen had never been inside the White House. He knew it only by reputation and floor plan. He stopped beside a uniformed social aide and asked, "Where's the men's room, please?"

"Through the library, on your right."

Owen followed the gesture into a room lined with books on four sides, a room made for historic fireside chats. The entrance to the men's room was set into the east wall, through a green door with a brass marker.

He emerged after a few minutes, nodded to the aide, and followed the red carpet up a brass-banistered stairway to the state level of the mansion. He turned into the glittering gold and white East Room, where equally glittering guests drank and danced and chatted under the stern faces of George Washington and John Quincy Adams. There were a few hundred of them, men done up in black tie and women in fluttering gowns.

Crashing the White House, Owen decided, was a time for sheer bravado, and for an old rule of thumb—the less said, the better. He took a Scotch from a passing waiter and wandered through the crowd, stopping only where good manners required him to, then moving quickly on. He wandered through the Green Room, the Blue Room, the Red Room, admiring the period antiques and the paintings, the priceless curios public guests were never allowed to touch. Then he took his place in the receiving line in the Cross Hall, waiting to shake hands with the President.

And the President's guest of honor.

ELIZABETH EASTON stood in the receiving line for ten minutes before she knew she couldn't stand it a minute more. She made her escape, and went back upstairs to the relative privacy of the family quarters.

Vanessa Nichols found her in Anne's room, dry-eyed, motionless, staring down at the bed's smooth surface.

Vanessa paused in the doorway. "Elizabeth?"

The First Lady looked up. Her voice was as numb as her eyes. "Hi, Vanessa. Come in."

"What are you doing?" Vanessa crossed the room and put an arm around Elizabeth's shoulders. "This is the last place you should be."

"I keep thinking she'll be here."

Vanessa smiled sympathetically, but remained firm. "Come away with me. You're torturing yourself."

"I know. Even Mrs. Haskins asked to be moved down the hall. She said she couldn't stand it here."

"How is Mrs. Haskins?"

"All right physically. But she's blaming herself." Elizabeth closed her eyes. "Oh, Vanessa, I blame myself, too!"

"That's nonsense! How could it be your fault?"

"If I hadn't gone to Mexico and sent Anne to Michigan—"

"They'd have done it another way. Professionals make opportunities if they have to. I know that much about Ed's work."

Elizabeth wasn't convinced. She picked up a doll resting against the pillow, smoothing the yarn hair back from the painted face. "What am I going to do?" she said softly.

Vanessa's arm tightened around her shoulder. "I know what you're going through. But they're going to find her. There are thousands of people looking for her right now."

"But it's been two days! And they haven't found anything!" Elizabeth's eyes were no longer just numb. They were dark and tormented. "I'd give anything . . ." Suddenly, she clutched the doll to her breast and burst into tears.

OWEN WAS one of a few hundred people in the receiving line. The President shook his hand. "I'm glad you could come," he said. "And have you met the maestro?"

Owen's eyes shifted to the small, white-haired violinist. "This is a very great pleasure, Herr Heinemann. I've enjoyed your music for years."

Franz Heinemann smiled. "Thank you. I'm pleased to hear it."

"I believe we have a mutual friend," Owen added. "Anna Schurz."

For a moment, Heinemann only looked back at him. Then his eyes showed an emotion very close to fear. Perspiration broke out on his forehead.

"Perhaps we should talk later," Owen said.

"Yes, I think we should."

Owen nodded. Then he turned and disappeared into the crowd.

Half an hour later he was alone with Franz Heinemann in the White House library. Heinemann, his eyes cold, his face a mask of arrogance, looked at Owen as he might have looked at an insect or a crippled child—or a Jew.

"Anna Schurz," Owen said. "Your conduit to the SS."

"Who are you?" Heinemann said. "Israeli?"

Owen laughed. "No, but I suspect they'd like to know about you in Tel Aviv. They've scoured the world for lesser men."

Heinemann smiled, but his eyes remained cold. "If you're not Israeli, who are you? Who else could care?"

"There are one or two people outside Israel who disapprove of mass slaughter," Owen replied. "But don't worry, your secret is safe with me. I'm not going to tell a soul."

Heinemann sat down in a chair by the fireplace and looked up at Owen with eyes that were coldly impassive. Auschwitz and Dachau meant less to him now than they had forty years ago. To him, their only significance had been their function; that gone, they mattered no more.

"Perhaps you should tell me what you know," Heinemann said.

Owen remained standing. "Nineteen thirty-eight," he said. "You were a young violinist, with a growing international reputation and a friend named Anna Schurz. Then the Nazis annexed Austria, and suddenly passports could be revoked at will."

62

Heinemann glared at him scornfully. "History. My own and the Third Reich's. Both are well known."

"Quite so," Owen replied. "But history never recorded a meeting between you and Anna in the fall of '39. *Who's Who* doesn't tell us how willingly you paid the price for preserving your own passport—how quickly you agreed to inform on your own friends in Vienna's artistic community—"

"Not friends," Heinemann broke in. "Jews."

"Jews in hiding," Owen said. "You betrayed whole families of them. Who could have known it was you, a young violinist— arrogant, perhaps, but no Nazi. You kept your true feelings a secret. But you believed in the Nazis."

"I supported the Nazi *cause*," Heinemann said. Then he dismissed the point with a gesture. "None of this matters today. They are gone; the cause is not. What matters is how you know this. Anna died more than thirty years ago."

"Anna died *two* years ago," Owen said. "She took her own life. In Brazil. After she had signed this."

He reached into the jacket of his tuxedo and brought out several sheets of folded paper. Heinemann took them, glanced at them. Then he looked up at Owen, his eyes burning with hatred. Anna's confession told it all.

"What do you want?" he demanded.

"The same thing the Nazis wanted. Your cooperation."

Owen glanced at the door as a swell of voices rose outside in the hall. "You can call for help. Or you can come with me."

Heinemann hesitated a moment. Then, reluctantly, he got up and followed Owen through the green door with the brass marker.

The old man seemed suddenly smaller under the bright light reflecting off the bathroom tiles. There was no time to waste now. The guest of honor was bound to be missed eventually. Owen reached into his pocket and brought out a fountain pen. He pulled off the cap and the pen point.

Heinemann saw the sharp needle inside. His mouth twisted into a kind of smile. "My cooperation?" he said. Then the smile was replaced by a look of utter contempt. "Swine! My life will speak for itself!"

"I daresay," Owen replied. He plunged the needle into Heinemann's arm, through the cloth of jacket and shirt, straight into the flesh. The old man did not resist. Franz Heinemann died as he lived. Proud. Arrogant. And without a trace of remorse.

Chapter Seven

Owen left Washington on a morning shuttle bound for New York City. His papers identified him as a French antique dealer. In New York, he would change identity once more, to become an Austrian businessman on his way home to Vienna.

The morning papers carried the story of Heinemann's death. The *Times* gave it a properly serious tone, but the tabloids were full of melodrama: an old man alone, his heart failing, in the men's room—at the White House, for heaven's sake.

If only they'd known the truth, Owen thought, the tabloids would have gone berserk.

In any case, the White House had issued a statement expressing regret over the loss of a great artist and dismay that it happened there. The President had ordered a military transport to take the maestro home. The military jet, in fact, was taking off from Andrews Air Force Base shortly after Owen's commercial flight departed JFK. The President had also appointed an official party as escort—a former ambassador to Austria, a prominent American pianist, and the Secretary of State.

And one other distinguished passenger, Owen thought with a smile—small but distinguished, and of far greater interest than anyone else on that plane.

ED NICHOLS had been thinking about Franz Heinemann all day. Officially, it wasn't his concern. Unofficially, it interested him greatly. He wasn't sure why. Instinct, perhaps. Or the timing. . . .

The timing. My God!

He pressed the button on his desk and almost shouted into the intercom. "Get the White House physician for me," he said, "and tell Fleming to get in here on the double."

Nichols was on the phone when Fleming came through the door, breathing heavily.

"Then it's possible," Nichols was saying. He nodded. "Thank you, Doctor. That's what I wanted to know."

He replaced the receiver and looked across at Fleming, eyes bright behind the wire-framed glasses. "Here's a theory for you, Paul. I think Franz Heinemann was murdered."

"Murdered!" Fleming stared back, astonished. "But why?"

"For a US military transport and no customs search."

"But that's all standard procedure—"

"Not when someone's got the President's daughter and may be trying to smuggle her out of the country."

Nichols didn't wait for Fleming's mouth to close. "Get on the horn to our station chief in Vienna," he said. "I want everything covered—airports, railroad stations, border crossings."

Fleming got quickly to his feet. At the door, he stopped. "Ed, let *me* go to Vienna. This may be the break we've needed. We can't trust this to a station chief alone."

Nichols hesitated. Then he pressed the button on his desk. "Call Andrews," he said into the intercom. "Tell them to have a plane ready to leave for Vienna in thirty minutes."

"For you, sir?"

"No, for Paul Fleming."

TRAFFIC WAS HEAVY around Vienna's Schwechat Airport as evening settled over the city. Simon made his way slowly toward a drive where public cars were banned. He flashed his pass at the guard and was let through.

The American jet was sitting on the concrete apron, about two hundred yards beyond the terminal. Simon pulled up near a cluster of people, got out, and opened the rear door of the hearse. Then he waited while a baggage lift was rolled into place alongside the plane. Four men in coveralls positioned the coffin on the lift. They rode down with it and carried it to the waiting hearse. Pallbearing was no regular chore for the baggagemen. If any of them noticed the cavity in the floor of the hearse, it was there, they thought, to prevent the coffin from shifting during the ride.

Simon closed the rear door and climbed back in behind the wheel. He started the engine and pulled up behind the police escort. Then he pressed a lever under the dashboard. Behind him, locks disengaged. Heinemann's coffin and a separate secret compartment which fitted into the cavity beneath it were no longer fastened together.

He followed the escort car through the streets of Vienna to a mortuary near the banks of the Danube. When the coffin was lifted out, no one but Simon noticed that the cavity was no longer there. The floor of the hearse was now perfectly flat.

He watched the coffin being carried up the steps, then started the engine again and slipped away. After a while, he turned into a drab, industrial street of the city. As he swung into a garage, the door lowered behind him. A woman came forward, young and blonde. She smiled prettily. "Any problems?"

"None." Simon got out and handed over the keys. "She's all yours from here," he said. "I've got a plane to catch."

OWEN'S PLANE touched down at Schwechat an hour after the American jet. As he left the terminal, he took out the parking stub that had come with his Austrian passport. The stub was for a blue Volkswagen, and the keys were under the floor mat.

He bypassed Vienna, skirted the village of Grinzing, and turned west, into the Vienna Woods. The directions that came with the passport were explicit. He had no trouble finding the small road that led off the autobahn into the thick forest, where the cottage was hidden from view. He nosed the Volkswagen into a wooded path. From there, he set off on foot.

Owen could just see the gingerbread cottage through the thickness of green. A quaint little scene, like something from Hansel and Gretel.

The door swung open as Owen approached, but the woman who stood there was not the witch of the fairy tale. She was slender, with delicate coloring and blonde hair pulled back in a knot at her neck. The chic black dress of the Athens bar was gone, replaced by slacks and a sweater. She was herself now, not the American beauty who had so captivated the German back in the Grande Bretagne. But it was the same woman. Blondie!

Without a word she led Owen upstairs to a loft where a small, pajama-clad figure was lying on an eiderdown mattress. In its arm was a needle, attached by tube to a bottle hanging overhead.

Glucose water with vitamins and minerals added. Even unconscious, Anne Easton had to eat.

Owen nodded his approval. This was not the dark curly top he had stolen out of the house at Indian Springs. Her hair was straight now, and cut in a boyish style, with a long fringe.

Blondie came up behind him. "Well?"

"Excellent," Owen replied. Once they got Anne into the right clothes, she could easily pass for his son. He bent down to check her pulse and breath rate.

"How long can you keep her drugged?" Blondie asked.

"A few more days won't hurt." He looked at Blondie. "What do I call you?"

"Erica." She flashed her familiar sweet smile. That, at least, hadn't been part of the act in Athens. "Erica Foley, of course." She picked up a manila envelope and handed it to him.

Inside, he found three green US passports, for the father, the mother, and the four-year-old child. The Foleys of St. Louis, Missouri—a happy family threesome on holiday in Europe.

"What about my things?" Owen asked.

"You'll find everything you need in the bedroom."

"Good." Owen smiled. "We have nothing to do, then, until it's time to cross the border."

"I don't think I'll mind waiting," Erica replied.

THE MORTUARY director bowed deferentially and closed the door behind the American, wondering if he and the maestro had been personal friends. The man from the foreign ministry had told him only that the visitor was an important US government official who had requested a private viewing.

Inside the candlelit chapel, Paul Fleming, deputy director of the CIA, moved quickly to the superbly-crafted walnut casket that had been America's contribution to Franz Heinemann's final rest. He looked down at the old violinist, body rigid against a cushion of white satin. Only the Stradivarius looked real, carefully arranged in a pair of lifeless hands.

Fleming bent down to examine the coffin, running his fingers along the polished wood, rapping occasionally with his knuckles. Nothing. Nothing to suggest Anne Easton had been here.

She had been. He knew it. Attached to this casket somehow. But he had to have concrete evidence. Proof.

Then it caught his eye: a tiny scratch in the bronze trim that edged the bottom of the casket. Not just a scratch, but several, all perfectly spaced at exact intervals.

A smile crossed Fleming's face. He reached into his pocket for the camera and began to record the evidence on film.

ED NICHOLS leaned forward, excited. "Good work, Paul!" he said into the phone. "You're convinced she was transferred inside the hearse?"

"Had to be. Nothing came off that plane but the coffin and the official party with their hand luggage. The mortuary director supervised the arrival at the other end, along with about thirty people. It had to be inside the hearse, Ed, but the driver has vanished."

"As long as Anne doesn't vanish," Nichols said. "I want that country blanketed with people who know what to look for."

"It is. I'm using all our people and half the military intelligence agents in Europe. And I've alerted the borders. I don't want any slip-ups. Airports and railroads?"

"They're covered."

"Good." Nichols nodded. "They may have smuggled her into Austria," he said, "but they won't get her out!"

NICHOLS watched the last part of the welcoming ceremony from the inside of the hedge. The Marine band was playing the national anthem. A color guard presented the flags of both countries, and to a flourish of trumpets the President escorted the Belgian prime minister toward a waiting limousine.

The ceremony was over. Matt Easton turned toward the break in the hedge. There his smile vanished. The public man was gone.

"Ed, you're here. Good."

Nichols smiled as he fell into step along the covered colonnade that faced the Rose Garden. "I was already on my way when I got your message to come," he said. "I've got some good news. We know Anne is in Austria."

The President looked up sharply. "What makes you think so?"

Quickly, Nichols explained. He was watching Matt, watching for a change in the eyes—for a new look of hope, even gratitude. Instead, he saw only confusion.

"The point is," Nichols finished, "now we know where to look. Where to concentrate our resources."

The President stared at him for a moment. "I'm not sure we do. I called you here because we've had contact."

"From the kidnappers? From Vienna?"

"From Berlin."

The President pushed open the glass-paned doors that led into the Oval Office. Sam Wycoff, the Secret Service director, was waiting inside. "Show him," the President said to Wycoff.

Wycoff held out a locket, small and gold, engraved with the single initial A. Nichols recognized it instantly. He and Vanessa had given it to Anne on her third birthday.

He looked up at Wycoff. "How did it get here?"

"Through the mail, addressed to the President. It was sent air special two days ago from West Berlin. This was in the package, too." Wycoff held out a piece of paper.

Nichols read it, and his face went pale. Four words: "Cannon the Racy Bar."

Slowly, he said to the President, "Could I see you alone?" To Wycoff, he said, "I'm sorry, Sam, it's a matter of national security."

The President nodded, and Wycoff left the room.

Nichols dropped into a chair. "The Racy Bar is a nightclub in West Berlin," he began. "It's called The Resi, actually. American GIs renamed it after the war."

"And Cannon?" the President asked.

"Cannon's one of my agents in the Soviet sector. I assume the message means we should send him into The Resi and wait for a move from them."

The President leaned forward. "Then send him!"

"It's not that simple. Cannon's a code name. He's under deepest cover. He's a high-ranking military official in the Soviet's East German Command."

"Hell, Ed! A *Russian?*"

"More or less. He was born in Omaha, but the CIA sent him

into the USSR years ago, and created a background. He worked his way up through their military doing a damn good job—until he got near the top. That's when we started cashing in. Matt, he's our primary source of intelligence on Soviet activities in East Germany. We can't risk his cover!"

The President sat back. "It seems his cover is already blown."

"Not necessarily," Nichols said. "Cannon is the code name we use. But they may not know who he really is."

"And they will if he goes to The Resi."

"Yes."

Silence fell over the room as the two men looked at each other. Finally, the President said, "With Anne's life at stake, we can't take any chances. We have to send Cannon in."

Nichols nodded. They didn't have any choice.

THE RESI was a cavern of a place, with two hundred tables connected by telephones and pneumatic message tubes. It was jammed. Hell of a spot for a secret meeting, Cannon thought. If only he weren't quite so conspicuous here, a Russian colonel sampling a taste of western decadence. He found an empty table and ordered a glass of vodka.

The tables were arranged in a semicircle around a large dance floor, where the orchestra was holding forth with Broadway show tunes. Behind it fountains danced to the music. Cannon spotted the CIA agent called Zebra at a table across the floor. Now he could only wait. For what? For whom?

The waiter returned with his drink, and Cannon paid the tab. Then he tasted his vodka and let his eyes scan the room.

He'd already spent an hour talking possibilities with Fleming. West German intelligence? No. West Germany was America's strongest ally, economically if not culturally. West Germany would not kidnap Anne Easton.

Cannon felt a dull ache forming at the back of his head. Tension, he decided, and took another drink of vodka.

One of the superterrorist organizations? They wouldn't mind the risk, but if they were going to kidnap Anne Easton, they would move in with a commando squad and kill everyone in sight. Nothing as cunning as a single man walking out through the front door with the US President's daughter tucked under his arm.

The headache was getting worse, spreading across his temples and around behind his eyes. Pounding, true pain now, making it hard to think. Damn! This was no time to be sick. Cannon looked for Zebra on the other side of the room, but could no longer see her. He couldn't see anyone, just a splash of color and light. The music from the orchestra pounded painfully in his head.

He had to make contact. He had to let Zebra know. Something was wrong. He fumbled for the telephone on his table, tried to raise it to his ear. What was Zebra's table number?

Cannon tried to remember, but the pain was agony! He wanted to sleep. If only he could put his head down. And sleep.

On the other side of the room, Zebra saw Cannon collapse against the table, like a man who'd had too much to drink. She got up and moved casually through the room, walking past Cannon's table. Then, curiously, she turned back.

"Hello there, honey." Brightly. "What's the matter?"

Cannon didn't move.

"Are you sick?" She bent over him, placed a hand against his neck. Then, suddenly, she stood up and summoned a waiter. "This man needs an ambulance!"

As the waiter leaned over Cannon, the woman raised her hand to her own neck. It was the signal they used. The others would know what it meant.

Cannon was dead.

Chapter Eight

They approached the Austrian border. Erica eased the blue Volkswagen into the line of cars waiting to cross into Italy.

The US passports that belonged to the Foleys of St. Louis were in the glove compartment. Their story was set. It was time to make it work.

The man in the seat beside her was about thirty-five, with a fresh American face. He turned to look at the child sleeping across the back seat. Johnny Foley wasn't well. Chicken pox—it had to happen now!

71

A customs inspector approached them on Erica's side. "*Buon giorno.* Your passports, *per favore.*"

Erica smiled as she handed them through the window.

The inspector's eyes shifted to the back seat. "What is the purpose of your visit to Italy, Madame Foley?" he said sharply.

Erica looked back at the stern dark eyes and suddenly her mind went blank! She remembered none of the questions and answers she and Owen had practiced. No destination. No purpose.

But the inspector didn't notice. His attention had been diverted by the clatter of an old pickup truck that rolled into place in the adjacent line. With it came squeals and grunts—and an unmistakable odor. The truck was full of pigs.

Erica relaxed against the seat. The inspector sniffed the air with distaste. Then he turned back to the passports in his hands. "Yes, Madame Foley, the purpose of your visit."

"We're on vacation," Erica replied evenly.

A swell of voices rose from the truck. Questions—impatient, Italian. The driver of the truck climbed down. He was an Italian peasant, small and stooped, with wisps of gray hair showing under an ancient cap. He hobbled toward the back of the pickup on uneven legs. Three customs agents clustered around as he showed them a metal tag wired to a leg of one of the pigs.

The inspector forced his concentration back to the passports. Behind him, the squeals and grunts grew louder as the agents moved in to check the rest of the truckload.

Finally, he could stand it no more. He turned. "What's the delay here?" he demanded. "Are the pigs tagged?"

"Yes, sir."

"Then get them out of here." The inspector turned back to Erica. "Please, your car papers."

Erica produced the car rental forms. He examined them while behind him the truck pulled away. Suddenly, it was very quiet.

The inspector bent over, his eyes probing deep into the car. They lingered on the sleeping child. T-shirt and jeans. American tennis shoes. And red spots on the face.

"Your son has a rash, Madame Foley."

"Yes, chicken pox."

"Chicken pox?" The inspector was clearly dubious. He opened

72

the rear door of the car and gently touched the child's face. Suddenly, he straightened up. His face was grim. "I'm sorry, Madame, but you'll have to come with me."

Erica's gaze shifted to the customs building. "Is something wrong?" she said.

"These are *not* chicken pox. Come with me. You, too, sir. And, please, bring the child."

NICHOLS' fist turned white as he gripped the telephone harder. "What do you mean, Cannon is dead?"

"I'm telling you, Ed, it's as if someone set this up to flush out Cannon and kill him," Fleming replied.

"But who? The Russians wouldn't kill him without knowing exactly what information he had passed on to us. Who else would want Cannon dead?" The answer was simple. No one.

Nichols brought his other fist down on the desk. Damn! Even brought home with his cover blown, Cannon would have been an invaluable resource. Now he was dead, murdered in plain view of CIA's deputy director and several crack agents. And what had they learned about the President's daughter? Nothing!

Nichols sighed heavily. "Are you sure no one made contact with him before he died?"

"I'm positive," Fleming replied. "I was there the whole time. No one got near him but the waiter."

"The waiter! Paul, if the poison was in the vodka—"

"That didn't escape me," Fleming broke in dryly. "The waiter has disappeared. He was filling in for a buddy who was sick."

"And the buddy?"

"Gone, too."

"Look, Paul, use the whole damn army if you have to. I want that waiter found. It's possible they've slipped Anne over the border, in spite of our precautions. And if they have"—he paused —"it must not happen again."

"NOT *real* chicken pox," Erica said. She glanced nervously at her husband, then down at the sleepy child between them. "It was a joke," she went on. "Johnny drew the spots on himself. It's indelible ink. It won't wash off."

"Why didn't you tell me the truth about the rash?"

"You didn't give me a chance. I was going to tell you."

"Madame Foley," the inspector said, "we have a border alert to detain anyone with a child if the circumstances are suspicious. False chicken pox are suspicious."

Richard Foley leaned forward across the desk. "Are you suggesting that we've kidnapped our own son?"

"I'm suggesting nothing, sir. I am only saying you can't leave until we've verified your identity."

Foley was quiet for a moment. Then he said, "I insist on placing a call to the nearest American embassy."

OWEN had grown used to the odor of pigs. He was driving south through Italy, watching in the rearview mirror for Erica on the road behind him. An hour had passed since he crossed the border with his truckload of pigs, but still no blue Volkswagen. Obviously, she had been stopped at the border, just as they had planned.

Owen smiled. He wasn't worried about Erica. Of course the American embassy would make the identification. The man in the car *was* Richard Foley of St. Louis, Missouri. He worked for the CIA. And the boy in the back was his son. Only Erica had a part to play, and Owen had no doubt she could do it.

He drove on, picking up speed. North of Venice, he turned off the highway and followed a winding road into the countryside. The farm lay just ahead, nestled against the gentle slope of a hill.

Owen pulled off the cap and gray wig as he drove into the barn. Then he peeled away the thin layers of rubber that had added forty years to his age. He looked at himself in the mirror, saw a new version of the man he had been—an Italian peasant, but younger, his hair still black like Edward Drake's.

Then he climbed down from the seat and pressed a hidden button. The seat opened up like a coffin, revealing the child inside. The President's daughter was a boy now, in peasant clothes like Owen's, with the straight dark hair not unlike his own.

He checked her pulse and breath rate, and noted the time. She wasn't due for a feeding for two hours. He closed the compartment. Fifteen minutes later he drove out of the barn with new license plates and papers, but leaving the pigs behind.

THE PRESIDENT'S eyes turned progressively colder as Nichols described what had happened in Berlin. When the CIA director finished, Matt Easton pushed himself up out of the chair and began to pace off the anger he was feeling.

"Damn it!" he exploded finally. "My daughter's been missing for six days. I've given you every power of this office, and what do you have to show for it? Nothing except one top-secret agent murdered." He raised his hands in a gesture of futility. "I'm surrounded by bunglers. First the Secret Service. Now you. You, Ed, of all people! I thought I could surely trust you!"

Nichols did not flinch. "You know you can trust me."

A buzzer sounded. The President pressed a button. "Yes?"

"The Secret Service director is here, Mr. President."

"Send him in."

Sam Wycoff closed the door behind him. In his eyes, a look of defeat. He was holding a box in his hand. "This arrived in today's mail," he said. "From Johannesburg, South Africa." He put the box down on the President's desk.

Matt Easton lifted the lid. A pair of child's pajamas.

"Mrs. Haskins has identified them," Wycoff said. "They're the pajamas Anne was wearing the night she disappeared."

The President took the pajamas in his hands. A sharp look of pain crossed his face.

Nichols pulled out a piece of paper from the box: "Sherman Old South Church."

The same thing, all over again.

PAUL FLEMING glanced at his watch. It was midnight. He focused his binoculars on the black man standing in the shadow of a tree across from the church, his dark skin and clothing hardly separate from the darkness of shadow and night. It was Sherman.

Frankie Sherman. Baseball superstar, retired. An American in Johannesburg on a State Department goodwill exchange, setting up Little League ball teams. Simple. Noncontroversial.

Only Frankie Sherman was also on assignment for the CIA. His job: to act as contact with the black South African underground. He was important, but the President's daughter was more important. In spite of Berlin, they had to take the risk. Again.

This time, though, there would be a large team of agents to protect Sherman.

As Fleming watched, Sherman hurried across the street into the church. Inside, there was darkness and total silence. Sherman moved forward toward a dim light in the sanctuary.

Old South was a Methodist church. There were no frills here, just a bare wooden floor under rows of uncushioned pews. Walls plain, painted white. No stained glass in the tall windows.

And, Sherman thought, no sign of the backup team Fleming had promised. He crept down the side aisle, ducking low under the windows. At the front, steps leading up to the simple altar. Like the floor, bare wood. And on the steps, a white envelope. Not dropped by accident. Balanced, in plain view.

Sherman bent down to pick up the envelope. Then, as he straightened up, he heard a sound. High and to his right. A window. A sharp crack. A whining through the air.

In that instant he knew what the sound was, but his reflexes weren't fast enough. Sherman's head exploded as the bullet penetrated his brain. His body reeled sideways and crashed into a pew.

Inside the church, the sound of footsteps on the wooden stairs. Too late. Out front, Fleming heard a motor start up, a car driving away. Then someone was running his way. Not Sherman, but Zebra.

Fleming knew before she told him. Frankie Sherman was dead.

THE CAR FERRY from Brindisi was twenty hours at sea. Owen booked the cheapest passage, no bed or food. He brought his own peasant fare—bread and cheese. Like his passenger under the seat, he would sleep in the truck—if he slept at all.

The ferry would dock at Patras on the northern coast of the Peloponnesus. From there he would drive east to Piraeus, the port of Athens. Another change of identity and transportation. Another car ferry. South this time. To Heraklion, on the island of Crete.

Crete, a parched and rugged island where people valued their independence above all else. Owen smiled. As long as he kept to the countryside, no one would bother him or the peasant boy who was really the President's daughter.

77

IT WAS a warm spring day in Washington, sun bright, banks of red azaleas in bloom. The President climbed out of the White House pool and pulled on a terry cloth robe. A poolside table was set for coffee. He gestured for Nichols to join him.

"You've read my report?" Nichols said.

"Yes, I've read your report," the President replied calmly. Too calmly. "Tell me, Ed. When we send people like Frankie Sherman into foreign countries on a State Department exchange, do we or do we not guarantee their diplomatic immunity?"

"State does. I don't. Intelligence out of South Africa is critical right now."

"I know that. But there's also the matter of you and me both being accountable to the law. Or had you forgotten?"

Nichols didn't reply.

"You've put me in a hell of a spot," the President added angrily. "If this thing blows open, I'll have a credibility crisis that could affect our relations with every country in the world. And Congress!" His eyes turned a shade colder as he fired off the questions. "Who kidnapped my daughter? Why? What do they want? And"—he leaned forward across the table—"where is she?"

Nichols felt a new, uneasy tightening in his chest. He and Matt had had their disagreements, but never anything like this. Matt was furious. And he had good reason to be.

"I don't know," Nichols said nervously. "But I'm beginning to get some ideas."

"Ideas! Damn it! I don't want ideas—I want facts!"

Nichols didn't reply. He knew the spot he was in.

The President stared at him. Then, finally, he leaned back in his chair. "All right, let's hear your ideas."

"Two things," Nichols began. "First, the motive. Not a specific ransom demand, something far more complex. We've lost two valuable agents, but if the kidnappers were after Cannon and Sherman alone, there would be easier ways to get them."

The President shrugged, without committing himself.

"So there's more," Nichols said. "They're after something or someone bigger. And, Matt, I think it's me. Me as CIA director. Or maybe it's bigger than that. Maybe it's you they're after. Maybe the whole damn government!"

The ice melted. The President was fully interested now.

"I feel as if I'm being manipulated," Nichols explained, "and through me, you are, too. There can be little doubt of it. The kidnappers have an informant. Someone on our side."

"Good God!"

"You see," Nichols explained, "the kidnappers couldn't have known how long it would take us to make the arrangements with Cannon and Sherman. In Cannon's case, we signaled and he made contact as soon as he could. But we didn't know how long that would take. A couple of hours? A couple of days? Then we set up a time for Cannon to go to The Resi. Yet the waiter also knew the right day and the right time that Cannon would be there.

"Sherman, too," he went on. "He was killed from a tree outside the church. I suppose it's possible someone sat in that tree for two days, waiting for him to show up, but I doubt it. Once again, the killer was there at the precise right time."

The President was stunned. "Do you have any idea who the informant is?"

Nichols shook his head. "No idea at all. But," he added, "next time I'm going to find out."

The President looked at him for a moment. Then his face changed. "You may be glad to know that the next time is here." He turned and nodded to a Secret Service agent standing out of earshot near a West Wing door. The agent signaled someone else. An aide appeared, handed an envelope to the President, and disappeared back the way he had come. The President handed the envelope to Nichols.

Nichols glanced at the postmark: Washington, DC. In the envelope was a sheet of paper. On it, a small footprint. And four words. He looked up.

"The footprint is Anne's?" he asked.

The President nodded.

Four words: "Shelley Curtis The Rotunda."

This time Nichols was beyond reaction. Another key agent who worked under deep cover for the CIA.

The President's eyes asked the question.

"Shelley Curtis," Nichols said, as much to himself as to Matt. "My agent in place inside the US Congress."

Chapter Nine

 Shelley Curtis watched the vote totals as they added up on the light board built into the gallery rail over the House floor. She smiled. They were winning by a large margin.

An agriculture bill. Appropriations. Routine. And in it, secretly —unknown even to most of the voting members—money that had nothing to do with agriculture. Money to buy planes, to build airfields, to pay the soldiers who worked for the CIA. Intelligence did not always accommodate democracy. Some things had to be kept off the record if the enemy wasn't to know.

Congresswoman Curtis, not yet forty, had cast her yea vote and was now free to go home. It was nearly eleven p.m., but for Shelley the night had just started. She had a late date of sorts at the club called The Rotunda.

The Rotunda could mean one of two places—the great domed hall of the Capitol, or the private political club on Ivy Street. Paul Fleming had opted for the latter, and warned her to be careful.

Shelley didn't need the warning and was prepared to take any risk. She was a graduate of CIA's training school and had spent five years in the field before she retired to a desk job at Langley. There she became dissatisfied with certain CIA methods and took her complaints to public hearings in Congress. Her testimony made Shelley an overnight celebrity. Two years later she ran for Congress and won. With her obvious credentials, she had no trouble acquiring a seat on Intelligence Oversight.

It was an ideal spot for a loyal former agent—an agent who never did object to the way things were run at Langley. Shelley had been set up for her testimony on the Hill. Her election had been financed in part by covert government funds. In truth, she never had stopped working for the CIA.

Shelley left the chamber by the east exit and waited for the elevator. The door opened. She stepped through and it started to close again, but a hand reached forward to block it. A man entered the elevator. He was tall and blond.

"Simon! What are *you* doing here?"

"We've got to talk," Simon replied. He pushed the button for the first floor. "Follow me, but remember, we're not together."

Shelley nodded and asked no more questions. She knew Simon worked for the CIA. Something must have gone wrong.

The door opened again; Simon got off first. He flashed a card at a guard and moved off down the hall. The guard recognized Shelley. "Late night," he observed.

"Aren't they all?" She smiled and headed down the hall, keeping distance between herself and Simon ahead. They were in the Crypt, one floor below the House chamber. Here there were no people, only giant statues carved out of marble and bronze. She knew where Simon was going—to the tiny chamber in the basement of the building, designed to be George Washington's tomb. She'd had meetings there before.

Shelley followed a flight of circular stairs down to a corridor that wound its way into the heart of the building. Simon was waiting for her at a gate. On the other side were white walls molded into cathedral-like arches, and a long box draped in fringed black velvet. The Lincoln catafalque, unused between state funerals, was stored here in this appropriate place.

Shelley looked at Simon and said, "What's wrong?"

"Nothing." Simon dropped his hands into his pockets and turned away. His steps were slow and easy. Then, abruptly, he stopped and turned back to her. His scar showed up clearly under a harsh overhead light. So did the small automatic he was holding.

Shelley froze. "What *is* this? What are you doing?"

The voice was calm. "I'm going to kill you," he said.

Simon? But they were on the same side! Her hands pushed deep into her coat pockets. "Fleming didn't send you," she said.

"It doesn't matter who sent me." He pulled back the safety.

Shelley smiled uneasily. "Look, Simon, put the gun away. If you don't, I'm going to scream so they'll hear me from here to the White House."

Simon laughed. "A lot of good that will do," he said, gesturing with his automatic to the thick stone walls. For an instant, his eyes turned away.

Shelley fired.

The bullet exploded out of her coat pocket and straight into Simon's chest. His hand lost its grip on the automatic, which fell

81

to the floor with a clatter much louder than the soft splat that had killed him. Then his knees gave way to his own deadweight.

Shelley's hand released the gun still in her coat pocket. My God! She had to find Fleming, and fast.

PAUL FLEMING was waiting in a car on Ivy Street. He saw Shelley approaching the club, and softly called her name.

She turned and came running to the car. There was a powder-burn hole in the pocket of her coat. Her eyes were wide and dark with panic, and her hands were shaking as she jumped in beside him.

"What's the matter?" Fleming asked urgently.

"Simon! I just killed him!"

Fleming stared back, astonished. "Simon?"

"Our Simon," Shelley confirmed. The rest came out in a rush.

Fleming listened in stunned silence. "Simon," he said when she finished. "Did he tell you why?"

Shelley shook her head. "I'm sorry, I know I should have tried to find out, but I couldn't think—"

"It's all right," Fleming assured her. "Take it easy. I'm just glad you're alive. Did you leave him there?"

"I hid him under the catafalque."

Fleming gave a dry little laugh. "Handy," he said.

"Do you still want me to go into the club?" she asked.

"I don't think it will come to anything, but let's find out. I'll talk to Nichols in the meantime and get back to you here."

Shelley got out of the car.

The interior of The Rotunda was like a baronial hall scaled down in size. A wide staircase with heavily carved wooden banisters branched off at the entrance, climbing two ways to the balcony that served as a gallery for presidential portraits. A third branch of the stairway led down to tables clustered under dim lights. Dinner was over; this was the drinking crowd, mostly congressional staff unwinding after a long day on the Hill.

The bartender recognized Shelley. "Hi, Miss Curtis. What can I get you?"

"Brandy, please."

After her first sip Shelley could feel herself starting to relax.

82

The scene with Simon seemed far away. Then she realized she was more numb than relaxed. It was a long time since she'd been involved in anything like this.

But nothing would happen here.

THERE WAS no one stationed at The Rotunda's front door. Proof of membership was required only to buy food or drink. Graham pushed open the door and stepped in. That fool Simon had botched the job. Now he would have to take care of the Curtis woman himself.

He glanced down the stairs to the bar, then turned to the steps on his left and made his way up to the balcony. He stood there alone, listening for the sound of the telephone.

"Phone call for you, Miss Curtis," the bartender said. "You can take it by the coatroom."

Shelley nodded. It was probably Paul Fleming telling her to go home. She crossed the room to the phone near the stairs.

"Hello?"

"Miss Curtis?"

A man. Not Fleming. "Yes?"

The answer came from above, a sharp whine through the air. The bullet hit at the back of her head and escaped again through her mouth.

A waitress screamed. Faces at the bar turned around. Incredulity gave way to shock, to frozen silence. No one moved.

And in that instant of horrified inaction, a man raced down the stairs from the balcony level. A man in a shapeless raincoat, with a hat pulled low on his head. He burst through the door and into the darkness outside.

Graham had made his escape.

OWEN FELT an enormous sense of relief. He had successfully eluded the searchers and was here now, on the island of Crete—the fox leaving the hounds with no scent to follow and a whole world to search.

The sun was bright on the dark Cretan sea and turned the leaves of the olive grove a shimmering silver. Through gnarled tree trunks he could see the rocky coastline awash with foam as the treacherous waves broke against the shore. The air was cool, full of the scent of mint and lemon.

He turned and walked back into the house, a small two-story bungalow with whitewashed walls. It was set back from the coast road that ran east from Heraklion and was protected from its nearest neighbor by distance and the wild growth of the island.

Owen climbed the stairs to the second floor and unlocked a door. The room inside was spotless and sparsely furnished. Anne Easton lay motionless on the bed. Owen pulled up a chair.

Her lashes fluttered. She opened her eyes and lay staring at the unfamiliar room. Then her eyes brightened as they fell on one thing she recognized. The face of Edward Drake.

Owen smiled. "Just lie still for a while," he said.

"Where's Haskie?"

"She had to go away for a few days. She asked me to keep you until she gets back."

"Is this your house?"

"For now, yes."

It was explanation enough. No distrust showed in the big dark eyes. She was used to strange places and people, this cosmo-politan child. And in any case, Edward Drake was no stranger; he was Mrs. Haskins' friend. Anne looked at him and smiled.

Owen smiled back. Then he glanced at his watch. It was still night in Washington. He wondered how the President was sleeping these days.

MATT EASTON lay quietly on his back, eyes open, staring up into the darkness over the bed. Beside him, Elizabeth, asleep at last, her breath soft against the pillow. But not even sleep smoothed the deep lines of tension on her face.

Dear God, what had he done to her? What had he done to Anne?

He got up quietly and made his way across the thick carpet to the bathroom door. Inside, he switched on the light and sat down on the wide edge of the tub, elbows on knees, face in hands. The bathroom—one of the few places in the White House where he ever felt truly alone. It was almost comical.

Closing his eyes, he thought back to election night. Victory. Total joy. He might not have considered that night an occasion to

84

celebrate if he had known it would come to this. His wife distraught with fear. His daughter the victim of power out of control. His best friend a stranger. And himself?

He smiled wryly. The President of the United States, perched on the edge of a bathtub, wishing he'd never been caught by the lure of the White House at its terrible price.

"Matt? Are you all right?" Elizabeth was awake.

He got up and opened the door. A path of light fell on her, sitting up in bed, her expression concerned.

"No," he said. Then, "I'm not all right."

He moved back to the bed and put his arms around her, pulling her close, seeking comfort as much as he sought to give it.

"Matt—"

He placed his fingers lightly against her lips. "Please don't talk. Just listen."

She nodded.

"This whole thing is my fault," he said quietly. "I've been trying to make up my mind all week. And now I've made a decision." He looked down at the dark eyes staring at him. "I have something to tell you," he said.

PAUL FLEMING drove straight to Langley, only to learn that Nichols had left for home. A call to the house got Vanessa. Ed wasn't there yet.

"Have him call me the minute he gets in," Fleming said.

He kept a nervous eye on the time as he turned to the other matter. Simon dead, his body stashed under the Lincoln catafalque. There was irony in that. CIA heroes rarely got their just honors when they died. Neither did CIA traitors.

Fleming reached for the phone again. Renovation on the old Capitol building was an ongoing thing. No one would notice an extra crew of painters with an official job order and their equipment loaded onto a hand cart. No one would know Simon had ever been there. That much was under control.

A knock came at the door. A messenger entered and handed Fleming a sealed envelope. It was red for ultra-urgent and marked EYES ONLY for him. Fleming tore it open and read the telex inside. Then he grabbed up the phone and dialed Nichols again.

"I'm sorry," Vanessa Nichols said. "He's still not back."

Fleming switched on the scrambler attached to his telephone. "Look, Vanessa, tell him I can't wait. We've had a telex from Athens. An agent there says she's seen Anne Easton. I can't explain it now. But tell Ed I'm leaving for Athens right away."

"Tonight?"

"As soon as I hang up." Fleming's finger hovered over the disconnect button. "One more thing. Tell him I left Shelley Curtis down at The Rotunda. She's got a hell of a story. Make sure Ed calls her as soon as you hear from him."

"I will."

"Thanks." Fleming disconnected the line without a good-by.

NICHOLS didn't have to be told about Shelley Curtis. He was sitting in his car outside The Rotunda, where the police were at work in swarms. Like Cannon and Sherman before her, Shelley Curtis was dead. The killer had been there at the precise right time. He had to have been tipped off. By someone on the inside.

But who had known when Shelley was going to go to the club? He, Nichols, did. He and Fleming had set this up, which meant that Fleming knew, too. And one other person whom Nichols reported to. Matt Easton.

Beyond that, Nichols' directions had been clear: tell no one. Limit knowledge this time to the three people who are above suspicion. And yet, the killer was there.

Suddenly, Nichols' mind reeled against a blow more stunning than any physical force. The informant! The insider who had tipped off a killer in Berlin and Johannesberg, in Washington, DC. It had to be Paul or Matt!

Nichols felt something far worse than shock. The President of the United States permitting his daughter's abduction? Impossible! But Paul? That was almost as bad. The deputy director of the CIA involved in a plot to kidnap the President's daughter? What would either of them have to gain?

Nichols switched on the ignition and started to drive aimlessly. His mind was a jumble, his heart pounding inside his chest. He had never had to deal with anything like this before. A problem of staggering proportions—beyond precedent.

Matt. It couldn't be Matt. It was out of the question, defied everything sane. It had to be Paul.

Nichols took a deep breath and forced himself to relax against the seat. His mind was beginning to clear. He was starting to see himself from an entirely new perspective—and he wondered, for the first time, how much he really controlled the CIA.

He was the director, yes, but an outsider brought in at the top by the President. Because of that, he had never fully subscribed to the unwritten motto at Langley: What's good for the CIA is probably good for the country.

But Fleming was not an outsider. He was a CIA professional who had come up through the ranks. Presidents came and went; so, too, their appointed directors. But professionals like Fleming stayed on through political change. Among the other professionals, it was Fleming who had the standing, Fleming who had earned their loyalty, Fleming who controlled the CIA.

Nichols turned the car into the southwest freeway. He felt stranded, isolated, cut off from both sources of what was supposed to be his own far-reaching power—the White House and the CIA. He had to find out what Paul Fleming was doing, but he couldn't go to Matt. Not until he was sure Matt wasn't involved. And he couldn't go to the CIA—to the people who worked for him—either. That left one choice: he had to get outside help.

But he did want to talk to Fleming. He turned off the freeway and found a phone booth. He dialed the agency switchboard.

"I'm sorry, sir," the night duty officer said. "The deputy director has left, but he said to tell you to call your wife."

Nichols hung up and dialed his home.

"Ed, where are you?" Vanessa asked.

"Never mind that. Did Paul leave a message for me?"

"Is the line safe?"

"You'd better switch on the scrambler there."

Vanessa found the switch. Now her voice had a hollow sound. The scrambler was working. "There was a telex. Someone in Athens saw Anne!" she said. "Paul's on his way there now."

"Paul is!" Where did this fit in?

"He also said you're supposed to call Congresswoman Shelley Curtis. Immediately. She's down at The Rotunda."

"That won't be necessary," Nichols replied dryly.

"Is something wrong?" Vanessa asked, worry clear in her voice.

"Not something, everything," Nichols replied.

He replaced the receiver and sat there thinking over his plan. A dangerous plan. A huge risk. But unless Paul Fleming was cleared of suspicion, he couldn't trust anyone Fleming might control. And there was nowhere else to turn on this side. He reached for the phone again and dialed another number.

The man who answered was named Kolonov. He was special assistant to the vice-consul at the Soviet embassy in Washington. He was also the senior KGB resident in the United States.

Chapter Ten

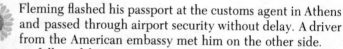 Fleming flashed his passport at the customs agent in Athens and passed through airport security without delay. A driver from the American embassy met him on the other side.

Fleming followed him out into the bright sunshine. Waiting by the curb was a black Pontiac, some buses, a throng of people. And one face Fleming recognized!

His step didn't falter; his eyes showed no sign of surprise. He climbed into the back seat of the big American car. The driver pulled away into the flow of traffic. Fleming glanced back toward the terminal building and caught the gray Mercedes in his peripheral view. It, too, was pulling away from the curb. There was no mistaking the wide face, the broad Slavic features of the driver.

Svitsky!

Fleming leaned forward and spoke to the driver. "There's a taxi behind us. Can you lose it?"

The driver looked in his rearview mirror. "You bet I can."

"Then do it."

SPRING in Washington had taken a sudden backslide, giving way to a gray sky and a wet, chilling mist. Nichols glanced at his watch—it was five p.m.—and quickened his pace across the footbridge that connected the Virginia shore with Roosevelt Island. He knew the park closed at sundown, by the combined demands of the National Park Service and the rising tide of the Potomac river. The meeting would have to be short.

The bridge gave way to a path that cut through tall trees to a clearing. Nichols walked quickly along it and stopped in the deepening shadows of the trees on the other side of the clearing. From behind came the snapping of a twig.

Nichols turned. It was Kolonov, his overcoat turned up against the damp chill of the air, his mouth set in a firm, tense line.

Nichols moved toward him. "Well?"

"I did my best," the Russian replied. "I put Boris Svitsky on Fleming. He's our top agent in Europe."

"And?"

"Your Fleming's no fool. He spotted Svitsky and lost him."

"Lost him!"

The Russian shrugged. "It's not so surprising. Two good field agents, pretty evenly matched."

"Except that Fleming's a retired agent." Nichols glared at him. "I won't accept that. I want Fleming found."

The Russian laughed uneasily. "Isn't that a little unreasonable at this point?"

"Not half as unreasonable as I'm going to be," Nichols replied. He turned away in frustration. Boris Svitsky, of all people! Fleming would recognize him in an instant.

Then, suddenly, a new thought struck him. One thought and another, they all fell into place. He knew now who had ordered the kidnapping of Anne Easton. He also thought he knew why.

OWEN watched Anne's face as he opened the brown paper package from the market. Her curiosity gave way to disgust.

"What's that?"

Owen laughed. "It's octopus. Want a bite?"

Anne shook her head decisively. "Peanut butter, please."

"I thought you'd say that. Sit down. I'll fix a sandwich."

She did as she was told, and Owen was grateful. If he had to play Mary Poppins, he'd just as soon do it opposite a bright, well-behaved child. He made the sandwich and poured Anne a glass of milk. It had been a week since she left the United States, drugged, in the false compartment under Franz Heinemann's coffin, two days since they'd arrived on Crete. Good food and fresh air had done their work. Anne's dark eyes were shining out of a pink face.

The phone rang. Startled, Owen gestured for silence. Then he crossed into the next room and picked it up.

A woman's voice: *"The promised hour is come at last."*

Dryden. The signal from Graham.

"The present age of wit obscures the past," Owen replied. He smiled, having recognized the voice. "How are you?"

"Busy," Erica said. "I have a message from Graham. It's midnight tonight. At Knossos. Sunflower is going home."

"Tonight! Graham said I'd be here two weeks or more. What's gone wrong?"

"Nothing I know of."

Owen was silent a moment. Then he said, "What's the plan?"

"Simple. You'll turn Sunflower over to Graham, and he'll take her home."

"There are night guards at Knossos," he said.

"Two men—one at the gate, one inside the grounds. Graham wants you to see to them before he arrives."

"Will you be there?" Owen asked.

"I doubt it. But I could be available after this is over."

Owen could feel the familiar smile at the other end of the line. "I'll keep that in mind," he said.

Owen hung up. He knew he should be relieved. He would turn Anne over to Graham and be done with it. But he felt a vague sense of concern. The signal had come too soon; they'd been two days on Crete, not two weeks. He turned back to the kitchen.

"Was that Haskie?" Anne asked.

Owen looked at the small, unhappy face. "No, it wasn't. But you'll be seeing her soon," he said. "Your parents, too."

Unhappiness faded to a look of total joy. "When?"

"I don't know yet. Soon. Now please be quiet and let me read the paper." Owen sat down and picked up the *Herald Tribune*.

But Anne could not remain silent. "Look, it's Uncle Ed!"

Owen turned the paper around. It was a picture of Ed Nichols, flanked by a couple of diplomats at some embassy affair in Washington. Uncle Ed, was it? He turned the page.

Anne took a drink of her milk, and then cocked her head to one side. "When is Uncle Ed going to be vice-president?" she asked.

Owen sighed. Reading, obviously, was out of the question for now. He dropped the paper. "What makes you think he's going to be vice-president?"

"Daddy said so. He told Mommy. I heard him." She looked out the window at the sunny day. "Can we go swimming now?"

"After your nap," Owen said. He was studying Anne. He was surprised by her natural use of an official government title. But then, the language of government and politics was as common to the President's daughter as the language of nursery rhymes. "Did your father say when Uncle Ed was going to be vice-president?"

Anne shrugged. She didn't remember. Perhaps she never knew. "Why can't we go swimming now?"

"Because you haven't finished your lunch or had your nap." Owen reached for his newspaper again.

"After the next election."

He glanced up. "What?"

"Daddy said Uncle Ed will be vice-president after the next election." Anne's face creased into an earnest frown. "When's the next election?"

Owen ignored the question, but he was interested now. "Your father said that? You're sure he said that?"

"I heard him."

"When?"

"I don't know."

Owen kept his voice calm. "This is very important," he said. "Think hard. What were you doing when your father and mother were talking?"

Anne closed her eyes tightly. Then they popped open again. "I was opening a present."

"What kind of present?"

"A book. It was for my trip."

"When was that?"

Anne stared back at him. Then, suddenly, her face broke into a grin. "The day we went to Michigan!"

"You're sure?" Owen said, more urgently now.

"I remember, Mr. Drake. I put my book by my suitcase, and we went on the plane the same day."

The day Anne left for Michigan. A full week after Owen's meeting with Graham in New York.

He sat quite still, staring at the child. She had no idea of the significance of what she had said. If the President thought Ed Nichols might be guilty of treason, he would hardly be thinking of making him his running mate! And that meant Graham had lied! The President had authorized nothing!

Owen leaned back in the chair without taking his eyes off Anne. He had kidnapped her with her father's permission. So he thought. Now, in a flash of memory, that sanction was gone. It had never existed!

If the President hadn't authorized the kidnapping, then he couldn't have known about it. He could not be working with Graham. He must be distraught with fear for his daughter's safety. President and father, a man of enormous power and extraordinary motivation—all of it now aimed at Owen.

A tightness was spreading across Owen's chest. Fear, a new sensation. A threat, not to life, but to freedom. Freedom was life. Without it, he would rather be dead.

"Mr. Drake!" Anne was at his side, tugging at his sleeve for attention. She looked frightened. "What's the matter?"

Owen touched her cheek. "I'm sorry," he said. "Nothing's wrong. Up to bed now. We've got a swim on for later."

A grin of pure delight spread across Anne's face as she scampered out of the room.

Owen began to pace the floor. The fear was gone; he felt anger. Graham had used him, had led him into the worst kind of danger—without warning, with a lie.

Then, in an instant, the anger disappeared. There was no time now for emotion, only for careful thinking and planning. Had Graham lied about Nichols, too? If so, why the kidnapping? *Why* the kidnapping.

Owen was sure of one thing, that Graham had a lot of explaining to do. And he'd better be convincing, or there wasn't a chance Owen would relinquish Anne.

The rendezvous was set—midnight tonight at Knossos. Sunflower was going home.

Or was she?

AFTER HIS MEETING with Kolonov, Nichols drove straight to the White House, bringing the car to a halt at the West Wing entrance. He hurried to an ante-room that bordered the Oval Office.

Matt's secretary, red-eyed and worried, was sitting behind her desk. A man was pacing the floor in extreme agitation. He was the appointments secretary, gatekeeper to the President. He looked up sharply as Nichols strode into the room. "Where have you been?" he demanded. "We've been trying to find you for over an hour!"

Nichols ignored the question. "I've got to see the President," he said, and moved toward the heavy carved door.

The other man blocked him. "You can't see him now. He's on his way over to the Executive Office building. He's called a press conference. He's going to resign!"

Nichols stared at him, stunned. "But why?"

"Heaven only knows! He's got some crazy notion that this whole thing with Anne is his fault. And that if he resigns, they won't want her anymore."

Nichols' eyes narrowed. "You've got to stop him."

"I've tried. We all tried."

"I didn't say try, I said stop him! He's making a huge mistake. You get him back here right now. Tell him his wife died, anything, but get him back here."

The appointments secretary left the room in a hurry.

Nichols looked at the red-eyed woman behind the desk. "Pull yourself together," he said. "It's going to be a long night."

THERE WERE two cars in the paved lot cut out of the trees that lined the approach to Knossos. A modern chain-link fence enclosed the ancient ruins. It was ten p.m. Daylight was gone, and so were the tourists who came here in droves at this time of year.

Owen could not see the ruins from where he stood surrounded by trees, only the bright glow of floodlights from the top of the hill. But he could see the small house that gave overnight shelter to the guard on duty at the gate.

The smell of coffee and the sound of bouzouki music floated across to Owen. He moved quietly out of the trees, keeping to the soft earth that bordered the gravel path. At the door of the gatehouse, he stood for a moment listening. Then he picked up a handful of gravel and threw it against the fence.

There was a soft staccato of sound. The guard heard it, shut the radio off. Footsteps came toward the door. Owen stood flush with the wall, his hand moving to his waist to check the revolver in his belt. Then the guard stepped through the door.

Owen gave him no time to turn around. The edge of one hand struck the man's neck sharply as the other hand clamped across his mouth. He dragged the unconscious guard back into the gatehouse and laid him out on the floor. Then he produced a plastic syringe; in it, enough Valium to keep a grown man sleeping through the night.

Next, he let his eyes scan the walls of the room. The fuse box was behind the door. He yanked it open, studied the wiring inside, and pulled the master switch. The guardroom fell dark and with it the floodlights at the top of the hill.

Owen stepped behind the door and waited. In less than five minutes he heard footsteps approaching on the far side of the gate. The other guard was coming to investigate.

The second guard unlocked the gate from inside. There were more footsteps and then the beam of a flashlight moved into the guardroom. The man came just behind it.

"Niko!" He dropped to his knees beside the prone body.

Owen sprang forward, his hand coming down hard against the man's neck. The second guard collapsed beside the first. Owen plunged a dose of Valium into his arm. Then he taped the mouths of both men, tied their arms behind their backs, lashed their legs together. He stood back to study his work. For the first time in four millenia Knossos had been secured.

Owen left the guardroom and made his way through the gate and up the hill to where the Palace of Minos once stood above the banks of the river Kairatos. A sprawling, multi-level structure that covered more than five square acres and had housed as many as eighty thousand people. An architectural miracle built in the days of prehistory, when even ancient Greece was yet to come.

Death had found Knossos without warning. The river was still there, but the palace had been leveled to rock-strewn rubble by a sudden catastrophe—a massive earthquake probably—that obliterated this and every trace of Minoan civilization for nearly four thousand years.

Now it had been laid bare by the archaeologist's spade. The structure of the ground floor was a large central courtyard surrounded by the foundations of what had been hundreds of rooms. There were only patches of restoration to whet the imagination. A few reconstructed walls, some small buildings rebuilt with old stone, two restored columned porches. And bulls' horns everywhere, the stylized stone bulls' horns as tall as a man, that once edged the palace walls like turrets on a medieval castle.

Owen listened to the crickets in the trees, to the flow of the river nearby. In the distance lay the lights of a city, Heraklion. Otherwise, there was no manmade light to counteract nature's own pale moonlight. Knossos remained as it had been through thousands of years. Isolated. Inviolate.

Knossos was a place where history merged with myth. The legendary home of Minos, king of Crete, son of the mighty Zeus. And of Minos' son Androgeus, whose murder by the king of Athens sent Minos into a rage of blood and lust. Minos demanded his price, the finest youth of Athens for sacrifice to the Minotaur—a fearsome beast, half man, half bull, who dwelled in the fabled labyrinth beneath the Minoan palace.

The retribution continued for twenty-seven years, until the Athenian king sent his son Theseus to slay the Minotaur. Theseus succeeded, and escaped with the help of Ariadne, who led him through the twisting labyrinth with her ball of thread.

All legend—until the excavations at Knossos gave the myth a home. A prehistoric civilization beyond anything dreamed of on Crete. A culture where the bull was revered above all other creatures. Artistic renderings of a ritual called the bull dance, pitting unarmed youth against a massive beast. All of this and the ruins of a structure so vast, so intricate in design, that one conclusion was clear.

Whatever its history, Knossos didn't only house a labyrinth. It *was* one.

Owen's gaze swept the ruined remains of the upper levels of the palace. He knew that beneath all this rock, underground passages still wound their way in a maze, and that even today a visitor could lose his way without a guide, without Ariadne's thread.

Then, abruptly, he turned away. There was work to be done, and the night was wearing on.

NICHOLS sat in the President's chair, looking at the President's phone. It was the most secure phone in the world—debugged daily. That was why Nichols had come here. And thank heavens he had! Matt Easton could not be allowed to resign.

Nichols stood up as the President entered the room. Matt's face was haggard, his eyes burning with a quiet intensity.

"What is it, Ed?" the President asked.

"I've figured it out," Nichols said. "And we've got a hell of a problem."

THE BRITISH ambassador to Washington hung up the phone and sat staring into space. It was the strangest request he had ever received from the White House—and perhaps the most urgent.

Then he quickly pressed down his intercom. "Get me a scrambled line to the Foreign Office," the ambassador said.

Within the hour, the same request had been posed to four other parties. International operators stayed busy through the night as calls flew back and forth across the ocean—to and from London, Paris, Bonn, Athens, Tel Aviv.

Nichols had pulled out the stops. Everywhere except Langley. The one agency he didn't press into service was the CIA.

A LONE MAN dressed in black appeared through the restored gate of the palace where the tours of Knossos began. He paused there a moment, then quickly moved up the open steps that led to the central courtyard. It was Graham.

Owen stepped forward to meet him. "It's not like you to be late," he said. It was twenty minutes past midnight.

"I expected you to meet me at the gate."

Owen shrugged. "This seemed more historically pure. Besides, we need to talk."

"Talk! There's no time for talking! Where's the girl?"

"She's here," Owen said.

"Where? Damn it!"

Owen gestured toward a flat-roofed structure that covered the grand staircase, five flights of steps descending into the underground levels of the palace. "She's down there somewhere. I daresay you could find her on your own inside of a week."

"What is this, Owen? What do you think you're doing?"

"Just this: I've got the girl. You want her. And you can have her. But first I want to know why you have cut this short. What's the rush? What's the real story?"

Eyes furious, Graham said, "All right, you want to know? I'll tell you. Fast. Sit down."

Owen preferred to stand. But he leaned back, letting a shoulder rest against one of the sculptured bulls' horns.

"I am in a hurry," Graham said, "and with good reason. For one thing, Simon is no longer available to plant the false clues."

"He's dead?"

"Not just dead, killed—by one of Nichols' agents. There's no more doubt about Nichols. He's done everything I expected him to and more. Three of our key agents are dead because of him, and in each case a scandal is brewing." Graham shook his head. "I think Simon was working for Nichols all along."

Owen's mouth dropped open as he stared at Graham. "Simon working for Nichols? Then Nichols knows—"

"Yes, Nichols has to know about you. And where you are. But there's more," Graham went on. "Nichols did go to the Russians. Soviet agents are on your trail. We've proved our case. We've got to get that girl back to the White House before—"

Graham didn't finish the sentence. He swung around, horrified. In that instant, the lights had come on at Knossos. Floodlights everywhere. Followed by the sharp crack of a pistol. The tip of one of the bulls' horns burst away in an explosion of dust, and the bullet smashed into the courtyard behind them.

Graham dived for cover behind the low wall of a nearby foundation. Owen grabbed his revolver and ducked down near Graham. Then a voice came to them from the south end of the courtyard. A thick accent. Russian.

"That was a warning shot, Fleming. You know we can do better. Come out with your hands in the air."

Graham turned to Owen, his eyes wide with shock.

"Here's another warning, Fleming."

A second bullet, fired from a different position, smashed into a wall on the opposite side of the courtyard. Graham produced a pistol and peered cautiously over the wall.

"I can't figure out where they are," he whispered.

Owen shrugged. "You said the Russians were after *me*."

"Don't split hairs with me, Owen. They've got us cornered here!"

"Us?" Owen said. He smiled. "I believe the voice said Fleming."

Graham turned slowly back to Owen. He went pale. He was staring into the barrel of Owen's revolver, inches in front of his face.

Graham, the code name Fleming had used when he worked in the field, a name he retained at Langley for the key agents he supervised directly. Owen was one of these few. Owen had always known both names, and that they were one person, but he had never before referred to Fleming as Fleming.

Nor had he ever held Fleming at the end of a revolver.

Fleming dropped his pistol to the ground. His face was contorted by a mixture of rage and fear.

"Come out now, Fleming. We don't want to kill you. We want to take you home."

"Why don't you do what they say," Owen said. "They're your colleagues, not mine."

"That's insane! What are you talking about?"

"You, Mr. Deputy Director." Owen smiled. "There was only one thing wrong with your story. It wasn't Nichols, it was you. From the beginning. You're the leak to the Russians. You're the traitor. And now you've dragged me in with you."

Fleming stared at Owen, his face turned cold, hardly admitting defeat. Then he laughed wryly. "I knew I should never have trusted you. Until this I never used you for anything but CIA jobs, because, frankly, I was afraid to. You're too damn smart."

"It's a tough game you play," Owen said. "An agent in place, especially at your level. Pressure from Moscow, pressure in Washington, having to please both sides. But why?"

"You said it—pressure from Moscow. They couldn't be content to have me where I was. I had to get Nichols' job."

So that was it. Nichols' job. Suddenly, it all made sense. Kidnap the President's daughter, and count on the President to rely on his best friend. Then lead Nichols on a wild-goose chase halfway around the world. Dangle a clue in his face, then snatch it back just as he starts to pounce. Make Nichols look like a bungler.

"And then you would rescue the victim and take her home in triumph," Owen said. "Brilliant. It might have worked."

"Are you going to kill me?"

"Of course not."

A look passed between them, like the silent exchange of two doctors who agree on a simple diagnosis. Fleming was a Soviet agent of considerable rank. The knowledge he carried in his head was far too valuable to lose. No agent loyal to the CIA would willingly let that die.

Another bullet hit the pavement on the other side of the wall. *"That was our last warning, Fleming. Come out now, or . . ."*

The Russian voice suddenly lost its power, ground to a halt. Silence. Then darkness. The lights went out overhead.

Owen jumped to his feet, his astonishment genuine. He kept the gun pointed at Fleming as his eyes swept the ruins.

Suddenly, a voice came from behind. "Drop the gun, Owen."

He stood there a moment. Then he slowly opened his hand and the revolver fell to the ground.

Erica was standing by the bulls' horns, her face a pattern of light and shadow under the pale moon. She was holding an automatic in one hand. In the other, a small electronic device—the master switch from which Owen had controlled the lights, the tape deck and amplifier, and the guns he had positioned precisely to avoid their line of fire.

Fleming glanced at the switch, and now he understood. He turned on Owen, glaring. "Tapes! I should have known!"

Owen shrugged. "I found out what I had to."

"You were guessing!"

"But now I know. You're a Soviet agent. So's she."

Erica smiled sweetly. "You're surprised?" she said.

"No. It happens." Owen turned back to Fleming, who was now aiming his pistol at him. Owen would not kill Fleming, but he knew the same restriction did not work in reverse.

"We're wasting time," Fleming said. "Where's the girl?"

Owen stood for a long moment saying nothing. Then his shoulders sagged, his eyes went flat, his expression admitted defeat.

"Follow me," he said. "I'll show you."

Chapter Eleven

"I blackmailed Kolonov," Nichols said.

The President looked up sharply. "You what?"

"Kolonov made a mistake once, an affair with a woman. That's nothing, but the woman in this case was a Red Chinese agent." Nichols smiled. "Kolonov didn't know it, and by the time he found out, the affair was a *fait accompli*. I knew they hadn't heard about it in Moscow, or Kolonov would have been recalled. So when Fleming took off for Athens, I went to Kolonov for help."

"You went to the Russians for help?" The President passed a hand across his eyes. "I'm glad I didn't know it at the time."

"I told you why I couldn't come to you."

"Yes, I know. You thought I'd kidnapped Anne."

"I never believed it, but I had to find out."

"Under the circumstances, I won't argue the point."

"I told Kolonov to put the best agent he had on Paul Fleming and report every move to me. He could hardly say no. He did it —an agent by the name of Svitsky. Fleming spotted Svitsky. And lost him. And that, I knew, was impossible."

"Why?"

"Because Svitsky's too good to let himself be seen—unless he wanted to be, unless he'd been ordered to let Fleming see him. And that could mean only one thing: Kolonov, a high-ranking KGB officer, didn't want Fleming tailed.

"I asked myself why. Who would want Cannon dead? Only the Russians. But the Russians wouldn't kill Cannon without grilling him first to find out what he knew. Unless they already knew, through their own agent inside the hierarchy of the CIA!"

"Fleming."

"Yes, Paul Fleming. A traitor of the worst kind."

"But why would he kidnap Anne?"

"Diversion?" Nichols said. "With Anne, perhaps they hoped

101

to make us think someone else was behind the killing of my three key agents. Perhaps they hoped to avoid retaliation."

A buzzer sounded. The President picked up the phone, listened a moment, hung up. "The French have agreed," he said.

Nichols nodded. "Good. That just leaves the Israelis."

"They'll cooperate," the President said with a grim certainty. "If they don't, they'll never get another cent from this government, not while I'm minding the purse."

Nichols smiled. This was the Matt Easton he knew and admired. "Still sorry you didn't resign?" he said.

"I don't know. Nothing's changed because we now suspect Paul Fleming. If I weren't President, Anne would not have been kidnapped. And Elizabeth wouldn't be suffering this ordeal. They're paying the price for my ambition. And it's far too much to pay."

Nichols understood. "This will be over soon," he said. "Fleming can't get away from us now, not with half the world's intelligence agents on his tail."

FLEMING stayed above as Owen descended the grand staircase with Erica behind, her automatic close to his back. She switched on a flashlight and pointed its beam into the darkness below.

The staircase had been rebuilt, with huge wooden beams and inverted Minoan-style columns supporting its weight. At the bottom of the stairs, they came to the east wing of the palace, the area of the restored royal apartments. Owen turned left into a long passageway that led to the workshop. Here the suddenness of the final destruction was made vivid by work left in progress, by tools cast aside in their users' haste to flee.

Owen moved on, turning right, turning left, winding his way through the maze. The air became steadily damper; beyond the light in Erica's hand the darkness was intense.

Erica spoke only once, from anger more than concern. "What are you doing?" she demanded. "There must be a shorter route."

"Sorry," Owen replied. "There is no such thing down here."

They moved around to the west wing—an area full of long, narrow storage rooms. There were mounds of earth, modern tools left here by archaeologists. They passed through a door, made a turn to the left. Another door lay just ahead.

"Watch it here," Owen warned. "There's scaffolding overhead."

He ducked as he crossed the threshold. Erica swung the light up, keeping Owen in view under the crisscrossed beams of modern metal and wood. He grabbed a bar overhead as his feet found another below. And Erica stepped through the door.

Into nothing! An open shaft of stone. A pit with a floor thirty feet below. Owen had seen it before. A large slab of stone at the bottom suggested the pit's ancient purpose. A temple, for sacrifice.

Erica's gun and flashlight flew from her hands and her arms flailed the air. Owen stood on the scaffolding that rose up from below. His eyes met hers—full of terror, an instant of recognition, a futile moment of hope.

Erica's arms reached out to him. A scream began. Owen felt a rush of air as her shadow fell past him and became a free-floating silhouette against the dim flashlight beam farther down. A metallic crash echoed back up through the pit as the gun hit the floor below. A second crash brought total darkness. Then came the crush of bones against rock. The screaming ceased. There was silence.

Owen jumped back through the door. He retrieved the extra revolver and flashlight he had hidden earlier, and ran.

FLEMING stiffened at the muffled scream from deep inside the ruins. A woman's scream? A man's? Impossible to tell.

He was sure of one thing: Anne Easton was essential to his plan. Anne was his trump card, to be played at the end of the game. Rescue. The triumphant return, just as Owen had guessed. A personal success in contrast to Nichols' bungling. A simple request, the directorship. And why not? Nichols would be finished.

But without Anne, Fleming's whole plan caved in. He would be a bungler, along with Nichols. Failure in Washington. Worse than that, failure in Moscow.

Fleming crossed the courtyard, jumped up on a wall that gave a clear view of the ruins. Wherever Owen emerged, with or without Erica, with or without Anne Easton, Fleming would see him. And he had to come up. There was no other way out.

But there were footsteps at the far end of the courtyard! Someone moving in stealth up the open steps from the gate where Fleming himself had entered the ruins over an hour ago.

Owen? Impossible! But still—one of Owen's tricks, maybe? Fleming dropped to a crouch, raised the pistol.

A whistle. A signal. A switch pulled at the bottom of the hill. The lights flared on overhead. Then a voice broke the silence. "Police! Drop your weapon and come out."

Greek, this time. Through a bull horn!

Fleming shouted across the courtyard, "Forget it, Owen!"

The voice switched to English. "Heraklion police! Come out with your hands in the air!"

Fleming was silent. He waited. Then a man appeared at the top of the steps. White shirt, gold and black epaulets. A black cap with a sharp, shining bill. In his hand, a police revolver. Fleming waited no longer. He fired.

The policeman's body rose up in the air, then toppled backward down the stairs. Suddenly, there were two more figures in white shirts and black hats. Crouching, running, ducking behind cover. Three, four, a whole damn battalion. Real cops!

Fleming jumped, landing on his feet on the far side of the wall. A volley of gunfire followed him, bullets gouging holes in ancient stone. He zigzagged across open pavement, leaping over foundations. There was no time for strategy now, only speed.

He ran for the fence at the north end of the grounds and threw himself over into the grassy meadow on the other side. He ran to the car he'd left parked down the road. A new volley of bullets missed his tires as he took off at high speed toward Heraklion.

A mile or so down the road, he made a sudden sharp turn into a drive that wound back to a farmhouse. The barn door was standing open. He drove in, cut the engine and slammed the barn door shut. He heard two police cars roar by.

Fleming's body trembled with exhaustion. Erica had secured this place beforehand. He had left his clothes here, a second car, a radio set, a telephone. If Erica had the girl, she would find her way here. But now, with a moment to think, Fleming had to be realistic. He knew that the scream had not been Owen's.

Fleming was heading for the barn door when a sound came from behind. He drew his pistol.

"Don't fire!"

A man moved out of the shadows. Broad, Slavic features.

"Svitsky! What are you doing here?"

"I'm making contact with you."

"What's this about? I don't have time—"

"You'll make time, Comrade. We've got a big problem."

Fleming's eyes narrowed. "What?"

"Nichols is on to you."

OWEN HAD ALMOST reached the foot of the grand staircase when the lights came on and shouting broke out overhead.

Police! Where had they come from?

He cut across a corridor into the royal apartments. From behind came the murmur of voices in Greek and footsteps pounding on stone. The police were descending the stairs now.

Owen's eyes scanned the room where he stood, a private sanctuary with four walls and ceiling and no place to hide. He moved quickly into a corridor that led to a smaller chamber, with blue dolphins painted in fresco along the upper walls. A gay room designed for the queen of Crete.

Beyond the queen's room, a short corridor and one last refuge—the tiny chamber that had been the queen's bath. There was no light here, just a deep clay tub, once complete with running water, and still intact four thousand years after the last royal soaking. Owen flattened himself on the floor behind the tub.

He listened in silence as footsteps came closer—from the sanctuary into the queen's room on the other side of the wall. They stopped there a moment, then came on. Not one man, but two.

Owen lay where he was, hardly daring to breathe. The footsteps entered the corridor to the bath, approached the doorway. They stopped. Two policemen were standing less than five feet from where Owen lay. A flashlight beam probed the corners of the tiny room, passing over the rim of the tub. Then the light swung back sharply and aimed at a spot on the floor.

"What's that?"

A moment of silence. One of the men came forward into the room. His hand brushed the floor at the edge of the tub.

"A coin. American."

The other man laughed. "So what? There were hundreds of tourists here today. There's no one here now. Let's go."

The light flicked off. The footsteps moved away. Owen took a deep breath. Then he sat up and looked down into the tub. A dark blanket covered the bottom. Owen pulled it back.

Anne Easton lay where he'd left her, in the deep curve of the tub, her eyes closed against a peaceful face. She was unconscious again, oblivious to danger, and Owen was glad for that. The drug, in a way, was her protection—as her life was his. He checked her pulse, strong and steady. Then he pulled the blanket around her, lifted her up, and carried her out of the room.

Outside the sanctuary, Owen moved quickly down a corridor to a small arching doorway. He had removed its lock earlier and re-placed it with one of his own. Now he opened the door and stepped inside an excavation filled with dirt and wheelbarrows. There was no electricity here, only battery-operated lamps strung across the carved-out roof overhead. And the latest "find" at Knossos: a sub-terranean tunnel leading down the hill, away from the domestic quarters of the palace, to the river Kairatos.

Owen carried Anne into the tunnel, making his way easily along the declining stone floor. Minutes later he emerged into open air. Lights glowed from the top of the hill behind him, but ahead there was only the night—a patchwork of moonlight and shadow. More digging tools. Cypress trees lining the riverbank.

And a boat, a simple rowboat.

Owen had planned it that way. He laid the girl on the blanket in the grass and pushed the boat quietly into the water. He re-trieved the oars from their hiding place in the brush and slipped them into place. Then he picked up Anne, climbed into the boat, and pushed off from the riverbank.

The oars sliced the water, making less sound than the flow of the river. Slow and strong, downstream. Away from Knossos. Away from the police and Paul Fleming. To a waiting car.

IT WAS DAWN, Fleming stood at a window of the farmhouse, watching the sun come up over the mountains of Crete. On a table nearby, the radio set remained silent. No report from the agents he had posted along the road on each side of Knossos. There was nothing to report. Behind him a door opened.

"I've just been in touch with Moscow," Svitsky said.

Fleming felt a tightening in his chest that he recognized as fear. "I'd call that a bit premature."

"Perhaps." Svitsky shrugged. "Nonetheless, they're not very happy with you. You're a liability now. They're cutting the ties."

"That's a death sentence! What do they want? I've given them Cannon, Sherman, Shelley Curtis."

"True. But you've failed the assignment they gave you: a KGB agent in place at the head of the CIA. And you've probably blown your cover. You've got nothing to bargain with now."

Fleming turned away in deep frustration. "It's a tough game you play," Owen had said. "Having to please both sides." Now he had failed both sides—not only Moscow, but Langley.

Svitsky had spelled it all out during the night. Fleming had succeeded too well. He had forced Nichols to go to the Russians for help, an ironic twist—to Kolonov at the embassy. And Kolonov, of course, had reported to Moscow that Nichols was suspicious; that was enough.

There had to be a way out. He stood there thinking, and an idea came to mind. He turned to Svitsky.

"Tell Moscow I can salvage this yet," he said.

"How?"

"Same as before. I rescue the girl and take her home."

"But you've been out of contact with Nichols too long. How will you handle him?"

"How will he handle me when I come home with Anne?" Fleming said. "Nichols suspects, but he doesn't know for sure. I defuse his suspicions by giving Anne back to her parents. Then I blame the kidnapping on Owen. I simply say that once I found out Owen was alive and had Anne, I purposely cut myself off from the CIA. Owen's a CIA agent! I didn't know what to think."

Svitsky smiled. "It might work. Of course, it means you've got to find Owen."

"I can do that with time. I've still got contacts inside the CIA. The agents I've turned. They're still loyal to me."

Svitsky was silent. Then he shrugged. "I'll see what they say."

Fleming felt enormous relief. But now he had to get Owen. It was vital! He also had to get Anne Easton. She was more than a trump card now. She was Fleming's only chance for survival.

THE DIRECTOR of Greek intelligence was in his office as the sun came up over Athens. A report lay on his desk. He picked up the phone and in minutes reached Nichols at the White House.

"We've located Paul Fleming," the Greek said, and quickly explained what had happened.

A fisherman setting nets in the river Kairatos, on the island of Crete, had noticed lights going on and off at the nearby ruins of Knossos. Then he heard gunshots and angry voices and decided to call the police. When the officers arrived, they found the night guards unconscious. A radio call went out for more help.

The Greek described the scene at Knossos—one man, alone, killing an officer, escaping over the fence. "But," the Greek said, "the man has been identified from photographs. It was Paul Fleming. I'm sorry to say he got away in a car and we don't know where he is now." Then he added, "There is something else. Another man must have been inside the ruins. Before Fleming escaped, he called out a name. That name was Owen."

Nichols frowned. Owen? Suddenly, his face went white. *Owen!*

Of course. Richard Owen! A man who could have walked into the house at Indian Springs and back out with the President's daughter. A man who could have and would have.

Fleming had been Owen's case officer for years. It was Fleming who went to Oslo, where Richard Owen had died, Fleming who confirmed the identification. Dental records. Fingerprints. All in Owen's file. And who had instant access to that file? Who could substitute other records for Owen's own? Paul Fleming.

Richard Owen wasn't dead!

Nichols hung up the phone and looked across at the President. "I hate to say this," he said, "but we've got serious trouble. I know who has your daughter—a monster of our own making."

Chapter Twelve

Owen pulled into the driveway of Harry Goldman's bachelor quarters in Heraklion. Harry had been divorced for nearly a year now. Owen hadn't seen him since Harry had left the CIA and returned to the US air force. It ought to be a happy reunion. Owen checked the condition of his passenger in the back of the car, then went to the front door and rang the bell.

Lights came on in the house and in a few moments, the door opened. Harry Goldman stood there, legs bare under an old bathrobe. He looked exactly the same. Hair dark, eyes a little distant, and, yes, the beard as full as ever.

Harry's jaw dropped. "Richard Owen!" He grabbed Owen with both arms. "I can't believe it! They said you'd been killed!"

"They were wrong," Owen replied.

"Yes, I guess they were!" Grinning, Harry pulled Owen into the house. "What are you doing here at this hour?"

"It's a long story. Do you have a coffee pot?"

"Right next to my Glenfiddich. Man, I'm glad to see you!"

They settled themselves in the kitchen over cups of hot coffee and talk of old times. It was a strange friendship, thought Owen, who rarely allowed himself friends. A friendship where serious questions were asked cautiously, if at all, and where answers were never required. A friendship based on shared experience, shared danger, shared confidence.

"How's Barbara?" Owen finally asked.

"Barbara! At the moment I seem to be paying for a world tour." Harry was rubbing his eyes with both hands. Then he got up, rummaged in a kitchen cabinet and produced a bottle of aspirin.

"You mention Barbara, and I get a headache," he said. "I'll tell you this. I'm never going to get rich unless she gets married again." He popped two aspirin into his mouth and washed them down with more coffee. Turning back to the table, he stumbled.

"Hell, what's the matter with me?"

Owen smiled. "Keeping late hours again?"

Harry managed a sheepish grin but no reply.

"How do you like your job here?" Owen asked.

Harry shrugged. "Softest tour I've had, but frankly I won't mind when they decide to move me on."

Owen nodded. "Enjoy it while it lasts."

"Yeah." Harry shook his head. "Damn! What's going on?"

Then, suddenly, he looked at Owen and knew. He stared across the table without moving, his mind lunging at Owen but his body refusing to budge out of the chair.

"The coffee?" His eyes were growing distant. "What's in it?"

"Nothing permanent." Owen reached into his pocket and produced a plastic vial of tiny white pills. "Diatol. Enough to make you sleep for a couple of days."

Harry's head was starting to sag. "Why?"

"I'm sorry. Harry. Trust me. It's important."

"It better be," Harry replied thickly. Then his head dropped, and he slumped forward across the table.

Owen carried him upstairs and laid him on the bed. He found Harry's keys and went out to his garage. The car inside was a small white Fiat. Owen backed it out and drove his car in. Then he carried Anne Easton into the house.

Two hours later he telephoned a local number. "This is Captain Goldman. I won't be in today. I think I've got the flu."

"I'm sorry to hear that, sir," came the voice at the other end. "I'll notify your section."

"Thanks." Owen hung up. Then he carried Anne out to Harry's waiting Fiat and drove away.

THE WOMAN behind the Olympic Airways ticket counter smiled at the man on the other side. She'd seen her share of US officers in this job, but never one with a beard like this.

"Here you are, Captain Goldman," she said. "One seat on our flight to Athens, departing in forty minutes. I've left the return date open."

Owen smiled. "Thank you."

He'd booked the return flight on purpose. He'd spotted two British MI6 agents outside. There were bound to be more. He knew they'd be checking everything, including one-way trips out of here.

"Do you have any luggage to check?" the woman asked.

Owen glanced down at the garment bag he was holding. "No, thanks," he said. "I think I'll keep this with me."

HARRY GOLDMAN'S secretary was a young airman, nineteen years old and a new recruit to the air force. He had joined up to see the world, and Heraklion was surely that. Unfortunately, he spent most of his time at his desk.

110

"I'm sorry, but Captain Goldman is sick," he told the commanding officer's secretary. "He took the NATO report home last night, and he's not coming in today."

The woman's rank was higher than his. "Then someone will have to go get it," she replied coolly. "The CO must see the report today."

Someone. The airman knew who that meant.

"Yes, ma'm," he said. "I'll leave right away."

When he reached Captain Goldman's house, the young airman rang the doorbell several times. There was no answer. The morning paper was lying on the front steps. Apparently, the captain had spent the night elsewhere.

Terrific.

He started to return to his car. Then he stopped. If the captain wasn't in the house, the NATO report might be. He walked around to the back.

A kitchen window gave to a little pressure. He pushed it up. Surely the captain wouldn't care. If he had to return to the base without the report, after all, he would also have to reveal the captain's white lie. Sick with the flu? Sure he was!

The airman climbed through the open window.

THE AIRPORT IN Athens was full of West German agents. Owen recognized three. Where had they come from? he wondered. They were on the wrong side for Fleming. Nichols? That made better sense. Nichols and the President in tandem, drawing on global resources. The world, it seemed, was against him.

He took a cab to Omonia Square, where he set off on foot by a roundabout route to the Xenophon Gallery. A bell tinkled as he pushed open the door.

"May I help you?" a handsome, gray-haired woman asked.

"Yes, I'm Harry Goldman. I'm here to see Molly."

"Molly." A pause. Then, "Follow me, please."

Molly was the gallery's bookkeeper and sat in an office at the back. She also handled CIA identification at the Athens station.

Molly had known Harry, but not too well, Owen hoped. Dark hair, dark beard, in uniform—he was Harry Goldman, but he didn't want to press the issue with an intimate friend.

"Harry! What are you doing here?"

He had passed. Owen hung the garment bag on a metal rack. "I came by to say hello."

"After all this time?" Molly gave him a doubtful glance. Then she grinned. "Never mind. How's the air force?"

"Busy in the wild blue yonder." It was the kind of thing Harry would have said. Cute.

"You look different somehow." She frowned. Then her face broke into a smile. "The glasses!"

"You had to notice."

Molly laughed. "Vain as ever. How long will you be here?"

"That depends on how much red tape you can cut. You may have heard, I'm assigned to air force intelligence."

"No, I hadn't, but it figures."

Owen nodded. "And I'm on *the* priority assignment."

Molly looked back at him without saying anything.

"Anne Easton," Owen added. "If we don't find her soon—" He sliced his throat with his finger and left the sentence unfinished.

Molly nodded grimly. "I knew something was up when Paul Fleming arrived here. Have you seen him?"

Owen nodded. "In Heraklion. But listen, there's a file I need to see. I can go through channels if I have to. I was hoping you'd save me the trouble."

"Which file?"

"Erich Parsons."

"Sure," Molly said. "He's not even classified."

Owen knew that. It was one reason he had picked Parsons.

"And anyway," Molly added, "you know enough to blow this place sky-high anytime you want to. Come with me."

"Thanks," Owen said. "I appreciate this." He picked up the garment bag. "And so, I hope, will the President."

MOLLY didn't leave him alone with the files for long. But it was just long enough for him to get what he needed.

Two hours and several stops later Captain Harry Goldman checked into the Hotel Pandora. It was a clean place that offered minimum service at rates to match. Anne would be safe here.

He lifted her out of the garment bag and laid her gently on

112

the bed. She was nothing but a liability now. As long as he kept her with him, capture was too real a threat.

He dropped down in a chair by the bed to think through the alternatives. On the one hand, Paul Fleming, a man with the power to unleash the worst of both worlds—the CIA and the KGB —working toward a common goal: get Owen! That threat was bad enough.

The other threat was worse. Ed Nichols and all he represented. Capture. Extradition and justice.

Owen knew what he should do: dump Anne with some local authorities and disappear. Anything else would be foolish. An unerring instinct for his own safety had kept him alive up to now. And a free man. He could not go against that instinct.

But there was also the question of pride. Professional pride. And commitment. He wanted to defeat Fleming, to finish the job, do it right. Yes, the toughest assignment of his career had gone sour, becoming tougher still. He had money and his own ingenuity. Nothing more. He couldn't trust anyone now. He was wanted on both sides of a bipolar world, by the law and the lawless. He was entirely on his own.

He glanced at the small child sleeping comfortably on the pillow, and he smiled with a new sense of exhilaration. It was an enormous risk, but also an enormous challenge. Against all of that, whatever it meant, he would take Anne Easton home.

And then he would walk away. Richard Owen would simply cease to exist. Forever.

THE HARRY GOLDMAN incident came to Ed Nichols' attention via defense intelligence, where they considered a drugged air force officer, recently with the CIA, well within the limits of the unusual circumstances they'd been told to report without delay. Especially when the officer's passport was missing, along with his wallet and one uniform.

Nichols knew Goldman's name, as he knew everything in Richard Owen's file—including all friendships, however distant. And now, settled into the President's study, on the phone again to Athens, Nichols knew something else: the incident had been reported too late.

"Captain Harry Goldman is still unconscious," the Greek intelligence officer reported over the phone. "Yet he left Heraklion this morning on an Olympic flight to Athens."

"You're sure it was the same Harry Goldman?"

"Unless you have two air force captains of the same name and description with identical passport numbers."

Nichols sighed. It had to be Owen. He and Goldman had known each other for years. And friendship notwithstanding, the style of the escape was strictly Owen's own.

"Were you able to pick up his trail in Athens?" Nichols asked.

"Sorry. He took a taxi into the city and got out at Omonia Square. From there, nothing."

Nichols hung up and leaned back in his chair to think about Richard Owen. Professionally, he knew Owen as well as anyone could. He had studied his past assignments. He had analyzed his techniques and motivation. And he had come to one conclusion —that Owen would not intentionally betray the CIA.

Owen's loyalty was dictated not by idealism but by the kind of person he was. He would never work for the Soviets; he valued his freedom too highly. He was also the best of his kind, and he had to work for the best.

Good intentions were no defense according to the law—Owen was guilty of kidnapping, probably murder, and possibly treason —but he could not have known that Fleming was a traitor. Or could he have?

A new thought struck Nichols, and he frowned. Owen had been with Fleming at Knossos. Before Fleming escaped, he had called out to Owen. In anger? He had probably thought the policeman was Owen. It was Owen he'd tried to kill!

Had Owen discovered the truth? Had he split from Fleming?

A smile spread across Nichols' face as the theory grew toward conviction. If there had been a split, it was Owen who had Anne Easton. That was good news, because Owen would not hurt Anne. Not if he could avoid it.

A delicate balance, Nichols thought. He wanted Fleming with a vengeance, but now he wanted Owen more. Because Owen had Anne. Yet caution was needed.

Then another thought struck Nichols, and the smile disappeared.

If Owen had split with Fleming, then Fleming must want him as badly as Nichols did! This wasn't a chase, but a contest. He not only had to find Owen—now he had to do it before Fleming did.

MOLLY LEFT the Xenophon Gallery at the usual time. At home, she started to pour a drink, then changed her mind and made coffee. This was no time to blunt her nerves. She had to make contact with Graham. But how? She could only wait.

Then the telephone rang.

"Hello?"

"Is Stephanos there?"

Molly's face showed enormous relief, her voice only a mild interest.

"You must have the wrong number."

The line disconnected at the other end. Molly hurried out the door. Ten minutes later she was waiting inside a phone booth and picked up the phone as it rang.

"Thank God, it's you, Graham," Molly said.

"What's wrong?"

"Do you remember Harry Goldman?"

"Of course. Why?"

"He was in the gallery today and talking about Sunflower."

Paul Fleming was clearly astonished. "Harry Goldman was?"

"That's just it. I don't think it was Harry at all," Molly said. "He looked like Harry, talked like him, moved like him. But after he left, I remembered. Harry was allergic to roses. There were roses on my desk, but he didn't react at all."

Fleming's voice turned cold.

"Repeat every word he said."

Molly left nothing out. The air force. The glasses. Anne Easton. The Erich Parsons file.

"Did he give any clues to where he was going?" Fleming asked.

"No," Molly said. "But once I realized he might be an imposter, I made a few phone calls. There's a Harry Goldman registered at the Hotel Pandora in Athens."

After Molly hung up, she smiled. She'd given Graham the head start he needed. Still, she'd delay a little longer. Then she'd report Goldman's visit to her CIA control.

A REPRIEVE had come from Moscow. Fleming had returned to Athens with Svitsky aboard an unscheduled plane. He felt sure Owen would come here, too—to the bigger city, with its crowds of tourists for camouflage and its many routes of escape. Now he knew he'd been right.

Fleming had gone straight to the home of a Soviet diplomat who was the local KGB resident. He used the secure phone to call his people inside the CIA; he had three at the embassy and one at the local station. The call to Molly had paid off.

He'd hung up the phone, turned to Svitsky, and said, "Owen's at the Hotel Pandora."

Svitsky nodded. Twenty minutes later the two of them were standing outside Owen's door. A strip of light showed across the bottom. A radio played softly inside.

Fleming raised his pistol as Svitsky flung himself at the door. It flew open. It hadn't even been locked!

And no wonder. Fleming stared into the empty room. Harry Goldman was there, what was left of him—a uniform hanging neatly in the closet. Richard Owen had left him behind. He was gone, and so was the President's daughter.

On his way out of town, Owen had stopped by a mailbox and deposited a package. In it were Harry's passport and wallet, with two hundred dollars to cover the cost of the uniform and the parking charge Harry would have to pay to get his Fiat out of the airport at Heraklion.

It was, Owen thought, the least he could do for a friend.

Chapter Thirteen

 Evangelos Panayotides dipped a piece of bread into the *tzatziki* and popped it into his mouth, without taking his eyes off his visitor from New York.

"Some distributors are passing off their Mexican crops for Colombian," the visitor was saying. "That makes all crops suspect. No one's buying our shipments until this blows over."

"Which distributors?"

"The Italians."

"I see." Panayotides nodded his toadlike head. Then he washed down the *tzatziki* with a glass of ouzo and strolled over to the edge of the terrace. His house was perched on the slope of Mount Parnassus, above the village of Delphi. The view spread far beyond the village, to the Temple of Apollo, stark and awesome by moonlight, to the smaller, more serene Temple of Athene Prothene, to the olive grove spreading down the side of the mountain.

It was from Parnassus that Apollo once routed the Persian army by heaving boulders down on the advancing troops—and from this peak that Evangelos Panayotides ran an empire so prosperous that he could afford to be generous.

Let the Mexican government spray its fields to poison the marijuana; he had no holdings there. The Italians did and were trying to pass their tainted crops off as Colombian. Let them. Panayotides didn't feel like war. He turned to his visitor. "Store our stuff," he said. "It'll be worth twice as much next year."

Then he glanced up as a servant appeared.

"There's a priest to see you, *Kyrie*."

The toadlike face wrinkled into a scowl. "I don't want to see anyone now. Send him away."

But the servant persisted. "He said to tell you his name is Father Phoebus and he knew you five years ago."

Panayotides' expression froze somewhere between rage and fear. Father Phoebus, was it? What did they want now?

He dismissed the visitor with a gesture and turned back to the servant. "Tell the good father I'll see him," Panayotides said.

Project Phoebus had been a CIA operation with the goal of dropping an agent behind the Iron Curtain into the Karelian Isthmus area, where the Soviets maintained several top-secret defense systems. The drop had to be made with no trace back to the CIA. Evangelos Panayotides had obliged with a pilot and a small jet from his private fleet of planes. He did not do it by choice. The CIA had the goods on him—signed documents and photographs. Enough to send Panayotides to jail for the rest of his life.

That was five years ago. And he had believed their promise that they would never use him again. Now they were back.

He looked at the man who came across the terrace, a man wearing the black beard and full robes of a Greek Orthodox priest.

117

"Father Phoebus?" Panayotides said.

Owen nodded.

"What do you want from me?"

"The same thing we wanted before."

The Greek sat down. "The Karelian Isthmus again?"

"Hardly," Owen replied. "No, this time the target is Newark."

"Newark!" Panayotides stared at him, incredulous. "You're joking! Newark, New Jersey?"

"Newark, New Jersey," Owen confirmed. "Your regular port of entry to the United States. You have certain officials there on your payroll and can come and go pretty much as you please."

The Greek smiled, impressed by the thoroughness of this man. "That's true," he said. "I have had my way at Newark."

"And with you on the plane," Owen said, "so can I."

But the Greek shook his head. "No. I never travel by plane."

"I know." Owen smiled. "A near crash. You haven't flown in three years."

The Greek stared at him. There was little, it seemed, that the CIA didn't know.

"I'm prepared to pay a rather good price," Owen added.

"I hardly think money will change my mind!"

"Not money. A name. The name of the man who betrayed you to the CIA. A man who is still a part of your organization."

Panayotides leaned forward. The question had plagued him for all these five years. Disloyalty, the worst of all possible treachery! He spat the words out. "Who is it?"

"Will you go with me to Newark?"

The Greek hesitated a moment. Then he said, "When do you want to leave?"

"Right now."

ED NICHOLS replaced the phone in the President's study. He knew now where Owen had gone after Omonia Square. He had walked into the CIA station in Athens and back out again!

And this time he'd made a mistake.

He had left a clue. The answer had to be there, in a file drawer marked *P*. Something Owen wanted, and not in the Parsons file. Something else in the drawer with Parsons.

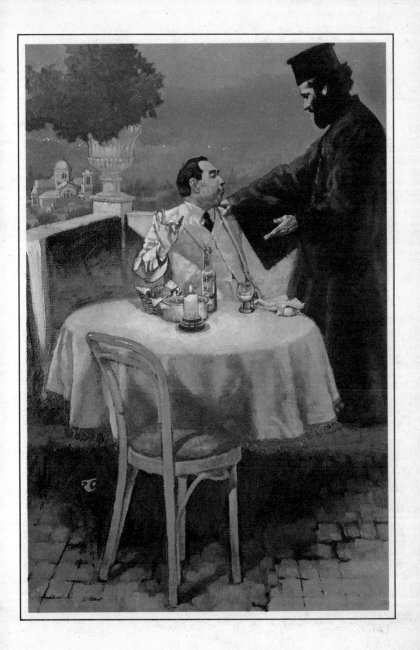

Those same files existed on computer tape at Langley. Whatever it was, if it took him all night, Nichols knew he would find it.

He had to find it. Owen had made one mistake; he wouldn't make another.

FLEMING knew it the minute he saw the file drawer in the Athens office—not Parsons, but Panayotides! Even a page was missing.

Molly had then checked with the CIA man inside Panayotides' organization. One of their jets had taken off from an airstrip north of Delphi less than an hour ago. The Greek himself was on board. With him, two bodyguards and a Greek Orthodox priest.

The plane's destination: Newark, New Jersey.

Fleming knew it was risky going back to the United States before he had Anne Easton. But Owen had to be aboard that plane. And if Owen was there, Anne had to be, too.

Fleming also knew he had to move fast, get a larger, more powerful plane—one that would not have to put down to refuel. He dialed Aeroflot, asked for a specific agent. And he smiled. It was Project Phoebus all over again. But this time Panayotides was delivering Richard Owen.

THERE WAS a rumble of thunder as Nichols climbed down from the helicopter, then a burst of lightning that lit up the army trucks parked near the terminal building at Newark airport.

A man ran from the terminal to meet him, leaning into the wind. "Mr. Nichols? I'm John Temple of the Federal Aviation Administration. Some day, isn't it?"

Nichols nodded grimly as he shook Temple's hand. "Do you think the plane will have to be diverted?" he asked.

Temple glanced at the sky and shrugged. "Can't say yet. It's hard to predict what a storm will do."

Nichols fell into step with Temple, hurrying across the pavement toward the terminal building. Another flash of lightning jagged down through the sky and in that instant, Nichols could see faces peering out of the army trucks—troops from Fort Dix ready for action. Nichols wasn't expecting war. But he needed bodies to create a tight security shield in the critical areas of the airport when Owen came off the plane with Anne Easton.

"Meantime," Temple added as they neared the door, "you may have a problem with the general manager. He's got trouble enough with the weather, he says. Air traffic backed up all over. He's not wild about your plan."

"He doesn't have to be wild about it," Nichols replied. "He just has to do it."

Seymour Scott was sitting behind his desk when Nichols walked in. Scott was a man of about forty, with receding black hair and eyes that were coldly penetrating.

"Mr. Scott. I'm Ed Nichols."

"I know who you are," the manager replied.

"Then you know I expect your full cooperation," Nichols said.

"I know this," Scott replied. "I don't take orders from the CIA. I don't have the time or inclination to close this airport down. I've got a call into Washington now."

"Oh, you do." Nichols was not surprised. "I'm not here in my capacity as director of the CIA. I'm here as a federal marshal. I also have legal sanction to nationalize this airport if necessary, under the Emergency Powers Act."

Nichols produced the letters that verified his statement. Then he reached for the telephone and started dialing.

"What are you doing?" Scott asked.

"I'm expediting your call." Nichols listened as the phone rang. Then he identified himself and waited a moment more.

"I'd like you to speak to the airport manager," Nichols said into the phone. Then he held it out to Scott. "It's the President."

PANAYOTIDES' servant leaned down to look out a starboard window. "It's American," he confirmed. "It looks like an F-15."

Panayotides nodded. He turned, resigned, to the man in the seat beside him. "What do we do now?" he said.

The priest shrugged and glanced through his own portside window. "Pray?" Then he added, "There's another one over here."

"Escorts! Just what we needed!" Panayotides said.

FLEMING raised a pair of powerful binoculars to his eyes. He focused on the army trucks at the back of the terminal building.

He turned to Svitsky, who was standing at another window. The two men were in a high-rise apartment, a mile from Newark airport. They'd arrived there by way of New York, disguised as Soviet crewmen on a regular Aeroflot flight.

But Nichols was at the airport, and the whole army with him!

"We can hardly go in there," Svitsky said.

Fleming nodded and raised the binoculars again. "We will," he replied. "But for now, we'll just have to wait."

TRAFFIC in and out of Newark airport had come to a halt. Thirteen planes were waiting at the ramps for taxi clearance—and they would wait until Nichols gave the sign to go. Eight more, circling overhead, were being diverted to nearby airports. The terminal was crammed with irate passengers.

Nichols was standing at a window on the observation deck, looking out at the sheets of wind-driven rain which were sweeping across the pavement. Temple, the FAA man, was at his side.

"It's still too soon to know if the weather's going to be a problem," Temple said. "We've got forty minutes at least. And in any case, I gather you have contingency plans."

Nichols nodded. The air force escorts had been his idea, his plan to prevent Owen from bailing out unobserved over the eastern shore. And the F-15s provided another kind of insurance. If Owen's plane were diverted by weather, they would stay with it. Federal agents and troops were on alert all along the Atlantic seaboard; they could be mobilized with practically no delay.

Yes, Owen was covered. He would not get away.

PANAYOTIDES' pilot switched on his radio. "Newark Approach Control, this is *Charioteer Six*. Do you read me?"

There was a crackling of static before the reply came. "This is Newark. We read you, *Charioteer*. How's the weather up there?"

"Nothing we can't handle." Then he made it official. "*Charioteer Six* requesting final approach to Newark on instruments."

There was a long moment of silence before the response came back. "Right, *Charioteer*. Turn left three six zero."

"Left thirty-six," the pilot acknowledged.

"We're handing you off to the tower now."

"Roger, Approach Control. This is *Charioteer Six* out."

The plane began its descent, down through rain-swollen clouds and turbulence. Panayotides' knuckles whitened as his hands gripped the armrests on both sides of the seat. His eyes shifted to the window on the left. There was no visibility! Only dark clouds!

In the tower, Nichols watched the speck of light turning more to the right with each new sweep of the radarscope. The man in the headset in front of the scope said. "We're charting you, *Charioteer*. Right heading two zero. You're cleared for runway 4E."

"Right, Newark. Descending to one thousand feet."

"Brake system?" It was the pilot talking to the co-pilot.

"Okay," came the reply.

"Landing gear?"

"In place and locked."

Then the pilot: "We're at two thousand feet, Newark."

"And cleared for final approach," the man in the headset said. "Bring her on in."

Nichols and John Temple pulled on a couple of oilskins and hurried downstairs by private elevator. Outside, they jumped aboard a waiting baggage truck and sped toward runway 4E. Nichols wiped the rain from his glasses. His face was flushed with excitement. He could see the troops in position along the runway. Just a few minutes more and he would have Anne Easton.

The plane appeared through the low-hanging clouds. It was coming down fast and strong, lined up in a perfect approach to the runway. "Faster!" Nichols shouted. He glanced at Temple, who smiled with anticipation.

Then, suddenly, the smile faded. Temple's eyes widened, his jaw dropped. Nichols' heart lurched in fear, and he leaned forward as his gaze shifted back to the sky.

The plane was dropping too fast! It was coming down at a sharp angle to the pavement.

Nichols heard Temple's cry, two agonized words against a great roar of sound as the pilot put on extra power. Wind shear! A dramatic shift in wind speed or direction that struck with no warning.

The pilot tried to pull up, but the plane was too close to the ground. It was listing to port. He brought the left wing up sharply, and the right wing dipped too low. The plane rolled back and forth as it roared in close to the runway.

123

It touched down hard on the pavement. But the nose was up. The struts that held the wheels snapped off, and the plane came down on its belly. It skidded across the concrete, sending up a huge spray of sparks.

Nichols' heart stopped. The troops were running for cover. From behind came the shrill pitch of sirens as fire trucks raced toward the plane. And the plane continued to skid, smashing signal lights on the runway as it slid off the pavement. Finally, it came to a stop in a deep patch of mud and grass.

The sparks had been doused by the rain. There was no explosion or fire. *Charioteer* was on the ground and safe.

Nichols fell back against the seat, weak from fear, and relieved. Then, quickly, he pulled himself together. The hatch was opening. A chute was dropped, and the passengers pushed toward it.

Nichols ran toward the plane as Evangelos Panayotides came sliding to the ground. The toadlike face was totally drained of color. His eyes were wide and staring in terror. A man in a black suit came next, then another.

Nichols glanced up. A priest in black robes was standing in the open hatch. Their eyes met, exchanged nothing. Then the priest, too, came sliding to the ground.

BEN KAUFMANN turned to his seatmate as the Eastern jet rolled to a stop at the ramp. "Nice talking to you," he said.

"My pleasure." The other man grinned. "I have to admit, I never met a professional golfer. Good luck at the PGA."

"Thanks."

Kaufmann merged with the line in the aisle. The doors opened and people began filing off the plane.

A stewardess had already retrieved his golf bag, a large professional model, from the closet that divided the first- and tourist-class cabins. She smiled as Kaufmann approached.

"I guess you never check these as baggage," she said.

"No, ma'am." Kaufmann returned the smile. "These clubs are my livelihood."

Outside, palm trees swayed to a gentle wind under a sunlit sky. Miami. The temperature was eighty degrees.

Richard Owen took a deep breath. Then he moved forward,

124

supporting the weight of the golf bag against his back. He headed for customs.

The clubs in the oversize bag were genuine; they could be—well might be—removed. The outside pouches, unzipped, would reveal golf balls, wooden tees, pigskin gloves. Only by reaching down into the bag could anyone discover why it weighed a bit more than it might have.

Owen smiled as he thought of Newark and the priest who was a servant of Panayotides'. Owen had never been near the plane called *Charioteer*, and neither had Anne Easton.

"THEY WANT YOU at the embassy, now," Svitsky said.

Fleming studied his face. It told him nothing. But nothing said a great deal. The assignment was over, a failure. Newark had been the end. In Moscow, patience had run out.

Fleming stalled. "Why?"

Svitsky shrugged. "They're probably sending you home."

Home? Where was that? Moscow? A dacha on the Black Sea? Unlikely.

Fleming had no delusions. His value had ceased with his cover. Moscow could not let him live.

He nodded. "I'll pack a bag."

After Newark, he and Svitsky had driven to an apartment in Washington. They had tried to pick up Owen's trail, without success. But it didn't matter much now. Fleming had been out of contact too long to simply explain it away to Nichols. Langley was no longer his home any more than Moscow was.

He stepped into the next room, threw the few things he had with him into a suitcase. Then he picked up his pistol.

Svitsky was scanning a magazine when Fleming returned. He started to get to his feet. Fleming fired.

He allowed no time for shock or recognition. The bullet entered neatly between Svitsky's eyes, and the force of the shot slammed him down into the chair. Svitsky died there, without knowing what had happened.

Fleming picked up the bag and left the apartment, not sure where he was going, knowing only what he had to do. Anne Easton was still his only chance for survival. With the President's daughter as hostage, he could negotiate his own future. Amnesty from the United States and protection from the Soviet Union.

But to find Anne Easton, he first had to find Richard Owen.

NICHOLS nodded to the secretary outside the Oval Office, then opened the door and walked in. Matt was behind his desk.

Nichols crossed the room and dropped into a chair. "Get Elizabeth on the phone," he said. "I need to see both of you."

The President frowned. "Why?"

"Because I've got an idea," Nichols said. "A plan to trap Owen."

Chapter Fourteen

George Zvinczk was a middle-aged man and balding. His face was deeply lined, with skin hanging loose at his jaw-line, the result of drink more than age. He had been drinking when Owen arrived on his doorstep in Gaithersburg, Maryland.

"Who did you say you were?"

"I'm Jack Rogers of the American Guild of Variety Artists," Owen repeated. "I'd have called, but we don't have your number."

Zvinczk smiled as he stepped back from the door. "That's because I don't have a phone. Come on in."

"Thank you." Owen moved a pair of socks from a chair and sat down. "I have some bad news," he said.

Zvinczk picked up his glass. "Let me have it."

"The picnic has been canceled."

A flicker of disappointment settled into a look of resignation. Zvinczk nodded. "It figures."

"But," Owen added quickly. "I have another offer for you. It pays twice as much, plus expenses."

The reddened eyes didn't change. "I'll take it," Zvinczk said, and downed the last of his drink.

"I thought you would." Owen reached into a pocket, then tossed an airline ticket folder onto the bare table between them. He added ten one-hundred-dollar bills.

Zvinczk stared wide-eyed at the money. "Are you serious?"

"Quite serious."

Zvinczk opened the ticket folder. "Nairobi?"

"A six-week engagement with a circus there."

"But me? Why me?"

Owen shrugged. "They need a star clown who's not under contract elsewhere." He leaned forward. "That's just a down payment, of course. Half is expenses. The rest is your first week's pay. You have to leave tonight," Owen went on. "Can you do it?"

"Can I do it!" Zvinczk grinned. "Are you kidding? For that kind of money, I could go to the moon!"

FLEMING STROLLED into a bar on Fourteenth Street, north of the White House. He was dressed in faded jeans and an old shirt. He ordered a beer and glanced across at the phone booth. Someone was inside; his calls would have to wait.

The same calls again, to a handful of former employees who were still loyal to him. They were all he had, and not much. So far they had turned up nothing to help him find Richard Owen.

He paid for the beer and picked up the newspaper he'd bought at a corner news stand. A late edition of the Washington *Post*. As always, he turned to the classifieds.

And there something caught his eye. A display ad in the help wanteds. A name in boldface type: BLACKJACK.

Blackjack. A CIA project he had once assigned to Owen. A project for which they used the classified pages as a means of communication. A code name known only to Owen and Fleming.

The format of the ad was as it had been then, but the words were slightly different: "Dealers wanted for BLACKJACK. Excellent opportunity. Moon Rock Casino. Apply now Box 745P."

Fleming smiled. Did Owen want to make a deal? If so, it might be legitimate. Or it might be another trick. Fleming didn't care. Either way, it would lead him to Owen.

Apply now meant tonight at seven forty-five.

THE National Air and Space Museum was one of several museums that lined both sides of the Mall between the Capitol and the Washington Monument. Owen pushed through a revolving door and walked in. It was seven thirty.

127

The ceiling of the central exhibit hall was as high as the building itself, with airplanes suspended from it, hanging in mid-air, as if caught in a moment of flight. Among them, the Wright Brothers' *Flyer*, Lindbergh's *Spirit of St. Louis*, the Bell X-1—the first plane to fly at the speed of sound. Other exhibits, on the floor, brought history up to date—*Friendship 7* and *Gemini 4*. In another huge hall to the right were early passenger planes. To the left, NASA rockets and a lunar landing craft.

In between, there were hundreds and hundreds of people. Owen moved through the throngs at his leisure, hands in pockets. When roughly ten minutes had passed, he turned back toward the central hall to an exhibit much older than anything else in the building. A lunar sample, a triangle of smooth black basalt brought to earth by astronauts and dating back four billion years. He took his place in the line of people waiting to pass by the moon rock.

Fleming had arrived early and had taken an escalator up to the mezzanine. A black X-15 high-altitude research plane hung even with the balcony level—good cover, Fleming thought.

He raised a camera to his eyes and began snapping pictures as he studied the faces in the central hall through the camera's telescopic lens. He could hardly have missed Owen. A young man in jeans and sneakers, his hair a mass of tight curls, his eyes covered by tinted glasses. And on the back of his T-shirt, a bright yellow flower that might have been a daisy, or a sunflower.

Fleming smiled. He stepped back from the rail into the shadows.

Below, Owen waited as long as he dared, but Fleming did not make contact. At eight fifteen he looked at his watch. Then he turned and walked out of the museum. His car was where he'd left it, behind the building. He pulled into the traffic, driving east toward the ground-floor apartment he had rented on Capitol Hill.

Stars were starting to show over the lights of the city. The weather reports were good, a beautiful day tomorrow. Warm and sunny, with no chance of rain. A perfect day for a picnic.

But that was tomorrow.

Owen turned into Duddington Place, where trees and townhouses lined both sides of the street. He locked the car, climbed the steps to a front door, then turned around. There was no one on the street. He unlocked the door and went in.

ELIZABETH EASTON glanced at her husband, then at Ed Nichols. "Do you really think this will work?" she said.

They were upstairs in the White House, in the Lincoln Sitting Room, small and cozy with its paisley drapes and rosewood chairs.

Nichols shrugged. "I can only repeat what I've told you before," he said. "I think Owen is trying to bring Anne home."

Elizabeth sighed. "I wish I could know that—"

"Yes, so do I, but we're moving in a realm of conjecture here. Frankly, the idea is just outrageous enough to appeal to Owen. Returning Anne to the White House? And getting away with it? That fits Owen, all right. But we'll be waiting for him."

Elizabeth glanced down at the guest list in her hand. "Which one do you think he will be?"

"It's impossible to guess. The Speaker? A Cabinet secretary?" Nichols looked at the President. "It wouldn't surprise me, Matt, if he came disguised as you."

"Surely he's not that good," Elizabeth said.

"Almost."

The President glared at both of them. "I don't care how good he is. I want Owen caught. And tried. And sent up for life. The man's a kidnapper. A murderer. He may be a Soviet spy."

Nichols shook his head firmly. "You're wrong about that. Owen doesn't work for the Russians. And he will be caught."

IT WAS nearly two a.m. when Fleming finally approached Owen's window from the outside. He ran a hand gently around the frame, looking for hidden wires.

They were there—an electric alarm system. Owen was always prepared. There was bound to be at least one more set of wires on the inside. These wires couldn't be cut or dismantled. They had to be shut off. Fleming turned away toward the basement door.

Owen awoke with a start.

There was no sound from the single window that opened to the outside, just a soft buzz from the plug in Owen's ear. And that meant the window was open.

He lay quite still, then turned his eyes to the clock on the bedside table. The lighted dial was gone. Someone had cut off the house's electricity.

Owen had anticipated electrical failure. He had installed another system, undetectable even to a professional eye, operated by battery and activated by movement. It was that alarm that set off the buzz in his ear. A warning, no more. But enough.

Owen's hand found the switch that was lying under his pillow, then closed around the revolver as a voice came from behind. "Don't move, Owen, I have a gun."

Fleming. Owen didn't move.

A flashlight came on. "All right, now turn over. Slowly."

Owen turned over on his back and looked up into the powerful beam of light. "Hands where I can see them," Fleming said.

Owen released the revolver and brought his hands out.

"Where's the girl?"

"You do have a one-track mind," Owen said. "I'm sorry, she isn't here. She's not even in Washington."

"Do you think I believe that?" Fleming said.

Owen shrugged. "Believe what you like. It's not my concern."

Then, suddenly, his eyes shifted to a door in the opposite wall. A moan came from the other side of the door! The sound of a child crying out softly in sleep.

A slow smile spread across Fleming's face. He chuckled. Then he started to back away, his eyes and pistol still aimed at Owen.

"Don't go in there," Owen said.

"Be quiet!" Fleming glared at him and kept backing up, a step at a time, until he was next to the door, solid oak with a brass knob. He stuck the flashlight under the arm with the gun, holding it firm, still on Owen. Then his free hand reached for the knob.

It came close, but did not touch. In that fraction of time and space before contact was made, a giant spark was released, a flash of blue fire like the flame from a welder's torch. A sudden, sharp hum filled the room as thousands of volts of electric power surged up through Fleming's arm. His body convulsed. His hair actually stood on end. And his heart stopped cold. Then the spark disappeared, the hum ceased, and Fleming fell to the floor.

Four blocks away, the lights of the Capitol dome flickered and dimmed. In between, everything went dark. Radios, TVs, the crime lights. A complete power outage.

Owen jumped out of bed and dropped down beside Fleming's

body. He raised his hand and gave a sharp rap against Fleming's chest. The heartbeat resumed. Fleming was alive, but unconscious. He would not come out of it soon.

Owen sat back on the rug he had wet down to act as a grounder. It was damp, but only that, not enough to make Fleming notice, A wire ran down from the brass knob to the rug. A second wire ran under the outside door to a manhole, where Owen had tapped it into the main power lines underground.

There was no need for caution; the power lines had gone dead. Owen retrieved the wire and used it to tie Fleming up. Then he crossed the room. The brass knob was harmless now and turned at his touch. He stepped into the room where Anne was sleeping.

She had slept through it all, as Owen had known she would when he gave her the last injection. The drug would be easing up soon. She would be awake in the morning.

He glanced down at the tape recorder he had switched on from under his pillow. It was still running on a table beside the bed. The only sound on the tape was long past, that single childish moan that had summoned Fleming far more effectively than Owen himself could have done.

Chapter Fifteen

Elizabeth Easton glanced out over the crowd as she descended the steps that curved to ground level from the balcony of the White House. The sun shone on striped awnings, under which waiters in white jackets served hot dogs and hamburgers, ice cream and cotton candy. There were children everywhere, sons and daughters of congressmen—running, climbing trees, playing softball.

Elizabeth watched the children, and the dull ache in her heart sharpened to a stab of pain. Her own child wasn't here. Yet the mood was festive. Square dancers performed a lively routine on a raised platform to the music of a country band. Across the lawn, a steam organ was parked on the curving blacktop drive. In between, a magician, a puppet show, clowns roaming the grounds. And hundreds of guests.

131

Was one of them Richard Owen? Was he here? With Anne? There was only a chance that Owen would choose this occasion to bring Anne home. A picnic for congressional families, with minimum security and swarms of children. Ed had planned it as an invitation to the man who had kidnapped Anne.

But Ed gave no guarantees. There was only a chance this would work. Elizabeth knew she could not let herself think beyond the moment. She must be natural. Behave as if nothing were wrong.

She stepped into the crowd. Matt was standing close by, chatting with friends. His presence had been reassurance so many times in the past, in crowded rooms with people pressing in. She wanted to be beside him. But there might as well have been an ocean between them. Voices pulled her one way, another.

"And how is Anne?" someone said.

Elizabeth smiled. "She's fine."

Someone else. "But I read somewhere she was sick."

"Yes, well—"

Elizabeth's eyes sought Matt but couldn't find him now. Panic was setting in. "Anne's fine. Really. She's much better."

Sympathetic smiles were distorted by point of view.

"A sick child needs her mother."

"Don't you wish you were there?"

"I've been needed here," Elizabeth answered feebly.

Tears stung her eyes. The smile on her face turned painful. Her cheeks hurt. More than that, her control was about to collapse. She wanted to scream.

She took a breath and fell back on an old technique. "You'll have to excuse me. I have something I must tell Matt."

The bodies parted. She could see Matt again. He turned and saw her, smiled, extended an arm. Elizabeth hurried to him.

"I was looking for you," he said, and his arm closed around her waist. Gentle pressure, more important than words. "You remember Les and Susan."

Elizabeth began to relax. She smiled at the congressman and his wife. "Yes, of course. How are you?"

At some point while they talked, Elizabeth noticed a clown standing near the ice cream tent, surrounded by dozens of children. She didn't know him by name, only by his familiar appearance—

the plaid suit that clashed with the orange hair, the white face, the red putty nose, and the huge, painted-on grin. Her eyes shifted from the clown to the children around him. And she smiled. They were enchanted. The star clown was as good as she'd heard.

Then a new stab of pain reminded her of her purpose. She turned back to the conversation.

The orange-haired clown stayed near the ice-cream tent. Once again Elizabeth watched him. The cluster of children shifted, and for the first time she saw another clown. A traditional tramp clown, done up in a tattered black suit, with soulful eyes painted into a melancholy face. Familiar again, but different. And a clever idea, she thought. The tramp clown was tiny. A midget!

Without knowing why, Elizabeth looked back at the big clown. His eyes met hers; his expression remained painted in place. But his hand moved. He touched the midget's shoulder with a gentleness that seemed out of place. The tramp clown looked up, then followed the big clown's gaze. The sad face turned to Elizabeth.

The little tramp stood there a moment, then jumped into the air with a suddenness that sent the children into peals of laughter. He was running, leaping, this way.

Elizabeth stood still in a moment of confusion at the sight of the sad little clown moving with such obvious joy. Moving this way, clearly. To her. And she didn't know why.

Then a voice broke over the general din of the party. "*Mommy!*"

Elizabeth caught her breath as the truth of the moment broke through. She was still afraid to believe. She stared at the painted face, at the familiar motion of the small body in the unfamiliar tattered black suit. Then she dropped to her knees and held open her arms. It was Anne! It was *Anne!*

The crowd stood back, stunned to silence, but Elizabeth no longer cared about public display. She was laughing and crying as her arms closed around her daughter, holding Anne tightly, as if she feared that wishing had caused an illusion, that Anne might fade except for her embrace.

Then Matt was there, too, his arms around both of them. His face mirrored his wife's. Tears and laughter. No thoughts for image. The crowd simply didn't exist.

Elizabeth caught Anne's face between her hands. Happy tears

poured out of the soulful eyes and melted the makeup. Then Elizabeth glanced up at Matt. Words failed. A look passed between them. Utter joy. Intense love. Inexpressible relief.

Beside them, a Secret Service agent switched on his microphone, barked an order. Across the lawn, guards fanned out quickly to preassigned positions. But it was already too late.

The big clown had disappeared.

RICHARD Owen emerged from a door behind his steam organ. The clown suit was gone now; he was wearing a business suit.

A flurry of excitement arose on the lawn behind him. Owen turned, saw Anne in her mother's arms. And her father's. *Reunion.* His job was done. But he didn't feel free; he had no idea where he would go from here.

He moved toward the gate, nodding to one of the guards, passing through to the outside. He picked up his pace. Then, from behind, came the sound of footsteps running this way. Owen did not look around. It was a clown they wanted.

He rounded the corner onto Seventeenth Street, where he'd left the Fiat 124 Spyder, a small sports car with a powerful engine. Owen stepped down from the curb and came around from the back of the Spyder to the driver's side.

But someone else had stepped off the sidewalk in front of the car—a man in a dark suit, his hand in his pocket and obviously holding a gun. Two more men approached from behind.

Then a black car came to a stop beside him. The driver hopped out and came around to open the door. The man in the back seat smiled, but Owen did not smile back. His shoulders sagged, his face went pale, and life disappeared from his eyes.

This was it, capture. The man in the car was Nichols.

"Get in," he said.

Owen did as he was told. He was unarmed against three armed men, and he didn't much care anymore. He felt numb.

The driver pulled into the traffic, heading away from the White House. Nichols pressed a button in the armrest at his side. A glass partition rose from the back of the driver's seat.

Nichols pointed to the partition. "It's soundproof," he said. "We can talk."

134

"What's the point?"

Nichols smiled. "I ought to explain. The picnic was a trap."

"So I gathered."

"You'll forgive my preening a bit. It's not every day I set a trap for a prey as elusive as you and see it work."

"Congratulations."

Nichols produced a handkerchief, took off his glasses, and rubbed at a spot on one lens. "I couldn't let them have you back there," he said. "The President wants your head on a tray."

No doubt, Owen thought. He wished Nichols would drop the postmortem.

"For myself," Nichols said, "I prefer one piece."

Signs of life showed in Owen's face. He turned and caught Nichols' eyes in direct gaze. "What are you telling me?"

Nichols did not turn away. "That I was wrong when I thought Richard Owen kidnapped Anne Easton. Owen died in Oslo. As for who kidnapped Anne . . ." He shrugged. "I don't know. It might have been Boris Svitsky. Whoever it was got away."

Owen stared back, incredulous, but he felt alive again.

Nichols gave a confirming nod. "They have a department for justice down the street from the White House," he said. "Justice is not my job. I've got other problems, like an agency full of people I can't trust. That's why I can't let them put you in jail. I need you now, more than ever. We've got to rebuild."

Owen laughed softly. "We've been on the same side all along."

"Not quite all along. But since Knossos, yes, we've had an identical goal—to get Anne safely home and you out of reach." Nichols' eyes were full of admiration. "You did a hell of a job."

Owen dismissed the compliment with a shrug. He had done his job, simply that.

"But that's all past history," Nichols said with a dismissing gesture. "Your new assignment is Fleming."

Owen smiled. He reached into a pocket, brought out a key, and tossed it across to Nichols. "I was going to mail this to you."

"A key?"

"Fleming."

Nichols stared at the key. "You've got Fleming locked up?"

Owen nodded. "Trussed up like a turkey and, I daresay, ready

135

to talk." He gave Nichols the address on Duddington Place.

A smile broke over Nichols' face. "In that case," he said, "you can have the night off. We'll start first thing tomorrow."

He handed Owen a different key. Owen glanced at the plastic tag. Room 302, the Executive House Hotel on Rhode Island Avenue.

Nichols pressed a button in the armrest, a prearranged signal. The driver pulled in to the curb. Nichols extended his hand.

Owen shook it. "There is one loose end," he said. "I promised a clown six weeks' work at five hundred a week, and I only paid him for one."

"All right, where is he?"

"In Nairobi by now."

"Nairobi!"

Owen grinned and got out of the car.

The hotel was a five-block walk. Owen entered the lobby and rode the elevator up to the third floor. He unlocked the door to room 302, stepped in, and closed it behind him.

The room looked as if he'd been staying there for days. Clothes, his own size and taste, in the closets and the bureau drawers. Shaving gear in the bathroom. An attaché case.

In the attaché case, new papers. A wallet. Credit cards. A passport. Everything he needed to become a new person.

He picked up the passport and opened it to the photo page. And he smiled. A likeness of his own face stared back at him, but nothing else was the same. Richard Owen was dead.

Very thorough. And very funny. Nichols had become an insider. He had demonstrated the irreverence necessary for dealing with an insane world.

The name on the passport was Graham.

"It's great fun to write a thriller, because I love to let my imagination wander," Marilyn Sharp told us. "Since I had no inside information on the CIA, it took me a long time to figure out just how Richard Owen would kidnap a President's daughter. Obviously, only a superhero like Owen could pull off such an impossible feat!"

Marilyn Sharp

Sunflower is Marilyn Sharp's first novel, and she spent seven years at it. Married to a United States congressman, she has had a hectic life helping him in three political campaigns, as well as raising their young son, Jeremy, and trying to snatch time in between to write. "People think being a congressman's wife should be the sum total of my existence. But like my character Elizabeth Easton, I place a high value on time spent with my child and on my own career." Since *Sunflower* was published, Mrs. Sharp has established her identity as a successful author.

Although she believes in leaving politics to her husband, she enjoys living in Washington, DC. When attending White House functions, she occasionally scribbles quick notes that are invaluable for plot details. Of course, there are places she is not allowed. She asked her husband to take a close look at the men's room off the White House library; he found that since there were no guards there, it would make a plausible setting for a murder scene in her book.

Marilyn Sharp is already at work on her next thriller, which she promises will have more high intrigue in foreign places and, naturally, plenty of surprises.

THE
PASSING BELLS

A CONDENSATION OF THE BOOK BY

Phillip Rock

Illustrated by Cecil Vieweg

PUBLISHED BY HODDER AND STOUGHTON

Now, God be thanked,
  Who has matched us with His hour,
And caught our youth,
  and wakened us from sleeping. . . .

Summer, 1914. England slept.

Beneath sunlit skies Abington Pryory slumbered. To the earl and his family and friends it seemed that the easy days would never end: below stairs too there was contentment with a way of life that must surely last for ever.

Then came the war. The dream broke. The illusion shattered.

The Passing Bells is a brilliant and deeply moving evocation of that last peaceful summer, and of the unimaginable horrors of war that followed. There is dramatic involvement in the lives of a vivid cast of memorable characters. And there is understanding, too, of the changes wrought in people's hearts when an old order ends and a new one is born.

By any standards, *The Passing Bells* is a remarkable achievement.

PART ONE

1

The dawn came early, tinting a cloudless sky the palest shade of green. On Burgate Hill woodcutters paused to rest after the steep climb to the top, lit their pipes and watched the sun rise behind the brick chimneys of Abington Pryory, the great house itself shrouded from view by the dense foliage of oak and birch wood. Beyond them the men could see a thin plume of smoke rise from the gentle hollows of the heath: a goods train bearing the rich harvests of Surrey to the London markets.

Anthony Greville, ninth Earl of Stanmore, heard the distant sound of the train as he lay drowsily in bed. He turned his head and glanced at the bedside clock: 5:23. The great house was coming alive. He stretched his long, leanly-muscled body under the quilt and listened to the muted sounds: the murmur of pipes as the scullery maids drew water for the cooks; the faraway ring of shovels as coal buckets were filled; scurrying footsteps as the housemaids brought hot water for the early risers. There were forty servants in that summer of 1914, counting stableboys and grooms, and they could make a fair amount of noise as they began the day. It was a sound that the earl found comforting.

He shaved himself, standing before the mirror in his stockinged feet, while his valet, Fisher, held towels and a bottle of bay rum.

The earl studied his face in the glass. "Do you think the moustache is getting a bit too military, Fisher?"

"It is rather martial, if you'll permit me to say so, m'lord."

"We shall trim it later, Fisher." The earl dropped his razor into the shaving bowl. "My brown tweed today after my ride . . . and black tie for dinner."

"Very good, m'lord."

The morning ride was the earl's unfailing ritual, in the heat of summer or the dark, frosty mornings of winter. He dressed for it in old whipcord breeches and a Norfolk jacket. There were thirty pairs of riding boots in the dressing-room wardrobe, but his choice for the morning ride was a pair of Irish hunting boots, supple as gloves, the tan leather creased into fine lines like the face of an ancient, weatherbeaten man. He was getting into the boots with Fisher's help when after a discreet tap Coatsworth entered the room followed by one of the maids bearing a large, silver tray on which stood a teapot, milk, sugar, a basket of scones, a pot of marmalade and a dish of butter. The elderly butler walked slowly, his dark trousers almost obscuring his slippered feet.

"Good morning, m'lord."

"'Morning to you, Coatsworth. How's the gout this morning?"

"Better, m'lord. Soaked my feet in hot vinegar last night. It was Mr. Banks's suggestion. Works wonders with the horses, he says."

"Indeed."

The butler cleared a table and motioned the maid to set the tray down. She was a young girl, slender and dark-haired, with high cheekbones and a thin, uptilted nose. She lingered, looking about the room. A very pretty girl, the earl thought as he smiled at her. "Thank you, Mary."

"Ivy, m'lord," the girl whispered.

"Of course, Ivy." One of the new ones.

"You may go, lass," Coatsworth murmured. He poured tea, then split a hot scone and buttered it. "I think you will find the scones to be quite delicious m'lord. Mrs. Dalrymple changed the recipe. Ross says they remind him of the scones his mother baked when he was a lad in Aberdeen."

"Gets about a bit, doesn't he? Told me he came from Perth."

The butler chuckled. "I'd say Glasgow was nearer the truth." Jamie Ross was a brash young man, but a first-rate chauffeur and mechanic. He was badly needed now that the number of motor cars in the family had increased from one to four.

142

The earl did not linger over his breakfast. He could feel the tug of field and wood. His only regret was that he would be riding alone on this glorious June morning. William was not yet down from Eton, and Charles had lost his zest for riding. The thought of his eldest son cast a momentary shadow over his mood. Charles's record at Cambridge had been most gratifying, and the lad's direction seemed clear enough to Lord Stanmore. As the eldest, he should now apply himself to understanding the complex structure of the family property, not merely Abington Pryory with its score of tenant farms, but the land in Wiltshire, Northumberland, and Kent, as well as the various parcels of London commercial properties. A job enough for any man, but when the earl had tried to discuss his son's future with him he had drawn a total blank.

"I'm off," he said, getting abruptly to his feet. He strode across to the door that connected his rooms with those of his wife, Hanna. It was a source of satisfaction that never in twenty-five years of married life had that door been locked, a symbol of love that quelled the dark predictions of his friends, who had said that the marriage could not last, *American women being what they are*. He had never understood the meaning of that remark.

The contrast between the two sets of rooms symbolized the difference between men and women, as the earl saw it. His rooms were panelled with dark oak and spartanly furnished, while the rooms of Hanna Rilke Greville were those of a warm and sensuous woman. They had deep pile carpets, gilt-framed paintings, mirrors and rococo furniture. Silk curtains diffused the light, bathing the rooms with a softly feminine glow.

The countess was still asleep, her long, blonde hair tied into two thick coils that lay across the pillow like strands of spun gold. The earl did not intrude. He stood for a moment looking at her, then closed the door quietly and walked briskly towards the hall.

He left the house through the glass-domed conservatory and strode out across the west terrace, where two under-gardeners were sweeping flagstones. The men paused in their work to touch their caps; he acknowledged their gesture by a slight nod. Beyond the walled rose garden several long, low greenhouses marked the edge of the vast kitchen gardens. A tree-shaded gravel path wound past the gardeners' cottages and the storage sheds to the stable area, separated from the garden by a high stone wall.

This world of paddocks and stables was his and he was intensely proud of it. The new wooden buildings with their slate roofs were painted in his colours, buff with accents of dull orange. They were the finest stables in England and his twenty-five hunters and steeplechasers were the best that could be bought, bartered or begged. His favourite, Jupiter, a seven-year-old chestnut gelding, was being walked in the paddock by a groom while a stocky, bandy-legged man watched the horse with a practised eye.

"Good morning, Banks," Lord Stanmore called out cheerily. "Have a saddle on him, I see."

George Banks, the head groom, removed a knobby briar pipe from between his teeth and tapped out the ash against his palm.

"Fit as a fiddle, m'lord. As good as new."

The earl peered intently at the horse's left front leg as the groom walked the horse towards him. "Not favouring the leg at all?"

"No, m'lord," said Banks. "It's the hot packs what done the job. He's full of mustard. He watched Tinker go and I reckon he's eager to be catching up with him."

"Tinker? Who on earth has taken . . . ?"

"Why, Captain Wood-Lacy m'lord. Came down from London late last night. He was up with the lark and eager for a ride."

The earl swung up into Jupiter's saddle. "Damn. Wish I'd known. Which direction did he take?"

"Towards Burgate," the groom said.

"Thank you, Banks. Perhaps I can catch up with him."

He tapped the big gelding with his heels and the horse responded eagerly, breaking into a canter down the hard-packed, sandy path.

CAPTAIN FENTON WOOD-LACY, Coldstream Guards, rode slowly and morosely through the dappled shadows of a beech wood. He was a tall, square-shouldered man of twenty-five, with dark, deep-set eyes, a prominent, high-bridged nose and thin lips. It was a face which, when angered, could reduce incompetent subalterns to twitching terror. But that was his parade-ground face; with friends, women, small children, and the meek of the earth, the hard line of the mouth softened and the eyes became warm. At the moment, the face was troubled. A passing stranger seeing this man seated on a magnificent bay, dressed in fine, London-cut riding clothes, would have taken him for a rich squire. In actuality, he carried in his pocket a letter from Cox's Bank, informing him respectfully that his account was seriously overdrawn.

The beauty of the morning, with the sun filtering through the leaves, mocked his mood. Something had to be done, but he couldn't for the life of him figure out what. A hundred pounds would clear his present debts—and he could probably borrow that amount easily enough from Lord Stanmore as he had done in the past—but a hundred quid would merely delay the inevitable. His share of his late father's estate came to an inflexible six hundred pounds a year. That and his captain's pay were not enough to maintain him in a regiment that prided itself on the tone of its officers. His early promotion to captain had merely hastened his ruin. An unmarried officer in the Guards was expected to maintain suitable lodgings in Knightsbridge or Belgravia—the higher the rank the better the address. And on top of all the other expenditure, his clothing had to be of the most stylish cut. His tailor's bill had been outrageous.

"Dash it to hell," he whispered to the trees. He gave his mount Tinker a tap and the graceful animal trotted briskly on, out of the wood into a meadow thick with buttercups. There Fenton reined in and gazed ahead. Far off, partially obscured by willows, rose the Gothic façade of Burgate House, where there was a permanent solution to his problems—but at a cost that he had so far been reluctant to accept. Archie Foxe lived in Burgate House with his daughter, Lydia. It was a hideous building, built by a duke in Queen Anne's time. It looked more like a cathedral than a house. Yet Archie Foxe loved the place. Archie Foxe of the East End and the dropped aitches, of Foxe's Fancy Tinned Goods and the ubiquitous White Manor Tea Shops. Archie's offer of a place in his firm was of long standing. One thousand pounds a year to start. Not a trifling offer that, except of course that it would mean chucking in his commission.

The captain's personal Rubicon lay in front of him. A thousand quid a year. And Lydia? That little question eluded an answer.

145

Lydia Foxe would make up her own mind about that. She was beautiful, twenty-one, and with the world's most indulgent father. It had been her suggestion in the first place that Fenton join "Daddy's shop", as she so quaintly understated the firm of Foxe Ltd. She was helping to choose furnishings for his flat, her taste far exceeding his budget. "You're a man who should live among beautiful things," she had said. "You're wasted in the army."

"Oh, damn," he whispered fervently. It just wasn't that simple. A man's regiment became something a little sacred. When the regimental band struck up and the long scarlet-and-blue-clad column swung up Birdcage Walk from Wellington Barracks, he felt an almost indescribable sense of pride. Fife and drum, the colours streaming. Boyhood dreamings . . . a *Guards officer* and thus set apart. To give that up, to be merely Mr. Wood-Lacy of Foxe Ltd., purveyors of cheap food in tins, tea shops strategically placed on busy corners in major towns, was to reduce himself to the level of the general herd. And if that be snobbery, then make the most of it!

He leaned sideways in the saddle and sabre-cut a tall weed with his riding crop, a vicious, backhanded slash. On straightening up he heard a distant hallooing and glanced idly over his shoulder to see Lord Stanmore, several fields away, coming on at a gallop, the chestnut gliding over hedges with the grace of a swallow.

The Earl of Stanmore in his proper element, Fenton mused. This had been his initial view of the man when first visiting Abington Pryory at the age of nine. Indeed it had been Lord Stanmore who had taught him then the proper way to sit a horse, in that summer of 1898, the year his architect father had begun the restoration of Abington Pryory. The house had then become a second home for the Wood-Lacy family, and a bond of friendship and respect had been created between the older man and himself. He watched the earl galloping towards him and his spirits lifted.

"Dash it all, Fenton," the earl cried out as he drew alongside. "You could have waited for me."

"Sorry, sir. Didn't think you'd be up that early."

"Not up? What the deuce do you mean? You know my habits."

The captain smiled. "My apologies."

"Accepted. Well, now, caught up with you at least. Did you see

146

how the old boy took that last hedge?" He patted his horse on the neck. "Damn, but it's a fine morning. That crowd at the house don't know what they're missing. I suppose you know your brother Roger's here with Charles. Dashed if I can understand those two lads. In my day chaps came down from Cambridge with a damned clear idea of where they were going in life. Neither Roger nor my dear son have the foggiest."

"It's just a phase," Fenton said abstractedly.

"Damned if I can see it. Last night Roger and Charles were deep in conversation about editing a new poetry magazine with Rupert Brooke. Rupert Brooke! Have you ever seen him? The chap walks around with his hair down to his shoulders and no shoes on his feet. I ask you . . . !" His voice ended on a note of heartfelt exasperation.

"Can you lend me another hundred pounds?"

Lord Stanmore tugged at his moustache. "Can I what?"

"Lend me a hundred pounds." Fenton was gazing stolidly ahead. "I know that I still owe you . . ."

"Nonsense! No talk of that, my dear fellow. Of course I'll lend it to you, if you need it badly enough."

Fenton's smile was faint. "I suppose I'll always need it badly enough."

"You're in the worst possible regiment for a man of your means. I've a suggestion, Fenton. I hope you won't take offence."

"I'm sure that I won't."

"It's quite simple, really. Marry money. Be honest, lad, is it such a crime to rescue a Manchester mill-owner's daughter from marrying some pasty-faced solicitor?"

The captain laughed for the first time in weeks. "I suppose it isn't, not when you put it that way."

"Precisely. Look, we'll be opening the Park Lane house next week for the season, and Hanna has half a dozen parties in the works to get Alexandra launched. We could kill two birds with one stone. Find my daughter the right husband and you the proper wife. Dammit, man, you might enjoy it." He pointed his crop towards Burgate House. "By Harry, there's a pretty butterfly in that place I'd like to see taken off the market . . . for reasons I'm sure you understand."

"I believe so, yes," Fenton said quietly.

The ninth Earl of Stanmore frowned and looked away from the great monstrosity of a house. "Dash it, Fenton, I've been more than accommodating over the years, permitted Charles his puppy love for the girl when he was sixteen, but, by God, he's twenty-three now, time he got over it and found a more suitable mate." He dug his heels into his horse's flanks. "Let's ride!"

More suitable to *him*, Fenton was thinking as he kicked his own mount into a gallop, meaning, of course, that Archie Foxe's daughter, despite her Paris clothes and Benz motorcar, was still Archie Foxe's daughter, and fated by her class to wed someone far less noble than a Greville. The soldier son of an architect perhaps? Fenton wondered: the late lamented Sir Harold Wood-Lacy, refurbisher of old buildings, to the delight of such clients as Queen Victoria for his work at Sandringham, and the Earl of Stanmore for his painstaking restoration of Abington Pryory. Yet the earl had paid him with part of his wife's dowry, the million dollars that Adolph Sebastian Rilke had gladly handed over to see his daughter wed to a nobleman; dollars that had been earned in Chicago, by the brewing of beer. And there'd been no loss of social status in *that* union. Money was the American peerage: an American heiress ranked with a Hapsburg. Yes, one could so easily understand the difference between Adolph Rilke and Archie Foxe, even if one found the hypocrisy of it all slightly amusing.

2

"Mr. Coatsworth informed me how satisfied he was with you this morning, Ivy. But you must remember about dawdling and staring."

"Yes, Mrs. Broome," Ivy Thaxton whispered.

Mrs. Broome, for all her formidable size and regal bearing, was not unkind. She prided herself on her ability to so train the servants that reprimands were rare. There were some house-keepers who were veritable ogres, constantly bullying and punishing the staff. She looked approvingly at the slender, dark-haired girl and then reached out and touched her gently. "Now

148

run off with you, Ivy, and have your breakfast; then give a hand
with the linen."

"Thank you, Mrs. Broome," she said, curtsying respectfully
before hurrying down the passage towards the servants' hall. Ivy
Thaxton was seventeen and this was her first week away from
home. She had grown up in a comfortable but crowded house near
Norwich, the eldest of five children. And with another child on the
way, the older birds must make room for the fledglings, her father had
said. Her first week of service had been bewildering. She was not
unhappy, it was just that there was so much to remember. There
were so many corridors, stairs and rooms that sometimes she got
lost.

In the servants' hall there were a dozen or more servants seated
at the long table having their breakfast—valets, footmen and the
kitchenmaids mostly. The amount and quality of the food still
astonished her. Her plate was heaped with bacon rashers, eggs,
and a thick piece of bread, fried golden crisp. There had always
been enough food on the table at home, but it had been plain fare,
heavy on boiled greens, carrots and soup. She found a place at the
end of the table and ate her breakfast with single-minded purpose. Conscious of someone staring at her across the table, she
glanced up into the amused face of a freckled young man with
sandy hair, who was nursing a mug of tea and smoking a cigarette.
He was dressed in a tight black jacket with pearl-grey buttons.

"You don't 'alf put your grub away," the young man said.
"Where does it go? You can't weigh more'n a half-starved cat."

"It's rude to stare," she said, her face burning.

"Sorry, lass, but it was either look at you or at one of them ugly
mugs up the table. I'd rather glim a comely lass any old day in the
week. Jamie Ross is my name. What's yours?"

"Ivy," she said, almost inaudibly. "Ivy Thaxton."

He smiled warmly at her. "You've only been here a week,
haven't you?" he said. "You from London?"

"Norwich. Are you from London?"

He tilted his head and blew a perfect smoke ring. "I'm from
everywhere if you want to know the truth. Aberdeen, Liverpool,
Leeds, London. Like to keep on the go. That's why I took up
chauffeuring."

"Is that what you do?"

"Can't you tell from the uniform? I'm his lordship's and her ladyship's driver. The poor dears couldn't go anywhere without me."

One of the valets, a large, portly man, glanced down the table. "Oh, put a cork in it, Ross."

The chauffeur leaned across the table and spoke in a harsh stage whisper. "They're all jealous of me, see. 'Cause I've a proper trade and they don't know nothin' but how to polish a bloody pair of boots. I can do anything with a motor. I can pull it apart, scatter the pieces and then put it back together again blindfold."

"Can you really do that?" Ivy asked.

"Of course I can; an' make it run better than it did before. I'm somewhat of an inventor, see. I think up all sorts of things."

"Think up a muzzle for your mouth," the valet said. There was a wave of laughter from the others at the table.

Ivy stood up. "I really must go. I've got to help with the linen."

The chauffeur walked her down the passage that led to the linen room. No one appeared sorry to see him leave, but Ivy thought he looked very grand in his black breeches and black leather gaiters.

"Do you like it here?" she asked.

"Oh, it's not so bad. The cars are right beauties, and his lordship's a proper sort."

They reached the linen-room door and Ivy held out her hand. "It's been awfully nice talking with you, Mr. Ross."

"Jamie," he said, taking her hand and giving it a slight squeeze. "When's your afternoon?"

"Next Wednesday."

"Well, if I'm off duty I'll take you into Guildford on me motorbike, treat you to the pictures." He walked off jauntily.

ROGER WOOD-LACY walked abstractedly along the corridor towards the breakfast room. He had been awake since dawn, seated on the windowseat in his bedroom, watching the sun rise. The fifth stanza of his latest poem was beginning to take shape in his head.

"Now hold the brittle garment of the night in jest . . . and scoff the wearing of day's bright mantle rare."

151

Not bad, he mused, not bad at all. Outside the door of the breakfast room he paused in front of an ornately-framed mirror to look at himself. The image pleased him. Tall, slender, the paleness of his face accentuated by his dark, unruly hair, he was the image of a poet if he ever saw one.

"Good morning, all," he said, making an entrance. But only his brother Fenton was seated at the table.

"Well, Roger," he said. "And how are you?"

"Fine thanks. When did you get here?"

"Last night." He eyed his younger brother critically. "Your hair wants cutting."

Roger turned his back and walked stiffly to the sideboard on which stood half a dozen silver serving dishes, their contents kept warm by tiny spirit lamps burning bluely beneath them. He helped himself to kidneys, scrambled eggs and a slice of gammon.

"Anyone staying here that I know?" asked Fenton.

"House is rather empty for a change. Just that biddy Lady Dexford and her daughter. You know, Winifred Sutton. And I hear one of Charles's cousins is due in tomorrow from Chicago."

"And that's it?"

Roger nodded as he chewed. "Bit of a scene brewing, if you ask me. His nibs and Hanna are as keen as paint about joining the Grevilles to the Suttons. They keep pushing poor Charles and Winifred into the rose gardens every night to walk under the moon. Not a thing's come of it. Charles has . . . well, other matters on his mind."

The door opened and the Marchioness of Dexford swept into the room, her plump daughter trailing after her.

"Ah! Both brothers Wood-Lacy! How nice! Fenton, you handsome rogue! I hear such naughty stories from my nephew Albert. He's in the Guards, you know. Well, here you are and I shall get at the truth, never fear. Say hello to Fenton, Winifred."

"Hello, Fenton," Winifred said, almost in a whisper. "It's very nice seeing you again." Her soft, unhappy eyes met Fenton's and then she dropped her gaze quickly.

Pretty, Fenton was thinking. A bit too buxom, but she would slim down. Just turned eighteen. Ripe for the marriage block. He smiled pleasantly at her. "I'm happy that you remember me."

152

"How could she ever forget!" her mother cried. "Gave the child her first kiss! Sweet sixteen! Most gallant of you, Fenton!"

He could barely recall the incident. An avuncular peck on the cheek at her birthday party. He felt sorry for her. The walks in the moon-drenched rose garden with Charles must be agony for her. A young woman longing to be loved. Charles, silent and moody, wishing that he were walking beside Lydia Foxe.

"That's a charming frock, Winifred," he said. "It's very becoming."

"Th . . . thank you," she stammered.

Fenton could understand Lord Stanmore's desire for the match. The Marquess of Dexford was a rich man with an ancient title. Fenton smiled again at Winifred and she smiled shyly back. An easy bit of fruit to pluck, but not of course until Charles informed his parents that he would never marry the girl.

Fenton stood up and gave a slight bow. "I leave you to breakfast. Perhaps we can form teams later for croquet."

IVY HURRIED UP the back stairs cradling a pile of linen in her arms. The stairs were steep and the sheets and pillowslips felt like a ton by the time she reached the first floor. She opened the door slowly and peered hesitantly around it. The rules were emphatic: should family or guests be seen, she should draw discreetly out of sight until the corridor was empty. There were so many rules that Ivy's head spun trying to keep track of them all.

The corridor, an outer passage with tall, mullioned windows on one side, was empty. She remembered those windows from the day before, when she had come this way to help Doris make up Lady Alexandra's bed. The room that she was now looking for was past Lady Alexandra's rooms. She stepped out resolutely, but as she passed Lady Alexandra's bedroom, the door flew open and the earl's daughter poked her head out.

"Velda?"

"No, m'lady."

"I can see *that*," the girl said petulantly. "Where's Velda?"

"I don't know, m'lady." She had never heard of Velda.

Lady Alexandra Greville took a step into the corridor and glanced up and down. "Oh, bother!"

153

Ivy stared at her in awe. So pretty, like the portrait on a box of chocolates. A slim, oval face, blue eyes, thick, blonde hair.

"*You* must help me," Alexandra said. "Don't just stand there! Help fasten. . . ." The sound of a car horn cut off her words and she whirled back to her room. "She's here! Quickly! Quickly! Just drop what you're carrying and do me up."

"Yes, m'lady," Ivy blurted. The clean linen fell to the floor with a dull thump. She hurried into the room to find Alexandra standing impatiently in front of a mirror. Her dress was open down the back, revealing silk lingerie fringed with frothy lace.

"Do up the buttons quickly, but don't miss any."

"No, m'lady." There seemed to be dozens of them, tiny ivory ones. She began to button them, her fingers trembling. It was a beige wool challis, of such fine quality that it felt like silk.

The young woman turned around and smiled. "You're new, aren't you? What's your name?"

"Ivy, m'lady. Ivy Thaxton."

"Well, Ivy," Alexandra began, then stopped as a middle-aged maid hurried into the room. "It's about time, Velda. Wherever did you get to?"

"I am sorry, m'lady. I . . ." The woman hesitated when she saw Ivy and gave her a withering look.

"It doesn't matter," Alexandra said with a shrug. "I'm buttoned now. But do hurry and get my hat. I'm in a most awful rush."

"Yes, m'lady."

Alexandra bent quickly towards the mirror and gave her cheeks a pinch to redden them. "I shall ask one final favour of you, Ivy. Please hurry downstairs as fast as you can and tell the lady who just arrived, Miss Foxe, that I shall be down in a few minutes and that we must drive like the wind or we shall miss the London train."

Ivy backed towards the door. "A . . . Miss Foxe?"

"Yes, yes. Quickly, quickly."

Ivy flew out of the room and down the corridor. She gave no thought to taking the back stairs. There couldn't possibly be time for that. She ran full tilt, clutching her little cap to keep it from flying off her head, to the main staircase, nearly colliding with a footman on the upper landing.

"Sorry!" she called out, descending the stairs two steps at a

154

time. The startled man stared after her, his astonishment shared by the butler and two other footmen standing in the entrance hall.

"What on earth. . . ?" Mr. Coatsworth blurted.

Ivy came to a skidding, momentary halt in front of the butler.

"I . . . I must find a Miss Foxe. Have you seen her?"

Mr. Coatsworth pointed in the direction of the open front doors. Ivy could see a shiny blue motorcar parked on the drive, a red-haired young woman behind the wheel, a tall, dark-haired man in riding clothes standing beside the car, talking to her.

"Thanks ever so," Ivy said, making a dash for the door.

"Now, see here . . ." the butler stammered. "See here. . . ."

Out on the gravel drive Ivy slowed, and walked demurely towards the car. "Are you Miss Foxe?" she asked respectfully.

The young woman looked at her past the tall, angular form of Captain Wood-Lacy. "Yes, I am."

"I have a message for you, miss . . . it's from Lady Alexandra, miss . . . she says for me to tell you that she shan't be but a minute and that . . . and that you will have to drive . . . like the wind to keep from missing the train."

"Oh, did she?" Miss Foxe gave a husky laugh. "Dear Alex," she said to Captain Wood-Lacy. "That girl would forget her head if it weren't firmly rooted to her neck. I *told* her we were driving up to London."

"Bit of a rough trip, isn't it?" Fenton said.

"Oh, Lord, no. Not in the Benz. And the road's quite decent once you're past Dorking."

"Going shopping?"

"Alex has some dress fittings at Ferris's and I have to see Daddy."

Ivy was at a loss over what to do. Stand listening to the conversation until dismissed, or just turn and walk away? Not that she was in any hurry to leave. The woman in the car fascinated her. She had a hypnotizing, sensual beauty. Her red hair was coiled on top of her head and secured by a green velvet band. Her face was long, with high cheekbones, luminous green eyes and a full-lipped mouth. Ivy pulled herself out of her trance.

"Is . . . is there any message for Lady Alexandra, miss?"

A second throaty laugh. "Oh, good heavens, no."

"Yes, miss . . . very good, miss." Ivy turned away.

"What an odd little creature," Lydia said as she watched the maid walk back to the house. "Did you notice her staring at me?"

"No, but then I was staring at you myself so I can't blame her."

Lydia's fingers toyed with the heavy wooden steering wheel. "Please, Fenton, we promised to talk only in generalities."

He touched her shoulder, sensing the warm flesh beneath the linen motoring coat and silk dress. "I find that impossible."

She looked away. "Don't make it difficult, Fenton. You know how fond I am of you. You've been like a brother to me . . ."

His fingers tightened. "You can't look at me and say that, Lydia. But I shan't press you. I know what you're hoping to accomplish and I wish you luck. You'll need it."

IVY MADE HER SLOW WAY to the first floor, taking the back stairs. When she reached Lady Alexandra's room there was a small crowd standing in the corridor: Mr. Coatsworth, one of the footmen, the maid, Velda—and the housekeeper, Mrs. Broome.

"There she is, the little baggage," Velda said, sniffing back tears. "Oh, I'd give her such a thrashing if it was up to me."

Mrs. Broome only sighed wearily. "That will do, Velda. Kindly go about your duties."

"Yes, Mrs. Broome." She glared at Ivy before turning away and going into the room.

"If you need any assistance, Mrs. Broome," the butler said gravely, "I would be most happy to lend a hand."

"Thank you, no, Mr. Coatsworth."

"As you wish, Mrs. Broome. Come along, Peterson."

Ivy was left alone with the housekeeper who was now pointing down at the floor where the pile of linen was lying.

"We do not toss clean linen on the floor. Pick it up, Ivy."

"Yes, Mrs. Broome," Ivy whispered. She bent and gathered the linen into her arms. "I . . . I'm sorry . . . it's just that . . . that. . . ." Events had taken place so quickly. Dropping the sheets had been the only thing to do at the time, but how could she make that clear to Mrs. Broome?

"You were sent to make a bed. Now go and make it, child. I wish to see you do it. I wish to make sure that you have not forgotten *everything* that you have been taught."

Ivy walked down the corridor, her face burning, while the house-keeper kept a slow, measured pace behind her. The bed that needed making was a large four-poster. Ivy made it with pains-taking care, while Mrs. Broome stood silently watching. Then Ivy stepped back and waited anxiously.

"Very well done, Ivy. Now, you were hired as a housemaid, not as a lady's maid, not as a messenger." Ivy opened her mouth as though to speak and Mrs. Broome raised a hand in admonishment. "It would pain me greatly to give you notice. But there is, apparently, something that you are not aware of yet, and that is *place*. Everyone has his or her place in life, Ivy. Your place, at least for the time being, is that of a housemaid at Abington Pryory. It would be a queer sort of world, Ivy, if none of us knew our place. Can you imagine Mr. Coatsworth making beds, or me being told to empty chamber pots? Mr. Coatsworth nearly had a stroke when he saw you leaping down the main stairs."

"But, Lady Alexandra said . . ." Ivy stammered.

Mrs. Broome stiffened. "Lady Alexandra is very young and inclined to dramatics. I cannot admonish Lady Alexandra, but I can, and must, admonish you. In the future, when asked to do *anything* that is not a regular part of your duties you shall decline in a respectful manner, and immediately convey the request to one of your superiors. Do you understand, Ivy?"

Ivy could only nod her head numbly. Mrs. Broome then reached out and patted the trembling girl on the cheek.

"I shall not give you notice, Ivy, if there are no more unfortunate lapses. Now, finish tidying up here. Her ladyship's nephew is arriving from America tomorrow and will occupy this room. We wish it to be nice and pleasant."

And then she was gone, moving majestically out of the room. Ivy held her breath until she was safely out of sight, then sank down on the windowseat and buried her face in her hands. She had come so close to losing her position, her place, and then what would have become of her? She couldn't go home, not with the baby due any minute and Da having enough trouble putting food on the table and paying the rent and seeing to it that her brothers and sisters had decent clothes and sturdy shoes to wear to school. She felt like blubbering. Resting her feverish face against the cool window glass, she could see the drive. The shiny blue car came suddenly into view, going very fast, Miss Foxe clutching the steering wheel. Lady Alexandra was looking back and waving, one hand clamped on top of her straw sailor, its long, brown velvet ribbons fluttering in the wind. "Goodbye," she was shouting happily to someone. "Goodbye . . . goodbye."

So that was *their* place, Ivy thought with a sharp pang of regret. It *was* a queer sort of world, come to think of it.

3

Hanna Greville, Countess of Stanmore, sat at her oval writing desk facing a bay window in her sitting room. The window overlooked a formal garden where ranks of boxwood and roses formed precise geometric patterns. The countess was wearing a green silk peignoir. She had retained the golden good looks of her youth, and her blonde hair cascaded in shiny waves over her shoulders.

The top of the oval desk was nearly obscured by piles of papers filled with her almost microscopic handwriting—the guest lists for the many extravaganzas planned for the "season" in London. The last two weeks in June and all of July would be spent at Stanmore House, the Greville mansion in Park Lane. The earl, of course, would have preferred to stay in the country, and in previous years he had managed to avoid going up to London for the season. But Alexandra had not been coming out then. This year the countess had insisted firmly that he should attend every function, meet every guest, for the name of his daughter's future husband lay somewhere among the papers before her.

"Who?" she wondered, her finger moving slowly down list after list. "The Honourable Percy Holmes; Paget Lockwood; Thomas Duff-Wilson." She paused at that name. A barrister, wealthy from inherited money, a fine sportsman.

"Terribly busy, my darling?"

She gave a little jump of surprise and turned to see the earl standing behind her. "Oh, Anthony, you startled me."

He bent his head and kissed her softly on the nape of the neck. "I'm skilled at sneaking into boudoirs."

"That isn't a skill a *gentleman* brags about." She gave his hand a quick squeeze and then turned back to her work. "Pull that armchair over, and let me go through these guest lists with you."

"Heaven forbid! That's your province, Hanna."

"It's a little more important this year and you know it."

Lord Stanmore frowned and walked slowly to the window. He gazed down at the garden. "I'm not concerned about Alexandra. I know that you will pluck the right fellow out of the pack and that she will be happy. No, it's Charles who disturbs me."

Hanna picked up a gold pencil and tapped it lightly against the edge of the desk. "He's just going through a phase, Tony."

The earl smiled wryly. "That's what Fenton said. Why is it that I can talk to Fenton and yet I can't talk to my own son?"

"You were chatting away together at dinner last night."

"Oh, we open our mouths and words come out, but a wall is there and we both know what—or who—it is."

Hanna stood up and walked over to stand next to her husband.

"How wonderfully neat the garden is," she said quietly. "It's a pity that lives can't be so arranged, but they can't. We can merely guide people, train them, and I believe that we've trained Charles very well. He's infatuated with Lydia and always has been, but I know in my heart that when it comes to a decision he will make the right and proper one."

"Perhaps." His eyes were on the geometric plantings below.

"But we mustn't press him. . . . It was a mistake inviting Mary and Winifred. I told you that."

"Winifred's father is . . ."

"A fine and honourable man," she cut in. "Yes, I know all that, and it would be wonderful if Charles fell in love with the girl and married her. But let me put in a little Yankee commonsense. Charles feels nothing for Winifred. I shall have a heart-to-heart talk with Mary and explain the facts. She'll understand Charles's position and she won't resent it one bit."

"Well, all right," he said in a pained manner. "Perhaps you're doing the right thing."

"I will be doing the *only* thing." She touched him gently on the shoulder. "I understand Charles far better than you do at this period in his life. And what's more, I understand Lydia."

"OH, I FEEL SO GLORIOUS!" Alexandra shouted, clutching her hat and bouncing up and down on the car seat.

"Sit still," Lydia shouted back, "or you'll fall out." Frowning slightly, she concentrated on the controls. They were racing along a narrow road which curved in lazy S's through dense woods and sunlit patches of hedgerowed fields.

"Gloriously happy!" Alexandra cried into the slipstream of wind buffeting her face. "Oh, Lydia, do you realize that by this time next year I might be having a baby! Mamma's inviting every devastatingly handsome bachelor in London."

"How do you know they're *devastatingly* handsome?"

"I just know. Not a one under six feet, all destined for greatness —and one of them will sweep me off my feet and into his arms. And I can't wait to have babies, five at least. I shall stroll into the nursery every night with my devastatingly handsome husband and nanny shall parade them in front of us."

"Are you planning on having all five at one swoop?"

"No, silly, one at a time. But seriously, I believe marriage and babies to be a holiness. I truly do."

The countryside gave way to the suburbs: Merton and Wimbledon, rows and rows of little brick houses. Then, as they reached London, the traffic became heavier with buses and ponderous horse-drawn wagons. Lydia stopped in front of an elegant Georgian edifice in Hanover Square, the House of Ferris, couturier. A doorman hurried from the entrance to open the car door, touching the brim of his hat.

Alexandra sprang from the car. "Lydia, don't you dare pick me up before three. I don't want you to see my gowns until they're free of basting stitches. Promise?"

"Promise," Lydia said flatly. When the doorman closed the car door she put the Benz into gear and roared off towards Oxford Street and her father's office.

Foxe House, a tall limestone-faced building near Oxford Circus, was one of the largest and most modern office buildings in England, completed in the spring of 1912. Archie Foxe now had all the departments of his vast enterprise under one roof, in what he called "the Yank method".

Lydia turned into the garage entrance, where a boy in a smart

160

blue uniform took over the car. She removed her linen motoring coat and left it on the seat, then walked to a lift which whisked her up to her father's office. "Is my father about?" she asked the pretty young receptionist.

"He went downstairs, Miss Foxe," the woman said. "But I'm sure we can find him for you." Archie Foxe was a compulsive roamer, going from office to office and desk to desk, overseeing, criticizing and praising every one of his employees.

"Oh, that's all right," said Lydia. "But if you do hear from him, tell him I'm in his office or I'll be waiting for ever!"

"Of course, Miss Foxe."

Lydia liked her father's office. The walls were lined with oak, the flooring oak as well, polished to a satin lustre, with a fine old Oriental carpet to add the proper touch of warmth to the room. Comfortable leather chairs. A grand old desk that had belonged to the Duke of Wellington. A few pictures on the walls. A landscape by Constable. Two modern paintings of London by Walter Sickert. And on the desk two photographs in silver frames.

These photographs, enthusiastically inscribed by Herbert Asquith, and David Lloyd George, made Lydia smile. The nearly bottomless bankbook of Archie Foxe had been of great help to the Liberal Party in the General Election of 1906 and the prime minister and his chancellor of the exchequer would never forget it. She wondered what Lord Stanmore would do if he were confronted with the images of *those* men. Smash them with his riding crop in righteous Tory rage?

Archie Foxe had been born in the East End in 1854. "Hard work and a bloody good idea" was his business philosophy. He would not talk about his childhood to anyone, not even his own daughter, nor to the upper-class woman he had married late in life and who had died when Lydia was a child. His childhood had been one of stinking hovels and workhouses, of a father drifting away in despair to gin-caused madness and a mother dying of consumption in a freezing attic. He could see the place of his childhood from the top-floor windows of Foxe House. It was not a distance that could be measured in miles.

At the age of nine he had been apprenticed to a butcher, and Archie's job was to chop up scraps of near-putrid beef which the owner turned into gelatinous meat pies. The vileness of those pies inspired Archie to make better ones. After finishing his apprenticeship at seventeen, he entered into partnership with a middle-aged widow who owned a tiny bakery near Covent Garden. The two of them made pies at night, good ones, which Archie sold during the day to various eating establishments and public houses. Within a year they had ten meat cutters and pastry men working for them. The widow sold her share of the partnership to Archie in 1880 and spent the rest of her days comfortably in the country.

"I could then do what I ruddy well wanted," Archie would tell a journalist many years later. What he wanted then were shops, clean, well-lighted places on corners of major thoroughfares, where ordinary blokes could have a cup of tea and something good and filling to eat for very little money and be waited on by a pretty young woman dressed in a blue uniform with a starched white apron and a white cap. The first of all the subsequent hundreds of White Manor Tea Shops opened its door on the northwest corner of Ludgate Circus on June 3, 1883.

"Men must eat, you see, that's only nature. That's why you can't 'elp but make a bit o' money caterin'. The only trick to it is in givin' ordinary people decent grub at a fair price, because there's a lot more of them than there are rich people. Of course, it grew a bit from that, you see. Got a bit more posh, you might say. There are White Manors where a navvy can hop in for his tea and there's White Manors that have got ruddy six-piece orchestras and a duke couldn't find fault with the Dover sole. But the price stays fair, you see. . . ."

There were some magazines on a table and Lydia sat down and leafed through a copy of the *Illustrated London News*. There were pictures of the King and Queen at Cowes and several pages on German army manoeuvres in East Prussia: ranks of drab uniformed men, with *Picklehaube* helmets, marching across fields. How operatic they all looked. She turned the page. . . .

"Well, this is a welcome surprise."

She looked up and there was her father coming into the room, full tilt as usual. He rocked back on his heels and gazed at his daughter with obvious pleasure. He was a stocky man who looked younger than his years, with reddish hair combed carefully to help conceal a round bald spot. His puckish features were those of a street imp grown old—and wiser.

She was examining him critically. "You promised not to wear checked suits. They make you look like a bookmaker."

He touched the loudly patterned jacket with his heavy, blunt hands. "I like checks . . . an' bookmakers."

"Oh, Daddy," she sighed. "You're quite impossible." She stood up and walked over to him, kissing him on the cheek. "I've missed you. Can't you come down for a few days?"

"There's been too much to do, but I'll try and manage. You keepin' busy?"

"Oh, yes, with one thing or another. I drove Alexandra up for a dress fitting. She hopes to be married any minute."

"Oh? Who's the lucky gent?"

"She hasn't met him yet, but I gather any man will do as long as he's tall, handsome and can walk on water."

"Seems to me that walkin' on water is your ruddy standard, too."

She turned away from him and went stiffly to the windows. London had never looked so beautiful, almost like a picture post-card, a too-blue sky, a perfectly-formed nimbus of white, fleecy cloud framing the dome of St. Paul's.

"I find your impatience for my marriage depressing, Daddy."

"Oh, do you?" he snorted. "Well, my girl, it's normal for a man to want grandkids."

He came up behind her and rubbed the side of his hand against her neck. She turned back with a smile and put her arms around him, inhaling his scent of fine woollens and good tobacco. "You're a dear. I'll give you lots of little nippers one day, I promise."

"I've never doubted it, but I wish you'd hurry up."

"I have plans," she said quietly. "Really quite wonderful plans."

HANNA gave some thought to her nephew from America as her maid brushed and combed her hair.

The telegram was in the centre of her dressing-table. "Will arrive Cunard S.S. *Laconia* . . . docking Southampton Friday June 12. . . . Give my regards to all . . . Martin Rilke."

The telegram made her smile. It was so *American*. So filled with uninhibited friendliness. *Give my regards to all.* Only a midwesterner would cherish such presumptions towards people he had never met, simply because they were family. She could understand his attitude, although she had left Chicago at the age of nineteen, but her husband and her children would have been bewildered by it; so she had merely said after receiving the telegram, "My nephew will be arriving on the twelfth. Charles, it would be nice if you went down to the docks to fetch him."

After her hair was arranged to her satisfaction, the maid helped her into a morning dress of white lawn and she started down for her breakfast, passing her elder son's room on the way. She hesitated, then rapped gently and opened the door.

Charles was fully dressed on the bed, his back against the headboard. A breakfast tray, the food barely touched, was on the bedside table. He put down the book he had been reading and smiled.

"Good morning, Mother."

"Don't you feel well? You look a bit pale."

"I'm fine."

How gaunt he has become, she was thinking. He was her firstborn and the unhappiness in his eyes hurt her deeply.

"Can we have a little talk, Charles?"

He looked away from her. "What about?"

"Winifred Sutton, among other things."

"Ah," he said with a thin smile. "Winifred."

"I convinced your father this morning that there is no possible chance of your becoming attracted to the girl. I intend to be equally candid about it with Winifred's mother."

"Well, that's a step in the right direction, I must say." He sat on the edge of the bed and placed his hands on his knees, a pose that always reminded her of her husband. They were so alike in looks and mannerisms, the same slenderness, the same clean features, and yet so opposite in character. The room reflected Charles's tastes, just as her husband's rooms reflected his. Books were everywhere, stacked, piled—books of history and poetry.

"You look instantly better," she said.

"Yes, as a matter of fact I am." He grinned at her. "And I'm quite sure that Winnie will feel better as well. I frighten her. There's quite a simple, passionate soul beneath all that *embonpoint*. I'm not the man to bring it out and she knows it."

164

"That's a pity, in some ways."

He nodded. "The dynastic blending of two fine old names. I feel a bit of a rotter disappointing everyone—except Winnie, of course. I'll break the terrible news to her myself. In a day or two she and her mother will depart seeking more receptive game. I'm sure that Lady Dexford has a list that beggars the one you've compiled for Alex."

"Charles! What an awful thing to say!" Her indignation was so patently artificial that they both laughed.

She walked farther into the room and stood looking about with a wistful expression. "You used to keep this room so neat. I think it now reflects your state of mind, Charles. A topsy-turvey confusion."

Their eyes met and he looked away. "I sense the preamble to a motherly lecture. I'd rather you didn't get started. Not till I get it all clear in my mind as to just what I want to say."

Hanna felt suddenly tired as she looked at her son. "I can hear every word of it, Charles, and I can hear your father's reply. He's an inflexible man. I should like to leave you with just one thought and I want you to face it honestly. Will you promise me that?"

"Of course," he said.

"I've known Lydia since she was a child and I'm fond of her. But the question I must raise is this. Should you marry Lydia, your father might publicly disavow her as his daughter-in-law. The social implications of such an action would be devastating. I ask you in all honesty, Charles—if Lydia knew that for certain would she have quite the same affection for you as she does now?"

IT HAD BEEN a long day. Lord Stanmore leaned back in his chair and waited for Coatsworth to pass the cigars around the table. The ladies had left for the drawing room, the younger women to the music room where Alexandra kept her gramophone. He felt satisfied, with just a small tinge of regret over the way things had turned out between Charles and Winifred. Still, Charles had been a little less moody, and Winifred had acted as though a great weight had been lifted from her shoulders. The young knew what they wanted, he supposed. Still, it would have been a damned fine match.

Coatsworth placed the crystal port decanter on the table to the earl's left, where Mr. Cavendish, a local squire, was seated. Cavendish filled his glass and passed the decanter on to Fenton, who filled his glass and handed it down to a retired brigadier and one of the leading horsebreeders in the country. And so the port went the rounds of the ten men at the table.

"I'd gladly have the government double my taxes," the brigadier was saying, "if it meant another Dreadnought or two."

"Nonsense," a man who was Conservative MP for Caterham said. "Let Germany pour millions into sabre-rattling. We have the most powerful merchant navy on earth and it's getting more powerful minute by minute."

An elderly surgeon from Guildford cleared his throat. "Still, it isn't simply a question of merchant bottoms, is it? It's a question of production. Fritz out-produces us in steel and chemicals."

"Yes, quite so," the earl said. "A cousin of my wife's, Baron Heinrich von Rilke, a scientific chap, told me of some truly remarkable things that they were doing at his laboratory in Koblenz. One mustn't sell the Germans short."

Fenton let his attention wander. The distant gramophone was playing a fast two-step. His right foot began a soundless tap-tap-tap on the carpet. He stifled a yawn. "I say, sir," he said, hoping to sidetrack any further discussion of English industrialization, or the lack of it, "Roger tells me that one of Lady Stanmore's relations is arriving from America tomorrow."

"Quite so," Lord Stanmore said without enthusiasm. "From Chicago. Newspaper wallah of some kind. Never met him." He stood up sharply. "Gentlemen, let's join the ladies."

Roger, Fenton and Charles lingered in the dining room until the older men had left, trailing cigar smoke down the corridor towards the drawing room. Charles drew a watch from his waistcoat. "A master stroke, Fenton. Without it we'd have been stuck in here for another half hour at least."

Fenton looked puzzled. "What are you talking about?"

"My cousin from Chicago. Father wished to avoid any probing questions about the fellow."

"What on earth for?"

"There's some kind of skeleton in mother's cupboard, the chap's father, her brother William. All I know is that he died years ago. . . .

Let's hop it now before someone insists we form bridge fours."

They left the dining room by way of the French windows that led onto the terrace. The gramophone grew louder, playing a frantic Texas Tommy. In the music room Alexandra and Lydia were dancing together. Winifred stood beside the gramophone, one hand on the crank.

"Charming!" Fenton murmured, watching the prancing girls.

The syncopated music came to an end and they broke apart, flushed and laughing. "Oh, I did enjoy that," Alexandra said. "I could do the Texas Tommy all night."

"I prefer a waltz myself," Roger said.

"That's because you're staid and dull."

"*Staid!*" Roger stiffened with indignation. "I'll show you! Play a tango—I dance the tango with a great deal of *sensuality*."

Fenton helped Winifred find a tango record.

Alexandra held out her arms. "Come on, Roger, and try not to step on my toes."

Charles bowed to Lydia with exaggerated formality. "Miss Foxe, may I have the pleasure?"

She curtsyed. "You may indeed, Lord Amberley."

He put an arm about her waist and she moved closer. Their hips touched and his body became tense. "Relax," she said softly.

The Latin rhythm began and Charles stumbled slightly. She had to lead for a moment until he was able to co-ordinate his body to the pulsating sound.

Fenton took Winifred by the hand. "Shall we try it?"

Her smile was wan. "I . . . never learned to tango. I don't think I can."

"Nonsense." He held her firmly, one hand in the small of her back. "It's simply a question of practise. I can teach you."

She was really quite pretty, he was thinking, smiling down at her. She smiled back, shyly, a pink glow spreading across her cheeks and throat. He guided her expertly through the steps, the sensual movements of the dance.

"You're doing very well," he said. "Just follow me."

She had little grace, but that was probably nervousness. Her eyes were hazel, he noted, and her hair the palest shade of brown. Yes, a very pretty girl, and if she lost weight she would have a

167

quite fetching figure. Lady Winifred Sutton, only daughter of the Marquess of Dexford. A dowry of . . . ten thousand pounds?

"Are you going up to London for the season, Winifred?"

"Oh, yes," she blurted, staring down at her feet. "Mamma will open the house in Cadogan Square next week." She looked up at him wistfully. "That isn't very far from the barracks, is it?"

"No. And it's just a short walk from my flat."

He detected a sudden change in her breathing. "Perhaps you could attend one of our . . . entertainments," she said hesitantly. "My coming-out ball is on the twenty-second of next month. I know that Mamma would be pleased if you could come."

He appeared to think about it. "I believe I could. You can tell your mother that I'd be honoured to receive an invitation."

Across the room Charles had bent closer to Lydia. "Let's dance out onto the terrace," he said. They tangoed out of the music room, and along to a stone bench. Charles pulled her down beside him. "You look so beautiful tonight, Lydia—that dress, your hair. . . . But you knew I wanted to talk to you alone and you deliberately stayed in . . . in *groups!*"

"It would have been rude not to mingle."

"So much has happened today," he said excitedly, running a hand through his hair. "I told Winnie that I could never become *emotionally* involved with her. She took it quite well."

"So I noticed," she said stonily.

"But that doesn't solve anything, darling. I'm afraid Father's going to be as intractable as ever."

She smoothed her dress over her knees. It was pale green silk embroidered with seed pearls, the bodice cut with a discreet plunge. "Charles, I think that the time has come to be honest with each other. I love you and I *think* you love me."

He stared at her with his mouth open. "You *think*? Good God! You dominate my thoughts day and night. There's not another woman that I would care to even *look* at." He put his arms around her and pressed her close to him.

She pulled back from him slightly and placed a slim, cool hand on the side of his face. "Tell me, Charles, are you ever direct with your father about us?"

He looked away from her, towards the house. Most of the rooms were lighted, and yellow squares of light fell across the terrace.

"I . . . I intend to have a long talk with him."

"You might begin by reminding him that we're living in the twentieth century. He wouldn't be ostracized if I married into the family. After all, it would be apparent to everyone that I hadn't *bought* my way into the peerage. There are a number of impoverished peers in this country, Charles. You'd be utterly amazed at how easily I could marry one of them if that was all I wanted."

He was staring at her with a look of dread. "Lydia, you wouldn't. . . ."

"Of course I wouldn't." She draped her arms about his neck and pulled him gently down to her. Her lips roamed teasingly across his face. "You're my own, sweet darling and I love you very much. I want to experience all the joys of marriage, and I want to experience them with you, no one else."

He held her tightly, kissing her lips, her neck, the soft hollow of her throat. He could feel her firm breasts against his chest.

"Lydia . . . Lydia . . ." he murmured.

She traced a fingertip across his earlobes. He was really such a boy, she was thinking, so torn between duty and desire. "I've thought of a way to approach your father, Charles," she said quietly, stroking his hair, "but we must talk it over thoroughly first. Spend the day with me tomorrow. Perhaps we can take a luncheon basket to Leith Wood and talk."

"Lovely," he murmured, "Lovely. . . ." Then suddenly he stiffened and pulled away. "Oh, God! I can't . . . I . . . I have to go to Southampton and greet some cousin from America. Oh, damn. I'm sorry, darling."

"I understand." Her smile was cryptic. "There's no need to explain. I quite understand."

4

The chauffeur, Ross, had managed to find a place to park the big Lanchester touring car, but they were a good distance from the Cunard dock. A solid line of lorries, taxicabs and lumbering horse-drawn wagons jammed the narrow approaches to the pier.

"A thought just struck me," Roger Wood-Lacy said as he and Charles walked away from the car, Ross keeping a respectful six paces behind. "Have you any idea what this chap looks like?"

"Haven't a clue. My age, a bit Germanic, I expect." Charles glared balefully ahead. He was in a bitter mood. But for Martin Rilke's inopportune arrival, he would have been resting his back against an oak tree in the cool glades of Leith Wood while Lydia served him watercress and ham sandwiches from a wicker basket. Damn!

Both young men found the jumble of large wooden buildings bewildering. Beyond the roofs they could see the tall funnels of the *Laconia*, wisps of smoke still trailing after them. Ross stepped forward and suggested that they head for an enormous, open-sided structure which bore a sign marked "BAGGAGE DISPERSAL". Hundreds of people could be seen inside, milling about under metal signboards that dangled from the roof with the letters of the alphabet painted on them.

"Good thinking, Ross," Charles said.

There were a great many people under the "R" sign, roaming through canyons of trunks. "Is that him, do you suppose?" Roger asked, pointing discreetly down one of the aisles of luggage.

Charles saw a man with a Kodak folding camera, in his early twenties, of medium height and stocky build, blond haired and square jawed, the eyes blue. He certainly had the Rilke mouth, wide, and quick to smile—as it was smiling now in his direction.

"Say," the man called out, "you wouldn't happen to be Lord Charles Amberley, would you?"

"Yes, I am," Charles said.

Martin came towards him with his right hand thrust forward. "You look just like I thought you'd look." He pumped his cousin's hand vigorously. "Gosh, it's nice of you to meet me. Is Aunt Hanna with you?"

"No," Charles said. "I came down with my friend, Roger Wood-Lacy. Roger . . . my cousin from America, Martin Rilke."

Roger took a step forward. "How do you do?"

"Very well, thanks," Martin said. "Had a swell trip, a bit rough for a few days, but all the passengers were good eggs."

"Glad to hear it," Roger said. A pleasant-looking fellow, he was thinking, although on the boisterous side—like most Americans.

Martin's luggage was soon located and, with the help of a porter, was safely strapped on the back of the Lanchester.

"Beautiful scenery," Martin said as they left Southampton and drove into the countryside. "I hope you won't mind if I ask your driver to stop now and then. I'd sure like to take some pictures."

Oh, God, Charles groaned silently. "Well, it's rather a long drive and we'd like to get there before dark. But we shall stop soon at Taverhurst for lunch. A quite ancient inn, the Three Talbards, and you can take all the pictures you want."

"That'd be fine. Where are we now? Near Hardy country?"

"The edge of it, yes," Charles said. "Hampshire rather than Dorset."

Roger arched one eyebrow. "I suppose Hardy's novels are required reading everywhere. *Tess of the D'Urbervilles* and *Jude the Obscure.*"

Martin nodded. "That's right, but to be honest, I prefer Hardy the poet."

"Oh, I say," Roger said with exuberance. "I feel the same way about him. Have you read 'Channel Firing' yet?"

"Yes, just before I left home. I especially liked the last stanza where he talks about Stonehenge." He glanced wistfully at the green hills of the South Downs. "I'd sure like to see that place."

"But you shall, old boy," Roger cried. "We'll see to that, won't we, Charles? Oh, I say, this is absolutely marvellous. Think of old Hardy's poems being read in *Chicago. . . .*"

Their accents and mannerisms had begun to grate on Martin's nerves a little. They seemed so affected, though they were, in the slang of his newspaper's city room, "genuine articles". He knew enough about England to recognize that. They could have been set down in rags in the middle of the Arabian desert and it would have been apparent to the lowliest Bedouin that they were English gentlemen, just as it was apparent to the young woman who waited upon them at the Three Talbards. This was what the English called *class*, and it was not an exportable commodity.

"Here you are, sirs," the barmaid said, and she placed a steaming steak and kidney pie on the table along with mugs of dark brown ale..

171

"Has my man been taken care of?" Charles asked.

"Oh, yes, sir," the barmaid said. "He's out back, sir."

"I understand you work on a newspaper, Rilke," Roger said after a few minutes of silent eating.

"That's right, the Chicago *Express*. I joined it when I left college last June. I'd like to become a novelist and I thought a year or two of seeing the seamier side of life would be a help."

"What are your plans now?" Charles asked.

"Well, let's see. Three weeks here in England, then I go to Paris, Berlin, and Rome. Six weeks in all. Not exactly the grand tour, but the limit I could afford."

"Charles and I may go to Greece in July," Roger said. "Pity you couldn't hop over for a week or two and join us."

THEY ARRIVED at Abington in time for tea on the terrace. It was a hectic moment for both Martin and Hanna, he trying to remember the names of the dozen or so people his aunt had invited, all of whom studied him with unabashed curiosity, and she trying to greet him in an "auntly" manner while not neglecting her guests. Two of them were leaving for London, a Lady Something and her daughter Winifred. Their departure added to the confusion.

"We shall have a long talk later," Hanna whispered to Martin, giving his arm a little squeeze. "Meanwhile I'm sure you'd like some time to yourself before dinner."

He excused himself gratefully and a footman ushered him to his room. His trunk and suitcase looked shabby against the pristine furnishings, but he only had eyes for the bed and flopped wearily onto it. He was closing his eyes when someone coughed to draw his attention. A middle-aged man, wearing a black linen jacket and grey striped trousers, stood just inside the room.

"Beg pardon, sir," the man said. "I'm Eagles, your valet. If I may have the trunk keys, sir, I shall unpack and see to your clothes."

He wanted to tell the man not to bother, but his aunt had obviously ordered the valet to come so he got off the bed and searched his pockets for his keys and handed them over.

"Thank you, sir. Shan't take but a moment. Sea travel is terrible hard on clothing, sir. The salt air sets the creases."

It was embarrassing to Martin to watch a total stranger sort through his luggage. The valet did not actually cluck his tongue, but his lips remained pursed as he sorted out the dirty clothes and removed wrinkled suits and jackets. He singled out his tuxedo for immediate attention.

"I shall give this a sponge and press immediately, sir. Dinner is always black tie, at least."

The *at least* had an ominous ring. The tuxedo was his only article of formal wear, and it was two years old.

"Thank you . . . Eagles?"

"Eagles, yes, sir. I shall get right on to this, sir, and have the rest of your clothing back in the morning."

After the valet had gone, Martin sat on the edge of the bed and debated whether to take a hot shower. A shower sounded good, but it was obvious that his quarters didn't include a bathroom. He recalled all the tales he had heard about primitive British plumbing. An English mansion might have thirty bedrooms but only two baths and a couple of water closets. He was puzzling over that dilemma when there came a gentle knock on the door.

"Come in," he called out.

The door opened and a slender, dark-haired girl in a maid's uniform came into the room carrying flowers in a glass vase. She seemed to shrink into the room like a scared doe, and barely glanced at Martin as she set the vase down and turned to go.

Martin stood up. "Wait a minute, maybe you can help me."

"Help you, sir?" the girl whispered.

"Well, I'd like to take a shower. Where's the bathroom?"

"Yes, sir," the girl said. "The bathroom is the third door on your left . . . no . . . on your *right* as you leave the room, sir."

She was a daisy of a girl, Martin thought. Seventeen or eighteen, skin like peaches and cream and eyes that were almost violet, with the thickest and longest lashes he had ever seen.

"My name's Martin Rilke," he said impulsively. "What's yours?"

"Ivy, sir. Ivy Thaxton."

"Thaxton." He repeated the name slowly, savouring it. "That's really a good *English* name, isn't it?"

She was looking squarely at him for the first time and a smile appeared to linger just below the surface of her face. "Yes, sir."

174

The smile came, faint, curious. "You're from America, aren't you?"

"That's right. Chicago."

She nodded. "Chicago, the state of Illinois, situated on Lake Michigan, railways and cattlemarkets. . . ."

"Say, you've really done your homework, haven't you?"

"I was very good at geography, sir, at school. It . . . it was my favourite subject . . . that and arithmetic."

"Arithmetic? You're the first good-looking girl I've ever met who liked arithmetic."

A crimson glow appeared suddenly on her cheeks. Lowering her eyes she went past him and out of the door.

The bathroom he found was large, totally out of proportion to its use. There was nothing in it but a mammoth porcelain-enamelled tub, and an oak cabinet containing fresh soap and extra towels. On the other hand, the WC next door was a dark, evil little place no larger than a cupboard. There was no shower. The hot water came in fits and starts, rattling the pipes and belching occasional puffs of steam, but eventually the water rose in the tub and Martin sank gratefully into its warmth. The English were an odd race. No question about that.

Back in his bedroom, Martin eyed his tuxedo dubiously. Its appearance had been bettered by the valet, but not by much. He was struggling with a black tie when there came a tap on the door. It was one of the liveried footmen informing him that sherry would be served in the library at six thirty.

A tall, ruddy-faced man with iron-grey hair walked towards the door as Martin entered the room.

"My dear fellow," he said, advancing with hand outstretched in greeting. "I'm delighted to meet you."

Martin could only assume that the man was his uncle. "How do you do, sir?" he said, shaking the man's hand. The grip was strong, friendly.

"Come," said the earl, placing an arm about his shoulders. "You know my son and his friend, Roger. . . . Let me introduce you to my daughter, Alexandra, and Captain Fenton Wood-Lacy."

The dinner jackets, Martin noted with a touch of envy, were faultless.

His aunt touched his arm. "Now, Martin dear," she said. "We

have so many functions planned for later this month. I don't believe you'd find all of them interesting, but I've written your name down on every list containing lots of pretty girls."

"That's swell of you, Aunt Hanna, but, you see, I'm only planning to be in England for three weeks or so and I . . . well . . . I was hoping to see as much of the place as possible, travel around." He felt embarrassed, hoping he wasn't insulting her.

Then she smiled, almost with relief it seemed to him. "That's a wonderful idea, Martin!"

"Yes, it is," the earl agreed, nodding his head vigorously. "A capital idea, my boy. The London season may be heaven for the ladies, but it's hell on us men."

"Now, Anthony," Hanna chided, laughing. "I think your plans are splendid, Martin. When do you want to get started?"

"The sooner the better. I thought I might take the train up to London tomorrow and make arrangements with Cook's . . . you know, join a tour group of some kind."

"I'll go with you, then, in the morning," said Fenton. "The adjutant needs me back."

"Are you stationed in London?"

"Yes. Coldstream Guards."

"That must be exciting. Don't you get to serve a good deal of time in India?"

"No such luck. The Guards are the King's household troops and he does not want to squander us on the Northwest Frontier."

"Saving them for something really big," Roger said.

Fenton nodded sombrely. "Right you are."

AFTER DINNER, Martin played one game of snooker with Fenton and then excused himself and went up to his room. The cover had been removed from the bed and the sheets neatly turned down. His last clean pair of pyjamas had been laid across a chair. The quiet efficiency of the house impressed him.

There was a good bedside lamp, and he sat in bed and placed his leather attaché case beside him, opening it and rummaging through it for one of the new notebooks he had brought along.

"Write down your observations every day for reference later." The famous novelist Theodore Dreiser had told him that when he had been guest speaker at the university, their common heritage as German-Americans creating an instant bond. It had also been the big, slow-speaking, gloomy-faced author who had advised him to work on a newspaper.

He took a notebook and a fountain pen from his case. Opening the notebook to the first page, he began to write.

"*Observations and reflections. Friday night, June 12, 1914.* Here I sit, feeling like a country cousin come to stay with rich relatives.

The house is magnificent, a mixture of architectural types. But there is a unifying cohesion to the style, the entire façade having been reconstructed by the Wood-Lacys' father, a prominent architect, now dead. Charles told me the Normans built a priory here in the eleventh century and it was written into the Domesday Book as pryory, with a "y" instead of an "i". The structure was torn down in the fourteenth century and a manor house was built here retaining the name, poor spelling and all. . . .

Aunt Hanna has three children. William—named after my father —is sixteen and at Eton. Charles is my age. He seems nice enough, but indecisive. I have no idea what he wants to do in life, but I gather that that isn't terribly important. Young men of his class— he will inherit the title one day—are not expected to do anything except ride a horse and look after the lands and the tenants. This class structure contains a million and one taboos. But I shall fathom it out in time. Alexandra is eighteen and just about the prettiest girl I've ever seen. Angelic face. Not too much behind it, I'm afraid. The kind of girl who has no room in her head for anything but boys, clothes and parties.

Aunt Hanna took me aside after dinner and we talked about my father, her beloved Willie, and how much I reminded her of him. Perhaps we were alike when she last saw him, but her image of him is vastly different from my own. She referred to him as *le beau Bohème*, as though his act of leaving home at twenty and finally being disinherited had been romantic. She should have come to Paris and seen him in his final days, drugged with absinthe, our apartment filled with mad paintings that would never sell. God forgive me, but his death was a blessing. . . ."

His eyes began to blur and he closed the notebook. He turned off the lamp and sat in the darkness watching the curtains float gently in the night wind. The silence was almost unnerving. He wasn't used to it. He missed the muted thunder of Chicago's traffic, the distant rumble of trains. He felt a pang of homesickness for Clark Street, the pool and the poker games, the hard-boiled talk of newspaper men.

He had debated with himself about coming to Europe, blowing the bulk of his savings, putting his job in jeopardy (for there was no guarantee that Briggs would take him back after being away from the *Express* for six weeks), but maybe this was the perspective he needed as a writer. Nothing stood still in Chicago: the city was bursting outward and upward. Whereas Europe was the past, changeless and drowsy, content with the old glories. . . .

5

Captain Fenton Wood-Lacy walked across a stubbled field, a gun under his arm, a game bag dangling from his shoulder.

"I might try and bag some pigeons," he had told the earl after their early morning ride. It was the type of shooting that Lord Stanmore felt was beneath his dignity, but he did not discourage other men from killing the grain-scavenging birds.

Fenton, however, had brought no cartridges.

He was walking slowly and it was nearly nine o'clock when he reached the edge of the formal gardens that were spread out on both sides of Burgate House. A gate was open and he sauntered through, leaving the gun and the game bag on a carved stone seat. He followed a path to the broad stone terrace encircling the house. A maid washing an upstairs window waved at him and he waved back. The servants at Burgate House reflected their master. They were all Londoners, as cheery and cheeky as sparrows.

As he approached the windows of the morning room he could see Lydia inside, just as he had hoped, seated at a table having her morning coffee. She was wearing a pale yellow peignoir and her hair hung loosely to her shoulders.

He tapped gently on the glass and she got up from the table and opened a window.

"Good morning," he said.

178

"What on earth are you doing here? Don't they serve breakfast at the Pryory?"

"They do, but the company can't compare. May I come in?"

She stepped back. "By all means. But take care Harker doesn't mistake you for a burglar and put buckshot into you."

"I'll take the chance." The casement window was narrow but he managed to climb through. "*Voilà!*" he cried, stumbling down into the room. "Amazing the skills one learns in the army."

He could tell that she was not overjoyed to see him. She would be polite, of course. Lydia was always polite even when she was on the verge of being her most shrewish.

He straddled a chair and folded his arms along the back of it. "I just happened to be passing by . . ."

"Please, Fenton, don't be any more ridiculous than you are already." She cut him a slice of seed cake and sipped her coffee without looking at him. "The Rilke cousin get in all right?"

"Yes. Pleasant chap. Open-faced and honest, hardly your type."

She finished her coffee and set the cup down. "That was a crude remark, Fenton. Quite beneath you."

"I feel a bit crude this morning. Had a rotten sleep. Is your father here?"

"You do jump around, don't you?" She was looking at him now. "What's Daddy got to do with it?"

"I wanted to tell him that I'm serious about joining the old firm. I sat up most of the night writing my resignation-of-commission letter." He smiled into her narrowed, questioning eyes. "It's a great deal easier getting out of the Guards than getting in. It took Uncle Julian at least six letters to get me posted from Sandhurst, and God alone knows how many lunches at his club."

The telephone began to ring far down one of the corridors, the sound muted by the walls. Lydia sat motionless, one hand toying with a silver spoon. The ringing stopped and after a few moments there was a tap on the door and the butler appeared.

"Lord Amberley on the line, Miss Lydia."

Lydia played with the spoon. "Thank you, Spears. Tell him . . . tell him that I'm still sleeping."

"Very good, miss."

They sat in silence until the butler's footsteps receded down the

179

hall, then Fenton stood up. "So you are letting him dangle on the hook?"

"That's unkind," she said stiffly.

"Perhaps, but I know the game. He tried to telephone you at least five times last night. When *are* you going to speak to him?"

"I'm going to invite him for dinner tonight," she said. "Not that it's any of your bloody business."

"My, my, aren't we touchy this morning . . . and after I walked all the way over here to ask you to marry me."

He was standing very close to her, and he noticed that her hand was trembling slightly.

"No, Fenton," she said softly. "Please go away."

He placed his hands gently on her shoulders. "Give up on Charles," he said. "Nothing can ever come of it. You know that, if you're honest."

"He'll marry me." She spoke so quietly that he could barely hear the words.

"I'm sure he *wants* to, but his nibs is an obstacle you'll never get around. And Charles will never take any step that isn't according to the unwritten code of the Grevilles. Is marrying into the peerage so damned important to you? Of course, you could always pick up a lord on the cheap, and pay off his debts. But you don't want that, do you? People would only make jokes about how one can buy anything at a White Manor Tea Shop these days."

She jerked her head away and turned quickly, lashing out at his face with her right hand. He grabbed her wrist in full swing and pulled her roughly to her feet, knocking the chair over.

"You bastard!" Her lips were taut, bloodless.

He held tightly to her wrist and pulled her against him, bent his head and kissed her. She didn't struggle—he hadn't expected that she would—and he could feel her body submit to him.

"Marry me," he said, pulling gently away. She shook her head, eyes closed, lips parted. "You love me and you damn well know it. But then love doesn't count, does it? Marriage is too important."

She stiffened and stepped back, rage in her eyes.

"You're a fine one to talk. You and Winnie Sutton . . . what a fine exhibition that was. The Wood-Lacy prelude to seduction." She mimicked his voice. "*Just follow me.*"

180

"I felt sorry for her."

"Don't insult my intelligence. You weigh your charities very carefully. You looked at that dowdy creature as just so many pounds sterling to the ounce. Is that how you look at me?"

"I admit I'm in a rather nasty spot at the moment, but I'm not after your father's money. If I thought you'd be content living on my army pay I'd never ask the old boy for a farthing. But you couldn't live on it and so I'm willing to go to work on civvy street. It's as simple as that. I'd make you a damned good husband, in bed and out, and you know that, too."

She nodded solemnly. "Yes, I know it."

He placed his hands on her hips, feeling the softness of the flesh beneath the silk.

"We're very much alike. We both want things that are just a shade beyond our grasp. I'm in a regiment that I can't afford and you want a social standing that all the money in the world won't buy. But there has to be more to life than becoming a countess one day, or strutting around Buckingham Palace in a red coat. Do you remember when you were nine and my father was working at the Pryory? You used to follow me up the scaffolding and do every dangerous thing I did. Well, I wish you'd follow me now."

He was very strong, very handsome, in a dark piratical way. It would have been so easy to succumb, but it wasn't what she wanted. It wasn't enough.

"I'm sorry, Fenton. I'm not a little girl any more."

He let go of her hips. Not with any obvious reluctance. He simply allowed his hands to drop away from her body.

"No need to apologize. It was a forlorn hope anyway." He held out his hand. "I'm off back to London with the Rilke cousin at ten. Are we still friends?"

Her fingers brushed his. "Always. Are you horribly in debt?"

"That's one way of putting it. But I have some plans afoot."

She winced and looked away from him. She had a vivid mental picture of Fenton and some featureless débutante walking beneath an arch of drawn swords, rose petals strewn at their feet. The image pained her.

"Let's wish each other good fortune," she said tonelessly. "And much happiness."

181

FENTON SAT in a moody silence halfway to London. Martin contented himself with watching the scenery.

Then, as the train entered the suburbs, Fenton emitted a deep sigh and reached into his pocket for cigarettes.

"Do you smoke, Rilke?"

"Yes, thanks." He preferred cigars, but he took the offered cigarette, grateful for the breaking of the ice.

"Rather a blistered landscape, isn't it?" Fenton said, gesturing towards the window. "I suppose all England will be like that one day, every hill crawling with brick villas. I detest progress."

"So do I, sometimes. Chicago's growing like a weed."

"Yes, I dare say. Still, in America there is so much land to expand into. All those prairies." He puffed on his cigarette and eyed Martin narrowly. "I really hate to bring this up, Rilke, but that jacket doesn't fit you at all. Who the devil is your tailor?"

"Marshall Field," he blurted. Marshall Field was a big American department store.

"The man should be shot. Look here, old chap, I hope you won't take offence, but my tailor could make you a couple of outfits in no time at all. What do you say we pop around?"

Martin squirmed, but the jacket *was* terrible, there was no question of that.

"Of course," he said. "But don't you have to report to your unit?"

"As a matter of fact, I pulled a slight deception. I just felt like getting back to London for . . . personal reasons."

They took a taxi from Waterloo station to the Strand. At Thomas Cook & Sons arrangements were made for Martin to join a ten-day tour of the beauties of the British Isles. They had lunch. Afterwards, at Savile Row, Fenton's tailors, Mr. Purdy and Mr. Beame, looked on Martin as a challenge. They exchanged knowing glances and raised eyebrows over the shoddiness of Yankee cloth and workmanship. Three new outfits, which according to Fenton, would see him through the day in style, would be ready on Wednesday afternoon.

"Two fittings on Tuesday, Mr. Rilke, in the morning and again in the afternoon. It is not customary for Purdy and Beame to work under pressure of time, but we will be, we can assure you, equal to the task."

"A decent bowler and umbrella and you'll be fine," said Fenton as they stepped out of the shop. "My hatter's in Old Bond Street." Then suddenly he stiffened, and faced about to peer intently into a window displaying pipes.

"Oh, Lord," he said under his breath. "Perhaps he'll pass by."

A young man was coming towards them. His body was slim, almost willowy, and black, curly hair framed a narrow, high-cheekboned face, the skin a pale olive-ivory. The Jewish nose was thin but prominent, the eyes were large, oval and brown like the eyes of a fawn. But the fawn-like characteristics were negated by his mouth, a wide slash that seemed to be fixed in a permanent sneer.

"Captain Fenton Wood-Lacy, I presume," the man said. "And companion."

"Why, hello, Golden," Fenton said, doing a poor job of imitating surprise. "Fancy running into you."

The man's lips curled even tighter in derision. "Fancy! I never knew you to be taken by pipes."

"I'm not, as a matter of fact, but any port in a storm."

The man threw his head back and laughed. "Oh, Fenton, I do admire you. You are the most candid man I've ever known. But do introduce me."

"Golden . . . Martin Rilke from Chicago. Rilke, Jacob Golden, the Fleet Street gadfly. Rilke is a fellow journalist, by the way."

"Oh?" Golden said, peering at Martin intently. "What paper?"

"Chicago *Express*."

Golden closed his eyes for a second. "*Express*. . . . Republican, hostile to President Wilson, distrustful of organized labour. . . ."

"Hey," Martin said with a laugh. "Lay off. I only write book reviews."

"That's what you should be doing, Golden," Fenton said dryly. "Might keep you out of mischief."

Golden sighed. "My father feels the same way, I'm afraid. No more reporting on Balkan intrigues. It's nothing but murders now. One must cater to the public tastes, or even create tastes to cater to." He winked at Martin. "But then I'm sure my father knows what he's doing. And he *does* own the paper."

"Same old Golden. No wonder your friends duck into shop

183

doorways." Fenton pulled a watch from his waistcoat pocket. "Time for tea. Let's hail a cab and go to the Guards' Club."

"My dear Fenton," Golden said, "they don't like Jews there."

"I know. An odious rule. It should merely be *certain* Jews. Where do you suggest?"

"A White Manor. The two shilling de luxe. And speaking of White Manors, I saw the beautiful Lydia Foxe in Paris two months ago. At the opera, clinging to the arm of a major in the *cuirassiers*. She seems to have a penchant for military men."

He turned away, blithely innocent. "Ah," he cried, dashing suddenly into the street, "there's a cab. . . . Taxi! Taxi!"

MARTIN ARRIVED BACK at Abington Pryory at ten thirty that night, taking a rattletrap taxi from the station to the house. The butler informed him that his lordship and her ladyship had retired early. "But if you care for supper, sir . . ."

"Perhaps a sandwich, in my room, if you don't mind."

"Not at all, sir," Coatsworth said with genuine understanding. "A trip up to London is always most fatiguing."

He wasn't sure if it had been the trip or the company that had been fatiguing. A bewildering day, he decided as he put on his pyjamas. A footman brought ham sandwiches and a tankard of pale ale which Martin wolfed down before getting into bed, placing his attaché case on his knees and taking from it a notebook and pen.

"*Observations and Reflections. Saturday night, June 13, 1914.* Had tea at a White Manor near Marble Arch. It was a huge, multi-storied place with several dining rooms, a string orchestra, and bakery shop. The food—small sandwiches and a variety of cakes—was both good and inexpensive. The service is first-rate, hordes of young women in crisply-starched blue uniforms taking orders, all of them pretty and cheerful. I wonder if Ivy Thaxton has ever heard of the White Manors? Probably must have. It seems to me that it would be a far better place for a young girl to work—being a maid in a place like Abington must be gruelling.

Jacob Golden is twenty-four, but wise beyond his years, as the saying goes. He's the only son of the great Lord Trewe, publisher of the London *Daily Post*, largest daily circulation in the world.

184

Yellow journalism at its most blatant. Jingoism and sensationalism in a heady mixture.

Jacob and Fenton went to school together. From what I could gather, there were only a couple of Jews in the school and Jacob had a miserable time until Fenton took him under his wing. After Oxford, his father gave him a job as a roving correspondent and he has been to a great many places. I felt a pang of envy as he talked about the Balkan Wars.

Jacob said that his paper might be interested in half a dozen articles about England as seen through a visitor's eyes—"A Yank's View of Britain", he suggested as a title. Advised me to make the pieces short and laudatory, although a gently chiding humour would be OK. Five pounds per article. That won't pay for my trip, but it will make a slight dent in the tailor's bill. . . ."

A gentle tapping at the door interrupted his train of thought. He was surprised when Charles stepped into the room, dressed in evening clothes and carrying a bottle of champagne.

"I hope I'm not disturbing you," Charles said.

"No, not at all." He capped the pen and closed the notebook.

"I saw your light as I came up from the garage. Thought you might enjoy a nightcap."

Martin got out of bed and put on his dressing-gown. Charles found two glasses on the chest-of-drawers, one with a toothbrush in it.

"Just right for swizzing out the bubbles," Charles remarked as he undid the wire around the cork. There was a tiny, satisfying pop and then the pale amber wine flowed into the tumblers. "Enjoy your trip up to town?"

"Yes," Martin said, taking one of the glasses. "I'm going on a Cook's tour of England next week. Leave on Thursday morning."

"That should be pleasant. You'll probably see a good deal more of old England than I've ever seen. But that's always the way, isn't it? The traveller sees more than the native."

It seemed to Martin that something was troubling his cousin, but what it could be or why he had come in was a mystery.

"Odd, come to think of it," Charles said. "Here we are cousins, and yet I know next to nothing about you."

"I know very little about you," Martin said.

"There isn't that much to know. I went to Eton and Cambridge. Would like to be an historian. Enjoy good music. Have been to Italy and France. You were born in Paris, weren't you?"

"In Montparnasse."

"Is your mother French?"

"Was. She died four years ago."

"I'm sorry. That's my point. I should have known that."

"I don't know why you should," Martin said, sitting on the edge of the bed. "Her death wasn't really a family matter."

"The disinheritance, you mean?"

So he knows about that, Martin thought without bitterness. The midnight conversation was becoming curiouser and curiouser.

"Yes, the disinheritance. That took place before I was born, so I don't know too much about it. I never knew my grandfather, but I gather he was a tough old bird, very old-fashioned and puritanical." Charles was watching him, hanging on every word. "I guess my father was a rebel. He didn't want any part of the family business. He wanted to paint. Anyway, when my grandfather died he'd cut my father out of his will."

Charles wet his lips with champagne. "It seems so cruel to be disinherited, just for wanting to be an artist."

"Well, my father alienated people, I guess. It seems he had a terrible reputation in Paris and I don't think anyone was sorry when he died."

"How did he die?"

Martin took his time answering. He filled his glass and drank half of it. "He cut his wrists," he said.

"That's horrible," Charles whispered. He stood up, clearly shaken by what he had heard. "If only there had been someone in the family to take your father's side, to conciliate . . . ."

"But there wasn't. Anyway, that was a long time ago. There's not much point in talking about what could or could not have been done. Or is there? You won't mind if I'm blunt, will you? Is there anything bothering you?"

Charles stood very still, eyes fixed on the windows, then he returned to the chair and slumped wearily into it.

"Tonight I asked a woman to marry me. . . ."

"Congratulations. But you don't look very happy about it."

Charles stared down at his hands folded tightly in his lap. "It's something we both want, but the final decision rests with me . . . in facing my father squarely. I'm terribly afraid that he might withhold his blessing. It's not the girl—father likes her—it's what her father does that my father finds unacceptable. Having him as an in-law would be a constant source of embarrassment." Charles looked up, his expression carved into a mask of firm resolution. "I intend to tell my father in a few weeks, on my birthday."

Martin bent down for the champagne. "I think I understand what you've been driving at. Are you trying to say that your father might disinherit you?"

"No, I can't be legally disinherited, but there's nothing to prevent him from turning his back on me. Except my mother; she's always had a great influence over him."

Martin took a swallow of champagne. "Maybe you'd better talk to her first."

"No. She'd just tell me to think it over, to wait. She's hoping my feelings for Lydia will undergo a change, or hers for me. That won't happen." He drained his glass and leaned forward. "When you get back from your trip I want you to meet her. Then you'll understand my feelings. Lydia Foxe is the most beautiful, most captivating, most exquisite creature that God ever gave the breath of life."

Martin avoided looking Charles in the eye. He drank his champagne, the wine tasting musty all of a sudden. He was thinking of Jacob Golden and his remark to Fenton about seeing Lydia Foxe in Paris with a French officer.

"I sure hope it all works out for the best."

"I have a strong feeling that it will," Charles said a little too fervently. "Yes, I really believe it will."

After Charles had gone, Martin flopped wearily into bed, but it was impossible to get to sleep. He tossed and turned for a long time and then got out of bed and stood in front of the open window. He gazed down at the gardens, so ordered and geometric, so faultlessly pruned. The serenity seemed a paradox. Perhaps that was symbolic of England. A carefully-nurtured façade of grace and tranquillity behind which emotions seethed as strongly as they did in New York or Chicago.

6

Jamie Ross was happy to be in London. London was motorcars and the company of his true peers, the men who drove those cars and made them run, where chauffeurs and mechanics met over a pint and talked seriously about magnetos, carburettors, fuel pumps and horsepower. London was also pretty girls, droves of housemaids, typists and God knows what else in Hyde Park, Piccadilly and the Strand. It was heaven for a bloke like him, he was thinking as he walked up and down the narrow cobblestoned mews behind Stanmore House, the heels of his boots ringing sharply on the stones. He was wearing a new uniform of dove-grey serge, black boots and leggings, a grey cap with a black leather peak and tight-fitting black leather gloves. He strutted a little, feeling certain that a maid or two would be peering through the curtains of the big house. Ivy Thaxton was forgotten. Up and down he walked, past the old buildings that had once been coach houses but were now garages with living quarters above them for the servants. The rear of Stanmore House rose four storeys on the other side of the mews, its marble-columned front facing Park Lane.

One of the garages was open, its doors folded back to reveal the Stanmores' silver Rolls-Royce. Ross paused for a moment to look at it. A good car. Fine bit of machinery beneath the bonnet, but it could be better. He had written a letter to the Rolls-Royce company suggesting a method for improving the carburation system. He wondered idly if anything would come of it.

"'Morning, Ross. Care for a fag?" One of the elderly footmen was coming towards him. The man was in his braces and wore carpet slippers. Ross took the offered Woodbine.

"Keepin' banker's hours, aren't you?"

The footman made a sour face. "Didn't get to me bed till after three this mornin'. They had thirty-five people for dinner."

The footman sat down on a stone step and unfolded a newspaper. Ross looked over his shoulder.

"What happened at Newmarket yesterday?"

The footman turned the pages. "Let's see . . . Ah. Kennymore took the Princess of Wales Stakes, no surprises there. But did you hear about the Austrian archduke?"

"What about him?"

"Got scuppered yesterday. Him and his missus. Anarchists tossed a bomb at him, then shot the two poor blighters dead."

"Get off it," Ross said with disbelief.

"It's in the paper. See. Archduke Franz Ferdinand, heir to the Austrian throne—and his consort—murdered in Sarajevo."

"Where's Sarajevo?"

"Bosnia."

"Never heard of it. One of them queer penny farthing countries. Couldn't happen here. Too bloody civilized."

Ross took a drag on his Woodbine. It was starting to get hot, the sun bouncing off the walls of the old stable houses. His hands felt sweaty in the gloves. Well, what the hell did he expect on the twenty-ninth of June, snowflakes? The church in South Audley Street began to toll the hour of ten.

Ross flipped the cigarette away, walked quickly to the open garage and got into the Rolls. Before the bell had finished striking the hour he had driven out of the mews and had turned into Park Lane. Lord Stanmore was just coming out of the front door.

Ross drew the car up to the kerb, a footman opened the rear door and the earl got in.

"Good morning, Ross."

"Good morning, m'lord."

Lord Stanmore sank back against the seat with an audible sigh. "Ah, a perfect morning, Ross."

"Indeed it is, m'lord," he said, waiting for his moment to slip the car into the traffic streaming down from Marble Arch.

"I have to go to the House, Ross—shan't be too long, though. Drafting a message of condolence . . . that beastly assassination of the Austrian archduke."

"I was just now reading about it, m'lord. Told Mr. Picker that it would never have happened in England."

Lord Stanmore leaned forward to make conversation easier over the hum of the traffic. He was fond of young Ross. Bit of a rough diamond. But a bright, intelligent man. A good example of what was admirable among the lower classes.

"Jolly well put. We may have our anarchists in England, but they have a sense of fair play. Shooting the man on a Sunday, too."

After driving the earl to the Houses of Parliament, Ross spent an enjoyable time in conversation with the other chauffeurs and told them about the carburettor device he had thought of and of the letter he had written to the Rolls-Royce company.

"Did you take out a patent?" Lord Curzon's chauffeur asked.

"No. Why?"

"Why? To keep anyone from stealing your idea. I hope you didn't send a set of drawings."

"No . . . just wrote to 'em." He was beginning to feel a bit uneasy. "Told 'em enough to wet their whistle, like."

"Good." The man drew a piece of paper and pencil from his coat and leaned against a mudguard to write. "I'm going to give you the name of my brother-in-law. He's chief clerk for a firm of solicitors. He'll tell you how to get a patent."

Ross wondered for a moment if the older man was making fun of him, but there was no hint of mockery in his eyes as he handed him the slip of paper.

"Thanks, mate," Ross murmured.

"Think nothing of it. And good luck to you."

"Hop to it, lads," a driver warned. "Here they come."

Lord Stanmore and a dozen other peers could be seen crossing Palace Yard, all of them smoking cigars and chatting away in high spirits. Hardly the proper mood for men who had just drafted a message of condolence, Ross was thinking. He straightened his cap and walked towards his car.

Lord Stanmore got into the back of the Rolls. "Pall Mall, Ross. Drop me at the club and then see to her ladyship's needs, or my daughter's." He chuckled wryly. "I can well imagine how they've been keeping you hopping the past ten days or so."

Ross estimated that he had been on duty an average of fourteen hours a day since the family had moved up from Abington. Her ladyship's passion for hand-delivered invitations meant driving all over London with one of the footmen, in full livery, powdered wig and all, seated beside him, to the hooting delight of every passing lorry driver. Lady Alexandra was party mad, which meant long hours waiting outside big houses in Mayfair and Belgravia,

190

jawing with other chauffeurs while tango music drifted into the street. It was such a bloody waste of time. Somehow he had to find a spare hour to visit the solicitors' office. A patent with his name on it. The thought awed him. Of course, it would take a bit of money. He might be forced to sell his motorbike. Still. . . .

As they came to Trafalgar Square, Lord Stanmore called out, "I say, Ross, turn into the Strand."

He obeyed without question, although it meant cutting in front of other cars, ignoring the squeal of brakes and the irate blowing of horns. Lord Stanmore was leaning forward and pointing. "There, Ross, in front of Cook's. Yes, by Jove, thought I'd spotted the fellow. Pull up."

Ross sliced neatly through the traffic and parked behind a touring bus.

"Martin!" The earl rolled down his window and poked his head out. "Martin, dear boy!"

Martin Rilke was standing on the pavement talking to the tour director, his attaché case and suitcase beside his feet. He turned at the sound of his name and walked over to the car. "Hello, sir. This is a surprise."

Lord Stanmore extended his hand through the window and squeezed Martin's arm. "And a very pleasant one. All done with your tour?"

"There are two more days—the sights of London, but I'd rather see those on my own. I was just saying goodbye to the guide."

Lord Stanmore opened the door. "Hop in, lad, and we'll take you to the house. All your gear's up from the country as promised and there's a room waiting for you."

Martin hesitated. "Thank you, sir, but I must take a cab to the *Daily Post*. I've written a few articles about the trip for them."

"Good for you, but hop in anyway. I'm just going to my club and then Ross will drive you there." He shifted over on the seat. "Won't hurt your chances of a sale if you arrive in style."

THE *DAILY POST* building in Fleet Street was an architectural fusion of Gothic cathedral and Victorian railway station. Slender Ionic columns of soot-blackened stone and dull green copper flutings bound myriad windows into an awesome monolith.

"Do you want me to wait for you, sir?" Ross asked as he stopped at the main entrance.

"No, thanks," Martin said. "I'll get a cab. Fifty-seven Park Lane. Is that right?"

"Yes, sir. Stanmore House."

Clutching his attaché case, Martin entered the palatial lobby. A uniformed page escorted him up to the second floor, to a vast room filled with oak desks and shirt-sleeved men. Taut steel wires were suspended horizontally from the ceiling, crossing and criss-crossing the room. Small metal message-containers rocketed back and forth on the wires like artillery shells. Typewriters clattered, men shouted over telephones or cried out for the copy boys, and a tickertape machine added to the din. It was a room that made the editorial offices of the Chicago *Express* seem like the interior of a funeral parlour.

"Mr. Golden's down there, sir," the page said. "Fourth desk."

Martin thanked the boy and made his way through the aisles, walking ankle deep in scrap paper.

"Hello, Rilke," Golden called out cheerfully. He was bent over a desk, a green eyeshade pulled low on his forehead. "Pull up a wastepaper basket and sit down."

"I think I'm intruding. You guys seem pretty busy."

"Not me, *they*." He leaned back in the chair and locked his hands behind his head. "I'm polishing an item about a clerk who made off with five thousand pounds of his firm's money. The other lads in this room are not so much busy as *confused*. Austro-Hungarian internal affairs have never been their forte and my dear old man is demanding reams of articulate, incisive prose to explain Bosnian political aspirations to a multitude of unlettered readers. I have my own views on that dark corner of the world, but no one here wants them expressed."

"That assassination was a terrible thing. But there doesn't seem to be any major crisis over it."

Golden's slash of a mouth twisted in derision. "A bit backward in our knowledge of the European ant heap, are we?"

"A bit, yes."

"A common enough fault, I'm afraid, but don't despair, Professor Golden is at hand." He reached to the desk for a tin of

192

cigarettes. "The Austro-Hungarian Empire, a simple tin of Abdullah smokes—a hodge-podge of Germans, Magyars, Croats, Slavs, exceeded in stupidity and monumental corruption only by the Russians who border them to the east." He shifted an inkwell into position. "The mighty Russian inkwell, murky with serfs, Cossacks, mystics and dark plots."

"I'm not totally ignorant of European politics," Martin murmured.

"No, I'm sure you're not, Rilke, but you've watched it all from a long distance. I've seen it from the gutters of every capital. Hate. That's the binding word on the Continent. And to see true hatred one must go to Serbia, to the little cafés in Belgrade, and, casually, over a glass of slivovitz, bring up the subject of Austria and whether or not she has a legitimate right to keep Slavic people enfolded in the Hapsburg wing. Then you'll see hate. A violent people, those Serbs—nine years ago they sliced up one of their kings like dog meat. . . . But we love them because they're so small and plucky and Austria is such a big bully."

Golden moved a small box of paper clips into position below the flat tin of cigarettes. "Serbia. On Austria's southern flank. That's why the Russians love them. They keep the Austrians off balance and tie up half their army. Well now, what have we got right now? One dead Hapsburg archduke. Not much of a loss. . . . But his death will give the Austrians an excuse to crush Serbia if they can prove it was a Serbian activist who committed the crime and there's no doubt in my mind that one did." He pushed the cigarette tin sharply against the box of clips. "Austria moves against Serbia, but not in swift anger—they'll never cross the Danube unless they can be assured that Germany will keep the Russians in check, and they'll be given that assurance in due time. That will anger the Russians no end and so we can move the inkwell against the smokes. And what will France do? She has a treaty with Russia, just the excuse she needs to avenge 1870—the loss of Alsace and Lorraine. With the Russian bear scaring the wits out of the Germans in East Prussia, the French will attack across the Rhine and storm to Berlin."

He leaned forward with a gleeful smirk. "But the Germans are such clever chaps. They know all this; they worked it out on paper years ago. The Germans prize and honour generals with brains while we despise ours. They have a plan to deal with French moves.

It calls for a massive flanking sweep through Belgium in order to fold the French armies into a net before the Russian bear can even stumble out of its cage. It's a plan that might well work. The French refuse to believe that Germany would violate Belgian neutrality. So do we. It wouldn't be sporting, would it? Belgium is inviolate. There's a paper to prove it signed by all the great powers years ago: just one more holy relic to toss on the scrap heap." Golden tidied up the European scene by moving the ink-well to its proper place and dropping the box of paper clips into the top drawer. "But back to more pleasant subjects. How did the Yankee tripper find little Britain?"

"I had a grand time," Martin laughed. He placed the attaché case on the desk top. "Wrote half a dozen sketches."

"Good. Leave your copy and wander about for a bit. You'll find a canteen of sorts down that corridor. Ta-ta and leave me to it."

Martin sat at a small table next to the canteen window with a view of the Temple gardens and the river. He was finishing his second mug of tea and his third bun when Golden came in with the travel copy papers rolled into a tight cylinder. He sat down and tapped the roll against the edge of the table.

"They're damned good, Rilke. I laughed out loud over the Yorkshire cattle-show piece. The judges were right out of Dickens. Just the ticket." He looked thoughtful. "Is it absolutely vital that you should go on to the Continent?"

"No, I guess not. Why?"

"Because perhaps you could postpone it for a bit. I think your style of writing would go over very well with our readers. A Yank's-eye view of Britain, with the emphasis on the upper-middle-class, mildly satirized like the Yorkshire squires. Being a roving feature writer for the *Post* would be jolly good experience. Or do you have to be back in Chicago by any fixed date?"

"No. In fact, I don't know even if I'll have a job when I get back."

"Does that mean you're interested?"

"Sure."

The sardonic mouth softened into a warm smile. "Jolly good. Let's hop upstairs and I'll introduce you to the chief."

The top floor of the building was in awesome contrast to the lower depths. Deep carpets and oak-panelled walls subdued all

194

sound. A broad corridor ended in a double set of doors which opened into a vestibule in which a male secretary sat behind a small desk adjacent to another set of double oak doors.

"Is he busy?" Golden asked.

"Naturally," the secretary drawled. "Is it important?"

"It is," Golden said. He leaned towards the man and spoke in a stage whisper. "The chap I'm with fired the fatal shot yesterday and is willing to tell all for fifty quid."

The secretary faked a yawn. "Go in, Jacob, and take your assassin with you."

Beyond the doors was a cavernous room that seemed to be part office and part museum. Glass cases filled with Egyptian artifacts stood next to a tickertape machine. Paintings by Gainsborough and Turner competed for wall space with shilling maps of sections of the world. Typists scurried in and out of glass-enclosed cubicles. At the far end of the room was a broad oak table, and behind it sat Harry Golden, Lord Trewe.

"Guv'nor," Jacob said, "meet Martin Rilke, from Chicago. An eminent journalist on the *Express*."

Martin extended his hand across the table. There wasn't even the remotest family resemblance. If Jacob was a willow, his father was an oak, a dark brown trunk of a man. The hand that reached out and took hold of his own was hard and horny.

"Rilke, did you say?" The deep voice fitted the man. "Then you'd be Hanna Stanmore's nephew. I can see the likeness."

Jacob leaned across the table and placed the tightly-rolled sheaf of articles in front of the press lord. "Rilke took a Cook's tour of jolly old England and came back with some very amusing observations of about a thousand words each. I'd like you to read them."

Lord Trewe merely glanced at them. "If you say they're good, Jacob, give them to Blakely."

Jacob scooped up the articles and shoved the roll under his arm. "Right. My idea is to run a short column every day by Rilke, his unjaundiced view of the London social and sporting scene. He's staying with the Stanmores, which gives him an inside look at society—thus he should use a *nom de plume*—can't have you being accused of biting the hand that feeds you, can we, Rilke?"

"He can feed himself," Lord Trewe rumbled. "We've never been accused of underpaying our correspondents."

A harassed-looking man darted up with handfuls of paper. "Berlin and St. Petersburg reports, sir."

Lord Trewe snatched them from the man's hand and read through them rapidly. His face was expressionless, the carved figurehead on a ship's prow. When he was through with them he tossed them casually aside and looked at his son with a faint smile. "All your fears are proving groundless. The world is used to Hapsburgs getting themselves murdered. Not a ripple in the European pond."

"Still waters run deep," Jacob said, "I do believe."

Lord Trewe settled back in his chair. "Get on with your work, Jacob." The interview was clearly over and Jacob led Martin back towards the bedlam of the news room.

"Well, Rilke," Jacob said. "How does it feel to be writing for the most powerful newspaper in the world?"

"Good, but I can't very well stay with the Stanmores. It wouldn't be right."

"You'll have a hard time finding suitable lodgings, old boy. This is the height of the season. Tell you what, I have more rooms than I know what to do with, a big old flat in Soho above the finest Hungarian restaurant this side of the Danube."

BY LEANING OUT of the garret window and craning her head Ivy Thaxton had a fine view of Mayfair. A bit lopsided, more roofs than streets to be seen, but, still, it *was* London and she *was* there.

Just below the window there was a flat, secluded spot near the base of a tall chimney. Her happiest moments of the long day were the few minutes she could sneak in total solitude by popping out of the window to sit there, her face turned up to the sun.

She had so little time to herself. Velda Jessup had thrown a fit of some kind shortly after they arrived in London and had been carried out of the house on a stretcher; so Lady Alexandra was left without a lady's maid. Mrs. Broome had decided to give the job to Ivy.

"It's a big step up the ladder, my girl."

It was also hard work. Lady Alexandra was in a perpetual fever of activity, her days and nights spent at balls, luncheons, garden party teas, riding in Rotten Row, attending fashion shows and plays. Each activity required a new costume from shoes to hat and she could never make up her mind about just what she wanted to wear. And talk! A constant stream of chatter about this boy and that boy, and should she marry a barrister or should she give her hand to a dashing Hussar who was the youngest son of a duke?

Ivy smiled in the blessed, sun-filled tranquillity of the rooftop, lulled by the muted rumble of traffic and the cooing of a pigeon preening itself on a chimneypot. *A step up the ladder. . . .*

Was it? She stared thoughtfully into space. A lady's maid. Ironing and sewing, folding things into drawers and hanging things in cupboards all day and half the night, too. Lady Alexandra never put so much as a stocking in its proper place, but then one didn't keep a dog and expect to do the barking.

On her one afternoon off she had sat in Hyde Park, watching the boats on the Serpentine. She had sat on a bench in her plain brown dress, one hand pressed to the crown of her straw sailor hat to keep it from spinning away across the pond in the wind. Three girls about her age had come along the path sharing a bag of sweets between them, nice-looking girls, well-dressed. They had sat for a moment on the bench, talking and laughing, and then one of them had drawn a silver watch on a chain from a small pocket and had glanced at it and said, "Oh my, we'd best get back to the office or Mr. Parrot will be ever so upset."

The other two girls had laughed and one of them had replied, cheeky as can be, "Well, you know what Mr. Parrot can do!"

Then they had walked on, not hurrying one bit, down the path towards Stanhope Gate, off to work in an office somewhere, typing, she supposed.

They hadn't taught typing at school. Hadn't taught much of anything, if it came to that. The library in Norwich had been her real school. She had begun with the A's—Jane Austen, the historical romances of William Harrison Ainsworth, the collected essays of Addison. "Don't you think they're a bit too deep for you, Ivy?" The librarian had held rigid views on what was proper reading for young girls. But Ivy had persisted doggedly, volume after volume: Dickens, Galsworthy, Shakespeare. Well-read, but nothing learned of any practical value.

"Ivy? Jane, where is Ivy Thaxton?" Mrs. Broome's voice.

"Out the window, Mrs. Broome. I told her. I said, Ivy, I said . . ."

Ivy sighed and looked up to see Mrs. Broome's incredulous face in the garret window.

"Ivy Thaxton! You come in from there this instant, before you fall to your death!"

"It's impossible to fall, Mrs. Broome."

"Perhaps. It is also impossible to permit his lordship's staff to scamper across the rooftops like common chimney-sweeps! Come up! *At once!*"

She climbed back into the small, stuffy garret she shared with four other girls. Mrs. Broome stared coldly at her.

"Honestly, Ivy, you are incorrigible. Never let me see you out there again."

"No, Mrs. Broome, you won't."

The housekeeper appeared dubious. "Well, we shall see what we shall see. At least I won't have to concern myself with your extraordinary behaviour for the next few days. Lady Alexandra has been invited to Somerset. You will go with her, of course. So hurry along and begin packing her clothes."

"Yes, Mrs. Broome."

"Take an extra dress for yourself and plenty of clean aprons and caps. You will be leaving first thing in the morning, the eight-thirty from Paddington."

The occasion was a house party at the Duke of Avon's ancient castle. Lady Alexandra was more bubbly and talkative than ever as she agonized over her selection of clothing, but by eleven o'clock that night the clothes had been carefully packed. The cream-coloured leather trunks with the Greville coat-of-arms embossed upon them in gold leaf were closed and ready for the footmen to take downstairs in the morning.

"Goodnight, Ivy. Be up bright and early in the morning."

"Yes, m'lady."

She walked wearily down the corridor towards a narrow stairway that led to the garret rooms. As she passed one of the doors it opened and Martin Rilke stepped out. He was wearing a dressing-gown and was holding a toothbrush.

"Ivy . . . Thaxton?" he asked, smiling.

"Yes, sir," she said, looking away from him.

"Don't you remember me?"

She nodded. "Yes, sir. Mr. Rilke from Chicago."

"Right! Cattlemarkets and railways." She was looking at him curiously and he suddenly was lost for words. He felt silly standing in the corridor in his dressing-gown. He wanted to say that he'd been hoping to run into her again, that she was just about the prettiest girl he'd ever seen, but he knew that would only embarrass her. In England gentlemen didn't speak to maids that way.

"Are you going back to America soon?" she asked.

"No," he said quickly, glad that she had broken the impasse. "I've got a job on the *Daily Post*. I'll be in England for another couple of months, but I'll be leaving here tomorrow, moving in with a friend in Soho."

"That should be nice. I'm going down to Somerset tomorrow with Lady Alexandra."

"That should be nice, too."

"Yes, sir," she said, starting off towards the stairs. "Goodnight, sir."

Up in the garret room Ivy stood by the window. He is quite taken by me, she thought, but he will never say so. After all he knows his place—and mine.

"Damn," she said softly, staring out across the shadowed roof, the sleeping city. "Damn . . . damn . . . damn."

7

Charles Amberley emerged from the coolness of the Carlton Club and waited patiently in the afternoon heat for the doorman to signal a taxi. To anyone passing by he looked elegant, cool and detached—inside, he was seething. He had just left his father. They had had lunch together, Scotch salmon and a superb bottle of hock followed by fruit, cheese and a hundred-year-old brandy, his father waiting for the brandy before toasting his birthday.

"To July twenty-third. May it always be a day of sunshine."

His father had been in a good mood. The season was beginning to wind down, more and more people were moving out of London, back to their country estates. He could decently do the same.

"I tell you, Charles, I miss the horses, damned if I don't. And speaking of getting away, I thought you and Roger were intending to go to Greece this month."

"We decided against it. Roger is preparing a book of his poems for publication."

"A fruitful summer, what? Did Alex tell you that she's finally made a choice?"

"No. How did she do it? Stick a pin into a list?"

"Something like that, I'd say. The chap's name is Saunders. He's in the Foreign Office, Lord Esher's nephew. Of course, that's her choice for *this* week, but I hope she stays with it."

"So do I. And, Father, I've made up my mind to marry Lydia."

How soft those words sounded to his ears, a melody. They had rung a different tune for his father, but he had said little. Sipped his brandy, lit a cigarette.

"Oh? You know my feelings on that subject, Charles. The thought of your being Archie Foxe's son-in-law is most painful to me."

"Because Archie's in trade?"

The earl had cradled his glass between his hands. "I don't hold that against him. What I simply cannot abide is his contempt for the British class structure. Damned if I don't believe the man's a socialist at heart. And his closeness to Lloyd George and all that scruffy bunch of Liberals is repellent to me. I'm sorry. Lydia has been welcome in my house since she was a child. But marriage? That is out of the question."

"And if I marry her anyway, Father?" His voice had sounded tinny and ineffectual in the vastness of the dining room.

"I do not wish to discuss the matter any further, Charles." He had set his glass on the table and reached for the bottle. "Have another drop of Napoleon. Do you good."

The taxi arrived and Charles slumped onto the back seat. God, he agonized, what was he going to do? His father couldn't actually stop him from marrying Lydia, but he might let the world know that as far as he was concerned the marriage did not exist. Would Mother forbid him from taking such baleful measures? And if she did, would Father be swayed by any of her arguments? He squeezed his hands tightly until the knuckles ached. Everything was in doubt. His parents' game was to evade the issue, play for time. And what of Lydia? No woman would wish to marry a man ostracized by his own father. He didn't quite believe her assurances that he was all she wanted. Acceptance by society was important to her. What doors would not open for Lydia *Amberley* that no amount of Archie's millions could ever have breached? That name meant acceptance at even the most rarefied levels of society—provided, of course, that their union had been socially blessed.

"God," he whispered fiercely. What would she say if he had to tell her that it would not be blessed? Would she smile, kiss him, tell him that it didn't matter? He knew in his heart what her reaction would be. Lydia loved him, but her love was based, at least in some measure, on his position in life. The thought turned his blood to ice. But what if he were wrong? What if she wanted the marriage, blessed or not? What then? Could he defy his father? Toss away every vestige of his sense of obligation?

He felt that he was in the grip of a nightmare. His emotions were still in a whirl when he arrived at Fenton Wood-Lacy's flat, which Roger was sharing while in London.

The captain's batman opened the door. Roger was in the drawing room, seated on the floor surrounded by printed proofs of his poems. Sprawled next to him was Rupert Brooke, his open tennis shirt revealing an expanse of tanned chest.

"Hello, Rupert," Charles said. It was good to see him again. The poet had already left King's College when he and Roger had gone up to Cambridge, but Brooke had lived for a time near by, at the Old Vicarage in Grantchester. Charles and Roger had spent hours there talking endlessly about books and poetry, or swimming in the dam above Byron's Pool. . . . *Yet stands the church clock at ten to three? And is there honey still for tea?*

"Hello, Charles," Brooke said with a lazy smile. "Many happy returns of the day."

"I gather Roger's been advertising the fact," Charles said.

Brooke nodded. "In the hope we can all persuade you to give a party for the occasion, at some small, but epicurean restaurant."

"My pleasure," he said thickly.

Roger looked up for the first time and noticed the sickly pallor of his friend's face. "I say, Charles, do you feel all right?"

"I'm fine, thanks. It's just the heat and petrol fumes. God," he blurted, "I'd like to get away for a month or two. Can't you postpone that blasted book? Let's go to Greece."

"I'd stay away from that section of the world for a few months," Brooke said. "There's bound to be another Balkan war. We were just discussing it before you arrived. Austria's just sent a perfectly shocking demand to Serbia."

IT WAS ALL very proper, Fenton Wood-Lacy was thinking as he walked slowly towards 24 Cadogan Square. It was the day after Winifred Sutton's coming-out ball and it was socially correct to return and thank the hostess for a splendid time. He had come to do more than that. He had had only one dance with Winifred, but it had been the final one, a waltz, and after it was over he had overheard a woman mention to Lady Dexford that ". . . they make such a lovely couple". Lady Dexford had beamed radiantly. He had then brought Winifred a final cup of punch and had asked her if he might call the next day and perhaps, if she wasn't too tired from the exertions of the ball, go for a walk.

"I am so glad you asked," she had said. "And I shall let you in on a secret. Mamma will be pleased as well."

And so now he stood on the front steps of the Dexfords' London house feeling, he thought ruefully, very *suitorish*, with a box of chocolates from Fortnum and Mason under his left arm.

A butler opened the door. "Good afternoon, sir."

He was ushered, almost reverently, into the drawing room where Winifred was seated demurely on a divan. "Well, Winifred," he said, "your ball was a total success."

"Mother was so pleased that you came." She looked down at her hands twisted tightly in her lap. "And happy that you are calling on me today."

"Well," he said, clearing his throat, "it's my pleasure, Winifred. A chance for us to . . . talk."

202

"Could we go for a walk? It's so stuffy in the house."

A few moments later they were going down the front steps into the golden sunshine.

Winifred put a hand on his arm. "Let's walk slowly to the river. I love Chelsea, don't you?"

He admitted that he did. He also told her that she looked lovely.

She blushed fiercely and her hand tightened on his arm. "Thank you. Is it wrong for me to say that you look lovely, too? That's not the proper thing to say to a man, I know, but it happens to be true. I feel very proud walking beside you."

Her usual reticence vanished once they were away from the house. She was candid about herself, aware of her shortcomings.

"One of my problems has always been a sweet tooth, but if one hopes to achieve slenderness, one must firmly resist such treats. I shall treasure your box of chocolates, but I shan't eat them."

"I'm sorry. My next present to you will not be edible."

"Thank you. Food will be the death of me. On my tombstone they will write, 'Here lies Lady Winifred Sutton, fasting at last'."

She slipped her arm through his. Her intimacy was childlike. He felt like a favourite uncle. Lord, he thought, how terribly young she is.

The Thames was sluggish in the afternoon heat and their conversation began to wear thin. Yet she seemed content just to be with him, walking decorously by his side. A tug ploughed up-river pulling a string of empty coal barges. Some grey birds rose from the mud flats in the shadow of Albert Bridge and flew off across the river towards Battersea. They walked on, leaving the Embankment and turning in the direction of Sloane Square. A sentry standing by the gates of the Duke of York's barracks tapped his rifle butt against the pavement as they walked past.

"Why did he do that?"

"Because he recognized me as an officer," Fenton said after acknowledging the salute with a slight nod of his head. "I've been to those barracks a few times. Perhaps he remembered my face."

"No. You just look like a captain in the Coldstream Guards. I think it's the way you wear your boater. It's the way I imagine Kitchener would wear his."

He stooped and whispered in her ear. "Don't tell anyone, but

Lord Kitchener doesn't own a straw hat. Nothing but uniforms, even his pyjamas are scarlet, with rows and rows of medals."

Her laugh was throaty and rich.

He was enjoying her company. Was, in fact, beginning to like the girl. She was on the dowdy side, no question about that, but her hair was pretty in the sun and her complexion clear and rosy. Good teeth. Lips that looked soft and kissable. She was easy to be with and one could, in a sense, relax.

He hailed a cab and asked the driver to take a long way back to Cadogan Square.

"This has been the most wonderful afternoon of my life."

"I'm glad you enjoyed yourself, Winifred."

She turned to look at him. "Can we do it again sometime?"

She was his for the asking. Hooked, netted and placed in the creel. He felt a nagging sense of shame for being so cold-blooded about it, but, damn it all, he *did* like her.

"May I ask your father for formal permission to call on you?"

She seemed to stop breathing for a moment, then she let out a tiny cry and leaned against him, her lips brushing the side of his face. "Oh, yes, yes. Oh, my dearest, *dearest* Fenton. May God bless you and keep you always . . . *always*. . . ."

IT WAS MIDNIGHT and Martin Rilke had just got in from meeting his deadline for the *Post*. Jacob Golden's flat in Beak Street smelled of furniture polish. The charwoman had been in during the day, not that she could have found much to do from her last visit. Jacob had been sent hurrying to Belgrade as the Serbian crisis grew, and with him away the spacious rooms remained clean and orderly. Martin found he missed Jacob's untidy presence: the blue haze of his strong Turkish cigarettes, the torrent of his conversation which was mordant, exasperating, seditious and profane —but always worth listening to.

There was nothing much to eat in the kitchen except for tinned Strasbourg pâté, water biscuits, thick glass jars of Russian caviare and a cupboard stacked with champagne. More substantial meals were eaten out or brought up on trays from the Hungarian restaurant below, Jacob doing the ordering by shouting out of the back window into the alley where the cooks and waiters lounged during their breaks, playing cards on an upturned milk crate. The restaurant closed at eleven and so Martin was now stuck with appetizers.

He poured a glass of champagne, spread a thick layer of pâté on a water biscuit and then leafed through the stack of mail on the desk. Dunning letters for Jacob mostly. One envelope addressed to him. Guards' Club stationery:

> Dear Rilke,
>
> I have the unfortunate honour to be assigned Captain of the Guard over the Bank Holiday. The inner workings of Buck duty might make an item for the penny press. If you are not otherwise engaged, I look forward to your joining me and a few friends for dinner in Guards quarters, St. James's, Tuesday evening, August 4, 7 p.m. Black tie.
>
> Sincerely, Fenton Wood-Lacy

He made a mental note to reply in the morning. It should be interesting. He could probably squeeze two articles out of it.

His notebooks lay piled on the desk, but he felt too weary to write and too keyed-up to sleep. One singular event, a couple of weeks before, stuck in his mind, lingering with a peculiar poignancy: a picnic beside the Thames at Henley with the Stanmores and their guests, a scene belonging to another age, suspended in time and misted by a golden light. The Royal Regatta held on the smooth green water of the river; gleaming, highly varnished rowing boats gliding as noiselessly as the royal swans; great bowers of willow trailing leafy tendrils in the stream; women in white dresses and large hats strolling along the banks; a band playing in a gingerbread pavilion.

Jacob's last dispatch from Serbia had triggered the remembrance of that day. *One can see Austrian gunboats prowling the Danube. . . .* The squat iron hulls became superimposed over the delicate pageant on the Thames. There had been no talk of crisis that day as they sat on the grass and ate strawberries and cream. Now Austria-Hungary prepared for war. What would Russia do? France? England? Treaties and alliances bound country to country like bands of steel.

Strawberries and cream, and white wine served by the Stanmore butler—for of course there were servants even at a picnic in a meadow—from a silver bucket filled with ice. He had met Lydia Foxe. What had they talked about? He couldn't remember. A stunningly beautiful woman. Easy to understand Charles's infatuation, but he had detected a toughness behind the lovely face. She was bright, charming, and yet once he had happened to glance at her while she was watching the earl and Hanna eat their strawberries. The woman's eyes had been pure steel. . . .

THEY ALL SEEMED to be watching the clock, although Roger Wood-Lacy, who had also been invited, tried to keep the conversation going by telling a few jokes. Uniformed mess attendants removed the dinner plates. There was, Martin noted, a good deal of uneaten food. But not on his plate. The rack of lamb had been delicious.

"You have good cooking in the army," he said.

Fenton sat at the head of the long table in his scarlet jacket, brass buttons reflecting the candlelight.

"Our own chaps don't do too badly in the mess, but the palace chefs provide this dinner. It's the generous legacy of King George the Fourth, the great Prinny, a lover of fine food and blowsy women. Unfortunately, he only willed the Captain of the King's Guards provision for the former."

Charles Amberley checked the time again. "Ten thirty."

"That makes it two minutes later than when you last looked," Fenton remarked drily.

One of Fenton's mountaineering friends, a ruddy-faced barrister named Galesby, frowned and shook his head slowly. "You're taking all this very lightly, Fenton. After all, what happens or does not happen in the next hour and a half concerns you a good deal more than it concerns any of us."

One of the messmen brought around a box of cigars. Fenton selected one and passed it slowly under his nose. "We have a rule here against talking shop. War, my dear Galesby, is shop."

"To you. I never took the king's shilling so I'm entitled to speak my mind. I ask you straight out, Fenton. Do you believe Germany will back down by midnight and refrain from marching into Belgium?"

Fenton lit his cigar. It was so silent in the room they could all hear the hissing of the match. "We are long past the moment when

anyone can back down. The Germans are in front of Liège and
God himself couldn't turn their troop trains around. The politicians, the statesmen, the kings and emperors have done their jobs
and now the soldiers take over. It's simply come down to that."

Martin could visualize the trains in the night . . . hundreds upon
hundreds of them rolling west across Germany, rolling east across
France. Along the Danube there had been war for six days. By
rights it should stay there, toe to toe between Austria and Serbia,
if no one rushed to the aid of either side.

The minute hand jumped. In the silence they could hear the
soft whirring of the clock's gears. The port was passed along.
Glasses were refilled.

Fenton had to inspect the guard at Buckingham Palace at midnight and so the guests left shortly before, a gravely formal
parting in the austere, treeless courtyard of St. James's.

Charles took a deep breath of the clean night air. "I could do
with a walk."

"Good idea," said Galesby. "Think I'll join you. Heading down
to Whitehall, I suppose?"

"We might as well be among the first to know," Charles said.

They all walked in silence to The Mall. St. James's Park was
shadowed and gloomy across the wide, tree-lined road.

"Yes," Galesby said, almost to himself. "Quite odd. One would
have thought that intelligent men could have settled issues across
a conference table."

"That would be contrary to fate," Roger said, his tone strangely
fervid. "War is a form of rebirth. A rite as old as time. I was talking to Rupert this morning. I've never heard him so enthusiastic.
To go shining to war in defence of little Belgium has all the nobility
of Arthurian quests, he said."

"I don't know about that," the barrister said, tossing his half-
smoked cigar into the gutter. "All I bloody well know for sure is
that nothing will be quite the same again."

"That might be a blessing," Charles said quietly.

They paused at the end of The Mall, the lights in Admiralty
House twinkling through the trees at the edge of the park. Big
Ben tolled the hour, twelve hollow iron peals. They could hear
distant cheering and then the sound of a rushing crowd, hundreds

of feet ringing on the pavements. Shadows streamed across the wide expanse of Horse Guards Parade. Men, mostly young, running with a wild exuberance.

"War!" they were yelling. "It's war!"

Martin and Galesby stepped back to keep from being bowled over by the frantic rush towards Buckingham Palace, now blazing with lights. Roger grabbed Charles excitedly by the arm.

"Come on, Charles! Come on!"

The crowd swallowed them. They were one with it, borne along.

A middle-aged man, red-faced and puffing, ran out of the shadows of Waterloo Place.

"Is it war?" he shouted. "Is it war?"

"Yes, you damned fool," Galesby said. "Yes, it is."

PART TWO

1

The fairyland château at Longueville shone silvery white under the August moon. It was the temporary headquarters of the Third Division, Second Corps, of the British Expeditionary Force, and the cobblestoned courtyard was crowded with staff cars, tethered horses and motorcycles. Captain Fenton Wood-Lacy walked stiffly up the steps of the château and into the entrance hall.

It was bedlam—signallers were struggling to set up telephone equipment and staff officers hurried up and down a baroque marble staircase, while clusters of battalion commanders stood about in glowering impatience. Fenton felt conspicuous among so many majors, colonels and brigadiers, even more so when Colonel Blythe, his uncle's ADC, spotted him and cut through the crowd.

"Ah, Captain," the colonel said, pumping Fenton's hand. "The general's most anxious to talk to you. Come upstairs."

The elderly colonel led him up the winding staircase to the second floor and ushered him into a large room. "His nibs'll be along in time," he said.

Fenton made a futile dab at his dust-streaked khaki.

"Don't worry. Dusty uniforms are strictly *de rigueur* in this

division. I believe your uncle would court-martial any officer who showed up in clean kit." He gave Fenton a pat on the arm. "I'll send up a whisky."

Fenton walked slowly around the room, a gallery filled with bucolic paintings and *objets d'art*. A soldier brought whisky and Vichy water. Fenton made himself a stiff drink and sat down on an impossibly delicate Louis XIV chair. He was several degrees past weariness, having been in the saddle since dawn.

When the general came striding into the room Fenton jumped to his feet and made a proper, if hasty, salute.

"At ease, boy, at ease." Sir Julian Wood-Lacy, VC, DSO, smiled broadly at his nephew. "By thunder, but you're a sight to behold. Dirty as a collier." He clapped Fenton on the shoulders with both hands. "How's young Roger?"

"Hurrying to enlist, last I saw of him."

The general tugged at his walrus moustache. "This flap'll be over by the time he gets his uniform. Our Teutonic friends will be scurrying back across the Rhine before the leaves fall."

"Do you think so, sir?"

The general leaned forward and lowered his voice. "I *know* so. They've been taking fearful losses at Liège. By God, I hope we get a crack at 'em, but I'm afraid they'll pull in their horns and rush back to cover their centre. Those Belgians are fighting like terriers, and the Frogs have been on the attack since this morning. They should be deep into Lorraine by this time tomorrow." He rocked slowly back and forth on his heels. "I must be brief, Fenton. I've just arranged your transfer to my staff."

Fenton glanced away from his uncle's bright, piercing eyes. "That smacks a bit of nepotism, wouldn't you say?"

"Good Lord, it positively reeks of it. We are on the move north into Belgium, the entire army. I suppose you can visualize what that means: ninety thousand men and hardly one decent map among all of 'em. I need a trustworthy liaison officer, someone who won't rub my fellow divisional commanders the wrong way. You're just the chap for the job. I hope you don't resent my turning you into a messenger boy?"

"No, sir, not at all."

Colonel Blythe appeared in the doorway and coughed discreetly for attention. "The battalion commanders are assembled, sir. . . ."

"Right," the general said. "Take our new young thruster in hand, there's a good chap." He turned abruptly and strode out of the room, his spurred boots pounding a brisk tattoo on the landing.

Colonel Blythe smiled faintly. "Comforting sound."

"He certainly exudes confidence."

"Yes, and we should be grateful for that. The troops are cocky as hell, but the high command is as nervous as a maiden aunt in a men's smoking room." He poured himself a whisky and downed it neat. "The French Fifth Army is off to our right somewhere, but there's no communication between them and us. No one knows for sure what they're doing. Nor do we have the foggiest idea what Fritz is up to." He drew a map from a leather case fastened to his belt and handed it to Fenton. "Our corps area goes along the canal from Condé to Mons. Fifth Division HQ will be at Élouges. We want you up there tomorrow to liaise with their advance party. The maps are bloody useless." He ran a hand through his thinning hair. "Lord, what a way to go to war."

FENTON found it impossible to sleep in his billet that night. Thoughts swirled in a vivid hodge-podge. It seemed unbelievable that six days ago he had been in Southampton waiting to board the transport ship. Lord Dexford had brought gifts to the docks for his future son-in-law: a box of tinned delicacies from Harrods, Abdullah cigarettes, a bottle of whisky, and a letter from Winifred:

My dearest Fenton,

God protect you in this hour of trial. I know you will be brave and daring and help achieve a quick and glorious victory. All of the newspapers predict that the war will be over by Christmas. I pray they are correct and that we will be tangoing at a victory ball on New Year's Eve.

Ever . . . Your Winifred

My Winifred! Fenton groaned. Here, it was a struggle for him to recall her face.

At noon he walked towards the crossroads where a staff car was waiting. Private Webber, his batman, trailed along behind him carrying the bags and whistling softly to himself. He would be pleased at the idea of his officer being attached to staff. No more thirty-miles-a-day marches, no more sleeping on the ground.

"What's that, sir?" Webber stood still, head cocked to one side. Something had moved against the dark woods that bordered the field, a pulse of air that was not wind. Then sound came, dull, persistent thuds to the northeast, like thunder.

"Blimey," Webber said, sniffing the air. "Don't smell like rain."

Fenton walked slowly on. The heavy guns were miles east. They could be French or Belgian and the Germans might be reeling back from those withering blasts, but doubt gnawed at him.

"I'M AFRAID I'M LOST, SIR," the driver said. The staff car was halted at a crossroads.

"It's not your fault," Fenton said. "This map's a bloody work of fiction."

It was an eerie feeling being alone in the middle of God knew where. The road ahead might lead them straight into the German army for all they knew. Ninety thousand British troops in France and Belgium, and not a man to be seen. It was damned discomfiting. Fenton glared at the map. He removed his cap and wiped his forehead with a handkerchief. Lord, it was hot. The sun beat down from a cloudless sky. Poor old Webber was groggy from the heat, slumped sideways in a listless, soggy bundle. The driver, Lance-Corporal Ackroyd, was a thin, wiry Londoner of the Middlesex Regiment. He'd hold up all right. Fenton reached into his pocket and took out a tin of cigarettes.

"Care for a fag, Corporal?"

"Thank you, sir," the driver said, perking up noticeably. "Been dyin' for a smoke, sir. Blimey. Abdullahs."

"Might just spoil your taste for Woodbines."

"Might at that, sir."

Fenton smiled and the man grinned back. A certain amount of familiarity was unavoidable. They were, in a manner of speaking, in the same boat.

"Bloody dismal country."

"Yes, sir. Mucked up a bit."

It was an ominous landscape, chilling even in the brightness of an August day. Dank patches of woodland, untilled fields, the sour smell of neglect. Weed-dotted slag heaps and conical structures of rotting timber marked the sites of abandoned coal shafts.

Fenton folded the map and slipped it into its case. "Drive east another couple of miles. We're bound to reach some sort of village that'll give us a fix."

Ackroyd put the car into gear, and drove on along the narrow road. Suddenly he braked and pointed ahead.

"Aeroplane, sir! Comin' straight for us."

It had side-slipped over a line of poplars and was flying towards them no more than thirty feet off the ground. It banked sharply and the pilot leaned out of the cockpit.

"One of ours," Fenton said, studying the slow moving machine carefully. "Avro, I think. What the hell keeps them in the air?"

"Looks like a Chinese laundry cart, don't it, sir?"

The plane's tiny engine popped and the ungainly contraption of canvas, wood and wire made a sickening lurch, straightened up feet from the surface of the field, then glided to a perfect landing.

Fenton and the corporal got out of the car and ran across the field. The pilot was climbing carefully out of the cockpit, threading his way through the maze of wires connecting the bottom wing with the top.

"Hello, chaps," the pilot called out. "Can you spare some petrol? I'm down to my last few drops."

"There's a five-gallon tin in the boot," Fenton said.

"Thank the Lord. I can get to Le Cateau on that."

The corporal ran back towards the car and the pilot leaned wearily against the edge of the plane's lower wing. "Nice of you to help me, Captain. I shall do you a good service. Turn your car around. There's absolutely nothing ahead of you but Huns. Bloody hordes of 'em, about ten miles away. Never seen anything like it."

Fenton drew out his map. "Where are they exactly?"

"Oh, Lord, *everywhere*." He drew his finger across the map, leaving a faint smear of oil. "From Charleroi all across to just north of Mons. There must be two hundred thousand of 'em. Looks like a grey river from the air. And artillery, miles and miles of horse-drawn gun transport. Big fight this morning all along the canal. We did well, I think, but the corps is in full retirement nonetheless. I've got to get my report to HQ if I can ruddy well find it."

"Yes," Fenton said dryly. "I think they might be interested. See any French troops on our right?"

"Well, some of their cavalry—tossing plumes, breastplates shining in the sun—all that fancy dress rot. A few infantry, all going south. If our chaps are still at Mons, their flank is in the air."

"What about us? We're trying to reach Élouges."

"Well, the road to the south will take you there, eventually. But the place is an unholy mess, jam-packed with transport and all of it moving back into France."

The pilot ate some cheese and bread from the hamper in the car while Ackroyd refuelled his plane. He then instructed the corporal on how to spin the propeller without decapitating himself and flew off, the little plane rising as effortlessly as a swallow from the field. They stood in the road and watched until it was lost to view.

"Rather a pleasant way to travel," Fenton said quietly.

"Where to now, sir?" Ackroyd said as he opened the car door.

"South," said Fenton. "Fast."

The road went south then curved due west and the scarlet ball of the sinking sun seemed to touch the road ahead of them. Shadows flickered across it.

"Horses," Ackroyd muttered as he stepped on the brakes.

"Lancers," Webber said, squinting into the glare.

Fenton caught a glimpse of the riders' headgear silhouetted against the sun: small helmets with a flat projection on top. "No. Uhlans," he said with remarkable control, considering the chilling quality of that name. "Back up."

Private Webber was a batman, but every guardsman went through an extensive musketry course. He stood up, braced his body, raised the Lee-Enfield to his shoulder and squeezed off a shot. One of the shadowy figures toppled to the road and a rider-less horse careered wildly past the car. His second shot went wide as the car roared back down the road, weaving from side to side. There was a burst of machine-gun fire from the fringe of the woods ahead of them and bullets splattered the car. The front tyres blew and the car lurched violently off the road into a ditch. Fenton caught a glimpse of Webber toppling backwards with blood sheeting his face and then he was flying out of the back of the car, crashing through branches and landing heavily in a drift of leaves.

Fenton blacked out, and when he opened his eyes he could see nothing but dancing red lights. He struggled to breathe, but something was pressing against his face, and the barely audible voice of Lance-Corporal Ackroyd said: "Don't move, sir . . . don't move."

Ackroyd's hand was over his mouth. His eyes came into proper focus and he could see that there were billows of flame shooting up from the car, about thirty yards away. He was well into the beech woods, his view of the fire fragmented by slender black trunks. Ackroyd must have dragged him. By Harry, he'd see that the man was made sergeant. He nodded slowly, signalling Ackroyd that restraint was no longer necessary.

"Where are they?" he whispered.

"Bleedin' everywhere, sir."

He could hear them now, the soft thud of horses' hooves, the crack and splinter of young trees, guttural German curses. Then someone shouted, "*Achtung! Die Engländer kommen!*"

A British bugle call from far down the road, the distant thunder of galloping horses. The Uhlans who were searching the wood crashed back towards the road. A machine gun began to clatter from a position near the still-blazing car, a pyre more than likely, because poor old Webber was probably being consumed by it.

"Can you walk, sir?"

"I . . . don't know."

"Try, sir, *try*." There was an edge of desperation in Ackroyd's voice. Fenton got slowly to his feet. There was a dull pain in the small of his back, but nothing seemed to be broken.

"Keep low, sir, and run like hell."

The direction seemed unimportant at the moment, the only factor being to get as far away as possible from the Germans. Bending nearly double they began to run, Ackroyd in the lead, racing through the undergrowth, not stopping until exhaustion brought them to the ground. Fenton vomited and rolled onto his back under a hawthorn bush. Ackroyd lay on his face as though dead. They were deep in the forest and there was no sound but the rustling of leaves, a nightingale's lilting notes, and their own tortured breaths.

THEY HID BY DAY and moved by night, working their way slowly southward. The German army was all around them, but not in a solid mass. They ate apples and wild berries and what little food they could find in the many abandoned cottages. The weather was good, hot by day and balmy at night, with cloudless skies and enough moonlight to make walking cross-country easy. A sudden thunderstorm struck during the second night of their journey and forced them to seek shelter in a barn. The rain stopped at dawn but a different thunder continued all day—the bombardment was ten miles or so away, near Le Cateau, as far as Fenton could judge.

They set out again as soon as it got dark. The moon rose early and they made swift progress, reaching a railway line before midnight. Fires ringed the northern horizon, a dull glow as though some strange dawn were breaking. They walked along the railway track until at four in the morning they reached the first scattered houses of a small town. Transport wagons were parked along a narrow road leading into it, and draught horses were grazing in a nearby field.

"Ours," said Fenton, spotting the distinctive field cookers.

The two men paused to dab at their mud-caked, bramble-torn uniforms then marched on smartly. Ackroyd whistled "Tipperary" to alert any sentries, but they were challenged neither when they walked along the station platform nor when they went through the deserted ticket office to the street beyond.

"A bit queer," Fenton said. "There should have been a sentry."

"Ruddy town seems to be empty, sir."

They walked on, their boots ringing loudly on the cobblestones. The street curved and led to a town square dominated by a stone fountain. There, around the fountain and spread out across virtually every inch of the paved square, were the sprawled figures of soldiers, three hundred or more, lying like dead men. Fenton noticed the badges of half a dozen regiments. A sergeant in the Gordon Highlanders lay on his back in the gutter with his head resting on his pack. His left hand was swathed in a dirty, blood-caked bandage. Fenton nudged him in the side with his foot.

"On your feet, Sergeant."

The man stared stupidly at Fenton for a moment, then stood up with a groan.

216

"What the hell is going on?" Fenton said sharply. "It looks like a beggars' army."

The sergeant's red-rimmed eyes moved from Fenton's face to the pips on his sleeve. He pulled himself to rigid attention.

"All the lads is just worn down, sir."

"I can understand that, Sergeant. But why are there no pickets out? Good Lord, man, Fritz'll be here by dawn."

"Yes, sir. Colonel Hampton told us to stack arms and get some sleep, sir. Told us we were out of the war, sir."

"*Your* colonel, Sergeant?"

"No, sir. From the Winchesters, sir."

"Where is Colonel Hampton?"

"Town hall, sir, just across the square."

"Do you believe you're out of the war, Sergeant?"

The muscles in the tall sergeant's jaw tightened. "I canna argue with a colonel, sir . . . even a colonel in the bluidy Winchesters."

The foyer of the town hall was crowded with wounded men being attended to by a couple of medical orderlies and a French civilian. The wounded were well bandaged and heavily anaesthetized. Fenton was impressed. "You men are doing a good job."

"Thank you, sir," one of the orderlies said, then nodded towards the Frenchman. "Thanks to 'im. He's the local vet. Brung over bundles of 'orse bandage and plenty of morphine."

"Can any of the men be moved?"

The man rubbed the side of his face and looked thoughtful. His eyes were sunken and there were deep shadows under the sockets.

"A dozen maybe, if they're kept flat. Most are in rum shape, sir. Them bloody shells tear 'ell out of a man."

"Sort out the men you can move, then you and your mate decide which one of you will stay behind with the rest. One of you must stay, I'm afraid. It won't do for the Germans to say we abandon our wounded." The man nodded gravely. "Now where can I find Colonel Hampton?"

The orderly pointed down the corridor. "Down there, sir."

"Any other officers present?"

"Yes, sir, two lieutenants." He lowered his voice and looked earnestly into Fenton's face. "There's something a bit odd about the colonel, sir. I think he's losin' control of himself."

217

Oh, God, Fenton thought, what a bloody awful situation. The sight of the stuporous men in the square made him realize how deathly tired he was himself. It would have been the most natural act in the world to lie down on the floor and close his eyes—and if a German boot woke him in a few hours, so be it. And down the hall there was a regimental commander, most probably a man who had seen long and honourable service, who was just as tired.

He found the three officers in the mayor's office, the two lieutenants lying on the floor and the colonel stretched out on a leather couch. There was an oil lamp on the desk, glowing feebly. Fenton turned up the wick, but no one moved a muscle as the sudden light fell upon them. He kicked the two younger officers until they were on their feet, groaning and mumbling, then shook the colonel vigorously. He was white-haired with a long, cadaverous face. Sixty at least with a faded ribbon from the South African war on his tunic. Off the reserve list, yanked from his London club to lead a regiment into battle. Fenton felt sorry for the man.

"Wake up, sir. Wake up. Time to move out."

The colonel stared glassy-eyed at Fenton. "What? Move out?" The old man struggled feebly to sit up. "What the deuce you talkin' about, sir? By Harry, the men've earned their rest, sir . . . fifty-two hours without sleep . . . they've done all they can do."

"Not quite, sir," Fenton said quietly.

The lieutenants seemed unsure, tensely aware that some sort of clash was developing between two superior officers.

"Stay for a moment," Fenton told them. "I'll need you as witnesses. I am about to request that the colonel should place himself on the sick list."

The colonel's face turned a mottled shade of purple. "Sick list? Who the hell d'you think you are, talkin' to me like that, tellin' me what to do? Ill? I'm not *ill*, sir!"

"There must be something the matter with you, to permit your command to fall asleep and be captured by the enemy. You are either ill or a coward, sir."

The colonel seemed to stop breathing, then the staring eyes rolled back and he slumped forward.

"Fetch the medical orderly and be damned quick about it," Fenton said sharply to one of the lieutenants.

The other officer lurched almost drunkenly towards the couch. "Is he all right?"

"Yes. Get out on the square. Rouse the men. Blow bugles, ring bells, kick posteriors, but get 'em on their feet."

"I'll try, sir."

Fenton glared at him. "I didn't ask you to *try*."

He glared the lieutenant out of the room and then pressed his fingers against the colonel's wrist. The flesh was clammy, but there was a faint pulse. He would be all right. Or would he? How could he ever be *all right* again? The man might live to be a hundred but he had died in France just as surely as poor old Webber.

Out in the square, roughly one quarter of the men were standing up, but they looked like tramps crawling out from under bridges. The two lieutenants were swearing and pleading with them, tugging at their belts and straps, kicking them. Some men rose, others lay half stupefied, muttering curses and threats. Time was running out. The Germans would be stirring at dawn. Fenton spotted three Cameronian privates buckling on their equipment near the fountain. One of them had a canvas sack slung over one shoulder, bagpipes jutting up from it.

"You there!" Fenton shouted at the man. "Blow us a tune."

"He dinna 'ave the breath, sir," one of his mates called back.

"He'd better bloody well find some!"

The piper grinned sheepishly and took his pipes from the bag. There was a slow howl and then the skirling of "Blue Bonnets Over the Border" issued forth, clear and stirring, with just that hint of sadness which all pipe music seemed to contain.

"Walk around, man, walk around."

Slowly the exhausted men began to stand up. There was a distant neighing of horses and the clatter and creak of the transport wagons. A few men cheered feebly, then they started to form fours and move slowly out of the square. They knew which way to go—south across the railway, dark poplars marking the road.

Fenton remained in the square until the last man, wagon and horse had left the town. It was dawn, the dark stone of the church steeple turning to a pale rose. Swallows dived from the sun-tinged belfry into the dark folds of a chestnut tree. It reminded Fenton of Abington on any summer morning.

He turned to go, pausing for a moment to look at the orderly who was staying with the wounded. The man stood on the steps of the town hall, seemingly unconcerned. Perhaps he was relieved that for him the war was over. "Good luck, sir," he called out.

Fenton raised his arm in a gesture of farewell and limped away, the cobblestones painful to his feet, following the droning bagpipes out of the little town.

Over by Christmas. . . . That was what everyone had been saying. *Home before the leaves fall.* A damned good joke that.

2

The grass crackled with frost, snapping under Jupiter's hooves as Lord Stanmore cantered out of a leafless copse and headed back towards the Pryory. A black February day with slate-grey clouds lowering against the frozen earth. The earl could feel the chill penetrate to his bones and he was grateful when the stables came in sight; an elderly groom was waiting to take the horse.

The earl left the stables in a hurry. It pained him more than anyone knew to see the rows of empty stalls. Cavalry losses had been heavy at the Battle of the Marne and all but two of the horses had been given to the army. It was, the earl thought, the least he could do. Yet the call to the colours had not stopped there. Banks had taken a commission in the veterinary corps and the stableboys had joined up too. No one was left at Abington Pryory but the middle-aged and the elderly. Even the young maids had departed, answering their country's call for women to take over the jobs that men were leaving. Men and more men. Kitchener had asked for one hundred thousand volunteers. Over a million responded.

Fully two thirds of Abington Pryory was closed off, the furniture covered with white sheets. A house embalmed and awaiting resurrection. The earl complained of neglect, the lack of help.

"*It's the war, Anthony,*" was Hanna's reply. As if he had to be told! Charles in uniform, Roger Wood-Lacy as well. Not in France —yet. *In France.* What an ugly sound . . . ominous as the casualty lists on the first page of *The Times* to be scanned over breakfast.

220

Fifty-eight thousand names of the dead, wounded and missing after Ypres alone. So many names that he recognized. No, he didn't need Hanna to remind him that there was a war.

Coatsworth shuffled in with the breakfast. He set the dish before the earl and removed the silver cover.

"Ross is leaving us, m'lord," he said.

"Ross? What a bloody bore. Send him in after breakfast."

The earl lit his first cigar of the day. "Well, Ross, I hear you're rushing off to take the king's shilling."

Jamie Ross looked pained. "I wanted to join the army, m'lord, but the fact of the matter is I received a letter this morning from the Rolls-Royce company. I took out a patent on a carburation system, and they think that my system will make their aeroplane engines run much more efficiently."

Lord Stanmore drew the cigar slowly from his mouth. He was quite mystified. "*Aeroplane* engines?"

"Yes, m'lord," Ross said with great patience. "The army has ordered a great many aeroplanes, m'lord. What they have now are terribly slow and the engine conks out if the machine turns upside down. Same sort of trouble we used to have driving up Box Hill, a tendency for the engine to stall on steep gradients."

"Upside down? Why on earth would they want to fly upside down?"

"I suppose they can't help it sometimes. Well, m'lord, the Rolls-Royce people say I can do more to crush the Hun working with their engineers than by enlisting in the ranks."

The earl studied him through plumes of grey-blue smoke. Curious. *Ross* of all people. Of course, he had known that the lad was mechanically clever. Still, he probably had little education —yet he was considered too valuable to go to France. While Charles had left Cambridge with first-class honours and no one could find a greater use for him than a second lieutenancy in the Fusiliers.

"Dashed inconvenient, you leaving us. Where on earth shall I find another driver?"

Jamie Ross shifted his feet uncomfortably. "Begging your lordship's pardon, why don't you do your own driving? I could teach you in just a few hours. It's really quite simple."

"I'm sure it is," he said stiffly, "but I prefer to be driven."

221

The earl found Hanna in the library on the telephone to Mary Dexford, whose eldest son had just been killed. She hung up and dabbed at her eyes with a lace handkerchief.

"She's taking it so wonderfully. Andrew was terribly brave, led his troops against a machine gun. Mary seemed so resigned, so fatalistic about it. And she has no fears for her other son. She told me that she senses an aura of invincibility around him. She believes there is a greater force than our modern conception of God, an ancient spirit that the Druids knew well."

"Utter rot," the earl muttered.

"Perhaps, but it comforts her." She twisted the handkerchief into a lace string. "So many are gone in such a short time. Ours and theirs. I wonder if any of the German Rilkes . . . ?"

She could not complete the thought. She could expect no words of sympathy from her husband over the fate of her relatives in Germany. Anti-German feeling ran like a virulent fever throughout the entire country. Mr. Koepke, the baker who had sold his bread and cakes in Guildford for the past twenty years, had been hauled off in a police van like a common criminal. Poor Adolph Koepke, who had always kept a small barrel of broken biscuits and jam tarts by the door for passing children to take free of charge. Those same children had stood in the street and jeered.

She pulled and twisted the handkerchief abstractedly. She had always been proud of her German blood, of the plodding, early rising, thoughtful, God-fearing folk. Not perfect by any means, but not a nation of red-eyed monsters either. German soldiers did not rape Belgian nuns, did not spit Belgian babies on bayonets and tie Belgian virgins to the clappers of church bells. That was propaganda nonsense, but it was believed, the ugly rumours spawned by the factual brutality of the German army's march through Belgium. Martin, who had been authorized at the beginning of the war to be European correspondent of the Chicago *Express*, had witnessed some of it. At Louvain, soldiers infuriated by snipers had lost their heads and run amok, shooting innocent civilians and setting fire to a few buildings. An appalling incident, but that was war. Still, there was no point in trying to speak rationally about the war, or about the Germans. Any chance of that had been buried in November, with the British dead at Ypres.

"Mamma, Papa, close your eyes!" Alexandra's voice from beyond the library door. It was easy for Hanna to comply. Her eyes were already closed, her lips moving slightly in a soundless prayer.

The door opened. "You can look now!"

Alexandra in a nurse's uniform, pirouetting so that the long white skirt swirled, the white veil floating from beneath a white headband, red crosses on the sides of it.

The earl looked bemused. "What on earth . . . ?"

"I've joined the Voluntary Aid Detachment of the Red Cross," cried Alexandra happily. "Jennifer, Cecily, Jane and I all joined up together." She made another mannequin's turn. "Do you like it? This is the summer uniform. The winter one is a pale blue serge with accents of red, but it doesn't fit properly. I shall have to return it to Ferris for alterations."

"What on earth do you know about nursing?" the earl asked.

"Oh, we shan't be doing that awful bedpan type of thing. They have proper nurses for that. Our jobs will be to look after men who are convalescing . . . push them in their wheelchairs, write letters for them, read to them if the poor dears have been blinded. There will be ever so much to do."

"Will you be leaving home?" Hanna asked slowly, not trusting her voice.

"Yes, but I shan't be far off. The Hargreaves gave their house at Roehampton to the Red Cross as a convalescent hospital for officers." She made a final pirouette. "Isn't it chic?"

"Dashed smart," the earl said without conviction. "Are you sure you can do that sort of work? Some of those poor fellows will be quite badly shot up, you know."

Alexandra glanced at her image in a mirror. The headband and veil made her look like an especially pretty young nun. Not too concealing, though. One could still see her blonde hair. She drew herself up proudly. "It might be difficult at first, but this is war and one must be prepared for some degree of self-sacrifice."

AT THE WINDSOR DEPOT seething rain turned the drill ground into a morass. The platoon moved across it, ankle-deep in mud. Barely half of the men were in uniform, the rest struggled along in cheap mackintoshes. A bowler hat or two; cloth caps mostly. The working poor, soldiering for a shilling a day. Only ten men had rifles.

"Platoon, halt! Dismissed!"

They streamed towards the barracks in a sodden mass.

Second-Lieutenant The Viscount Amberley watched them go. He was properly dressed for a soldier of King and Country—a well fitting uniform, decent boots, a British Warm—but these clothes were not provided by the government. They came from Hanesbury & Peake, Military Tailors.

Charles walked on to the mess, hurrying his steps in anticipation of a whisky and hot water. The mess was crowded, the Royal Windsor Fusiliers sharing it with a new battalion of the London Rifles— "Quite unthinkable before the war," the Royal Windsors' adjutant had remarked sourly when the London's officers had first entered the mess. The breaking of traditions didn't bother the younger officers of either regiment. They were all civilians in uniform, a few short months removed from Oxford, Cambridge, Eton, the Inns of Court, budding business careers. Sharing the mess gave them the opportunity to share their uncertainties at what they were trying to do.

"I wish to hell I had just one NCO who knew the ropes," a London Rifles lieutenant remarked moodily. "I feel such a bloody fool drilling the men with a book in my hand."

Roger Wood-Lacy of the Royal Windsors sipped his drink. "The men don't mind. I told mine straight out that I didn't know a thing about drilling and we muddled through together."

"When are they going to instruct us on trenches?" a downy-cheeked subaltern asked.

"When we get to France," Charles said as he joined the group at the bar. "I understand they are building a training base at Harfleur and they'll run us through it for a week or two before sending us up to the line."

"With half our lads in macks, bowlers and brollies?" Roger scoffed. "Fritz'll die from laughing."

"All of the men will be in uniform by next week, and they'll have Lee-Enfields by then, too. The colonel told me this morning."

"I hope you're right," a London Rifles officer said. "The lads find it hard to feel like soldiers when they don't look like them."

"What are you up to this afternoon, Charles?" Roger asked.

224

Charles looked at his wristwatch. "Meeting Lydia in London, if I don't miss the train. I've got noon to midnight off."

"Lucky devil! Where are you taking her?"

"To dinner. I don't much care what we do. Lounging around on a sofa with a brandy and soda would suit me fine."

"Typical thinking of the active service officer," Roger said. "By the way, got a note from Fenton. They upped him to major. He's in trenches. He says they're quite snug and enjoying the winter sports. Only a hangman would appreciate Fenton's humour."

"Well," Charles answered, glancing at his watch again, "you know your brother."

DID HE? CHARLES WONDERED, seated in the train as it skirted the freezing Thames. Would they ever know Fenton again? *In trenches.* . . . Those two words separated him from the majority of mankind as completely as though he were on the far side of the moon. Those few survivors of the First Battalion who had drifted back from Ypres to the Fusilier depot at Windsor never talked about their experiences, not even to each other. Fenton would be the same, withdrawing behind his gift for sardonic understatement to blot out the horrors. Charles tried to imagine what they must be like, but that was a mystery that must await his own initiation.

"How grand you look," Lydia said as he pushed his way through the crowded station to meet her.

"You look rather grand yourself," he said with a grin of pure joy. She looked so beautiful in a Russian sable coat that he felt like sweeping her into his arms and kissing her right there—not that anyone would have even noticed—there were soldiers kissing girls everywhere one looked, a battalion was waiting to board a train, their packs and rifles stacked in momentarily neglected rows down the platform, and yet he pecked at her cheek almost furtively.

"How demonstrative you are, Charles." Her smile was cryptic. "Have you missed me terribly?"

He took hold of her gloved hands and squeezed them as though to prove his sincerity. "You know I have, but it's been almost impossible to write. We've been on the go eighteen hours a day, trying to learn soldiering and teach it to the men. Still, we're starting to shape up now and I'll be able to come to London more

often." He was about to add, "before they ship us to France", but thought better of it. There was no point in putting a damper on the evening.

They went for dinner to the Café Royal, which was jammed with men in uniform (most of them with the red tabs of staff officers on their lapels), businessmen, government officials and droves of elegant women. It was not a place where second lieutenants took their girls on a second lieutenant's pay. But he had left those modest trappings back at Windsor along with his muddy boots. In the Café Royal he was the heir to an earldom.

The food was ambrosial after regimental boiled beef and greens, the Pouilly Fumé pure nectar, but the orchestral thumpings and wailings became too much to bear. Charles smiled ruefully and raised his voice above the din. "Rather difficult to talk here."

"Yes," Lydia agreed. "Let's go."

They drove to her father's house in Grosvenor Square, twenty rooms of Regency elegance. "Don't you feel cramped?" Charles asked, eyeing the domed ceiling in the foyer with its skylight of stained glass, the long marble corridors.

"We do a great deal of entertaining," she said defensively, handing her coat to a maid. "This place is really more for Daddy's friends at the ministry than it is for us."

"Archie Foxe in the government! I couldn't believe it when I saw the announcement in *The Times*. What exactly is he doing?"

"Applying the Foxe Method to the war effort: advertising, efficiency and quality. He started by criticizing the recruiting posters. Kitchener sticking his fat finger in one's face will be replaced by more subtle inducements. And then there's the problem of army rations. The system is quite inadequate. Food distribution is Daddy's game, you know, and the whole purpose of Langham's war ministry is to get experts to handle the planning problems of the war."

"David Langham's ministry is it?"

"Yes. The Liberal fighting cock, sharp of spur and tongue, soothing half of Parliament and irritating the rest."

A fire burned in the drawing room, reflecting off highly polished wood, silver and glass. It was an eighteenth-century room, large but warmly intimate. A butler brought brandy in a crystal decanter.

227

"And yourself?" Charles asked. "How are you keeping busy?"

"I arrange small dinners here for Daddy. Dining-room politics, capital and labour breaking bread and resolving to pull together for a change. I suppose it sounds rather silly and frivolous to you, but more things are accomplished over a fine port than one could possibly realize."

Charles sat next to her.

"Lydia, you know what I'd like to accomplish—and I will."

She looked at him intently and placed a cool hand against the side of his face. "Please, Charles. Don't spoil a perfectly wonderful day by making promises that you're in no position to keep. It isn't fair to me, or you."

He drained his brandy and set the bulbous glass on a side table.

"That's all in the past, Lydia. Don't you feel a great change in the air? I dread the thought of going to France and having shells tossed at my head, and yet I'm happy to be a part of something new: a clean start for a tired old world. The ranks are aware of it too—they know that the war will change their lives utterly, that's why they're so uncomplaining." He took hold of her hand and kissed the palm of it. "When I get back I shall marry you. If my father threatens to disavow you, I shall shame him in front of his peers. By God, it's young men who are fighting this war and it's young men who must benefit from the victory. *I* shall not back off on *my* rights. *That* I promise you, Lydia."

He made an attempt to get down on one knee in front of her, but stumbled in doing so. The rich food of the Café Royal, the wine, the brandy, the glow of the fire, the fact that he had been up before dawn, conspired to rob him of grace. His head spun and he sat at her feet and rested his brow against her knees.

"Lord," he muttered. "I feel as if I've been drugged."

"Poor darling." She kissed the top of his head. "You must be exhausted. Would you like to take a nap on the couch?"

"Yes, I think so. For an hour or so. I have to be back by midnight."

"I know. I arranged with Daddy to have Simmons drive you. The night train is so horrid."

He nestled his head in her lap and sighed with contentment. "Oh, Lydia, I feel such peace with you."

228

"And I with you, my darling."

She helped him out of his jacket, laughing at the complexities of the Sam Browne belt. Finally he was lying down.

"I feel such a fool," he muttered drowsily. "With the prettiest girl in England and I . . . take a nap on her couch." He fell asleep almost instantly. She stood for a moment looking down at him, so boyishly vulnerable. Maternally she brushed a lock of hair from his eyes and tiptoed from the room, closing the door quietly behind her.

Would he stand up to his father? She thought about it, seated in the morning room, staring at the tall windows. She lit a cigarette. Yes. She had the feeling that *this* time he would. It was the uniform, being part of something that his father was not. *In the war*. Their respective statures had been reversed.

There was a rumble of voices in the hall and then her father stepped into the room followed by David Langham.

"Good weather for ducks," Archie Foxe growled. "Is that Charles sleepin' in the drawing room? Anything the matter?"

"No. Just tired," Lydia said, snuffing out her cigarette. Archie did not approve of women smoking.

"I have some telephone calls to make. Will you look after Mr. Langham?"

"Of course. How are you, Mr. Langham?"

"Wet, Miss Foxe. Quite damp to the bone."

He was not, of course, at all wet, having stepped from a motor-car to the front door under a large umbrella. David Selkirk Langham, neat as a pin in striped trousers and morning coat: the Tory papers often caricatured him as the Prince of Darkness whispering into Asquith's ear. There *was* something devilish about his dark, piercing eyes, Lydia decided. He had a narrow, spade-shaped face, thin eyebrows like a pencil line and a trim Van Dyck beard. Salacious stories had been whispered about this self-educated Merseyside solicitor since the day he had entered parliament in 1908. Women, it was said, were hypnotized by his air of virility. Tory lies, her father had said, but she wasn't so sure. She had merely to look into his eyes to read the challenge there.

"The young man on the couch, is that Charles Amberley?"

229

"Yes."

"His father referred to me as a blackguard once during a speech in the House of Lords. Is the son as Tory as the father?"

"No. He has no political feelings one way or the other."

"Foolish of him. Doesn't he know it's politics that make the world go round? The way some of these lads talk, you'd think they were going off in suits of armour to fight the King of France. It's going to be a long and bitter war, a political war. . . ."

Her laugh interrupted him. "Mr. Langham, you're not in the Commons making a speech."

He bowed slightly. "My apologies. There are more enjoyable things to talk about with a beautiful young woman than European politics." He eyed her boldly, and she felt a vague excitement. Her hand went idly to her throat and she looked away from him. Rain drummed against the windows.

"Where were you and Father off to this evening?"

Langham smiled. "A meeting with the prime minister and Kitchener to discuss this Dardanelles business."

"What do you think about it?"

"Brilliant in concept, just what one would expect from young Churchill. My own mind is not made up. Should the enterprise fail, the political repercussions could be disastrous."

"You don't strike me as a man who would be afraid of risk."

There was a sound in his throat, like muffled laughter. His hand brushed her arm. "Some games are always worth the candle and some are not. Don't you think that's true, Lydia Foxe?"

She ignored his touch. "I'm not certain, Mr. Langham. It's not candles I care about in games, only prizes."

3

Jacob Golden was lying outstretched on the living-room couch staring at the ceiling. It was a position he had been in, almost without interruption, since returning from Serbia in January. He had said little, and written less, about his experiences there.

"Enjoy the April sunshine?" he drawled as Martin hung up his coat in the tiny hall.

"Yes. Went up to the park and fed the ducks."

"Reach any firm decision?"

A letter for Martin had arrived that morning from Chicago and had contained a small cheque from the *Express* and some words of advice from his editor, Comstock Harrington Briggs:

Dear Rilke,

The enclosed check does not reflect your worth but does measure pretty accurately the extent of your usefulness to us at this time. Your Belgium sketches were good and fair, but your current things on wartime Britain are becoming too overtly Anglophile to suit our readers. The good folk in the midwest are getting a bit irritated at England, France and Russia—especially England—for conducting what they feel is a crush-German-trade war. So I can't think of any good reason for you to stay in London any longer. There is an opening on the police beat. The job is yours if you'll send a cable. . . .

Martin slumped into a chair. "Go back to Chicago, I guess."

Jacob yawned and sat up. He had lost a good deal of weight and looked skeletal. "Why don't you rejoin the *Daily Post*? You could take my spot and cover the Dardanelles expedition. I intend to leave the paper."

Martin mulled that information over for a few seconds. "What happened in Serbia, Jacob?"

Golden ran his hands through his hair. "Nothing that I hadn't expected. I saw what the Austrians did to Serbian villagers and I saw what Serbians did to Austrians—rape, torture, butchery. My dispatches detailed the atrocities on both sides, but only the Austrian outrages were printed, of course." He smiled sardonically. "There's something hideously wrong about this war. It's going to be a mindless, pointless, chaotic slaughter and I don't wish to be involved in it."

"It's difficult not to be involved. Where will you go?"

"Why, into the army, of course. Best place in the world to avoid emotional involvements of any kind. Chap I knew at Oxford is in the Royal Signals Corps. He's offered me a commission. Back-room job in Whitehall, thinking up codes and ciphers."

"You seem to be a bit more cheerful all of a sudden."

"It's getting it off my chest. You're a marvellous chap, Martin. You let people speak without clucking your tongue. I truly think you'd have lent a sympathetic ear to Attila the Hun."

"I suppose that's a compliment," Martin said dubiously. "But I'm not without some strong views."

"Of course you're not, it's just that you're far more objective about things than I am. This war is going to need a few unbiased witnesses. Would you like to go to the Dardanelles?"

"If I can, sure."

"Right! I'll get on the blower and fix it up. Fetch some bubbly while I mend a fence or two with the guv'nor."

Jacob was on the telephone to his father when Martin came back from the kitchen with champagne and two glasses.

"It just seemed the decent thing to do," Jacob was saying, his tone unctuously patriotic. "No reasonably healthy Englishman should be out of uniform and so. . . . I'm glad you understand, Father. . . . Now, as for this Mediterranean business, I can't think of anyone more suited to take my place than Martin Rilke. . . ."

HE STAYED APART from the other newspaper correspondents, elderly men who had covered military affairs since the Boer War and even beyond. He was an outsider—"that American chap"— tolerated but resented. .The number of press representatives allowed to join the Mediterranean Expeditionary Force was limited to a scant half dozen by General Sir Ian Hamilton, commanding the expedition.

The advisability of a neutral going along had been questioned by the War Office, but Lord Trewe argued that Martin should be allowed to accompany the expedition precisely *because* he was a neutral. American sentiment towards the British war effort was at a low ebb; so America must be made aware of the scope and grandeur of the British assault on the Gallipoli peninsula.

And so he was part of the host gathering in Egypt. Yet little of what he wrote was passed uncensored by GHQ and none of his photographs had been stamped with the censor's seal. It seemed curious to Martin that the British would be so touchy about what could be sent back to London. The smallest and most ragged Egyptian shoeshine boy knew that the English were preparing to sail for Gallipoli by the last week in April—so surely did the Turks.

"*Observations and reflections. Alexandria. April 10, 1915.* It is curious here. An air of almost unbearable excitement permeates every aspect of the expedition as though nothing but great honours wait over the horizon. Gallipoli apparently is a waterless and desolate peninsula, a mountainous spit of land dividing Europe from Asia. Are there many beaches? No one seems to know. . . . Maps of the place are impossible to find. Will it be heavily defended? Probably. . . . A month or so ago the British and French fleets attempted to force a passage through the Dardanelles. But several ships were lost and it was decided that the navy would not try again until the peninsula was in British hands so that the Turks couldn't enfilade the warships from batteries on shore. I know nothing of military strategy, but that seems to make sense.

Charles Amberley is here! We met by accident in the lobby of Shepheard's Hotel in Cairo and I spent a day with him, Roger Wood-Lacy and Rupert Brooke. Brooke is a fine fellow with the ability to talk for hours without boring anyone. The most mundane things fill him with poetic delight—the narrow, crowded, dirty streets of Cairo, the *fellaheen* working their fields, oblivious to the boom of guns as the artillery send practice rounds howling across the desert. *Now, God be thanked Who has matched us with His hour, And caught our youth, and wakened us from sleeping*—Everyone in Egypt seems to know that poem of his. Don't care for it myself. Too romantic in concept. I can't look on war as being a blessing. . . .

April 12, 1915. Rupert Brooke is ill . . . a touch of the sun. He's being taken aboard a hospital ship. He will miss the Gallipoli landings which must be a blow to him. I went with Charles and Roger to the dockyard to see a ship that the Royal Windsors will board next week for the landings. It's a rusty old collier, the *River Clyde*. Two thousand men will be aboard her for the assault.

Two hundred or more ships will be sailing from Egypt, heading first for the island of Lemnos fifty miles off the southwestern tip of Gallipoli. Mudros Bay on Lemnos is large enough to contain every vessel in sight. I assume the final sorting out for the assault will be done there. Everything appears to be so smoothly handled, so efficiently worked out that success must be assured. . . ."

THE *RIVER CLYDE* drifted slowly at anchor in the dead calm waters of Mudros Bay, the sun hammering down on the deck plates. Charles Amberley stood in the bows and watched the men of his platoon stack sandbags to form a loopholed wall, four feet high and many layers thick, turning the fo'c'sle into a small fort where twelve machine guns could be emplaced. Leaning against one of the sandbag walls, he gazed out over the vast harbour at the host of ships floating so serenely on Homer's "wine-dark sea", and he thanked God for his mercy in not sending him to France.

"Ah, Charles," Lieutenant-Colonel Askins stood timber straight, one large brown hand toying with his sun-streaked moustache. "Damned fine job of sandbagging there."

"Thank you, sir."

"What the deuce is wrong with Captain Talbot? That's his bloody job, y'know. Told me he had the cramps. Don't believe a word of it. Shirking, I call it. I'm putting him ashore and making you acting captain and battalion chatter-gunner."

"Thank you, sir."

The colonel's eyes became distant and he looked away. "You're a friend of that poet chap, Rupert Brooke?"

Charles felt his stomach contract. "Yes, sir."

"Wood-Lacy more than you."

"Yes, sir."

"Chap died yesterday. Sorry to be so blunt about it. I thought I'd better tell you. Break the news to young W-L after we're safely ashore. He has a damned important job to do tomorrow and I don't want his thoughts wandering about. I'm sorry about this, Charles. I know what it is to lose a friend."

The sun seemed to lose its heat as though the light had gone from the sky. The sea turned sullen and oily. Charles looked down at the lighters now coming alongside with their dense cargoes of men. Over two thousand for V beach alone. Only General Hamilton knew how many for the five others. There seemed little point in grieving for one dead poet.

IT LAY AHEAD of him in the darkness, unseen except in the mind's eye, the sharp semicircle of Sedd-el-Bahr bay, V beach. Memorized map statistics: four hundred yards of narrow sand just

234

west of the ruins of a mediaeval castle, the land rising gently behind the beach in a series of terraced slopes, a village of stone huts beyond the old fort. He peered through a sandbag embrasure, his cheek resting against the Vickers gun. Nothing to be seen but the dark bulk of the land, nothing to be heard but the throb of the *River Clyde*'s engines and the rush of water past the prow. He straightened and glanced towards the stern. The two empty lighters that would form a causeway to the shore were in tow, dark shapes in the phosphorescent wake. Behind them, unseen, were twenty cutters filled with Dublin Fusiliers. They would secure the beach while the *River Clyde* grounded herself in the bay and the lighters were warped round from the stern to make the bridge. Fifteen minutes after grounding the whistles would blow and the two thousand men in the collier's hold would pour out of the sallyports cut in the hull, race down wooden platforms, jump onto the lighters and run onto the beach without getting their feet wet.

One hour till morning. A bell clanged and the ship slowed. Then the first heavy shells of the fleet roared overhead and screamed in their plunge to the land. The half-moon coast from Sedd-el-Bahr to the tip of Cape Helles exploded in flame.

"Stuff it to 'em!" someone called out in the gloom.

For nearly an hour the guns of the fleet fired steadily. The pale sky was sullied by sheets of dun-coloured cloud. Grit settled on the deck, the soil of Gallipoli uprooted by the hammering shells. Explosions blinked and twinkled, sharp points of fire beneath fountains of yellow earth.

Charles held his wrist close to his face and looked at his watch. Six o'clock. Nothing, not a mouse, could be alive in that boiling, churning, cordite-reeking stretch of land.

"God pity them," he murmured.

Clang, clang! Clang, clang!

The ship trembled as the engines went full speed. The hazy sunlit bay drew closer.

"Load all guns!" he called. "Open sights, one hundred yards!"

There was the clatter of ammunition boxes being opened, the sharp snap and clang as the coiled belts were locked into the breeches.

They would fire at ghosts, at pulverized bone.

235

The shelling ceased as suddenly as it had begun. The shore drew closer, heavy with silence.

"Away all boats!" an impetuous midshipman called out, his boyish voice thin as a curlew's cry. "Onto the beach!"

The navy cutters headed in a long line for the shore. The Dubliners were standing, bayonets fixed, the early sun catching the blades.

"Blimey," a machine gunner said as he glared past the barrel of his gun. "The shellin' didn't touch the wire."

Charles bent his head to a loophole in the sandbag wall. The man was correct. Thickets of barbed wire stretched the length of the cove and up the slopes.

"The Dubliners will have to cut it," he said. "I hope they—" The keel grated against the bottom and the ship came to a stop thirty yards from the beach. Footsteps hammered on the deck as sailors ran towards the stern to haul the big lighters around to bridge the gap of deep water. Charles looked through one of the side embrasures. It was so quiet he could hear the officers on the cutters relaying commands. Thirty yards to go . . . twenty . . . ten. A bluejacket clutching a boat hook jumped into the surf.

Was that a bugle? A faint, brassy, two-note call coming from the ruins of the village above the cove? Charles couldn't be certain.

"Did anyone hear . . ." he started to ask and then a haze of smoke sheeted the entire curve of the bay and the surface of the water was suddenly whipped into a white froth by the first blast of Turkish rifle and machine-gun fire. The soldiers packed into the boats began to scream as the bullets scythed into them.

"Fire!" Charles yelled. The Vickers guns exploded, their noise drowning the cries of the dying Dubliners. Spouts of sand and clay traversed hillside and beach but the Turkish fusillade didn't slacken. There were no targets, Charles thought wildly. Not a Turk could be seen. There must be well concealed trenches all along the slopes. The men had probably stayed back in the hills until the shelling had ceased and then rushed down to their positions. There were only five beaches at this end of the peninsula where troops could land. The Turks knew that and had had a month to fortify them and to rehearse their defence. They had learned well.

236

Bullets clanged against the steel plates of the *River Clyde* and thudded ceaselessly against the sandbags. The sailors trying to drag the lighters around from the stern were shot off the decks and catwalks. Other men took their places to haul on the tow ropes for a few seconds before the bullet storm dropped them where they stood or sent them flopping over the side.

Charles slammed a fist against a bag and cursed under his breath. Why the hell didn't they back off and signal the fleet to start shooting again? He tapped the broad neck of a Fusilier sergeant and shouted loudly to be heard, "Going to the bridge. Take charge."

He dropped down the hatch and half-ran through the fo'c'sle, brushing past the sweating ammunition handlers. Out on the well deck a platoon of the Hampshires were kneeling in tight masses against the high iron sides as bullets passed over them cracking like steel whips.

The wooden ramps were being lowered over the sides, the operation directed by Lieutenant-Colonel Askins from the bridge, exposed to the fire storm and totally oblivious to it.

"What the hell are you doin' here?" Colonel Askins said as Charles reached the bridge. The colonel was staring at the shore, lips compressed, tight and bloodless.

"We can't dampen that fire with the machine guns, sir. Need artillery . . . the fleet. . . ."

"Too late for that . . . committed now. Bloody ship's fast on the sands. Second wave coming in now." He moved his right arm in a jerky fashion, pointing over his left shoulder.

Charles glanced aft. A string of launches and cutters packed with men was fanning into the bay.

"General Napier's leading 'em. Every one of them wants the VC today." He looked at Charles with distant eyes. "It's a bloody mess, Amberley, but we have to stick it. Get the men ashore, bayonet the Turk up the beach. No other bloody way to—"

And then he was dead, the top half of his skull spinning away towards the ship's funnel, hair and cap neatly together. Charles dropped to his knees and pressed his hands to his eyes. Anyone seeing him would have mistaken his cringing attitude for cowardice, but he was far beyond fear. Terror created its own form of courage. It was just that the colonel's death had come with such explosive suddenness he hadn't been prepared for it. He glanced at the long, sprawled, blood-draining body and stood up.

Charles saw the lighters had been lashed together in front of the bows. The men of the first platoon, A Company, the Royal Windsors, had started running down the disembarking platforms.

Charles caught a glimpse of Roger, revolver in hand, whistle in his mouth, leading his men down. Bullets slapped against the ship or ricocheted off with a whirring howl. It was like standing in a blizzard of lead. Then suddenly the ramp was empty, the platoon gone, a few men lying in the lighter in a bloody heap, the others in the water, motionless clumps of dark brown, sinking slowly, trailing plumes of scarlet. A whistle blew. The second platoon of A Company ran the gauntlet and withered away to six lone men before they reached the lighter.

Dead. Roger was dead. One of the corpses in the lighter, or one of the bobbing sacks of khaki in the water. Gone without a parting word. The realization numbed him. Oblivious to the fire, he made his way slowly back to the fo'c'sle and took his position again amid the steaming, clattering Vickers guns. They were safe here, Charles thought dully, pressing the triggers aimlessly while Turkish bullets thudded into the heavy sacks of white Egyptian sand.

A major in the Hampshires crawled up from the well deck and shouted to Charles over the stuttering roar of the machine guns. "No more chaps going in. . . . Waiting till nightfall. Keep the Vickers . . . firing."

Charles nodded and rested his head against the sun-heated bags. Through a peephole he could see the bay, the drifting boats filled with dead, countless bodies rolling in the surf, blood staining the water a Burgundy red. God, he thought, old Homer had been right. It was a wine-dark sea.

4

London sweltered in the July heat, but it felt cool to Martin after the heat of Gallipoli.

In the *Daily Post* offices nothing had changed. The message capsules still hummed over the ceiling wires, copy boys raced back and forth and the presses rumbled in the distance like the engines of some great ship. There were still shilling maps pinned to the walls of Lord Trewe's sumptuous office, a map of the Western Front next to a landscape by Constable. "Well, Rilke, I'm glad to see you back."

"I'm glad to be here, sir. I have quite a few things for you to read. Journals I've been keeping. . . ."

Lord Trewe folded his heavy hands across his waistcoat.

"I don't like reading journals, Rilke. I like to read your writing on the fourth page of the *Daily Post*. Let me tell you something that you may not know. Those who wish to read about the high strategy of this war read *The Times*. Those who wish to read about the men who are doing the dangerous jobs at the front read the *Daily Post*. Specifically, they read 'Gallipoli Sketches' by Martin Rilke, as do the readers of five American newspapers, three Canadian and two Australian. You've come back a famous man. I do not hesitate to say that you've invented a new form of war reporting. Human interest, Rilke, that's your forte. Now you're back and I'd like your next byline to read 'Western Front Sketches' by Martin Rilke."

Lord Trewe rested his hand on Martin's journals. "I know what's in these, Rilke. They contain everything that the censors would have tossed out." His gaze was direct. "I know what's going on out there: a brilliant concept bungled, the insanity of the Anzac corps, those men jammed on a cliff not fit for goats. What can you teach me in your journals that I don't already know?"

"Apparently nothing. But tell me, what does the average man on the street know? Let him read this." He tapped the journals with stiff, persistent fingers. "This is the *real* story of Gallipoli. It's a bloody mess and the public have a right to know. If you people expect to win this war—"

The press lord's fist came down on the stack of journals like a hammer. "We *will* win. We'll win because the men in the street are resolved that this war shall be won. They know how many died at Aubers Ridge, at Neuve Chapelle, and are dying now in Gallipoli, and would hang any newspaperman who told them that these men died for nothing. So this newspaper will report the war, without eroding the people's faith that the army will win through, eventually.''

He leaned back in his chair and toyed abstractedly with his gold watch chain, threading the heavy links through his fingers. "I'll tell you something, Rilke. This Gallipoli fiasco will topple many men: Asquith, Churchill, Kitchener. The conduct of the war will be taking a new turn. Lloyd George and David Langham are on the rise. We're all feeling our way, though. There has never been a war to compare this with. It will go on until one side or the other breaks. You write of the day-to-day business of fighting the war very well, Rilke. I want you to continue. Will you?''

"I guess I must. It has to be witnessed, doesn't it?''

"Yes. You may not be writing *all* the truth, but by God you're writing enough of it so that you should feel no shame. Your descriptions of Gallipoli made every Englishman who read them weep at the bravery and the heartbreak of it." He pushed the notebooks towards Martin. "Keep these to yourself, and don't look so glum, lad. A man can do only so much in these times.''

MARTIN TOOK A SEAT on the upper deck of a bus from Fleet Street to the Strand. That a war was on was evident by the number of men in uniform, and the recruiting posters on every pillar-box, but the crowds that he looked down upon from the open-topped bus were anything but glum. Lord Trewe had been right, of course. The war had to go on even if it shambled forward at the moment, over-burdened with inept commanders. A kind of vacuum existed between the front and the headquarters. Operations were planned on maps at Lemnos without the staff officers having any clear idea of what those operations entailed. Fifty yards looked a tiny distance on a map, if one ignored the fact that every inch was barren of cover and under the sights of Turkish guns. The staff never talked of *the men*, the tired, dirty, lice-infested, fly-plagued soldiers, but always in terms of *the regiment*. "The Royal Windsors can do it. . . .'' as though those dun-coloured ranks living like moles were scarlet-clad phalanxes of immortals. He felt guilty, sitting in safety on a London bus, while the men he had written about, the thirst-plagued infantrymen clinging to their toehold in the Aegean, might at this moment be corpses turning

240

black on the dead ground below Achi Baba or Chunuk Bair—
Charles Amberley perhaps among them.

The face of a woman in the crowd as the bus turned off the
Strand into Charing Cross Road, a slim, ivory-pale face, black hair.
She had been in a maid's uniform when he had seen her last, she
was in a uniform now, the blue and red of an army nurse. The bus
slowed as a torrent of pedestrians crossed the street, heading for
Trafalgar Square. Clutching his briefcase he dashed down the
aisle, half fell down the narrow, curving steps to the bottom deck
and then leaped past an astonished conductor into the street.

"Get killed that way, mate," the man yelled after him.

The blue and red figure was standing in front of a dress shop,
gazing reflectively at the display in the window.

"Ivy Thaxton?"

She looked at him curiously and then smiled.

"Why, if it isn't Mr. Rilke . . . from Chicago, Illinois."

"That's right," he said, grinning broadly. "Railways and
cattlemarkets. I spotted you from a bus. How are you?"

"Fine. And yourself?"

"Swell, just swell."

"You certainly look fit." Her violet eyes were innocent enough,
but he felt disquieted by their steady gaze.

"Say," he said nervously, "you're not going to hand me a white
feather, are you? I guess I look too healthy to be out of uniform."

She touched his hand and smiled again. "I was just teasing. We
all read your articles in the *Post*. The men in the ward say you're
the only one who knows what the soldier goes through. I'm
terribly proud of you, Mr. Rilke, and I do brag a bit about knowing you. Fancy! I used to make your bed!"

He fingered the soft fabric of her uniform sleeve. "You've sure
found something better to do with your time."

"Yes. I joined the QAs last September. I'm a probationer, training at All Souls Hospital."

"When do you have to be back today?"

"Eight o'clock."

"It's only four thirty. Will you join me for tea? I met a dozen
QA sisters on Lemnos and I owe every one of them a good cup of
tea. There's a White Manor in Charing Cross Road."

"It's very posh," she said doubtfully. "An orchestra and everything. I wouldn't want you to go to any expense."

"You're special, Ivy. And anyway, I've got three months' pay burning holes in my pocket."

They walked slowly towards Charing Cross. "Will they be sending you to France?" he asked.

"Not until I'm qualified to work on a surgical team, in about a year. I hope the war will be over by then. Do you think it will?"

"No, I'm afraid I don't."

"Oh, dear," she sighed. "Neither do most of the men in the wards. But one lad placed a little sign behind his bed. He lettered it himself. 'Peace be with us in 1916'. Not that it will make much difference to him. He lost both legs and an arm at Festubert."

Her sombre, reflective mood changed as they walked into the plush elegance of the Grand Tea Salon in the White Manor. An orchestra was playing a tango and couples were dancing.

"Oh my, isn't it grand!"

The tea was lavish, *petits-fours* and éclairs, Madeira cake and ices. Martin toyed with a piece of cake and watched Ivy eat.

"How old are you, Ivy?"

"I turned eighteen in March. Getting on in life. And—do you know, this is the first time I've ever been out to tea with a man."

"Make the most of it then. Would you care to dance?"

"I never learned how," she said dubiously, "but I'll try."

The first touch of her slender body made his legs feel weak. It seemed incredible how neatly she fitted against him.

They danced until the *thé dansant* ended at six thirty. It had been the most enjoyable couple of hours Martin had spent for a long time, the most enjoyable she had ever spent, she said as they walked towards St. James's Park. "And, oh, how beautiful some of those women looked in their gowns! I never went to a dance before. Da didn't approve."

"What does he do for a living?"

"Works in a shoe factory. He's doing very well. Times were so hard before the war but now he's making ever so much money, making army boots. Odd, if you stop to think about it."

This hour was the loveliest of the day, the sun catching the tops

242

of the trees and all the buildings along Whitehall, the park crowded with soldiers and their girls.

"I feel kind of silly carrying this briefcase, like some sort of door-to-door salesman," he said.

"I think it makes you look distinguished. I'm sure people think you just left Parliament and are on your way to see the King." She suddenly spread her arms wide. "Oh, I do love green parks!"

He took her hand and led her away from the path towards a grove of trees.

"You're such a happy soul, Ivy."

"I'm not really. I'm a bit on the glum side most of the time. I'm in the amputee ward, you see, and there's such a terrible amount of sadness there . . . though you have to keep cheery, matron insists on that. But I am enjoying myself with you."

He dropped the briefcase and took her impulsively into his arms, pressing her to him, his hands strong against her back. There were couples all around them under the trees, strolling by the dark green lake, and no one paid the slightest attention as he kissed her firmly on the lips. All the horrors of Gallipoli lay in the leather briefcase at his feet, but all thought of them vanished for a moment in the sweetness of her mouth.

HANNA STANMORE lingered over her tea on the terrace of Abington Pryory. Across the balustrade she could see William and four of his friends making a mockery of a tennis game, slamming balls into the grass to see how high they would bounce.

William was growing so tall. The apple of his father's eye. So much like Anthony; fine rider, good shot.

Seventeen. A difficult age, not quite a boy, not yet a man.

She felt a sense of dread the moment she saw Coatsworth walk onto the terrace. The man's leaden countenance foretold doom. The pale blue envelope on the small silver tray confirmed it.

"Thank you, Coatsworth," she said.

She held the envelope in her hand until he had gone. War Office stationery. It was addressed to her, but then they always addressed the letter to the mothers. She slit the envelope with a knife, her hand sure, only her heart racing, a throbbing pain behind the eyes.

Dear Lady Stanmore,

It is with regret that I have received word today that your son, Captain The Viscount Amberley, has sustained wounds during the recent fighting at Cape Helles. He has been taken aboard a hospital ship. Accounts as to the extent and severity of his injuries are necessarily sketchy at this time. We wish him well.

Yours sincerely, T. Pike, Brig. Gen.

THERE HAD BEEN a great many men wounded or taken sick during the July battles. Finding the exact particulars about one man was next to impossible. Lord Stanmore haunted the War Office and Martin sent messages through press channels to Alexandria. Nothing. It took two weeks for information to get through, fourteen days and nights that moved in a timeless vacuum of nightmare for Hanna. Her husband's assurances that Charles was bound to be all right, *probably no more than a flesh wound,* sounded forced. She spent the days working on needlepoint to try to keep her mind occupied, but there was nothing she could do at night except lie in bed and imagine her son's mutilated body. . . . She felt on the verge of madness. And then the afternoon came when William ran whooping into her sewing room yelling, "Old Charlie's all right! Only a fractured hip and pelvis. That chap from the army just rang up Father and told him!"

She was weeping uncontrollably when her husband came into the room.

August 9, '15.

My dearest Mother, Father, William and Alex,

This short letter is for you all. I was almost literally hit by a Turk shell, the ugly thing landed right next to me but failed to explode. Broke my right hip and pelvis, but the bones are mending. I should be fit for duty within four months.

I am in the French naval hospital in Toulon, very pretty French nurses and a doctor who believes that half a litre of wine a day never hurt a man. I could not ask for more sympathetic care and will be evacuated to a hospital in England in about three weeks' time. It will seem odd coming home. So much will have changed. I don't quite know how to put it, but I am not the same man who left just a few short months ago. But we shall talk about that when I arrive.

My warmest regards to Coatsworth, Mrs. Broome and all the staff. Also, please convey to the vicar that God has been kind to me and I much regret filching pears from the vicarage garden when I was eleven.

All my love, Charles

The earl scowled at the broken top of his boiled egg.

"What do you think he means about change? Of course he's changed. A man can't get hit by a shell and not be affected by it somewhat."

"I suppose he means . . . many things," Hanna said quietly. She read the letter through again silently. "I could weep."

"Oh, mother, *please*," William muttered, then glanced quickly towards his father. The earl did not admonish him. They both shared a horror of emotional outbursts.

"I was thinking of poor Roger," she said. "If only God had showed a little kindness to him as well."

She was not being entirely honest. She grieved for Roger Wood-Lacy, but what truly distressed her was Charles's assurance that he would be *fit for duty within four months*.

She reflected on her husband's attitude as she sat in the drawing room working on a tapestry. She knew how he had suffered for the past two weeks, had noticed the hint of pain in his eyes. Yet he had followed his normal routines to the letter; riding in the morning, inspecting the estate, going up to London. To the casual observer his attitude might have appeared uncaring, but she understood his inner torment and knew that the only way he had been able to cope with it had been to pretend that it didn't exist. But it *had* existed and his repressed suffering must leave some mark on him, alter him in some way.

"Miss Foxe on the line, your ladyship."

"Thank you, Coatsworth." She carefully finished a stitch. Lydia had obviously received a letter as well and she had a strong feeling that she knew what Charles had written to her. Change. Yes, many things would change.

"I didn't mean to disturb you, Lady Stanmore," Lydia said. "I thought that you'd like to know I received a letter from Charles this morning."

"We received one, too, my dear."

"Yes, I felt certain you would have. If you and Lord Stanmore intended to visit him in France, I could arrange it. That's really why I called. You could leave this weekend—via army transport from Portsmouth and then by train to Marseilles. Perhaps we could meet to discuss it."

Hanna held the receiver very tightly. "How easily you can manage things, Lydia. Could we have luncheon tomorrow? Say at the Savoy? One thirty?"

There was a moment's pause and then Lydia's voice, accepting—a calm, self-assured voice, the tone of a chess player who knows the exact number of moves to checkmate.

HANNA HAD NOT BEEN up to London for months, and the crowds in the Savoy amazed her. It had always been so quiet, now it was bedlam, swirling with officers and young women. Many of the officers were from the Canadian divisions, tall, boisterous, back-slapping men with flat, almost American accents. It was like being back in Chicago. At last she spotted Lydia and moved imperiously through the throng like the countess she was.

"How lovely you look, my dear. Your dress is most becoming. Not Ferris, surely."

"No, from Worth. I'm glad you like it."

"Very much. The shorter skirts suit you." Her compliments were genuine. She had certain reservations about Lydia, but none for her taste in clothes. "How hot it is here. Must be the crowd."

"I meant to warn you," Lydia said with a laugh. "The Savoy these days is rather like Waterloo station on Bank Holiday, but I did manage to reserve a table on the terrace. It's relatively quiet."

Waiters hovered. They ordered lobster and Liebfraumilch—now labelled, the *sommelier* remarked patriotically, Alsatian White.

"I brought my letter from Charles," Lydia said. "You can read it if you'd like."

"You want me to, don't you, Lydia?"

"Yes," she replied evenly. "I very much want you to read it. I . . . I think it might explain a good deal."

246

"About you and Charles? I don't think so. Such letters are not meant to be read by a third party."

The lobsters came and the two women ate, talking of generalities. When the coffee arrived Lydia poured two cups from the silver pot. "Was Lord Stanmore pleased at the thought of going to see Charles?"

"I didn't mention our conversation," Hanna said, sipping her coffee. "He would only resent special treatment. No, we will wait until Charles is sent home, but I am most grateful for the gesture. Might I ask how you could have arranged things?"

"Through David Langham."

Hanna looked away and watched the river traffic moving under Waterloo Bridge. "Mr. Langham has become a most powerful man. Or so I gather from the newspapers."

"Yes," Lydia said. "His ministry has become quite vital. The shell shortage at Neuve Chapelle spurred its importance. The ministry sees to it that if the army needs a million rounds of machine-gun ammunition in September, those million rounds will be available."

"Fascinating," Hanna murmured. "It must employ a great many people." She averted her eyes from the river and studied Lydia as though seeing her for the first time. Charles's infatuation was easy to understand, but she doubted if he had ever looked much beyond the shiny chestnut hair and the faultless skin. There were depths in the green eyes that were impenetrable.

"Charles is determined to marry you, Lydia, come what may. That's the crux of his letter, isn't it?"

"Yes."

"I can understand his feelings." She looked down at her cup and ran a finger around the thin porcelain rim. "Both Lord Stanmore and I want Charles to be happy. I understand my husband very well and I know that he would now be willing to soften certain attitudes that he once had towards you and Charles. To be blunt, I could induce him to give his blessing."

"And would you?"

"Not if it means seeing Charles go back to the front a few short months after his honeymoon. I'm sure that you find that just as painful to contemplate as I do."

"Yes, I do." Lydia set down her cup and glanced around for a waiter. "Would you care for a brandy, Lady Stanmore? Daddy keeps a private stock here of some wonderful sixty-year-old cognac."

"He must dine here often."

"Late suppers mainly, with Mr. Langham."

"I'd enjoy a glass. I find brandy settles the nerves."

The waiter caught Lydia's eye and moved to the table. She told him to ask the wine waiter for a bottle of 1865 Otard.

"Mr. Langham was telling me only this morning about a new branch of the ministry that's being formed to deal with the testing and procurement of new equipment for the army. Major-General Sir Thomas Haldane will head it and he's looking for bright men to staff it, preferably officers who have seen the war at first hand. I thought of Charles right away."

"Yes," Hanna said, speaking slowly so as to keep any tremor of emotion from her voice. "Would he take such a job?"

"He would have no choice. General Haldane can order the transfer of any line officer he wishes to have."

"It sounds like a satisfying and worthwhile task."

"Very. The prime minister and Lord Kitchener are terribly enthusiastic about it. Charles would be doing far more for his country in Whitehall than he could ever do in the trenches."

Hanna felt faint as the weeks of unending tension suddenly eased. She was grateful for the brandy when it arrived and inhaled the heady fumes before taking a sip.

"To Charles," she said. "And to you."

Lydia smiled. "Thank you, Lady Stanmore. I know everything will work out for the best. I shall make Charles a very good wife."

"I'm sure you will, my dear," Hanna said with the barest trace of a smile. "He's a fortunate young man."

And she meant that from the very bottom of her heart.

5

Number Seven Red Cross Hospital at Chartres occupied a large limestone château overlooking the River Eure. The heavy casualties during the spring offensives had flooded it with every conceivable type of injury. Fortunately, there had been minimal activity on the Western Front during the summer, but the *médecin-chef*, Dr. Gilles Jary, had just received notice from Paris that he could expect a marked increase in patients.

"Such stupidity!" he stormed, pacing his small, crowded, untidy office. "*Merde!* That is all I can say, *merde!*"

His matron of nurses, a stout, middle-aged Englishwoman watched him impassively.

"Now then, matron, what problems do *you* have for me today?"

"None . . . a small pleasure. Three VADs have arrived from England."

"Ah," he sighed, "English girls. All of them blonde and willowy?"

"Only one is blonde and rather more *voluptueuse* than willowy, I would say. Shall I send them up?"

"No, I shall meet them in Ward D. They can follow me on rounds."

Alexandra Greville walked gravely behind the English matron. The other two VADs stood as close to the doctor as they could, both of them jotting down what he said in notebooks. Their eagerness pleased the doctor and he complimented them extravagantly. He then turned to face Alexandra. Yes, he thought, *voluptueuse* was certainly the word to describe this blonde beauty. He felt a momentary regret at not being thirty years younger.

"Miss Greville, you seem, if you will pardon me, abstracted. Is anything the matter with our little hospital?"

"Oh, no, doctor," she said quickly. "It's just that I had hoped to be sent to the hospital at Toulon. My brother is there."

"Well, one must make the best of it, no? *C'est la guerre*. Come with me, child, we shall walk through Ward C together. Half a hundred *blessés*. All of them, as you can see, gravely injured. All far from their loved ones." He stopped by a bed. "Young Rialland here, nineteen years of age. Think of *him* as your brother."

The young man on the bed was staring at Alexandra as though a vision had appeared before him. "*Quel ange!*" he whispered.

"*Merci*," she murmured shyly.

"You see!" The doctor patted her on the shoulder. "You are an angel to him, and a French nurse will be an angel to your brother. You will be happy here and we will be happy to have you."

THEY ALL SAW the airman fall. It was on a Saturday morning and the aeroplane flew low over the hospital, its motor stuttering. The windowpanes rattled and everyone who could move rushed out of doors to see the fragile machine clip the top of a tree and go spinning towards the ground like a bird with a broken wing.

"Well, he's dead, poor man," matron said.

Ambulance drivers brought the airman to the hospital. He was unconscious, and both legs were broken, but he was very much alive. Dr. Jary went to work on him immediately.

"Young bones are a miracle," Jary remarked as he emerged from the operating theatre two hours later. Alexandra helped him remove his blood-specked apron and filled a basin with hot water. "Yes, Miss Greville, a miracle. Clean breaks, like good wood."

"Will he walk again, doctor?"

"Walk? He will run, fly. I must telephone the Royal Flying Corps and tell them that their Lieutenant Dennis Mackendric will be as good as new."

It was not long before the twenty-year-old airman was known as "Merry Dennis" by all the nurses. He was Scottish, sandy haired and ruddy faced, his athlete's torso always on display, for he refused to wear a nightshirt. Alexandra fell in love with him, as did every other nurse.

One morning, a week after the accident, Alexandra sat rolling bandages at a table in the cool entrance hall of the château. Her thoughts were drifting and she did not hear the man as he crossed the floor from the front door. His voice startled her.

"Excuse me. I'm Major Mackendric. I'm looking for my brother, a Lieutenant Dennis Mackendric."

A tall, gaunt-faced officer of the RAMC stood facing her. He was perhaps thirty. The mouth had a youthful quality, but the eyes, dark brown and deeply recessed in shadowed sockets, were ageless.

"I'll take you to him." Her voice registered surprise. No two men could have been more opposite in looks and manner.

"Thank you. By the way, who's in charge of this hospital?"

"Dr. Jary."

"Gilles Jary? Thank heaven for that. Some of these Red Cross surgeons couldn't set a watch, let alone a fracture."

He seemed an arrogant man. Even his brother did not appear to be overjoyed at seeing him. "Oh, Lord, Robbie!" he said.

"Hello, Dennis. Took a tumble, I gather." Major Mackendric eyed him sourly and then turned on Alexandra. "Do you permit all your patients to lie about half naked?"

"No," she blurted. "It's just that . . ."

"It's bluidy hot, man," Dennis protested.

"One is as liable to catch pneumonia on a hot day as on a cold one. Must be mad to let you lie about uncovered." He nodded curtly at Alexandra. "Where will I find Dr. Jary?"

"In his office. Down the corridor to your left."

"What do you want to see him for?" Dennis asked. "Don't go leapin' on the poor man because of my bluidy flannel!"

"I want to study the X-ray plates."

"Lord! Wasn't there enough to keep you busy up at Ypres?"

"Yes," the major said with intensity. "More than enough."

The younger Mackendric sucked in his breath. "I didn't mean that, Robbie. And I'm really *damned* glad to see your ugly mug."

"And I yours. Put your pyjama top on, that's the lad. I'll be back." He strode off, boots clicking briskly.

"Well!" Alexandra said, letting her pent up sense of outrage underline the word. "Well! What an exasperating man!"

"That he is," Dennis said with a grin. "He'd drive a saint to drink. The annoying thing about Robbie, though, is that he's always right." He sat up and held out his arms. "Slip the smelly old flannel on. There's no point in sendin' him into a bluidy rage."

She saw Major Mackendric later in the day with Dr. Jary. He smiled at her, but she made a point of ignoring him.

"There are two or three cases you could perhaps help us with," Dr. Jary was saying. "Abdominals, fecal abscesses . . ."

"I only have a few days' leave."

"I can have them prepared right now, cut after lunch. You were Sir Osbert's pupil, after all."

"I'm supposed to be on leave, but—oh, what the hell!"

THEY WHEELED the last patient from the operating room at one o'clock in the morning, matron told them at breakfast next day.

"He must have been very tired," Alexandra said.

Matron nodded. "He was. The colour of paste. Doctor Jary pressed a bottle of whisky on him and sent him into town."

Alexandra felt a compulsion to see him again. He had an *interesting* face, she decided, the face of a man who had seen much. She volunteered for double duty in order not to miss him. He arrived in the afternoon looking pale and drawn.

"Your brother's sleeping," she said, meeting him at the top of the stairs to the wards. "In a pyjama top."

"Sorry I made such a strafe about it." He removed a hand-kerchief from his pocket and wiped a sheen of sweat from his forehead. "Do you have such a thing as a cool drink, Miss . . . I'm sorry, I don't know your name."

"Alexandra Greville," she said simply.

"Robin Mackendric, now formally introduced." He held out his hand. The palm was damp, the fingers icy.

"Do you feel all right, Major?"

"A bit under the weather. I could use that drink . . . some lemonade, perhaps, and a couple of aspirin tablets."

She brought the glass to him. He took the aspirins from her hand and drank the lemonade. "Tell me," he said. "What time do you get off duty?"

She looked at him blankly. "Get off? At six thirty."

"Will you have supper with me in town?"

She could only stare at him. The invitation was totally unexpected. The man was at least ten years her senior. Her instinct was to murmur a polite no, but there was a look in his eyes that made her hesitate. She saw pain there, an almost desperate appeal.

"All right, Major. Will you pick me up or shall I meet you somewhere?"

"It's a pleasant walk. I could meet you by the river at seven."

THEY WALKED slowly along the towpath, the sun turning the poplars to slim columns of brass. Barges moved up the river, pulled by plodding horses while the bargemen sat cross-legged on the decks.

"France is such a lovely country, don't you agree, Major?"

"Yes, quite beautiful."

"And so historic. Chartres cathedral is one of the finest examples of Gothic architecture. I developed a passion for Gothic architec-

252

ture when I was about eleven years old. It didn't last of course. . . ."

She was talking too much and too rapidly. She took a deep breath in an attempt to calm herself. She found the taciturn doctor disconcerting. He paused for a moment to light a short briar pipe. She noticed that his hand holding the match trembled slightly. That only disconcerted her more and loosened her tongue once again. "I do love your brother. He's such a . . . bonny Scot! You . . . you're a bit older than he is, I take it."

"I'm thirty-two. Dennis is twenty."

"I'm nineteen, but I feel a good deal older. I suppose it must be the war. Have you been out here long, Major Mackendric?"

"Since last October . . . first Ypres."

"What a dreadful battle that must have been. And you're assigned to a casualty clearing station?"

"Yes." He stopped and faced her. "Let's not talk about it."

"What would you like to talk about?"

"You, good food, and barge horses. In roughly that order."

"Food then," she said a little too brightly. "All I've eaten for weeks is lentil soup and something grey and stringy boiled with turnips. Matron said there are some fine restaurants in Chartres."

There were indeed several elegant restaurants in the town, all of them with staff cars parked in front. He took her to an inn that had a garden at the back which sloped down to the river. There were tables under the trees, lanterns suspended from the lower branches, their soft lights glowing yellow on the placid waters. He ordered duckling, strawberries, and a bottle of Montrachet.

After dinner they walked back towards the hospital, barges still moving along the river, cabin lights twinkling in the darkness.

"Thank you so much, Major Mackendric," she said when they reached the lane that led to the château. "I enjoyed the meal thoroughly."

"And I enjoyed your company, thoroughly." He stepped closer to her and placed a firm, sure hand on her arm.

"Miss . . . Alexandra . . . I believe in being candid. I've become rather obsessed by you—from the moment I saw you rolling bandages in that sepulchral entrance hall."

"Major Mackendric . . ." she said haltingly. "I'm sure I . . ."

God knows, she had been kissed before, any number of times.

But now a warmth she had never felt before swept through her veins and her legs felt waxen. He released her.

"I'm leaving for Paris in the morning. Will you come with me?"

"Impossible," she said weakly. "Quite impossible. You must be mad, Major Mackendric."

He bent his head slightly and kissed her throat. "Mad as a March hare. All right, come up on the Friday train, the one that leaves at noon. You can take the evening train back on Sunday."

She tried to laugh, but only an odd, husky sound emerged. "Really, quite impossible, Major . . ."

"Dr. Jary encourages leaves now and then. He told me." He took hold of her arm again, a brief, taut-fingered squeeze. "I ask only that you think about it."

"I . . . I'll think about it."

He let go of her arm reluctantly. "Thank you, Alexandra. I shall be at the Gare Montparnasse when the train arrives."

CLICKITY-CLICK . . . *clickity-click* . . . The train to Paris took three hours. It seemed to Alexandra like an endless journey.

She had tried as discreetly as possible to find out all she could about Robin Mackendric, asking his brother oblique questions. "Robbie and I were never very close. He was more like an uncle than a brother. But after he got married . . ."

"Married?"

"Oh, yes." Not noticing the note of dismay. "The poor fellow. A thin-lipped Aberdeen woman who doesn't take kindly to Robbie's views. He's a fellow of the Royal College of Surgeons, but chose to work in a Liverpool charity hospital. Now he's coiled up like a steel spring about to snap. I saw him at Ypres in May and he looked like death. I told him to chuck it in and go back for a month. But no, wouldn't think of it. I said, you're not the only sawbones in Flanders . . . but what's the bluidy use! Robbie's Robbie."

Clickity-click, clickity-click, the wheels sang to the rails, the outskirts of Paris whipped past the window. She had been to Paris many times as a girl—to visit the Louvre, the shops on the Rue St. Honoré with mamma. Now she was coming to Paris alone to confront a man, a *married* man thirteen years older than herself!

254

She felt like a sleepwalker as the crowd of passengers propelled her along the platform. And then she saw him. He stood with his back to a kiosk, anxiously examining the flow of people, and she knew, watching him, that she had been right in coming.

"Good afternoon, Major Mackendric."

He had not seen her approach. He let out a sigh.

"And a very good afternoon to you. How nice you look."

She was wearing a pale blue uniform with a short, darker blue cape trimmed in red, made for her by Ferris. Suddenly she was afraid it made her look like an actress playing the role of a nurse.

"Are you surprised that I came?"

"A bit, yes. But delighted. May I carry your suitcase?"

She handed him her small, leather overnight bag.

"I had a long talk about you with your brother. He told me that you're married, among other things."

"Yes," he said quietly. "Been married for several years."

"Dennis is concerned about you. He feels that you're . . . well, reaching the end of your tether, so to speak. When we first met, you made me think of a man clinging to a cliff by his fingertips."

"What picturesque imagery."

"I think you're just horribly lonely and need companionship, someone to talk to, to share a good meal with."

"That's very kind of you."

"It's really no trouble at all. We can be together until Sunday evening, visit the Louvre. I can stay at the YWCA."

"Yes," he said thoughtfully, "I suppose you could at that."

She had been rehearsing what she would say all the way up from Chartres, trying to anticipate his response. She had expected more reaction. His bland acceptance threw her off balance.

There was a pavement café on the Rue de Vaugirard, green-painted iron tables and chairs under brightly-striped umbrellas. The place was crowded, but three young men, wearing soiled white jackets over their shirts, stood up with their glasses of beer.

"Kindly take our table," one of them said in halting English.

"*Merci.*" He watched them stroll off. "Medical students. There's a training hospital around the corner. I attended a seminar there in 1910. Your Dr. Jary conducted it."

That comment made her painfully aware of the difference in

255

their ages. She had been a schoolgirl in 1910, struggling with Latin verbs. He had been a qualified doctor.

He ordered Chablis and soda for both of them and she watched him rolling the cool glass between his palms.

He was so unlike any man she had ever known that it was pointless even to try to find points of similarity. To begin with, he didn't try to impress her, no stories of great deeds done on the cricket field, or point-to-point races. And no funny stories to make her laugh. He was simply . . . himself. Moody, introspective, and yet capable of breaking out of his thoughts from time to time to tell her one thing or another. He knew a great deal about architecture, engineering, music, literature and botany and touched on all of these subjects as they talked. Later he took her to a restaurant by the Seine.

"One thing you have not talked about," she said, spearing a truffle with her fork, "is medicine. One has the feeling that you're ashamed of being a doctor."

"I'm ashamed at the burden mankind has thrust on us in the last year. No. Let me retract that. Not ashamed, angry."

Yes, she thought, studying his face in the glow of the candles, it wasn't pain that she had seen in his eyes at all, but anger— deep smouldering fury. The realization shocked and puzzled her and she was unable to finish her meal.

He noticed. "Shall we go?" he said. "I'll call for a taxi."

"Is a taxi necessary?"

"Lord, yes. The YWCA is the other side of Paris."

She shifted a tomato with her fork, from one side of her plate to the other. "I don't think I wish to stay at the YWCA. I . . . I'm certain that where you are staying is far more pleasant."

"It's . . . a nice old hotel, yes."

"Can we walk there?"

"I suppose so. But are you *absolutely* sure you want to go at all?"

She nodded and looked up, meeting his eyes, holding her gaze without flinching. "Yes. Quite sure. But not in a taxi. There's something rather . . . *sordid* about going to an assignation in a taxicab."

His smile was slight, almost sad. "It's not an *assignation* if we go together."

256

SHE HAD NO possible way of knowing what to expect. Every novel she had read had concluded the seduction scene with a series of dots. She lay naked in a wide bed, vulnerable to violent assault by a man as naked as herself. But of course she wasn't assaulted and had known she wouldn't be. He didn't *pull her passionately into his arms* the way Elinor Glyn would have described it. His hand simply moved slowly over her body in the darkness, fingers stroking the hollow of her throat, straying across her breasts. "How lovely you are, Alexandra," he said in quiet wonder.

She wanted to tell him that she loved him for his gentleness and for the pleasure he was giving her, but she was incapable of speech. She touched his body, pulling him closer to her.

"I shan't hurt you," he whispered.

When normal senses returned she noticed the patch of light on the ceiling, heard the trumpeting klaxon horns from the street below. Her hands lingered on his long body. "Robbie," she murmured. "Robbie."

THE THOUGHT OF HIS LEAVING her filled her with dread. The world seemed bleak on Sunday morning, despite the sun flooding the room. He must return to duty.

"Take me with you."

"No," he said, kissing her. "Quite impossible."

"Why?" she pouted. "I'm a nurse, I can work by your side."

"You're a volunteer girl, fluffing pillows and sponging brows."

"And working the autoclave machine. I'd be useful. And there would be nights when we could be together in some country inn."

He moved away from her and sat with his back against the headboard. "There are no country inns in the salient. Nothing but shelled-out villages, shelled-out woods, shelled-out roads. And troops, troops everywhere. No, you'll go back to Chartres and I'll take the night train to St. Omer." He cupped her chin in both hands and bent forward to kiss her softly. "Alex, these have been the most wondrous two days of my life. When things get too bad, I'll hold on to my sanity by remembering you."

"May I write to you? I write marvellous letters."

"I can't stop you, Alex, but do you think it's wise?" He took both of her hands into his. "Alex, you're a beautiful, passionate,

257

nineteen-year-old woman. When you step off the train in Chartres you will probably meet a handsome, gallant twenty-year-old man. You'll be married in a church and forget all about me. That's as it should be. You shared two days of your life with me and you could never comprehend how much it's meant to me."

"Oh, Robbie," she whispered, kissing his hands. "We must see each other again. Maybe this silly war will end tomorrow."

IT WAS IMPOSSIBLE to get him out of her mind. If there had been someone to share her thoughts with, it might have been halfway bearable. Even Dennis Mackendric was gone, moved to Rouen. The days dragged and the nights became eternities. She yearned to drown Robbie's image in work, but the hospital was half empty now. The next great offensive was beginning in this last week of September. It would be some time before the wounded filtered down to Chartres.

Impulsively Alexandra took French leave, catching the morning train for Paris and then the train to St. Omer. Wearing her winter cape, she looked suitably like an army nurse, and the military policeman at St. Omer barely glanced at her identity papers.

"Going to Number Fourteen General, Sister?"

"No, Number Twenty CCS, near Kemmel."

He whistled softly through his teeth. "Might be a bit difficult. Terrible amount of traffic on the roads. You could try your luck with the ambulance transport officer. He's in the Rue Hericat. Little whitewashed stone house; can't miss it."

The narrow, dingy streets were clogged with British soldiers on their way to the front, silent streams of rain-darkened khaki, the men hunched under their heavy packs. They reminded her of cattle plodding wearily through a market town.

A convoy of thirty empty ambulances was leaving for Flanders, six of them marked for Kemmel. The transport officer didn't question her right to go there and rubber-stamped her papers.

In the ambulance she began to experience a growing sense of dread, which became more pervasive the closer they came to the front. That evening she could see distant stabs and flickers of flame, and when they stopped in a village for tea and bully beef sandwiches she could hear the muttering thunder of the guns. A

Royal Engineer officer sloshed through the mud to tell the drivers that the road to Kemmel and Ypres had been heavily shelled that morning and would be impassable until daybreak. She huddled in the ambulance, not able to sleep, listening to the driver snore. Her depression deepened with the night.

It was eight in the morning when the ambulances pulled into the CCS compound, rows of wooden buildings with dirty brown canvas roofs, connected to each other by duckboards laid across a sea of mud. Beyond a sagging barbed-wire fence lay the remains of an orchard, a few stumps of shattered trees amid interlocking craters.

A tall, sharp-faced English nurse eyed her coldly. "VAD? What on earth are you doing up here?"

"I . . . I wish to see Major Mackendric."

The nurse studied the forlorn-looking girl standing in front of her desk and her expression softened. "He's in surgery at the moment. Have you had your breakfast?"

"No, Sister."

"Well, come along and I'll take you to the mess tent. You're a friend of the major's, I take it?"

"Yes. I . . . I nursed his brother."

A tiny smile tugged at the woman's firm mouth. "Oh, you nursed his brother, did you? Well, I never."

She sipped her tea, holding the mug tightly with both hands to keep it from spilling. A battery of heavy British guns a mile away were firing and the noise was nerve-jarring. The salt and pepper shakers on the mess table bounced and slid at every sound.

And suddenly he was seated across from her, his uniform jacket hastily buttoned, his tie askew. He looked at her, bemused. "What on earth am I going to do with you, Alex?"

She stared into the murky depths of her tea, not trusting herself to look at him. She felt close to tears. "I shan't go back."

"But you can't stay here. Surely you can see that?"

She shook her head like an obdurate child. "I'll be useful."

"Alex, all nurses here are QAs, some with twenty years of service. There are no VAD girls beyond St. Omer. You don't have the slightest conception of what we do here."

She set her tea down and looked at him for the first time, her longing for him so evident in her eyes that his firmness wilted.

"Oh, Alex . . . Alex . . ." He reached across the table and touched her hand. "You're making this so difficult."

"I don't mean to, Robbie. But I'm not very experienced at . . . love affairs. Perhaps there are some girls who can have one and then forget all about it. I can't. I tried very hard. Believe me, I did. But the fact is . . . the fact is . . ."

He squeezed her wrist and glanced away. Two orderlies at a nearby table were casting sidelong looks at them. At casualty clearing station everyone knew everything about everybody and anything not known for certain was grist for endless speculation.

"Don't cry," he said firmly.

"I won't. It's just that I'm so happy to see you and I want so badly to stay. I know I can be useful."

He took out his pipe and filled it slowly and deliberately to give himself time to think.

"Alex," he said, "like you I can't have a love affair and then forget about it. But we must be sensible. You have some sort of romantic notion of playing nurse to my doctor. But there are no pillows to fluff here. If you're serious about wanting to become a nurse then join the QAs. . . . Oh, Lord, here comes Vale."

A thin, fair-haired officer, wearing a white jacket over his uniform, walked towards their table, smoothing his moustache with one finger. Without being invited he drew up a wooden chair.

"Parsons needs your touch in Number Six right away, Major. It's the Gurkha sergeant. Gas gangrene in the right leg."

"Damn."

"Oh, well, can't be helped, can it? Have to chop-chop quick-quick, or the poor fellow's done for."

Robin stood up with obvious reluctance. "I suppose you want a formal introduction, Vale?"

Vale grinned. "If you don't mind, old chap."

"Alexandra Greville, Captain Vale. Captain Vale, Alexandra Greville." He tapped out his pipe in a shell-case ashtray. "I'll be an hour. Show Miss Greville around, will you, Vale?"

"Be delighted, positively delighted."

Her nagging sense of trepidation returned when Captain Vale showed her through the wards. They were coldly functional, row upon row of canvas cots, wheeled carts piled high with dressings, bottles of anti-tetanus serum and hypodermic needles.

"It's a bit on the empty side at the moment," said Vale. "We cleared shop this morning, ready for the next batch. Rather like old Waterloo station. Chappies come and go." He led the way across duckboards past a drystone structure that might once have been a stable. "That's where we operate, move the chappies in, move 'em out . . . cut, cut, cut. Tommy calls this place Mendinghem. The French hospital at Hazebrouck is Endinghem."

A bell rang, four loud clangs . . . pause . . . four more.

Captain Vale's expression hardened slightly, a tense thinning of the lips. "Staff call. Get the news of what we're in for today. Nasty bit of firing since dawn. Won't be pleasant, I'm afraid."

Alexandra stood at the end of the mess tent, out of everyone's way. Doctors, nurses and orderlies stood about in groups. Finally Mackendric came in, a surgical gown over his uniform.

"All right," he said. "The Bedfords and Suffolks were in it this morning. Half their wounded are on the way down to us now, three to four hundred. They were badly shelled so prepare for extreme multiples. The bearers found thirty or so Cameronians who had been lying out in the wire since Wednesday. We know what to expect there, so be sure to have chloroform handy."

The nurse Alexandra had met that morning came up to her as she sat dejectedly in the mess tent. "Feel a bit lost, do you?"

"Yes, a bit."

"Well, can't have that, can we? Have you been taught anything useful? If I told you to inject five hundred units of ATS, would you know how to go about it? Or set up a Carrel drip?"

"No . . . I . . ." She could feel her face burning. The woman's grey eyes seemed to bore right through her.

"I'm matron here," she went on, not unkindly. "Major Mackendric asked me if there was any possibility of my using you. I'm afraid there isn't. You'll have to go back to St. Omer tomorrow. But I can certainly find something useful for you to do this afternoon. You can give the orderlies a hand."

The orderlies were tense but friendly, offering her tea and practical advice. "Speed's the ticket," Corporal Hyde said, a cigarette pasted to his lower lip. "It's like a ruddy factory when we get movin'. We have to turn the lads over to the sisters as un-mucky as possible. Cut the old dressin's off and if there's lots of mud we wash it off with soap and antiseptic."

At three forty-five the first mud-encrusted ambulances drew up in front of the admitting tent. Orderlies ran to open the doors and to get the wounded. Coming from them was a sound that Alexandra could not associate with anything she had ever heard before—a muttering, groaning, muted howl. All the men had been hastily bandaged at their regimental aid posts, given morphine pellets, but the effects were wearing off.

She glanced at the sisters standing by two dressing carts. Their faces were impassive. "Hop to it, girl," one of them said.

Alexandra had been among the wounded before, but she had seen them only as they had arrived at the Hôpital Croix Rouge, clean, well-bandaged men. Here, horror piled on horror; a man with his eyeballs blown out, dirty cottonwool stuffed into the sockets; sheared off legs and arms, the stumps wound with soiled puttees; a man screaming and twisting like an animal in a trap, hands pressed against a bulge of intestines that were slipping through his fingers.

Her legs shook and she sank to her knees beside a stretcher, staring down at a blackened, muddy bandage covering a man's upper thigh. As she cut hesitantly at the bandage the man screamed and cursed and tried to sit up. Corporal Hyde held him down. "Cut them bloody rags off, miss!" he said.

She cut, her hand shaking so violently she almost dropped the scissors. Beneath the bandage lay a bloody puddle with bits of hip bone jutting from the ooze. Vomit rose in her throat and she clamped her teeth to hold it back.

"Keep them moving along, for God's sake," a sister called out in exasperation.

Her nausea came in wave after wave. There seemed to be no end to the writhing, grunting, animal-like creatures who were laid in front of her. The nightmare only deepened.

"Cameronian," an orderly muttered as a mud-encrusted form was set down in front of her. He placed a bottle of chloroform on the floor beside her. "Just douse the little bastards."

The man had been four days in a shell hole between the wire, four days of sun and rain. A self-applied dressing under his right armpit bulged over the festering wound beneath. She cut the dressing away with difficulty. Then, boiling up out of the suppurating depths of the shell-chewed cavity, came a mass of fat, white maggots, creeping onto her fingers along the scissor blades.

She screamed and could not stop screaming as she staggered, retching, towards the door. A sister grabbed her, slapped her hard across the face. She felt nothing, just slipped down into darkness.

IT WAS PEACEFUL in the ambulance. Around her in the blackness were silent forms, drugged, still as death. Yet someone was calling her name, she could hear it softly, softly. . . . *"Alex, Alex . . ."* out there in the inky night. She stared fixedly at a stretcher on the brackets above her.

Alex, Alex . . .

The ambulance began to move, creaking and lurching slowly across the compound. Taking away the wounded. Yes, she thought dully. And she was one of them . . . just one of the wounded. Perhaps even one of the dead.

PART THREE

1

It was a December day of arctic winds and pale heatless sun. Lady Winifred Sutton had been walking for two hours through Chelsea and along the river before returning to Cadogan Square.

The war had touched half a million English homes, an avalanche of telegrams pushed through pillar-boxes telling of dead or wounded, missing, captured men. Twenty-four Cadogan Square, with two dead sons, was such a home.

She approached it with the usual feeling of dread. She hated London, but her father had donated his country home to the Red Cross for the duration of the war. She yearned for the quiet fields of Dorset, and knew too that her mother would have been less frenetic there, more reconciled to the finality of the deaths of her two sons. Here there was nothing to be done about her mystical conviction that their spirits could be enticed back from eternity.

The ladies of her mother's séance group were just descending to the pavement when she got home. She had hoped to avoid them and broke away as soon as she could and hurried up to her bedroom. This was her private refuge. She sat at her dressing table, feeling a dull pity for all those poor women who tried so desperately to bring back their loved ones.

There was a gentle knock and a maid looked in. "Colonel Wood-Lacy on the telephone, m'lady. Shall he ring back?"

"Thank you, Daphne. Yes, he may ring back in half an hour."

Fenton in London. She hadn't seen him since the war started . . . fifteen months. He had never taken a leave in England, but he had written to her once in a while. The slender pile of his letters was in her dressing-table drawer.

Today we moved up to the line and took over the trenches recently held by the French. Quite messy, I'm afraid. . . .

Not love letters by any means, and yet she had kept them neatly together as though they were. They all began *Dear Winifred* and were signed *Affectionately.* Like letters from an uncle.

Now he was Lieutenant-Colonel Wood-Lacy, DSO. She had read of his new rank and his decoration. One always read the lists —the dead, the wounded, the missing—and the promoted.

His voice on the telephone was as she remembered it. "Ah, Winifred, I hope I'm not inconveniencing you."

"Not at all, Fenton. How nice to hear your voice."

"I got in last night . . . staying at the Guards' Club."

"Do you have a long leave?"

"A few weeks." There was a slight pause. "I thought we might have tea together . . . that is, if you're free this afternoon."

"I would enjoy that, yes."

"Shall we say four thirty?"

How correct he was, she thought bitterly as she hung up. Honour-bound at least to see her. After all, he had taken the first step in the ritual of courtship in that long-ago July. That ritual was now archaic, one of the lesser casualties of the war, but he was too much of a gentleman to ignore it totally. So he would take her to tea—not to dinner and the theatre, but to *tea!*

265

FENTON COULDN'T KEEP from staring at her as they drove towards Mayfair in a taxi. The change in her was dramatic. He had remembered her, with twinges of shame, as a plump schoolgirl whose gratitude for his attentions had been almost embarrassing. He barely recognized the tall, slim, beautiful woman at his side.

"Why are you staring at me?" she said.

"I'm sorry, I was trying to recall the Winifred I knew."

"Have I changed that much?"

"Well, you're older, of course. You're also a very lovely young woman, Winifred."

"Thank you." She glanced out of the side window. It was getting dark and crowds streamed across Hyde Park Corner. "Must we go to tea? I would really like to go to Madame Tussauds. I've always wanted to see the Chamber of Horrors. I had a friend at school who's seen it several times. Her uncle used to take her."

His hearing was not so numbed by shell fire that he couldn't detect sarcasm. "You feel that I'm being patronizing?" he asked.

"No. I think you're just being noble. A less considerate man would have ignored the situation and simply not called on me."

He tapped on the glass. "Stop here, driver."

They walked along Piccadilly in silence, the wind driving grains of ice into their faces. He took hold of her arm and led her into the warm, spacious lobby of the Torrington Hotel.

"Did your friend's uncle ever buy the child a pink gin?"

"He may have," she said thoughtfully.

"May I buy you one, or will it slow your growth?"

"You're angry, aren't you?"

"Don't you think I have a right to be?"

"Yes, and no. Let's just say, that we both have a right."

The bar was crowded with officers and well-dressed women. There was a tiny dance floor—every hotel bar had a dance floor now—and a four-piece ragtime band was playing the Castle Walk. Fenton ordered a pink gin and a whisky and soda.

Winifred took a sip of her gin. "Odd. Us having a drink together in a public place. Quite unthinkable a year ago."

"Yes, times change, but human emotions do not. If I've hurt you, Winifred, I'm deeply sorry."

"You have nothing to apologize for. The war has changed

everyone's plans. I suppose we'd be married by now if Germany hadn't marched into Belgium. I wonder if we'd be happy? Probably. I would have a handsome husband and you would have . . . what? Why did you choose me, Fenton? It wasn't love. I was never under that illusion. Fundamentally monetary, I suppose. Or is that an uncalled-for remark?"

"No. You deserve to know. It's true I needed money to stay in the regiment. But it wasn't just money . . . I enjoyed your company. I enjoy it now."

She toyed absently with her drink, turning the slender glass between her fingers. "I have difficulty sometimes in remembering what I was like that summer, or what you were like. We're different people now, aren't we? So much has happened in our lives. But I recall how infatuated I was. Also I was desperate to be engaged. I felt I owed it to my mother, that it was all my fault Charles hadn't dropped on one knee. And then, out of the blue, you strolled into my life with a box of chocolates under your arm. No man's timing could have been more perfect."

He took a hefty pull at his drink. "You certainly don't need to feel grateful now if a man looks at you."

"And you don't need a rich wife to stay in the army. The slate has been wiped clean, Fenton. It's like meeting for the first time."

"My feelings exactly. What say we make a proper evening of it? Dinner at Romano's or upstairs at the Café Royal. . . ."

"Sounds like fun, but I really don't feel up to celebrating. Will you be in London long?"

He felt a twinge of disappointment, of having been deliberately cut by her. How deeply did she resent him? "On and off for the next two weeks," he said. "I'm going to Abington for the weekend. May I telephone you next week?"

She looked at him with a cautious, deliberating gaze. "Yes," she said with a slight nod. "If you really want to."

THERE WAS a bleakness to the countryside that Fenton had never seen before. A shabbiness that was not attributable to the weather. Roofs needed repair, walls thirsted for whitewashing, orchards were unpruned. The train was delayed at Abbotswood Junction to permit some troops to double time across the tracks. Their grey-haired officer rode his horse with taut-bodied fury, mentally cursing the shambling mob of recruits. He saw only a thousand green troops; Fenton saw one thousand bricklayers, carpenters, and butchers' boys: the heart's blood of the shire running into the misted, sleet-covered fields beyond.

Yet, but for the lack of footmen, at Abington Pryory that evening it could have been any gathering for dinner at any time. The candles in their silver holders were reflected in the highly polished surface of the long table and the war was snugly tucked away as Lord Stanmore carved the roast mutton and Coatsworth uncorked the wine. It seemed to Fenton that he had but to close his eyes for a second and when he opened them again Roger would be arguing with Charles about modern poetry and Alexandra and Lydia Foxe would be chattering away about Paris frocks. But time did not come back. Roger was dead. Alexandra hadn't opened her mouth all evening. Charles was a married man and Lydia was Lydia *Amberley*.

Fenton was seated opposite her and it was impossible for their eyes not to meet. When toasts had been offered he had raised his glass to her and she had smiled at him as though saying, "I told you I would do it." The future Countess of Stanmore. It seemed incredible, but there she sat, looking to the manner born.

"So the fighting has wound down for the winter and what have we got to show for it?" The earl tapped his wine glass with a spoon. "1915 is not a year I'd like to see again."

Hanna rose majestically. "Anthony, you may talk of the war all you wish over the port. We ladies would prefer to be spared."

Alexandra stood up with the other women and then walked to her father and kissed him. "Goodnight, Papa. I'm going to bed." She turned to Fenton and placed a hand on his shoulder. "Goodnight, Fenton. It's so good to see you again."

He touched her hand. It was cold and her face was waxen.

"Alexandra not well?" he asked after the women had left.

"She was with the Red Cross in France," Charles said. "Came back in October quite ill."

The earl lit a cigar. "So Sir John French is out and Haig is in. So much for the politics of the high command. You're in Whitehall these days, Charles. What sort of wild tales there?"

268

"Not too many filter down to my office," Charles replied. "I'm rather a new boy. But I understand that Haig would like to end the war next year with one huge blow in late summer, up at Ypres. Joffre would prefer to launch an offensive along the Somme. Either way, it's going to be a big push and 1916 might just be victory year."

"Don't bet on it," Fenton said. "They're just getting light-headed up at GHQ, seeing all these New Army battalions come into being. A million men under arms. They're mesmerized by the figures, but it doesn't change the formula. At Loos *ten* million would have still been stopped by the wire and the Boche machine gunners. The Hun defence is simple and works like a bloody charm. We have to make a radical change in our strategy and Haig is not the man to do it."

Charles coughed discreetly. "Let's play some snooker. I agree with Mother . . . must we talk of the war?"

By midnight, only Fenton and Charles remained in the billiard room. Fenton watched Charles miss an easy shot.

"You haven't said much about Whitehall."

Charles glared at the tip of his cue. "Just started really so I don't quite know what it'll be like. We're an odd group: dons from London University, scientists with Viennese accents, eccentrics talking to eccentrics. People come to us with mad ideas on how to win the war—death rays, stuff like that."

Fenton sank the blue ball, scanned the table. "Don't exaggerate. Sounds like a worthwhile place to me."

"I suppose it is. It's just that . . . well, dammit, I feel I should be helping to drill the new battalions, not talking to farmers about caterpillar tread tractors. Someone, somewhere, came up with the whimsical idea for a land battleship, a sort of enormous, armoured tractor. Bound to be a washout. Even if we did develop it, we don't have the generals who would know what to do with the bloody thing."

"If you feel so strongly about it you shouldn't have volunteered for the job."

Charles fluffed another shot. "I was *ordered* to report to General Haldane as soon as I could walk without crutches. He told me that he wanted me to work in NS5, and that was that."

"Well, at least you have a lovely young wife to go home to every night. Count your blessings."

"I do," he said gravely. "I feel guilty about having so many."

"Remind me to send you a hair shirt. Be sensible, old boy. I've been watching you. You walk rather painfully."

"All the breaks have knitted well," Charles said defensively.

"Perhaps they have, but you'd be bloody useless marching. Keep working on your land battleship, and remember that there's a chap just like you in Berlin trying to beat you to the punch."

FENTON BECAME fully awake before the first pale light tinted the windows. It was from force of habit, the morning stand-to of the trenches, the men alert and tense, waiting for the sun to rise behind the German lines. The time of greatest tension. His heart was beating faster and he felt sweaty under the eiderdown. He sat on the edge of the bed and lit a cigarette, wondering if he would ever be able to enjoy dawn again, or even enjoy sleep for that matter. His dreams had been bad ones. There was a tremor in his right hand. He cursed it softly, and slapped it against his leg. He lived in dread that one day his body would betray him and he would suddenly begin to tremble all over.

Downstairs the cooks were making breakfast for the staff—only twelve now where once there had been forty. They were seated in the kitchen when Fenton walked in.

Coatsworth poked his feet into a pair of carpet slippers. "Shall I inform his lordship that you're up and dressed, sir?"

"Yes, please, tell him I'll be in the stables."

The old groom was happy to have company and the horses were eager to be saddled. The two men had just finished tightening the saddle girths when the earl hurried towards them.

"Why in blazes didn't you tell me you weren't going to sleep late? Thought a returned soldier would lie abed to all hours."

"Rather hoped I could, to tell the truth."

Time seemed to slip backwards again in the exhilaration of the ride, memories brought alive by the thudding of the hooves on frosty ground. But the illusion faded. There was nothing to sustain it. His horse was old and in poor shape. The earl was old and embittered. They rode back in silence, along a rutted path. When the house came into view the earl reined in and lit a cigarette.

"Giving it up, Fenton." He waved his cigarette at the distant house. "Moving to London. I'm lending all this to the army. Well, I shan't miss it. It's only a house now, you see. The life I lived in it's gone and all I'm left with is a ruddy big building. I shan't come back here until the war's over." He smoked silently for a moment. "I'm not deluding myself, Fenton. A door's been slammed shut and it will never open again. Even if the war should end tomorrow nothing would ever be the same."

When the earl went in for his breakfast Fenton walked sadly along the weed-dotted terrace. The Pryory was as neglected as everything else, the Italian garden a tangle of unpruned shrubs. It had been a mistake to come down to Abington, a yearning perhaps to recapture something that he knew in his heart was irretrievably gone. The door to the conservatory opened and Charles hurried out. He was in uniform, and he looked harassed.

"I have to take the eight-forty to Salisbury. My so-called commander just rang down and ordered me to Wiltshire, to commandeer some farmer's ruddy tractor and arrange for its shipment to Newbury. Will you drive me to the station?"

As he drove the Rolls-Royce back to the house, Fenton thought up various excuses for going up to London. There didn't seem to be much point in staying on. He found Lydia and Hanna having coffee in the breakfast room.

"Did he make his train?" Lydia asked.

"Just. He asked me to tell you he'll get back to London some time on Monday." He made a show of looking at his watch. "And speaking of London, I'll get the three forty-two. Sorry to cut my stay short, but I've got a devil of a lot of things to do."

"No point in your taking the train," Lydia said casually. "I'm driving up in an hour."

"Oh?" Hanna said.

"Yes. I thought Charles told you. The upholsterer's man is due in this afternoon to measure the windows." She glanced at Fenton. "Charles and I have bought a house in Bristol Street. I'm in the middle of redecorating it."

And that was that. He was grateful to be gone.

Lydia no longer dared drive a German car, but her Napier Six was suitably rakish and powerful. She said nothing until the house was far behind.

"I can't tolerate being alone there without Charles."

"No upholsterer's man?"

"A white lie. I could stand it if Alex was up and about, but she's pretty much taken to her bed. I'm not sure what the matter is. Something happened when she was in France but I can't get a word out of her. Very curious. She used to overwhelm me with confidences." She concentrated on the road. There was little civilian traffic but a good deal of army transport, most of it horse-drawn. "I find you a bit curious as well," she said. "You haven't said one word about Charles and me."

"What am I supposed to say? Are you happy?"

She hesitated slightly. "Yes."

"Do you love him at all?"

"He loves me. That's all that matters."

"Did you get him his job with NS5?"

"I talked to a few people. Is there anything wrong in that?"

"No, but he'll hate you for it if he finds out."

"He will survive. That's all I care about."

"With coronet in place?"

She brushed a loose strand of hair from her forehead, then smiled.

"Please don't play the bastard with me, Fenton."

Lydia parked in front of a narrow, three-storey house that had been built during the reign of George II. The windowsills had been freshly painted white, shutters and front door a gleaming black.

"Handsome-looking place," Fenton said.

"It's quite charming on the inside, too. Care for a drink?"

"I could do with a whisky, yes."

There were ladders in the hall and a smell of turpentine.

"It's more ordered on the upper floors," Lydia said. She led the way up a gently curving staircase to the first-floor landing and into a large room furnished in the Oriental manner, with black and red lacquered cabinets and low divans covered in pale green silk.

"There's whisky in the cabinet. Help yourself while I change."

272

An elderly maid came in to light the fire while Fenton poured himself a whisky. He found himself thinking of Winifred. He was still thinking of her when Lydia came back into the room, her travelling suit replaced by a silk gown in shades of blue and green. There was certainly an air of chic about Lydia that Winifred would never acquire. She closed the doors and walked over to the fire, the glow of the flames turning her loose hair a shimmering copper. He poured her a brandy, then sat beside her on a divan facing the fire.

"How long will you be in England?" she asked.

"Four or five months. I go up to Leeds after the New Year and start training a battalion. One of those old pals conglomerations, all the lads enlisting together. I'll feel a rank outsider."

"I'm sure they'll be proud having a Guards officer commanding them. I know I'd be."

"I can just see myself ordering *you* about."

"That," she said tautly, "would depend on what you ordered me to do."

She set her drink on a low table and turned to him. He moved his arms around her, feeling the warmth of her body beneath the gown.

"I want you, Fenton."

"You *have* Charles."

She undid the middle buttons of his shirt and slipped a hand through the gap. "His love is ethereal. Passion shocks him."

"You'll have to teach him. Be patient."

She kissed him. "I don't feel very patient at the moment," she whispered. "Please, Fenton . . ."

She was warm, vibrant, passionate. Infinitely desirable. But there was a taste of brass in his mouth. The taste of tarnish.

"No." He pushed her gently away from him and stood up. "We're much too late for this, darling Lydia. We quite missed the boat."

She lay back, staring at him. "Charles would never know."

He buttoned his shirt and straightened his tie. "I wasn't thinking of Charles. I was thinking of myself. Everything is becoming so shabby these days. I just don't feel like joining the trend."

"You bastard," she said quietly as he walked out of the room.

273

2

Martin Rilke struggled along Oxford Street, the wind threatening to tear his umbrella from his hand. A middle-aged woman waiting at a bus stop stared at him without sympathy.

"Strong chap like you," she said in a thick Cockney accent. "Slacker."

He was used to them, the insults and the white feathers handed to those out of uniform.

He entered the White Manor at Marble Arch and removed his raincoat and hat. An orchestra upstairs was playing a waltz, fragmented by the clatter of plates. He looked around and finally spotted Ivy seated at a table next to a column. He felt like shouting at the sight of her—he hadn't seen her for three weeks.

"Ivy!" He slid into the chair opposite her and reached across the table to touch her hand. "Gosh, it's good to see you."

She smiled warmly, her hand clenching his, then frowned slightly. "You look pale."

"I know you've been capped, but don't play nurse with me, honey. I'm just weak from hunger."

"So am I."

She could eat, bless her. He felt almost paternal, watching her devour what was placed before her—a pork pie, ham and cress sandwiches, a slice of cake and cup after cup of tea. And yet she was as thin as a waif. She amazed him.

"I have a little something for you. A Christmas present."

She looked at him sternly. "That's not fair. We made a promise not to exchange gifts."

"OK, I welshed on the deal. But I saw this item in Regent Street and I knew you'd like it." He toyed with his cup. "You'll be going soon, won't you?"

"Yes." She crumbled a bit of cake between her fingers. "On January third . . . Number Nine Stationary Hospital in Boulogne."

"Will I be able to see you before you leave?"

"I doubt it. Sorry, Martin, but this is our last . . . *date?* I must remember that word."

"I could come there with you, write an article about Num-

274

ber Nine Stationary Hospital and Sister Ivy Thaxton of the QAs."

"Please don't. It's going to be a difficult time for me. I would be terribly distracted if you were there."

"Would you really?"

"Don't look so pleased with yourself. I shall miss you, Martin."

"I'll sure as heck miss you. Funny, we hardly see each other, except when I get back from France. Yet just knowing that you're in London is a comfort to me. You're my best girl."

Ivy blushed. "You must meet so many girls in . . . well, Paris, places like that."

"Look, you're a daisy and my heart jumps into my throat whenever I see you. OK? Do you believe that?"

"If you say so, yes." Something clearly was troubling her and he wasn't sure what it was. Simple anxiety, he hoped. She had never been out of England before and the idea of going across the Channel to France must be unnerving.

"Let's go over to the flat," he said, "and I'll give you your Christmas present."

The flat was tidy for a change because Jacob rarely spent any time in it. The first time he had brought Ivy there she had spent half an hour, over his protests, tidying things up.

"How about a glass of sherry?"

"No, thank you." She sat stiffly on the edge of the sofa. "Sherry makes me feel tipsy."

"Well," he said lamely, "have it your own way." He clapped his hands with a forced cheerfulness, "Santa Claus has come to town, so close your eyes and don't open them until I say so."

He ducked into the hall and brought out a large package, wrapped in bright paper and tied with a red ribbon. He placed it next to her. "You can open your eyes now."

She had never received a present in her life, at least not one that came wrapped up—just a rag doll and three pennyworth of rock in a Christmas stocking. She looked at the parcel in awe.

"Open it. Go on."

She undid it carefully so as not to tear the paper. A large white box was revealed. She opened it gingerly and stared at the large, glove-leather carrying bag inside, with IVY THAXTON stamped on it in gold.

"Oh, my," she whispered, stroking the leather. "It must have cost a fortune. It's just beautiful."

He kissed the side of her neck. "So are you, Ivy."

She half turned and seemed about to say something, but he stopped her with his lips. She resisted at first and then she suddenly responded with a degree of passion that left them both a little shaken.

"Oh, Ivy, Ivy . . ." he whispered hoarsely, his lips against her cheek, one hand lightly stroking the curve of a breast felt through the serge of her winter uniform.

She moved his hand away with regret. "No, we mustn't . . ."

"Marry me, Ivy."

She drew away from him. "No. You shouldn't ask me."

"Why not? You know how I feel about you. I've done everything but advertise in the papers that I love you."

"And I love you, Martin, really I do, but it wouldn't be right. What would Lady Stanmore say?"

He sensed a bitterness in her tone as she looked away from him. So that was it. The upstairs maid. He put an arm about her shoulders and gave her a hug.

"Aunt Hanna would love you as much as I do. Underneath her English airs she's Hanna Rilke from Prairie Avenue. She wouldn't bat an eye if I told her you were the girl for me."

"I saw her this morning," she said quietly. "She came to hand out little Christmas presents in the convalescent ward. I tried to be inconspicuous, but she spotted me right off."

"And?"

"Oh, she was very gracious, held out her hand and asked me how I was getting along. I don't know what I said. And Lady Alexandra just stood behind her mother, staring, not saying a word. Perhaps she was a bit shocked to see me shaking her mother's hand. There was something in her eyes, a coldness . . . I just don't know how to explain it, Martin."

He attempted to draw her closer to him, but her body was rigid. "Look here, Ivy. That's got nothing to do with us."

"Perhaps not, but you'd still be marrying Lady Alexandra's maid. Can't you just see Mr. Coatsworth's face if he had to serve me at the table?" She smiled to herself and then turned to

Martin and rested her head on his shoulder. "Oh, I know I'm being silly. I really shouldn't care about that. We'd live in America, wouldn't we, Martin? In Chicago, Illinois, railways and cattlemarkets."

"Anywhere you wanted to live," he said, stroking her hair. "The Associated Press want me to leave the *Post* and work for them. AP men go all over the world, and any place they sent me you'd be right there with me."

She nestled closer to him and was silent for a time. Then she said, "I could never marry you until this horror is over."

"I know," he said quietly.

"I've been nursing gas cases the past five weeks. There's so little you can do for them, and they're so terrified."

"Shush," he whispered, holding her tight. "Don't talk about it."

"We lose sixty per cent of them. And they're not the worst ones. The really bad cases are left in Boulogne. They're the ones my team will be nursing. They need me more than you do at the moment, Martin."

He thought of the stumbling, retching men he had seen at Hulluch, their brass buttons turned a vivid green by gas. He held her closer. "I understand," he said.

SHE FELT LIKE walking even though it was dark and the wind was bitter. It wasn't that far and they enjoyed striding briskly side by side along to the sprawling hospital, lights glowing from myriad windows—no blackouts tonight, no fear of Zeppelin raids in this wind. The leather bag hung from Ivy's shoulder on its broad, sheepskin-padded strap and, looking at her out of the corner of his eye, at the smartness of it and her obvious pride of ownership, he couldn't have felt more pleased if he had bought her a diamond ring—although he would have much preferred *that* expense.

"Well, here we are," she said, facing him. The brick building of All Souls Hospital rose behind her like a cliff. "I shall write to you when I get settled and give you my exact address."

He wanted to embrace her, but a great many people were walking past them in and out of the hospital. He bent forward and kissed the tip of her nose. "Take care of yourself." And then he was gone.

She stood for a moment watching him walk away and then she turned and entered the building. A group of sisters passed her on their way out. A tall girl stopped and touched the bag.

"I say, Thaxton. Wherever did you get it?"

"It was a present. From my young man. Isn't it grand?"

"Lovely! Oh, by the way, your friend has been waiting for ages, in the sisters' lounge in D wing."

Friend? What friend? But when Ivy reached the sisters' lounge, there she was, Lady Alexandra.

Ivy was momentarily stunned. "Hello, m'lady,"

Alexandra looked up, her eyes blank. Then she smiled slightly. "Hello, Ivy. I suppose you're surprised to see me."

"Yes." She stood stiffly not knowing what to say. "Have you been here long?"

"A couple of hours I suppose."

"I go back on duty at nine."

Alexandra glanced at a wall clock. "That gives us half an hour. That is, if you can spare me the time."

"Time for what, m'lady?"

"To talk." She reached out and took Ivy gently by the hand. Her fingers were icy. "And please don't keep calling me m'lady. You're not my maid any longer."

No, not a maid any longer, yet she still felt awkward. She could almost hear Mrs. Broome whispering over her shoulder, "Stand up straight, Ivy, and for heaven's sake don't stammer." She felt vaguely sick. How wrong Martin was. But how could an American understand?

She sat on the very edge of the couch. Alexandra still had hold of her hand. "I was surprised to see you this morning, Ivy. I had quite forgotten that you had joined the QAs. You must be very proud." She released her grip and folded her hands in her lap. "I haven't been very well and I didn't want to visit All Souls, but mother insisted that I should come."

"I see." This was not the same Alexandra Greville, Ivy was thinking. Certainly as pretty as ever, and as smartly dressed, but the manner had changed. The bubbling, talkative girl had turned into a sombre, introspective woman. Her eyes looked troubled.

"Mother was quite upset after touring the wards, Ivy. We had

278

lunch at Claridge's and she cried all the way through it." She looked up and her eyes were bitter. "Odd to be so moved. It was a nice ward, wasn't it?"

"A . . . nice ward?"

"I think you know what I mean, Ivy. A show ward. All the lads so cheerful, despite their wounds. And all the wounds so trivial and so neatly bandaged."

"The staff chiefs . . . don't like to upset important visitors."

"You resent my coming here, don't you?" Alexandra asked.

Well, Ivy thought, an honest question deserves an honest answer. "Yes. I don't wish to hurt your feelings, but we really don't have that much to talk about, do we?"

"The reason I came, Ivy, was simply to ask you a few questions. You see, I want to join the QAs."

Her stare was rude, frankly incredulous. "You? I just can't see you going through the training. It's a lot of hard, dirty, exhausting work. There's a Red Cross VAD unit here for ladies—writing letters, rolling bandages—why don't you join that?"

"Oh, dear," Alexandra said, drawing in her breath sharply. "What an awful little snob you turned out to be."

And she was gone, half running down the corridor. Ivy's resentment turned to cheek-burning shame. "Wait!"

She caught up with Alexandra, grabbed her by one arm and pulled her back into the lounge. "I'm *not* a snob," she said.

Alexandra stood stiffly, her face taut and pale. "Yes, you are. It would be like my saying that all *you're* suited for is making beds."

They studied each other like two strangers. But there was a bond of sorts.

"I'm sorry," Ivy said. "I'm sure you didn't wait hours just to tell me that you wanted to join up. You wanted to talk."

"Thank you, Ivy. I joined the Red Cross, you know. I even went to France. Something happened to me there—a kind of breakdown —and although I want very badly to become a military nurse, I have this fear that I might break down again."

It was so quiet that Ivy could hear the thumping of her heart. "Tell me about it," she said.

As Alexandra told of her trip to the casualty clearing station at Kemmel, Ivy kept her eyes on her face, seeing pain and honesty mirrored there. She could visualize the Alexandra she had known, play-acting the role of a nurse in her elegant, expensive uniforms from the House of Ferris. Reaching out, she took Alexandra by the hand and pressed firmly. "You don't have to tell me what happened there. I can guess."

"They needed help so badly," she whispered. "Hundreds of men, Ivy, men without arms, legs, faces. I failed them. . . ."

"You didn't fail anyone," Ivy said sternly. "You can't fail at something that you weren't equipped to do in the first place."

A nearby church bell pealed the first stroke of nine.

They walked slowly down the corridor towards the main entrance. Nurses and doctors passed them, some nodding in recognition to Ivy, all eyeing Alexandra in her sable coat with varying degrees of curiosity.

"I look out of place," Alexandra said.

"Do you feel out of place? I mean . . . will you be comfortable in the QAs? Or are you just trying to prove something?"

"I want to be useful," she said flatly.

Ivy stopped and faced her. "We all have a certain amount of fear every time we walk into a ward. The only courage you need is the courage to stick out twelve months of training." She paused. "I must go. Perhaps we can talk again tomorrow."

Alexandra bent quickly forward and kissed her on the cheek. "I'll be joining up tomorrow. Goodnight, *Sister* Thaxton."

"Well, I never," Ivy murmured, holding one hand to her cheek. She watched Alexandra cross the vast entrance hall, crowded now with departing visitors, and, stretched above the door, a sign lettered by the ambulatory patients: PEACE ON EARTH, GOOD WILL TOWARDS MEN.

FENTON WOOD-LACY spent Christmas with his parents in Suffolk, and returned to London on the Thursday before New Year. It was dark when the train pulled into King's Cross. He took a taxi to Cadogan Square. Number Twenty-four.

If the butler was surprised at the lateness of the call he did not show it by so much as a blink of the eye. "Lady Winifred, sir? I do believe she has retired for the night."

"Who the devil's at the door, Peterson?" Lord Dexford emerged from the gloom in maroon smoking jacket and carpet slippers. "Fenton, by Gad! What the devil you doin' here at this hour?"

"I was . . . in the neighbourhood," he said lamely. "Sorry if I woke up the household. I didn't realize it was so late."

"Nonsense." The marquess dismissed the butler with a gesture. "It's good to have company. Just goin' to have a nightcap."

A shaft of light fell on the dark stairs as a door opened on the first floor, and Fenton looked up at the figure standing by the balustrade. "I'm sorry, Winifred. I intended to telephone. . . ."

Lord Dexford scowled at Fenton and then glared up at his daughter. "Either come down or go back to bed, Winnie. As for me, I'm going to the library and closin' the door."

She came down the stairs, clad in a long, quilted satin dressing gown, her hair loose about her shoulders, and sat on the third step from the bottom. "What an odd man you are, Fenton."

"Impulsive . . . also a bit reflective." He leaned beside her, hands in his trenchcoat pockets. "I've been doing a lot of thinking the past few days. You said we're different people now, but essentially I don't think anything will ever change us."

She folded her arms about her knees. "You came to propose, didn't you?"

"Yes."

"That'll make Father very happy."

"It's not your father I care about pleasing."

"It'll make me happy, too. I love you, Fenton. I fell in love with you when I was sixteen. Or was it your scarlet jacket I fell in love with then? Difficult to say. I don't love you for your jacket now." She looked at him in silence, then hugged her knees tighter to her body. "One thing has been left unsaid. Do you love me?"

"If wanting to be with you is loving you, if feeling at peace is loving, then, yes, I love you."

She nodded sombrely. "How honest you are. Where shall we be married?"

"I thought we could . . . well, go up to Scotland tomorrow and get married in Gretna Green. That is, if you don't mind."

"Oh, Lord," she laughed. "What will Mother say?"

"She won't have a chance to say anything." Lord Dexford stepped into the hall, a bottle of champagne under each arm.

"Knew how the wind was blowin', Fenton. Put the bottles in your kit bag. The Royal Mail leaves Euston at midnight. You have plenty of time to make it if you can hurry your packin', Winnie."

3

It had been raining steadily in Yorkshire and the factory on the outskirts of Huddersfield was surrounded by a lake of mud. When the army car which had brought Charles from Leeds pulled up in front of the main building he saw a small sign on one of the doors: ROLLS-ROYCE MOTOR WORKS—EXPERIMENTAL. The War Office had decided that the caterpillar-tread landship, now called "tank" MkI, or Big Willie, was low on power. Charles was here to check out specifications on a new engine.

A gangling young man wearing a blue work smock stepped outside to meet him. "Lord Amberley? My name's Wilson. I'm plant manager here. Our Mr. Ross is over in shed Number Four."

Big Willie was inside a large corrugated iron building, electric lights shining off its steel-plated sides, a great, rhomboid-shaped monster. There was the dull boom of heavy hammers from inside the hull. Charles and Wilson climbed onto the back of the tank and peered into the open hatch.

"Is Mr. Ross there?" Wilson yelled.

The hammering ceased and a tousled-haired man in grease-stained overalls emerged from the hull. Charles stared at him in disbelief. "But . . . you're *our* Ross!"

Jamie Ross grinned and pulled himself out of the hatch. "Not exactly *your* Ross any longer, m'lord." He wiped his fingers on a cloth and held out his right hand. "But it's fair good to see you."

"I'm quite flabbergasted, Ross. I knew you'd gone to the Rolls-Royce company, but to find you here . . . ."

"I've been at this factory the past three months." He folded his arms and looked Charles up and down. "Major now. You one of the chaps responsible for this clanking dragon of a thing?"

"Not really. Just sort of an overseer."

"I talked to one of your bunch in London the other day. He said the machine was underpowered. That's a bit of a laugh, you know.

282

This must weigh thirty tons and its got a hundred and five horse-power engine in it. Doubt if you'd get more'n three miles to the hour on a dead flat, hard-paved road."

"Do you have a better engine?" Charles asked.

"Oh, yes. We have a three fifty horsepower in the testing stage. Aircraft engine. But we won't have them on the factory line for at least four months."

"They can't wait four months for a new engine," Charles said. "Can you coax more power from what we've got?"

Ross closed his eyes and clasped his hands behind his back. He rocked slowly on his heels for a minute and then said, "If you could give my lads three days, round the clock. . . ."

"Of course," Charles said.

"Modifications with available parts. It would make a ruddy big difference in performance."

"Sounds good," Charles said.

"Fine. We'll get on with it then. Like a mug of tea?"

"Yes . . . I would, please."

It seemed odd to be walking beside Jamie Ross, odder still to be seated across from him in the tiny engineering office. Ross poured two mugs of sweet, milky tea and then seated himself behind a battered desk.

"I read about Mr. Wood-Lacy dyin' at Gallipoli. Sorry. He was a nice chap. How's his lordship and her ladyship?"

"They're fine, thank you."

"And Lady Alexandra?"

"She's in London, training as a nurse . . . at All Souls Hospital."

Ross shook his head. "Hard to believe. She was tango-mad last time I saw her. The world do change a bit, don't it?"

Charles stared into his tea. "Yes, it does."

"Been changin' a bit for me, too. I got seven patents on this new engine. The company's sendin' me to America at the end of the month. The Yanks are going to build the bulk of 'em under licence for us, Lor', think of it. Me, Jamie Ross, goin' to America." He sipped reflectively at his tea. "I never knew you were interested in mechanical things."

"No. And I'm still not terribly interested."

Ross smiled. "I get the picture. The army chaps turn deaf when a man with grease on his hands speaks to 'em. I suppose you tell the brass. Is that it?"

"Something like that."

CHARLES STAYED at the factory for the next two days, forty-eight hours with virtually no sleep. He kept meticulous notes of each procedure. When the job was completed to Ross's satisfaction, the men from the test centre at Hatfield Park, who had brought the tank, drove it onto a wagon on the railway siding. They then covered it with canvas so that not an inch of its metal body could be seen.

"And that's that," Ross said. "What do you do now?"

"Follow it down to the test ground and demonstrate it for some generals and war ministers. Rather like selling a terribly expensive motorcar to people who don't really want to buy one. Above all, I keep cheerful, even if the damned thing runs off its tracks."

Ross shook his head in wonder. "Queer way to fight a war."

"Yes. I think it is." Charles held out his hand. "Good luck in America, Ross. You know what you can do and you do it to perfection. I admire that. You must be a very happy man."

Ross frowned slightly. "Well, I don't know about that, but I'm satisfied. Is that what you mean?"

"Yes. I suppose it is, Ross. I suppose it is."

LYDIA WAS DRESSING for a dinner engagement when he came home after the demonstration, dried mud on his boots.

"Charles! You could at least have telephoned."

He slumped into a small velvet chair in her dressing room.

She glanced over a white, powdered shoulder. "Are you tipsy?"

"God, no. Just worn to the bone. Big Willie did himself proud for a change. Even knocked over a small tree. Went seven miles at four miles per hour and didn't break down once. General Haldane was so pleased he smiled, at least I think it was a smile. He thanked me and I told him I was chucking it in, resigning from NS5. He wasn't the least bit surprised."

"That's ridiculous. You can't resign. You don't have medical clearance. Don't make gestures, Charles."

"It's not a gesture. I want to be doing something that fits my

284

abilities for a change—and my temperament. I want something . . . manly. I want to be a company commander and take my chance in the line like everyone else."

She turned in her chair and looked at him. "I fail to see anything *manly* in wanting to get killed."

"I don't expect to be killed. I expect to serve a few tours in trenches and then be given a battalion to train, like Fenton."

"Really, Charles, your conception of duty belongs to another century! What about your duty to me? There are more than enough widows these days without you going out of your way to create another one!"

"There's no point in our talking about it," he said, getting to his feet. "You simply wouldn't understand."

"Why? Because I'm not of your class? For God's sake, Charles, don't turn your *noble heritage* into high bloody farce!"

He left quietly. He did not slam the door, but there was a finality about his departure. She looked at herself in the mirror. Lydia Amberley, future Countess of Stanmore, *German bullets permitting*. Her childhood dream. A dream from an age rapidly fading. No, she thought, an age already gone.

4

"*Observations and Reflections. June 24, 1916*. In a front-line observation post with Fenton Wood-Lacy. The barrage began today—one man to every seventeen yards of German trench. A day-and-night bombardment for a week before the *Big Push* right along the River Somme. This is the New Army for the most part, battalions of chums joining up together. A people's army.

There is simply no way to describe the power of this barrage. Birds flutter in confusion above Aveluy Wood. The earth rocks and the air reeks—battle reporting cliché number 346—but, dammit, the earth *does* rock and the air *does* reek. Not a shred of cloud and the heat is intense. One can see a twinkle of brassy specks in the sky as the howitzer shells pause in their arcs before plunging to earth. Bolts of flame erupt from the German lines. It seems inconceivable that so much as a rat could be alive over there.

June 27. Fenton and several other officers checking the effect of the bombardment on the German wire. The belts of wire with their inch-long barbs are a hundred yards deep in some places. A jungle of steel brambles. Eighteen-pounder guns fire shrapnel to cut the thickets. Not too effective. To compound their concern, one of those freak summer rainstorms has swept in and the churned-up ground will make tough going for the infantry.

July 1. Men packed into the forward trenches five hundred yards from where I sit in what had once been a fine old wood. Barrage has been continuous all night. Suddenly ceases at 7.30. Silence catches at the heart and I can clearly hear the whistles blowing up and down the line. One hundred and fifty thousand Englishmen climb out of their trenches and start across. Twinkle of sunlight off bayonets for as far as the eye can see in both directions. The men are heavily laden and walk slowly, almost casually, in lines, nearly shoulder to shoulder. A Highland battalion off to my right is being piped across.

Machine guns at a distance sound ineffectual, a metallic, rattling sound, like a marble shaken in a tin can, but the lines of walking men begin to melt away. Some begin to run towards the German wire. They do not get far. Others waver, turn in confusion and drop. The second wave plods on, the third wave follows the second. There may not be many Germans left alive in the shell-pulverised trenches, but there are enough. Their machine guns scythe the middle ground and the Tommies die where they stand. Difficult to write . . . hands shaking badly. The generals were quite wrong . . . battle of the Somme will not be won today —or tomorrow, or the day after that. . . ."

COLONEL ROBIN MACKENDRIC was taking his turn as marshalling officer at the casualty clearing station at Corbie, examining each stretcher case that was brought in, sorting out those men who needed immediate surgery and might live because of it; those who would die no matter what was done; and those who could be dealt with at one of the base hospitals in Rouen. The number of men in the second group seemed to increase daily.

He was checking his sixtieth case when Major Vale came into the ward. His fellow surgeon was not drunk, but he was far from

286

being sober. He slumped happily into a canvas chair. "Met some Australian chaps in Corbie, marvellous fellows, knew of an *estaminet* near the junction that serves real English beer. Sat, talked, watched the trains go by."

"I'm glad you enjoyed yourself."

Vale got clumsily to his feet, yawning. "And I spotted an absolutely smashing QA in the junction off one of the hospital trains. Blonde stunner . . . seen her before. I'd swear it was the same girl who went bonkers on us at Kemmel. Remember?"

"Yes."

"Friend of yours or something, wasn't she?"

"Something like that."

That night, Robbie stayed awake, trying to read. There were sounds all about him—the rattle of the dressing carts in the corridor, the rumble of gunfire from Delville Wood—but he heard nothing. He was miles away, walking hand-in-hand with her along the Rue Saint Honoré. Had that really been him? He felt old and tired. His fingers ached constantly from clenching instruments for too many hours a day, too many days. Burning himself out. Thirty-three and he felt like an old man. She would be what now? Twenty? She had taken his advice and undertaken the training to become a nurse. Perhaps she had taken the rest of his advice as well and had met a man of her own age and forgotten all about him. He would never know unless he talked to her.

THE TRAINS came empty into Corbie, were shunted onto a spur where the ambulances and the walking wounded were waiting. He spotted her among a score of nurses with two hundred New Zealanders lying patiently on their stretchers. She was giving ATS shots with cool proficiency, checking dressings, telling the bearers in which carriage to place the men whom she had tagged. Rain thudded off the corrugated iron roof of the platform.

"Your efficiency is to be commended, Sister."

She paused, but did not look up at him. "Hello, Robbie."

Her hands were sure and knowing on a dirty scrap of bandage covering a mud-encrusted leg. He watched her wash an area of flesh around the jagged holes in the calf with soap solution, then wrap a clean bandage around the leg. She made a motion with one hand and the bearers lifted the stretcher and carried it into the train.

"Next," she said, straightening up. Her eyes met his for the first time. It was like an embrace. "You're good to see, Robbie."

"Do you mean that, Alex?" His voice was solemn.

She nodded fiercely. "Yes, yes, I do. Now please go or I shan't be able to concentrate. If . . . if you can get away this Saturday . . . ."

"I will," he said flatly.

"AND THERE WOULD be nights when we could be together, in some country inn."

He could remember her saying that in Paris. No country inns in the Ypres salient. But this was Normandy. Apple trees and rich earth between the great loops of the Seine. Clusters of villages with stone houses. Inns with clean linen and feather beds. He held her tightly, watching the sunset through the windows, one hand drifting idly down her naked back. She turned slightly in his arms and moved her lips across his chest.

"I shall never give you up," she whispered.

"I won't talk you out of it, although I should at least try."

"It would only be a gesture. You want me, Robbie."

"Yes. I want you." He held her silently, then he said, "I didn't tell you about Dennis. He's in Ottawa . . . flying instructor. He wrote me a long letter about Canada—quite a different world. If this war ever does end, I'd go there. I want a new sort of life. I've asked my wife for a divorce, but she could deny it."

"It won't matter," she said, her voice husky. "I don't care. I'll go with you, Robbie, married or not."

"You might regret that one day, Alex."

"Never . . . ."

THE RUNNER from brigade HQ came along Ale trench, paused for a second and then turned into Stout, moving swiftly at a half crouch like a large and wily rat. A bullet cracked loudly as it passed over the narrow trench. Sniper's corner; but he had been this way before and knew the bad spots. Stout was a horrible trench, tumbled in from shelling, full of deep, muddy sumps and broken duckboards. It meandered in and around the shattered trunks of blackened trees. Cadavers had been spaded into the

288

parapet and bony fingers and legs mingled with the snaky roots of the trees. The stench on a hot day was enough to stifle a man, but it was September now, and cold; the smell wasn't too bad.

The shriek of a five point nine sent him head first to the trench bottom and he hugged the crumbling sides as the shell exploded ten yards behind the trench. He got up and ran on, turning sharply to his right into Watling trench. There he rested and lit a cigarette. Watling was deep and the sandbagging in good repair. A sentry kneeled against the parados above him, so caked with mud the runner didn't see him until he turned his head.

"Can you spare a fag, chum?"

The runner handed up his cigarette and lit another for himself. "This the Second Windsors?"

"You got it, chum. Which comp'ny you lookin' for?"

"Battalion commander."

"Major Amberley. First communication trench and back fifty yards. Can't bloody well miss it. Thanks for the smoke."

"Think nothin' of it, mate." The runner scurried on his way. He was not surprised to find a major commanding the battalion. There was a rumour that after Delville Wood only a lance corporal was left to lead one of the battalions.

Charles slit the flimsy envelope the runner had brought and read the contents, holding the paper under the hissing pressure lamp which dangled from the ceiling of the dugout.

"No reply," he said crisply. "Tell the storeman to give you a double tot of rum."

The adjutant stirred on his wire mesh bunk. "What's up?"

Charles stared at the paper. "We're to attack Hanoverian redoubt at 0800 tomorrow with A and B. No whimsy about taking the ruddy place. We're to draw fire, while the New Zealanders go in.

The adjutant lay back with a groan. "Bloody waste."

Charles sat down at the table and sipped his tea. It was ice cold and tasted of kerosene. The stupidity of the order caused his hand to tremble with rage. The battalion had lost nine officers and two hundred men in their last attack, half the casualties occurring as the men went through their own wire. One corporal had managed to get close enough to the German positions to hurl a Mills bomb and he had died throwing it. And now they wanted another attack on a totally impregnable position carried out in broad daylight.

The adjutant swung his legs off the bed and scratched his chest. "Do you realize something, Charles? We've pushed the Germans four miles since the first of July. Young Baker figured it out last night. By his calculations we'll have 'em over the Rhine by 1938."

"I think Baker's an idiot," he said savagely. "If he had told me, I'd have put him on a charge."

DAWN CAME in misty rain. Charles put a whistle between his teeth and looked at his wristwatch—0757, 58, 59—he knew that if he survived the war he would never be able to wear a wristwatch again—0800. He blew a shrill blast on the whistle, and two hundred men from A Company scrambled up the ladders, bunching through the pre-cut gaps in their own wire. Ten yards, twenty; they were scrambling in and out of old craters, bayonets gleaming through the mist; thirty yards now, forty; almost to the German wire, fifty yards deep. Signal rockets hissed upwards from the enemy lines, bursting yellow and green against the low clouds.

"Damn . . . oh, damn," Charles whispered as he heard the drone of howitzer shells, the drones turning to shrieks, the shrieks to thunderbolts and vomiting geysers of earth and flame. Clods of earth and truncated men hung motionless for a split second against the grey sky. What was left of A Company scattered away from the wire and dived for the steaming shell holes.

0810. Charles blew his whistle with a dry mouth. B Company was slow to leave the trench. Whistles were blowing furiously and the platoon leaders were cursing and shouting. The men went up the ladders and through the wire, keeping low. Then heavy German machine guns started to hammer through slits in the thick concrete revetments ahead, catching the men waist high and ripping along the top of the sandbagged parados.

"You rotten little coward!" Lieutenant Baker's voice, high pitched with hysteria. "I should damn well shoot you!"

Charles hurried out of the observation gap into the front trench, to where Baker was standing flourishing a revolver.

"What's the matter?" Charles shouted.

The lieutenant pointed his weapon at a private who sat slumped against the fire step. Blood poured from under the soldier's right

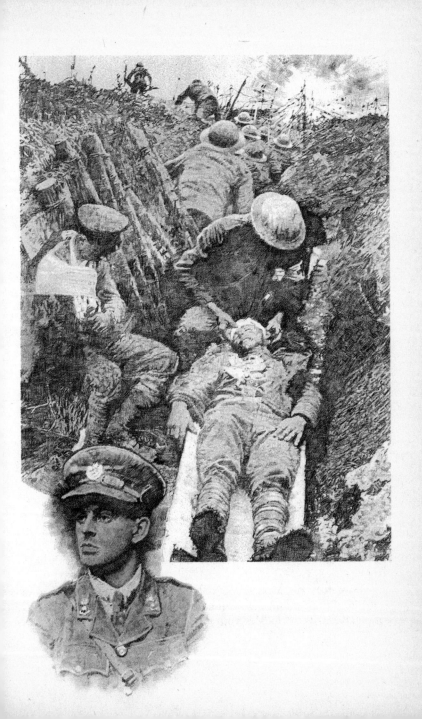

boot. "Shot himself in the foot! Ordered him up the ladder and he just reversed his rifle and gave himself a Blighty." He waved the revolver under the man's nose. "It's a firing squad for you!"

"Get him back to the aid post," Charles ordered.

"Under guard?"

He looked at the soldier. His eyes were dull, uncaring, oblivious even to the pain of his wound. He was no more than eighteen.

"Yes," Charles said dully. "Under guard, of course."

They would tie him to a post more than likely, shoot him by firing squad. Damn, he thought, clenching and unclenching his fists, why hadn't the man been clever enough not to shoot himself in front of his lieutenant! But what was one more corpse?

The Boche machine-gun fire had ceased. Out between the wire somewhere a man was screaming, ragged shrieks and sobs. The sound went on and on, rising and falling, dwindling at times but never ending. 0830. When night came he would send out the stretcher bearers. He prayed fervently that the shrieking man would be hours dead by then.

PARIS (AP) December 12, 1916. Martin Rilke of the Paris bureau of the Associated Press has been released from the Hôpital St. Antoine after suffering severe wounds on the Somme front in September. He is recuperating satisfactorily at St. Germain en Laye outside Paris.

The house that Martin Rilke had rented was set in the middle of a well-cultivated garden, surrounded by dense groves of beech and pine. It was a small, two-storey house of weathered limestone, and had stood empty since the Germans threatened Paris in the first weeks of the war.

Ivy Thaxton arrived four days before Christmas, walking the three kilometres from the railway station to the house, her leather carrying bag slung over one shoulder. Martin came out to meet her on the path, walking stiffly with two canes.

"Why didn't you take a taxi?" he called. "You shouldn't have walked."

"I love to walk! And it was only a mile or two." Ivy stopped in front of him, smiling, brushing a strand of black hair from her forehead. "Oh my, look at you, the wounded warrior."

"Just a shell-scratched scribe," Martin said, forgetting the pain in his hip at the sight of her. "Gosh, but you're a tonic, Ivy."

She held out her hands to him. "Come on, in you get. I want you on the bed with your trousers down."

"What?"

"You heard me. I want to take a look at your wound."

After some protestations he led the way into his downstairs bedroom, lay on the bed and glowered at the ceiling as Ivy took down his trousers. The red weal traversed the right hip and dipped down across the upper thigh. He closed his eyes and clenched his jaw as her gentle fingers traced the scar.

"No inflammation," she said. "You're a lucky man, Martin. You missed emasculation by an inch. Do you have any unguent? It looks puckered and must itch badly."

"I itch all over, Ivy. It's called yearning-for-Ivy-Thaxton disease and it's curable."

"Where's the unguent?" she asked crisply. He told her where to find it, and she rubbed the yellow ointment into the edges of the scar. "You can pull up your trousers now."

He did so gratefully, letting his breath out through his mouth. "This is a hell of a time to propose, Ivy, but I wish you'd give it some thought. I wouldn't expect you to quit nursing any more than you'd expect me to give up reporting the war, but you have two weeks of leave, and two weeks of happiness isn't a bad deal in these times."

"Well, if you really *want* to take on the obligation of a wife . . ."

"Oh, boy, do I!" He pulled himself up. "Call for a taxi! Alert the mayor that he's got a wedding to perform!"

"Will it be legal?" Ivy asked, looking worried.

"Of course it's legal! What kind of a guy do you take me for? *Monsieur le Maire* can marry anyone. We can always have a church ceremony one day, Ivy, if you'd like that."

She leaned forward and kissed him. "I don't care, Martin, just so long as I can write to Mum and Da with a clear conscience."

There was no taxi, but there was a wheelchair and no lack of strong arms at the local inn, willing to push *le bon Americain* into town, especially for such a purpose. Ivy walked beside the wheelchair as two stablehands pushed him. After a brief ceremony and

293

celebration in the town hall, the mayor drove them back to the house in his wheezing Renault.

"I am happy," Martin sighed. "Drunk with joy."

"And champagne."

"'Fill every glass, for wine inspires us, and fires us with courage, love and joy . . .' *The Beggar's Opera.* There's more to it— something about women being the most desirable things on earth. But only one woman, Ivy."

"Observations and reflections. The House. December 25, 1916. The House, *our* House. Ivy cut a small pine tree and dragged it through the snow, the first real snowfall of the winter; soft, wet flakes drifting from the grey sky. I helped her set it in a wooden keg filled with sandy soil, and we decorated the branches with strips of red and yellow cloth, tiny silver teaspoons tied on with thread, holly berries from a bush in the garden, tin foil from cigarettes. It's beautiful.

After lunch I was able to mount the stairs with no problem. I sat down on the bed to ease my leg and Ivy sat beside me. We made love, she protesting at first that making love in the middle of the day is wicked. Pale sun through large windows. Is there anything more lovely than her body tinged with such a light?

Distant thunder growled and bumped along the horizon making us both think of the Somme barrage. But now the Somme battles are bogged down in mud, snow and freezing rain, the armies more exhausted than spent lovers could ever hope to be.

She goes back soon for re-assignment, most probably to London —which is how my luck runs. Still, I'll be able to wangle a trip to Blighty every month or so and we can use Jacob's flat. . . ."

CHARLES AMBERLEY studied the lists placed on his desk by the adjutant. The names of the living and the names of the dead. Few of the names were familiar to him. The battalion had received far too many replacements for that. Names without faces.

Roster—2nd Royal Windsor Fusiliers
Duty strength July 18, 1916: Officers 36; Other ranks 1005
Duty strength January 3, 1917: Officers 8; Other ranks 325

He signed his name on the bottom of the typewritten sheet. "And that's that, I suppose." The signing of the roster was his last official act. The new battalion commander would be arriving from St. Omer in a day or two.

"Well, Charles," the adjutant said, holding out his hand. "You did a bloody fine job."

And that was that. Charles's leave papers were in his pocket. Lorry to Amiens, train to Rouen, leave boat to Southampton, train to London. Twenty-four hours after shaking the adjutant's hand he was walking through Waterloo station with a thousand other men back in Blighty on leave.

"Charles! Charles!"

Her voice was thin against the clatter of hobnail boots. He hadn't expected her to meet him at the station, but there she was, beautiful in dark furs, waving to him from the far end of the platform.

"Hello, Lydia."

"Charles." She kissed his cheek. He took her firmly in his arms and kissed her hard on the mouth.

"That's the way, ol' sport," a passing sergeant called out.

"It's good to have you back, Charles." She touched his face with a gloved hand. "Are you all right?"

"I'm fine. Not a scratch."

He couldn't tell her how he felt because he couldn't explain; disembodied, as though he were two people walking side by side. Flesh and shadow, and difficult to know which of the two was *him*.

The house in Bristol Street seemed alien to him when they got there. A stranger's house. He was afraid to touch anything. It was all too clean and too fragile. His bath was drawn by a maid he could not remember ever having met, although she seemed to know him.

"So nice to have you back, m'lord."

Back where?

The bath was warm and pleasantly scented. He sat tautly in its steamy murk and ran his hands lightly across the surface of the water. The palest of light filtered through the curtains and glowed against the bathroom walls. He was not there. He was floating off in some vast distance of time and space. Silent shells burst in a wasteland of pollarded trees. A man writhed against ripped sand-bags mouthing silent screams. He was above it all. An impassive watcher. Beyond feelings of any sort. The shadows of the platoon slipped through curtains of rain, became lost to view, then re-emerged beyond the wire. Half a dozen bent figures.

Christ! Where's the rest of them?

Whose voice was that, he wondered? It hardly mattered. They were dead, of course. Foolish of the chap to have even asked.

"Charles? Are you all right?" Lydia tapping at the door and calling his name.

"Perfectly," he said in a flat, tired voice.

WATCHING HIS FATHER carve the sirloin of beef made Charles think of the parable of the prodigal son. "Alex not home?" he asked.

The earl paused in his carving to swipe the knife against the steel. "No. Decided to spend her leave in Paris. And your brother William's training with the Public Schools' Battalion. He gets passed out as a second lieutenant next week."

"Difficult to believe," Charles said as Coatsworth bent forward to serve him. The slices of beef sent rivulets of scarlet juice across the white plate.

His mother seemed to be sending signals to him, and so when she excused herself right after dinner, complaining of a sudden headache, he dutifully escorted her up to her room.

"Is your headache better?" he asked as he closed her door behind him.

"Much." She faced him, her face pale. "May I be blunt with you, Charles?"

"By all means."

"William has become a terrible concern to me. I can understand his anxiety to join up. He's eighteen now, big, strong, fiercely patriotic. I can't fault that, can I?"

"No." He thought of young Baker waving his pistol at the infantryman who had shot himself in the foot. Baker was in hospital now. Both eyes blown out by a German shell. "It's becoming a boys' war now, Mother."

Her hand darted to her throat, fingers worrying a string of beads. "William is such a superb horseman. It would please your

296

father if he took a commission in the Queen's Bays. One was offered."

"Oh. Naturally he's turned the offer down?"

"Why *naturally*? It's one of the most prestigious regiments."

"The cavalry's a joke. All dressed up and nowhere to go."

"If . . . if he were *ordered* into the Bays . . ."

"As I was *ordered* into NS5?" He smiled and shook his head. "It won't work, Mother. You and Lydia should know better."

"What has Lydia got to do with it?" she asked cautiously.

"You know perfectly well, Mother. Lydia has *entrée*. Now more than ever with Lloyd George in Downing Street, and David Langham as . . . what? The grey eminence? I'm sure Lydia could get Willie posted to the Bays—ordered, if you will—but he'd only slip out of it, by resigning his commission, and then re-enlist as a private in an infantry regiment. He'd be commissioned by that regiment the same day. Officers with fighting spirit are ducking out of the cavalry every day using that dodge."

Hanna's laugh was like a wail. "Fighting spirit! William is too young to have *fighting spirit*. He thinks the war's a game."

"I'm sorry, Mother, but we must all take our chances."

IT WAS MORNING, shopkeepers opening their shutters, the day bright and clear. Patches of snow in the street, dirty grey piles in the gutters. Charles walked slowly until he came to Conduit Street before daring to stop and look back. No one was behind him, and yet he could have sworn someone had been following him. Odd. Shadow and substance. Which was which? He continued walking, more quickly than before and he was quite alone this time. Just Charles Amberley in uniform, his trench coat well buttoned up against the wind. He turned sharply, a drill turn, into Burlington Street and then into Savile Row. In the window of one shop he spotted a small, neatly printed sign which read: OFFICERS' TRENCH ACCESSORIES. He went in, the door ringing a copper bell as he opened it.

He selected what he wanted from a display case and the clerk nodded his approval. "A fine choice, if I may say so, sir. Would you also be interested in a truly first-rate trench compass?"

"No. This will suffice. Thank you for your patience."

"No trouble at all, Major. We are here to serve."

He swung onto a bus leaving Piccadilly Circus and got out at Wimbledon. He walked to the Common, towards neat rows of canvas-roofed wooden and tarpaper huts. A sentry from the Public Schools' Battalion standing on guard at the entrance to the camp presented arms as Charles walked through the gate.

"Dashed nice of you to drop in, Major," the second-in-command said, leaning back against his desk. "I believe we met in France last August, at Albert."

"Perhaps. There was another Public Schools' Battalion at High Wood."

Charles looked out of the window of the hut. He could see squads of men marching in lines, a group far away spearing straw dummies with bayonets.

There was a crisp knock on the door and then William stepped into the hut, his boots and puttees covered with mud. He saluted his own major smartly and then grinned at Charles.

"Major Lord Amberley, sir!"

"Hello, Willie," Charles said. "I've brought you something useful to have in the trenches."

The duty clerks heard the quick splatter of shots and burst into the room from the outer office. Acrid blue smoke hung in spirals, drifting down towards the figure writhing on the floor, clutching a bullet-splintered knee. They hurled themselves on the trench-coated man holding a pocket pistol. He did not offer any resistance as he let the gun fall from his hand.

"What in God's name did you do?" the second-in-command shouted, coming out of his momentary paralysis.

"I gave him a Blighty," Charles said calmly. "He didn't shoot himself . . . he didn't shoot himself."

5

The rain had ceased, but ominous banks of cloud obscured the peaks of the Welsh mountains and slipped like dark smoke into the valleys. The ivy-covered façade of Llandinam War Hospital was shrouded in mist.

"Ugly-looking place," Fenton muttered as his driver pulled up in front of the iron gates.

Martin, seated beside Fenton in the back, leaned forward to peer through the windscreen. "An old castle?"

"No, just some Victorian coal baron's idea of a fitting house for himself. Wales is littered with such monstrosities. All of them," he added bitterly, "eminently suitable as lunatic asylums."

The sprawling house became less forbidding when they drove up to it. It could have been the clubhouse of some ancient and noble golf club if it hadn't been for the ambulances parked in front of it.

"I shall wait for you, shall I?" the driver asked in a sing-song voice.

"Yes," Fenton said. "We want to catch the London train at Llangollen at six thirty. I'm sure you can get a cup of tea if you can find the kitchens."

Martin walked slowly beside Fenton to the front door, leaning on his cane—only one cane now, a major advance in his recovery.

In the hall a corporal in the RAMC led them to a locked security door and told them to go along the passage to the office of the resident doctor on duty. Once they stepped into the corridor the oak and steel door closed with a thud behind them.

"I don't like one damned thing about this," Fenton muttered.

The doctor was a jovial, heavy-set man of fifty who introduced himself as Major Wainbearing. "A specialist in brain disease and psycho-analytic science. Learning a great deal from this war, quite a gold mine of neurasthenic ailments." He leaned back in his comfortable chair in his pleasant office and smiled affably. "Now, then, you are Mr. Rilke, I take it . . . Lord Amberley's cousin."

"Yes, that's right."

"And you, of course, are Colonel Wood-Lacy." The doctor folded his hands across his stomach, a sudden frown appearing on his elderly cherub's face. "Lord Amberley was brought here as a clearly diagnosed neurasthenic. He was passive, but he was hallucinating: deep in conversation with a certain Second-Lieutenant Baker, a rambling monologue on Blighty wounds and firing squads. Are either of you familiar with a Lieutenant Baker?" They shook their heads. "No matter. He was quite normal within a week. He has remained so. We walked out of the grounds last Monday and played a round of golf."

"How nice," Fenton murmured.

"He did damned well, considering the appalling state of the greens. I told him that I was prepared to release him from here and to recommend a medical discharge from the army. Cured, you understand, but obviously too . . . *carefully* balanced to risk further military duties. I told him to go to some quiet spot and avoid stress of all sorts."

"Sound advice," Fenton said with thinly-veiled sarcasm.

"He told me, in his gentle way, that if I did such a thing he would contrive, in some unspecified manner, to kill himself."

"Do you think he was being serious?" Martin asked.

"Oh, no doubt in my mind at all."

"Perhaps if we talk to him . . . ." Fenton said.

"Yes, by all means do. He's been looking forward to your visit, the only two people he wishes to see. His mother and his wife came here last month but he refused to talk to them." He reached out and pushed a button on his desk. "One of the orderlies will take you to him. He'll be in the rec room. And do stay for tea. We have a wizard pastry chef here."

The recreation room was large and airy with an untidy collection of sofas, chairs, card tables and benches. A dozen men in grey dressing-gowns and pyjamas were reading or playing whist. One player's hands shook so violently that he could barely hold his cards.

"Lord Amberley is over there," the orderly said. "At the corner table."

He was in uniform, bent studiously over a writing tablet, and did not look up until they stood in front of him.

"Hello, chaps," he said quietly. "Good of you both to come."

"The least we could do," Fenton said with forced affability.

"You look good, Charles," Martin said.

"I feel very well," he said gravely. "They say that I'm cured. Of course, they don't say exactly what one has been cured *of.* They do some quite remarkable things here in their quiet way. All through the gentle art of conversation. One simply talks. It supposedly clears the mind."

300

Fenton pulled two chairs up to the table. "And now you may talk to us, if you'll permit me to get right to the point."

Charles capped his pen and set it down beside the writing pad. "I'm sure you feel uncomfortable being here, but you can both help me, if you will." He sorted through some neatly-inscribed envelopes. "I wrote a long letter to my father and one to William at Charing Cross Hospital. Both were sent back to me unopened. There's not much point in writing to William again. I doubt if he will understand, or forgive, what I did. Perhaps he will one day, but not now. I've written a shorter explanation to Father which I would appreciate your handing to him, Martin. He might feel obliged to at least open it if he receives it from you. The other letter is for Lydia. It's an apology—of sorts—for all manner of things. But I shan't bore you two with that. As for you, Fenton, I ask a favour."

"Anything at all, old chap."

Charles picked up the pen and toyed with it. "I was committed without a hearing. The medical officer of Willie's battalion judged me unsound of mind, and I was sent here. Now, six weeks later, I am to be handed a medical discharge and put quietly out to pasture. I'm sure that will please the War Office. They're no more anxious to know why I shot Willie than my father is. The act of a temporary maniac. So be it."

Fenton leaned forward and folded his arms on the table. "I don't believe it was the act of a maniac and neither does anyone who has been in trenches. You snapped with the strain, Charles. You didn't know what you were doing and the very best course of action at the moment would be for you to accept a medical discharge and regain your full strength of mind."

"I have that now, Fenton. What I don't have is any *peace* of mind. I may not have been very lucid after I shot Willie, but I knew why I shot him. It was a deliberate, premeditated act, and I want the reasons for it to be made a matter of record."

"What sort of record are you talking about?"

"I want a transcript—the official transcript of my court-martial for the maiming of a brother officer."

Fenton could merely stare at him. Martin gripped his cane and tapped it gently against the floor. A tall, ruddy-faced man with a

Kitchener moustache who had been pacing restlessly, suddenly strode up to the table, hands jammed into the pockets of his dressing-gown.

"Now look here, Randall," he shouted, staring hard at Charles. "Get brigade artillery on the blower right away. Tell the bastards that they're fifty yards short and are hitting D Company. Quite wasting the attack, quite wasting it, sir!"

"I'll do it right away, Colonel," Charles said in a tired voice.

"See that you do!" the man said. "Bloody skrimshankers!"

"We get a lot of that here," Charles said after the man had strolled away, apparently satisfied and at peace. "There's a young chap in my room who spends most of his time seated with his bed cover over his head. Still in his dug-out and won't come out until the shelling stops. Not much older than William. Only thing is, Fenton, Willie would never have broken down. Willie would have gone over the top like a shot. He might have cleared our wire, gone ten, perhaps fifteen yards and then died, for absolutely no purpose at all, just like Roger."

Fenton licked dry lips, reached out and gripped Charles by the wrist. "Tell all that to Martin. Tell him everything that went through your mind before you pulled the trigger. Tell him everything that happened on the Somme, every damned horror. He'll send it to America and a newspaper will print it. That's the only record you need. Don't ask for a court-martial because you'll never get it."

Charles shook his head stubbornly.

"No. I doubt if many newspapers would want to print it. Too defeatist. And even if it were printed in some anti-war paper, what would happen after it was read? Yesterday's news, just an old scrap of newspaper blowing about in the gutters. I want a hearing, at least. A hearing to see if a court-martial would be justified. They would keep a transcript of it: War Office document number whatever."

Fenton sat back stiffly in his chair. "I think you're bonkers, Charles. A man can't ask for his own court-martial."

"No," Charles said, "of course not, but *you* could demand that one should be held. Technically you were my superior officer at the time. The Windsors were attached to your brigade."

"Christ," Fenton said, pushing back his chair and standing up. "You're asking a lot of me."

"Yes."

"As a soldier I should turn you down flat, but if it will give you some kind of peace then I'll do it, as your friend. Of course, this won't change a damned thing. It's just a gesture that no one is going to appreciate."

"Thank you," Charles said. "I knew you wouldn't let me down."

FENTON SAT in brooding silence during the ride to Llangollen station, and after they had got on the London train.

"I suppose you had no choice," Martin said after a while. "If you had turned him down . . ."

"He might have killed himself. That thought had some slight effect on my decision!"

"What happens now?"

Fenton drummed his fingers on the window ledge and stared at his own reflection in the rain-streaked glass.

"I send in my demand through the proper channels and a hearing date will be set. Before that happens there will be a few gentlemanly calls from various brigadiers in Whitehall, asking me to reconsider my actions. I shall decline to do so on the grounds that I consider the shooting of one officer by another bad form. There will be a hearing and Charles will be permitted to talk for as long as he wishes in order to justify his act. The panel will then deliberate for a second or two and rule that no court-martial is warranted because of the mental condition of the accused. Charles will then be sent back to the hospital and quietly discharged from the service. Rather a waste of time for everyone, isn't it?"

"Charles is seeking some kind of peace. If this hearing will give it to him it won't be a waste of *everyone's* time."

"No, I suppose you're right."

"Please write to me how it turns out, care of AP, Rue Chambord. I'm going back to Paris sometime tomorrow."

WALES HAD BEEN corrosive to the spirit. So had writing up the request for court-martial. Both were behind Fenton now as he arrived at his mother's house in Suffolk where Winifred was staying. He found solace lying on the bed with her, his hands moving gently over the great bulge of her womb.

"We're going to have a forty-pound baby. I swear it."

"Twins," she said. "I can feel two distinct pairs of kicks."

"Clever girl," he murmured, kissing the tautness of her skin.

"Do you want sons very badly?"

"I want children very badly, sons or daughters. I'll leave that up to you. Surprise me."

They clung tightly to each other as the March winds moaned across the river and hammered at the casement window.

"You haven't said a word about Charles," she said softly.

"There isn't a great deal to say. A sad man in a sad place. Just one more casualty of the Somme. Charles and four hundred thousand other men."

He didn't tell her about the request for the court-martial, nor the fact that Charles had contemplated suicide. Winifred had enough to think about, being with child.

"Does Lydia see him often?"

"He doesn't want to see her—or his mother. There's nothing he wants to talk about except the war."

There was nothing Fenton wanted to talk about less, but there was no escaping it. On the third morning home the telephone rang, a Brigadier Tynan calling from London. "About this court-martial request of yours for Lord Amberley. Sticky business, don't you know. Be much better all round if you reconsidered it."

"I can't do that, sir."

"Can't, eh? Rather delicate. Peer's son and all that."

"I'm sorry, but I insist on a hearing."

"I see. Well, won't interfere with your rights as the lad's superior officer, although I strongly disapprove of your insistence. Very well then. Hearing set for Thursday next at Llandinam."

"Make certain a shorthand clerk is along."

"We're quite capable of conducting a proper hearing," the brigadier said stiffly. "Good day, sir."

LUGGING A PORTMANTEAU from his apartment in Paris on the Rue Pigalle, Jacob Golden hired a taxi to take him out to Martin's house in the suburbs, the driver grumbling because it was a long

304

way. He dipped into his coat and gave the man double the fare in advance. Money was not a problem—yet. It would be once the paper he was planning went into production, but there was no point in worrying about it now and so he leaned back in the taxi and watched the gaunt winter woods flash by.

Martin sat propped up on a couch. He was surprised and delighted to see Jacob stroll into the room.

"Jacob! I don't believe it." He struggled to get to his feet, but Jacob made a gesture of restraint.

"Don't get up, for God's sake. Where do you keep the champagne?"

"In the pantry."

"Well, we shall crack a bottle or two later." He removed his coat and pulled the chair closer to the couch.

Martin leaned back against the pillows and looked him up and down. "How come you're not in uniform?"

"Oh, I resigned my commission."

"You can do that in the middle of a war?"

"They're beginning to close the loopholes now, but, oh yes, officers serve King and Country on a strictly volunteer basis. Men of breeding simply do not resign, do they? But I did. I fulfilled the requirements of the new law and registered as a conscientious objector and then skipped over here before I could be rounded up and put to hard labour on some sugarbeet farm in Suffolk."

"You sound awfully damned breezy about it. I never knew you to have strong religious beliefs."

"I don't, but I do have strong, conscientious objections to this war. I consider it to be a foul joke played on mankind, a monstrous deceit. I've decided to try and do something about it by publishing a newspaper which will print the unvarnished truth."

Martin whistled softly between his teeth. "You won't get away with it. They close down pacifist newspapers all the time, here and in England. I'd think twice about this if I were you, Jacob."

"I've thought a thousand times about it. My mind is made up. If I can cause just one person to stop singing 'Rule Britannia' or the 'Marseillaise' every time they read an official communiqué from the front, and to begin thinking truly about this war, then going to gaol would be a pleasure."

Jacob moped around the house for two days, debating with himself how to put out his paper. His depression was palpable. It was on the morning of the third day that Danny, a breezy New Yorker who was the Paris bureau's copy boy, arrived on his battered motorcycle. Along with a few letters, he carried a bulky package in his canvas knapsack.

"A Limey officer dropped this off at the office, Mr. Rilke. Said he was doing a favour for a Colonel Wood-Lacy and that it was to be given to you personal."

"Thanks, Danny. Anything new on the wires?"

"U-boats sank another American ship; Congress looks ripe for voting for war in a few weeks; and McGraw predicts that the Giants will take the pennant this year."

"Good for McGraw. At least there's some sanity left in the world."

There was a letter attached to the brown paper parcel.

Dear Martin,

Enclosed is a copy of the transcript which I managed to get hold of. Charles's agonized reflections on the war deserve something more than a filing cabinet in Whitehall. Just what you can do with it I do not know, but I want you to have it nonetheless.

The proceedings went just the way I said they would go. Charles spoke for two hours or more in front of three impassive Whitehall warriors. Their findings were foregone—no court-martial justified and Charles to remain at the hospital.

Best wishes, Fenton

"What is it?" Jacob asked, glancing over Martin's shoulder as he sat reading the typed document. "Copy of a lawsuit?"

"More of an indictment, Jacob. Charles Amberley shot his brother in the leg while home on leave."

"Good God! Why?"

Martin touched the loose pages he had already read. "You can discover that reason for yourself."

Jacob drew a chair up to the desk beside Martin. The first paragraph of Charles's statement held his attention as nothing had ever held it before.

"I entered this war with the highest of ideals and the firmest of faith in the rightness and justness of my patriotism . . . ."

They read through the document several times, Martin lying on the sofa, Jacob slowly pacing the room.

"It took guts for Fenton to get this hearing," Jacob said. "I can see why the War Office was content to just let things lie. A pretty damning statement."

"I couldn't get this published, you know that. It's too critical of the high command's handling of the Somme attacks. Too outraged at the battle being turned into nothing more than bloody attrition. Even if I took it back to the States in my pocket, I doubt if I could find a paper that would touch it. They've got war fever over there now. No editor wants to print a cold shower."

Jacob began to stalk the room in agitation. "Hell, if the newspapers won't touch it, let's print it ourselves—a thousand copies or more, well printed and bound—send copies to every member of Parliament, every churchman, every intelligent human being we can think of."

"Have you been at the brandy?"

"No. I'm drunk with purpose all of a sudden. I feel like flashing a bright light into dark corners. I'd like to see some MP with guts stand up in the House with this statement in his hand and cry out, 'What in the name of God is going on over there? Let's find some generals who aren't dead from the neck up!'"

Martin stared at the ceiling. "*Could* we print it?"

"Not here, unless you care to see the inside of a French prison. Could be done easily enough in London, of course."

"Why *of course?*"

"My mother's brother, my Uncle Ben, prints foreign books and has a fine letterpress business in Whitechapel. Used to go there sometimes as a kid. I can still smell the ink he used."

Martin scowled. "You'd be running a risk going back to England, wouldn't you, Jacob?"

"Well, all that can happen to me in England is that they give me a choice, go back into the army or get tucked away in a CO camp. It's a risk I'm willing to run. Fenton faces a bigger one. I wonder how much will come down on his head?"

Martin swung his legs off the sofa, then bent towards the table where the transcript lay scattered. He sorted the pages together with firm purpose.

"He would never have sent this to me if he were afraid of repercussions. Come on, Jacob, if we hurry we can catch the night train to Le Havre."

"Observations and reflections. London. March 25, 1917. There is a great sense of satisfaction in setting type. For me, it is a return to print shop—10 point Baskerville—cranking out the Lincoln High School yearbook on the platen press. A copy of the slim, paperbound book that we have worked so hard on lies before me. Title page reads:-

AFTER THE SOMME

An inquiry into the advisability of court-martial
of Major The Viscount Amberley, 2nd Royal Windsor
Fusiliers, conducted at Llandinam War Hospital.
With an introduction by
Martin Rilke, Associated Press

God willing, I will have grandchildren one day and they may wish to know why the old man stuck his neck out and put his name on the document. Jacob argued that the book needed a touch of authenticating, and so I wrote an introduction, explaining who I was and what I had seen of this war to date and who Charles Amberley was to me. My cousin's story, perhaps your son's story, or your brother's or father's story . . . .

March 28. Hyde Park. Ivy managed to get a night off from All Souls and Jacob discreetly left the flat to us and took a hotel room. She has been curious about my stay in London and I told her the truth. She read the little book, not saying anything until she had turned the final page. It is nothing new to her, the self-inflicted wounds, the intense gratitude that once-strong men feel when they are carried out of the line with a crushed leg or a shattered hand or arm. She knows I may get into trouble when this thing is sent around. May even lose my English visa and my French *permis de séjour.* Everyone very touchy at the moment. British battle casualties well over the seven hundred thousand mark, the

French a great deal more, America trembling on the brink of jumping into this war with closed eyes. Lousy timing for an indictment of Western Front generalship and the callousness of slaughter. But my Ivy does not try to dissuade me. She is blunt about it. "I have my job and you have yours. Do what you feel is right." Solid Norfolk speech. She may go back to the hospital trains soon so I give her the key to Rilke Manor just in case AP ships me to Timbuktu. . . ."

HAROLD DAVIDSON, Liberal member for Coventry, began the book at breakfast and finished it at the Commons before the debate began on the railway expansion bill. He skimmed through most of it because he was a very busy man, but he read enough to stoke more fuel on his already burning distrust of General Sir Douglas Haig. After the first debate on the railway bill had been concluded to no one's satisfaction, he launched into a tirade about Haig's mismanagement of the Somme offensives.

"I 'ave in my 'and a book . . ." he shouted as he began his thirty-five minute speech—but hardly anyone remained to listen.

DAVID LANGHAM left his usual afternoon meeting with the prime minister, and told his driver to take him to Bristol Street. Lydia gave him a gin and French vermouth and then sat down on the divan.

"I suppose you've come to bring me a copy of poor Charles's book."

"Yes," he said. "Care to read it?"

"Not if I can avoid it, but people have been ringing me up all day to tell me about it."

He reached out his hand and touched her lightly on the face. "You look very drawn and beautiful. I am leaving for Paris on Monday to have a private chat with Georges Clemenceau. Why don't we meet at the Crillon—say, Thursday next?"

"That might be nice," she said. "London is so tiresome."

LIEUTENANT-GENERAL SIR JULIAN WOOD-LACY stalked the tiny office in Whitehall, slapping his booted leg with a leather swagger stick. "I can't tell you how painful this is, Fenton."

"I'm sure it must be, sir."

"For the life of me, I can't fathom your obstinacy in requesting a court-martial. Damnedest thing I ever heard of! Well, what's done is done. How did that newspaper wallah get hold of the transcript?"

"I gave it to him."

The old general nodded, almost sadly. "Always said I'd thrash you if you ever lied to your uncle. Well, dash it, the truth hurts."

"What happens now? A court of inquiry, I suppose."

"Great Scot, no! The less done about this matter from now on the better. But it means a decided setback in your career, Fenton."

JACOB GOLDEN carried the cardboard box through the streets of Whitechapel until he spotted a bus heading for Charing Cross. He sat on the open top deck, savouring the sunshine and the wind, the heavy box resting on the seat beside him. Traffic was heavy along the Strand, the huge War Savings rally in Trafalgar Square spilling over into the adjacent streets. He got off the bus and pushed his way slowly through the crowd, moving towards the throbbing drums and shrilling fifes of the London Rifle Brigade band. The sun glinted off fifes and the drum major's baton, the strains of "The British Grenadiers" stirring the crowd to cheers. Tiny Union Jacks held in a thousand hands were being waved in time to the music. Artillery pieces were ranged wheel-to-wheel in a square below the platform. Attached to each gun was a sign giving its price to the taxpayer in pounds, shillings and pence.

"INVEST IN WAR SAVINGS!" a voice appealed over a loudspeaker. "HELP THE BOYS DO THE JOB! YOUR KING AND YOUR COUNTRY NEED . . . YOU!"

Jacob stood by one giant, olive-painted iron wheel, the barrel of the howitzer looming above him. Raising the box above his head, he placed it on an iron-flanged tread at the top of the wheel and then quickly climbed up the spokes and straddled the breech.

"'Ere, now!" a sergeant gunner called out. "Get off there."

Jacob reached down for the box and held it in front of him. The gunner made a grab at him but he propelled himself upwards, thighs gripping the sun-warmed barrel. On the lip of the barrel now, he reached into the box and sent book after book flying out

310

into the crowd. Half a dozen constables shouldered their way through the people. When the final book was gone, he waited contentedly for the bobbies to climb up and get him.

THE TELEPHONE CALL was expected. Martin had already been on the phone for half an hour with Bradshaw, the London bureau chief.

"Martin Rilke?"

"Speaking."

"Ah, yes, Davengarth here, Ministry of Information. You caused a bit of a flap here. Do wish you'd taken the trouble to clear the document with the press censor's office. Well, look here, Rilke, no point in your coming in here now. Your Mr. Bradshaw phoned us and said you were being re-assigned. Going back to America, I take it."

"That's right. New York."

"Well, *bon voyage* and we hope to have you back here again one day. Perhaps after the war."

"Yes," Martin said, hanging up. "After the war."

He took a taxi to All Souls. The hospital had never seemed so huge, or so crowded, and he felt a momentary panic that he wouldn't be able to find her, but he was soon walking quickly down a long corridor towards the multiple amputee ward where she was on duty. She was his wife and he wanted her with him, but he knew the impossibility of that, couldn't even ask her as he held her hands tightly in an aisle between rows of beds, the mutilated men watching them with drugged eyes. He held her hands and kissed her on the cheek and then the matron called for her impatiently from the far end of the ward.

He could still feel the softness of her skin against his lips as he sat in the back of the taxi, the driver speeding through a maze of streets towards Waterloo station. Crowds streaming away from Trafalgar Square suddenly blocked their progress like a wall.

"Sorry, guv'nor," the driver said. "Can't be helped. But you won't miss your train."

He didn't really care if he missed it or not. "Going home," the AP man had told him. A wry joke. He felt that he was home now and on his way to a strange and alien place. He sat stiffly on the seat, not seeing the crowds or the line of big guns being hauled slowly out of the square, the great iron wheels churning up paper-bound books, the wind taking the scraps and blowing them like pale leaves across the pavement—unnoticed, disregarded.

EPILOGUE

"Observations and reflections. Hazebrouck. November 11, 1920. Heaven knows there has been enough soul searching about it, but now it has been done and the rightness of it must wait for the verdict of history. It seems, somehow, right to have waited for the second anniversary. Last year was too soon, the armies barely demobilized, the shock of the war still too numbing for any quiet reflection on it to be possible.

Anyway, the deed has been done. Two days ago, just up the road from here in Flanders, plain wood coffins containing the remains of six nameless Tommies, chosen at random from a forest of graves marked "Unknown" that stretch from Ypres to the Marne, were placed in a hut. A British officer was blindfolded and led inside. The coffin that he touched at random was carried out and taken to Boulogne. There it was placed in a giant casket of oak, the lid bound with iron straps and attached to it was a great seal which is inscribed:

A British Warrior
Who fell in the Great War
1914–1918
For King and Country

A warrior familiar only to God. Today that poor flesh will be taken through the streets of London for burial in Westminster Abbey on Armistice Day, the gun carriage trailed by admirals and field marshals and the dead man's king.

AP suggested that I go to London, but I preferred to stay on this side of the Channel and gather notes for my own elegy.

Brief impressions. Convoys of trucks, filled with bricks, bags of sand and lime, on the road to Albert, a wasteland of dead ground, a moonscape of craters and tumbled-in trenches. Salvage crews work baling the miles of wire and demolition men explode or defuse shells.

The splintered trees have been cleared and new ones planted. In time there will be glades and leafy paths on those scarred hills and in time there will be cottages on the patches of brick dust where the villages had been. How short these distances seem now, how vast they were then—paths of eternity. Such a small wedge of ground to have changed so many lives . . . .

Odd how peaceful it is. No major stories to be gathered here. The storms have shifted. Jacob is in those winds, a special observer for an agency of the League of Nations, keeping an eye on political developments in the new nations carved from the old empires between here and Siberia. "Watching the new hatreds grow," as he puts it.

All of us scattered. Strange to think of Alexandra living in Canada and working in a clinic for war wounded with a doctor who may or may not be her husband. She seemed so much a part of the ambience of Abington Pryory and Park Lane. Now the Pryory is sold. All is changed.

The army is sending Fenton to Iraq. Every job he gets is tough. The army would be happy to accept his resignation, but he says it is too late to leave it now. Still, I see they have given him a battalion, and at least he has Winifred and their twins.

Lydia is in Paris. Apparently David Langham has induced her to buy a house, so that he can have a place of quiet retreat during the interminable months of the "Peace" Conference at Versailles. Her closeness to him has not gone unnoticed. In this post-war world, money is desirable, but influence is everything.

Charles was not discharged as cured. He is still in Wales. He says that he must stay and "watch the shadows on the hill in case the men come back."

Still, Charles, the dead who remain here are not forgotten. The Commonwealth War Graves Commission has spared no expense to lay out cemeteries. Low walls surround them and trees and shrubbery soften the lines of stone. They are like English gardens

313

and the caretakers dedicated men. It takes only minutes for them to locate any grave for visitors—the neat rows of white crosses, the names on each. On one of them, Ivy Thaxton Rilke. Beneath the name are the initials of the military nursing service and a date, October 9, 1917.

There are at least a hundred thousand other graves from Passchendaele; not that that's any comfort. She lies in a special plot beside twenty of her patients who died with her when the shell hit. Alexandra saw to that.

A grave in Flanders. Far from the places she had hoped to see. Chicago, Illinois, on Lake Michigan; railways and cattlemarkets.

No. I couldn't face going to London and witnessing the pomp at the Abbey, not with her on this side of the channel. A quiet spot. Just the wind and a blackbird swaying on a cypress tree and then, at eleven, the distant tolling of a bell.''

Phillip Rock first came to live in England in 1934, when his father, Joe Rock, a well-known Hollywood producer, came here to run a film studio at Elstree. The family lived in Stanmore, and Phillip went to a boarding school near Hertford. He remembers his time there with great fondness. "I had a typical English boyhood," he says. "I played cricket with more zest than skill, and collected conkers by the pailful to be soaked in brine, dried, drilled, and dangled from pieces of string."

Phillip Rock

The outbreak of war brought difficult days to the film industry, and eventually Joe Rock lost his film studio. In August 1940 Phillip and his sister were sent back to America to stay with a variety of relatives while his parents remained in Britain, his father to join a Home Guard unit composed of Americans, and his mother to work for an Americans-to-Aid-Britain committee. They lived in London and were bombed out of their flat during the blitz.

Phillip Rock joined the US navy in 1944, and served in the South Pacific. After his discharge, his ambition to become a writer took him to Hollywood where he soon sold his first screenplay to MGM. He has since written numerous novels, screenplays, articles and short stories, and has also taught screenplay writing.

His interest in the Great War, so movingly shown in *The Passing Bells*, goes back to the years before 1939. "It began in London," he recalls, "when I first observed the silent crowds on Armistice Day. I was puzzled by them, and awed. And then a neighbour in Stanmore, an illustrator famous for his drawings of RAF aeroplanes, took me to see the Imperial War Museum and explained to me the history of that most tragic of wars."

It is not surprising that Phillip Rock, a true Anglophile, married an English girl, from Surrey, where much of the action of *The Passing Bells* is set. Their twenty-year-old son is now working in the British film industry.

Today the Rocks live in a rambling Hollywood house complete with dog, cat, and a multitude of pigeons. There *The Passing Bells* was written, Phillip immersing himself in all the Great War classic novels, together with authoritative war histories and magazines of the period. Although the actual writing of the book took only nine months, it is a story that he feels he has lived with all his life.

John Cooke

THE EDUCATION OF
LITTLE TREE

A CONDENSATION OF THE BOOK BY

FORREST CARTER

TITLE-PAGE ILLUSTRATION BY JOHN COOKE
DRAWINGS BY MICHAEL HAMPSHIRE

PUBLISHED BY FUTURA PUBLICATIONS

Forrest Carter was a five-year-old
orphan in the 1930s when he went to live
with his Cherokee Indian grandparents
in their Tennessee mountain home.
They called him Little Tree.

Little Tree's story of his education is
realistic and moving. It reaches its climax
as he endures a brief, harsh stay in
a sanctimonious church orphanage
and returns home to share the touching
dignity and tranquillity of his grandparents' old age.

This remarkable, true account
captures with gentle humour all the love
and simple, natural wisdom which were
the legacy of a very unusual boyhood.

LITTLE TREE

M<small>A</small> L<small>ASTED</small> a year after Pa was gone. That's how I came to live with Granpa and Granma when I was five years old.

The kinfolk had raised some mortal fuss about it, according to Granma, after the funeral. There in the gullied backyard of our hillside shack, they had stood around in a group and thrashed it out proper as to where I was to go, while they divided up the painted bedstead and the table and chairs.

Granpa had not said anything. He stood back at the edge of the yard, Granma behind him. Granpa was half Cherokee and Granma full blood. They was the pa and ma of my ma.

He stood above the rest of the folks; tall, six foot four with his big black hat and shiny black suit that was only worn to church and funerals. Granma had kept her eyes on the ground, but Granpa had looked at me, over the crowd, and so I had edged across to him and held on to his leg and wouldn't turn loose even when they tried to take me away.

Granma said I didn't cry one bit, just held on; and after a long time, them tugging and me holding, Granpa had placed his big hand on my head.

"Leave him be," he had said. So they left me be. Granpa seldom spoke in a crowd, but when he did, Granma said, folks listened.

We walked down the hillside in the dark winter afternoon and onto the road into town. Granpa led the way, my clothes slung over his shoulder in a tow sack. I learned right off that when you walked behind Granpa, you trotted; and Granma, behind me, occasionally lifted her skirts to keep up.

When we reached the town, we walked to the back of the bus station. Granma read the lettering on the front of the buses as they came and went. Granpa said that Granma could read fancy as anybody. She picked out our bus, just as dusk was settin' in.

We waited until all the people were on the bus, and it was a good thing, because trouble set up the minute we set foot inside the door. Granpa pulled his snap purse from his forward pants pocket and stood ready to pay.

"Where's your tickets?" the bus driver said real loud, and everybody set up to take notice of us. This didn't bother Granpa one bit. He told the bus driver we stood ready to pay, and Granma whispered for Granpa to tell where we were going. Granpa told him.

The bus driver told Granpa how much it was, and while Granpa counted out the money real careful, the bus driver turned around to the crowd in the bus and lifted his hand and said, "*How!*" and laughed, and all the people laughed. I felt better, knowing they was friendly and didn't take offense because we didn't have a ticket.

Then we walked to the back of the bus, and I sat in the middle between Granma and Granpa. Granma reached across and patted Granpa on the hand, and he held her hand across my lap. It felt good, and so I slept.

It was deep into the night when we got off the bus on the side of a gravel road. Granpa set off walking, me and Granma behind. It was cracking cold. The moon was out, like half of a fat watermelon, silvering the road ahead.

It wasn't until we turned off the road, onto wagon ruts with grass in the middle, that I noticed the mountains. Dark and shadowed, they were, with a ridge that lifted so high it bent your head back to look. I shivered at the blackness.

Granma spoke from behind me, "Wales, he's tiring out."

Granpa stopped and looked down at me. "It's better to wear out when ye've lost something," he said. He set off again, but now it was easier to keep up.

320

After a long time we turned off the wagon ruts onto a foot trail and headed dead set into the mountains. As we walked, whispers and sighs began to feather through the trees like everything had come alive. There was a bobble and a swishing beside us, a mountain branch rolling over rocks and making pools where it paused and rushed on again. We were into the hollows of the mountains.

Granma began to hum a tune behind me and I knew it was Indian and needed no words for its meaning to be clear, and it made me feel safe.

A hound bayed so sudden I jumped. Granpa chuckled. "That'd be ol' Maud—ain't got the smell sense of a lapdog—dependent on her ears." In a minute we were covered up with hounds, whining around Granpa and sniffing at me to get the new scent.

We crossed a footlog over the branch of a spring and there was the cabin, logged, set back under big trees with the mountain at its back and a porch running clear across the front.

The cabin had a wide hall separating the rooms. The hall was open on both ends. Some people call it a gallery, but mountainfolk call it a dogtrot, because the hounds trotted through there. On one side was a big room for cooking, eating and settin', and across the dogtrot were two bedrooms. One was Granpa and Granma's. The other was to be mine.

I laid out on the springy softness of deer-hide webbing, stretched in the frame of hickory posts. Through the open window I could see the trees across the spring branch, dark in the ghost light. The thought of Ma came rushing on me and the strangeness of where I was.

A hand brushed my head. It was Granma sitting beside me, on the floor; her full skirts around her, the plaited hair streaked with silver falling forward of her shoulders and into her lap. Low and soft she began to sing:

> "They now have sensed him coming
>   The forest and the woodwind
> Father mountain makes him welcome with his song.
>   They have no fear of Little Tree
>   They know his heart is kindness
> And they sing, 'Little Tree is not alone.'

Even silly little Lay-nah
  With her babbling, talking waters
Is dancing through the mountains with her cheer
  'Oh listen to my singing,
  Of a brother come amongst us
Little Tree is our brother, and Little Tree is here.'"

Granma sang and rocked slowly back and forth. And I could hear the wind talking, and Lay-nah, the spring branch, singing about me and telling all my brothers.

I knew I was Little Tree, and I was happy that they loved me and wanted me. And so I slept, and I did not cry.

THE WAY

It HAD taken Granma a week of evenings to make the boot moccasins. With a hook knife, she had cut the deer leather and made the strips that she wove around the edges. When she finished, she soaked the moccasins in water and I put them on wet and walked them dry, until they fitted soft and giving, light as air.

This morning I slipped the moccasins on last, after I had jumped into my overalls and buttoned my jacket. Granpa had said I could go with him on the high trail, if I got up, and he had said he would not wake me.

"A man rises of his own will in the morning," he had spoken down to me. But Granpa had made many noises in his rising, bumping the wall of my room and talking loud to Granma. So I had heard, and I was first out, waiting with the hounds in the darkness.

"So. Ye're here." Granpa sounded surprised.

"Yes, sir," I said, and kept the proud out of my voice.

Granpa pointed his finger at the hounds jumping around us. "Ye'll stay," he ordered. They tucked in their tails and whined and begged, but they didn't follow us.

I had been up the low trail that followed the bank of the spring branch, twisting and turning until it broke out into a meadow where Granpa had his barn and kept his mule. But this was the high trail that took to the side of the mountain, sloping upward as it traveled along the hollow. I trotted behind Granpa and I could feel the upward slant of the trail.

I could feel something more. Mon-o-lah, the earth mother, came to me through my moccasins. I could feel her push and swell here, and sway and give there. She was warm and springy and bounced me on her breast, as Granma said she would.

The cold air steamed my breath in clouds. Bare tree branches dripped water from ice prongs that teethed their sides, and as we walked higher, gray light eased the darkness away.

Granpa stopped and pointed by the side of the trail. "There she is—turkey run—see?" I dropped to my knees and saw the tracks: little sticklike impressions coming from a center hub.

"Now," Granpa said, "we'll fix the trap." And he moved off the trail until he found a stump hole.

We cleaned it out, first the leaves, and then Granpa cut into the spongy ground with his long knife and we scooped up the dirt, scattering it among the leaves. When the hole was deep enough, Granpa pulled me out and we dragged tree branches to cover it and, over these, spread armfuls of leaves. Then Granpa dug a trail sloping downward into the hole and back toward the turkey run. He took grains of red Indian corn from his pocket and scattered them down the trail, and threw a handful into the hole.

"Now we will go," he said, and set off again up the high trail. Ice, spewed from the earth like frosting, crackled under our feet. The mountain opposite us moved closer as the hollow far below became a narrow slit, showing the spring branch like the edge of a steel knife. We sat down in the leaves, off the trail, just as the first sun touched the top of the mountain across the hollow. From his pocket Granpa pulled out some sour biscuits and deer meat, and we watched the mountain while we ate.

The sun hit the top like an explosion, sending showers of glitter into the air. The sparkling of the icy trees hurt the eyes to look, and the light moved down the mountain like a wave as the sun backed the night shadow down and down.

And now the mountain popped and gave breathing sighs that sent little puffs of steam into the air. She pinged and murmured as the sun released the trees from their armor of ice.

Granpa watched, same as me, and listened as the sounds grew with the morning wind that set up a low whistle in the trees. "She's coming alive," he said, soft and low, without taking his eyes from the mountain.

"Yes, sir," I said. "She's coming alive." And I knew right then that me and Granpa had us an understanding that most folks didn't know.

The night shadow backed down and across a little meadow shining in the sun bath. The meadow was set into the side of the mountain. Granpa pointed to a covey of quail fluttering and jumping in the heavy grass, feeding on the seeds. Then he pointed up toward the icy blue sky.

There were no clouds, but at first I didn't see the speck that came over the rim. It grew larger. Facing into the sun, the bird sped down the side of the mountain; a skier on the treetops, wings half folded—like a brown bullet—toward the quail.

Granpa chuckled. "It's ol' Tal-con, the hawk."

The quail rose in a rush and sped into the trees—but one was slow. The hawk hit. Feathers flew into the air, and then the quail was on the ground; the hawk's head rising and falling with the death blows. In a moment he rose with the dead bird clutched in his claws, back up the mountain and over the rim.

I didn't cry, but I know I looked sad, because Granpa said, "Don't feel sad, Little Tree. Tal-con caught the slow, and so the slow will raise no children who are also slow. Tal-con eats a thousand ground rats who eat the eggs of the quail, and so he helps the quail."

Granpa dug a sweetroot from the ground with his knife and peeled it, so that it dripped with its juicy winter cache of life. He cut it in half and handed me the heavy end.

"It is The Way," he said softly. "Take only what ye need. When ye take the deer, do not take the best. Take the small and the slow, and the deer will grow strong and always give you meat."

And he laughed. "Only Ti-bi, the bee, stores more than he can use . . . and so he is robbed by the bear and the coon . . . and the Cherokee. It is so with people who store and fat themselves with more than their share. They will have it taken from them. And

there will be wars over it . . . and men will die, but they will not change the rules of The Way."

We went back down the trail, and the sun was high over us when we reached the turkey trap. We could hear them in there, gobbling and making loud whistles of alarm.

Granpa stretched full length into the hole. In a little while he had six turkeys laid out on the ground, legs tied with thongs. "They're all about the same age—ye can tell by the thickness of the combs. We only need three, so now ye choose, Little Tree."

I walked around and studied them. I had to be careful. I got down on my hands and knees and crawled among them, until I had pulled out the three smallest I could find.

Granpa said nothing. He untied the legs of the others and they took to wing. He slung two of the turkeys over his shoulder. "Can ye carry the other?" he asked.

"Yes, sir," I said, not sure that I had done right.

A slow grin broke on Granpa's bony face. "If ye was not Little Tree . . . I would call ye Little Hawk."

The turkey was heavy, but it felt good over my shoulder. The sun drifted through the branches of the trees beside the trail, making burnt gold patterns where we walked. I heard Granpa, ahead of me, humming a tune. I would have liked to live that time forever, for I knew I had pleased Granpa. I had learned The Way.

SHADOWS ON A CABIN WALL

IN THE evenings of that winter we sat in front of the stone fireplace. Pine knots sputtered and flickered, throwing shadows that jumped and contracted, making the walls come alive with fantastic etchings. There were long silences while we watched the flames and the dancing shadows. Then Granpa would break the silence with some comments on the "readings."

Every Saturday and Sunday night Granma lit the coal-oil lamp and read to us. Lighting the lamp was a luxury, for we had to be careful of the coal oil. Once a month me and Granpa walked to the settlement, and I carried the coal-oil can with a root stuck in its snout, so that not a drop was spilled on the way back. It cost a nickel to fill it, and Granpa showed a lot of trust in me, letting me carry it back to the cabin.

When we went, we always carried a list of books made out by Granma. Granpa presented the list to the librarian, and turned in the books that Granma had sent back. The list always had the name of Mr. Shakespeare (anything we hadn't read by him, for Granma didn't know all the titles). Sometimes this caused Granpa trouble with the librarian. She would pull out different stories by Mr. Shakespeare and read the titles. If Granpa couldn't remember by the title, she would have to read a page. Sometimes I would recognize the story before Granpa, and I would pull on his pants leg and nod at him that we had read that one.

The librarian asked Granpa what he wanted with books if he couldn't *read*, and Granpa explained that Granma read us the books. After that she kept her own list of what we had read. She was nice, and smiled when we came in the door. Once she gave me a stick of red-striped candy, which I broke in two and split with Granpa. He would only take the little piece, as I didn't break it exactly even.

We kept the dictionary checked out all the time, as I had to learn five words a week, starting at the front. And there were other books; one was *The Decline and Fall of the Roman Empire* . . . and there were authors like Shelley and Byron that Granma hadn't known about, but the librarian sent them along.

Granma read slowly, bending her head to the book with her long hair plaits trailing to the floor. Granpa rocked with a slow creak, and when we got to an exciting place, I always knew, because Granpa stopped rocking.

When Granma read about Macbeth, I could see the castle and the witches taking shape in the shadows, and I'd edge closer to Granpa. He'd stop rocking when Granma got to the stabbings and the blood and all. Granpa said none of it would have come about if Lady Macbeth had kept her nose out of the business that ought to have been done by Mr. Macbeth, and besides, she wasn't much of a lady, and he couldn't figure out why she was called such.

Granpa also taken the side of Julius Caesar in his killing. He said he couldn't put his stamp on everything Mr. Caesar done. But he said that was the low-downest bunch he'd ever heard of, Brutus and the others, slipping up on a feller, outnumbering him and stabbing him to death. He said if they had a difference with Mr. Caesar, they'd ought to made theirselves known and settled it square out. He got so het up about it that Granma had to quiet him down. She said we was all in support of Mr. Caesar at his killing, so there wasn't anybody for him to argue with.

But where we run into real trouble was over George Washington. To understand what it meant to Granpa, you have to know something of the background.

Granpa had all the natural enemies of a mountain man. Add on to that, he was poor without saying and more Indian than not. I suppose today the enemies would be called

the establishment, but to Granpa, whether sheriff, revenue agent or politician of any stripe, he called them the law. It was politicians, Granpa said, who were responsible for just about all the killings in history if you could check up on it.

In reading the old history book in later years, I discovered that Granma had skipped the chapters about George Washington fighting the Indians, and had read only the good about George Washington to give Granpa someone to look to and admire. After listening to Granma's readings, Granpa began to refer to George Washington in many of his comments, holding him out as the hope that there *could* be a good man in politics. Until Granma slipped up and read about the whiskey tax.

She read where George Washington was going to put a tax on whiskey makers and decide who could make whiskey and who couldn't. She read where Mr. Thomas Jefferson told George Washington that it was the wrong thing to do; that poor mountain farmers didn't have nothing but little hillside patches, and couldn't raise much corn like the big landowners did. Mr. Jefferson warned that the only way the mountainfolk had of realizing a profit from their corn was to make it into whiskey. But George Washington wouldn't listen, and he put on the whiskey tax.

It hit Granpa deep. He didn't say anything, just stared into the fire with a lost look in his eyes. Granma felt sorry about it, for after the reading she patted Granpa on his shoulder and slipped her arm around his waist as they went off to bed.

It was a month later, when me and Granpa was on the way to the settlement, that I realized how he had been taken under. Every once in a while a car passed us on the road but Granpa never looked around, for he never accepted a ride. But of a sudden an open car with a canvas top pulled up beside us, and I got a surprise.

The feller inside was dressed like a politician. He leaned over and hollered, "Want a ride?"

Granpa stood for a minute, then said, "Thankee," and got in, motioning for me to get in the back. Down the road we went, and it was exciting to me at how fast we covered ground.

"Are you a farmer?" the feller asked.

"Some," Granpa said.

"I'm a professor at State Teachers College," the feller said. I was pleased that he wasn't a politician.

Of a sudden Granpa whirled toward the professor and said, "What do you know about George Washington puttin' on the whiskey tax?"

"The whiskey tax?" The professor looked nervous. "I don't know," he said. "I don't know anything about it." Granpa was studying the road ahead through the windshield, and I knew right then why we had taken the ride.

Granpa spoke again, but his tone didn't hold much hope, "Do ye know if General Washington ever got a lick on the head—I mean in all them battles maybe a rifle ball hit him?"

"I . . . that is," the professor stuttered, "I teach English and I don't know *anything* about George Washington."

We reached the settlement and Granpa said we would get out. When we got on the road, Granpa taken off his hat to thank the professor, but he didn't hardly wait for us to hit the ground before he spun off in a cloud of dust.

Then Granpa said he figured George Washington took a lick on the head some way or other in all his fighting, which accounted for an action like the whiskey tax. He said he had an uncle once that was kicked in the head by a mule and never was quite right after that. That sounded reasonable to me and could of accounted for some of George Washington's troubles.

TO KNOW THE PAST

GRANMA and Granpa wanted me to know of the past, for "If ye don't know where your people have been, then ye won't know where your people are going." And so they told me most of it.

How the Cherokee had farmed the rich valleys and held their mating dances in the spring, when life was planted in the ground. How their harvest festivals were held in the villages as frost turned the pumpkins, reddened the persimmon and hardened the corn. How they had prepared for the winter hunts and pledged themselves to The Way.

How the government soldiers came and told them to sign the

paper. Told them the paper meant that the new white settlers would know where they could settle and where they would not take land of the Cherokee. And after they had signed it, more government soldiers came with guns and said the paper had changed its words. The words now said that the Cherokee must give up his valleys, his homes and his mountains. He must go far toward the setting sun, where the government had other land for the Cherokee, land that the white man did not want.

How the government soldiers ringed a big valley with their guns, and at night with their campfires. They brought Cherokees from other mountains and valleys, in bunches like cattle, and put them in the ring.

After they had most of the Cherokees, they brought wagons and mules and told the Cherokees they could ride to the land of the setting sun. The Cherokees had nothing left. But they would not ride, and so they saved something. You could not see it or wear it or eat it, but they saved something. They walked. The wagons could not steal the soul of the Cherokee.

Government soldiers rode before them, on each side of them, behind them. The Cherokees looked straight ahead and would not look down, nor at the soldiers. Far behind them the empty wagons rattled and rumbled and served no use.

As they passed the villages of the white man, people lined the trail to watch them pass. At first they laughed at how foolish was the Cherokee to walk with the empty wagons rattling behind him. The Cherokee did not turn his head, and soon there was no laughter.

And as the Cherokee walked farther from his mountains, he began to die—starting with the very young and the very old and the sick.

At first the soldiers let them stop to bury their dead, but then more died. By the hundreds, by the thousands. More than a third of them were to die on the trail. The soldiers said they could bury their dead every three days, for the soldiers wished to hurry and be finished with the Cherokee. The soldiers said the wagons would carry the dead, but the Cherokee would not put his dead in the wagons. He carried them. Walking.

The little boy carried his dead baby sister. The husband carried his dead wife. The son carried his dead mother, his father. And they did not turn their heads to look at the people who lined the sides of the trail. Some of those people cried. But the Cherokee did not cry. Not on the outside, for the Cherokee would not let them see his soul.

And so they called it the Trail of Tears. Not because the Cherokee cried. They called it the Trail of Tears for it speaks of the sorrow of those who stood by the trail.

All of the Cherokee did not go. Some, skilled in the ways of mountains, fled far back into the bosom of the hollows and lived with their women and children, always moving.

They set traps for game but sometimes dared not go back to the traps, for the soldiers had come. They dug the sweetroot from the ground and pounded the acorn into meal. They fished with their hands under the banks of the cold creeks and moved silent as shadows, a people who were there but not seen, not heard.

Here and there they found friends, like the people of Granpa's pa. They were white folk, but mountain bred. They did not lust for land or profit, but loved the freedom of the Tennessee mountains, as did the Cherokee.

Granma told how Granpa's pa had met his wife and her people. He had seen the faintest of signs on the banks of a creek. He brought a haunch of deer and laid it there in a little clearing. With it he had laid his gun and his knife. The next morning the deer haunch was gone, but the gun and the knife were there, and lying beside them was a long Indian knife and a tomahawk. He did not take them. Instead he brought ears of corn and laid them by the weapons; he stood and waited a long time.

They came slowly in the late afternoon. Moving through the trees and halting and then coming forward again. Granpa's pa reached out his hands, and they, a dozen of them—men, women, children—reached out their hands and they touched. Granma said they each had to reach across a long way to do it, but they did.

Granpa's pa grew up tall and married the youngest of the daughters. They held the hickory marriage stick together and put it in their cabin, and neither of them broke it as long as they lived.

She wore the feather of the redwing blackbird in her hair, and so was called Red Wing. Granma said she was slender as a willow wand and sang in the evenings.

Granma and Granpa spoke of his pa in his last years. He was an old warrior who had joined the Confederate raider, John Hunt Morgan, to fight the faraway monster of "guvmint" that threatened his people and his cabin.

His beard was white. Age was overtaking his gauntness; and now when the winter wind bit through the cracks of his cabin, the old hurts came to life. The saber slash that ran the length of his left arm; the ankle, big and cumbersome, where the minnie ball had chewed it in the wild exuberance of a cavalry charge in Ohio. He relished thinking of that charge. The memory of it softened his hatred for the cane—and the limp.

The worst of the hurts was in the gut, where the lead was never taken out. It gnawed, like a rat chewing at a corncrib, night and day. Soon now they would stretch him out on the floor of the mountain cabin and cut him open. The gangrene would come out, and he would die there on the floor, in his blood. No last words; but as they held his arms and legs in the death throes, the old sinewy body would bow up from the floor, and the wild scream of the exulting rebel would come from his throat. Forty years it had taken the guvmint lead to kill him.

The century was dying. The time of blood and fighting and death, the time by which he had been measured. There would be a new century, with other people marching and carrying their dead, but he knew only the past—of the Cherokee.

I have been many times to the graves of Granpa's pa and ma. They are close together, high on a ridge of white oak, where the leaves fall knee-deep in autumn. Where only the hardiest Indian violets poke tiny and blue around them in the spring.

The marriage stick is there, hickory and gnarled, unbroken still, and filled with the notches they carved in it each time they had a sorrow, a happiness, a quarrel they had mended. It rests at their heads, holding them together.

And so small are the carved names in the stick, you must get down on your knees to read: Ethan and Red Wing.

332

THE SECRET PLACE

I RECKIN a million little critters lived along the spring branch. If you could be a giant and could look down on its bends and curves, you would know the spring branch is a river of life.

I was the giant. Being over two feet tall, I squatted, giantlike, to study the little marshes where trickles of the stream eddied off into low places. Rock minnows darted to chase musk bugs scuttering across the stream. When you held a musk bug in your hand, it smelled real sweet and thick.

Once I spent a whole afternoon collecting some musk bugs, for they are hard to catch. I took them to Granma, as I knew she loved sweet smells. She said she had never smelled anything so sweet and couldn't figger how she had missed knowing about musk bugs.

Granma said I had done right, for when you come on something good, first thing to do is share it with whoever you can find; that way, the good spreads out to no telling where it will go.

I got pretty wet, splashing in the spring branch, but Granma never said anything. Cherokees never scolded their children for having anything to do with the woods.

I would go far up the spring branch, wading the clear water, bending low through the green feather curtains of weeping willows that hung down, trailing branch tips in the current. Water ferns made green lace that curved over the stream and offered holding places for the little umbrella spiders.

These little fellers would tie one end of a thin cable to the fern branch, then leap into the air, spilling out more cable in an umbrella and try to make it across to a branch on the other side. If he made it, he would tie the cable and jump back and forth until he had a pearly looking net spread over the spring. They were gritty little fellers. If one fell in the water, he'd get swept downstream, crawl out on the bank and come back to that same fern. Then he'd try again.

I got to know the spring branch, following it up the hollow: the dip swallows that hung sack nests in the willows and fussed at me until they got to know me; the frogs that sang along the

banks, but would hush when I moved close, until Granpa told me that frogs can feel the ground shake when you walk. He showed me how the Cherokee walks, not heel down, but toe down, slipping the moccasins on the ground. Then I could come up and set down beside a frog, and he would keep singing.

Following the spring branch was how I found the secret place. It was a little ways up the side of the mountain and hemmed in with laurel—a grass knoll with an old sweet gum tree bending down. When I saw it, I knew it was my secret place, and so I went there a lot. Ol' Maud taken to going with me, and we would sit under the sweet gum and listen—and watch.

Once in the late afternoon me and ol' Maud was watching when I saw a flicker of something move a ways off. It was Granma. She was root gathering, and I caught up to help. I reckined I was too young to keep a secret, for I had to tell Granma about my place. She wasn't surprised—which surprised me.

Granma said all Cherokees had a secret place. She told me she had one and Granpa had one. Granma said it was necessary. Which made me feel right good about having one.

Granma said everybody has two minds. One of the minds has

to do with body living. You used it to figure how to get shelter and eating and to mate and have young'uns and such. But she said we had a spirit mind that had nothing atall to do with such.

Granma said that when your body died, the body-living mind died with it. She said if you used the body-living mind to think greedy or mean all your life, you would shrink up your spirit mind to a size no bigger'n a hickor'nut. Then, when you was born back —as you was bound to be—you was born with a hickor'nut spirit mind that had practical no understanding of anything.

If the body-living mind took over total, that's how you become dead people. Granma said dead people, when they looked at other people, saw nothing but bad; when they looked at a tree they saw nothing but lumber and profit; never beauty.

Granma said the only way that the spirit mind got bigger and stronger was using it to understand. Natural, she said, understanding and love was the same thing.

Granma's name was Bonnie Bee. I knew when I heard Granpa late at night say to Granma, "I kin ye, Bonnie Bee," he was saying, "I love ye," for the feeling was in the words.

And when they would be talking and Granma would say, "Do you kin me, Wales?" and he would answer, "I kin ye," it meant, "I understand ye."

Granpa and Granma had an understanding, and so they had a love. Granma said the understanding run deeper as the years went by, and she reckined it would get beyond anything mortal folks could explain. And so they called it kin. Kinfolk meant any folks that you understood, so it meant loved folks. People brought it down to mean just blood relatives, but actually it was never meant to mean that. Right out I seen that I was going to commence trying to understand practical everybody, for I sure didn't want to come up with a hickor'nut spirit.

Granma said that the old sweet gum tree in my secret place had a spirit too. Not a spirit of humans, but a tree spirit. She said her pa had taught her all about it.

Granma's pa was called Brown Hawk. She said his understanding was deep. He could feel the tree-thought. Once, she said, when she was a little girl, her pa said the white oaks on the mountain

335

near them was excited and scared. They were of much beauty, tall and straight. They wasn't selfish, allowing ground for sumac and persimmon, and hickory and chestnut to feed the wild things.

Then one morning Brown Hawk watched while lumbermen moved through the white oaks, marking and figuring how to cut all of them down. When they left, Brown Hawk said, the white oaks commenced to cry. And he could not sleep. He watched the lumbermen build a road up to the mountain to bring their wagons.

Granma said the Cherokees determined to save the white oaks. She said at night, when the lumbermen would go back to the settlement, the Cherokees would dig up the road, hacking deep trenches across it. The women and children helped.

The next morning the lumbermen came back and spent all day fixing the road. But that night the Cherokees dug it up again. This went on for two days and nights. Granma said it was a hard struggle and they grew very tired. Then one day, as the lumbermen were working on the road, a giant white oak fell across a wagon. It killed two mules and smashed the wagon. She said it was a fine, healthy white oak and had no reason to fall, but it did. The lumbermen gave up trying to build the road.

Granma said the moon waxed full, and they held a celebration in the great stand of white oaks. They danced, and the white oaks sang and touched their branches together, and touched the Cherokee. Granma said they sang a death chant for the white oak who had given his life to save others.

"Little Tree," she said, "these things you must not tell, for it will not help to tell them in this world that is the white man's. But you must know. And so I have told you."

I knew then why we only used the logs that the spirit had left for our fireplace. I knew the life of the forest . . . and the mountains.

GRANPA'S TRADE

In all his seventy-odd years, Granpa never held a job in public works. Public works, to mountainfolk, meant *any* job that paid for hire. Granpa couldn't tolerate regular hire. He said all it done was use up time without satisfaction. Which is reasonable.

In 1930, when I was five years old, a bushel of corn sold for twenty-five cents; that is, if you could find anybody that would buy a bushel of corn. Which was not likely. Even if it had sold for ten dollars a bushel, me and Granpa could not have made·a living at it. Our corn patch was too little.

But Granpa said every man ought to have a trade and take pride in it. His trade was handed down on the Scotch side of his family for several hundred years. Granpa was a whiskey maker.

Most folks outside the mountains give whiskey making a bad name. But their judgments are arrived at on big-city criminals who hire fellers to run off a lot of whiskey fast, not caring what kind it is. Such men will use potash or lye to "turn" their mash quick. They'll run their whiskey through sheet iron and truck radiators, which has all kinds of poisons and can kill a man.

Granpa would never put anything in his whiskey, not even sugar to stretch it out. Granpa made pure whiskey; nothing but corn in the makin's.

He also had no patience atall with aging whiskey. Granpa said he had heard all his life about how much better aged whiskey was. He said he tried it oncet. Said he let some fresh whiskey set for a week, and it didn't taste one lick different from all the other whiskey he made.

Granpa said that where folks got that at was letting whiskey set in barrels for a long time, until it picked up the scent and color of the barrels. He said if a fool wanted to smell of a barrel, he'd ought to go stick his head in one and smell of it, then go git hisself a drink of honest whiskey.

Granpa's still was up in the Narrows, set back in laurels and honeysuckle so thick that a bird couldn't find it. Granpa was proud of it, for it was pure copper: the pot and the cap arm and the coil, which ran around in circles and was called a worm.

Granpa made one run a month, which always come out to eleven gallons. We sold nine gallons to Mr. Jenkins, who run the store at the crossroads, at two dollars a gallon. It bought all the necessaries and put a little money back besides.

We kept two gallons. Granpa liked to have some in his jug, and Granma used considerable of it in her cough medicine. Granpa said it was also necessary for spider bite, heel bruises and things like that.

Most people making whiskey used white corn. We used Indian corn, the only kind we grew, which give our whiskey a light red tint. We was proud of our color. Everybody knew it when they saw it. At Mr. Jenkins' store, there was men who would not buy any other whiskey but Granpa's.

We would shell the corn, and some of it we put in a tow sack. We poured warm water over the sack and let it lay in the sun or in the winter by the fireplace. In four or five days the corn had long sprouts. The other shelled corn we ground up into meal.

Me and Granpa would tote the meal up the Narrows to the still. We had a wood trough that we stuck in the spring branch and ran water to the pot 'til it was three-quarters full. Then we poured the meal in and started a fire under the pot. We used ash wood, for ash makes no smoke. Granpa said there was no sense in taking a chance. Which was right.

Granpa fixed me a box which we set on a stump by the pot. I stood on the box and stirred the meal water while it cooked. I couldn't see over the top and never seen exactly what I was stirring, but Granpa said I done good and never let a batch scorch. Even when my arms got tired.

After we cooked it, we drawed it off through a slop arm in the bottom, into a barrel, and added the sprout corn, which we had ground up. Then we covered the barrel and let it set. After four or five days there would be a hard crust on it. We would break up the crust, and then we was ready to make a run.

Granpa had a big bucket and I had a little one. We dipped out the barrel and poured the beer—that's what Granpa called it—into the pot. Granpa set the cap on the pot, and we put wood to fire under it. When the beer boiled, it sent steam up through the cap arm, which was connected to the hollow tubing of the worm. The steam ran through the worm, which was set in a barrel that had cold water from the spring branch running through it. The water made the steam turn back to liquid. At the bottom of the barrel, where the worm come out, we had hickory coals to strain off the bardy grease, which would make you sick if you drank it.

After all of this you would think we would get a lot of whiskey, but we only got about two gallons of what Granpa called singles. He said they was over two hundred proof. We set the two gallons aside and drained off the "backings," which didn't turn to steam, in the pot.

Then we had to scrub the whole thing down. We put the backings and the singles back in the pot and done it all over again, adding some water. This time we got our eleven gallons.

I seen right off that stillin'—if you done it proper—was hard work. Whiskey can be ruined a lot of ways. The fire can be too hot. If you let the workings lay too long, vinegar sets up; if you run early, it's too weak. You must be able to read a "bead" and judge its proofing. I seen why Granpa taken such pride in his trade, and I tried to learn.

Granpa had a maker's mark for his whiskey, scratched on top of every fruit-jar lid. It was shaped like a tomahawk, and nobody else in the mountains used it. Granpa said that since me and him was partners now, half of the mark was owned by me. I was right proud, and seen to it, as much as Granpa, that we never turned out bad whiskey under our mark.

When me and Granpa was at the still, Granma kept the dogs locked up. Granpa said if anybody was to come up the hollow, then Granma was to turn loose Blue Boy—up and comin' to have the best nose in the mountains—and send him to the still. Then we would know somebody was on the trail.

I guess one of the scaredest times of my life come about while making whiskey. It was late winter. Me and Granpa was finishing up our last run and was putting the half-gallon fruit jars in the tow sacks. We put leaves in the sacks too, for this helped us to keep from breaking our jars.

Granpa always carried two big tow sacks with most of the whiskey. I carried a little tow sack with three half-gallon jars. It was a pretty big load for me, toting it back down the trail. I would have to stop considerable to set it down and rest.

We was just finishing our sacking when Granpa said, "Damn! There's Blue Boy!"

There he was, laying by the side of the still with his tongue

339

hanging out. He had come up without a word and laid down. I said "Damn!" too. (Me and Granpa occasional cussed when we wasn't around Granma.)

Granpa said, "Ye take your sack and head back down. Iff'n ye see somebody, step off the trail 'til they pass. I'll hide the still and go down t'other mountainside. I'll meet ye at the cabin."

I grabbed up my sack and wobbled out, fast as I could. I was scared . . . but I knew this was necessary. The still come first.

Flatlanders could never understand what it meant to bust up a mountain man's still. Granpa's still had been handed down to him, and now, at his age, he could never replace it. To have it busted would put me and him and Granma where it would be practical intolerable to make a living.

Granpa sent Blue Boy with me. We had come maybe halfway down the Narrows when we heard a big racket break out down on the hollow trail. Granma had turned all the dogs loose and they was howling and baying up toward us. Something was wrong. Blue Boy raised his ears and tail and sniffed the air; hairs ruffled on his back, and he started walking stiff-legged ahead of me. I sure appreciated ol' Blue Boy right then.

Then there they was. They come around the bend and stopped and stared at me. They were the biggest four fellers I had ever seen, and they had badges shining on their shirts. My mouth got clacker dry and my knees commenced to wobble.

"Hey!" one of them hollered. "A damn Indian kid!" Another one said, "What'cha got in that sack, kid?" And one hollered, "Look out for that hound!"

Blue Boy was walking real slow toward them. He was growling low and showing his teeth. Blue Boy meant business.

They started walking, cautious, up the trail toward me. I seen that I could not get around them. If I jumped in the spring branch they would catch me, and if I run back up the trail I would be leading them to the still. I taken to the side of the mountain.

There is a way to run up a mountain. Granpa had showed me the way Cherokees do it. You don't run straight up, you run along the side and angle up as you go. Instead of angling up away from the men—which would have taken me back up the Narrows—I

340

headed up the side that led down the trail, toward the men.

This made me pass right over their heads. They broke off the trail, thrashing in the brush, and one of them nearly reached my foot as I passed. He was so close I knew he was going to kill me right off. But Blue Boy bit him in the leg. He hollered and fell back'ard, and I kept running—fast as I could—which wasn't too fast as the fruit jars was slowing me up.

I heard the men clambering up the mountain behind me, and about that time the rest of the hounds hit. It all sounded pretty fearful, mixed in with the men yelling and hollering and cussing.

I kept running as long as I could. After a while I had to stop. I felt like I would bust; but I didn't stop long. I kept going until I was settin' right on top of the mountain. The last part of the climbing I had to drag my fruit jars, I was that wore out.

I could still hear the dogs and men. They were moving back down the Narrows trail, and then the hollow trail. It was a continuous squalling and yelling all the way. Though I was so tired I couldn't stand up, I felt right good about it, for they didn't go near the still, and I knew Granpa would be pleased. My legs was weak, and so I laid down in the leaves and slept.

When I woke up, it was dark. The moon had come up over the far mountain. Then I heard the hounds. I knew Granpa had sent them after me, for they sounded kind of whining, like they was trying to get me to answer. I whistled and heard them yelp and bark. In a minute they was covering me up, licking my face and jumping all over me.

Me and the hounds come down off the mountain. Ol' Maud couldn't stand it, and run ahead barking and howling to tell Granma and Granpa I had been found. Aiming to take all the credit herself, I reckined, though she couldn't smell a lick.

As I come down the hollow I saw Granma out in the trail. She had lit the lamp to guide me home. Granpa was with her. They stood and watched as I come along with the dogs. I felt good about it. I still had my fruit jars and had not broke any of them.

Granma knelt to meet me. She grabbed me so hard she nearly made me drop my fruit jars. Granpa said that he couldn't have done any better hisself. He said that I was likely coming on to be the finest whiskey maker in the mountains.

Granma never said anything. She toted me the rest of the way home. But I could of made it, more than likely.

TRADING WITH A CHRISTIAN

I ALWAYS looked forward to me and Granpa delivering our wares over the cutoff trail to Mr. Jenkins' crossroads store. Wares is what Granpa called our whiskey.

The cutoff trail ran over mountain ridges that sloped toward the valley like big fingers pushing out and resting in the flatlands. It was several miles long, passing through stands of pine and cedar on the slopes, persimmon trees and honeysuckle vine. In the fall I would stop on the way back and fill my pockets with hickor'nuts, chinkapins, walnuts and chestnuts, and then run to catch up with Granpa. In the spring I done the same thing, picking blackberries.

Totin' our wares was a pretty good job. I would sometimes fall far behind Granpa, carrying my three fruit jars in the sack. I was still learning five words a week out of the dictionary, and Granma would have me put the words in sentences. I used my sentences considerable on the way to the store. This would get Granpa to stop while he figured out what I was saying, and I could catch up and rest.

When we got to the last ridge, me and Granpa always looked for the pickle barrel in front of Mr. Jenkins' store. If the barrel was settin' out front that meant the law, and we was not to deliver our wares. I never saw the barrel settin' out front, but I never failed to look for it. I had learned that the whiskey-making trade had a lot of complications to it.

I liked Mr. Jenkins. He was big and fat and had a white beard that hung down over the bib of his overalls, but his head was near totally without hair; it shined like a pine knob.

He had all kinds of things in the store: racks of shirts and overalls and boxes of shoes. There was barrels with crackers in them, and on a counter he had a big hoop of cheese and a glass case which had candy laid on the shelves.

Every time we delivered our wares Mr. Jenkins asked me if I would go to his woodpile and pick up a sack of wood chips for the stove in the store. I always did. The first time he offered me a big stick of striped candy, but I couldn't rightly take it just for picking up wood chips, which wasn't hardly no trouble atall. He found another piece of candy which was old and which he was going to throw away. Granpa said that it was all right to take it, seeing as how it would not be of benefit to anybody. Every month Mr. Jenkins came across another old stick, and I guess I might near cleaned out his old candy. Which he said helped him a lot.

It was at the crossroads store where I got slickered out of my fifty cents. It had taken me a long time to accumulate. Granma would put aside a nickel or dime in a fruit jar for me each time we delivered our wares. It was my part of the trade. I liked to carry it, all in nickels and dimes, in my pocket when we went to the crossroads store. I never spent it, and when we got home I put it back in the fruit jar.

I kind of had my eye on a big red and green box which was in the candy case. I didn't know how much it cost, but I was figuring that maybe next Christmas I would buy it for Granma . . . and then we would eat what was in it.

It was about dinnertime of a day when we had delivered our wares. The sun was overhead, and me and Granpa was resting, squattin' down under the store shed with our backs against the store. I always finished off the stick of old candy while we set. It was a good time.

Men commenced to come to the store in twos and threes. We listened to them talking about things. They said a politician was coming to make a speech. Some of them said there was a depression, and fellers was jumping out of winders in New York and shootin' theirselves in the head about it. Granpa told me that New York was crowded with people who didn't have enough land to live on, and likely half of them was run crazy from living thataway, which accounted for the shootin's and the winder jumping.

I don't know that Granpa would have stayed, but before we got rested here come the politician. He shook everybody's hand; though he didn't shake mine nor Granpa's. Granpa said this was because we looked like Indians and didn't vote nohow, so we was of no use whatsoever to the politician. Which sounds reasonable.

He wore a black coat and had a white shirt with a ribbon tied at his neck. He laughed a lot and 'peared to be mighty happy. That is until he got mad.

He got up on a box and commenced to get worked up about conditions in Washington City, which he said was total going to hell. He said the rotten Catholics was behind every bit of it, and was aiming to put Mr. Pope in the White House. He got to hollerin'

344

pretty loud about it, and said if it wasn't for him puttin' up a fight agin' them, that they would be in total control . . . which sounded pretty bad.

While the politician was talking, a feller walked up to the fringe of the crowd, leading a little brown calf on a rope. The calf stood spraddle-legged behind him with its head down. I got up and edged over to it. I petted it oncet, but it wouldn't lift its head. The feller looked down at me with sharp eyes that crinkled nearly shut when he smiled.

"Like my calf, boy?"

"Yes, sir," I said, and stepped back, as I didn't want him to think I was bothering it.

"Go ahead," he said, real cheerful. "Pet the calf. Ye won't hurt 'em." I petted the calf.

The feller spit tobacco juice over the calf's back. "I can see," he said, "that my calf takes to ye . . . more'n anybody he's ever taken up with. Seems he wants to go with ye." I couldn't tell that the calf looked that way, but he ought to know. The feller knelt down in front of me. "You got any money, boy?"

"Yes, sir," I said. "I got fifty cents."

The feller frowned. After a minute he said, "Well, this here calf is worth more'n a hundred times that much."

"Yes, sir," I said. "I wasn't figuring to buy it." The feller frowned again. "Well," he said, "I'm a Christian man. Even costing me all that this here calf is worth, I feel in my heart ye'd ought to have it—the way it's taken up with ye."

"I ain't—wouldn't take him atall, mister," I said.

But the feller held up his hand to stop me. He sighed. "I'm a'goin' to let ye have the calf, son, fer fifty cents, fer I feel it's my Christian duty, and I won't take no fer an answer."

Since he put it thataway, I couldn't hardly turn him down. I taken out all my nickels and dimes and give them to him. He passed the calf's rope to me, and walked off so quick I didn't know which way he went.

But I felt mighty proud of my calf, even though I had more or less taken advantage of the feller—him being a Christian, which, as he said, handicapped him somewhat. I pulled my calf around to show Granpa. He didn't seem as proud as I was. I told him he could have half of it, seeing as how we was partners in the whiskey-making trade. But Granpa just grunted.

We was ready to set out for home, so I led my calf behind Granpa. It was pretty hard going. My calf couldn't hardly walk. It stumbled along, and I pulled on the rope best I could.

By the time I got to the top of the first ridge, Granpa was nearly at the bottom. I seen I would be left behind, so I yelled, "Granpa, do ye know any Catholics?" Granpa stopped. I pulled harder on my calf and commenced to catch up.

"I seen one, oncet," Granpa said, "at the county seat. He 'peared to be peaceful enough."

Granpa set down on a rock, and I seen he was going to give some thought to it, for which I was glad. My calf was pantin' pretty hard. "Howsoever," Granpa said, "iff'n ye taken a knife and cut into that politician's gizzard, ye'd have a hard time finding a kernel of truth. Ye'll notice he didn't say a thing about gittin' the whiskey tax taken off . . . 'er the price of corn . . . 'er nothin' else fer that matter." Which was right.

Granpa said the politicians was all crooked in Washington City; that they was so many trying to git control, it was a continual dog-fight. Granpa said they was only one thing certain. The Indian was not never going to git control.

While Granpa was talking, my calf laid down and died. I was standing in front of Granpa, holding onto the rope, and Granpa pointed behind me and said, "Yer calf is dead." He never owned to half of it being his.

I squatted down and looked at my calf. It was close to being as bad a time as I could remember. My fifty cents was gone, and the red and green box of candy. And now my calf—being worth a hundred times what I paid for it.

Granpa pulled his long knife from his moccasin boot and cut the calf open. He pointed at its liver. "It's speckled and diseased. We can't eat it."

I didn't cry—but I might near did. Granpa knelt and skinned the calf. "Likely Granma would give ye a dime fer the skin," he said. "And we'll send the dogs back. They can eat the calf." Reckin that was all that could be made of it. I followed Granpa down the trail—carrying the hide of my calf all the way to the cabin.

I told Granma I couldn't put my fifty cents back in the jar, for I had spent it for a calf—which I didn't have. Granma give me a dime for the hide and I put that in the jar.

It was hard to eat that night, though I liked ground peas and corn bread. Granpa looked at me and said, "Ye see, Little Tree, ain't no way of learning, except by letting ye do. Iff'n I had stopped ye from buying the calf, ye'd have always thought ye'd ought to had it. Ye'll have to learn as ye go."

"Yes, sir," I said.

"Now," Granpa said, "what did ye learn?"

"Well," I said, "I reckin I learned not to trade with Christians."

Granma commenced to laugh. Granpa looked dumbstruck, then laughed so hard he choked on his corn bread. I figgered I had learned something funny, but I didn't know what it was.

Granma said, "What ye mean, Little Tree, is that ye'll have caution at the next feller who tells you how good he is."

"Yes, ma'am," I said. "I reckin."

That night I dreamed about a big Christian who had a red and green box of candy and said it was worth a hundred times as much, but I could have it for fifty cents. Which I didn't have; and so could not buy it.

A DANGEROUS ADVENTURE

INDIAN violets come first in the mountain springtime. Just when you figure there won't be a spring, there they are. Icy blue as the March wind, they lie against the ground, so tiny that you'll miss them unless you look close. I helped Granma pick them until our fingers would get numb in the raw wind. Granma made a tonic tea from them.

On the high trail, where ice still crunched beneath our moccasins, we got evergreen needles. Granma put them in hot water and we drank that too. It is better for you than any fruit, and makes you feel good. Also the roots and seeds of skunk cabbage.

Once I learned how, I was the best at acorn gathering. Granma ground them up into a yellow-gold meal and mixed in hickor'nuts and walnuts and made bread fritters; which there has never been anything to taste like. Sometimes she had an accident in the kitchen and spilled sugar. "Durn me, Little Tree," she would say. "I spilt sugar in the acorn meal." I never said anything, but when she did that I always got an extra fritter.

Then sometime in late March we would be gathering acorns on the mountain, and the wind, raw and mean, would change for just a second. It would touch your face as soft as a feather. It had an earth smell. You knew springtime was on the way.

Ice would break and melt on the high ridges, swelling the ground and running little fingers of water down into the spring branch. Then the yellow dandelions poked up everywhere along the lower hollow, and we picked them for greens—which are good when you mix them with fireweed greens, poke salad and nettles. Nettles make the best greens, but have tiny hairs that sting you when you're picking. Granpa said he had never knowed anything in life that, being pleasurable, didn't have a catch to it—somewheres.

Mustard comes through on the mountainside in patches that look like yellow blankets. It grows little bright canary heads with peppery leaves. Granma mixed it with other greens and sometimes ground the seeds into paste and made a table mustard.

Everything growing wild is a hundred times stronger than tame things. We pulled the wild onions from the ground and just a handful would carry more flavor than a bushel of tame onions.

As the air warms, and rains come, the flowers pop colors out like paint buckets have been spilled all over the mountainsides. Firecracker flowers have long, rounded red blooms that are so bright they look like painted paper. The harebell pushes little bluebells from among the crevices. Bitterroot has big lavender-pink faces with yellow centers that hug the ground, while moonflowers are hidden deep in the hollow, long-stemmed and swaying like willows with pink-red fringes on top.

When the air gets heavy so it's hard to breathe, you know what's coming. The birds fly down from the ridges and hide in the hollows and in the pines. Heavy black clouds float over the mountain, and you run for the cabin.

From the porch we would watch the big bars of light that stand for a full second, maybe two, on the mountaintop, running out lightning wire in all directions. Cracking claps of sound, so sharp you know something has split wide open—then the thunder rumbles over the ridges and back through the hollows. The trees whip and bend in sudden rushes of wind, and the sweep of rain comes thunking from the clouds in big drops, letting you know there's some real frog-strangling sheets of water close behind.

Folks who laugh and say that Nature don't have a soul spirit have never been in a mountain spring storm. When she's birthing spring, she gets right down to it, tearing at the mountains like a birthing woman clawing at the bed quilts.

If a tree has been hanging on, having weathered the winter winds, and she figures it needs cleaning out, she whips it up out of the ground and flings it down the mountain. She goes over the branches of every bush and tree with her wind fingers, then she whips them clean and proper of anything that is weak. Granpa said she was tidying up from last year, so her new birthing would be clean and strong.

When the storm is over, the new growth, tiny and timid green, starts edging out on the bushes and tree limbs. Then Nature brings April rain. It whispers down soft and lonesome, making mists in the hollows and on the trails where you walk under the drippings from hanging branches.

It is a good feeling, exciting—but sad too—in April rain. Granpa said he always got a mixed-up feeling. He said it was exciting because something new was being born, and it was sad, because you knowed you can't hold on to it. It will pass too quick.

Then, when April gets its warmest, all of a sudden the cold hits you for four or five days. This is called blackberry winter. The blackberries will not bloom without it. When it ends, that's when the dogwoods bloom out like snowballs over the mountainside.

The white farmers gathered out of their gardens in late summer, but the Indian gathers from early spring, when the first greens start growing. Granpa said the woods would feed you, if you lived with the woods instead of tearing them up. However, there is a right smart bit of work to it. I figured I was more than likely best at

349

berry picking, for I could get in the middle of a patch and never have to bend down to reach the berries. I never got much tired of picking berries.

There were dewberries, blackberries, elderberries, which Granpa said makes the best wine; huckleberries and the red bearberries, which Granma used in cooking. I et berries fairly regular while I was picking them. Granpa did too. But he said it wasn't like he was wasting them, because we would eventually eat them anyway. Which was right. Poke salad berries, however, are poison and will knock you deader than last year's cornstalk. Any berries you see the birds don't eat, you had better not eat.

Along about July, when the sun would have been on the cherries just enough, Granpa and me would set down in the shade of a cherry tree to watch the birds.

One time a robin got to feeling so good from cherry eating, that he wobbled right up to Granpa and lit upon his knee. He fussed and told him what he thought about the whole thing. He eventually decided to sing, but his voice squeaked and he give it up. He staggered off into the brush, with me and Granpa practical laughing ourselves sick. And we saw a red cardinal eat so many cherries that he keeled over and passed out on the ground. We put him in the crotch of a tree so he wouldn't get killed by something during the night.

Every bird that comes around your cabin in the mountains is a sign of something. Granpa knew all the bird signs. It is good luck to have a house wren live in your cabin. Granma had a little square cut out of the top corner in the kitchen door, and our house wren

flew in and out, building her nest on the eave log over the stove.

House wrens like to be around people who love birds. She would cozy down in her nest and watch us in the kitchen with little black bead eyes that shined in the lamplight. When I would drag a chair close and stand on it so I could get a better look, she would fuss at me; but she wouldn't leave her nest.

Whippoorwills start singing at dusk. If you light the lamp, they will move closer to the cabin and eventually sing you to sleep. They are a sign of peace and good dreams, Granpa said. The screech owl hollers at night, and is a complainer. There's only one way to shut up a screech owl; you lay a broom across the open kitchen door. Granma done this and I've never seen it fail.

The blue jay playing around the cabin means you are going to have good times and fun. The red cardinal means you are going to get some money, and when you hear a turtledove, it means that somebody loves you and has sent the turtledove to tell you.

The mourning dove calls late at night from far back in the mountain, and it is a long, lonesome call. Granpa said if a mountain man died and didn't have anybody in the world to cry for him, the mourning dove would remember and mourn. He said it lent a matter of peace to a feller's mind, knowing that. Which I know it did for my mind.

We stopped trapping in the spring and summer. Granpa said that there was no way in the world that a feller could mate and fight at the same time. He said animals couldn't either. Even if they could mate and you hunting them, they could not raise their young,

and you would eventual starve to death. So we taken pretty heavy to fishing.

First we wove fish baskets out of willows. At the mouth of the basket we turned the willow ends down and sharpened them into points. This way the fish could swim into the basket, and the little ones could swim back out, but the big fish couldn't come out through the sharp points. Granma baited the baskets with meal balls and sometimes with worms.

We toted the baskets up the Narrows to the creek. There we tied them with a line to a tree and lowered them into the water. The next day we would come back; and there would be big catfish and bass . . . and once I got a trout in my basket.

Granpa taught me to handfish. This was how, the second time in my five years of living, I nearly got killed. The first time, of course, was in the whiskey trade when the tax law might near caught me. This time, however, Granpa nearly got killed too.

It was in the middle of the day, which is the best time to hand-fish. The sun hits the middle of the creek and the fish move back under the banks to lie in the cool and doze.

This is when you lay down on the bank and ease your hands into the water and feel for the fish holes. When you find one, you bring your hands in easy and slow, until you feel the fish. If you are patient, he will lie in the water while you rub him along the sides. Then you take one hold behind his head, the other on his tail, and lift him out. It takes some time to learn.

This day Granpa was laying on the bank and had already pulled a catfish out of the water. I was a ways down, feeling for a fish hole. I heard a sound right by me. It was a dry rustle that started slow and got faster until it made a whirring noise.

I turned my head toward the sound. It was a rattlesnake. He was coiled to strike, his head in the air, not six inches from my face. I froze stiff. He was bigger around than my leg and I could see ripples moving under his skin. Me and the snake stared at each other. He was flicking out his tongue, and his eyes was slitted—red and mean. I knew he was about to strike me, but I couldn't move.

A shadow fell on the ground, over me and the snake. I hadn't heard him coming, but I knew it was Granpa. Soft and easy he said,

"Don't move, Little Tree. Don't blink yer eyes." Which I didn't.

Then of a sudden Granpa's big hand come between my face and the snake's head. The rattler drew up higher. He begun to hiss, and rattled a solid whirring sound. But the hand stayed steady as a rock. I could see beads of sweat shining against the copper skin.

The rattler struck fast and hard. I saw the needle fangs bury up in the meat as the rattler's jaws took up half Granpa's hand.

Granpa moved his other hand and grabbed the rattler behind the head and squeezed. The rattler come up off the ground and wrapped himself around Granpa's arm. He thrashed at Granpa's head and face with his rattling end. But Granpa wouldn't turn loose. He choked that snake to death with one hand, until I heard the crack of backbone. Then he throwed him on the ground.

Granpa set down and whipped out his long knife. He cut big slashes in his hand where the snake had bit. I crawled over to Granpa, for I was weak as dishwater. He was sucking the blood from the knife slashes and spitting it out. I didn't know what to do, so I said, "Thankee, Granpa." He looked at me and grinned.

"Helldamnfire!" Granpa said. "We showed him, didn't we?"

"Yes, sir," I said. Though I couldn't recall as having much to do with the showing.

Granpa's hand commenced to get bigger and bigger. He taken his knife and split the sleeve of his deer shirt. The arm was twice as big as his other one, and was turning blue. I got scared.

"I'm going for Granma," I said. Granpa looked at me and his eyes stared off, faraway. His face looked funny.

"Reckin I'll rest a spell," he said, calm as syrup.

I run down the Narrows trail, and nothing but my toes touched the ground. I couldn't see good, for my eyes was blinded with tears, though I didn't cry. I fell down, running along the hollow trail, sometimes in the spring branch, but I scrambled right up again. I knew Granpa was dying.

The cabin looked crazy and tilted when I run into the clearing, and I tried to yell for Granma . . . but nothing would come out. I fell through the kitchen door and right into Granma's arms. She held me, looked at me steady and said, "What happened?" I whispered, "Granpa's dying. . . . Rattlesnake . . . creek bank." Granma dropped me flat on the floor, which knocked the rest of the wind out of me.

She grabbed a sack and was gone. I can see her now; full skirt, with hair braids flying behind, and her tiny moccasin feet flying over the ground. She could run! I screamed as loud as I could, and it echoed up the hollow, "Don't let him die, Granma!"

I turned the dogs out and they took off after Granma, howling and baying up the trail. I ran behind them. When I got to the creek bank, Granpa was laying flat out. Granma had propped his head up, and the dogs was circling around, whining. Granpa's eyes was closed and his arm was nearly black.

Granma had slashed his hand again and was sucking on it, spitting blood on the ground. When I stumbled up, she pointed to a birch tree. "Pull the bark off, Little Tree."

I grabbed Granpa's long knife and stripped the bark. Granma built a fire, using the birch bark to start it. She dipped water out of the creek and hung a can over the fire and put roots and seeds into it, and some leaves that she had taken from the sack. The leaves was lobelia, for Granma said that Granpa had to have it to help him breathe.

Granpa's chest was moving slow and hard. While the can was heating, Granma looked around. Fifty yards off, there was a quail nesting on the ground. Granma undid her big skirt and let it drop on the ground. She tied the top of the skirt together, and tied rocks around in the bottom. Then she moved on the quail's nest like a wind whisper. Just at the right time—she knew—the quail rose off the nest, and she threw the skirt over it.

She brought the quail back, split it from breastbone to tail, and spraddled it over Granpa's snakebite. She held the bird on Granpa's hand for a long time, and when she took it off, the quail had turned green all over its inside. It was poison from the snake.

The evening wore on, and Granma worked over Granpa. The dogs set around us in a circle, watching. Nighttime fell, and Granma had me build up the fire. She said we had to keep Granpa warm. She taken her skirt and laid it over him. I taken off my deer shirt and laid it on him too.

I kept the fire going. Granma laid down by Granpa, holding

354

close to him, for she said her body heat would help. So I laid by Granpa on the other side, though I reckined my body wasn't big enough to heat up much of Granpa. But Granma said I helped.

Granpa commenced to talk. He was a boy again, running through the mountains, and he told all about it. He talked, off and on, all night. Just before dawn he quietened and begun to breathe regular. I told Granma the way I see it, there wasn't any way atall that Granpa could die now. She said he wasn't going to. So I went to sleep in the crook of his arm.

I woke at sunup . . . just as the first light topped the mountain. Granpa set up, all of a sudden. He looked down at me, and then at Granma. He said, "By God! Bonnie Bee, a feller can't lay his body down nowheres without you stripping buck naked and hunching at 'em."

Granma slapped Granpa's face and laughed. She rose and put on her skirt. I knew Granpa was all right. He wouldn't leave for home until he had skinned the rattler. He said Granma would make a belt for me from its skin. Which she did.

We headed down the Narrows trail, the dogs running ahead. Granpa was a little weak-kneed, and held Granma close. I trotted along behind them, feeling might near the best I had ever felt since coming to the mountains.

Though Granpa never mentioned putting his hand between me and the snake, I figured, next to Granma, more than likely he kinned me more than anybody else in the world, even Blue Boy.

A NIGHT ON THE MOUNTAIN

Granpa was half Scot, but he thought Indian. Indians gave themselves to nature, not trying to subdue it or pervert it, but to live with it. And so they could not think as the white man.

Granpa told me when the Indian brought something to trade and laid it at the white man's feet, if he saw nothing he wanted, he picked up his wares and walked off. The white man, not understanding, called him an Indian giver, meaning one who gives and then takes back. This is not so.

Granpa said the Indian held his palm up to show "peace," that he held no weapon. He said the white man meant the same thing by shaking hands, except his words was so crooked, he had to try to shake a weapon out of the sleeve of the feller who claimed he was a friend. Granpa said it was total distrustful of a man's word. Which is reasonable.

As to folks saying, "*How!*" and then laughing when they see an Indian, Granpa said it come about over a couple of hundred years. He said every time the Indian met a white man, the white man commenced to ask: *How* are you feeling, or *How* are your people, or *How* is the game where you come from, and so on. He said the Indian come to believe that the white man's favorite subject was *how;* and so, being polite, he figured he would just say *how,* and let the white man talk about whichever *how* he wanted to.

Granpa said I thought Indian too. He said it would always carry me through . . . which it has; like the time the big-city men made a trip to our mountains.

We had delivered our wares to the crossroads store, and Mr. Jenkins said two men from Chattanooga had been there, and they wanted to talk to Granpa.

Granpa looked at Mr. Jenkins from under his hat. "Tax law?"

"No," Mr. Jenkins said. "Said they was in the whiskey trade. Said they heard tell you was a good maker and they wanted to put you in a big still, and that you could get rich working for them."

Granpa didn't say anything. He bought some coffee and sugar for Granma. I picked up wood chips and taken the old candy off Mr. Jenkins' hands. Then we walked out, and didn't hang around the store; but headed straight off up the trail. Granpa walked fast.

When we got to the cabin, Granpa told Granma about the big-city men. He said, "You stay here, Little Tree. I'm going to the still and lay some more covering branches over it. If they come, you let me know."

I set on the front porch watching for the big-city men. Granpa had not hardly gone from sight when I saw them coming across the footlog. They had fine clothes like politicians. The big fat man wore a lavender suit and white tie. The skinny man had on a white suit and black shirt which shined.

They walked right up to the porch. The big man was sweating

pretty bad. He looked at Granma. "We want to see the old man," he said.

Granma didn't say anything. The big man turned to the skinny man. "The old squaw don't understand English, Slick."

Mr. Slick had a high voice. "To hell with the old squaw," he said. "I don't like this place, Chunk—too far back in the mountains. Let's get outa here."

"Shut up," Mr. Chunk said. "The boy looks like a breed. Do you understand English, boy?"

I said, "I reckin."

Mr. Chunk looked at Mr. Slick. "Hear that? He reckins." They laughed right loud about it. I saw Granma move back and turn Blue Boy out. He headed up the hollow for Granpa.

Mr. Chunk said, "Where's your pa, boy?" I told him I didn't recollect my pa; that I lived here with Granpa and Granma. Mr. Chunk wanted to know where Granpa was, and I pointed back up the trail. He took a whole dollar from his pocket and held it out. "You can have this dollar, boy, if you take us to your granpa."

He had big rings on his fingers. I seen right off that he was rich and more than likely could afford the dollar. I taken it and put it in my pocket. Even splitting with Granpa, I would get back the fifty cents which I had been slickered out of by the Christian.

I felt pretty good about the whole thing, leading them up the trail. But as we walked, I commenced to think. I couldn't take them to the still. I began to lead them up the high trail, although I didn't have any idea in the world what I was going to do. They pulled off their coats and walked along behind me. Each one had a pistol in his belt.

Mr. Slick said, "Don't remember your pa, huh, kid?" I said I hadn't no recollection of him atall. Mr. Slick said, "That would make you a bastard, wouldn't it?" I said I reckined, though I had not got to the B's in the dictionary and had not studied that word. They both laughed. They seemed like happy fellers.

Mr. Chunk said, "Hell, they're all a bunch of animals." I said we had lots of animals in the mountains—wildcats and wild hogs; and me and Granpa had seen a black bear oncet.

Mr. Slick wanted to know if we had seen one lately. I pointed

to a poplar tree where a bear had taken a claw swipe. Mr. Chunk jumped like a snake had struck at him. He bumped into Mr. Slick and knocked him down. Mr. Slick got mad. "Damn, Chunk! If you had knocked me down there . . ." He pointed down into the hollow. You could barely see the spring branch, far below.

The higher we got, the more Mr. Chunk and Mr. Slick fell farther behind me. Once I come back down the trail looking for them, and they were sprawled out under a white oak. The white oak had poison ivy all around its roots. They was laying in the middle of it. I didn't say anything. They was already in the poison ivy, and I didn't want to make them feel worse about things. They was looking pretty bad.

Mr. Slick raised his head. "Listen, you bastard," he said, "how much farther we got to go?" I said we was nearly there.

I had been thinking. I knew Granma would send Granpa up the high trail after me, so when we got to the top, I was going to tell Mr. Slick and Mr. Chunk that we would just set down and wait; that Granpa would be along directly. Which he would. I figured it would work all right and I could keep the dollar, seeing as how I would have more or less taken them to Granpa.

Mr. Slick helped Mr. Chunk out of the poison ivy patch and they kind of staggered along behind me. I got to the top of the mountain a long time before they did. I set down under a bush where the trail made a fork. I figured I would wait on Mr. Chunk and Mr. Slick, and we would all set here until Granpa come.

When they finally come over the top of the mountain, Mr. Chunk had his arm over Mr. Slick's shoulders. He had hurt his foot, for he was limping pretty bad.

Mr. Chunk was saying that Mr. Slick was a bastard. Which surprised me, as Mr. Slick had not said anything about being a bastard too. Mr. Chunk was saying that Mr. Slick was the one who thought up the idea of putting mountain hicks to work for them.

They was talking so loud, they passed right by me. I didn't have a chance to tell them to wait, as Granpa had learned me not to interrupt when people was talking. They went on down the trail on the other side of the mountain, until they disappeared among the trees, heading into a deep cleft.

I didn't have to wait long for Granpa. Blue Boy come up first, tail wagging. In a minute I heard a whippoorwill ... but as it was not dusk dark yet, I knew it was Granpa. I whippoorwilled back. I saw his shadow slipping through the trees. He wasn't following the trail, and you could never hear him, if he didn't want to be heard. In a minute there he was.

I told Granpa that Mr. Slick and Mr. Chunk had gone on down the trail, and also everything I could remember they said. Granpa didn't say anything, but his eyes narrowed.

Granma had sent us corn pone and catfish in a sack, and me and Granpa set down under a cedar and ate. I showed Granpa the dollar, which I reckined if Mr. Chunk figured I had done my job I could keep. I told Granpa we could split it. Granpa said I could keep the whole dollar.

Far off we heard a yell down in the cleft of the mountain. We had plumb forgot about Mr. Chunk and Mr. Slick. It was getting dusk dark. Granpa stood up and cupped his hands around his mouth. "Whoooooooeeeeeeeee!" he hollered down the mountain. The sound bounced off another mountain; then into the cleft and on up the hollows, getting weaker and weaker. There wasn't any way of figuring where the sound had come from. Then we heard

359

three gunshots. "They're answering with pistol fire," Granpa said.

Granpa kept hollering. I did too. It was fun, listening to the echoes. Each time the pistol answered us, until it didn't answer the last time.

"They're out of bullets," Granpa said. It was dark now. Granpa stretched and yawned. "No need me and ye thrashing around down there tonight. We'll git 'em out tomorrow." Which suited me.

Me and Granpa pulled spring boughs under the cedar tree to sleep on. If you're going to sleep out in the mountains during spring and summer, you had better sleep on spring boughs. If you don't, red bugs from leaves and bushes will eat you up. This was a bad red-bug year. Blue Boy curled up on the soft and springy boughs by me and felt warm in the sharp air.

Me and Granpa clasped our hands behind our heads and watched the moon come up, full and yellow. We could see might near a hundred miles, Granpa said, mountains humping and dipping in the moon spray, making shadows and deep purples in their hollows. Fog drifted along in threads, far below us. One little patch of fog would come around the end of a mountain like a silver boat and bump into another one and they would melt together and take off. Granpa said the fog looked alive. Which it did.

Far back in the mountains we heard two wildcats mating. They sounded like they were screaming mad. Down below us a screech owl screeched, and then there was yells and more screams. Granpa said it was Mr. Chunk and Mr. Slick. He said if they didn't settle down, they would disturb practical all the animals on the mountainside. I went to sleep looking at the moon.

Me and Granpa woke at dawn. There is not anything like dawn from the top of the high mountain. The sky was a light gray, and the birds getting up for the new day made fusses and twitters in the trees. Granpa pointed to the east and said, "Watch."

Above the rim of the farthest mountain a pink streak whipped up, a paintbrush swept a million miles across the sky. The paintbrush run in streaks—red, yellow and blue. The mountain rim looked like it had caught fire; then the sun cleared the trees. It turned the fog into a pink ocean, heaving and moving down below.

The sun hit me and Granpa in the face. The world had got born all over again. Granpa said it had, and he taken off his hat and we watched it for a long time.

The sun cleared the mountain and floated free in the sky. Granpa sighed and stretched. "Well," he said, "ye and me have got work to do. Tell ye what"—Granpa scratched his head—"ye trot down to the cabin and tell Granma we'll be up here awhile. Tell her to fix ye and me something to eat and put it in a paper sack, and fix them two big-city fellers something to eat and put it in a tow sack. Can ye remember now—paper sack and tow sack?" I said I could. I started off.

Granpa stopped me. "And Little Tree," he said, grinning, "before Granma fixes the two fellers something to eat, ye tell everything that the two fellers said to ye." I said I would, and set off down the trail.

When I got to the cabin, I told Granma that Granpa wanted something to eat in a paper sack for me and him, and for Mr. Chunk and Mr. Slick, something to be put in a tow sack. Granma commenced to cook up the vittles.

She had fixed mine and Granpa's, and was frying fish for Mr. Chunk and Mr. Slick, when I recollected to tell her what they had said. While I was telling her, of a sudden she pulled the frying pan off the fire and got out a pot which she filled with water. She dropped Mr. Chunk and Mr. Slick's fish in the pot. I reckined she had decided to boil their fish instead of frying, but I had never seen her use the root powders that she put in their pot.

I told Granma Mr. Chunk and Mr. Slick 'peared to be good-spirited fellers. I told her that I originally thought we was all laughing because I was a bastard, but it turned out, what they was more than likely laughing at was Mr. Slick's being one too. Granma put some more root powders in the pot.

She boiled the fish until the steam got heavy. Then she put the fish for the big-city fellers in the tow sack, and I set off up the high trail. Granma turned the hounds out, and they went with me.

When I got to the top of the mountain, I didn't see Granpa. I whistled and he answered from halfway down the other side. I went along the trail. It was narrow and shaded over with trees. Granpa said he had practical called up Mr. Chunk and Mr. Slick out of the cleft. It taken him some time to get them to understanding which direction to take toward his voice, but they was finally coming, and they ought to be in sight pretty soon.

Granpa hung their sack of fish down from a tree limb, right over the trail where they couldn't miss it. Then me and him moved back up the trail a ways and set down under persimmon bushes to eat our dinner. The sun was might near straight up when we saw them.

If I had not known them right well, I couldn't have recollected as having ever seen them before. Their shirts was tore up complete. They had big cuts and scratches over their arms and faces. Granpa said it looked like they had run through brier patches. He couldn't figure how they got all the big red lumps on their faces, but I figured it was from laying in the poison ivy vines. Mr. Chunk had lost a shoe. They come up the trail slow and heads down.

When they saw the tow sack hanging over the trail, they taken it loose from the tree limb and set down. They ate all of Granma's fish, and argued pretty regular over which was getting the most of it. After they finished eating, they stretched out on the trail in the shade. Granpa said it was better to let them rest awhile. They didn't rest long.

Mr. Chunk jumped up. He was bent over and holding his stomach. He run into the bushes at the side of the trail and commenced to yell, "Oh! My insides is coming out!" Mr. Slick done the same thing. Both of them groaned and hollered and rolled on the ground. In a little while they crawled out of the bushes and laid down on the trail. They didn't lay down long, but jumped up and done it all over again. This went on for might near an hour. After that they laid flat out, resting up. Granpa said more than likely it was something they had ate which didn't agree with them.

Granpa stepped out in the trail and whistled. Both of them got on their hands and knees and looked up toward me and Granpa. Their eyes were swelled might near shut.

"Wait a minute," Mr. Chunk hollered. Mr. Slick kind of screamed, "Hold on, man—for God's sake!" They scrambled to their feet. Me and Granpa went on up the trail to the top of the mountain. When we looked back, they was limping behind us.

Granpa said we might as well go back down to the cabin, as

362

they could now find their way out, and would be along d'rectly. So we did.

We set on the back porch with Granma and waited for Mr. Chunk and Mr. Slick to come along. It was two hours later and dusk dark when they came into the clearing. They made a wide circle around the cabin, which surprised me, as I figured they wanted to see Granpa. I asked Granpa about keeping my dollar. He said I could, as I had done my part of the job. It was not my fault if they changed their minds. Which is reasonable.

I followed them around the cabin to the footlog and hollered and waved to them. "Good-by, Mr. Chunk. Good-by, Mr. Slick. I thankee for the dollar."

Mr. Chunk turned and 'peared to shake his fist at me. He fell off the footlog into the spring branch. As he crawled out, Mr. Chunk said that when he got back to Chattanooga he was going to kill Mr. Slick. Though I don't know why they had fell out with one another.

They passed out of sight down the hollow trail. Granma wanted to send the dogs after them, but Granpa said no. He said he reckined it all come about from a misunderstanding on their part, regarding me and Granpa working for them in the whiskey trade. I figured more than likely it was too.

WILLOW JOHN

PLANTING is a busy time. Granpa decided when we would begin. He would run his finger into the ground and feel for the warmth; then shake his head, which meant we wasn't going to start planting. So we would go fishing or berry picking or general woods rambling, if it wasn't the week to work at the whiskey trade.

Once you start planting, you have to be careful. Anything growing belowground, such as turnips or taters, has to be planted in the dark by the moon, otherwise they won't be any bigger than a pencil. Anything that grows aboveground, such as corn, beans and such, must be planted in the light of the moon. If it isn't, you'll not make much of a crop of it.

When you have figured this out, there are other things. Most people go by the signs in the almanac. Granpa, however, would study the stars d'rect.

We would set on the porch in the spring night, and Granpa would say, "Stars're right for running beans. We'll plant some tomorrow if the east wind ain't blowing." Then, of course, it could be too wet—or too dry—to plant. If the birds quietened, you didn't plant either. Planting is a pretty tedious proposition.

Granma said she suspicioned some of the signs had to do with Granpa's fishing feelings. But Granpa said women couldn't understand complications. He said women thought everything was simple and plain out. Which it wasn't.

When the day was just right, we planted corn mostly. That was our main crop, for we depended on it for eating and feeding ol' Sam, the mule, and it was our money crop in the whiskey trade.

Granpa laid off the rows with the plow and ol' Sam. Me and Granma dropped seeds in the rows and covered them up. On the sides of the mountain Granma planted the corn with a Cherokee planting stick. You just jab it in the ground and drop in the seed.

We planted lots of other things: beans, okra, taters, turnips. We planted peas near the woods. Deer are crazy about peas, and in the fall will come twenty miles through the mountains to a pea patch. We always got an easy deer for winter meat. We also planted watermelons.

Watermelons are might near the slowest growing things ever planted. They just lay there, continually green. Finding and testing out a ripe watermelon is might near as complicated as planting.

I checked the patch every morning and evening. Each time I suspicioned I had found a ripe watermelon, Granpa would check it out. It wouldn't be ready. One evening I told Granpa that I was near certain that I had found the watermelon we was looking for, and he said we would check it the next morning.

We got to the patch before sunup and I showed Granpa the watermelon. It was dark green and big. Me and Granpa squatted down and studied it. Granpa decided it looked near enough ripe to give it the thump test.

You have to know what you are doing to thump test a watermelon. If you thump it and it sounds like a—*think*—it is total green;

364

if it sounds—*thank*—it is green but is coming on; if it goes—*thunk*—then you have got you a ripe watermelon.

Granpa thumped the watermelon hard. He didn't shake his head, which was a good sign. He thumped again. He said as near as he could tell it was a borderline case. He said the sound was somewheres between a *thank* and a *thunk*. I said it sounded like that to me too, but it 'peared to lean pretty heavy toward the *thunk*. Granpa said there was another way we could check it out. He went and got a broom sedge straw.

If you lay a broom sedge straw crosswise on a watermelon and it just lays there, the watermelon is green. But if the straw turns from crosswise to lengthwise, then you have a ripe watermelon. Granpa laid the straw on the watermelon. It turned a ways and stopped. I told Granpa I believed the straw was too long, which made the ripe inside the watermelon have too much work turning it. Granpa shortened the straw, and we tried it again. This time it might near made it lengthwise. Granpa said if we let it lay until the sun was straight overhead, about dinnertime, then we could pick it from the vine. After that we would drop it in the spring branch to chill.

I kept a close check on the sun. Seemed like it just set on the mountain rim, determined to make a long morning of it. Granpa said the sun acted that way sometimes, but if we got busy doing something, the sun would git on with his business. Which we did.

We busied ourselves cutting okra. I moved along the row and cut all the okra that growed low on the stalk. Granpa followed me and cut the high okra. Granpa said he suspicioned that me and him was the only ones who had ever figured how to cut okra without bending over or pulling down the stalks. All morning we cut okra.

We reached the end of a row, and there was Granma. "Dinnertime," she said. Me and Granpa broke into a run for the watermelon patch. I got there first, and so got to pull the watermelon from the vine. But I couldn't lift it. Granpa carried it to the spring branch and let me roll it in—*splosh;* it was so heavy it sunk down beneath the cold water.

It was late sun before we got it out. Granpa carried it, me and

Granma following, to the shade of a great elm. There we sat in a circle, watching the cold water bead on the dark green skin. It was a ceremony.

Granpa held up his long knife and laughed at my open mouth and big eyes watching; then he cut—the watermelon splitting ahead of the knife, which means it is good. It was.

Granpa cut the slices. Granma and him laughed as the juice run down my mouth and over my shirt. It was my first watermelon.

Summer eased along. My birthday being in the summer made it my season; that is the custom of the Cherokee. And so my birthday lasted, not a day, but a summertime. Now I was six.

Granma said I was lucky, for I was born to nature—of Mon-a-lah, the earth mother—and so had all the brothers and sisters of which she had sung my first night in the mountains. Granma said very few was picked to have the total love of the trees, the birds, the waters—the rain and the wind. She said as long as I lived I could come home to them. Where other children would find their parents gone and would feel lonesome, I wouldn't ever be.

Maybe it was my birthday that reminded Granma time was passing. She lit the lamp nearly every evening and read, and pushed me on my dictionary studying. I was down into the B's, and one of the pages was torn out. Granma said that page was not important, and the next time me and Granpa went to the settlement, he paid for and bought the dictionary from the library. It cost seventy-five cents. But Granpa didn't begrudge the money. He said he had always wanted that kind of dictionary.

Every Sunday we went to church. We walked the same trail that me and Granpa used to deliver our wares, for the church was a mile past the crossroads store.

We had to leave at daybreak, for it was a long walk. Granpa put on his black suit and the meal-sack shirt that Granma had bleached white, and he wore his black shoes that he tallowed to shine. The shoes clumped when he walked. He was used to moccasins. I figured it was a painful walk for Granpa, but he never said anything. Me and Granma had it easier. We wore moccasins.

I was proud of how Granma looked. Every Sunday she wore a

dress that was orange and gold and blue and red. It struck her at the ankles and mushroomed out around her. She looked like a spring flower floating down the trail.

The church set back off the road in a scope of trees. When we walked into the church clearing, Granma stopped to talk to some women; but me and Granpa headed straight for Willow John.

He always stood back in the trees, away from the people. He was over eighty but was as tall as Granpa; full Cherokee with white plaited hair hanging below his shoulders, and a flat-brimmed hat pulled low to his eyes. His eyes were black open wounds; not angry wounds, but dead wounds that lay bare, without life.

Granpa said that long ago Willow John had gone to the Nations. (We always called Oklahoma the Nations, for that is what it was to be, until it was taken from the Indians and made a state.) He was gone three years and came back; but he would not talk of it. He would only say there was no Nation.

Granpa and Willow John always put their arms around each other and held each other for a long time—two tall old men with big hats—and they didn't say anything. Then Granma would come, and Willow John would stoop and they would hold each other.

Willow John lived far back in the mountains; and so, the church being about halfway between us, it was the place they could meet.

Maybe children know. I told Willow John that there would be lots of Cherokees before long. I told him I was going to be a Cherokee; that Granma said I was natural-born to the mountains and had the feeling of the trees. Willow John touched my shoulder and his eyes showed a twinkle. Granma said it was the first time he had looked like that in many years.

We would not go into the church until everybody else was in. We always sat on the back row; Willow John, then Granma, me, and Granpa set next to the aisle. Once I found a long knife laying where I set. It was as long as Granpa's and had a deerskin sheath that was fringed. Granma said Willow John gave it to me. That is the way Indians give gifts. They leave it for you to find. You would not get the gift if you didn't deserve it, and so it is foolish to thank somebody for something you deserve, or make a show of it. Which is reasonable.

I gave Willow John a nickel and a bullfrog. The Sunday I brought them, Willow John had hung his coat on a tree while he waited for us, so I slipped the bullfrog and nickel into his pocket.

Willow John put on his coat and went into church. The preacher called for us all to bow our heads. It was so quiet you could hear people breathing. The preacher said, "Lord . . ." and then the bullfrog said, "Larrrrrrrupp!" deep and loud. Everybody jumped. A feller hollered, "God Almighty!" and a woman screamed, "Praise the Lord!"

Willow John jumped too. He reached his hand in his pocket, but he didn't take out the frog. He looked over at me and the twinkle come again to his eyes. Then a smile broke across his face, wider and wider—and he laughed! A deep, booming laugh that made everybody look at him. Then tears commenced to water in his eyes and roll down the wrinkles of his face. Willow John cried.

Everybody got quiet. Willow John didn't make a sound, but his chest heaved and his shoulders shook, and he cried a long time. People looked away, but Willow John and Granpa and Granma looked straight ahead.

The preacher had a hard time getting started again. He had tried once before to preach a sermon regarding Willow John, on paying proper respect to the Lord's house. But Willow John would never bow his head for prayers or take off his hat.

I thought on it over the years. I figured it was Willow John's way of saying his people were broken and lost, scattered from these mountains that was their home and lived upon by the preacher and others there in the church. He couldn't fight, and so he wore his hat. May be when the frog said, "Larrrrrrrupp!" the frog was answering the preacher for Willow John. And so Willow John cried. It broke some of the bitterness. After that his eyes always twinkled when he looked at me.

Every Sunday, after church, we went into the trees near the clearing and spread our dinner. Willow John always brought game in a sack. Granma brought corn bread and vegetable fixings. We ate there in the shade of big elms and talked.

When the sun tilted and hazed the afternoon, we would get ready to leave. Granpa and Granma would hug Willow John, and he would touch my shoulder with his hand, shy.

Walking across the clearing toward our cutoff trail, I would turn to watch Willow John. He never looked back. He walked, arms not swinging, in a long, loping awkward step, misplaced somehow—touching this fringe of the white man's civilization. He would disappear into the trees, and I would hurry to catch up with Granpa and Granma. It was lonesome, walking back home in the dusk, and we did not talk.

MR. WINE

HE HAD come all through the winter and the spring, once a month, regular as sundown, and spent the night. Sometimes he would stay over with us a day and another night. Mr. Wine was a back peddler.

He lived in the settlement, but walked the mountain trails with his pack on his back. We always knew about the day he would come, and so when the hounds bayed, me and Granpa would go down the hollow trail to meet him. We would help him carry his pack to the cabin. He usually had a clock with him that he let me carry. He worked on clocks.

Mr. Wine was maybe a hundred years old. He had a long white beard and wore a black coat. He had a little round black cap that set on the back of his head. Mr. Wine was not his real name. His name started off with Wine, but it was so long and complicated we couldn't get it straight. Mr. Wine said it didn't matter.

He always had something in his coat pocket, usually an apple; one time he had an orange. But he could not remember anything.

We would eat supper in dusk evening; then, while Granma cleared the table, Mr. Wine and Granpa would set in rockers and talk. I would pull my chair between them and set too. Mr. Wine would stop talking and say, "It seems like I'm forgetting something, but I don't know what it is." He would scratch his head and comb his beard with his fingers. Finally he would look down at me and say, "Could you help me remember what it is, Little Tree?"

I would tell him, "Yes, sir, more than likely, you was totin' something in your pocket that you couldn't recollect."

Mr. Wine would jump straight up in his chair and slap at his pocket and say, "Whangdaggle me! Thank you, Little Tree. I'm gettin' so I can't think."

He would pull out a red apple that was bigger than any kind raised in the mountains. He said he run acrost it and picked it up, and was intending to throw it away, as he didn't like apples. I always told him I would take it off his hands. Which I did. I saved the seeds and planted them along the spring branch, intending to raise lots of trees that give up that kind of apple.

Mr. Wine learned me to tell time. He would twist the hands of the clock around and ask me what time it was, and would laugh when I missed. It didn't take me long before I knew everything.

Mr. Wine said I was getting a good education. He said hardly any young'uns my age knew about Mr. Macbeth or studied the dictionary. But it was he who learned me figures.

I could already figure money somewhat, being in the whiskey trade, but Mr. Wine would take out some paper and a little pencil and show me how to make the figures and how to add them, and take away, and multiply. Granpa said I was might near better than anybody he had ever seen, doing figures.

Mr. Wine gave me a pencil, so I could learn to do figuring all through the month. It was long and yeller. There was a certain way you sharpened it, so that you didn't make the point too thin. If you made the point too thin it would break, and you would have to sharpen it again; which used up the pencil for no need. Mr. Wine said the way he showed me to sharpen the pencil was the thrifty way. He said there was a difference between being stingy and being thrifty with money too. If you was thrifty, you used your money for what you had ought but you was not loose with it.

There was all kinds of things in Mr. Wine's pack: ribbons of every color, pretty cloth and stockings, thimbles and needles, and

370

little shiny tools. I would squat by the pack when he opened it on the floor, and he would hold up things and tell me what they was.

Once he brought a black box with him which he said was a Kodak. He could take pictures with it. He said some folks had ordered the Kodak and he was taking it to them, but it would not hurt it atall or show any use if he taken our picture.

He taken a picture of me, and of Granpa too. The box would not take the picture unless you was facing d'rect at the sun. Granpa was suspicious of the thing and would not stand but for one picture. Granpa said you never knowed about them things, and it was best not to use anything new like that until you found out what would happen over a period of time.

Mr. Wine wanted Granpa to take a picture of me and him. It took us practical all the day. Me and Mr. Wine would get all set. He would have his hand on my head, and we would both be grinning at the box. Granpa would say he couldn't see us through the little hole. Mr. Wine would go to Granpa and get the box leveled up and come back. We would stand again. Granpa would say he couldn't see anything but an arm.

Me and Mr. Wine faced the sun so long that neither one of us could see a thing before Granpa finally got the picture taken. It didn't work out though. The next month when Mr. Wine brought the pictures, mine and Granpa's showed up plain, but me and Mr. Wine was not even in the picture that Granpa had taken. We could make out the tops of some trees and some specks above the trees; which, after studying the picture awhile, Granpa said was birds.

Granpa was proud of the bird picture and I was too. He taken it to the crossroads store and showed it to Mr. Jenkins, and told him he had personally taken the picture of the birds.

Granma would not have her picture taken. She would not say why, but she was suspicious of the box and would not touch it. But after we got the pictures back, Granma was taken with them. She put them on the log over the fireplace, and was continually watching them. I believe she would have stood for a picture after that; but we didn't have the Kodak, as Mr. Wine had to deliver it to the people who had ordered it.

Summer was getting ready to die, dozing away the days at the ending. The sun commenced to change from the white heat of life, to a hazing of yeller and gold, blurring the afternoons. Getting ready, Granma said, for the big sleep.

Mr. Wine made his last trip. We didn't know it then, though me and Granpa had to help him across the footlog and up the steps of the porch. Maybe he knew.

When he unstrapped his pack, there on the cabin floor, he taken out a yeller coat. He held it up and the lamp shined on it like gold. Granma said it reminded her of wild canaries. It was the prettiest coat we had ever seen. Mr. Wine turned it round in the lamplight, and we all looked at it. Grandma touched it, but I didn't.

Mr. Wine said he didn't have any sense and was always forgetting things. He said he had made the coat for one of his great-grand young'uns which lived acrost the big waters, but he made the size for what his great-grand young'un was years ago. After he got it made, then he remembered that it was a total misfit. Now there wasn't anybody could wear it.

Mr. Wine said it was a sin to throw something away that could be used by somebody. He said he was *so* worried that he couldn't sleep. If he couldn't find somebody which would favor him by wearing the coat, he reckined he was total lost.

Mr. Wine had his head bowed and looked like he was done lost already. I told him I would try to wear it.

Mr. Wine looked up and his face broke out in a grin among the whiskers. He said he was so forgetful he had plumb forgot to ask me for the favor. He pulled hisself up and danced a little jig around, and said I had totally lifted a big load off of him.

Everybody put the coat on me. Granma pulled on the sleeve, Mr. Wine smoothed the back, and Granpa pulled the bottom down.

372

It fit perfect, as I was the same size as Mr. Wine had remembered his great-grand young'un. Mr. Wine was so happy that he cried.

I wore my coat when we et supper, and that night Granma hung it on the post of my bed so I could look at it. The moonlight coming through my winder made it shine even more.

Mr. Wine slept on a pallet quilt in the settin' room, across the dogtrot from our sleeping rooms. As I lay abed, somehow or other I got to thinking that even though I was doing Mr. Wine a favor, maybe I'd ought to thank him for the yeller coat. I got up and tiptoed across the dogtrot. Mr. Wine was kneeling on his pallet and had his head bowed. He was saying prayers, I figured.

He was giving thanks for a little boy who had brought him so much happiness; which I figured was his great-grand young'un acrost the big waters. He had a candle lit on the kitchen table. I stood quiet, for Granma had learned me not to make a noise while people was saying prayers.

In a minute Mr. Wine looked up. He told me to come in. I asked him why he had lit the candle, when we had a lamp.

Mr. Wine said all his folks was acrost the big waters. There was not but one way he could be with them. He said he only lit the candle at certain times, and they lit a candle at the same time, and that they was together when they did this, for their thoughts was together. Which sounds reasonable.

I told him we had folks scattered far off in the Nations, and had not figured such a way as that to be with them. I told him about Willow John and said I was going to tell him about the candle. Mr. Wine said Willow John would understand. I plumb forgot to thank Mr. Wine for the yeller coat.

He left the next morning. We helped him acrost the footlog and he went down the trail, hobbling slow, bent under the weight of his pack. He was out of sight when I remembered I had forgot. I run down the trail, but he was far below me, picking his way along. I hollered, "Thankee for the yeller coat, Mr. Wine." He didn't turn and so did not hear me. Mr. Wine was not only bad about forgettin'; he couldn't hear good either. I figured, coming back up the trail, that him always forgettin', he would understand how I forgot too.

FALL CAME EARLY to the mountains that year. First, along the rims high against the sky, the red and yellow leaves shook in a brisking wind. Each morning the frost worked its way farther down the mountain, letting you know that you couldn't hold on to summer, letting you know the winter dying was coming.

Fall is nature's grace time, giving you a chance to put things in order. The creatures who was to stay the winter worked harder putting up their stores. Blue jays flew back and forth to the high oaks, carrying acorns to their nests. Now they didn't play or call.

The last butterfly flew up the hollow and rested on a cornstalk. He didn't flex his wings, just set and waited. He was going to die, and he knew it. Granpa said he was wiser than a lot of people. He didn't fret about it.

Me and Granpa dragged dead tree trunks and heavy limbs from the mountainside into the clearing. Granpa's axe rang and echoed up the hollow. I toted in wood chips for the kitchen bin and racked the fireplace logs against the cabin side.

This is what we was doing when the politicians came. They said they was not politicians, but they was. A man and a woman.

They would not take the rockers offered to them, but set straight in the high-backed chairs. The man wore a gray suit and the woman wore a gray dress. The dress was choked so tight around her neck, I figured it made her look the way she did. The man kept his hat on his knees and was nervous, for he continually turned the hat round and round.

The woman said that I had ought to leave the room, but Granpa said I set in on everything. So I stayed and rocked in my little rocker.

The man cleared his throat and said people was concerned about my education, and that it ought to be looked after. Granpa said it was. He told them what Mr. Wine said about me studyin' Mr. Macbeth and the dictionary.

The woman asked Granpa who Mr. Wine was, and he told her all about Mr. Wine. The woman sniffed her nose. I seen right off she total discounted Mr. Wine; which she did us too. She give Granpa a paper which he give to Granma.

Granma lit the lamp at the kitchen table. She started to read out

374

loud, but she stopped. She read the rest to herself. When she finished, she leaned over—and blew out the lamp. The politicians knew what this meant. They stood up in the half light and stumbled out the door. They didn't say good-by.

We waited in the dark a long time after they left. Then Granma lit the lamp and I listened to her read.

The paper said some people had filed with the law. It said I was not being done right by, that Granma and Granpa was old and had no education. It said Granma was a Indian and Granpa was a half-breed who had a bad reputation.

The paper said Granma and Granpa was selfish, and was total hampering me for the rest of my continual life. That they just wanted comfort in their old age and was putting me out to give it to them. It said that Granpa and Granma had so many days in which they could come in court and give answer. Otherwise I was to be put in a orphanage.

Granpa was total stumped. He taken off his hat and laid it on the table, and his hand shook. He rubbed his hat with his hand and just set, looking at the hat.

I set in my rocker by the fireplace and rocked. I told Granma and Granpa that I figgered I could up my dictionary learning to practically ten words a week or even more—maybe to a hundred. I told them that I seen right off I was going to have to double up on my reading. I told Granpa I was in nowise hampered atall; that I was gittin' the uppers on just about everything. I couldn't stop talking. I tried to stop, but I couldn't. I rocked harder and harder, and talked faster and faster. Granpa would not answer me. Granma stared at the paper.

I seen they figgered they was what the paper said they was. I said they wasn't. I said it was the other way around; that they comforted me. I told Granpa I had burdened them up pretty heavy and they had not, in nowise, burdened me. I told them I stood ready to tell the law this very thing. But they wouldn't talk.

I said I was gittin' ahead otherwise too, learning a trade and all. Granpa looked at me for the first time. His eyes was dull. He said maybe, the law being like they was, that we had ought not to mention about the trade.

I went to the table and set on Granpa's leg. I told him and Granma I would not go with the law. I said I would go back in the mountains and stay with Willow John, until the law forgot about the whole thing. I asked Granma what a orphanage was.

Granma's eyes didn't look right either. She said a orphanage was where they kept young'uns who didn't have a pa and ma. She said the law would come looking if I went with Willow John.

I seen right off that the law might find our still if they taken to looking. I didn't mention Willow John again. Granpa said we would go to the settlement in the morning and see Mr. Wine.

We left at daybreak. When we got to the settlement, we turned down a side street. Mr. Wine lived over a feed store. We went up long steps that wobbled as we climbed. The door was locked. Granpa shook it and knocked on it . . . but nobody answered.

We walked slow back down the steps. I followed Granpa around to the front of the feed store, and we went in. A man was leaning against the counter.

"Howdy," he said. "What fer ye?" His stomach hung over the belt of his britches.

"Howdy," Granpa said. "We was looking for Mr. Wine."

"Mr. Wine ain't his name," the man said. "In fact, he ain't got *no* name no more. He's dead."

Me and Granpa was stumped. I felt hollow inside and my knees weakened. I had built up a pretty heavy dependence on Mr. Wine as handling our situation.

"Yer name be Weatherfoul Wales?" the fat man asked.

"It be," Granpa said. The fat man walked behind the counter and dragged out a tow sack. He swung it up on the counter. It was full of something.

"The old man left this here fer ye," he said. "See, the tag. Got yer name on it."

Granpa looked at the tag, though he couldn't read it.

"He had everything tagged," the fat man said. "Knew he was going to die. Even had a tag tied around his wrist telling where to ship the body. Knew exactly how much it cost too . . . left the money in an envelope . . . right down to the penny. Stingy. No money left over."

Granpa looked up, hard, from under his hat. "Paid his obligations, didn't he?"

The fat man got serious. "Oh yes ... yes ... I had nothin' against the old man."

Granpa swung the tow sack over his shoulder. "Could ye d'rect me to a lawyering man?" The fat man pointed across the street. "Right in front of ye, up the stairs."

"Thankee," Granpa said. We walked to the door.

"Funny thing," the fat man said after us, "the old peddler, when we found him; the only thing he hadn't tagged was a candle. The dern fool had it lit and burning right beside him."

I knew about the candle, but I didn't say anything.

We went across the street and up the steps. Granpa knocked on a door that had glass across the top and lettering on it.

"Come in ... come in!" The voice sounded like you wasn't supposed to knock. We went in.

A man was leaning back in a chair, behind a desk. He had white hair. Granpa taken off his hat and the man got up and stuck out his hand. "My name is Joe Taylor," he said.

"Wales," Granpa said. Granpa taken his hand, but didn't shake it. He handed Mr. Taylor our paper.

Mr. Taylor set down and taken eyeglasses out of a vest pocket. He leaned on the desk and read the paper. He frowned. He looked at the paper for a long time.

When he finished, he handed it back to Granpa. "You've been in jail—whiskey making?"

"Oncet," Granpa said.

Mr. Taylor got up and walked to a big window. He sighed. "I could take your money, but it wouldn't do any good. Government bureaucrats that run these things don't understand mountain people. Don't want to. I don't think the SOBs understand anything." He was looking a long way off at something out the window. He coughed. "Nor Indians. We'd lose. They'll take the boy."

Granpa put on his hat. He taken his purse from his forward pants pocket and laid a dollar on Mr. Taylor's desk. We left. Mr. Taylor was still looking out the window.

We walked out of the settlement, Granpa carryin' the tow sack.

I knew we had lost. It was the first time I could keep up easy with Granpa. He walked slow. His moccasins dragged in the dirt.

That night Granma lit the lamp and we opened the tow sack on the kitchen table. There was rolls of red and green and yeller cloth for Granma; needles, thimbles and spools of thread. I told Granma it looked like Mr. Wine had might near emptied his pack into the tow sack.

There was all manner of tools for Granpa. And books. A figuring book and a little black book that Granma said had valuing sayings in it for me. I figured Mr. Wine was going to bring them on his next trip, if he didn't forget. That was all, we thought.

Granpa picked up the empty sack and started to put it on the floor. Something bumped in the sack. Granpa turned it up. A red apple rolled out on the table. It was the first time that Mr. Wine had recollected the apple.

We didn't eat much supper. Granpa told Granma about what Mr. Taylor had said. Granma blew out the lamp and we set in the half dark of a new moon coming through the winder. We didn't light a fire.

I told Granma and Granpa not to feel bad about it. I said I didn't. More than likely I would like the orphanage, with all the young'uns being there. I said it would not take long to satisfy the law and I could come back.

Granma said we had three days, and then I was to be delivered up to the law. We didn't talk anymore. We all three rocked, our chairs creaking slow, far into the night.

When we went to bed, for the first time since Ma died I cried, but I put the blanket in my mouth and Granma and Granpa did not hear me.

We filled up the three days, living hard as we could. Granma went everywhere with me and Granpa. We taken Blue Boy and the hounds. One morning, early in the dark, we set on top of the mountain and watched day break over the rims. I showed Granpa and Granma my secret place.

Granma spilled sugar in practical everything she cooked. Me and Granpa et fairly heavy on meal cookies.

The day before I was to leave I slipped off over the cutoff trail to the crossroads store. Mr. Jenkins said the red and green box was old, and so he would sell it for sixty-five cents. I bought a box of red stick candy for Granpa, which cost a quarter. This left me a dime out of the dollar I had got from Mr. Chunk.

That night Granpa cut my hair. He said it might be hard on me, looking like a Indian. I told Granpa I didn't care. I said I had just as soon look like Willow John.

I was not to wear my moccasins. Granpa stretched my old shoes. He pushed a piece of iron into the shoes, punching the leather of the uppers out over the soles. My feet had growed.

I told Granma I would leave my moccasins under my bed, as I would more than likely be back pretty soon. I put my deer shirt on the bed as nobody would be sleeping there until I come back.

I hid the red and green box in Granma's meal bin, where she would find it in a day or two; and put the box of stick candy in Granpa's suit coat. He would find it Sunday. I had only taken out one piece to more or less prove it out. It was good.

Granma would not go to the settlement for the leaving. Granpa waited in the clearing, and Granma knelt and held me like she held Willow John. I tried not to cry, but I did, some. I wore my best overalls and my white shirt. I wore the yeller coat. In my tow sack Granma had put two more shirts and my other pair of overalls. I would not carry anything else, for I knew I would be back.

Kneeling there on the porch, Granma said, "Do ye recollect the Dog Star, Little Tree? The one we look at in the evening?" I said I did. And Granma said, "Wherever ye are, in the dusk of evening ye look at the Dog Star. Me and Granpa will be looking too. We will remember." I told her I would remember too. It was like Mr. Wine and his candle. I asked Granma to tell Willow John to look at the Dog Star. She said she would.

Granma held me by the shoulders and said, "The Cherokees married your pa and ma. Remember that, Little Tree. No matter what is said . . . remember."

I said I would. Granma turned me loose. I picked up my tow sack and followed Granpa out of the clearing. Across the footlog, I looked back. Granma raised her hand and touched her heart, and pushed the hand after me. I knew what she meant.

379

Granpa had on his black suit. He had his shoes on too, and we both kind of clumped along. Down the hollow trail, pine trees swept low and held my arms. The spring branch commenced to run harder and jump and fuss, and a crow cawed over and over. All of them was saying, "Don't go, Little Tree. . . ." My eyes blinded, and I stumbled along behind Granpa. The wind rose and moaned. A mourning dove called, long and lonesome—and I knew she was calling for me. Me and Granpa had a hard time making it down the hollow trail.

We waited in the bus station, setting on a bench. I held my tow sack in my lap. We was waiting for the law.

I told Granpa I didn't hardly see how he was going to make it in the whiskey trade, me not being there to help. Granpa said it would be hard. We didn't say much else.

The woman in the gray dress came in. When Granpa stood up, she handed him some papers. She said, "We don't want any fuss now. What has to be done, has to be done; best for everybody."

Which I didn't know what she was talking about. She taken a

string with a tag on it out of her purse and tied it around my neck. Me and Granpa followed her to the bus.

Granpa knelt there by the open door of the bus. He held me a long time, kneeling on the pavement. I whispered, "I'll more than likely be back, d'rectly." Granpa squeezed me that he heard.

The woman said, "You'll have to go now." Granpa stood up. He turned and walked off, and he didn't look back.

The woman picked me up and set me on the step of the bus, which I could have made it myself. I told the bus driver I didn't have a ticket or any money. He laughed and said the woman had give him my ticket and told him to read my tag. There wasn't but three people on the bus. I went and set down by a winder, where maybe I could see Granpa.

The bus started out of the station. We moved down the street and I couldn't find Granpa anywhere. Then I saw him, standing on the corner by the bus station. He had his hat pulled down low and his shoulders sloped. We went by him and I tried to raise the winder, but I didn't know how. I waved, but he didn't see me.

I run to the back of the bus and looked out the back winder. Granpa was still there, watching the bus. I waved and hollered, "Good-by Granpa. I'll be back more than likely pretty quick." He didn't see me. I hollered some more. "I'll be back d'rectly, Granpa." But he just stood. Getting smaller and smaller in the late evening sun.

THE DOG STAR

WHEN you don't know how far you are going, it is faraway. Nobody had told me. I reckin Granpa didn't know.

I couldn't see over the backs of the seats in front of me, and so I watched out the winder; the houses and trees going by, and then just trees. It got dark and I couldn't see anything.

We stopped at a bus station in a town, but I didn't get off. I figgered I was safer where I was. I kept my tow sack in my lap, for it felt like Granpa and Granma. It smelled kind of like Blue Boy. I dozed off.

The bus driver wakened me. It was morning and drizzling rain.

We had stopped in front of the orphanage, and when I got off the bus, a white-headed lady was waiting. She had on a black dress and she looked like the lady in the gray dress, but she wasn't. "Follow me," she said.

We went through iron gates with big elms on each side, which rustled and talked as we passed. The lady taken no notice, but I did. They had heard about me.

When we got to the door of a building, the lady said, "You are going to see the Reverend. Be quiet. Don't cry and be respectful. You can talk, but *only* when he asks a question."

I follered her down a dark hall and we went into a room. The Reverend was sittin' at a desk. He didn't look up. The lady set me down in a straight chair, and she tiptoed out of the room. I put my tow sack in my lap.

The Reverend was busy, reading papers. He had a pink face, which looked like he washed it fairly heavy, for it shined. He didn't have any hair to speak of, just some around his ears.

There was a clock on the wall, and I told the time. I didn't say it out loud. I could see rain running down the winder.

The Reverend looked up. "Stop swinging your legs," he said right hard. Which I did.

He laid the papers down and taken up a pencil, which he turned end over end in his hands. "These are hard times," he said. "The state hasn't money for these matters. Our denomination has agreed to take you—possibly against our better judgment."

I commenced to feel right bad about the denomination having to mess with the whole thing. I didn't say anything, as he had not asked me a question.

He turned the pencil over and over again; which was not sharpened thrifty, for the point was too thin. I suspicioned he was looser than he put hisself up to being. He commenced again. "We have a school you can attend. Everybody here does some work, something you are probably not accustomed to. You must follow the rules or you will be punished." He coughed. "We have no Indians here, half-breed or otherwise. Also, your mother and father were not married. You are the only bastard we have ever accepted."

I told him what Granma had said; that the Cherokees married

382

my pa and ma. He said what Cherokees done didn't count whatso-ever. He said he had not asked me a question. Which he hadn't.

He commenced to get worked up about the whole thing. He said his denomination believed in being kind to everybody, to animals and such. He said I did not have to go to the church services, as bastards, according to the Bible, could not be saved. He said he seen by the papers on his desk that Granpa was not fittin' to raise a young'un. He said Granpa had been in jail.

I said I might near got hung by the law oncet myself; but I got away on account of the hound dogs. I didn't tell him where the still was; as this might lead to puttin' me and Granpa out of the whiskey trade.

He put his face in his hands, like he was crying. "I *knew* this was the wrong thing to do," he said.

He set so long shaking his head in his hands that I was sorry I had brought up about might near being hung.

I told him not to cry. I told him I was not hurt in any way atall and was not worked up about it.

He raised up his head and said, "Shut up!" He taken up his papers. "We'll see . . . we'll try, with the Lord's help. It may be that you belong in a reform school."

He rung a little bell on his desk and the lady come jumping in the room. She told me to foller her. I taken up my tow sack and said, "Thankee," to the Reverend. The wind rose up as we left the room and rain spattered the winder hard. The lady stopped and looked. The Reverend turned and looked at the winder too. I knew word had come about me, from the mountains.

My cot set in a corner. It was a big room and had twenty or thirty boys who stayed there, most of them older than me. My job was to help sweep up the room every morning and evening.

Wilburn slept on the cot that was closest to mine. He was maybe eleven. He was tall and skinny, and had freckles all over his face. He said he would not ever get adopted and would have to stay there until he was eighteen. Wilburn said when he got out, he was going to come back and burn the orphanage down. Wilburn had a clubfoot.

Me and Wilburn didn't play in any games in the yard. Wilburn couldn't run, and I was too little and didn't know how to play. Wilburn said games was for babies. Which is right.

Me and Wilburn set under a big oak in the corner of the yard during playtime. I talked to the oak tree. Wilburn didn't know it, for I didn't use words. She was old. With winter coming on, she had lost most of her talking leaves, but she used her naked fingers in the wind.

She said she was going to send back to the mountain trees on the wind that I was here. I told her to tell Willow John, which she said she would do.

Every oncet in a while all the boys lined up in the hall by the office, and men and ladies come and looked for somebody to adopt. The white-headed lady said I was not to line up. Which I didn't. I watched them from the door. You could tell who got picked. They would stop in front of the one they wanted and talk to him; and then they would all go into the office.

Every time it was line-up day Wilburn put on a clean shirt and overalls. He always grinned at everybody that come by and hid his clubfoot behind his other leg. But nobody ever talked to Wilburn.

Chapel services was held at dusk, just before suppertime. I didn't go, and skipped supper too. This give me a chance to watch the Dog Star from a winder halfway down the room from my cot. I stayed by the winder every evening for an hour. The Dog Star rose with a bare twinkle and got brighter as night darkened. I knew Granma and Granpa was looking at it, and Willow John.

All I had to do was watch. Granpa sent me remembrance of me and him settin' on top of the mountain, watching the day birthing, with the sun hitting the ice and sparkling. I heard him plain as speaking. "She's coming alive!" And there by the winder, I would say, "Yes, sir, she's coming alive!"

Granma sent remembrances of the root gathering and the times she spilled sugar in the acorn meal. She sent me a picture of my secret place. The leaves was all fallen, brown and rust and yeller on the ground. Red sumac hemmed it like a ring of fire torches that would not let anybody in but me.

Willow John sent me pictures of the deer in the high ground. Me and Willow John laughed about the time I put the frog in

384

his coat pocket. Willow John's pictures would get fuzzy, for his feeling was strong on something. Willow John was mad.

I was put in a grade of school. A big fat lady headed up the learning. She meant business and would not tolerate any foolishness atall. One time she held up a picture that showed a deer herd coming out of a spring branch. They was jumping on one another, and it looked like they was pushing to get out of the water. She asked if anybody knew what they were doing.

One boy said they was running from something. Another said they didn't like water and was hurrying to get across. She said this was right. I raised my hand. I said I seen right off they was mating; also, I could tell by the bushes and trees that it was the time of the year when they done their mating.

The fat lady was total stumped. She opened her mouth, but didn't say anything. She slapped her hand on her forehead and staggered back a step or two. Then she run at me. She grabbed me by the neck and commenced to shake me and holler, "I should have *known*—filth . . . filth . . . would come out of you . . . you . . . little *bastard!*"

I hadn't no way of knowing what she was hollering about, and stood ready to set it right. She shaken me some more, and then clasped her hand behind my neck and pushed me out of the room.

We went down the hall to the Reverend's office. She made me wait outside.

In a few minutes she come out and walked off without looking at me. The Reverend was standing in the door. He said, real quiet, "Come in." I went in.

His lips was parted like he was going to grin, but he wasn't. He kept running his tongue over his lips. There was sweat on his face. He told me to take off my shirt. Which I did. The Reverend reached behind his desk and taken up a long stick.

He said, "You are born of evil, but praise God, you are going to be taught not to inflict your evil upon Christians. You can't repent . . . but you shall cry out!"

He cut loose with the big stick acrost my back. The first time it hurt, but I didn't cry. Granma had learned me oncet when I stumped off my toenail how the Indian bears pain. He lets his

body mind go to sleep, and with his spirit mind, he moves out of his body and *sees* the pain—instead of *feeling* the pain.

The stick splattered and splattered acrost my back. After a while it broke. The Reverend got another stick. He was panting hard. "Evil is stubborn," he said, "but right will prevail!"

He kept swinging his new stick until I fell down. I was wobbly, but I got up. Granpa said if ye could stay on yer feet, more than likely, ye would be all right.

The floor tilted a little, but I seen right off I could make it. The Reverend was out of breath. He told me to put my shirt on. Which I did. The shirt soaked up some of the blood. Most of it had run down into my shoes. This made my feet sticky.

The Reverend said I was to go back to my cot and I was not to eat supper for a week. Which I didn't eat supper anyway. He said I was not to leave the room for a week neither.

That evening at dusk I stood by the winder and watched the Dog Star. I told Granpa and Granma and Willow John I had no way of knowing how I made the lady sick; nor what come over the Reverend. I told them I stood ready to make amend, but the Reverend said I was born evil and would not know how. I told Granpa that I couldn't noway handle the situation. I said I wanted to come home.

It was the first time I ever went to sleep watching the Dog Star. Wilburn wakened me under the winder. He said he left supper early so as to see about me. I slept on my stomach.

Every evening after that, when dusk brought the Dog Star up, I told Granma and Granpa and Willow John I wanted to come home. I would not see the pictures they sent, nor listen. I told them I wanted to come home. Three nights later the Dog Star was hid by heavy clouds. Wind tore down a light pole and the orphanage was dark. I knew they had heard.

I commenced to expect them. Winter come on. Outside, I spent my time under the oak tree. She was supposed to be asleep, but she said she wasn't, on account of me. She talked slow—and low.

Late one evening, just before we was to go in, I thought I seen Granpa. It was a tall man, and he wore a big black hat. He was moving away from me down the street. I run to the iron fence and I hollered, "Granpa! Granpa!" But he didn't turn, and was gone.

The white-headed lady said Christmas was might near on us. She said everybody was to be happy and sing. Two men who had on suits like politicians brought in a tree. They laughed and said, "Looky here, boys. You have your very own Christmas tree!"

The white-headed lady told everybody to thank the two politicians. Which everybody did.

I didn't. There was no cause atall to cut the tree. It was a male pine and it died slow, there in the hall.

The white-headed lady said that tomorrow was Christmas Eve and that Sandy Claws would come with presents. Sure enough, the next day four or five cars come up to the door. Men and ladies got out and had packages in their arms. They rung bells and hollered, "Merry Christmas!" They said they was Sandy Claws's helpers. Sandy Claws come in last.

He had on a red suit and had pillers stuffed under his belt. His beard was not real, like Mr. Wine's. It didn't move when he talked. He hollered, "Ho! Ho! Ho!" over and over.

The white-headed lady said we was all to be happy and holler back "Merry Christmas!" Which everybody did. The ladies all commenced hollering, "Sandy Claws is going to give out the gifts! Gather round in a circle!"

When Sandy Claws called out your name, you had to step forward and get your gift from him.

My gift was a cardboard box with a picture of a lion on it. Wilburn said you was supposed to pull a string through the hole in the box, and it would sound like a lion. The string was broke, but I tied a knot in it, which made the lion not growl much. I told Wilburn it sounded more like a frog to me.

Wilburn got a water pistol, but it leaked. I told Wilburn we could more than likely fix it if we had some sweet gum; but I didn't know where there was a sweet gum tree thereabouts.

Sandy Claws started hollering, "Good-by everybody! See you next year! Have a Merry Christmas!" All the men and ladies started hollering the same thing and ringing their bells. They went out the front door and got in their cars and taken off.

Wilburn said they come out every year so they could feel good. Wilburn said he was tired of the whole thing, and when he got out of the orphanage, he was not never going to pay any attention to Christmas, whatsoever.

Just as dusk begun to fall, they all had to go to the chapel for Christmas Eve. I stayed by myself and stood by the winder. I watched the Dog Star rising bright. I told Granma and Granpa and Willow John I wanted to come home.

Christmas Day we had a big dinner. Each one of us got a chicken leg and either a neck or a gizzard. Wilburn said he figured they raised special chickens that didn't have nothing but legs, necks and gizzards. I liked mine and et it all.

After dinner we could do as we pleased. I went acrost the yard with my cardboard box and set under the oak tree for a long time. It was nearly dusk, and time for me to go in, when I looked up toward the building.

There was Granpa! He was coming out of the office and walking toward me. I dropped my cardboard box and run at him, hard as I could. Granpa knelt and we held each other. Granpa said he had come to see about me, but had to go back home. He said Granma couldn't come.

I wanted to go—worst I ever felt—but I was afraid it would cause Granpa trouble. So I didn't say I wanted to go home. I walked with him to the gate. We held one another again, but Granpa walked off. He walked slow.

I stood there, watching him go away in the dark. The thought come to me that Granpa might have trouble finding the bus station. I follered along, though I didn't know where the bus station was myself. I saw Granpa cross a street and come up behind the station. I hung around the corner where I was.

Being Christmas Day practical nobody was about. I hollered, "Granpa, more than likely I could help ye with the bus lettering." Granpa didn't act stumped atall. He waved for me to come on over.

I ran. We stood at the back of the station, but I couldn't make out which lettering was which.

In a little while a loudspeaker told Granpa which one was his bus. I walked over with him, and we stood there a minute. Granpa was looking off somewheres. I pulled on his pants leg. Granpa looked down. I said, "Granpa, I want to go home."

Granpa looked at me a long time. He reached down and swung me up in his arms and set me on top of the bus step. He come up the step and taken out his snap purse. "I'm paying for myself and my young'un," Granpa said, and he said it hard. The bus driver didn't laugh.

Me and Granpa walked to the back of the bus. I was hoping the driver would hurry and close the door. Eventually he did, and we started up.

Granpa lifted me onto his lap. I laid my head on his chest, but I didn't sleep. I watched the winder. It was frosted with ice. There wasn't any heat there in the back of the bus, but we didn't care.

Me and Granpa was going home.

HOME AGAIN

IT WAS early morning but still dark when me and Granpa got off the bus. We set out up the gravel road, and after a while we turned up the wagon ruts. I saw the mountains, big and dark around us. I might near broke into a run.

By the time we turned onto the hollow trail the dark was fading into gray. I told Grandpa that something was wrong.

He stopped. "What is it, Little Tree?"

I set down and pulled off my shoes. "I couldn't feel the trail, Granpa," I said. The ground felt warm and run up through my legs and over my body. Granpa laughed. He set down too. He pulled off his shoes. Then he throwed them back toward the road as far as he could.

"And ye can have them clobbers!" Granpa hollered. I throwed mine back and hollered the same thing; and me and Granpa commenced to laugh. We didn't know exactly what we was laughing at, but it was funnier than anything we had laughed at before.

As we come up the trail, the first pink touched the east rim. Pine boughs swept my face and run theirselves over me. Granpa said they was wanting to make sure it was me.

I heard the spring branch humming. I run and laid down and turned my face to the water, while Granpa waited. The spring branch run over my head and felt for me—and sung louder and louder.

It was good light when we saw the footlog. Blue Boy bayed, and then here come the hounds. They all hit me at once and knocked me down, and licked me all over the face. Blue Boy commenced to show out by jumping all four feet in the air and twisting at the top of his jump. He would yelp as he leaped. Another tried it and tumbled in the spring branch.

Me and Granpa was laughing and slapping at hounds as we come to the footlog. I looked to the porch, but Granma wasn't there. I got scared, for I couldn't see her. Something told me to turn around. There she was.

It was cold, but she only had on a deerskin dress and her hair shined in the morning sun. She stood beneath the bare branches of a white oak. She was watching like she wanted to look at me and Granpa without being seen.

I hollered, "Granma!" And fell off the footlog. I splashed in the water, and it was warm against the morning chill.

Granpa leaped in the air and spraddled out his legs. He hollered, "Whooooooooeeeeeeee!" and hit the water. Granma run down into the spring branch and dived at me, and we rolled, splashing and crying some, I reckin. The hounds all stood on the footlog and looked at us, total stumped at the whole thing. They figgered we was crazy, Granpa said. They jumped in too.

Back in the cabin, I went to my room and put on my deer shirt and my boot moccasins. I run out the door and up the hollow trail, all the way to Hangin' Gap. I didn't want to stop running. The wind sung along with me, and squirrels and coons and birds come out on tree limbs to holler at me as I passed.

I come back slow down the trail and found my secret place. It was just like the picture Granma had sent me. I laid on the ground a long time and listened to the wind. The pines whispered and the

390

wind picked up, and they commenced to sing, *"Little Tree is home. Listen to our song!"*

All through that short winter day I lay in my secret place. And my spirit didn't hurt anymore. I was washed clean by the song of the wind and the trees and the spring branch and the birds.

When the sun had set behind the rim, I walked back down the hollow trail. I saw Granma and Granpa settin' on the back porch, waiting, and as I come, they stooped and we held on to one another. We didn't need words. We knew. I was home.

When I pulled off my shirt that night, Granma saw the whip scars and asked me. I told her and Granpa, but I said it didn't hurt. Granpa said he would tell the high sheriff, and that nobody was to come for me again. I knew when Granpa set his mind, they would not come.

By the fireplace that night, Granpa told how they had commenced to have bad feelings, watching the Dog Star, and then one evening at dusk Willow John was standing at the door. He had walked to the cabin through the mountains. He didn't say anything, but et supper with them by the fire. Willow John slept in my bed that night, but in the morning, Granpa said, Willow John was gone.

That Sunday when him and Granma went to church, Willow John was not there. On a branch of a big elm, Granpa found a message. It said Willow John would be back, and that all was well. The Sunday after that Willow John was waiting for them. He didn't say where he had been, so Granpa didn't ask.

Granpa said the high sheriff sent him word that he was wanted at the orphanage, and he went. The Reverend looked sick and said he was signing give-up papers on me. He said he had been followed around for two days by a savage who eventually come into his office and said that Little Tree was to come home to the mountains. That was all the savage said, and walked off. The Reverend said he did not want any trouble with savages and pagans and such.

I knew then who it was I had seen walking away down the street that I had thought was Granpa.

Granpa said when he come out of the office and seen me, he

knew at the time I was to be given up; but he didn't know if I was taken with being around young'uns, or wanted to come home . . . so he let me decide.

I told Granpa I seen right off what I wanted to do the minute I got to the orphanage.

I told Granma and Granpa about Wilburn. I had left my cardboard box under the oak tree and I knew Wilburn would find it. Granma said she would send Wilburn a deer shirt. Which she did.

Granpa said he would send him a long knife, but I told Granpa more than likely Wilburn would stab the Reverend with it. Granpa didn't send it. We never heard nothing more of Wilburn.

When we went to church that Sunday, I was first across the clearing, way ahead of Granma and Granpa. Willow John was standing back in the trees, where I knew he would be; the old straight-brimmed black hat settin' on top of his head. I run as hard as I could and grabbed him around the legs and hugged him. I said, "Thankee, Willow John." He didn't say anything, but reached and touched my shoulder. When I looked up, his eyes was twinkling and shining, black deep.

WE WINTERED good; though me and Granpa was put to it to keep up with the woodcutting. Granpa had got behind and said that if I had not come back, they would likely have froze that winter. Which they would.

Spring come, and we upped our corn planting, figuring to make the run of our wares a little bigger in the fall. It was hard times, and Mr. Jenkins said the whiskey trade was picking up, while everything else was going down.

During the summer I come up to seven years. Granma give me the marriage stick of my ma and pa. It didn't have many notches on it, for they was not married long. I put it in my room, across the headboard of my bed.

Summer give way to fall, and one Sunday Willow John didn't come. I run far back into the trees and called, "Willow John!" He was not there. We didn't go to church. We come home.

Granma and Granpa was worried. He had left no sign, for we looked. Me and Granpa determined to go and find him.

We set out before day that Monday morning. By early light we was past the crossroads store and the church. After that we commenced to walk up the highest mountain I had ever walked. At the top, a little fold run into the side, not deep enough to be called a hollow. Trees grew on its sides and pine needles carpeted the floor. Willow John's lodge was there, set back in the trees.

We had brought Blue Boy with us. When he saw the lodge, he commenced to whine. It was not a good sign.

There was only one room in the lodge. Willow John lay on a bed of deer hides spread over spring boughs. He was naked. The long copper frame was withered like an old tree, and one hand lay limp on the dirt floor.

Granpa whispered, "Willow John!"

Willow John opened his eyes. They was faraway, but he grinned. "I knew you would come," he said, "and so I waited." Granpa found a iron pot and sent me for water. I found it, trickling from rocks behind the lodge.

Granpa built a fire and put the pot over it. He boiled strips of deer meat, and raised Willow John's head in the cradle of his arm and spooned the broth down him.

I got blankets from a corner and we covered Willow John. Night come on. Me and Granpa kept the fire going. The wind whined around the corners of the lodge.

Granpa set cross-legged before the fire and the light flickered over his face, changing it from old, to older . . . making it look like crags and clefts in the shadows of his cheekbones until all I could see was the eyes; burning black, like embers going out. I curled around the fire pit and slept.

It was morning when I woke. The fire was beating back fog drifting in the door. Granpa still set by the fire; like he hadn't moved atall, though I know he had kept it burning.

Willow John stirred. Me and Granpa went to his side. He raised his hand and pointed. "Take me outside."

"It's cold out," Granpa said.

"I know," Willow John whispered.

Granpa carried him out the door and I dragged the spring boughs behind them. Granpa clambered up the bank of the fold to a high point and we laid Willow John on the boughs. We wrapped him in blankets and put his boot moccasins on his feet.

The sun broke through behind us and chased the fog into the deeps. Willow John was looking west, across the wild mountains and deep hollows, toward the Nations.

Granpa put Willow John's long knife in his hand. Willow John raised the knife and pointed to an old fir pine. He said, "When I have gone, put the body close to her. She has warmed me and sheltered me. My food will give her two more seasons."

"We will," Granpa said. He set down by Willow John and taken his hand. I set on the other side and taken his other hand.

"I will wait for you," Willow John told Granpa.

"We will come," Granpa said.

I told Willow John that more than likely it was the flu; Granma had said that it was going around everywheres. I told him I was certain that we could get him down the mountain where he could stay with us; and then he could more than likely make it.

He squeezed my hand. "You have good heart, Little Tree; but I want to go. I will wait for you."

I cried. I told Willow John maybe he could go next year, when it would be warmer. I told him the hickor'nut crop would be good this winter.

He grinned, but he didn't answer me. He looked far out over the mountains, toward the west. He begun his passing song, telling the spirits he was coming. The death song.

It begun low in his throat and rose higher and commenced to get thinner. In a little while you couldn't tell if it was the wind or Willow John that you heard. Me and Granpa saw the spirit slipping away farther back in his eyes and we felt it leaving his body. Then he was gone.

The wind whooshed across us and bent the old fir pine. Granpa said it was Willow John, and he had a strong spirit. We watched it, moving down the side of the mountain and raising a flock of crows into the air. They cawed and set off down the mountain with Willow John. Me and Granpa set and watched them move out of sight over the rims of the mountains. We set a long time. Granpa said Willow John would be back, and that we would feel him in the wind and hear him on the talking fingers of the trees. Which we would.

Me and Granpa taken our long knives and dug the hole, as close to the old fir pine as we could get it. We dug it deep. Granpa wrapped another blanket around Willow John's body and we laid it in the hole. He put Willow John's hat in the hole too, and let the long knife stay in his hand; where he gripped it tight. We piled rocks heavy and deep over the body of Willow John. Granpa said the coons must be kept away, for Willow John was determined the tree was to have the food.

The sun was setting in the west when I follered Granpa down from the mountaintop. I heard a mourning dove far back, calling. I knew it called for Willow John.

Granma lit the lamp when we come in. Granpa did not say anything. Granma knew.

WE WAS to have two more years together; me and Granpa and Granma. Maybe we suspicioned time was getting close, but we didn't speak of it. We lived it full. We pointed out things like the reddest of leaves in the fall, the bluest violet in the spring, so we all tasted and shared the feeling together.

Granpa's step got slower. His moccasins dragged some when he

395

walked. I toted more of the fruit-jar wares and taken to handling more of the heavy work. We didn't mention it.

That last fall ol' Sam died. I told Granpa reckin we better see about another mule, and Granpa said it was long time 'til spring; let's wait and see.

We taken the high trail more regular; me and Granpa and Granma. The climb was slower for them, but they loved to set and watch the mountains.

It was on the high trail that Granpa slipped and fell. He didn't get up. Me and Granma sided him down the mountain and he kept saying, "I'll be all right d'rectly." But he wasn't. We put him abed.

Granpa's body mind commenced to stumble and sleep. His spirit mind taken over. He talked to Willow John a lot. Granma held his head in her arms and whispered in his ear.

Granpa come back to his body mind. He wanted his hat, which I got; and he put it on his head. I held his hand and he grinned. "It was good, Little Tree. Next time it will be better. I'll be seein' ye." And he slipped off, like Willow John had done.

I knew it was going to happen, but I didn't believe it. Granma laid on the bed by Granpa, holding him tight. I run out of the cabin. The hounds was baying and whining, for they knew. I walked down the hollow and taken the cutoff trail. I knew the world had come to an end.

I was blinded and fell and got up and walked and fell again. I don't know how many times. I come to the crossroads store and I told Mr. Jenkins Granpa was dead.

Mr. Jenkins was too old to walk and he sent his full-growed son back with me. Mr. Jenkins' son made the box. I tried to help. I recollected Granpa said you was obligated to pitch in when folks was trying to do for you; but I wasn't much account at it.

We carried Granpa up the high trail, Granma leading. The hounds come behind. I knew where Granma was taking Granpa. It was to his secret place; high on the mountain where he watched the day birth and never got tired of saying, "She's coming alive!" like each time was the first time he had ever seen it. It was the place he had taken me first, and so I knew Granpa kinned me.

Granma didn't look as we lowered Granpa in the ground. She

watched the mountains, far off, and she didn't cry. The wind was strong, there on the mountaintop, and it streamed her braids out behind her. Mr. Jenkins' son walked back down the trail. Me and the hounds watched Granma awhile, then we slipped away.

We waited, setting under a tree halfway down the trail, for Granma to come. It was dusk when she did.

I TRIED to pick up Granpa's load and mine too. I ran the still, but I know our wares was not as good.

Granma got out all Mr. Wine's figgering books and pushed me on learning. I went to the settlement alone and brought back other books. I read them now, by the fireplace, while Granma listened and watched the fire. She said I done good.

It was just before spring. I come from the Narrows down the hollow trail. I saw Granma setting on the back porch. She didn't watch me as I come down the hollow. She was looking up, toward the high trail. I knew she was gone.

She had put on the orange and gold and blue and red dress that Granpa loved. She had printed out a note and pinned it on her bosom. It said:

> Little Tree, I must go. Like you feel the trees, feel for us when you
> are listening. We will wait for you. Next time will be better. All
> is well. Granma.

I carried the tiny body in and put it on the bed and set with her through the day. Blue Boy and the hounds set too.

That evening I went and found Mr. Jenkins' son. He set up the night with me and Granma. We made the box next morning and carried her up the high trail and laid her beside Granpa.

I taken their old marriage stick and buried the ends in piles of stone at the head of each grave. I seen the notches they made for me, right down near the end of the stick. They was deep and happy notches.

I lasted out the winter; me and Blue Boy and the hounds, until spring. Then I went to Hangin' Gap and buried the still's copper pot and worm. I was not much good at it and had not learned the

397

trade as I ought to. I knew Granpa would not want anybody using it to turn out bad wares.

I took the whiskey-trade money that Granma had set out for me and determined I would head west, across the mountains to the Nations. Blue Boy went with me. We just closed the cabin door one morning and walked away.

At the farms I asked for work; if they would not let me keep Blue Boy, then I would move on. Granpa said a feller owed that much to his hounds. Which is right.

Me and Blue Boy made it to the Nations, where there was no Nation. We worked on the farms, going west, and then the ranches on the flats.

One evening, late, Blue Boy come aside my horse. He laid down and couldn't get up. He couldn't go anymore. I taken him up, acrost my saddle, and we turned our backs on the red settin' sun of the Cimarron. We headed east.

I would not get my job back, riding off this way, but I didn't care. I had bought the horse and saddle for fifteen dollars and they was mine. Me and Blue Boy was huntin' us a mountain.

Before day we found one. It wasn't much of a mountain, but Blue Boy whimpered when he seen it. I toted him to the top as the sun broke the east.

He couldn't raise his head, so I held it, settin' on the ground. He licked my hand, when he could. In a little while he passed on, easy, and dropped his head over my arm. I buried him deep and rocked his grave heavy against the creatures.

With his nose sense, I figgered more than likely Blue Boy was already halfway to the mountains.

He'd have no trouble atall catching up with Granpa.

From the time he left Tennessee at the age of ten, Forrest Carter has been on his own, working on farms and ranches throughout the South. A cowhand with almost no formal schooling, he pursued his "book learning" by reading in the libraries of towns wherever he found jobs. His main interest has al-

ways been history, particularly Indian lore, and in his years of travel he has come to know Indians all across the country.

Carter turned writer because of a visit to a Creek Indian settlement in Florida. The tribe needed money to buy Christmas gifts for the children,

Granpa Carter

and Carter wanted to help—so he decided to try writing and selling a story. The result was *Gone to Texas*, a novel based partly on his great-grand-mother's post-Civil War diary and partly on background help from his Indian friends. It found a publisher almost immediately, a rare accomplishment for a first novel, and was later made into a movie starring Clint Eastwood. A sequel, *The Vengeance Trail of Josey Wales*, soon followed.

Forrest Carter

The autobiographical *The Education of Little Tree* is his third book, and he is enthusiastic about plans for more.

Today Forrest Carter spends most of his time in Texas and Oklahoma. He has no hobbies, he says, only the usual human foibles. These include a "miserable poker game and an unfulfilled premonition that spots on dice will make me rich." He hasn't let his literary success take him too far from his origins. He still wears the blue jeans and western shirts of his cowboy days, and part of the earnings from each of his books still goes to various Indian groups.

Little Tree now has more than he needs, and he has not forgotten Granpa's lesson of The Way.

The Mountain Farm

A condensation of the book by
ERNEST RAYMOND

ILLUSTRATIONS BY NITA ENGLE
PORTRAITS BY BEN WOHLBERG

Published by Cassell

The delicate and poignant story,
set in a remote Cumberland valley,
of a beautiful farm girl and the
aristocratic young mountain
climber who loved her.
Inevitably their romance
encountered difficulties: social pressures,
conflicting family loyalties. But
these were quickly overcome, for
the lovers were strong and
confident of the happiness life
had in store for them.
Until, one stormy August day,
the innocence of their dream
was shattered. . . .

"A charming love story. Mr. Raymond's evocation of the Cumberland mountains is superbly well done."
—*Victoria Holt.*

ONE

The sun of an April morning looked down on the long, deepening trough of Sledden Valley in Cumberland's mountains. Sledden is one of many valleys that radiate from the central massif which geologists call the Central Dome, a stormy upland of ruthless crag faces and the greatest area of tumultuous fell country south of the Scottish border. A narrow waste of scattered rocks at its top end, the vale of Sledden dives down and slowly widens till it opens at last on the green meadows around lovely Goswater Lake.

The valley's lower half is thus pastoral, with a fair road winding up it from the lake, past a huddle of green slate cottages known as Little Sledden, past the tiny church and the small school, on up into the ever-narrowing vale—till it comes to the most remote farmstead in all these valleys, Old Sledden. The road ends at its gate. Thereafter one hay meadow beyond the barns, and one ploughed field, then acid moorland and a mere twisting pony track that climbs northwest through heath and stone to the saddle of the pass.

Now, this upper end of Sledden Valley is remarkable in Cumberland's mountain region because its west wall rises to a mile of high grey precipices, the famous Idle Crags. Most climbs here are listed as Very Severes and are assaulted only by the "tigers" of the rock-climbing brotherhood.

When the wandering pony track has attained the pass it branches in two, one branch going on over the top, the other swinging around in a hairpin bend to enter the valley of Sledden Dore. The Dore, as the natives call this green basin up in the clouds, has trees and a carpet of good turf, and a tarn that on such a morning as this

403

glistens in the sun. But the strangest thing about the Dore is that springing up from its farther side is another range of crags even more forbidding than the Idles. Climbers' maps call them the Upper Crags. Their wrinkled, knotted faces, rearing up sometimes to beetling overhangs, are broken here and there by cascading falls of grey-green volcanic rock. These Upper Crags reach to the mountain's crown, which is known as Sledden Seat—probably, as Dr. Hugo Pater liked to say, because the Norsemen who invaded Cumberland a thousand years ago regarded this exalted summit as a happy seat for their northern gods.

ON THIS APRIL morning Dr. Hugo Pater and his friend Canon Joseph Nickle, the new vicar of Goswater with Sledden, emerged from Little Sledden and walked speedily towards the pony track. A stranger might have been surprised at their pace, for one was white haired, the other grey, and both looked over seventy. But the tall one, Dr. Pater, was a rapid, enthusiastic talker, and his discourse, like a sweetly working engine, determined the steps of his thin, eager legs. Canon Nickle, shorter and heavier, though four years younger, kept abreast because he so enjoyed the chatter.

The doctor wore a battered jacket open to the wind, and a black felt hat that had doubtless been impressive in his teaching days, but now was limp from a thousand mountain rains. Its brim fell over his white hair protectively, like the eaves of a Swiss chalet, and from under it the old black eyes sparkled with mischief.

"Look," he said, without slowing his pace. "Look up there." They were at a point on the road where they could see something of the Upper Crags. Two white specks, one above the other, were visible. "Unless I'm wrong, they're on one of the most ghastly climbs in the Lake District," Dr. Pater said. "Sumner's Overhang."

"Have you ever done it, Hugo?"

"My God in heaven, no—if you'll forgive the expression. It's listed as a Very Severe, but it used to be a Very Impossible till Sumner found a way up it one wild and careless afternoon when his life didn't seem important. But surely there are more than *two* on a Very Impossible Severe? Yes. There's the leader, belayed on the overhang, drawing in the rope. Those crags face northeast, Vicar. Have you ever pondered on the significance of that?"

"No, I'm too new here. Is there a significance?"

"*Is* there a significance? My dear Joseph, in the ice ages the northeast faces lay out of the sun, so the ice didn't melt as it did on the south and sunnier faces. It stayed as ice, and, moving ever so slowly, it cut and ground those jagged crags. It spent, I suppose, a few million years on the job. And that's why one side of this upper end of Sledden is smooth and grassy and the other has those shocking Idles. Ah well, you and I are just existing for a brief period between one ice age and the next. So are those lambs." He nodded towards the little white Herdwicks with their coal-black faces and black-trousered legs gambolling in the meadow beside them. "Their spell is even shorter than ours, but they certainly appear to be enjoying it."

Dr. Pater talked like this; he was very much the scholar, thinking in millennia. As a master at Milton Close School in Yorkshire, he had taught both the classics and mountain climbing, and so popular had he become that after a while he was made headmaster. Retired at sixty-five and a widower, he had come to Little Sledden to spend his declining years among mountains he'd always loved. Today, at seventy-eight, he must be in some sort of decline but, save on his scored face, it was nowhere visible.

Canon Nickle, who'd been here less than a year after thirty years in a crowded industrial parish, had quickly discovered in his scattered flock this nimble, scholarly man and delighted in him as a companion. The doctor's mind—in Sledden, Dr. Pater, though no medical man, had come to be called the doctor—seemed at home in any epoch of man—or of earth itself, apparently.

Canon Nickle deplored his own lack of comparable learning. "Unlike you, I never had brains, Oxford or no Oxford."

"Perhaps you hadn't, Joseph. But your years with the classics have scarred you. Else why on earth do you listen to all my extravagances with such a kindly interest? Ah, here is our excellent Harry Whinlake. The Whinlakes have been sheep farming on these fells for centuries, since their Norse ancestors invaded Cumberland."

They had come to where the road stopped at the gate of Old Sledden. In the cobbled farmyard a big, gaunt man stood beside his tractor, its trailer laden with manure, which he was about to drop in heaps on a ploughed field. The warm reek of the piled wet dung came pleasantly towards them, the very spirit of the whole world's farming borne upon its breath.

"Splendid smell," said the doctor. "So rich." His hand rose, greeting the possessor of such richness. "Hard at work, Harry?"

"Aye. Theer's ollas a mort o' wark for a hill farmer." Harry looked up out of pale blue eyes (his Norse ancestors, the doctor would say) and grinned. "A sheep farmer's boots are nivver really coald, we say." Whinlake, in his late sixties, was old enough to speak naturally the "Cummerlan'" dialect, while his two children, educated at Caldmere High School, spoke with accents little different from well-to-do townspeople.

The doctor tried the dialect. "How's tha luv'ly daughter, Harry?"

"Oor Marjy? She's aw' reet. At wark in yon medder."

"An' the lad, Matt? How's our Matt?"

"Och! He's a tarrable girt feul. Ah call him the stanner-by. Likely he's gapin' outa window nah and thinkin' what a fine chap he is, while his oald man and his sister git on wi' wark. He cud adone wi' a sight mair larropin' fra me when he wur a lad. No trooble wi' Marjy, though. Wheer ye goin' this mornin', gem'men?"

"Up by the crags to Sledden Seat, where we'll lunch."

"Why fowks go oop theer at aw' if they hev'n't got to, Lord aloan knaws. It's aw' reet for oald Tam Godrigg"—Tam was Harry's shepherd—"and for me; it's a shippert's and a farmer's job to foller t'sheep. But them climmers! Theer's some oop theer nah. Choosin' the hardest way and then givin' us aw' a mort 'a trooble when they brak their silly necks. T'sheep hev mair sense; they find the easiest way. Well, maist men are feuls at times. Ah include mesel'."

The doctor laughed. "Well, we two fools must hurry on, Harry. Good day to you."

"Jist you keep off t'crags and stick to tracks t'sheep hev made. Good day to you, gem'men."

They left him behind and soon saw his Marjy in the stony hay field. She was making it ready for the harvest, raking away its stones and the grey flocks of wool dropped by sheep. Her lustrous blonde hair fell below her shoulders, lifting in the wind as she raked. Her feet were bare, and above the well-shaped legs her coarse skirt played also in the wind. She was singing to herself, slightly off key.

406

"Hail, our Margaret!" Dr. Pater stopped by the wire fence.

Instantly she ran towards the two old gentlemen, eyes ready with welcome. But she could find nothing to say, so she just smiled.

To put her at ease the vicar teased her. "Not *Margaret*, Hugo. 'Greta' you must say. Greta is the name of her choice."

"Oh, I don't mind Margaret. It's Daddy's Marjy I can't stand." Then she spoke of something which was evidently on the top of her mind. "We've got two climbers coming to stay with us. Today!"

"At the farm?" Surprise made the doctor speak quite simply. "Your father's always said he'd never take in tourists. He'd give them teas, he said, but never beds."

She laughed. "He says the sheep clip no longer makes enough, so he'll clip the tourists as well. I shall love it. We're going to take them whenever Mrs. Pauncey's guesthouse is full. I shall have to make dinners for them." She grasped the top of the fence with both hands and leaned back, lifting her face happily and letting the full, curving hair hang back. "It's going to be fun."

"Do you know these young men? Or perhaps they're a couple of ancients like Joseph and me."

"Oh, *no!*" She blushed, for she sometimes called these two "my Ancients". Could they have heard? She hurried on. "One of them, Mrs. Pauncey says, is a famous climber. His name is Kingharber."

"Norman Kingharber—Norry! Yes, he really *is* a climber. I've met him often at the Climbers' Club. He does big things in the Alps, Greta. In the Himalayas too."

"How thrilling! And he's Oxford and all, Mrs. Pauncey says. Is he nice? Like . . . like you and the vicar?" Reparation lest she had hurt them just now.

"All people who are crazed on mountains are nice. He's a schoolmaster. A dangerous young man. He'll probably want to drag you up some impossible climb. People with obsessions are dangerous. Still, for your comfort, he's a magnificent leader and won't let you fall. Who's the other lad?"

"Someone called Wallis. They're coming together."

"Don't know him. Probably another tiger. But give my love to Norry. Well, come along, Vicar. Goodbye, my dear."

Greta returned to her stone raking as the Ancients put themselves to the steepening pony track.

"'A girl of nineteen is an extraordinary thing, Joseph," the doctor observed. "A girl of that age, if she has her share of beauty like our Greta, symbolizes the beauty of youthful aspiration: all its hungers, hopes and visions."

The vicar said only "Yes". He had his secrets about Greta. She was a regular attendant at his little church and had already come to talk to him more than once. At the local school, and at Caldmere High School, she had been one of the brighter pupils. Then when she was seventeen her mother had died, her father had needed her at home and she had had to leave school. So there were conflicts within her, between her loving duty to an ageing father and her secret cravings to escape. Had there been something a little desperate in that assertion, "It's going to be fun"? The vicar stayed quiet, keeping these matters in his heart.

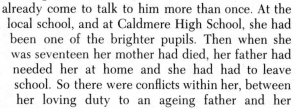

Greta

Walking up the pony track, they saw, high on the green fell that faced the Idle Crags, old Tam, Whinlake's shepherd, trailing behind a platoon of ewes and their lambs. These lambs were now strong enough to go up, after having Whinlake's red marks striped near their hind legs, to Old Sledden's allotted pasture. Two black-and-white collies ran round and round the flock, collecting the stragglers.

"I get the impression," the doctor remarked, "that the dogs really enjoy this bossing about of other creatures. Like men. How old is Tam?"

"Seventy-six, I think."

"And you're seventy-four. A mere lad. Great God—forgive me—I'm older than anyone living. The nearest thing in age to me is the mountains."

"Nonsense, Hugo. In some ways you're younger than us all."

"May you be forgiven, Joseph, for a kindly lie. Ever since my seventy-fifth birthday I've regarded each day as a bonus and got out of bed to enjoy it before the end. Let's join old Tam."

"Must we? Can't we stick to the track?"

"No. And you a mere lad! Dear me, no. As Harry says, sheep are the most sensible fell walkers in the world." The doctor, still talking vigorously, hurried up the steep gradient after the sheep.

Tam turned towards the voices, his long grey beard combed by the gathering wind. These high lean hills tend to breed high lean men, and if they are shepherds, whose work is largely on the solitary, majestic tops, they are often taciturn. Tam seemed to think that one word—or at a stretch three—was enough for most things.

"Good morning, Mr. Godrigg," the doctor said. "Quite a wind."

"Aye."

"Cold up here too."

"Aye, cold."

"How are you, Tam, these days?"

"Nobbut poorly."

"You look fine. Do the lambs go up as early as this?"

In answer Tam achieved quite a sentence. "Maister says they're oald enoof for t'fell yance they can joomp a gutter." But then he noticed one ewe limping behind the others, and an unreasonable dog barking at it. "Stop tha blether, tha feul dog." He dropped his shepherd's crook, picked up the clumsy, unshorn ewe and hung her around his shoulders. Head bowed by her weight, he muttered softly to the dog, "Pick oop stick, feul." Delighted, the dog gathered the long crook between his teeth and brought it behind his master. "That'll stop tha blether," Tam said.

Strangely it also seemed to stop Dr. Hugo Pater's flow of talk. Perhaps the old shepherd's taciturnity, now reassumed, made words unnecessary, or perhaps such terseness was a fitting acknowledgment of the silence and solitude on the tops they were now attaining. They came soon to the saddle where the pony track left them to wind away over the pass, and they swung around on the track that led into the Dore, the high valley beneath the Upper Crags.

GRETA, her raking done, dashed into the house to make sure it was perfect for Norry Kingharber and Mr. Wallis. The parlour was quite large and well furnished. Brightly patterned linoleum, newly polished by Greta, shone in the morning sunlight. On either side of an old deep window were two big leather chairs. There was a square dining table with an old-fashioned ball-fringed tablecloth, and on the walls a photograph of her father as a young man, another of her parents' wedding, and a large one of a magnificent sheep dog. She plumped up the cushions on the chairs, rearranged the daffodils and anemones she had put on the sideboard, and then stood looking out at the coarse, smelly yard, seeing little of it while she dreamed. Life was coming to the farm. Perhaps something fine would happen.

Greta, in her lonely years, had lived with two secret dreams. One grew from the inevitable longing for love, admiration, excitement, romance. She would bask in the sweet scent of some impossible happiness wherein she saw herself married to someone of wealth and position who would take her to wonderful places. She knew from her success at school that she had intelligence, and she could not but know that she also had some beauty to offer.

The other dream, even more completely private, was no less than a desire for goodness—a goodness of rather exceptional quality. This desire was a young plant raised in her by Canon Nickle's predecessor in the tiny Sledden church. It was being tended now by the Canon himself. And though it might seem at times in conflict with her first dream, it was quite a firm plant nowadays, and she truly wanted to nurture it.

Past twelve o'clock now. Any moment they might come. She leaned into the bow window and looked over a window box of flowers down the silent empty road.

TWO

"Shap Fell!" cried the young man in the red MGB as the road began to climb. He exulted in the name. "Shap Fell, Pug! It's the beginning of the mountains. The outskirts of paradise. Lovely, haggard country!" A silence, and he said more seriously, "I love Shap—it's the first promise of an escape into loneliness."

Pug Wallis did not notice that this might have been a strange sentence to come from a young man so apparently lively and happy, revealing perhaps a hidden melancholy. It was seven hours since they had left Brentham School in Buckinghamshire at five in the morning, and Norry had overtaken every car on the road with a merry wave. Pug had not been in the Lake District before, and Norry was determined to convert him to worship of mountains. Mountains were Norry's faith, and Pug could be a most promising convert, because he was a fine athlete, swift and hardy.

"By gock, as we say in Cumberland, I'm going to make a climber of you, Pug. Before we go home you'll be a tiger. You're coming up some Very Severes. The grades go: Moderate, Difficult, Very Difficult, Severe and Very Severe. Only the geniuses do the Excessively Severes, or Impossibles, as we modest men call them."

"Couldn't we settle for a Difficult this first time?"

"Certainly not. You're hot stuff at all team games. This is a game where we play a mountain, and a noble opponent he is, knowing every blasted trick for beating you. But when you've beaten him you'll love him for the rest of your life." Norry's zeal was rushing to the accelerator. The car was now doing seventy.

"But what," asked Pug, "if he beats you? What if you fall?"

"Depends, I imagine, on your former life. On the whole, I think we'd better keep you alive. I'm glad Ma Pauncey's guesthouse was full and we're being parked at the farm. There's a girl there, Pug, who's nothing less than a knockout."

Norry had never spoken to Greta, but he had often noticed her at Old Sledden, at work in the fields, once leaning on her farmyard gate, and each sight of her had disturbed him. When Mrs. Pauncey had written suggesting rooms at the farmhouse, his heart had quickened. He and that girl in the same house, she perhaps ready to fall in love . . . but, no—just a dream, exquisite and agitating . . . . He was not a heartless seducer; he could not want to hurt anyone, neither this pretty creature, nor the other young woman in his life. It was just that, like a thousand other young men, he indulged at times in thoughts he must hide.

The little red car went rocketing into the cottage-lined street of Little Sledden and stopped, Norry leaning on the horn, before the only large house in the village, Mrs. Pauncey's famous guesthouse —famous at least to climbers. Norry's loud greeting brought Mrs. Pauncey out of her door to respond in a delighted scream. "Ah! It's Norry. The deserter. How can you sit there and face me?"

411

Mrs. Pauncey was a broad-hipped, big-breasted woman with a girlish face. It was her ample body, her ample voice and her more than ample laugh that encouraged her guests to call her Pauncey to her face and Ma Paunchy behind her back.

"Norry, you traitor! We love you no more. Was it my fault you were too lazy to write in time? But the boy I've given your usual room to is a great improvement on you. You're very, very naughty."

"Not at all, Pauncey dear. It's you that's a wicked old woman. Turning me out into the street after all these years."

Norry

"Wicked!" And there was the famous Pauncey laugh, an uproar that resounded (so her young guests said) along the whole four miles of Sledden Valley. "Was it wicked to persuade Harry Whinlake to put you up, when he's never taken a guest in his life?"

"Nonsense, Pauncey. He needs the money. Pug and I—this is Pug Wallis—are going to be very happy there, away from all the rowdy kids at your house. I'm getting older and need quiet."

"*You* quiet! That's a good one! You'll be quiet in your grave, and not before. Don't you let him take you up anything really dangerous, Mr. Pug. Nobody should go up some of the places he climbs. He'll kill somebody one of these days."

"Grossly untrue, Pauncey. I'm the tenderest of teachers. But I'll forgive you this once."

"Forgive me! Now, Mr. Pug, don't you let him—"

But Norry had already started the car and was waving to her with his free hand. Almost at once they were out of Little Sledden, and then there were no further buildings in sight until they came to the farmstead gate. "There we are, Pug," he said. "There's nothing much after that farmhouse but God's own original chaos."

OLD SLEDDEN farmhouse was whitewashed stone, wide-fronted. Joining it was a roughly mortared cowhouse, with a hayloft above its broad door. Other barns stood beside the yard.

As the car stopped, some unseen sheep dogs opened an indignant protest. Norry heaved his long figure out of the car, and Harry, followed by two dogs, issued from a barn. "Aye," he said, opening the gate. "That'll be you."

Norry agreed that it was. "Yes, here we are, sir."

"Weel, it's first time we've tekken guests, but one's browt to onything these days. We're glad to hev you." Norry preserved his smile. "My lass'll mek you comfortable and cook you real gud fud. And that's what matters, is'na it?"

"Couldn't be more right, Mr. Whinlake. This is Mr. Wallis."

Harry agreed. "Aye. Mr. Wallis."

Norry said yes, agreeing with the agreement. And the rest was silence. Till Harry said, "Lass'll show you to yer rooms."

Norry descried her just within the door. She met his eye, and in shame at being caught peeping, leaned forward, standing now with a hand on each jamb—as if nothing had been farther from her mind than to halt in shyness. Her large, wide-spaced eyes offered their smile. Norry's heart quickened. Turning back to the car, he dragged out coiled ropes, two bulging bags and, most delightedly of all, his rock-climber's boots—whose sacred nails enshrined all his hopes and memories. One rope he tossed to Pug, the other he slung on his shoulder. "Shall we go in, Mr. Whinlake?"

"Heer, ah'll tek them bags."

"Oh, no, you won't, sir. We don't need any help. Come, Pug."

"This is my maid. Aye, heer's Marjy."

Her smile broke upon Norry and he saw the fascinated interest in her eyes, but the only words she could produce in her embarrassment were, "Would you like some lunch?" Wonderful the difference between her schoolgirl accent and her father's Cumbrian.

"No, thanks, my dear. We'll get straight out to the crags. Pug," he added, "this is our hostess. I don't know your name—"

"It's Margaret," her father said. "But she likes Greta."

The girl flushed, saying only, "This way, Mr. Kingharber."

So she had *his* name well enough. Pleasing. And to please her, he said, "Follow Greta, Pug."

413

Which caused her to turn and smile at him.

She took them to two small bedrooms, fresh and delightful with printed curtains and bedspreads, and bowls of forget-me-nots and primroses. "All lovely. Thank you, Greta," Norry said.

Hardly was she gone from hearing before Pug exclaimed, "My God! That girl!"

"Exactly. Disturbing. But forget her. She's not for you." From his bag Norry tossed onto the bed an Alpine jacket, thick Scottish socks and stout cord breeches—all heart-stirring garments. "I'm for the crags in twelve minutes. Go. Hurry."

It was twelve minutes later when Greta saw Norry standing outside the kitchen door in the sunlight. He was now in full climbing gear. His coiled rope was slung across his breast from one shoulder, and his other equipment was tied loosely around his waist. She suspected that he was displaying all this, in case she was watching.

WHEN THAT EVENING, after a brisk, warming-up walk, Norry and Pug sat down to dinner in the parlour, it was Greta's brother, Matt, who waited on them—if waited is not too generous a word for it. Dishes and plates bumped onto the table, unaccompanied by words of encouragement. Having dumped them, Matt stood staring out the window, presenting his back to the diners. Matt Whinlake was what his mother would have been content to call heavily built. His fat face was small-eyed enough for less partial observers to mention a potato.

Norry and Pug, full of goodwill, attempted to invade his massive silence. Norry, who rejoiced in friendliness, would have liked to call him Matt straightaway, but for the impenetrable aura round the young man. "Been a lovely day, Mr. Whinlake," he offered, hoping the "Mr." might please. But nothing would attract their waiter from the window. Norry could only grimace at Pug, and the two of them served themselves from the roast and vegetables.

When they were finished, Matt gathered up the crockery and departed. He came back with a fine browned apple pie, plopped it before them and went again to his window.

Pug said, "I think, Mr. Whinlake, your sister's calling you."

"Aye?" inquired Matt, turning around, and Pug found himself answering aye, probably for the first time in his life.

414

The call from his sister was for a bowl of rich cream that Matt had forgotten. He pushed it at them and then withdrew into the kitchen.

"Definitely a shade dim," said Pug, watching him go.

After Matt had cleared away the meal, Norry and Pug lit pipes, flung themselves into the two armchairs and were discussing how best to lure the daughter of the house into the room, when the father came in, his whole aspect implying a readiness for what he called "a rare old crack" with his visitors. Norry rose and offered him his chair, but Harry took a hard chair by the table. "Well, gud evenin', gem'men," he said. "Is there owt ah can tell you that you'd like to know?"

"Why, yes," said Norry, though in despair as he heard the girl humming in her kitchen. "Tell us how a hill farm is run."

No question could better have unloosed the farmer's tongue. "Weel, it's toof gangin' nah'days, and no mistek. Ah've nigh on a thousand acres, but it's mostly rough, high-level grazin'. Ah've nobbut ninety acres of inside land for crops and grass. Aye, it may be rough grazin' for t'sheep, but it's rough grazin' for t'farmer too, and t'farmer's family." And he was off on a full account of Marjy and Matt and the "tarrable gud woman" who had borne them and shared his life "back heer in this dyin' valley."

"*Dying*, did you say?"

"Aye. Ah mind when Sledden had its butcher and its cobbler and a blacksmith. But now—lads woan't stay in valley; they can git twice the wages in t'toons. Then, if a cottage comes on t'market, it's bought by people like you as a holiday place, and empty nine months o't'year. It's poor fun for Marjy. But she's a gud lass; goes to kirk and thinks t'worrld o' Canon Nickle. Ah'm glad t'lass listens to Mr. Nickle. It keeps her gud, which ah haven't the time to do. Matt's got hissel' sozzled wi' religion. He reads tracts, while the maid does the work. Not that she's perfect—she can be a worriment at times."

"But *how?*" Norry demanded, as if his host spoke of an impossibility, but happy to keep him talking about the girl.

"Weel, grummelin' about nivver seein' any life. Sometimes she'll sit and say nowt for hours. Odds-wods! If she's in a proper tantrum she'll gang off all trinked up, you know, powder an aw'. Theer's no so many young gommarels left around here now to play it soft with her, but them that do, do it well enough."

Norry was aware of a stab of jealousy, ludicrous since he could hardly be considered a rival.

"Does she encourage any of them?" he asked.

"Nivver a one. It's like she's ollas dreamin' o' somebody better than anyone here. Which I can understan', reely."

Greta's humming had long ceased. Hope of seeing her tonight having died, the young men's attention began to slacken. Perhaps the old man noticed this and was hurt, because he stirred and said, "Well, gud neet to you, gem'men. Ah'll be ga'in' now. You mun be riddy for bed, ah daresay."

AT THE DOOR of his bedroom Norry said, "Well, Pug, gud neet, as our host says. Tomorrow I'm going to haul you up a crag."

"Not a Severe, *please*," Pug begged, and with a lift of a hand went on down the long narrow passage, with thick black beams across the ceiling and thin black ones up the walls.

Norry had not been one minute in his bedroom when Greta came to his open door with two hot-water bottles on her arm. "Would you care for a hot-water bottle, sir?"

"Oh, my dear!" He saw shy pleasure in her eyes at these words. "Pauncey never gave us hot-water bottles. You're an angel."

A small smile. "I'll take Mr. Wallis his now, sir."

"No, don't go—and please have done with that 'sir'. Pauncey called me Norry when she wasn't calling me something much ruder. As for Mr. Wallis—Pug's the only possible name for Pug, you must surely see. Greta, you're a wonderful cook."

"Oh, no, sir—oh, I'm sorry." An apology for the "sir".

"You are. Though your brother's not too engaging a waiter."

"Oh, we're not sure he's all there," she suggested, laughing. "May I get you something? Milk? Or a pot of tea?"

"You're a sweetheart, but I don't need anything. You go to your bed and sleep."

Blushing at that "sweetheart", she departed down the passage to deliver Pug's hot-water bottle. Norry gazed after her slim youthful shape. It enchanted him, but it disordered his heart, intruding a fear there lest his control should break.

416

During the night the wind changed, and there fell a sheeting, shattering rain such as only these mountain kingdoms know. In the morning it was still pelting down. The brook was a foot higher than yesterday. The mountains showed in their every crease a narrow plunging white torrent.

"So?" said Norry, prospecting from the parlour window. "I know this valley; the sun'll be out before it's afternoon." And sure enough, the clouds split about noon and the sun came out for longer and longer stretches, pronouncing a benediction each time. Quickly they dressed for the fells, filled their rucksacks and hastened out. Norry wet a finger and held it up to feel the cold kiss of the wind. It was still in the dangerous west. "Risk it," he said.

At the gate they paused to watch a noisy procession coming up the road. Tam Godrigg was bringing ewes with their lambs to the folds behind the farmhouse for the lambs to be marked. Greta was running after errant ewes with her hair flying. Matt did his share solemnly, touching each silly vagrant with a stick. Strangely, Tam Godrigg, older by fifty years, was making the most noise, slapping his crook on the road and roaring orders at the dogs: "Gang ahint, feul," which meant fetch up laggards from behind, or "Fetch *on!* Coom *in* wid 'em." Which the dogs did with delight.

Greta waved to her laughing guests and spread despairing hands, feigning total exhaustion and breathlessness.

THE YOUNG MEN were perhaps halfway up the pony track when they saw two figures come down from the high valley called the Dore. They were Dr. Pater and Canon Nickle—both wet through, both shivering, and stumbling in their hurry to get home. But the doctor still talking.

"Nothing but a hot bath will save me from death," he was saying. "Hang it, I'm seventy-eight, and I await some terrible collapse every day. You're a mere chicken, Joseph, and I doubt if you're as wet as I am." The sodden brim of the doctor's hat now sagged down over his eyes. "You shall have a hot bath too. How

417

good to see my toy village down there, and my toy dwelling in its
midst. No, Joseph . . . not now. If I stop I shall die."

The vicar had stopped to drive into the peaty earth with his heel
some eggshell and orange peel which a luncher had dropped.
"Sorry, Hugo, but I can never leave these desecrations unremoved.
If I do, I feel in a state of sin."

"Quite agree. So do I. But not when I'm soaked to the skin. Just
pray next Sunday that the desecrater may be saved from hell. Now,
who are these men coming up the slope?"

".I think," said the vicar, straining his eyes, "that it could be your
Norry Kingharber and his friend."

"Could well be. But I beg you will not stay to chat with them,"
said the doctor, lifting a wet arm in salutation. "Perhaps we could
pass by quickly with a *Grüss Gott*, as we do in the Alps."

Norry had now recognized them and was waving.

"*Grüss Gott* and pass by," the doctor begged again. ". . . Good
day, Norry, my dear boy. We heard you were coming. And is this
your friend?" And far from passing by, the doctor engaged the
two young men in a friendly chat. He asked how they were faring
at the farm, and sought news of Norry's school. The vicar waited
there shivering until at last the doctor's own shivers defeated him.
"Well, good hunting, Norry . . . and Mr. Pug. Don't stop here
chattering, Vicar. If we don't keep moving we shall certainly die,"
and he took off down the track at breakneck speed.

By the time they moved into the village street, the doctor leading
the vicar by a pace and a half, the pair of them might have been
two competitors nearing a dead heat in a long-distance walk.

They hastened inside the doctor's cottage.

"Quickly into the caldarium, Joseph," urged the doctor. His
Roman name for his bathroom varied; often it was the tepidarium.
"As your host, I must let you use it first. You know where the neces-
sarium is, don't you? Thank your God I put it indoors. It used to
stand in the garden, in full view of Mrs. Pauncey's windows. Ah,
there is Johnny Blenco in the garden."

They were at the end of a passage whose door opened onto the
garden. Dr. Pater went out and resignedly the vicar followed him.

After all, thought the vicar, they had walked miles in a state of
saturation, so what mattered another cold minute or two?

419

Johnny Blenco, at work with his back to them, presented a curious shape in this square of walled garden bright with flowers. A small man, in his early thirties, Johnny was humpbacked and lame, with a head too large for his body. His hump and a shortened leg were probably congenital deformities left untreated by simple parents in a lonely valley. As doctor and vicar stepped into the garden, he looked up from the plant he was tying to a stake.

As always, the vicar felt a stab of sorrow to see the difference between that misshapen body and the remarkable beauty of the face, with its straight masculine nose, large brown eyes and strong mouth.

Johnny smiled, and this smile, turned on you suddenly, was like the sun on this morning breaking through cloud. "After last night's storm I thought I'd get a few stakes in," he said. In his accent there was no more trace of Cumbrian than in Greta's, though he too was a native of the vale.

Canon Nickle

"Wonderful fellow, isn't he, Vicar?" said the doctor. "Not only one of the world's best gardeners, but he has all the talents. He's Pauncey's electrician—Pauncey is bewildered by electricity—and he can plaster walls; he can even repair a dry stone wall, an art far beyond my understand—" He stopped with startling abruptness, perceiving the brief shake of Johnny's fine head at all these flatteries. "Did you have a go at the hypocausis, Johnny?"

"Yes. I stoked the boiler up when I realized that you and the vicar must be getting soaked."

"Good. Fine. And would you, my dear fellow, dash in and make us a fire in the scriptorium? Come in, Vicar, we can have boiling hot baths and possibly survive."

"Are you really telling me," the vicar asked inside, "that Johnny knows what you mean by a hypocausis and a scriptorium?"

"Of course. There's hardly a book on my shelves he hasn't read.

420

Do go and get that bath, Vicar, and don't dawdle. I'm cold."

When the vicar was in the bath he heard the doctor's voice. "You wouldn't be getting that bath now if Johnny didn't see to my pipes. And he can handle sheep as well as Tam."

"And you've not mentioned," said the vicar, splashing, "that besides looking after my churchyard, he's verger and sacristan."

"Look," said the doctor. "I wouldn't wish to hurry you, but apart from a towel like an archbishop's cope, I'm in a state of nature out here. There's the question of pneumonia."

THE SCRIPTORIUM, or study, overlooked the garden. Less than fifteen minutes later they were in it before a crackling fire, the doctor pacing up and down for greater fluency. He did not like yielding to the vicar in listing Johnny's talents.

"Look at him now. He's disbudding my rose trees and putting a mulch around them. I always say the lad has life in his fingers. But there are things about him I can't understand. It seems to be generally held that he has an odd gift for healing. Have you heard the story of old Tam Godrigg? You haven't?

Dr. Pater

"It was the winter before you came, when the snowfalls were heavy and Tam had to take hay up to his sheep. One day a freezing sleet was falling and chilled him so that he came down with pneumonia. For a time he was delirious, and Johnny went in day and night to look after him. We all help each other in this valley, so John's many employers set him free to do this. It was about the seventh day when the fever left old Tam . . . . But then, just when we thought all was going fine, complications set in and he was delirious again. Doctor Towney said this sort of attack was nearly always fatal. But Johnny just shook his head and from then on

421

stayed with Tam all the time. One evening I wandered in to see if I could help, and what I saw was Johnny holding one of old Tam's long thin arms, with his eyes fixed on Tam's face, while Tam moaned or tore at the bedclothes. Johnny signalled to me to keep still. I waited and waited, and ever so slowly the awful restlessness stopped and the hands clutching at the bedclothes became quite still. I whispered, 'Dead?' but Johnny smiled and shook his head. Later I asked, 'How do you manage to induce a peaceful sleep like that?' And what do you think his answer was?"

The vicar said, "I don't know."

"Exactly. That was his answer. 'I don't know, sir. I try to think of nothing—except wishing him well again.' Later he added, 'I feel a kind of confidence pouring out of me that the pain will go. And it seems to go.' Towney said he'd never heard of such a recovery. But no one ever speaks a word to Johnny about it, because he always looks as though he couldn't bear any mention of it. But it's not the only story they tell of his healings. He—" The doctor guillotined his sentence, and coughed.

Johnny had limped in. "I think I'll be going now, sir. I may come back this afternoon to ring the apple tree."

"Delighted if you do, Johnny; but what is ringing?"

"I strip away a half ring of bark from one side of the tree and another from the other side, lower down. It encourages the tree to produce more fruit and less wood."

"Could you apply a similar treatment to young Matt Whinlake, Greta's brother? Don't you think he'd do with a little less wood?"

Johnny accorded this only a nervous twitch-away of his head. The vicar, surprised, thought it was the mention of Greta's name that had provoked it. With a small smile, Johnny walked away.

"What does he do alone in that cottage?" the vicar asked.

"Reads. All my books." The doctor swung a hand towards the packed bookshelves on the walls. "Classics. Philosophy. But most of all, biographies of men who've achieved greatness. I sometimes wonder if he escapes from reality by dreams of being like them."

"Has he had any schooling?"

"Up to thirteen or so. I half suggested helping him, but he shies from help, just as he shies from praise. Resolved to stand on his own two feet, even if they don't match. And he's doing it. He makes

422

much better money as universal factotum than he would have done as a farm labourer. It's whispered that living quite alone he's amassed a pretty little pile."

"How is it he's never married?"

"*Married?* Surely he's too proud. He's not going to offer a girl a humped back and a game leg. Not to the only kind of girl he'd want. But who really knows a thing about our Johnny the Silent?"

Later the vicar walked by Johnny's cottage next door. It was set back from the road, with a dry-walled garden in front of it blooming in every cranny with alyssum, rock roses, lavender, saxifrages, gentians. The paint on the house shone like the glaze on porcelain. Even the usual doorstone of green volcanic slate shone hardly less. A japonica and a mallow draped themselves over the doorway. Everything showed the house-pride of the tenant. And the vicar wondered whether this house and garden were an unconscious extension of an unlovely body, they at least being beautiful.

FOUR

Inside the cottage Johnny Blenco sat with his elbows on a small round table. Before him was an open book, *Fridtjof Nansen: Explorer, Ambassador, Humanitarian.* Reading the Nansen, he had imagined himself an explorer. But now he was thinking, thinking on two secret matters he could tell to no one. And the first of them was this: in these last few years it had been impossible for him to look without hunger at Greta Whinlake, when helping her father, or passing her in the road and receiving her merry greeting. Like Norry, he would look after her slim retreating figure and draw from it pleasure, but for him the pleasure changed quickly into pain. She, the most beautiful girl in the valley, and he—he what he was. He, too, who in secret so prided himself on his intelligence.

And yet . . . and yet, this morning he had seen her in her doorway laughing with that splendid young man who was said to be a famous climber and the son of a wealthy family. He had seen the sparkle in her eyes as she looked up into his face—and pain thrust itself through his heart. When he had seen her talking to the sons of local farmers there had also been pain, smaller though, for he

423

was sure enough she would never content herself with one of these. But anyone could see how easily she might fall in love with this young man.

Or—wait—was it not more possible that in a lonely farmhouse a handsome young man might pluck the fruit of a girl's adoration and, having enjoyed it, disappear? To think this was to open a knifelike wound. Not a wound to his morality; a wound to his love.

The thought of morality carried him to the second of his extremely private matters. This cottage might touch Dr. Pater's wall and have the little home of the schoolmistress only three feet from its other side, but for Johnny at times it became a secret place where he could consider who or what was his God and where lay his duty to Him. Though never a word had he spoken to the vicar, he had come to believe that the whole of this transient material world, which offered him so little, was interpenetrated by something not material, but eternal, timeless. And *good*. Such was his God. Presumably it was a divinity far more ill-defined than the God of Canon Nickle, but it was near enough to the vicar's God for Johnny to be ready to serve in the yew-shadowed church along the road.

He had coined his own phrase for this God, three words he'd have been ashamed to uncover to anyone. He had summed Him up as "the three l's": life, light and love. If He was life, then His perfect expression in this world must be health, and one could strive to draw this from Him for oneself and perhaps for others. If He was light, then one could draw from Him ever-clearer understanding. And if He was love, then deformity mattered less than one thought, and one's business was to be a channel of that love to others. One's business and one's happiness.

Such then were the unspoken creed and chosen course of Johnny Blenco. And here this afternoon he was striving to draw from all this some power to quiet the ache of an impossible love and to keep himself sane and unselfseeking.

Without success . . . . However he'd been able to still the pains in old Tam Godrigg, he failed to temper his own heartsickness. It yielded to neither will nor trust nor prayer.

He looked around at the bookshelves on every wall, the flowered curtains in the windows, the high stone mantel above the deep fireplace. Nothing will ever change, he thought. Always you will be alone. No lover will ever sit in that chair, because the only one you want is not for you. Best accept it! Accept, accept—abandon absurd imaginings. There are other happinesses elsewhere.

Well . . . it was long after two and he had not yet had a meal. He decided to make himself a really good one. For Johnny had acquired from the doctor not only a love of books, but a love of good food and wines. Earning good money, he was able to indulge in this comforting luxury.

He moved his book off the table and laid out a knife and fork and a wineglass. Then, in his tiny kitchen, he cooked in butter some sliced carrots, onions and celery. In another pan he put more butter and a fillet of halibut. When the vegetables were cooked he added them, with a little stock and a touch of white wine, to the fish. A quarter of an hour later he poured a cream sauce over the fish and removed it to a plate on which a potato and some spinach were already laid. Then he carried the whole attractive dish to the table and sat down to enjoy it with the excellent bottle of chilled Riesling that it deserved.

NORRY AND GRETA were alone in the farmhouse, he in the parlour, she in the kitchen. Her father was out lambing with Tam Godrigg; Pug, whose parson father had long ago known Canon Nickle, had gone to supper at the vicarage; Matt was heaven knew where.

So silent was Norry that Greta, her curiosity rising, feigned a duty in the yard and passed the open parlour door. Her brief glance startled her. Norry was standing with his back to the fire, and on his face, staring sightlessly towards the door, there rested something like absolute despair. Norry, the impudent, stood there like a monument to dejection, arms fallen to his sides. Greta felt as if she'd trapped something that was not for her eyes. She returned to the kitchen.

But Norry, coming sharply to the surface, realized that Greta had twice passed the door. His heart pounded. At last he had his chance to talk with her instead of her father. There was so little time! This was their fourth day, and summer term began twelve days from now.

"Greta," he called.

Sounds of her rising from a chair and hurrying. "Yes, sir?"

"Greta, *damn* that 'sir'. My name is Norry. Now, Gretchen, I'm all alone here. Take a little pity on me and come and talk."

"I'd love to, sir." True—it sparked in her eyes.

"Let me hear that 'sir' again, and I'll beat you." A phrase which shook his heart. "Let me hear you say, 'Norry dear, I'm coming to sit with you.'" A shy smile. "Come on, say it."

A throw back of the head. "Norry, I'm coming to sit with you."

"Good. A bit forced, but you'll improve."

He walked to his usual armchair and threw himself into it. She entered hesitantly. Lord, she's beautiful, he thought.

"That's right," he said. "Now sit in Pug's chair. Do you like Pug?"

"He's very nice."

"I love old Pug. A marvellous athlete. We've only done five or six climbs, and he's already an expert. *You're* going to come with me one day, and I'll make *you* an expert."

"Oh, no. Even to see climbers on the crags turns me sick."

"You'd be on a rope, remember, and even if you should peel off the mountain, I'd never let you fall. I'd be roped to the mountain above you. If I fell, the mountain'd have to come too."

"I've no proper boots."

"That's no excuse. On the first fine day you'll be able to do it in bare feet." Even to think of her bare feet! "Wait till you get the feel of dry rock under your toes. It's exultation."

"Oh, shall I really try? Dare I?"

"You shall. There's no sense of achievement quite like balancing on your toes on an inch-deep foothold of rock, helped only by a glorious thank-God handhold above you. And there's no sense of triumph to equal arrival at the summit."

Norry was a hot gospeller for the mountains, his eyes on fire with his faith. He poured forth the faith with words that captured her interest. The mountains were escape, escape! You climbed high above the world of men, out of all their conventions, sins and cruelties, out of the hideous, polluted civilization they'd built with their sciences. But he had travelled too fast and too far for Greta. She brought him back.

"*Sins*"? What *could* he mean?

He lit a cheroot, leaned back and blew smoke rings towards the

426

ceiling. "How, when you stand so high, *can* you be anything but more or less what the Creator wants you to be? I tell you one's enlarged up there." Her eyes were fixed on him with heightened interest and much new understanding as he ran on. "Gretchen, have you ever been on Scafell Pike?"

"We leave that to you tourists. I've only been up to the Dore."

"Well, up on the pikes you feel you've escaped, not only out of the world of men, but out of time itself."

This clouded her eyes. She demanded what on earth he meant.

"Nothing on earth, my sweet. Earth is left behind. When the sun comes out suddenly up there, I know what Shelley meant when he wrote: *The great morning of the world when first God dawned on Chaos.* You've read Shelley, haven't you?"

She looked discomfited as she answered unwillingly, "No, but I've read Shakespeare and Tennyson and . . . and others."

He perceived that she wanted to show that she too had culture. To put her at ease he said, "Oh, there's buckets of time for you. Half of what I've read I only read because I had to teach it."

"Yes, but I really love reading," she assured him, rebuilding a wall of pride that had fallen. "I get books from the county library, and Canon Nickle has lent me some. So has Johnny Blenco. He's terribly clever. You must know him. . . . Do go on."

Sad, thought Norry, his ever-dominant desire to show off. He had to say something to impress her with his brilliance. He took to telling about his climbs in the Alps with guides and in the Himalayas with Sherpas. But only a little of this was vainglory; more was as serious as any ardent preacher could make his gospel. Then he caught himself, and ran from the subject. "Only a few more days," he lamented. "But I'll come again in September. Early August in the Alps, then Sledden."

"Oh, you *will* come again? And you'll come *here*?" she pleaded. And immediately flushed, thinking this eagerness had revealed too much.

"Yes, four whole weeks." Apparently he had noticed nothing.

"Oh, good." But she said this conventionally, as if to undo the previous fervour. Indeed, as a counterweight to that excess, she asked with a mischievous look as though prepared, herself, to be unselfish, "Don't you *ever* spend your holidays with your parents?"

427

This led him to talk of his home and family, which fascinated her. He described his family's eighteenth-century home in Grosvenor Square, which meant nothing to her till he said, laughing, that it was surrounded by embassies, whereupon she began to feel humble and afraid. He had two sisters, he said, one older than he and married, the other younger and engaged.

"Married to whom?" she asked, greatly interested.

"Well, Lucy's married to a baronet fellow, who's a barrister of sorts. We're rather mixed up with the law, you know."

"Baronet?" Greta's unease increased. "So she's a Lady Someone?" Oh, well. . . . "And your other sister?"

Marion, he explained, was engaged to a lieutenant in the Welsh Guards, which didn't frighten Greta as much but did nothing to lessen her awe. After a pause induced by fear, she ventured, "You've never told me what your father is."

"Oh, he's a judge, a lord of appeal in ordinary."

Her heart rocked. "Does that mean he's a lord?"

"Only since he was appointed to be. The law lords are the last court of appeal in the country, but they're only life peers."

"He is Lord Kingharber, though? And your mother's a baroness?" The heart which had rocked was now a deadweight.

"Of sorts, yes. But only since last year."

None of this was bragging, even if some of his earlier talk had been. What he had lived with for thirty years was so ordinary to him that he couldn't think of it as remarkable to anyone else. He had no cause to notice that Greta sat there stricken with the whole peerage. So it was not in apology but in affection that he said, "But I've talked enough about myself. Now tell me all about Greta. You're much more interesting than I am."

GRETA stood in her narrow bedroom, not beginning to undress. Seldom more saddened, she gazed before her and saw nothing. Had she not talked far too much about herself? Hadn't she bragged about her success at school? Hadn't she gone out of her way to imply that it had been rather splendid of her to give it all up so as to help her old father? Horrible braggings! It was true enough that she loved her old father and that she had longed to comfort and help him, but she should never have told a stranger, even laughingly, that her father had said it was *her* help he needed because she was twice the man that Matt was. Oh, dear, that could never be unsaid . . . .

At last, led by an old habit when sadness possessed her, she leaned her head against a wall and called herself a fool. What dreams had been hers about young guests who would come to the farm she could not say, because she had never clothed them in words. One small clouded dream there had certainly been, and Norry had enlarged it by his pleasure in her company and apparent unconsciousness of any class distinction. Now, after this talk about his family, that inflating balloon had sunk in emptiness to the ground. She had only to think of that stately mother, and she saw a remote farmhouse struggling for life at the beginning of nowhere. Silly, foolish dreaming. Why didn't one live with life as it was, and always would be? One was, after all, grown-up.

"Oh, well, oh, well. . . ." She lifted her forehead from the cold wall—a silly place to lean it, anyway—and began to undress. Norry clearly liked her, and that was something—or he had till this evening; but what now? Perhaps in the morning he'd have forgotten all her offensive talk and they'd have fun together for a few days. After that—well, nothing. Be done with dreams.

In her nightgown she thrust this new sensible creature fiercely into the narrow bed—where it lay worrying as before.

FIVE

On Saturday night Pug, who had thoughts of reading for holy orders, broke the news to Norry that he was going to church.

Norry exclaimed, "Oh, no! No, Pug. Not on a holiday."

"I'll only go to early service at eight o'clock. We'll have all day."

"*Eight?* But do they still have services in that microscopic church?"

"Of course. The vicar celebrates early Mass at Goswater one Sunday and at Sledden the next."

"OK. You go. But don't expect me to come."

"Of course you needn't come. I'll be back for breakfast."

But the word breakfast had recalled other words of Mr. Whinlake's: "A gud lass; goes to kirk and thinks t'worrld o' Canon Nickle." Norry on the whole preferred such girls. He felt safer with them. Pleasant to go to church when she would be there and to walk home with her. He got so few chances of talking to her.

And then she stood in the doorway as if his thoughts had drawn her there. "Excuse me. Would you mind breakfast a little late tomorrow? I try to go to church when there's a service."

"My dear sweet girl, I was just saying I would go to early service and was trying to persuade Pug to come too."

"Of all the foul lies!"—from Pug.

"Oh, well, perhaps it was the other way round. Anyhow, we'll all go like good children, and then walk home together. Or perhaps after church you have to meditate or something?"

"Oh, no. It'd be lovely to have you to come back with."

"Do you really go *every* Sunday?" he said, to keep her there.

"If I possibly can. Sometimes twice."

"Gretchen, my God!"

"Why?" She laughed, pleased to linger and take the chaff.

"Well, you must be so frightfully good after all that treatment. Though that may not follow. Pug does the same sort of thing and he's not all that better than I am. A little nicer, perhaps, but not much. Though he might be a lot worse if he didn't. Now, why don't you come in instead of standing in the doorway like that?"

"No, I mustn't. I've things to do."

"But Pug and I've got to go in a few days, and then you'll be sorry you didn't sit and chat with us. Remember, Gretchen, if you refuse to come and talk to me sometimes, I shall go back to Mrs. Pauncey's in September. At least she talks. Never stops. But I'd so much rather listen to you. I don't really love Pauncey."

So the flattering banter with its hidden love hints went on, but he couldn't hold her for long, though he could see she'd have liked to stay, had not doubt and discretion overcome her.

When she was gone he said, "Pug, I'm certainly going with you. I'm not having you walking home alone with Greta."

WITHIN its solemn guard of yew trees the church of Sledden seems, as you enter it, little more than a square, white-walled box. A few rows of dark wood pews face a small railed sanctuary, and over the altar is a tall, wide, pointed window of clear glass. If the interior is not unlike a sheephouse with pens, perhaps this has an aptness, because a sheephouse is a sanctuary for lost or helpless lambs.

Along a painted scroll above the window run the words, *I will lift up mine eyes unto the hills, from whence cometh my help.* This window was the creation of an eccentric Sledden vicar, who had cleared away three commonplace stained-glass windows and substituted this one tall width, declaring, "No man living can make a reredos to equal a vision of God's own mountains." Well, if as you kneel you see the highest summits of the Cumbrian massif, or if, better still, there is mist along the mountains and suddenly, as often happens here, the mist opens a gap for a moment and shows you mountain crowns lit with the sun and looking like the hills and precipices of God, you may begin to wonder if that old vicar was so eccentric after all.

It was clear and sunny when Greta set off for early service, not once looking back, but hoping her guests might come running out to join her. She had begun to "leave herself around" when she suspected they would be starting out for the day.

They did not come now and she walked to the church alone.

They came along the road many minutes later, in a hurry, for they had loved their beds. The church's single bell was still sounding, and by hurrying they hoped to be in time and not offend. When softly they entered the church they saw Greta in a pew second from the front, so they put themselves modestly in the last pew of all. Norry was surprised to see others in the church at such an early hour, but it was spring holidays for some, and one or two worshippers were from Mrs. Pauncey's—why, there was Pauncey herself!—and girls from the youth hostel in their jeans, ready for the hills. There was only one other man, dressed in his Sunday suit. Where was Matt Whinlake, said to be so preoccupied with religion?

The bell stopped. A silence, and then Canon Nickle, in full vestments, walked up the nave to the sanctuary, preceded by Johnny Blenco, his disfigurement covered by surplice and cassock. Having poetry in him and so great a love for these valleys, Norry was impressed by this picture: a celebrant in plain but beautiful robes, an active server, two candles gleaming on the altar, and above them, through that window, those living mountains in the sunlight.

431

But more often than at the hills his eyes were on the slender figure of Greta, with the arc of blonde hair lying across her back; and a wave of tenderness poured into him as he heard her—for the space between them was small—saying some response or prayer in a voice low but clear.

Greta had seen him come in, and she found her thoughts wandering more often than usual from the service. She had to struggle especially hard to hold them tight to their proper business. Yesterday she had seen on Norry's face for a second time that look of total melancholy. She had walked into the parlour to ask him a question and had seen him gazing out the window in seemingly desolate thought. When he realized she was in the room, he turned towards her with his merry, public face, but in that second she knew again that beneath the jubilant talk, the ardent enthusiasm, there lay some private heartache. And now, on her knees, she began to understand that his craving for hazardous climbs and solitudes was an escape from, or a rebellion against, this dark despondency within him.

But enough! Oh, God, forgive me for letting my thoughts wander like this. Help me to keep them on the service. I do want to always, but it is so difficult. Where are we now? Oh . . . And she said the responses fervently—just loud enough, though she did not know this, for Norry to hear and be touched by them.

But then again, soon after she was thinking about poor Johnny Blenco as he knelt on a step below the celebrant. She could see the sole of his orthopaedic boot extending from under his cassock. Dear Johnny! So solitary he always seemed. He too must live with secret sadness, and longings that in his case were really unlikely to be achieved. Often there was a smile on his so startlingly beautiful face, but, as with Norry, the sadness would be there when he thought no one was looking. There was, however, a difference, she thought, between the terrible melancholy on Norry's face and the frequent sadness on Johnny's. Norry's seemed empty of hope, Johnny's sad, certainly, but—perhaps the word was "wise". It seemed like a sad, wise confidence.

But here—really!—honestly!—they were at the Prayer of Consecration, the most sacred moment in the service, and she was worlds away. To strain for attention she sank her brow onto her two arms along the back of the pew in front of her. Outside the church

432

a cow lowed . . . no other sound anywhere . . . and the Prayer of Consecration went softly on.

When the service was over, Norry led Pug to the graves of two young mountaineers in the little churchyard. Like all the other graves, they had headstones of the local green slate, plain and homely, and stood among high, uncut grass with wild flowers bespattered everywhere like confetti.

The first stone told of a young climber who "fell while attempting the Greater Peregrine Buttress, hitherto unclimbed, and who now lies by the hills he loved." The parents had added, *A man's reach should exceed his grasp, Or what's a heaven for?* The grandeur of Robert Browning's words always dragged at Norry's heart. "Parents to love, those," he said. Then he turned away. "Come and look at this one."

This one recorded the death of a young man who, overtaken by a blizzard in the high valley under Sledden Seat, had broken an ankle as he struggled to descend. Norry knew his story. His two companions had made him comfortable under the lee of a great boulder, covering him with every garment they could spare, and then hastened down for help. But when they got back to him he was dead from cold and exposure.

Pug and Norry came away from this grave quietly, to see that Greta had emerged from the church and was waiting near the gate. Just as they came close to her, and as Norry said, "Good morning, beloved," Mrs. Pauncey issued from the door. "She must have been praying long and powerfully," Norry whispered. "Or else she's been talking her head off to the vicar."

Seeing him, she screamed, "Norry! I'm flabbergasted! I used to insist that you ought to come to church, but you'd only sit there making fun of me. Have you become holy all of a sudden?" And in that little churchyard the vociferous laugh seemed misplaced. Surely loud enough, thought Norry, to wake the dead. One imagined it stopping the flights of birds.

For once he could dredge up no impudent answer, and, anyhow, Pauncey was now eyeing Greta. "Aha! *Now* I see why you've come. An excellent reason."

Norry wished to heaven that the old cow would stop shouting her crude suggestions all over the valley. However true, it could offend Greta. "Do keep quiet, Pauncey," he begged. "Do remember you've been in church and ought to be behaving."

"I like that! Norry telling me how to behave! Greta dear, I hope you're keeping this young devil in order. I must hurry on. My guests want their breakfast. 'Bye, children."

When she was through the gate, after turning to telegraph a smile to them, Norry complained, "The frightful old cow! It always staggers me that anyone with so villainous a tongue can go so happily to church. If the Pauncey takes a dislike to you, you've *had* it. Just now she still loves me a little, but woe betide me if she changes her mind. Come along, Greta darling, and make me whole again. She's nearly ruined my morning."

As they went out of the gate Johnny Blenco came limping from the little vestry into the churchyard. He saw the happy three walking along the road, talking and laughing together, one of them that tall young climber, so perfect a pattern for a man. As he watched them go he saw that young man lay an arm along Greta's shoulder and draw her against him in affectionate fun. At the gate Johnny turned and walked towards his cottage. He did not turn to look at them again. All he did was to say to himself, I know my course. It was a habit of his, when hopelessness sank his heart, to repeat these words, over and over, so that they might take root in him.

But one of his dark moods had got him now—moods that fought with his course; ill-humoured moods in utter disharmony with his trust in that life and light and love for which it was his secret desire to become a channel. When such a mood gripped him he could only instruct himself—he did it now: *Hold*—and cry for help from the God who was nowhere in sight.

Whether these moods, emptied of all love, were getting less frequent in his solitary life he was not sure; he hoped they were. But he *was* sure that they would never beat him. Today he knew that either before he reached his cottage, or soon afterwards, he would emerge from this present assault. And be on course again.

GRETA, at Johnny's very moment of pain, was speaking of him to her companions. "Hasn't he the most marvellous face?" she said. "Everybody loves our Johnny—but just fancy having a face like

434

that on top of such a body! In a smaller way, I suppose, it's the same for everyone—if a girl's got a beautiful face, ten to one she's got thick ankles. Or if she's got marvellous ankles, she's got a nose like a horse. Why does nobody ever have everything perfect?"

Norry said significantly, "I can think of some who have." And giving Greta no chance to demur, he went on to announce that he was going to take her on a rock-climb very soon. Lord's Trod, it should be—a Moderate among the Upper Crags—and as easy as winking for a novice. "Now, don't be a silly kid, Gretchen. You'll be perfectly safe. You *will* come, won't you, sweet?" This was the point at which he'd given her the encouraging hug that Johnny Blenco had seen. "The Lord's Trod is easy, isn't it, Pug?"

Harry Whinlake

"Not too bad," said Pug, grimacing nevertheless.

"There you are. You can trust Pug. Come this evening and we'll explain it all to you."

But that evening after dinner, when Norry and Pug sat waiting for Greta, it was her father who appeared again, pipe aglow. "Weel, my young friends," he began genially. "Ivverything fine an' dandy for you, ah hope?"

"Lovely," said Norry in despair. "Won't you sit down, sir?"

"Aye, ah'll sit doon." And he sat with an elbow on the table and the pipe in his mouth, clearly settling in. "Marjy says you want to tek her climmin' tomorrow. Ah suppose that'll be aw' reet, but just you tek gud care of her. She's t'best thing ah got, and ah doan't want her hurt in any way. Nowt amiss in Marjy except a bit stubb'n offen-times."

"Stubborn, sir?" If all hope of an evening with Greta was gone, it was some consolation to talk about her. "Surely not with you."

"Mans, this varra day, when ah tell't her she mun't go climmin' wid you, by jing, ah got t'treatment. I might as well ha' bin talking

435

to my grindstone as to my dowter. When Marjy's in that mood ah just give in at the end. Oh, aye. It's best. Ah said, 'Aw' reet, aw' reet, go wid 'em, lass, wi' my blessin', but tek gud care o' thyself, because ah ain't got owt but thee,' an' at that she flings her arms around me and hugs and kisses me."

This statement his listeners greeted with the broadest smiles of understanding. It was not the way Norry had hoped to get Greta's answer, but it would do.

THEY STOOD at the foot of Lord's Trod, a towering buttress of the Upper Crags, so riven and ribbed by the weather of a million years that, while it looked like a frightening precipice, it offered many a foothold, handhold or belay. "I want you to feel the glory of dry rock under your feet and your fingers. That's the start in a terrific love story," Norry said.

Greta, looking up at the sheer cliff, acted out a shiver. "I've no love yet." She stood there in jeans, old climbing boots from Mrs. Pauncey's collection, and a vast Shetland sweater of Norry's, which he had rejoiced to pull over her.

"Don't tell her, Pug, but she looks quite adorable," he'd said. "Every inch a climber. A real tiger. Sweetheart, you don't know the joy that is coming to you."

Now he uncoiled the hundred-and-twenty-foot rope, fixed one end around his waist with a bowline and some half hitches, and then, about halfway down its length, tied it around her waist (enjoying this) with a simple overhand knot, simple in case she might have to adjust it. Meanwhile Pug, expert now, was hitching himself to the other end of the rope.

"There we are." Norry was a comforting teacher with any novice, but seldom so gentle as with this one. "Nothing to fear. I'm going to leave so little of the rope slack that it'll tauten if you slip and I shall have you tight. See, beautiful?"

"I see"—in a trembling voice.

"Mind you, it's also intended to look after me. Because in tying on this rope you agree that you're your brother's keeper. You could say it's a symbol of love between us both and Pug down below. Can't think why parsons don't use it in their sermons. If anything teaches you to watch over your neighbour, it's this bloody rope.

Now, the whole business is balance; physical strength is of no importance. You don't lug yourself up a rock face; you walk up it."

"*Walk* up it!"

"Yes, you just step from foothold to foothold, with your fingers in the handholds to help your balance. Ideally, only your feet and fingers touch the rock while you're climbing. Now, I'm going up the first pitch. A pitch, Miss Whinlake, is a succession of steps between one good belay—a secure tie to you—and the next. When I'm on the first good ledge I'll belay myself to the mountain. When I yell, 'Come on', you come just as slowly as you like, searching after each upward step for the next good holds. And as you come I'll be drawing in your rope, while the inactive rope comes up behind you like a long trail, with nice old Pug at its end. The inactive rope is the rope between climbers who are not moving: it becomes active directly they start. Here I go! . . . Oh, my darling, you're going to enjoy it so. God be with you till we meet again."

"I hope to heaven He will."

To see Norry go up from foothold to foothold made it look so easy that some of her fear lessened, but her heart thumped and her knees shook. Aware that she must be suffering like this, he kept singing as he stepped up and up, and wonderfully soon he was belaying himself on a shallow ledge, forty feet above her. The rope was now under one of his shoulders and over the other, so that his hands held it on his either side, and he could draw it around his back and over his shoulder as he brought her up. "Come, Gretel dear. I've got you."

She began in terror, but his voice encouraged her all the way. "Oh, good, *good!* Look, there's a superb handhold just above you on the left—that's it. Isn't this rather like ascending to heaven? Come on . . . You're *here!* You're *here!*"

She was there on the ledge with him, gasping, excited, proud.

He taught her then how to belay herself to a pinnacle and how to bring up Pug. He climbed the next pitch, moving neatly. The skill and grace of it! Then, "Bring up Pug," he shouted down.

"Come on, Pug," called Greta cheerfully, being securely tied to safety.

Pug from below answered, "Climbing."

And thus, pitch by pitch, they went up the nearly sheer face,

437

Greta getting more and more skilful, more and more exalted; and when Norry told her, "You're going superbly," she said, "Yes, I know. But I shall die if I look down."

To this he said nothing. But once, when she was halfway up a pitch, he drew the rope tight and said, "Now look down. You're tied to me, and I'm tied to a mountain that's stayed put for a million years. Look down. Just once. To learn something. I want you to learn that you can get used to any height."

"No, I shall die." But she did look down. "*Norry!* Don't let go!"

"As if I would, my heart. What a climber you'll make! Now you've another sense of triumph."

"A sense of the rope, you mean. *How* I love this rope!"

Higher and higher they went, into the first of the wind, she doing it more easily with every step. The crags wore away amid clumps of heather to become almost instantly the mossy grass of the long-undulating ridge. Now Norry was there, over the ridge. She had only to come up the last pitch while he stood glorying above her, both arms out-thrown to welcome her. "You've done it! *Now* how do you feel? Ever known such a sense of conquest?"

"Never, never," she answered breathlessly.

Whereupon—since this was victory—he drew her close and kissed her. Her kiss, in her excitement, was hardly less fervent than his. "Norry, I think I'm a little mad with it. Oh, thank you, thank you. I've never enjoyed anything so much in my life."

"Gretchen, I *lied*. It wasn't a Moderate. It was a Difficult. A climb is graded by its worst pitch. One pitch was difficult. Enough to be interesting."

"Norry, I'll never trust you again. *Interesting*," she scoffed.

At this point they remembered Pug, or Norry did; Pug waiting on a two-inch shelf forty feet below. "Gretchen! I'm ashamed of you. Bring up old Pug at once. He's your responsibility."

She obeyed, dragging up his rope like the expert she wanted to feel. But she had to say of Pug ascending, "Oh, he comes up with such *disgusting* ease."

He arrived on the grass ridge as if it were the top of the stairs at home in London. "Now," he said, "let's eat."

With Norry saying, "Pug thinks of nothing but food," they walked to the real crown of Sledden Seat and ate their lunches, gazing across ridge beyond ridge of mountains to the last pale silhouette against the sky, which was Helvellyn.

"You're not going to ask us to go *down* that climb?" said Pug.

"It's easy enough, if you face outward and look down."

A scream from Greta. "Oh, *no!* Let me keep this feeling of success. Not of ghastly fear. I'd fall and we'd all be dead."

"You shall go home thinking what a wonderful child you are. By an easy route. There are always grass routes off a grass-topped fell. I don't know them here, but we'll find one."

"I'll go and prospect," said Pug, getting up and wandering off over the tussocky grass.

Norry, who had been flat on his back bird-watching, sat up and rested a hand on Greta's. "Kiss me again. It was so lovely."

She did not answer, but the look in her eyes said something less than no; the eyes had opened wider as if doubts were at issue with pleasure in them; the brown lashes fell to veil this conflict; and her body leaned—or did it?—a fraction towards his, as he took her in his arms, her lips passive, perhaps, but not unwelcoming. It was at this kiss that his heart expanded in ecstasy as he knew he was no longer flirting but truly loving. Dismay as well as joy lay in this knowledge, for he was seeing the figure of his formidable mother and setting it against a rough-spoken farmer. He was also seeing one other figure.

Oh, what would the morrows be, if he loved like this? He looked down upon her face, tranced but smiling, and at her troubling beauty. More than troubling. It strained the heart to breaking. And it seemed the noblest emotion he'd ever felt—one huge expanding tenderness that burst all the limits of feeling, of self. Never anything like this before. This utter selfless bliss.

"Greta . . . Greta . . . *Gretchen* . . . *Gretel.* . . ."

Greta felt the strength of his love pouring over her, and, passive no longer, she knew she had fallen into a depth of helpless love. Her eyes closed.

"Do you know, Queen Greta, how beautiful you are?" she heard him whisper.

Opening her eyes and half smiling, she denied that she was beautiful, and he called her a little liar. And then they saw Pug coming back. Norry sprang to his feet and Greta started closing her rucksack. When Pug reached them they were both on their feet and ready. "Got a good route down?" asked Norry.

"Easy. I met some of Mrs. Pauncey's boys and girls coming off Sledden Dore. Do you know what a crag-fast sheep is?"

"Of course I know. It means a sheep stuck fast on a crag. Let's go and rescue it. Where is it?"

"On a ledge below the top of the Idles, the walkers said."

There being few more flattering roles to fill than that of rescuers, they hurried down Pug's route, two of them hiding from the other their remembered joy. From the brink of the Dore they saw a group of men and dogs on the green ridge above the crags, and one man on the rockfall many feet lower down. Between them, on a shelf not three feet wide, was the sheep, plaintively still. There was no traverse across the crag's steep face; the animal would have to be approached from above. Norry, seizing Greta's hand, pulled her back up towards the group on the ridge, and Pug followed. Drawing nearer, Greta cried, "Why it's my darling Ancients, and old Tam."

"And the man below is Johnny Blenco," said Norry. "He must have climbed up the rocks, but *how*, with no rope and a game leg?"

"He's miraculous," Greta said. "I've seen him do this before. He uses his orthopaedic boot as a lever."

"What a climber he'd make—small and light and strong."

Dr. Pater greeted them with the Alpine climber's *Grüss Gott* and assumed command of the situation. "Now, here are a couple of powerful young men and a shepherdess. These two young Samsons can lower Tam and pull him back up. Give us your rope, Norry."

With his old mountaineer's skill he tied the rope about Tam, one loop around the shepherd's waist and one around each leg to put him in a kind of seat. "Splendid. Now, mustn't lower him directly down to the foolish animal or it might be frightened and jump. Gently down. That's it. Step by step. Good boys!"

Tam, lowered to a level with the sheep and then guided onto the ledge, said, "Aw' reet," the first words they'd heard from him. With help from Johnny, now poised immediately below, he forced the sheep onto its side, tied forelegs and hind legs, and slung the animal around his neck. "Her's aw' reet," he called again, and Norry and Pug, using their bodies as belays, pulled shepherd and sheep onto the grass. "Aye. Thenks," said Tam. "Aye."

440

"Now bring Johnny up," the doctor called to Norry. "You'll have no difficulty; he weighs nothing."

Norry brought him up easily indeed. Johnny had a smile for all, but he would not stay to talk. As he walked silently away Greta said, "Doctor, you've hurt his feelings, saying how light he was."

"What's wrong with that? Oh, I see. Yes, sensitive. I've no more sense than that sheep—and where is it now, anyway? And Tam? Where's Tam? Tam's disappeared too. But Greta, my dearest, do you really think Johnny minds greatly being so slightly built?"

"I'm very sure he does."

"He shouldn't. Because the plain and obvious truth is he's a leprechaun. Leprechauns are often humpbacked. And Johnny's an extraordinary cook. He makes wonderful brews and soups, which is a suspicious sign—"

"No, no. Our Johnny's no leprechaun." The vicar grinned. "Leprechauns are evil."

"A Scandinavian troll then," insisted the doctor. "We're all Norsemen here. Don't forget he cobbles shoes, climbs like a fly—"

"But trolls are *ugly*," Greta protested, "and Johnny's not ugly. I could look at that face for ever."

"Lameness and a humpback, alas, are ugly, my dear. But I was only pointing out that our Johnny's something special. Now come, Joseph. Goodbye, my children." A wave to the young people, and the two old men continued homeward.

THAT SAME evening the house was empty again of all but Greta and Norry. Harry, Matt and Tam Godrigg were in the great barn marking the last of the lambs—impressing two red stripes down the side of each lamb's left buttock, and snipping a slit in its right ear. Pug, seated on a bale, looked as if he could watch this pastoral business for ever. There was little risk that any of them would return soon to the house. So Norry, recognizing a moment when he might have Greta to himself, had slipped quietly away.

Neither Norry, staring out the parlour window now, nor Greta, busy at her kitchen tasks, could see where this uprush of mounting love would lead them. Both could see endless barriers ahead, but so strong was Norry's longing to let this hour endure that he moved to the kitchen door.

"Gretel," he called softly.

Her thoughts had been wholly filled with that moment on the hillside when all the world was lit by the certainty that she was loved. It was an ecstacy tinged with hopelessness, but, at the sound of his voice, the pain seemed suddenly crowded aside by the greatness of the memory. When she came to the door she said, "Yes?" with lifted brow, as one not guessing why she was called.

"Come," he pleaded. And turned back to the parlour.

She came to the parlour and saw him standing before the window, looking out into the yard. Turning, he extended both arms in invitation, but said nothing. A hesitation on her part; then she responded, not without fear in her eyes, to the pleading in his. He sank into his customary chair, drawing her with him onto his knees, and held her tight against his breast, speechlessly, possessively. When he spoke it was to whisper, "I fell deeply in love with you today. Listen, my precious. I want to be truly honest, I never expected this. Tell me—did anything like that happen to you?"

"Yes . . . yes . . . something like that, but don't talk about it."

"Oh, my dearest! But why not talk about it?"

"Because I should have to think about it—and be sensible. And I don't want to be. I should know then that it's just a wonderful something that can't last. Anything more would be impossible."

"Why? Why impossible?" But he didn't deny it was.

"Oh, why do you make me say it? I . . . my home's so different from yours." This was the only way she could put it without too much pain. "I'm not educated enough for you—what am I but a sort of farmhand? What would your parents think?"

"My father would adore you." He gave her a reassuring squeeze. "You don't know the learned judge; he's quite a nice old thing."

"But why did you leave out your mother? That tells me a lot."

"I don't see why she shouldn't love you too."

"I can hear your doubt as you speak. There are your sisters too." It was his women of whom she was afraid.

"I'm sure they'd learn to love you. You're far more beautiful than either of them. I think I should be enormously proud of you."

"Learn to love me! And you *think* you'd be proud?"

"I *know* I should. And not only of your beauty. Everything you do and say makes me feel how fine and good you are."

442

"I'm not good. I'm weak and selfish. What can you have learned of me in ten days? And in only a few more days you'll be gone."

"To come back in the autumn, thank God."

"In four months. A thousand things can happen in four months." She shut her eyes. "Please don't talk. Just kiss me, Norry. Let's just stay like this for a little, as if it will go on for ever. Let me be a fool for a little."

With her eyes shut she seemed, as he kissed her again and again, to pass into a trance of happiness and peace. Once he spoke, but only to whisper, "Queen Greta"; at which, opening her eyes, she murmured, "Don't say anything . . . anything at all"; then closed her eyes again so that this hour beyond belief might endure.

SIX

There were two more days on the rock faces, with Norry leading. One of the climbs was a Very Difficult, and even on this climb Greta had been more happy than horrified, because of Norry's unfailing care and tenderness. That stretch of strong white rope, fifty feet of if, was like a tangible image of his protection. But it was also the sharp spice of fear in every climb that made the arrival so marvellous.

And then it was the last day. She now had a passionate desire to show him before he went in one long, lasting embrace, the fullness of her love, to plant in him a memory that could compete with other girls, girls of wealth and culture. Surely fate would give her time for this.

Five o'clock. Norry and Pug were back early from their climb to prepare for departure in the morning. But Pug sat in the parlour with Norry, and her father and Matt sat in the kitchen with her. A quarter to six. In an hour she must start preparing dinner. Desperate, desperate.

An idea. She looked out the kitchen window. The evening was as beautiful as a May evening could be. She cast off her apron, straightened her yellow dress and went out into the yard, passing the open door of the parlour and seeing that Norry was in his chair by the window. Hands lazily in pockets, she walked across the yard, stooping once to pick up a fictitious something, because she wanted to be seen, but not once did she look behind. With an acted carelessness she passed out of the gate, onto the pony track, then across the pasture. Her slow steps were heading through the bracken to a line of trees that marched with the brook. On and on, not once looking around.

But Norry had seen her, as planned. He took one glance at Pug, fortunately absorbed in a book, and then he was out of the room and following swiftly the flashes of her vivid yellow dress. It amused him to walk too softly to be heard, but perhaps it was the rushing of the brook that drowned his footfalls. At any rate, when he was close enough to say, "Where, miss, are you off to?" her gasped "Oh!" as she swung around showed genuine surprise.

In tune with that "miss" she answered, "I'm going, sir, to my own private waterfall. My refuge from you all. It's quite the most beautiful spot along the brook, and no one gives it any love but me. It has a whole series of waterfalls, and pools among the rocks to bathe in. On the whole, it's a pity you should know about it."

She led him along the stream, and he saw that headlands of grey rock beneath the spreading trees had forced the beck to carve deep canyons, so that there was the succession of cascades she spoke of and, embraced among fallen stones, the still, dark pools.

Norry exclaimed, "Yes! Good Lord, what a lovely place!"

"I always sit here." She pointed to a bald crown of rock under an oak's canopy. "And slip down into that pool. Or under the waterfall."

"But, Gretchen, you might be swept away. I can't have you swept away." He gathered her nearer hand out of its pocket, and it trembled as he took it, in a speech of its own. Then he took her into his arms, and if ever in their past embraces there had seemed to be giving of herself, it was here now. "I love you, Gretchen," he said. "You're the loveliest thing I've ever known."

"So you think now. But you'll see hundreds of others far more beautiful than me."

"There aren't any. There couldn't be. Precious, will you write to me often? Once every week? It'll be a letter from the two things I love best in the world. The mountains and Greta."

"So the mountains come first!"

444

"Only because I knew them first. Thank God I'm coming back."

"Not for months. Not till September. Must you go to those frightful old Alps?"

"If I could get out of it, I think I would now."

"Think? You always think; you never know. You don't really want me. Now, for a little, perhaps, but not for long."

"I've made promises that I can't escape from. Come, let's sit down. I want to sit where you always sit. And perhaps you'll think of me here, sometimes, till I come again."

They sat side by side on the round crown of rock, and at last Norry took her into his arms and drew her down. It was the world's hardest bed, but neither of them was conscious of it. "Gretel . . ." he murmured. "Dear Gretel . . ." And she: "I can't believe this. Norry, I've sat here dreaming of this. It's rather frightening. . . ."

He closed her lips on this doubt with a long, unmoving kiss. Desire mounting, the hand that was stroking her bare leg advanced towards her thigh, and he moved as if to lie upon her. She did not move, though she trembled beneath this touch. It was he who suddenly, with a shake of the head, said, "No," aloud, and drew his hand away. They lay there innocently, only kissing. For Greta nothing existed any more but the weight of his body upon her breast. She held him tightly against her.

NIGHT IN THE VALLEY. The lights along the hills had gone out one by one.

Past midnight now. But there were two who did not sleep. One, hearing the immemorial murmuring of the brook, saw always that little Niagara by Greta's favourite haunt. An unsparing temptation lay with Norry. A few hours and he would be gone from Greta. And his mind would not leave that moment on the round rock when he had turned to possess her, and she, though she had trembled, had done nothing to stay him. It was he who had stayed himself. That he had the whole of her love he was sure, and he more than half believed she would yield all to him. Yet the best of his love, an overwhelming tenderness, would persist. It was this that had forced that "No" on the rock and was stammering its "No" now. "She is only nineteen. If I were only certain we could marry but—" and now the conflict changed.

446

Now it was a battle between this new tenderness and a hundred social difficulties before him. Full love was but a few days old, and not ready yet to scorn all obstacles. And there was that old loyalty: that other one. "It's not fair to take her now. Or to hurt the other. These are mountainous obstacles. I don't know yet that I have the guts to scale them. So come, fool. Sleep."

One o'clock. Still trifling with the temptation, for the pleasure of merely contemplating it, he rose and opened the door to look along the passage. He was astonished to see a strip of light beneath her door. Could the light be her encouragement? He took a step—but no; he turned and shut his own door on it.

But back in bed, he was thinking, Wouldn't it be possible just to hold her close? Innocently, as on the rock? One last embrace. He shook his head. "How could I trust myself, loving her as I do? Perhaps if she came to me . . . of her own will. . . . If she saw a light from my room . . ."

So there were two lights waiting. Greta's was shining because— she could give no name to what she awaited. It was there to say, I am awake if you want to come to me. Just as *he* was thinking, so she thought, perhaps they could just lie together for a while . . . Though, as a farmer's daughter, she knew all about matings, she did not yet want this for herself. But if *he* wanted it, perhaps she would let him have all, though she knew her Church must call it very wrong. But right or wrong, if he came and needed her, wouldn't this love be stronger than any church? There was still a strange innocence in Greta's love; it was rather a passion of tenderness, an impatient readiness for sacrifice of self, than any animal instinct. Her hunger was more for his pleasure than for hers.

She lay waiting. And he did not come. Soon both were asleep.

MORNING was all along the mountaintops, but not yet down in the valley. Greta was up by lamplight, fixing an early breakfast. It was a hurried meal, with the little red car standing at the gate. And now they were piling bags into it. Matt, having helped with the bags, returned to the house without a word. Farmer and daughter remained to see their guests off.

"Ah, weel, gem'men," Harry said. "Ah'm real sorry you're goin'. Ah didna want to tek in guests, but ah've quite enjoyed it, and so has the lassie—eh, Marjy?" She nodded. "Aye, she's quite enjoyed it even though she's had to do aw' t'wark. Weel, we woan't keep you. Say goodbye to the gem'men, Marjy."

Norry was now in the driver's seat, and Greta, instead of saying goodbye, shut the car door on him abruptly, as if on an illusion.

Pug said, "Goodbye, Greta"; and Norry said, "Four weeks next time. I'll come the last week in August."

A strange little shake of the head was her only answer, and the car sped down the road towards Little Sledden.

FOUR SUMMER MONTHS to pass by. June brought the gathering in of all the sheep for their first washing and sulphuring. July, and they were rounded up again for shearing. She must help with that, and then with the haymaking. August, Tam fetched the sheep again for dipping. And all the time, in parlour or kitchen, in meadow or barn, her mind was away—first in an unimaginable school called Brentham, and then among all-too-imaginable snowcapped Alps. She had dreamed of, and wanted, the ecstatic agonies of being in love, and now she had them, among the sheep and the harvesters and the summer guests.

In June the guests had been few, even at Pauncey's. But August brought tea visitors who came pouring off the fells, and guests who stayed and needed cooking for, but Greta never came out of her kitchen, and they said what a quiet, grave girl she was.

In those full summer days she would long for bedtime. And quickly, in the darkness, she would be back with him on the top of Lord's Trod or lying by the falls. True, reminiscence might throw up moments when she'd said something foolish, and then she would gasp, "Oh!" aloud, clamping her hand over her mouth because the "Oh!" could be heard in the next room. Then she would rehearse the words of his letters to her: "Bless you, my adored . . . All my love . . . Buckets of love." How much did these gay phrases mean?

The thought that gave her most food for wonder was that the things she had dreamed of had come alive—even more wonderful than her dreams . . . with Norry so handsome, so clever, so famous. . . . It was, surely, too good to be true. Nevertheless, even while she tried, sanely, to deny the future like this, it was in happiness that she fell asleep.

448

The summer ripened her friendship with her new vicar. She could tell him—and only him—at least some of her thoughts. One June day after Morning Prayer she had waited and asked, as he came out, if she might come and see him about something.

"Why, yes, my dear," he said, smiling down on her. "That's what the Church is for. Tomorrow morning I shall be in Sledden again. We can chat on any subject you like, frivolous or serious."

And next day, a little before noon, they were sitting together in the front pew, the vicar with his legs stretched out on a hassock, Greta sideways towards him. "Now, Greta dear, open out."

She began by saying she was sad because in her lonely home she so seldom met any really well-educated people, and it was difficult to get any really *educating* books from the county library. Time was passing, she said. She'd be twenty in August.

The vicar laughed. "Good heavens! We must certainly do something before it's too late. What, particularly, do you want to read?"

"Shelley, I thought. I borrowed some Shelley from Mrs. Pauncey, but I want to read more."

"Ah! Pauncey. That reminds me of her neighbour. How dare you say, young woman, that you never meet educated people? Go and talk to Hugo Pater."

"I'd be terrified talking to him."

"My dear child, *he* does the talking. But it's often brilliant stuff. He'd love to have *you* listening."

"I couldn't. I'd never dare."

"Then how about Johnny Blenco? Another scholar."

"*Johnny* a scholar? But he only went to school in Caldmere."

"He's read almost all of Dr. Pater's books, and bought a lot of his own. They're about the only thing he spends his money on, apart from good food and wine, about which he also knows a great deal."

"I've never known all this about Johnny. He sounds much too clever for me. But he's so shy. He never says anything."

"Not about himself, no. But he'd talk to you about books. It'd be a kindness to him as well as to yourself. He's the boy for you, I'm sure."

Thus sprang up also that summer a strong friendship between Greta and Johnny Blenco. When they met in the street, instead of just greeting each other and passing, they stood and talked about

Shakespeare or Shelley, or some book that Johnny had loaned her. When she returned the book, she sat with him in his study for happy evenings, discussing topics worthy of Norry.

Neither the vicar nor Greta herself had any insight whatever into Johnny's caged love, and the pleasure, but heightened pain, that this sudden communion with her gave him. Johnny saw to it that these matters stayed invisible.

AT HARRY WHINLAKE'S FARM, the July sheep-shearing was almost as old-fashioned in its ways as the master himself. There were no shearing tables, no overhead shearing machine, nothing except the clipping stools, benches and hand shears. If the day was sunny the work was done in the open; one wanted the best light so that one did not cut and wound. Probably there was little difference between the shearings here and those in Genesis, Samuel and Isaiah.

This year the first day's clip was done in the barn because a fine rain was falling. It would take them three or four days to get through a thousand sheep. The clippers were Tam Godrigg, Harry, even Matt, who could hardly dodge this job, and Johnny Blenco, the universal handyman. Each man sat on a stool with a sheep across his knees. Swift and dexterous with the shears, they whipped off the whole fleece in one piece, as if it were a weatherproof over-coat on the animal's back—as indeed it was.

Greta's task was to hurry from clipper to clipper, pick up the fleeces as they dropped, then fold them and tie them in bundles.

Silence reigned in the barn as the men sheared, and the unfrocked sheep, transfigured into neat and nimble little creatures, went trotting daintily off to find their lambs.

So short of labour was Old Sledden Farm that Greta was also required to help with the sheep dipping. Early in August, Tam and his dogs brought some seven hundred of the sheep off the high fells again and penned them in the enclosure, and the next day Harry, Tam, Matt and Greta urged the crowded, shouldering animals into the trough of carbolic dip. While Greta mechanically urged a reluctant animal into the trough or helped an offended creature clamber out into the draining pen, her thoughts, like the sheep, were unruly. They were either in the Alps or seeking a rest in the fact that every hour brought September nearer.

450

EARLY AUGUST was greatly cheered for Greta by a new mischievous story from the vicar. He told it to her in the parlour, sitting cozily in Norry's chair by the window, while she sat on the edge of the opposite chair, wasting its comfort as surely as the vicar was making the utmost of his. He had come to ask if she could take as guests two friends of his in early September.

"Oh, no," she said hurriedly. "We've got people coming. We've got Mr. Kingharber and—probably someone with him."

"Too bad. My friends are not young, and I thought they'd be happier here than at Pauncey's. By the way, have you heard the latest about Pauncey?"

"No." Greta's interest brightened.

"Well, you know she's Dr. Pater's neighbour. What I mean is— Pauncey's a widow woman and Pater's a widower—"

Greta gave a shriek of delight. "But he's over seventy!"

"Dammit, child, so am I. But we're not dead yet."

"Oh, I didn't mean that! But . . . but she's only about fifty."

"Nonetheless, her eye is on Hugo. And the extraordinary thing is that he, who sees most things in heaven and earth, had never even glimpsed this. Until I directed his attention towards it."

"And whatever did he say?"

"*He*, of all people, couldn't speak. I've never seen a man more taken by surprise. When speech returned to him, he said, 'Joseph, it's ludicrous. I'd rather be dead and decently buried by you than married to Pauncey. Why, she'd never stop talking.'"

Greta at this gave a loud laugh which the vicar endorsed with one of his own. "Hugo does allow he's something of a talker, but I deduce that he considers his talk must be interesting because it deals with profundities. While hers, as he says, dealing with things that are blisteringly unfunny, looses those shattering laughs that curdle the marrow in his bones. Pauncey's very angry with Norry Kingharber, by the way. She won't like it that he's coming to you again. He preferred your place last spring, she said, and added that she knew why."

"Why?" asked Greta. You'd have thought she couldn't imagine the reason.

"Could it be, my dear, that the hostess at the farm is more attractive than the lady of the guesthouse?" The vicar's eyes were full of laughter. "She saw him with you in the churchyard one Sunday, and she says she heard him call you beloved."

"It's just the way he talks. She ought to know that."

"But then," pursued the vicar gaily and mercilessly, "some of her guests saw you climbing on the crags with him more than once."

"And she disapproved, did she? How dare she? Why shouldn't he take me . . . ? She's talked about it to everyone in the valley, I suppose?"

"To some, no doubt. She's quite a good creature really, Greta, but like most hearty women, she can never stop her tongue racing wherever it has a mind to go."

"She's a horrible old woman. What did she say to you?"

"Why . . . the ordinary things people say. . . . That it was wrong of him to take advantage of you."

"He *didn't* take advantage of me. We just liked each other. And why should it be wrong, if he liked me, to show it a little?" The vicar did not answer, and at once she saw why: it was because the obvious answer would hurt her. So she provided it herself. "You mean—because he might raise impossible ideas in a silly girl of nineteen. And that there could be nothing in common between a half-educated daughter of a poor farmer and a brilliant Oxford man whose father's a lord or something." Mounting tears in her throat stopped the rush of words.

"No, no, dear. Nothing like that." But the denial was so weak a thing that she knew she'd expressed what he was really thinking.

"Don't take it so to heart," the vicar chided. "It was just a gossiping woman's prattle." Perceiving he'd distressed a listener who was dear to him, and perhaps thinking he'd not been guiltless of some gossiping prattle himself, he said, "Well, my dear, I suppose I must be going now. Don't worry about Pauncey's silly talk. There's nothing in it." And, rising, he left her with an affectionate smile, but a little uneasily, guiltily.

GRETA'S INSTINCT had pierced straight to the certainty that it was the utter absurdity of a romance between Norry Kingharber and Harry Whinlake's daughter which was occupying the tongues of Mrs. Pauncey and her gossips. The more she was sure that they were calling it impossible, the more it seemed impossible to her too; and she was furious with them all, hating them all for persuading her of this—because it was a thought like death.

She set about gathering from other sources what Pauncey was saying. Her brother Matt, who preferred bad news to good, said, "Oh, aye! The old hen's fair set the valley talking."

Johnny Blenco said, "Yes, she did talk to me, of course, but I didn't want to listen."

As for the doctor, he, without knowing it, was simply offensive. He chose to be frivolous, affecting to see merely a delightful pastoral romance among the sheep. "I find it very natural that Norry should fall in love with you. If I were twenty years younger I should do precisely the same. And as for you, my dear, it's no good pretending he hasn't won some of your heart." And he touched her cheek affectionately, unaware that his touch was fire.

How dared he treat lightly something that hurt her so much? She had been happy to love him as one of her dear Ancients, but now she was hating him.

Then, with blithe innocence, he went on to lay waste whole days and nights for her: "I never supposed your Norry was capable of loving anything but his rocks, though I did hear once that he was half engaged to some girl in London."

Engaged. Half engaged. After learning this, Greta ran to her rock by the falls and lay on it face down, unseen among the full summer trees, with her brow resting on the cold stone, as she would sometimes rest it sadly against the wall of her room. Never such loneliness as this, and yet . . . she was almost welcoming the anguish because it was complete.

SEVEN

August drifted towards September; it was now but a few days before Norry would be with them again; and Greta, in spite of the ruin worked in her heart by the doctor's careless jocularity, began again to sing to herself. One morning she was thus singing in an oat field opposite the farmyard gate when she saw approaching a most magnificent grey car, long as a torpedo, with a grey-uniformed

453

chauffeur at its wheel and a large lady in the back. It was the most imposing car she'd ever seen come up the valley. As it drew near the gate, the lady looked through her window and considered Greta studiously, as if, it seemed to Greta, she were an interesting agricultural feature in this ultimate fringe of the habitable world, too primitive a creature to be sensitive to a stare. The chauffeur got out and went to the farmhouse door.

Next Matt came out looking for his sister, saw her standing in the field and hurried towards her. "There's a lady. Wants to see you. I'm putting her in the parlour."

The chauffeur was now ushering towards the house a tall, large-breasted, wide-haunched lady in flowered silk.

Did she want them to put her up? She was hardly their sort. Wondering, Greta crossed quickly from field to farmyard. In the narrow passage she dusted and smoothed her dress, passed her hands over her hair and then entered the parlour.

The lady was sitting in Norry's chair—and her face was *his* face. So this was his mother sitting there. Different from imagined pictures of her, but like them, clothed in silk and pearls, and authority. Comfortable authority lay printed in the lines around her lips. His mother here!

"You are Greta?" The lady smiled graciously. "I am Mr. Kingharber's mother."

"Yes. . . ." How did one address the wife of a lord? Must one say "your ladyship" or "milady"? "Madam"? No, she would *not* say "madam" to the mother of Norry, in whose arms she had lain. Best avoid all modes of address. "Yes. . . ." she said again.

"Have you a moment to spare? I saw you at work in the field."

Greta didn't like that "at work". How easily wealthy people gave themselves away. But one could smell that heaped dung through the window, open to a warm morning. So perhaps it was natural. "It's just that I help Father sometimes because we're shorthanded," she said. "Usually I keep house for him."

"I see. Do sit down, dear. I'd awfully like to talk to you."

"Yes?" Greta sat nervously on the edge of the other big chair.

"Mr. Kingharber's coming to stay with you again?"

Greta nodded. Mr. Kingharber! Doubtless this was the way his mother spoke of him to working-class people. Defiance rose. She said, "Yes, Norry comes on Monday." And saw that Lady King-harber had felt the prick of a bayonet.

"That was your brother who showed me in here?"

"That was my brother, yes." Though what's it to do with you? All the same—Matt *had* looked messy in his heavy muck-laden gum boots and a drooping hat almost as bad as the doctor's. Very different from this expensive visitor.

"I want to be frank with you, my dear. Norry is a careless boy, so while he's been away—he's been in the Alps, you know—"

"Yes, I know. He's written to me from Zermatt."

"Exactly. Written to you. So this week I've been tidying up his room for him, as he'll be at home a few nights before he comes to you, and—you must forgive me this, dear—I saw a pile of your letters to him. On top of a drawer."

A pile! All kept! And all taken with him to his real home. As if he loved them. Oh, good. But was this woman going to say she'd read them?

"And wondering if they were important, I glanced at them."

Lady Kingharber

"*At* them or *through* them?" Greta asked it dangerously. And not a doubt but Lady Kingharber disliked this abrupt tone from a girl of her class.

"I looked through one of them, yes, when I saw what they were, and glanced at others—but no more, no more—" (You expect me to believe that, dear lady?) "—and if you'll wait, I'll explain why I felt justified."

"If I wait a lifetime I shall still think it was wrong of you to read them." Praise heaven for anger, which gave one good words and the fierce courage to speak them. "Disgracefully wrong."

"Really! I . . ." Shocked at so insolent a rejoinder, but having no defence against it, Lady Kingharber could only look around the parlour—which to Greta suddenly appeared very small and trite and poor. "You must listen—and try not to be angry." With her eyes on Greta's face she seemed to soften a little. "Perhaps I was a little wrong, but I am his mother and I have his interests at heart. I must say I rather suspected something before I saw these letters. He seemed so remote from us all. As though he were living with some secret. There was one letter to you in his handwriting, which for some reason he had not sent you, and this I did feel entitled to glance through." She shook her head, as if at something in her mind, then touched Greta on the knee. "My dear, I don't wonder he's so attracted to you. You are very beautiful."

This softened Greta, but only for a moment. Anger instructed her to accept no flatteries if they were to be but a preamble to hard, wounding words. What was in that letter of Norry's? And which of *her* letters had she read? She only hoped they were the long ones in which she'd managed to work in some of the literary stuff she'd been getting from Johnny. That would have surprised her.

Maintaining the gentler tone, Lady Kingharber smiled and went on. "You can understand how I longed to see you. But I felt, too, that I ought to . . . to come and ask you if you knew one thing." (Engaged? Half engaged? The same deathly fear at the heart.) "I thought I ought to tell you that he's practically engaged."

(Yes, the blow . . . but her mind raced for relief to that word "practically".) "But what do you mean? How is one practically engaged?"

"Well, it's not final, though we all felt it was. We all love her. But of late he's changed towards her, more than ever since he came back from here in May. She's very unhappy."

"So can others be."

Lady Kingharber gave no heed to this. "She came and told me all about it. You see he's very attractive—and, well, in these days women sometimes give themselves to a man if they believe he's going to marry them. I don't know that I blame them, though it was all very different in *my* day. Girls seem to think it's all right pre-maritally—if you know what that means."

"I certainly know what premarital means. I've been to school."

"Oh, I didn't mean that, my dear. I just meant that you're so young, perhaps a little out of the world. You see, don't you, what I'm trying to say? He has a duty to her, don't you think?"

"How do you know he hasn't precisely the same duty to me?"

"I don't know. I wouldn't ask him. One's children must go their own ways. But I should be sorry to think it of you."

"But not to think it of her?"

"She's much older than you. And there's always been this thought of marriage."

Greta could not say, Whereas with me there can be no thought of marriage, which was all too plainly in her visitor's mind.

"If it were so, my dear," Lady Kingharber was going on, "I'm afraid I would have to give you a crude answer. It'd be a case of first there has first claim, wouldn't it?"

After a time Greta said in a low voice, "I don't know that that's always decisive. It depends . . . on many things."

"He has known her for years. I feel his duty is to her."

Fear held back an instant retort till at last anger won. "All you feel is that he should marry a girl of his own kind."

Lady Kingharber lifted two well-ringed hands from her lap and let them fall—as if in despair of denying this.

Silence. Till Greta stammered, "If he's grown rather quickly to love me, is that my fault? Are you suggesting that I made him love me? Haven't we to ask who started it?"

"I don't think it would be profitable to go into that."

"I should have thought it'd be extremely profitable."

A movement of the lady's head, as if irritated again at the way this girl spoke to *her*; and surprised, too, that a farmer's daughter should speak with such firmness, and in such an educated accent.

"You force me to be very frank. Surely you can see that a marriage between you and Norry would . . . hardly do."

"Hardly do" was so complete a statement of this visit's intent that Greta could only, at first, repeat it: "Hardly do?"

"Yes. . . . Oh, I don't want to say harsh things. But I feel I must."

"I don't quite see why you must." Greta's heart was now quivering within her breast like a plucked string. "I haven't asked him to marry me. That'll be *his* business, won't it? He'll have to ask me if ever he wants to. I ask no man to marry me."

"Is that your father out there?"

This was not meant cruelly. Curiosity had prompted it. But there was Greta's father passing through the yard in an old brown shirt and braces, with a pail in each hand.

457

"That is my father," said Greta, her heart sinking all the deeper for the weight of angry, furious love in it. "What was the harsh thing you didn't want to say? Or only half wanted to say?"

"Well, let us try to be reasonable, my dear. You're so young and lovely, I don't want to hurt you. No, don't toss your head. I can't bear to see a young creature hurt. I'm only suggesting, before Norry comes, that he's not really free. And I think it rests with you to help him to be loyal. You are clearly a sensible girl and will realize that these sudden attractions, especially at your age, are generally only passing infatuations."

"How do we know if anything is really love? Was *your* love for your husband a passing infatuation?"

Lady Kingharber shook her head at this impudence, but could answer only, "Let us keep to the matter in hand."

"I want to. I'm all for being reasonable, Lady Kingharber." At last the title had spoken itself, pray God, aright. "And I'm all for saying exactly what we mean. What you *really* mean is, not that Norry must be loyal, but that I'm nothing like good enough for him."

Lady Kingharber, since here was the truth, was incapable of an immediate answer, and the field for a time was Greta's. "I *know* I'm not, in some ways," she said. "But in other ways I might be. You think I'm nothing but a poor girl on a small farm, but my father has over a thousand sheep on the fells. And I'm not uneducated. I got prizes at school, and am now reading all I can. Our vicar, Canon Nickle, and Dr. Pater, who was the headmaster of a famous school, lend me books and help me."

"Well, I think that's a great credit to you, dear." Was there a weakening in Lady Kingharber's disapproval, a sense that she might have underrated Greta, even a beginning of something like affection? "Hardly do" remained, Greta was certain. Nevertheless, she thought, the battle's only just begun. I do love Norry, and if he loves me, I don't see why I shouldn't fight for him.

Something of this she stated to his mother, with a dignity and a calm of which she was unconscious, though she did feel she had aged ten years since this interview began. "I understand what you're feeling: that this has all been terribly sudden. I understand, too, that it's inevitable you should think of my not being of his class.

458

Nor am I. But I love Norry with all my heart, and I believe this gives me every right to try to keep him."

Lady Kingharber's lips moved to speak, but there was no stopping Greta now. "And if anything so wonderful were to happen as his wanting to marry me—though of course I can't think this likely —I should certainly say yes. I simply can't feel that I would be unworthy of him. I just can't feel it. But if it turns out that he doesn't *really* love me—well, I don't force myself on any man." So she repeated the proud statement that had pleased her earlier. Proud of her pride, of words spoken haughtily to a great lady: "I ask no man to marry me." The fine words danced in her mind.

Lady Kingharber could do nothing but rise, as one who could do no more here, but was surely intending to do much elsewhere. "Well, my dear," she said to Greta, who had risen too, "I was frank with you, and I can only thank you for being frank with me. You seem a good girl and I like you, and wish you all joy, whatever happens in this matter. You have all your life before you. I hope many, many good things, even wonderful things, will come to you."

"Thank you," Greta said with sincerity, for there really was kindness in the old lady's eyes. But she was thinking. And you're off now to make sure, if possible, that *one* wonderful thing doesn't happen to me. I don't know that I blame you. But I do know that all the fighting's not going to be left to you.

She went with her to the magnificent car, now turned about with its face towards the valley, towards the great world. As it drove away, the grey-uniformed chauffeur sitting with dignity in front and his large mistress in comfort behind, Greta thought, *She's* Norry's mother. And she began to be afraid again and sad. That whole unknown world: his mother, her daughters, their friends. . . .

And she, Greta, standing in this cobbled and muddy yard, beside a dung heap smelling richly, at a far edge of the inhabited world. It was all very fine to talk about fighting, but what hope, what hope? It all turned on if he really loved her. . . . Perhaps in a few days she would know . . . and *if* he did. . . .

THUS LADY KINGHARBER'S visit achieved the opposite of its intent: by bringing to Greta new hopes of her son's love, by stirring in her a fury of indignation at being written off as socially impossible, and by showing her one way she could put herself on a level with the other girl.

But this last? If the only thing she had on this earth to fight with was her body, should she not do this? What the other girl had done should *she* not be allowed? Surely it could be *sometimes* right, if it was love?

I don't know what to do. If only there were someone to ask!

But whom? Her father? Bless his dear heart, how could she even put such a question to him? He'd be bewildered, horrified, lost. Friends? Friends were scarce in the valley; where was there one whose intelligence, love and secrecy she would trust?

Johnny Blenco? I could ask him anything—except *this*.

Dr. Pater? Don't make me laugh!

Dear Canon Nickle? He would listen with understanding, but there was only one answer a clergyman could give. Still, if the Church's commandments were stern, its vicar would be gentle, and she found herself compelled to take him her trouble. For now, conflicting within her as never before were her passionate desires for love and a larger life, and that simple but strong desire for goodness. But her heart shook. Only with grievous trembling would she be able to speak.

Nevertheless, after early service that Sunday she waited in the churchyard until he left the vestry. "Oh, Vicar, I want to ask you something before Norry Kingharber comes."

He smiled, mystified. "Well, here I am."

Panic. "Oh, not now. It's going to be rather difficult."

"Come along then, after the eleven o'clock service. We'll talk."

Once again they sat together in that front pew. Greta leaning forward awkwardly, her hands fingering a prayer book. "You remember telling me about Pauncey's suggesting that Norry and I had been—flirting? Well, it's true we—we did get—terribly fond of each other. We hadn't known one another long, but does that necessarily make it silly?"

He smiled. "I don't think love has much to do with time, but I do feel one has to give oneself time to know that it's really love."

"I feel I know that already; is it very silly?"

"No, you may well be right. Does he feel the same?"

She fiddled with the prayer book. "I believe I could say yes, if

460

it weren't for that world of difference between us. Wonderful for me if—but a mass of difficulties for him." The prayer book was turned over and over. "His mother came to the farm yesterday, and asked me point-blank to let him alone."

"*Did* she? His mother? My dear, I see what you mean about difficulties." He stretched out a hand to cover hers. "I don't know, but I should have thought it'd be rather wonderful for any man to have your love."

"She said he was practically engaged. Do you know to whom?"

"Fiona Someone, the daughter of a retired commander in Brentham, Hugo says."

To one with no clear knowledge of naval ranks, commander sounded powerful indeed, like admiral. The thought raised her defiance, her despairing but fighting spirit, so that she didn't seem to care if her next words surprised and disconcerted him.

"I think I ought to tell you that, whether it was terribly wrong of me or not, I was ready, the last night he was with us, to let him —if he . . . came to my room—have anything he wanted of me. I longed to say, I'm all yours." The vicar shook his head, so she hurried on before he could speak. "Oh, he didn't come. It was just that I felt I was there for him if he wanted me."

"Greta, you mustn't do this. You mustn't."

"It's what I wanted to ask you about. His mother told me that the girl to whom he's practically engaged had done this, and that because of it he had a duty to her. He's coming now for four whole weeks, and I feel sure I shall be tempted to give myself the same chance as she has. Would it be terribly wrong of me?"

"Yes, it would be." He again put his hand over hers. "It's impossible for me to say anything else, my dear, as a parson. But even if I weren't, I don't believe I'd speak differently." He looked up at the wide altar window framing a view of the hills. "This church enshrines the wisdom of two thousand years. What you suggest has only one name, and that isn't love. Greta, I beseech you, keep yourself from this."

She looked down at the wooden floor. "I knew you'd have to say that. I don't know why I troubled you."

"Greta dear, you must pray for strength. I'll be praying too. If God means Norry and you to come together He'll bring it about."

461

Greta rose. "I mustn't keep you. It's Sunday and you're so busy. Thank you so much for listening to me."

He rose, too, and put a kiss on her forehead, the first time he'd ever done this; but there was no more he could say. And she went out of the church and along the road to home, with both hands in the deep pockets of her dress and her hair blowing like a tattered flag behind her in a strong valley wind. Once she looked back at the church and thought sadly, I wanted help, but there was none there.

And no one left now to whom she could say, I don't know what to do. I don't *really* know what's right.

ONE FAMOUS evening in that last week of August she dined with Johnny Blenco—no other word did justice to the meal he produced. It had meant seven or eight hours of joyous labour for him. First he had cycled into Caldmere to buy all that was required—a lot, for this would be the menu:

Scallops Poulette
Cumberland Guinea Hen with Bread Sauce
Pommes Frites   Red Currant Jelly   Braised Celery
Crêpes Suzette

Then there was the room to tidy, the fire to lay, the table to prepare with glasses, cutlery, the best china; flowers to bring from garden to living room. When it was time to cook, he was kept delightfully busy, basting the guinea hen with butter and water, simmering the scallops in wine with shallots, butter and mushrooms, then boiling down the liquid and adding cream. If there were many ingredients in these dishes, there were at least three mingled in Johnny's labour: abundant love, a large sprinkling of fun, and a small—but not too small—measure of pride.

When Greta came, dressed very carefully, into that living room, saw the flowers, the wine glasses, the gaily patterned plates, she gasped. "Johnny, what *have* you been doing? You shouldn't have gone to all that trouble for just me! You *are* a poppet—really."

Here was the praise he'd laboured for all day and now shuddered from, though loving it. He answered only, as he bent his face that its flush might not be noticed, "It's the first time you've ever had a

462

meal with me, so I thought I'd make an occasion of it. Also I think I'm showing off a little. Probably I'm being rather vulgar. Well, sit down and have some sherry." He poured it out. "I have a little more to do in the kitchen."

"Johnny, you must teach me how to cook as well as what to read. I can't think why our visitors put up with my plain fare."

"You cook splendidly. Pauncey says so."

"I don't. When you come to a meal with me, you'll be ashamed of me. Can't I help? I can't just sit here drinking while you work."

"But you can and will. There's no room for two in my kitchen."

"Johnny, you really are a dear."

Blushing hotly, he went away with his own glass in his hand.

While they shared the meal together, Greta giving gasps of admiration, they talked happily of a hundred things; but it was not till they were seated before the fire with glasses of port that their talk plunged into the deeps of her worries and his aspirations. The fact that the room was now in a deepening dusk, with only the leaping fire to light it, helped this descent into the mysteries.

It was amazing where they got to. Soon Johnny, leaning forward in his chair, was tell-

Johnny Blenco

ing her of his belief that men belonged to two different orders of existence—the one their temporal and passing world, the other a still, eternal world that had no part in time or death. Man woke up in the prison of a body that must die, but if he could apprehend this other dimension, he would know that it was all that mattered.

Much of this was too difficult for Greta to understand, but it held her eyes on him in fascination. Once she said, "Oh, Johnny, how wonderful to have a faith like yours."

"Faith?" he objected. "Faith's too firm a word. Call it a limping trust—" But as he uttered that word "limping" he faltered. Then, inspired by so enthusiastic a listener, he began to tell her all about his interpretation of God as life and light and love.

"Is it ridiculous," he asked, "that flowers suggest to me much the same things about God as brilliant or deeply spiritual people do? I once argued this with old Dr. Pater. He said I should have seen what his garden was like when he simply left it to God, before getting a gardener in. But I got the better of him—about the only time I ever did. I suggested that gardeners were God's creatures too, and the fact that it was they who produced the roses simply meant that God chose to channel this beauty through his creatures' hands. The old boy conceded that I had a point there."

"What a marvellous answer."

And Johnny proceeded, not without laughter and self-ridicule, to his conviction that a man's only sure happiness was to become, as far as he could, a channel of that life and light and love towards others. Smiling awkwardly, he said, "Just to trust that God is deep in one as the source of one's being can be a pretty happy business."

Now he was well within Greta's understanding, and her heart leaped to his every word. She longed to be a channel of life and light and love, and was astonished to find that while the vicar's religion seemed to tell her only what she *ought* to do, Johnny's sounded like something she longed to do. Or longed to be capable of doing. She said, "Johnny, you make me feel more alive. Is that what you mean by being a channel of life and light?"

It was not quite what he had meant, but he only smiled, and Greta was delighted to be an instant disciple of Johnny Blenco.

But for the present a disciple in theory only. Johnny's talk did not divert her heart from its course. Her mind told her that one day she might find happiness in renunciation of herself. But not yet, not yet! Not till she'd done battle for Norry on equal terms with that other, that shadow, far away.

EIGHT

The little red car came speeding, passionately speeding to where the road began to climb. Norry sat alone in it, and instead of all the fun and fooleries when Pug sat beside him four months ago, he drove with only melancholy as his companion; driving all the faster since this was a companion he was impatient to be rid of.

It was the melancholy whose presence Greta had detected when he supposed himself unseen. It sprang from a reflectiveness far deeper than his usual boisterous manner would suggest. Beneath the covering of laughter lay the despair of a nihilist who, try as he would, could discern no purpose in the universe, no ultimate good, nor any meaning for man. He would have liked to believe in a God, a progress towards something, but he could not. Science seemed to have finally destroyed the roots of such a faith and all the values that blossomed from it. Sometimes, in earlier years, he had attempted blind trust—but on deeper thought, this seemed weak-willed, unworthy. Nor in this atomic age could he believe that the quarrelsome human race, which regressed so easily into savagery, would not let loose, sooner or later, its violent end.

Yet to accept as certainty that everything was encompassed by emptiness was to sink into a black nightfall of the spirit. When one really arrived at this sense of an aimless universe, one could decide that the time might come when one claimed one's right to die.

But weak-willed, unworthy, the use of such words showed him that he did apparently believe in values—in courage, compassion, devotion. So thinking, he found himself examining, and hating, the shams in his life. One of these was the show of Christian belief which he put up at Brentham, simply because his ambition was to become a famous headmaster. Another was his continuing pretence of love to Fiona. After all she'd given him, he had neither the courage nor the cruelty to tell her that his love for her had long been dimming. He had meant only to flirt with Greta, but against the love she had lit in him, Fiona's poor little flame seemed hardly a lamp at all.

Ah, Shap Fell! Shap, the escape from despair! The high sport of climbing, conquest, exaltation—and Greta! If the true world is a nightmare, let us lower the blinds and sleep, dreaming livelier dreams.

GRETA did not see the car coming, though she had been watching for it from the room that would be Norry's. It was when she returned to straighten one last time the bed's bright new coverlet and to touch into perfection the flowers on the windowsill that she saw it, already there at the gate, with Norry unpacking. Down the narrow staircase at a rush, swaying around its bend and down its last treads. Dragging open the front door, she saw Norry crossing the yard with a bulging rucksack in one hand, a kit bag and coiled rope in the other. When he saw her he laid them down and spread his arms wide—first gesture of an embrace—but here in an open yard, one had to stop at this stage. He smiled all the rest and gathered up his packs again. "Good morning, my angel."

"Oh, you've arrived," she said foolishly.

"It looks like it," he said. "And four whole weeks this time. Have you any other loathsome guests in the house?"

"Not just yet."

"Oh, *good*. I've had awful pictures of some enormous old dowager filling half the parlour so that I'd never get you there alone."

Evading this with both eyes and words, she said, "We've had very few guests. Pauncey's turned people away rather than send them to us. And it's all your fault. She's mad at you for coming to us now, when she has room. And she's been rather imbecile about us climbing together."

"The frightful old cow! But not quite imbecile in what she's suspecting. Could be she's dead right."

Greta coloured at this, though it had pierced her with joy; and he, gazing down at her, said, "Woman, you're heart-rendingly lovely. How and where's Papa? And our Matt?"

"Matt's standing about somewhere, probably, instead of helping Daddy. He's decided he wants to be a preacher. The Reverend Matt, if you please."

At this instant her father emerged from the great barn. "Ah, gud to see you. Gud to see him back, isn't it, lassie?"

"Yes," she allowed, as if she were merely the polite hostess.

"Well, t'lass'll tek you oop to your room."

So she led him there. And Norry saw at once the flowers, the new bright curtains and coverlet, and understood their joyous welcome. "My pet, how beautiful you've made it. Now, come here, silly child, pretending to be all bashful. Come here at once."

"Why?"

He put out a hand and dragged her to him in a silent, rough answer to that ridiculous "Why?". And now was completed the invitation which had been stopped at stage one in the yard below. There was kissing and kissing, which gave her much joy, and though he spoke no word of love or marriage she was aware of the difficulties before him, and not disappointed.

She broke at last from the long embrace and, laughing, said, "I must go and make you some sort of lunch." But while her hands concocted his omelette, her thoughts were busy with the old argument. "It isn't as simple as the vicar says. Norry *does* love me, but he doesn't know what to do. And I love him with all my heart. I simply can't believe that if you really love each other and want to give each other everything God thinks it's always wicked. It's love, it's giving. . . ."

Then, she heard the vicar's voice, "Greta, I beseech you, keep yourself from this." And she answered, "Yes, and lose him, and stay here for ever."

BUT FOUR WEEKS they had before them, and this provided room for a gradualness that was easy and happy. Happy? Happier days than Norry had ever known. With his black cares left behind, with an ever-enlarging love so manifestly requited, he could wonder at times that such happiness was possible. Never had he felt an exultation at once so quiet and so voluptuous, so intoxicating and yet—so still.

Though he had come here to climb, Greta held him more than the mountains could, and he would hurry back from the crags to walk with her. They strolled, fingers linked and swinging, through Sledden Woods, their feet cracking acorns on the pine-needled path. "Is this as lovely for you as for me?" Norry asked, and got an "Oh, yes, *yes!*" Once they walked, not climbed, to sunlit ridges, where the mountains formed cauldrons of white mist beneath them. Another day he drove her to Goswater, and they wandered along the brink of a shining lake ribbed by a gentle wind. And so, fingers linked again, they drifted on between lakeland meads and mountains in a dream of happiness. In their mutual silence Norry told himself, I've never, never known happiness like this.

It was two days later that Norry took her on a climb with a friend

467

of his from Pauncey's, young Steven Ware, a dark, shock-haired eighteen-year-old who was an expert climber. The three of them did a Difficult among the Upper Crags; but at the top young Steven did not disappear as Pug had; and there was no kissing there that day. That night, however, there were snatched minutes in the parlour, but brief minutes only, because her father and brother were in and out.

All the next day the rain was in possession, such a rain as, it always seemed, only these valleys knew; but then the early evening unveiled a brilliant sun which flung broad scarves of light around the shoulders of the mountains. And Norry went out to play the trick she'd once played on him. He strolled into the farmyard, passing innocently by the kitchen window, and turned up the pony track. He hadn't long to wait. Together they walked to her waterfall and as before lay on the bald rock. Afterwards they came home openly, side by side, and Harry, seeing them, was untroubled and thought, "He seems to git on well wi't'lass. Ah'm gled of it; she sees aw' too few young people."

It was not till the fourteenth day that the pattern began to take its final shape. They had done three climbs that day with Steven Ware, two of them Severes, and she arrived on the tops aglow, exclaiming, "Oh, I'm happy, happy!" They could have borne Steven's absence for a while. Instead he sat with them on the last of the tops and told them all about Pauncey's latest insinuations. Greta clamoured for details.

"Oh, she said something like, 'I'd give a lot to know just what *is* going on,' and told me I'd no business to encourage you."

"Encourage *who* in *what?*"

The naïve boy flushed. "You two, in . . . cuddling a bit, I imagine she meant, but I agree it's no business of hers."

Greta could not speak. Norry was silent, too, in the presence of this charming devoted boy who, having been so instructed, still saw no reason to leave them alone.

At home that evening they learned that Harry and Matt would be out at a neighbour's party till late at night. The house would be theirs alone. Neither spoke of this, but after she'd cleared dinner away and he'd helped her for the first time in her kitchen, with laughter and fooling, and when the thought of that empty parlour

468

was silently present in both, he took her by the hand and led her towards it. With her fingers still gathered in his he dropped into his big chair and drew her down so that she lay on his lap and within his arms. Then it was lips upon lips till he lifted his face at last and said, "I suppose every horrible youth in Cumberland's in love with you?"

Her answer wasn't no. It was "I don't want any of them."

"Do you want me . . . a little?"

No answer; only a look, insecure, hesitant, into his eyes. He pretended to shake her. "Sweetheart, say something. Even if it's only that you hate me and are aching to go."

"I'm very happy with you, here, like this."

He gave himself to stroking the full column of her neck. "You've the loveliest throat I've ever seen." He passed his hand all around it: under the heavy hair, around beneath the chin, and down to the hollow above the breastbone. "And it's velvet."

Her eyes closed while his caressing hand sought other parts of her, but she put it gently aside. "No, let's just stay like this. It's so lovely. Just happiness and peace." But then, intending apology for a rejection, her heart dictated two words before her head considered them: "Not here."

He perceived at once what they might imply. "Darling, would you—one day—let me come to you in your room?"

Silence. If it was not yes, it was also not no. She gazed, defeated, into his eyes. And now she was frightened. Because when it came to the point, there was much more of the churchgoer in her than of the wanton.

Ever gentle, he spoke again. "I won't if you don't want me to."

Incapable alike of the yes and the no, she said, "I love you so."

He waited a while and then whispered, "Tonight?"

"Oh, no, not tonight." Postpone. Perhaps even prevent.

"Tomorrow night?"

Impossible to answer. But then she remembered that other girl. "Do you really want to come to me?"

"What do you imagine, my darling?"

A long pause, and the words that followed it were like a sigh. "Anything you want from me you can have. I love you. I can't help it. I love you."

No light burned in Greta's room that night. What she'd said was enough. Let the unencouraging darkness stand between them.

The house slept. A step in the passage? Yes. Her heart hammered in disarray. "Are you awake, my lovely?" A yes hardly to be heard, and she received him into her arms in the darkness. Now, lying at her side, he was smoothing back the hair from her brow that he might rest his lips on it, now kissing the whole length of her arm, its elbow, its shoulder, now finding her breasts. A whisper, "Dear Greta, am I the first to come to you like this?"

"Yes. Yes, of course."

He said, "Oh, *Gretchen* . . ." and later, "May I now?"

"Whatever you want."

"I don't want to hurt you."

In answer to which she only drew him closer and waited. There was pain and a gasp from her, so that he remained very still, just stroking her hair to comfort her. Then gradually he wrought for her the gathering ecstasy. . . . "Oh, my precious . . . oh, Norry, my beloved," while he gasped, "Gretchen, my dear love, my delight . . ."

Then back into the world of silence and darkness. Somehow an emptied world. What was this? Some deep sadness? Or no more than a loneliness now that he lay so quietly, unwanting? Suddenly, and terribly, all seemed to have meant too little to lead to more.

He asked, "Happy?"

"Oh, yes. Yes. . . ." But this was not the whole truth. Was this all? This? And this again? And then no more?

An hour later he rose in the bed to leave her. He said, "Darling, would you like me to come here again tomorrow?"

"Oh, yes." The ecstasy had been too great for her to refuse.

"Tomorrow then, my dear sweet." He kissed her gratefully. And left her lying there, happy for long minutes, but then musing. Had she paid a price required and bought much? Or nothing?

It was morning and they were back in the daylight, amid customary tasks. Norry and Steven were set upon climbing Thor's Face, in the Upper Crags, said by some to be more than a Very Severe; to be what they now named simply Excessive.

Thor's Face—smooth slab, some two hundred feet deep, it looked

470

almost vertical, though rounded like a swollen cheek. Above it, a grassy ledge with a dwarf ash tree, and a rowan, ablaze with scarlet berries despite its windy home. Except for a crack down the face like a sword slash, there seemed nowhere a pucker or crease to serve as handholds or stance for a climber. But to those who knew the only way up, there were weals in the lower half, and then this crack which could be negotiated by jammed handholds or footholds and pressure holds.

Its conquest was far beyond Greta, but Norry and Steven were eager to be at it. Then, as Norry dreamed over toast and marmalade, the room darkened. He leaped up and went to the window. In a moment the sky was one great thunder sheet, its colour matching the dreadful north faces of the mountains. The green of the valley intensified beneath an angry light.

Steven arrived from Pauncey's. He grimaced. "I hope we shan't have to put it off."

The words were barely uttered before thunder cracked and the farmhouse was enclosed within a thrashing rain that shut the world from view. Norry and Steven stood at the parlour window for perhaps a half hour until there was a quieting of the rain.

"Look!" Steven cried. "A patch of blue." And they went into the yard to watch as the storm went riding away down the valley.

"All clear, Steve. I'll get dressed," Norry said. He dashed indoors. As he dragged on his boots he said to himself, "We won't do Thor till the rock's dry." And having so decided, he allowed his thoughts to revert to where they had been all morning—the night just passed. A tenderness overwhelmed him—so great that he was dreaming now of whispering this night, "Gretchen, my darling, I want to marry you. Would you have me?" He could not but know she'd hear these words with extreme joy. He longed to give her this joy.

But there was so much to keep the words unsaid, if only for a while. The differences between Grosvenor Square and Old Sledden Farm seemed the least of the obstacles. Now that Greta was reading so avidly he could see little difference between her education and his sisters'. Damned if anyone at Brentham could parade a wife as beautiful as she. He'd be staggeringly proud of her. And better than her beauty was her warm adoration, her gay impudence and

472

even—strange thought in a professed unbeliever, or perhaps not so strange in a despairing one—her churchgoing. It gave him, if not belief in her creed, a belief in her. In humble moments he felt that Greta's love was a reward beyond his merit.

Yet there was Fiona. He had had, for her, nothing comparable to his exalting, exulting love for Greta. And they had agreed all along that either at any time could go free. Still, there had been enough between them to make him hate the pain he'd cause her almost as much as he loved the thought of giving Greta joy.

But here was old Steve in the yard, booted, roped and ready for Thor's Face—all unaware that his leader was mapping out a far more important climb. Never mind. Adjourn the debate with the decision *almost* reached—a decision that, even to contemplate, set his pulses jumping. Go out and be happy with Steve; all the happier for this enormous possibility dilating his heart. I love her. I love her. He snatched his rucksack, ran out, nearly colliding with Greta, seizing the chance to embrace her—"My dear sweet love"—then doubled down the stairs to join Steven and begin a great day.

NINE

At about fifteen minutes past five that evening, after a bright afternoon, there came a curious cloud formation over the valley and a violent gust that bowed the trees, set every blade of grass impotently bending, and whirled a hail of grit and gravel off the road with a stinging assault on Greta's cheeks as she, head bowed into the gust, was crossing the road from her orchard. More than a gust! Against a current that nearly overthrew her, Greta got indoors, and from here the wind seemed to be bombarding the house.

Perhaps a half hour of this. Then quiet again.

What they called the helm wind? But the helm wind was a strange cyclonic phenomenon that belonged as a rule to the valleys under Cross Fell, and the Pennine hills, miles away. And according to what Greta had heard, it was never as brief a thing as this astonishing, violent northeaster had been. It has seldom been known in summer months; usually at times between September and May—but it was September now. Mightn't it, though, she wondered, be a fringe wind—an escape from the helm? She felt rather thrilled at the idea. The helm could, so it was said, blow the beaks off the geese on the common.

In any case all was quiet now, so Greta began preparations for a dinner worthy of Norry. But whatever her hands did, her thoughts sang with the sound of his midnight voice. "Gretchen, my dear love, my delight," and she was daring to ask if . . . *if* those words could mean an incredibly perfect fulfilment of all her dreams.

IN THOSE minutes before the onset, out of a genial sky, of this icy, dry blizzard, Norry was walking homeward along the ridge under Sledden Seat. Steven, tired after the day, came many paces behind him. Near the ridge's brink there were two parallel tracks, beaten by the boots of climbers and shepherds, one of them some three feet nearer the brink than the other. Norry always called the inner track the cowardy-custard path, because it had so plainly been formed by persons who found the outer one too close to the downward dive of the mountain. Invariably he walked the outer, and advised his pupils to do the same, explaining that it made one indifferent to height.

In fact, the fall below the path was not at all precipitous until it veered around the top of Wry Barrow Combe, the scene of many famous climbs. As a rule, coming this way, Norry looked down at climbs he'd loved in the past. But he did not look down today; all his thoughts were given to Greta and his decision to ask her this night to marry him. And it was now, when he was walking easily home to her and to that moment, now when he was lost in joy, tranced by it, that Norry met the wind.

AS THE CLOCK in the kitchen ticked on, to six and more, Greta felt driven to go out and see if two figures were coming down the pony track. The path was empty to its top.

By the time the clock struck seven, anxiety clawed at her and she went out again. No one. . . . Yes—a distant figure. Limping. Badly. Trying to hurry. Steve? Yes, Steve alone, and staggering in pain. In terror she ran to him. "What is it?" she gasped. "Are you badly hurt?"

"Just a knee sprain." He took a deep breath. "Ligament's gone, I think. Not to worry. Not about *me*. But . . . Norry . . . has fallen."

"Is he hurt? Was it on that ghastly Thor's Face?"

"Hell, no. Norry doesn't fall climbing. He went up Thor's Face like a woodpecker up a tree trunk. No, he fell when he was simply walking home along the brinks of the Upper Crags; he loves to do that—the sight of them is so magnificent. But this time he wasn't looking; he seemed lost in some dream. And all of a sudden there was this awful rush of wind. It must have upset his balance, for he suddenly flung out an arm helplessly . . . and went down."

"Oh, Steve . . . oh, *no*! Did he fall far?"

"Not terribly far, thank God. He stopped himself somehow on a ledge. I managed to belay myself and get down to him. I . . . I was able to rope him to good anchors, but I didn't dare move him in case it was his spine."

"Oh, Steve . . . Steve! Was he in pain?"

"Not so much if he didn't move. I wrapped him in his sweaters, and mine, and put my parka over him in case of rain. Then I raced for home. I tried idiotically to do a shortcut down the Idles. That's where I fell."

"Oh, Steve, let me help you. What do we do, Steve? *What?*"

"Leave me. I can manage. Telephone the Caldmere police to call out the Mountain Rescue. Tell them he's lying on the Uppers above Wry Barrow Combe. I'll catch you up in a minute and give them the details."

So Greta ran home to the telephone. "Caldmere Police Station, please. I don't know the number, but quick! There's been . . . an accident." Voice breaking, she gave Steve's story. "He's coming in a minute."

The man's answering voice was comforting. "OK, my dear. The lads'll be there in no time. Don't worry too much. They've every possible thing in their ambulance and they're fine at their job. We'll have the first of them away in twenty minutes. . . . Old Sledden Farm? They may use your farm as the ambulance base, and you may be able to help them a bit."

"Yes, *yes*. Oh, thank you, thank you." And she laid down the receiver and stood there, unable to vent her anguish in anything but "Oh . . . oh . . ." like a child bereft of tears. Then she remem-

475

bered Steven struggling home and ran to help him in. Strange how the only easing for great mental pain was to help someone else. "Take it easy on that knee, Steve. They're calling the men now."

By the telephone, listening to him, she understood that he was getting some comfort from the knowledge that he was reporting as an expert climber should. "He is lying near Stour Buttress. He's covered with every garment I could put round him. I tried a distress signal three times, using his whistle, but as I was getting no OK signal, I guessed the mountains were empty, and hurried to phone. I've left my hundred-foot rope anchored and hanging to help chaps up. . . . My name? Steven Ware. Yes, near Thor's Face. What? Already? *And* Sir John Despencer? Oh, fine!" He turned to Greta. "The ambulance is there, and the first of the team are starting at once."

THE AMBULANCE, a square green Land-Rover, stood before the steps of the police station. A bold legend on a board above its windscreen read MOUNTAIN RESCUE, a blue lamp flashed at the board's side, and an alarm bell claimed priority. Within was every species of equipment that a rescue team might need. All the immediate first aid was in two swollen rucksacks, which would be carried on strong shoulders when the Land-Rover could get no farther.

On the pavement stood Sir John Despencer, a big, burly, red-faced man who was head of the family that owned a valley or two and the mountains around them. He was the perennial chairman of the Caldmere rescue team, and no chairborne position was that. Whether up mountain tracks or a near-vertical face, the vast seat of Sir John's old cord breeches led "his lads" to battle.

Inspector Sidney Olsen of the Cumberland and Westmorland constabulary stood beside Sir John, and several "lads", of any age from eighteen to forty-five, were now around the tail of the ambulance. One or two of them wore bright tangerine parkas easily descried at a distance; others wore on their shoulder the MOUNTAIN RESCUE patch—and one felt that they wore it with pride.

"Hop in, Hamish," Sir John ordered. "Get in, Colly, Pete, Hornly." Sir John had loaded himself also into the Land-Rover when he saw a very tall bespectacled man heading for them with a grin on his pleasing, scraggy face. "God save us, here's Dr. Bill," he said. "Lucky for that poor young man up there."

Dr. Bill Smythe was nearly fifty, but as good a climber as the youngest of the rescue team whose medical officer he was. Whenever he could, he answered their calls, and whenever he did, it was cause for rejoicing. "Pack in, Bill." Sir John somehow or other contracted his great body to make this possible. At once, encouraged by cheers and hand waves from spectators, the ambulance started off towards Old Sledden Farm.

AFTER LISTENING in an ache of despair to Steven telephoning his report, Greta helped him to Pauncey's, where Mrs. Pauncey, transformed at once into a quiet, mothering creature, dropped everything to make him comfortable. Her guests, temporarily without dinner, congregated outside in the last of the daylight, and so in minutes the whole of Little Sledden heard Steven's story.

Restless in her anxiety, Greta hurried home. Oh, why didn't they come? She stood at the gate, watching for them, and at last, at last she saw the Land-Rover, its blue lamp flashing as it sped through the dusk.

Pauncey

It stopped and Sir John clambered out, while the others drew out the swollen rucksacks from inside the van and the sledded stretcher off its roof. "Turn its nose round now, Ernie"—this to the young driver—"so we can hare away directly we get him in."

As the ambulance backed and turned its face towards Caldmere's cottage hospital, Mrs. Pauncey and her household arrived in force, carrying jugs, vacuum bottles, mugs and cups.

"We thought you all ought to have a quick cup of tea or coffee before you start," she said. "And some hot soup to take up with you. Greta and I'll have more ready when you come down."

477

"Dear lady," said Sir John, "you're goodness itself. Lap it up, boys, but don't take long. By the way, tell the other injured boy that Dr. Bill Smythe'll see him as soon—"

He stopped, because a tall old gentleman, presumably from Little Sledden, appeared to be giving instructions to the boys. "Here!" objected Sir John. "Thank you for your help, but *I'll* tell the lads what to do, please. Is this your husband, madam?"

Dr. Pater was not used to being spoken to—or of—like this. "No, I'm *not* Mrs. Pauncey's husband. I happen to be a lifelong friend of the injured man"—a shocking exaggeration—"and I should like to go with you. I've climbed all my life."

"Sir, our rule is, we take no strangers. Besides—I don't wish to be rude, sir—but this is no game for an old man."

"Old? What the hell about you?"

"I must have twenty-five years' advantage over you."

The doctor had no answer to this. There being no help he could give, he turned and walked sadly home.

But now Sir John saw another old man, tall, lean and bearded. "You, sir? You are—"

"Ah'm Mr. Whinlake's shippert," Tam Godrigg explained. "Happen ah cud help. Ah knaw Stour Buttress weel enoof."

Sir John was more impressed by this patriarch than by the other old party who'd bragged about his climbing, so he said only, "It's good of you, sir, but we've two young shepherds in our team and needn't trouble you."

"Ah weel, you'll git till 'im and help 'im, ah knaw," said Tam, accepting the decision and turning towards home.

"We will," Sir John assured that tall retreating figure. "Come on, lads. Come."

GRETA was already far ahead of them, up the pony track. Skilled rock-climbers all, the others would, she knew, get quickly up to the Dore by way of the Idle Crags, so she was hurrying with all the speed that love could put into her feet. Perhaps she could see him, call to him; perhaps she could walk at his side when they brought him down on the stretcher. What do I care what people say? I shall never, never care again.

It was a mile to the base of the Idles and many minutes before

478

she came in sight of them. Then, in the twilight, she distinguished a small figure high up on their craggy face and moving quickly higher. Running now, getting nearer, she recognized Johnny Blenco. Hearing the story, seeking no permission from Sir John, he had gone his way alone. Beyond belief, the way he was mounting that sheer rough wall. His movements had a skill, a grace not less than Norry's. A rucksack swayed on his back with every move.

"Johnny!" she shouted.

With the heavy boot secure on some infinitesimal shelf, he turned and called to her. "I'm going up to him. See if I can help."

"Oh, Johnny, *do*. They say you're wonderful at easing pain."

"Don't know about that, but I shall be company for him till the real people come. It must be pretty awful, lying there alone."

"They're coming up fast, and Dr. Bill is with them."

"Good, good. I'll climb quickly and tell him."

"Tell him I'll be on the Dore," she shouted. And tears crowded her throat. There was Norry in desperate need, and there was Johnny climbing sideways up that sheer slab to the rescue—a plain statement that men are responsible for one another. A controlled sob shook her and then she started running again.

THERE WAS LITTLE room on the broken ledge where Norry lay roped and still, so Johnny half sat at his side, held in position by the pressure of one foot on a splinter of rock below and a chain of slings cast over a rock anchor above. First he had drawn old sweaters from his rucksack and pressed them as cushions under Norry's knees and under his head, taking care not to move his body lest the spine were injured. Next he had taken Norry's left arm from under the wrappings Steven had folded around him, and after rolling back the sleeve, he was gently stroking it, upward towards the heart. Norry was conscious, but shock had worked some mercy, leaving the world vague for him. His arm was very cold, the pulse at its wrist weak and rapid. Sometimes he shut his eyes sharply as pain shot through him.

"Pain bad?" asked Johnny, still stroking.

"Cat-and-mouse . . . leaves me in peace and then pounces. Can't feel my legs. Afraid I know what that means. . . . Oh, God, if it *does*. . . . That stroking . . . helps. . . . What is it? Hypnotism?"

"I try to will the pain away. That's all I know."

Norry with an attempted smile asked, "Do you say prayers?"

Johnny laughed. "Only so far as that's the same thing, I suppose. But the morphine'll do it all much better than I can. Dr. Bill Smythe's coming. Are you thirsty?"

"Yes . . . yes, funnily so."

"One always is after shock." From the rucksack he drew a vacuum flask, filled its cup with hot sweet tea and, gently raising Norry's head, ministered the cup to him.

"Thanks," Norry said. "And that stroking *is* a comfort. *Oh!*"

Obviously another shot of pain. Johnny's hand tightened on the arm like a steel wrench. It was as if he would refuse all further power to the pain, or perhaps force into Norry the power to deflect it. As sometimes happened when he did this, his own tautened arm seemed to fill with pain. Johnny never understood this; perhaps it was caused by the impassioned rigidity with which he held the sufferer's arm, but it always felt as if, like a suction pump, his arm had drawn out some of the pain.

"Over?" he asked.

"Yes. . . ." A wait for breath. "God, but it's wonderful to have someone here. Tremendous of you to come up. . . ." Again a breathless sigh. And then, barely audible, "But God, oh God, if it *is*."

Instantly the steel wrench gripped the bare arm tight, this time to lessen, if possible, a great mental pain. Then gradually it opened and became a massaging hand again. "Greta is there." This did not penetrate at first. So Johnny repeated, "Greta is there."

"Where? What do you mean?"

"I saw her coming up before the rescue party. She loves you a lot, I think."

Norry could not know what these words cost his companion. But Johnny Blenco's healing instinct had taught him to surround a patient with thoughts of happiness and hope. Johnny, the reticent, would talk and talk when it was part of the business of healing. "She must be waiting below on the Dore by now. She told me to tell you. The others are just behind her."

Dramatically, as he said this, the whole of the valley below, and of the mountainside which held them, was flooded with light. "There they are! A ground flare to tell you they're here and

480

to let them see you. No, don't try to look, I'll tell you. There's one behind the leader with a rucksack. Then—yes, Dr. Smythe. They're all climbing well and they'll reach the rope your friend left there in a minute. Down below, Sir John Despencer seems to be giving orders to other chaps. . . . Oh, I see: he's sending them round with the stretcher to get onto Sledden Seat above us. Yes, Sir John's leading that lot. They're going to rope down to you from up there. But whatever they do, there's Greta waiting for you on the Dore."

As the first man arrived, Johnny, scrambling higher up the buttress, got himself out of his slings and offered them to this leader, Colly, who said, "Thanks, old boy. You safe there? You seem to have a good belay."

"You use it. I'll find another higher up."

Another ground flare, fired from below, floodlit the scene.

The physician in his large spectacles was climbing like a cat. Heedless of Steven's rope, he got himself onto a fairly safe stance immediately beneath Norry. Then he heaved himself up to an edgy seat by Norry's side while the leader set about securing him.

"Now we'll make you comfortable," Dr. Bill said, his bedside manner available even on a precipice. "Is he very cold?" he asked of Johnny above, though at the same time feeling Norry's arm. "Not too bad, after nearly three hours. Your pal did his job well with these sweaters and all. Colly, hand me the hypodermic."

In a moment the doctor had pinched together the loose skin on Norry's arm and injected the morphine, saying, "Here comes a spot of peace. And if one dose doesn't work I'll damned well give you another. Any ribs broken? Well, they don't matter much, even if they are. A few abrasions and lacerations, I see." A flare lifted his eyes to the men who were now on the green summit above the rocks. "They're lowering the stretcher now."

Up above, Sir John and those with him were anchoring fixed ropes to a stumpy birch tree and to one of the many strewn boulders. As they unfolded the stretcher and locked it in position, one explained, "Chief says, far the easiest thing will be to get him to the top of Thor's Face and lower him down it. It's smoother than anything else around, and has trees at the top for belays, so we could barrow-boy him down to the scree below."

All were safely belayed now, or held from above by the ropes,

481

and without much difficulty they got the stretcher beside Norry. The doctor, suspecting a fractured spine, said, "Place that down bag close to him, and gently, *gently* roll him onto it, face downward. Slowly—I don't want any pain. . . . Time doesn't matter. Cushion head and arms with blankets. . . ."

They strapped and lashed him, face downward, to the stretcher, so that save head and arms he was immobilized. A signal from the doctor, and those above hauled the stretcher slowly upward, Sir John directing its ascent. Dr. Bill, Johnny Blenco and Colly followed the stretcher up by means of a fixed rope.

Four men, two on either side, carried the stretcher, Sir John leading, to the top of the crags above Thor's Face. Here Dr. Bill gave Norry, who was still in pain, a second injection of morphine. A brief wait and, raising one of Norry's eyelids, he touched the white of the eye. "No longer conscious. Just as well."

Two men roped down to the grassy slope above the face, and those above lowered the stretcher gently to this green shelf; then all, except two who were dealing with the ropes, worked their way down and prepared for the barrow-boy descent.

"This'll be as easy as winking," said Sir John, looking down the rock face as a flare lit it. "Hamish, you're a light one. Job for you."

When the stretcher was upended, going down the face, there would be no danger to its unconscious passenger, because he was lashed and strapped to it at feet, fork and armpits. The doctor tested these straps and ropes. Then three long ropes were secured to the top crossbar of the stretcher's steel frame, and the anchor men took strong hold of them. With the ropes having friction belays around tree trunks and the men's bodies, the stretcher was held tight. Hamish, the light one, was then roped to the stretcher's lower crossbar. He took hold of the long steel handles, which, when extended, would enable him to see his footwork all the way down, and stepped carefully backwards over the sheer brink of the face. He then walked down it, drawing the stretcher after him as a barrow boy draws his barrow; with this difference, that instead of being upright as he walked, he was almost horizontal. And so, together, barrow boy and patient went down Thor's Face, the Very Severe, the Excessive. They had some difficulty because of the loose rocks under the face, but they fixed pitons from which ropes

482

controlled the stretcher over the scree down to the high valley, the easy ground of the Dore.

Greta, having watched it all by flare light, ran to receive them. "Norry, oh, Norry!" She stood there, looking down on him. No answer. Grey and unconscious. "Is he . . . ? He's not . . . ?"

"No, miss," said Hamish. "He's only unconscious. It's the morphine."

Then she remembered that these men might wonder what she was doing there. "He was our guest. I was the one who reported his fall to the police," she said to justify her presence, thinking at the same time, "What does it matter, anyway?"

Sir John said kindly, "There was no need for you to have come, my dear."

No need! "I only walked round by the pony track," she apologized, "to see if I could be of any help." This reminded her of Mrs. Pauncey's words, "Greta and I'll have soup for you all when you come back"—and here she had deserted, thinking only of her anguish. But Pauncey'll do it all, she told herself, and she had a sudden feeling that she'd like to fling herself on old Pauncey's breast and sob there.

Greta walked down the pony track at the side of the stretcher to which Norry's face was turned. She wanted, if he regained consciousness, to be seen at once by him. The men seemed content that she should walk there, but one of them, not suspecting her love, said with the unconscious satisfaction that runs with bad news, even among merciful men, "Dr. Bill's pretty sure it's his spine that's gone. He thinks there is paralysis in both legs. If so, it's a pretty poor lookout for him."

Another carelessly agreed. "Aye. Rather be dead, meself."

"Oh, don't—" she began. No. Walk on in silence. Walk on alone.

So, alone, she did not hear, "The odds are he'll die. And better so, I reckon."

Nor did she hear, "*Shut up!*" from an angry voice behind.

Johnny's voice. All the way, Johnny followed a few paces behind her, unnoticed. He didn't once approach her, unwilling to break in on her distress or to suggest that he had any special right to help her; and, tonight at least, feeling hopelessly unsupplied with any words of healing.

TEN

Two days, three days, nothing but rumours—usually dark. And Greta in her kitchen, in her fields, in her bedroom, praying, praying. She had come to believe that if she prayed passionately enough, she could hold him in life, rather as he had held her on the rocks with his taut rope; and that if her prayers wearied, she might be letting him slip down into death. Pray and pray, then, hardly daring to sleep lest that would loose her hold.

One morning she went into the church to pray, half believing that prayer in here might get through to heaven more easily. She knelt in the front pew and saw through the large window some of the climbs he had done with her as his companion. And in her dreaming mind she saw Lord's Trod and Goswater Lake too. With tears she dragged her thoughts back to their sole duty this morning. After a half hour in that quiet she came out into the churchyard, her eyes firmly turned away from the graves of those who had fallen on the mountains.

Johnny Blenco had seen her go in. Suspecting her purpose, he had waited for her, sitting on a meadow gate. His hope was to speak some words of comfort, but when at last she came out, her head was drooped, and he, gripped by diffidence and doubt, let her go by. Probably the only words he could have said would not have been comfort. For he had seen Norry in the hospital and was afraid for him.

When she was gone from sight he limped home. Not easy to watch the girl one loved suffering for desperate love of another, but such was life. His never-spoken love must clearly do all it could to help her, give her perhaps some telepathic power of support in her passion for this other—and suffer in doing so. Such was life too. One knew one's course.

On the third day after the fall Dr. Pater came to the farm's gate —not on his feet but in his ancient car. When Harry greeted him he asked, "Can I see your Greta, Harry?"

"Marjy? Is't bad news aboot poor laddie?"

"I would say it was grave. There seem to be infections as a result of the paralysis. But don't tell her that."

"Nay, nay. She's oopstairs preparin' his room for summun else, which is no gey easy for her, ah can tell you."

For Greta, unable to bear the suffering alone, had come at last to her father and, flinging her arms around him to sob against his breast, had told him all—except that visit of Norry to her room. "Daddy . . . I know he's dying," she had sobbed.

And he, who sometimes talked so much, had no words at first because he had suspected nothing and was amazed. He could say only, "My lass, my lass!" as she sobbed in his arms; and to himself, "Ah mun be gittin' daft as well as oald, knawin' nowt o' this. Ah just thought they got on well together, as young people will." Struggling for better words, he whispered, "Naw, if he wur goin' to die, he'd a done it at once, ah recken."

Now he said to the doctor, "Ah'll git her doon to thee."

"Do, Harry. He'd like to see her. I'll take her along."

"Ah weel, that'd be gud o' thee. Ah'll git her doon."

Dr. Pater had come straight from Norry's bedside. As an old acquaintance—if not a "lifelong friend"—he had easily gained permission to visit him, and when Norry had said, "Do you think you could get Greta?" it had been really no great surprise.

At the Caldmere cottage hospital he had gone into a shining white room so functional that he'd thought it humane and inhuman at once. Norry was lying immobile on a very high bed with a cradle holding up the bedclothes from the lower half of his body. His eyes had turned from the ceiling as Dr. Pater entered. He gave him a formal, sad smile. "They told me you were coming. Awfully nice of you."

The doctor for once was hard put to it for words. "Well—" he began, feebly indeed, he thought, "what can we all do for you?"

"Nothing." The answer rang with bitterness, but its tone was quickly amended. "They don't tell me, but I know. I've had friends who've busted their backs."

"So have I, Norry, and they've recovered."

"Some; as helpless burdens. Was it worth recovering?"

"Yes," declared the old doctor firmly. "One adjusts to anything. Blindness, lameness." But he did not speak the word "paralysis".

"I can't see myself adjusted to living as a totally helpless and rather disgusting burden. May I tell you exactly what I feel?"

485

"My dear boy, that's what I'm here for—if it helps."

"Thanks. It'd be good to talk to you." He smiled. "You're so terribly learned and wise."

"Learned is not the same as wise. I doubt my wisdom greatly. But say all you want to say, and I'll say what I can."

First, Norry said, he was bitterly ashamed at having fallen at all, and when the doctor interrupted, saying, "There was nothing to be ashamed of. That was a quite exceptional wind burst," Norry would not accept the excuse. "A decent mountaineer should be ready for anything. There are worse winds on the Eiger, but I—I was thinking of other things."

Then, as if a tap had been turned on, he poured forth his present state of mind with all the fervour of the ill, the loquacious doctor serving as listener and happy to be doing so. "I'm damned if I regret my climbing. I've always said to everyone, 'Life's at its best when you're gambling with it.' Well, I may have lost my gamble but I still think the same. Yet it's so difficult to lie here and know you're never now going to have the things you'd set your heart on —never, never, never. I keep coming back to that thought. Don't laugh, but with my Oxford scholarship and my reputation as a climber I had dreams of being a famous headmaster like you."

"Why should I laugh? Wasn't I your age once?"

"Then I had dreams of some wonderful wife and jolly kids and all that. Well—as you must know—that's now impossible for ever."

The doctor did know, so he hastened to deny the only part of it that wasn't true. "A wife is not impossible."

"To me, yes. I'm not offering myself as a lifelong burden to anyone. Do you know, that very night I was going to ask Greta to marry me."

"I knew you liked her."

"*Liked!* She still seems the only thing in the world that could make me want to go on living; but it wouldn't be fair to take her. She's made for a husband who could—*be* a husband to her."

"She loves *you*, of that I'm sure," said the doctor.

"So am I. But I'd want any wife of mine to have a life of her own. I've thought, lying here, that one course might be to marry Greta before the end—it's been done before—but there's Fiona, you know. It'd hurt her. Perhaps I ought to go without doing that.

Or I might live and Greta'd be stranded with me. No, it'd be best for them both if I died. They'd adjust."

"Don't talk about dying. Don't, please."

"But I must talk to myself about it. A lifetime of helplessness— I don't think I'm equal to that. Or that I propose to accept it. I've had a good run for my money—but it's funny to lie here thinking how soon life can be over. So soon. . . . Just ceasing to be."

The doctor had been searching for words without success, but he had found a few. "Norry, go into this fighting. That's the real *you*, isn't it? I remember a climber saying to me once, 'They don't come gamer than Norry Kingharber.' "

Norry smiled. "All my life I've told myself nothing was going to beat me, but I simply can't stir up that feeling any more."

"Only because you're still shocked and ill."

But Norry had withdrawn his eyes and was staring at the ceiling again. All he answered was, "Do you think you could get Greta? There's something I want to say to her."

And now, at the farm, Greta dropped everything and ran down to the doctor. "Oh, Dr. Pater, is he dying?"

"No, no, my dear." He kept doubts out of her sight. "He's very ill, naturally, but he's young and strong; everything's being done for him splendidly, and his mother has been with him."

"His mother! Will I have to see her?"

"I don't suppose so. She's gone back to her hotel. Anyhow, no reason you should be afraid of her. She seemed to me a dear, good woman. Are you ready to come at once?"

"Oh, yes." She smoothed her hair. "If I can come as I am."

"Of course." He had been about to say, "You're looking particularly charming," but decided that this was not the moment for gallantry.

In the car, driving fast to Caldmere, Dr. Pater was for the second time that day unable to find a word that didn't strike him as unworthy. It was she who ended the silence. "His mother came to see me. She more or less begged me to leave him alone. She didn't think I was good enough for him, and I understood how she felt."

"Rubbish," said the doctor. "You're good enough for anybody."

He parked his shabby old car, helped her out and led her down the hospital corridor. The smell of sternly-washed walls and floors, of distant drugs, of florists' shops, laid fear and heavy sadness on Greta's heart. Nervously, for one so self-assured, the doctor tapped on a door and a woman's voice answered, "Come in."

He went in and came out again to whisper, "His mother *is* there. But it's going to be quite all right." And he took her hand.

Lady Kingharber, large and alarming, was seated on the single chair at the high bed's side. Greta came only a few steps into the room and then stopped, her hands fingering one another. Norry said weakly, "Hello, Greta dear. This is my mother. I think you've met." Seemingly all had been confessed between them.

Lady Kingharber rose as Dr. Pater went quietly out. She put a hand on Greta's shoulder. "I'm going to leave you two together," she said. "God bless you, my dear."

Greta stood pressed against the bed. "Oh, Norry, Norry!" His face was so pale; his eyes so sunk in shadows.

He tried a smile. "Gretchen, my sweet. Well, here we are."

She clasped his limp hand. "Oh, darling!" The passionate sympathy weakened his control so that tears overspread his eyes.

She said, "Dare I talk much? Ought you to talk?"

This enabled a smile to override the tears. "Ought or not, I'm going to. Sit on the bed, my precious. There isn't much room with this cradle thing, but you'd seem so much nearer."

Sitting sideways, she maintained the consoling pressure on his hand, but did not know what to say. To love, to fear an end, and yet to have no words! At last she asked, "Was it *very* awful?"

And he, glad too of available words, answered, "Oddly enough, not too bad. Shock works wonders. Steve had been splendid at wrapping me up. Your humpbacked friend too. His healing business —it really seemed to help." Norry paused for breath. "He came to see me yesterday. He got old Dr. Hugo to bring him."

"To try and help again? In what way?"

There was a long pause. "How much do you know, sweet? About what happens if I live?"

"You'll live. Of course you'll live. What are you saying?"

"If I live, I'll be paralysed. A hopeless cripple."

"My beloved! I was told this, but I won't believe it."

"It's true. What your Johnny wanted to tell me was that it's not too bad, being a cripple. He said he'd always got a kind of joy in refusing to be beaten by it. I lay wondering for a while if I could manage to enjoy doing something like that. But, you see, my crippling's going to be very much worse than his."

All she could say, stupidly, was, "No! It'll be all right."

He shook his head. "I know all that they won't tell me. I know. I know. From now on I'm a useless burden, incapable of being husband or father. Gretchen sweet, I want you to know one thing. I asked Mother if it was right to tell you. She said you ought to know. It might"—he breathed heavily—"be good for you to remember. I'd made up my mind to ask you that night to marry me."

"Norry, Norry, my *darling*."

"Maybe you wouldn't have had me—it's too late now to ask—"

"No, no, no. Don't say such things. I—"

"I'd be no good to you—a more dreadful burden than you know."

With both hands she gripped his arm tempestuously, in a passion of pity. Somewhere she was conscious of the huge cracking of a dream, and it was no small wound, this breakup. But her love was all there, and she realized she must call it out in fullest power. The other, less selfish dream, the old aspiration after goodness, leaped to her aid, told her to offer herself, the whole of herself. She too could help and heal; *she* could bring back his desire for life. "But don't you see, I love you, I love you. I'll give my whole life to you. I'd love to—"

"No, precious, I'm not going to do that to you. Anyhow, I suspect I've had my day . . . and, as things are, all the day I want."

More fiercely she gripped his arm. "No, no, you're not to say that!" she cried. "We all love you. I love you so. We'll—"

The doorknob turned. Greta started, loosing her hold, as the nurse came in. "Perhaps he'd better rest now."

"Oh, no," Greta pleaded. "Not yet."

"Five minutes, then. We mustn't tire people, must we?" And she went out with an easy, unaware smile for both of them.

Five minutes in which to deal with questions of life or death! It inhibited thought and words. She could only say, holding tight to his arm as if to keep possession of him, "You've made me so terribly happy by what you've told me. I'll do *everything* for you. I *will!*"

489

But there were only pattings of her hand from him, and a great doubt, like denial, in his eyes. Once, too, the bitter reminder, "But the question may be solved *for* us, Gretchen."

And then the five minutes and more must have passed. "I suppose I have to go."

And he, "Yes, my darling. . . . God bless you always," which sounded like goodbye. Perhaps discerning her thought, he smiled. "Darling Gretchen . . ." almost as if giving her this to remember him by.

She backed towards the door, seeing his eyes watch her as if the thought behind them was, "So she goes. So it ends. This is all."

A smile of sad love, and she was gone from him.

AS THE DOOR closed Lady Kingharber rose from a chair in the corridor. Greta flung herself onto that large breast as to a place where she could sob convulsively and let the tears rush. "He doesn't *want* to live," she stuttered. "Why doesn't he?"

Lady Kingharber drew her close, but offered no answer beyond saying what was plainly a word of comfort and no more. "Perhaps he's very tired, that's all." With a light kiss on Greta's cheek, she murmured, "Thank you for loving him," and held her for the weeping to continue. But later, with a comforting arm still around the girl, and stroking her bent head, she said more. "Listen: he told me you'd given him the happiest hours of his life. Remember that. I want you to remember this too: if there's anything I can do to help you, ever, please, please let me do it. I feel you are one of us. Whatever happens, of this I am sure, my dear—there's a fine life for you somewhere."

Dr. Pater was sitting in his car as Greta came down the hospital steps. Quickly he got out and, speaking no word, put her in the seat beside his. Best perhaps to say no word. Best intrude not at all. He drove, thinking, "One dreams alone. And one's so alone with the dream when it dies." He began to recall loves and hungry dreams of his own, now fifty long years in the past. "They came to nothing, most of them, but I can think now that there's not one I'd have missed. They may have held as much pain as joy before they were over, but—oh, yes—they remain the dearest memories of my life. Memories that only youth can give, I fancy, because we feel

490

more deeply, some of us, then than ever afterwards. Life will brighten again for Greta. But what of Norry? Oh, God, be with him to whatever end awaits."

ELEVEN

Two days later Dr. Pater was again waiting outside the hospital, this time for the vicar to finish visiting patients. They had planned a walk around the lake. He saw him come out and went to meet him. "How is the boy?"

The vicar answered simply. "They tell me it can't be long before the end. They've sent for his sisters and his father."

"Ah, better so, perhaps. But why is it suddenly fatal?"

"There were infections from the first, and shock had left him too weak, it seems, to respond to treatment. At least, that's what they tell me. But I don't think that's the whole story. With all his liveliness and fun, and his magnificent courage, he could have put up a better fight. I think there was something in the possibility of death that he welcomed. His courage seems to have failed him."

The doctor shook a doubtful head, beginning to walk faster. "Joseph, there *was* courage. And I'm not sure that it's weak to recoil from a life of total deprivation and of some repellence to whoever's looking after you—forty or fifty years of it. A whole long life without dreams."

The vicar nodded—unspeaking.

"And beyond all that, a loss of the desire to live was helped by the fact that he was never able to believe that human existence had any final worth. A bleaker view than I can manage. But an honourable one. And not without its bravery. Ah well, to be sick and paralysed for ever is to be sick unto death, I imagine. I think it's not for two hale old men like us to speak a word."

IT WAS NOT in Dr. Pater to withhold news from his neighbours in Little Sledden, so Greta heard it too, but she resisted belief. So young, so strong; the shock would wear off; he would live. So she prayed and prayed, sometimes in the church. Johnny Blenco, seeing her go by, would fall to prayer too—for her. Half offering terms to God, Greta told no one the proud fact that Norry had been going to ask her to marry him; she had a half-formed hope that this little sacrifice might plead with God for his life.

Two mornings after his talk with the vicar, Dr. Pater, having seen her going towards the church, seized his chance of finding her father alone to tell him that Norry had died in the night. "Would you like me to break it to Greta, Harry?"

"Nay. She's my lass."

"Tell her he was unconscious and without pain."

"Aye. Leave me to it. Ah mun see her through it, if ah can."

"It'll hurt her rather terribly, I'm afraid."

"Aye, she'll soofer, poor bairn. But she woan't break. Leave her to me, an' thenk you for coomin'."

So Dr. Pater left him in his yard, and Harry walked the cobbles in thought, waiting for his Marjy to come home from the church. But when he saw her coming up the road he stepped back from her view, like a child evading a parent because he has a wrong to confess, and retreated, guiltily, to the kitchen. "Marjy," he called as she came in the house.

Surprised to see him there, she said, "Yes, Dad?"

"Ah've summat ah mun tell thee, lil' one. Dr. Pater's just bin. . . ."

Her eyes were on him; they were eyes that knew what was coming. "Yes, Dad . . . ? About Norry?"

"Aboot Norry; aye." He picked up her fingers and played with them lovingly, while repeated small shakings of his head spoke his sympathy. "Norry, aye. He's . . . he's awa' noo."

"Dead?"

"Aye. Awa'." Greta said nothing, but left her hand in his. "It's crool sad for thee, lass. He wur a good lad and tha wur reet to love him. Aye, an' the doctor said he passed awa' widoot pain. There wur no pain."

She bent her head. "Thanks, Daddy, I understand."

"Tha mun bear oop, Marjy lass. Thy pain'll pass. Ivverything gits bedder wi' time."

"Daddy," she said, "I can't feel anything. Is it because I daren't think? Shall I be able to feel it soon?"

"Aye, tha'll feel, aw' reet. But when tha does, coom an' tell me aw' aboot it. See? Th'art nivver aloan, lass."

GRETA ran from that room into a silence of days. Rather than speak she went fiercely into hard work of every kind. Let not her hands be idle lest her thoughts go free! Passionately she cleaned the house, helped her father get in the oats and barley, helped loose the rams among the ewes that they might drop their lambs in the spring. She did not sing at her work now, but sometimes hummed, and Harry would hear, with wordless pity, the pain and endurance in that low voice, humming.

Autumn had always troubled her with its beauty, but now it was not a sweet troubling; it was pain to see the oaks and limes and sycamores aflame, the bracken on the hills rust-red and gold. Once, on an afternoon when there was no work to do and she was alone with her wrecked thoughts, she went deliberately to her waterfall, that she might give herself there to an absolute pain. She flung herself face down on the rock, and, while the water rushed noisily past her, she inquired of Norry, "Wherever you are, can you feel my love? Or are you nowhere any more . . . nowhere any more?" Believing, or fearing, that this last was the truth, she indulged, lying prone on the rock, in a rebellion against faith and the treacherous dreams of youth. She plucked a bitter comfort from this contempt for her own two dreams, one of a wonderful love, one of being religious and good. Ha! Religious and good! The thought of the little church raised in her only a sick hostility to all it presumed to declare.

In the old days, lying in bed, she had announced to herself her ambition again and again: to have splendid sense, marvellous strength of character and terrific powers of love. Impossible to light these words with meaning when one's heart was dead. Rising then, she said only, "I love you still, wherever you are." She felt better, and a little proud, for having chosen this rebellion and despair.

Walking past the church next morning, she averted her head as if cutting a neighbour; but a movement in the churchyard snatched her eyes. Johnny Blenco was sweeping grass mowings from the turf between the graves. He did not see her, but this glimpse of him recalled the way he'd tried to comfort Norry. Having spoken to nobody for days, she felt a swelling desire to speak to Johnny. Thus it was that the little church, which she'd intended to cut, managed to call out to her as she went by.

But where could she talk to him? If only she could just happen to meet him in the road and say, "Can I come to see you, to ask you about Norry?" The next few days she walked past gardens where she knew he worked. But in vain, and it was in his own front garden that at last she saw him. His back towards her, he was planting bulbs for spring. And once again, looking over the dry stone wall, she was amazed at the flowers he could raise from this harsh soil.

"Johnny."

He stood up, turned, and dropped his trowel. His fine face radiated delight, but "Hello, Greta," was all he could say at first. And for awkward moments the stone wall was between them with nothing said—a symbol of rough embarrassment.

It was she who began. "Could I—I'm wondering if I could— come and see you one day?"

The big eyes opened with surprise. "Why, of course."

"Norry said you said things that comforted him."

"Not many, I'm afraid."

"If anyone could have, it would have been you. You know, I expect, that we were terribly in love? He told me he was going to ask me to marry him." She still took pleasure in this. But she'd spoken of it to no one except her father.

"I didn't know that," he said.

"I'd so love to talk to you about . . . him and . . . everything. Could I come some evening? If it wouldn't be a nuisance?"

"You mean *here?* I'd love it above all things."

These were words more demonstrative than any he'd allowed past his lips, but they had come out before he could modify them. Or perhaps consider them and stop them altogether.

To her the words were unremarkable. She said only, "I'd love it, too. I want a long talk."

"All right! Why wait? What about tomorrow?"

"Oh, thank you, yes, Johnny. Tomorrow evening."

SO THE NEXT evening she crossed that flower show of a garden and the door opened to her before she could touch the bell.

"Come in, dear." Again, in his pleasure, a word had spoken itself, but since it'd be unnoticed by her, why not utter it?

He had made a bright fire in the big stone fireplace, and on the

494

low table stood an oddly shaped bottle, two tiny glasses, an open box of chocolates and a dish of walnuts, raisins and almonds.

"Oh, you haven't been getting anything special for me?"

"No, I've had that liqueur for some time. It's one I like. Dr. Pater put me on to it." But he didn't tell her how he'd rushed to Caldmere to get chocolates and fruits that a girl might like.

They sat together before the fire and began the talk. It was a long talk, and as the evening darkened around them, Johnny lit candles in brass candlesticks on the mantel to add to the light from the fire. As always, Greta soon found herself at ease with him. She began, almost exuberant with relief, to describe her state of rebellion against all she'd once believed.

The talking was all hers. Johnny, ever quiet, listened and nodded when he could, or shook his head in smiling disagreement, or offered the briefest of comments. Once he filled up her glass, which she had sipped dry without really knowing it. Of the chocolates she was rather less unaware but not much.

She wanted to tell him how Norry had admired his assurance that one could get joy out of refusing to be beaten by a crippled state, but she knew how self-conscious his own deformity could make him. She managed to paraphrase it. "He told me all you said to him about how triumph over pains and disasters can have its own sweetness."

Here he nodded emphatically. "Yes, oh, yes. But go on."

She went on. And the strange thing was that, having found words for this idea, the words raised a flash of vision in herself. A flash, no more, doused by the rebellion she wanted to keep. Strange that it was her own words that had produced the healing flash. And as she talked on with this easiest of listeners, the flash came again—triumph over pain has its own sweetness—and she began to feel (but was annoyed to feel) an ache to surrender to it. She could see what surrender would imply: a loving, even joyous, return to goodness, the second of her private dreams. But for now the suffering was too much with her.

Though Johnny's part tonight in this dawning vision was at one remove—through what he had tried to do for Norry—his palpable interest and confident, endorsing nods had given Greta a sense of ease that hadn't been hers for weeks. She could see that he was

495

happy to have her there. She could not detect the hopeless, speechless love pouring towards her. She wasn't, this evening, listening to him, but to herself. How to lose, not the love ever, but the pain? One day, perhaps. Not yet. Not for a long time. But one day?

SNOW WAS ONLY a powdering along the crests that winter till the new year began. Then it fell heavily, but not heavily enough to endanger sheep at pasture. Until the blizzard in late January. The worst for years, and upon them before they could get the sheep to the enclosures. They tried to gather them off the tops, but a blizzard dulls the wits of the Herdwick sheep. Stubbornly, stupidly, they resist being driven down. They have to be forced, pulled or carried —and the sheep are many, the gatherers few and the days of January short. Tam Godrigg, Harry, Matt and Johnny Blenco worked from first light to dusk.

It was one such day when Greta, home alone, stoked the kitchen fire as usual to welcome and warm her men. Harry and Matt came in at dusk. Tam had stayed on the tops with two of the dogs to find some missing ewes. When the dusk became darkness and neither Tam nor the dogs had returned, Harry worried. "Wheer's oor Tam?" he said once or twice, then left the house to forge through the driving snow to Tam's cottage in Little Sledden. The cottage was dark. He went on to Johnny's.

"Johnny. Wheer's our Tam?" he asked on the doorstep.

"Probably sheltering somewhere with the dogs and the ewes."

This was possible. Tam knew every inch of his mountains.

In the morning they arose to the promise of a brilliant day. Harry went out into the yard, then returned to the house. "Dogs are no' back. If t'dogs are not hoam, Tam isna'."

Greta comforted him. "It's early yet. If Tam sheltered through that wicked night, he could be back any moment now."

When the sun was above the mountain ridge Johnny appeared. "Tam's not home yet," he said. "I'm going up to look for him."

Any alarm in Harry's heart he did not choose to show. "Aw' reet. Ah'm coomin', wi' dogs."

"I'm coming too," Greta said. "I'll bring some tea. If he's been out somewhere he'll be frozen stiff."

So Harry, Johnny, Greta and even Matt, two dogs accompanying

them, started their long clamber up the pony track. When they had reached the high valley, Greta's eyes swung to the Upper Crags and the long deep slab of Thor's Face. She heard Johnny suggesting that since the dogs were showing no excitement, it was unlikely Tam was near. Johnny would take the quickest route to Sledden Seat, up the crags, while the others, with the dogs, came around by the fell slope.

When Harry and his two children after a breathless ascent arrived on Sledden Seat, Greta could see Johnny limping along the ridge ahead, no prints but his in the virgin snow. Below where they stood, they could see the whole track, down to their farmstead, down the road to Little Sledden. If Tam was heading for home, they could not miss him.

No figures moved anywhere. All was one white desolation till Johnny stopped, shouted at them and pointed down. More than five hundred feet below something had moved: a dog had just sprung to its feet. "That's oor Gyp," said Harry. And another dog stood up. "Aye, an' Fan." The two dogs stayed where they were, but barked. And barked. "If them's Gyp and Fan," said Harry, "wheer's Tam?"

They came up to Johnny now, and stood in grim silence. Then Harry said, "Johnny—look at that." He pointed to where an overhang of snow seemed to have broken and then been snowed over again. "Could be sum'mun fell theer, lookin' down t'scarp just as we are."

Neither Johnny nor Matt made any reply, but Greta was unable to dam her alarm. "Daddy, if Tam fell, where *is* he?"

"Aye, wheer? He could'a slid a lang way."

Johnny said, "I'll get down to him if he's there."

"Ah's goan' doon," said Harry. "He wur my shippert." And as Greta and Johnny and Matt all protested, he sat himself on the brink of the steep descent and stretched down his long, gaunt legs to find footholds under the snow. "Ah've doon worse ner this in my time." Wherewith he charged himself, "Coom on, Harry Whinlake. Put thysel' togither." And, feeling for footholds, he began to ease himself down the scarp. He went seated all the way: an inelegant descent, lacking dignity—except the dignity of loyalty.

Johnny and Matt took the descent slowly, but more or less

upright, while Greta stood at the brink, dreading to follow them. Oh, for Norry's rope about her waist now! "I daren't," she told herself, looking down that near vertical slope. "I can't."

But in Greta, to whom admiration meant so much, the fear of being thought timid could be greater than the fear of death; and this fear, in its turn, became associated with the memory that she alone of this company had rock-climbed, instructed by an expert. Lastly, there was the uprush of affection for old Tam.

So—with tremors at her heart—she sat on the edge as her father had and felt for her first footholds. In the same position as her father, she went down from stretch to stretch, with awe and some-times panic. After a while it seemed easier. Almost enthusiastically, she went past her father; she heard him say, "Eh, lass?" Then, forgetting for a moment the reason for this descent, she was seized by a schoolgirl passion to pass the men and be first.

But Matt and Johnny, with the eager dogs panting beside them, were already kneeling and with their hands tossing snow away from one chosen place. Greta heard Johnny say, "*Quick!*" She was just above them when they uncovered Tam's marble-grey face; and tears sprang to her eyes as she saw Fan go promptly forward and lick that face.

"Dead?" she asked, since neither man spoke. They nodded.

Harry was with them by now, managing to stand and look down at his shepherd's dead face. "Awa', he is. Aye. Awa'." With a sigh, and putting his frozen hands in his pockets, he asked of the dead face, "And did tha' git drifted thysel', leuking for tha drifted yows? Tha's pack't it oop t'hard way, oald friend. But mebbe tha wud'na ha ask't owt else. Greta, lass, if tha's got heer, tha can get doon to hoose. Send for Sir John Despencer's lads, will ta, while we bide wi' oor Tam."

OLD TAM'S dying like this did a little to lessen the settled pain in Greta's heart. Another death so soon seemed to dilute the fact of Norry's death. In the liveliness of youth she had never given very much thought to the mysteries of life and death. But now she talked often with Johnny Blenco about these things, for he had become nearer than anyone else to her. Gradually even she began to catch something of what he meant about a sort of pleasure in the

499

acceptance of hostile odds, almost a joy in defeating them. So as the snow departed, except where it lay on the mountains high above, some of her grief melted with it and she was able to look without too much pain at places where she had been with Norry, or at rocks he had loved. But when it was April again and the lambs with their black-trousered legs were gambolling in the meadows; when in her small garden were the blue rosemary and speedwell she had picked for his table and must now pick for new young guests—then the pain came close again, and spring, with its merciless beauty, plunged her into the old abyss.

June witnessed a remarkable episode in the Whinlake family. Matt went from it. Ever a secret young man, he had not told them that for some time he'd been in correspondence with a sect, the Bible Christian Brethren. Now at last he informed them, not without pride, that the brethren had accepted him as what they called a leader, to oversee their meetinghouse on weekdays and preach on the Sabbath. Matt described this as a Call; obviously with a capital C. "Ah, weel, no girt loss," Harry said. "The girt ninnyhammer."

So Matt migrated to London, well pleased with himself. A month later Harry was more than sardonic about this new calling; he was bitter.

In July, just when his new young shepherd, Ed Kirby, wanted help with the clipping and there was the hay to reap, he had to come to Greta in the midst of a morning's work and concede with shame, "Ah'm feelin' middlin' poorly, as you might say, and your brudder's gang off to do better things than help his oald fadder."

This self-pity was so unlike him that she, too quick with alarm, exclaimed, "Daddy, what is it? Oh, you don't look good."

"Na, doan't git starty. It's pains in my legs maistly, an' an ache like a ton o' coal in my head. All ower by tomorrow."

She laid her hand on his forehead. "You'll go to your bed. You're feverish. We'll get help—there's Johnny and others."

Fever racked him that night and the next, and on the second morning, as she stood by the huge brass bed in which she had been conceived and born, she announced, "I'm getting a doctor to you."

"Na, na," he objected. "Whinlakes doan't need doctors."

But she decided nevertheless to call Dr. Bill Smythe, to whom she had felt a bond since Norry's death. He came that afternoon. Greta took him to his patient, and then went down to put on a kettle for tea. When Dr. Bill reappeared she led him into the empty parlour, where he spread his lank frame over the big chair she always thought of as Norry's.

"Greta dear," he said. "I'm in trouble with your father; I can't get him to accept that he's an old man now."

"He's sixty-nine in a few weeks."

"And pretty good for it. But if you've bent your back to toil that long—well, time sends in a bill. We've got to see that he has little now but rest and quiet. It was when I said this that I got into trouble. Is he, my dear, a hearty eater and drinker?"

"A very hearty eater and smoker, but not a drinker."

"Well, hardening of the arteries and perhaps some overeating and smoking has, I suspect, produced some kidney trouble. With care we can keep him reasonably well, but if it's not to get worse it means we must keep him warm in bed for a long time. Light diet. No exposure to chill. . . ." He began polishing his spectacles vigorously. "You see, Greta, with a condition like your father's there's always danger. I'm afraid his days as an active farmer are over. Is it possible to manage the farm without him?"

"We just must. I can do a lot. And there's Ed Kirby."

"Well, perhaps we can work something out. But, Greta, you've got to *make* him behave. And that, my dear—let's be frank—is much the same as saying keep him alive."

"I see," said Greta. "I'll do it."

DR. BILL'S diagnosis proved all too right. But in his bedfast weakness Harry accepted his fate far more easily than Greta had feared. A fortnight after the doctor's visit he said to Greta, "Ah weel, my lassie, we mun accept it—oald fadder's prapperly on t'shelf now and gud for nowt. Ah'll tell thee: we give oop t'farm and ah gang into some oald dodderer's hoam. The sheep'll fetch their price. Thoo mun hev tha life."

"Don't be silly, darling. You're not leaving this house. Don't forget we're a guesthouse now as well as a farm. With Matt gone we can have six guests." Here a heavy fall of the heart. "Oh, with the money I'm making with guests and teas we can hire labour to help Ed. You tell us what to do and I'll run the farm. You'll be the captain on the bridge, giving the orders."

"It's no job for a young maid."

"It's *the* job for thy daughter," she said.

TWELVE

Down in the kitchen, Greta walked back and forth, back and forth. Run both guesthouse and farm? Why not? A girl soon to be twenty-one? Of course I can do it. She was in a mood to show the world she could.

An end to her dream of escape, to her longing for an exciting life? Perhaps so. Self-sacrifice, was it? Very well, then, it was self-sacrifice, and she would give herself to it with a fierce joy. She remembered how her father used to say to Norry, "She's aw' ah've got, tha knows." Well, she vowed, the all he'd got should be there for him.

There was a sudden burst of sunlight through the broad window, and behold, the sky was now a canopy of blue after a day of dark clouds and moody showers. No need as yet to prepare the visitors' meal, so she took her coat from a hook and went out to enjoy the scents of a washed countryside. And she found as she climbed up the pony track that she was looking at the beauties of the valley below—Norry's valley—without pain. Here were the Idles up which Johnny had climbed alone to Norry, and all that, too, she could contemplate without pain.

And here, on their way home, were her Ancients—doctor and vicar. She went smiling towards them, and the doctor saw her and waved a welcoming stick violently. Many months having passed since her lover's death, he had supposed, of late, that it would be safe to jest with her again. Till this very hour the supposition would have been wrong.

"You can't start a climb as late as this," he called. "Walk back with us."

"With pleasure," she said. "I've got to get back and cook."

They asked after her father, and she told them all as they walked down the track.

502

"Oh, dear," the vicar said. "You'll have to get permanent help."

And the doctor, after pondering the problem, was delivered of an inspiration. "Greta," he said, "you must make a deal with Johnny Blenco. There's nothing he can't do. He has, indeed, a hundred other interests, but he'd fling them overboard for you."

"Why for me?"

"She's blind, Joseph. Unless this is a girl's mock-modest act."

"Hugo means that Johnny worships the ground you walk on."

"*Me?*" Greta exclaimed in unassumed surprise. "But he never—"

"Of course not. He's never said a word to me either," the doctor took it up again. "He only talks books and horticulture to me—and cooking occasionally; but when he asked me to take him to Norry in the hospital, he went on strangely long about *you*, and, God forgive me, it was only then that I perceived what I should have seen months before. But there it was: at last the cat was out of the cellar. *So*, Greta, go and suggest to Johnny that he become your bailiff, and his heart'll leap like a young ram on the mountains— whatever the quotation is. And don't imagine he'll trouble you about his love. Not our Johnny. Now, you see, I've solved your problem for you, and we can talk about something else."

Greta was silent, but with unforeseen flushes of happiness. It was true enough that she had never suspected an unspoken love in Johnny Blenco—but now she felt a rush of gratitude and affection to that slight, shy figure.

"Well," the doctor demanded, for they were now near the foot of the track, "what do you think of my idea?"

"I think it'd be quite wonderful, if it could only happen."

"And I suspect the doctor *has* solved something," the vicar said.

When they had parted from her at Old Sledden's gate, the doctor said to his companion, walking on, "I'm glad I did that. The boy will look after her. Just now she's probably longing to sacrifice herself to her father. Fair enough, but we mustn't let her overdo it."

BACK IN HER KITCHEN, Greta was astonished at the pleasure this unguessed news gave her. Always she'd been fond of Johnny, blending pity with admiration, and of late the ingredient of pity in her feeling had been drowned by the admiration. And now a flood of grateful affection joined the admiration. Astounding that within an hour of vowing to her father that she'd run the farm, the two wisest men in the valley, coming down from the mountains, should have met her on the hillside and put this plan before her. An act of God? Angels from on high with a message?

After she'd served her guests, two women teachers on their August holiday, sternly vigorous fell walkers, she went to her father's bedside and told him the doctor's idea, but without any mention of Johnny's love. In other words, she built a pleasing house before him, but omitted to put in the foundation.

"Ah'd nivver fash mesel' aboot any wark *he* wur leuking after," said her father. "But ah doot he'd give his time to us."

"I think he'd come," said Greta, and again offered no reason.

"Weel, you can only ask him. But it's askin' tarrable much. He makes gud money, and we could offer him only a little."

"Perhaps I'll ask him in the morning."

She walked to his cottage in the morning, saw his head through the window and lost her courage. This irresolution endured for days. At early service on Sunday she watched him with new interest and affection as he assisted the vicar. Should she ask him in the churchyard after the service? But perhaps that romantic old man had exaggerated his love. The depth of her disappointment at this idea shook her badly. When the service was over, she hesitated only a few seconds and then walked home.

It was the next day that a new idea swooped upon her like a bird of prey. It gripped all day. So unheralded it was and so unlikely it seemed at first; but with every hour that passed, it shed more of its unlikelihood, and by the end of the day it was filled with a strange joy. A quiet peace, the promise of a wholly unimagined happiness, even an expectation of enlargements and enrichments— all these seemed to lie in the heart of it. She could see the first of her old dreams changing before her eyes: it had been one of grandeurs and experiences far from Sledden; in this new form it had the excitement of something gay and adventurous here within the valley. And the joy she would *give!*

As her two dreams seemed to be merging into one, it was like a sudden enlightenment. She was in love with it. And she was impatient to put this idea, now aglow, before someone, to ask if it was sane. Not her sick father. And the vicar might not be in Sledden

504

for days. Who but the doctor? He'd always been very sweet to her, she told herself, longing to find reasons for going. And he'd so adore being asked for his advice.

That evening she wandered towards the doctor's cottage—and passed it. Then she turned around and this time, with a pounding heart, she touched the bell, as if it were red-hot.

The doctor opened to her, in a quilted smoking jacket of bottle-green velvet, a blackened pipe in his hand. "Why, *Greta!*" He spread out welcoming hands. "How very pleasant."

"If I might . . . only for a little . . . just to ask—"

"This is an honour. Come in, my dear. Come into the scriptorium. A bit frowsty and smelly with books. Should I open a window? No, it's only August but it might be a little cold. We'll have a fire and just sit and enjoy it together in a happy stuffiness."

Having lit a coal-and-log fire, the doctor dropped heavily into a corpulent leather chair and went on talking. "Appalling the benevolence with which I offered Johnny Blenco to you as a whole-time bailiff. Now who's going to raise me a garden like Johnny?"

"It was about Johnny that I wanted—"

"And who's going to sit in that chair and talk with me? There's no one else who knows who Herodotus was, unless it's Canon Nickle, and the good canon isn't as sound on these subjects now as Johnny is. Did you want to say something about Johnny?"

"Did you—did you really mean it when you said he was—kind of, well, in love with me?"

"Never meant anything more in my life. Why?"

"Well, you may think it's a funny idea, but I have got terribly fond of him, and . . . I wondered whether perhaps we could marry."

"*What?*" This jumped the doctor upright in his chair. He rose, walked a pace or two and looked at her again. "My dear girl! I never . . . You could surely . . . No, I'm not going to say that. I don't believe there's a better man than Johnny anywhere. But . . . there's his lameness—you know—his . . ."

"What does all that matter if I think he's a lovely person? Which I do. And it absolutely fills my heart to think he loves me. I've made up my mind to stay with Father and save our farm; Dr. Bill says he may live for years if we take care of him, so I thought it'd be marvellous if Johnny and I could work the farm together."

505

"But, dear lady, that needn't involve your marrying him. There's no compulsion to marry the bailiff."

"But I'd *like* to." She laughed as she said, "I think he'd be a marvellous husband."

"Lord, Lord! So he would. . . . But, Greta, will you forgive an old buffer for butting in?"

"I love your advice. I've come for it."

"You're very young and beautiful. You could have half the world to choose from."

The headshake with which she rejected this was so sharp that it whipped her hair around on her shoulders.

"Daydreams are over," she said. "I no longer want some wealthy young man whose life has been utterly different from mine. I'd rather stay home and be happy with Johnny. I *do* love Johnny; I know I do."

"Heavens, heavens, if only he could hear you! But, Greta, how is this interesting plan to come about? He'd never, never, offer his—his crippled body—to any woman."

"I suppose he wouldn't," Greta allowed with a sad smile.

"No. *That's* certain. I imagine you wouldn't let me suggest to him that, so far from your thinking it absurd, you'd—"

"Oh, no, no. You mustn't suggest anything like that."

"Then, my dear, I can see nothing but that you must do the asking. And why not? You'd give him the greatest hour of joy he's ever had in his life. Bear good Queen Victoria in mind. It was she who had to start the ball rolling with Prince Albert."

"I don't think I *could* ask him. You see, I know that in many ways I'm nothing compared with Johnny."

"And *he* won't ask *you*, so where are we? My dear, it'd be much easier for you than for him. I think, you know, you will go to him. And, oh, would I could be there when you say to him some of the things you've just told me!"

THE DOCTOR did, after all, in a small way and with Greta's consent, smooth her path for her. He was to tell Johnny only that she'd like to consult him about a scheme which he, the doctor, had suggested. "She thinks the world of you, you know," he began.

"Greta does? Do you know what she wants to say?"

"Indeed I do. I offered to submit it to you on her behalf, but she prefers to ask you herself."

But could she nevertheless do this? Her heart quivered within her as she went, one evening, through Johnny's garden to his rough green doorstone and narrow door. She heard, with fear, Johnny's rhythmic limp approaching on his old oak floorboards.

With a welcoming smile, as though he'd been watching for her, he said, "I've been looking forward to your coming since the doctor said you might. Will you have a glass of wine? I have a nice Château Carbonnieux right here. Or would you prefer a sweet wine?"

Greta had heard somewhere that people "with palates" preferred their wine dry. "Thank you, I'd rather have the dry one."

He brought her a glass and passed her some biscuits, and she sipped the wine and ate a biscuit, and could not speak. This silence is appalling, she thought.

He helped her after sipping his own wine. "You wanted to ask me something?"

"Yes. I did." She was sitting in the big wide chair with her legs drawn up beside her, and he in the equally capacious chair opposite, which made him look very small. "Yes, I . . . I do; and I don't know how to begin."

"Take your time. I can wait."

"I—you know I want to keep the farm going for Father—"

"Yes . . . yes. And we're all going to help."

"And the doctor—suggested I ought to have a—bailiff."

"Yes?" A light appeared in Johnny's eyes as if he'd guessed what was coming, guessed with surprise and delight.

"He—don't be horrified—he suggested you might think—"

"Greta, I've never had any suggestion put to me that pleased me so much. It's something I'd love to do. I've been wondering how best to help you, but I never thought of this. What a promotion! From odd-jobman to full-time farmer."

"He said you were so good at everything. And when I talked to Daddy, he said he'd trust you more than anyone."

"If you mean it, the answer is yes. Yes, a hundred times."

"But it wasn't all I've come to say."

"No? Well, go on."

"I can't. It's difficult."

"Have some more wine. It helps."

She sipped more wine and was not helped. "It's no good. I can't say it."

"But what are you afraid of?"

"You, of course. You may think I'm—oh, it's so difficult."

"Do you mean it would hurt me?"

"Oh, I don't think it would hurt you. But—you know what a talker the old doctor is—he . . . he said you were rather fond of me."

"He could have left out the rather." He added, looking at anything but her, "He could even have used a stronger word."

"Well, to tell the truth, he did use a rather stronger word."

"Love? He was so right. Though how he knew . . . Naturally I've never said a word to anyone."

"Why not? Why naturally?"

"Because some things sound so absurd."

"Was he really right?" With her deathless desire for love and admiration, she longed to hear him say yes more plainly.

Rising, he went to the window and said it rather to the flowers in the garden than to her. "Yes. I love you more than anything in the world. I have for years."

"Years? Then, Johnny—" But she could not continue.

"It's getting dark," he said. He lit the candle on the high mantel and sat again in the chair opposite her. "What were you going to say? You began, 'Then, Johnny—'"

"I wondered . . . if perhaps, then, we could marry."

"*Greta!*"

The amazement in his eyes, the joy unbelievable. What joy like giving joy? Johnny was staring at her. Speechless. Till he asked, "Greta, did you mean what you've just said? *Marry? Me?*"

"Perhaps it was a bit forward of me."

"But . . . but I thought you were in love with Norry."

"So I was. Terribly in love and unutterably miserable when he died. But one can love again. I do now. I love you."

"Not as you loved him."

For a moment only, the splendid wraith of Norry stood between her and him. Then, "Johnny, I *do* love you. As I loved Norry. I admit it was a surprise at first when I suddenly realized it; but I've

508

been living with it for days. I want *you* for a husband. You only. Will you marry me? Please?"

"Oh, dear God, Greta, wouldn't I give the whole world to marry you? But it wouldn't be fair, because . . . ." Even now he could not speak aloud of the back that shamed him. Instead, he provided a reason which could be spoken. "You're beautiful. You could marry someone better than me."

She surrounded the part he could not speak of with words that embraced it but hid it. "I love everything about you. I don't think I've ever been happier than sometimes when we've been together. It's funny, but I've felt then that I was *living* more fully than ever before. You're like that. Other people feel it too. Johnny, you just don't know what you are." She came to sit on the floor at his feet, resting a hand on his knee. "I know what you're thinking, Johnny; but can't you *see* that if it made any difference at all, which it doesn't, it could only make me love you *more*, not less, and long to make a fuss over you? Oh, men are silly, and you are clearly among the very silliest." She took one of his hands. "Mr. Blenco, could you, please, marry me?"

It was clear that he could at last see in her eyes the truth of her words. Bending down, he took her face between his two hands and kissed it, brow, cheek and lips. But the old shyness was still there. So she flung her arms around his neck. "Johnny, in many ways you're so much greater than most men, if you could only see it." Instantly she knew that she had chanced upon the finest words for his comfort. "*Dear* Johnny. We're going to be so marvellously happy." A kiss sealed the assurance.

He, when she took her lips away, shook his head over her upturned face and said, "It can't be happening."

THEY WILL TELL YOU today in the valley that their little church among the yews has never known a wedding like that of Harry Whinlake's lass and Johnny Blenco. Everyone who could be at the church was there. Harry was there, allowed out of his sickbed for the afternoon, and touching the hearts of all because his gaunt figure had to sit, bowed and frail, on a wooden chair while he gave his daughter away. The Mountain Rescue team were there as guard of honour because the bridegroom had been elected a member after that night when they'd found him alone by the fallen Norry's side. Sir John Despencer and Dr. Bill were with them, properly dressed in striped trousers and morning coats.

Canon Nickle said a few words from his altar step. In his long career, he said, he could remember no wedding which had given him greater happiness than this, nor one about which, knowing both of them so well, he could feel more confident. (Some say Dr. Pater forgot himself and murmured "Hear, hear," at this point.)

Dr. Pater, besides giving Johnny and Greta an expansive cheque, had had the wit to write to Lady Kingharber, saying, "I'm sure it would interest you to know," etc., and a handsome dinner set arrived "from Lord and Lady Kingharber with their great good wishes." Clearly a kind and sensitive lady had given thought to the young couple's guesthouse.

By the mercy of God, which, in the matter of sunshine or rain, is more badly needed among the mountains of Cumberland than anywhere else in Britain, the day was fine, so the wedding meats, largely prepared by Pauncey, were spread in Greta's flower garden. Is it necessary to state who proposed the health of bride and groom? Enough to say that the speech had wit, some classical allusions, and was too long.

"The girl farmer up at Old Sledden"—they are apt in the valley to call Greta for her father lasted less long than all hoped, and after his death Greta owned the farm with her husband and played a big part in its management. The farm flourished, as most things tended to do when handled by Johnny; and the guesthouse flourished too, earning a reputation for exceptional food. Visitors were surprised to learn that the more special meals were often cooked by the husband. This was not their only surprise. On arrival they could be astonished to see so attractive a hostess with a husband malformed, but they ceased to wonder at it when they found that she clearly admired and loved him, and that they both rejoiced in their children, who were straight and strong and beautiful.

As a young man my husband was an ordained priest, and served as a chaplain to the Forces in the First World War on many fronts, including Ypres, Russia, and at Gallipoli. It was this last experience that gave him the main theme for his first novel, *Tell England*. This became a best seller after the war, and remained in print for more than fifty years.

It was, however, only a beginning. Ernest lived to write books of even greater stature, particularly his masterpiece, *We, the Accused*, which is now under negotiation with the BBC for a television serial.

Two elements perhaps most greatly influenced my husband as a writer: his love for the Church (though he resigned his Orders, he never ceased to be a devout Christian); and the fact that he was the illegitimate son of a distinguished major-general to whom—though his father's presence was intermittent—Ernest gave all his childhood love.

Ernest Raymond

Although my own score of eighteen novels cannot match his of over fifty, during our thirty-four years of marriage he was my ever-ready adviser and sympathizer; and one of the best moments of the day was the six o'clock drink when we could relax from our writing and discuss the difficulties we had encountered. Patrick Raymond, Ernest's son by his first marriage, is also a successful novelist, and always welcomed our comments on his work. For myself, the sharing of Ernest's and my own work was a unique experience, which nothing can quite replace.

He was the essential novelist, with a profound interest in and curiosity about people. *The Mountain Farm* displays in particular his love and wide knowledge of the Lake District, especially the Borrowdale valley where we spent many happy holidays. We were keen hill climbers and even (though with little success) tried some rope climbing—with strenuous help from those more expert than ourselves.

It would give him great pleasure, I know, to think of *The Mountain Farm* going out to so many new readers.